"Had we not pursed the hydrogen bomb, there is a very real threat we would all be speaking Russian. I have no regrets."

-Edward Teller. Father of the thermonuclear hydrogen bomb.
Shot Ivy Mike. 1952.

MILESTONE

THE COMPLETE TRILOGY

Carl Lakeland

Published in Australia 2019

Copyright © Carl Lakeland 2018 Website: carllakeland.com
Typesetting: Carl Lakeland
Cover design: Carl Lakeland
Editing and Proof Reading: Jodie Payne and Anne Parry

ISBN number: 9780648587002 (paperback)

Distributed by:
Ingram Content: https://www.ingramcontent.com/
Australia: Phone +613 9765 4800 |Email: lsiaustralia@ingramcotent.com

Milton Keynes UK: Phone +44 (0)845 121 4567
Email: enquiries@ingramcontent.com

La Vergne, TN USA: Phone 1-800-509-4156 |
Email: inquiry@lightningsource.com

Gardners UK: https://www.gardners.com/
Phone: +44 (0)1323 521555 Email: sales@gardners.com

Bertrams UK: https://www.bertrams.com/BertWeb/index.jsp
Phone: +44 (0)1603 648400 Email: sales@bertrams.com

A catalogue record for this book is available from the National Library of Australia

DEDICATION

To all the friends I've made at the Australian Writers Centre. Special gratitude is extended to fellow writers, Carleton Chinner, Deb Eldridge, Ingrid Fry, and Nathan J Phillips.

I acknowledge the hard work and dedication of my editors and proof readers, Trent Maier, Anne Parry, Jodie Payne, and Sarah Endacott.

It may be he shall take my hand
And lead me into his dark land
And close my eyes and quench my breath—
It may be I shall pass him still.
I have a rendezvous with Death

And I to my pledged word am true,
I shall not fail that rendezvous.

~ *Alan Seeger. 1888-1916*

CONTENTS

BOOK ONE

Eagle

SHIELD

THE MILESTONE INCIDENT

CHAPTER ONE

Alice Springs 1996

SHE SAID NOTHING AFTER I PICKED her up from the safe house and drove her away. Heading south out of Alice Springs on the Stuart Highway, all I had for company was the constant rattle and whine of the diesel engine. Not that I minded so much. I had no experience making chit chat with a ten-year-old girl. Most kids I considered a right royal pain in the arse.

When she *did* say something meaningful, we were kicking up long dust trails, several hours south on the Oodnadatta Track.

"Hey, mate, slow down!"

Mate?

Did she just call me that?

I glimpsed her from the side for a second while the Land Rover bounced hard over the ruts and potholes. "What's the problem?" I yelled over the noise of rushing gravel.

"You're going too fast, and my bum hurts!"

My Land Rover wasn't all that forgiving in the suspension. A road like the Oodnadatta Track tended to show its weaknesses. I slowed things down a pace, considering my arse was also about to fall off.

"Where we going, mate?"

"Don't call me mate," I said. "Away . . . We're going away."

I checked the rear-view mirror for the umpteenth time. Nothing but dust. No cars. We were on our own. My brain thumped hard thinking about all the things that must get done. When we get there. South, to the big smoke. About as far south as we could get.

"Then, what do I call you?" she asked in what I thought was an annoyed undertone.

"You mean, who. I'm Nathan. And you're Angelique."

"Maggie said not to call me that anymore."

"Yeah. I know. Angel is your name from now on."

"You still haven't said where we're going. And what's wrong with your leg?"

"You ask a lot of questions," I said. But then I realised kids must be like that. I reached down and tapped my prosthetic limb with my knuckles, loud enough for her to recoil in her seat.

"Oh my god! You've got a wooden leg!"

"Yeah, just like a pirate. My leg is somewhere on the side of the road in Iraq. And we're going to Melbourne." I expected a barrage of questions, but she took it on board and went back to being silent. She didn't even bother to ask where Iraq was.

Thank you, Jesus . . .

I shot another quick sideways glance her way. Angel, with big, orange, foam headphones on her head, positioned her camera lens through the window at the rushing landscape. She took a few shots. The motor drive whirred. Then, she placed her camera in her lap as though poised for another opportunity to take it up again. Pentax 35mm. And she appeared to use it like a pro. A ten-year-old photographer. An artist in the making, I thought.

"What's that you're listening to?" I asked. She didn't respond. I leaned over and lifted an earpiece away and repeated my question.

She gave me eyes that said, 'as if you would know', before saying it was Metallica. I hadn't previously partaken in music by Metallica. *Now was the time*, I decided.

"Hey," I said. "Go ahead and share your music." I tapped the dash a couple of times, then went back to eyes on the road. Angel smiled for the first time in hours, getting out the compact disc from a rather large-looking portable device with the word Walkman written all over it in big letters. I figured maybe I'd get one of those. But I was no big music lover. My collection stretched across a couple of LPs by Supertramp and that was about it.

"How do I play it?" she asked.

"Feed it into the slot. You'll get it."

"Oh. Yeah, I see."

No sooner did she do that; I was greeted with a most awful sound. Screaming guitars. Yelling voices. No way could I make out any lyrics. She liked it?

I moved to turn the volume down. She flicked my hand away. "Don't, Nathan. It's Metallica. It's supposed to be loud."

I rolled my eyes. *What have I gotten myself into?* But I had to ask.

"You like it?"

"It's cool!"

"Figured you'd say that. And no. You're not getting any tattoos. Forget it."

"Tattoos? Gross!"

"We'll check back in ten years. I'll still have the same answer."

Angel giggled and began to bounce her head around in time to the noise I knew would stuff my speakers in a minute. Oddly, after a while, I began to . . . like the sound. I found myself bouncing my brain in my skull, the same as Angel.

"What's the name of the song," I said. "I can't make out the words."

"*The God that Failed.* It's my favourite. Will you take me to see Metallica one day?"

"You never know. That depends on if Metallica decides Melbourne has a big enough crowd. Do you reckon they'll come?"

"I know they will. I just know it."

* * *

A few more hours driving the dusty track saw us pulling up at William Creek. A hotel and a roadhouse in the middle of nowhere was a welcome sight, and an opportunity to fill up with food and get a tank of diesel. The sun sat low on the horizon. The track to the blacktop at Marree would have to be driven through the night. Heading inside to pay for the diesel, I noticed a sign behind the counter. 'Rooms 30 bucks mate.' That decided everything for me. A dusty track through the night wasn't on the radar if I could help it. If someone was tailing us, maybe they'd drive on past.

"I'll take a room," I said to the woman with no front teeth and a dirty pinafore that looked as though it'd been worn while slaughtering pigs. "And a bottle of bourbon in a paper bag."

After giving her hands a good wipe with what appeared to be a dishcloth coated in filth, she said flat, "No likka after three. Them's the rules."

Jesus . . .

I forgot about the local laws.

Figuring what the heck, I tossed her a lie. "I've got a sore throat and a killer of a headache. Gonna use it for medicinal."

"No booze after three," she said again. "Those bloody government fellas will have me head on a stick. It ain't so much for me not sellin' it to ya. God knows the few bucks I make from it, just ain't worth me losin' me licence, mate. Them's the rules. Can't 'elp ya. Sorry 'bout that."

"What'll it take then?" I asked.

"Bribin' me won't do nothin' neither. Take a look 'round outside, what do ya see? Nothin' but desert out there, mate. You reckon I got any other chance for makin' a livin'? If those government fellas get to knowin' I've sold anythin' illegal, they'll shut this place down. Then what?"

She huffed and rolled her eyes. I laughed a little under my breath. Here it comes, I thought. She reached under the counter and got a plain glass jar with a clear liquid. "Locals round 'ere call it rocket fuel. Government fellas 'ave got no record of this stuff. And it's 'alf the price."

Angel was gone by the time I got back to my Land Rover. I placed the jar of clear liquid down on the hood and scanned a full three-sixty. No sign of her anywhere. Where had she gone? Should I panic? Why didn't she stay in the car like I asked her to?

I looked inside the window and saw her camera on her seat. She hadn't gone to take pictures. Damn it! I specifically instructed.

Angel rushed past me, grabbed the door handle, opened the door, and hopped inside. Just like that. No nuisance. No concern.

"Didn't I tell you . . ."

"I had to go to the toilet, Nathan."

I put my head down and carried on.

A couple of minutes later, I opened the door to our motel room with a brown paper bag containing the jar of so-called rocket fuel tucked under my arm. Angel went through into the dirty, but somehow as-clean-as-it-could-get accommodation. Musty smelling. Mildew, but that didn't make sense. Mould doesn't grow in the desert unless there's something in the ground.

Dead bodies . . .

I pushed the thought out of my head, but still the mildew. How?

Angel came back from inspecting the bathroom. "There's no hot water. And there's water all over the floor."

There it was. Leaking pipes. I wondered how long those pipes had been leaking. In the middle of the desert, where fresh water meant life or death. Surely someone would fix it quickly.

"Figures. That's okay, Angel. It's like we're camping tonight."

She looked at me with a set of sad eyes as I sat on the edge of the lumpy bed, rubbing the itch away from my left thigh. "What happened?" she asked. "*How* did you lose your leg?"

In my mind I wondered how to answer. All the things I've done. All the things I've seen. There was no short answer, I realised. Only the long. But she was too young to hear it. Her little mind would never process it. There'd be the day when I'd have to 'fess up. She'd have to be much older than she was today. So, I did the thing I thought was best. I avoided it. I deflected. I gave her something else. The guilt at just doing that - no way could I be a parent. Now, the question was rushing up in my head. Why me? I couldn't do it. But before I knew it, it was time to get ready for sleep.

* * *

I heard a muted yelp from the bathroom. The girl had decided a cold shower was better than none. Something I chose to avoid. Not only that, she'd sorted herself out with no prompting. No fuss. No bother. It was in that moment I realised her determination. I admired that. I admired it even more in a ten-year-old girl. When she was out of the shower with her hair wrapped high in a towel, she said words that forced me to the edge of tears.

"My mum and dad are dead." She stated it without any emotional attachment, as though reading words from a dictionary.

"Yeah," I said, not able to add anything further. Not knowing how to respond.

"Did you know my mum and dad?"

"Yeah." Again, my words came in the multitudes. As she stood there intensely eyeing me, I thought back to the time I'd met Franco and Alisha. Basic training. Kapooka, 1980. Franco was a young recruit, the same as me. Alisha, a civilian nurse, who on occasion would show up at the base RAP to administer inoculations. They instantly hit it off. After they'd married, their relationship went toxic and I asked myself why I didn't bother to come between them. To stop them from making the worst mistake of their lives.

Shit . . . Why didn't I do anything? I had the power. I didn't see it . . .

But, as a seventeen-year-old boy soldier, I couldn't have known the future. I couldn't have foreseen Franco's demise and the damage he'd leave in his wake.

Angel never left my gaze as I reminisced. For a moment it seemed as if she knew what I was thinking about. That fiery stuff in the jar stopped me from saying the right words.

I had a small sip but couldn't bear to drink any more. It burned from my throat right down to my stomach. It tasted like vodka with a tequila aftertaste that blasted the taste buds into numbness. The rush to my head was almost immediate. No wonder it was kept under the counter. Maybe I'd have reacted better without it. Maybe I'd have been a bit more comforting to her. But somehow, she was doing well on her own. She reached over and placed a tiny finger on my cheek. "You're crying?"

"This place is dirty. I must've got dust in my eyes."

I felt her tiny arms around me, and her head, smelling of motel soap, resting on my shoulder. She was there for a couple of minutes. I couldn't have helped it if I tried. All the demons I kept locked in my head erupted, and I wept for just a second or two. A moment of weakness. I knew all about them.

So many nights I'd spent in my solace with a bottle of Wild Turkey and a loaded Beretta. The barrel at my lips. Only a small amount of pressure on the trigger and those demons would be gone for good. All those memories whirled at the back of my mind like a silent movie. All the while, Angel held me close and tapped on my back with her little hands. Could it be in that precise moment her purpose was to extract all my woes?

"Nathan, please don't cry. It makes me sad too," she said, sobbing a little.

"Sorry, Angel. I'll be sorted in a bit. I have a lot of stuff in my head, y'know?"

"What should I do to make it better for you?" she asked.

How can a girl so young ask such a grown-up question? I was taken aback and immediately rose from that place I'd been. I'd no business being there. It was a moment of complete openness. A place I tried hard over the years never to venture. This wasn't about me. How could I have been so selfish? My mission was Angel. My mission was Eagle Shield. I pulled my head out and got on with it.

Standing before me, with her little eyes gleaming, Angel gave me the warmest smile. "You're all better now, aren't you?"

Bowl me over with a wet sponge. Immediately, I felt lighter.

She reached and lightly tapped my prosthetic limb with a tiny knuckle, in the same way I'd done only an hour and a half before. "You were going to tell me what happened to your leg."

"Yeah, I was, wasn't I? But that's for later. Plenty of time, Angel. Time for sleep. We need to get going early." Another deflection. I wasn't happy.

The deflections will only last so long. One day, I'll man up.

There was the typical ten-year-old's displeasure. But again, her disappointment seemed fleeting and she left to get ready for sleep with no argument. I wondered how my mission would turn out. Angel was no longer the pain in the arse I thought her back in Alice Springs. Franco and Alisha's legacy was far from that. As I realised it, there was something else. I felt my heart being ripped from my chest. How was I to know that kid would take my heart away? Something I never expected, nor imagined possible. I was so far away from being paternally capable. I knew it. I felt it. With Angel, I could already tell it was going to be a different relationship than I at first assumed.

* * *

Late in the evening, occasionally, a road train thundered past. Exhaust brakes rattled anything not screwed down and could be heard a kilometre or so up the track. With the sounds of the thumping road trains and Angel's snoring, which was similar to a two-stroke lawn mower, I tried to sleep but failed.

Under a single, dim light bulb, at the crooked and aged TV table, I lifted the paperwork from the yellow folder Maggie had thrust into my hand. Among the papers was a fresh birth certificate bearing Angel's new name; I had to wonder how it was made possible. A bank passbook account had been set up. A new passport due to run out in five years. A blue computer floppy disk. The decryption codes for the disk were printed on a single sheet of silk and placed in a plastic sleeve.

A document entitled Eagle Shield, and a mission brief that had an attached address in Melbourne, accompanied with a set of keys. Acceptance papers to St Michael's Grammar School in Melbourne. I poured over the paperwork and navigated through the objectives in my head.

My mind drew back to Maggie before we left Alice Springs. I'd met her out on the street, in front of the safe house. Who'd know if even safe houses were safe? "Nathan, above all, keep her from harm," she'd said. "Your charge is of the utmost importance. Eagle Shield can never be taken for granted. You must never fall behind in your objectives. The agency will continue to fund Eagle Shield up until it's concluded, or until further notice."

"Concluded? You've made no mention of a conclusion."

"The day Angel steps into the Ben Chifley Building is when Eagle Shield is completed."

"Ben Chifley? Maggie, what makes you think Angel will even *want* to be an ASIS player? Don't you think that's being a little presumptuous?"

"We don't have the luxury of choice, my boy. It is what it is. You must make it happen. You must guide and direct her into position. Your mission brief explains all of your objectives. After she comes of age and starts her ASIS training, only then is Eagle Shield regarded as mission accomplished. I know you well, Nathan. Better than you might think. If there's anybody up for the job, it's you. Your package has had a close call. Much too close. We cannot risk that again. Her parents are gone. We've lost assets. We almost lost Angel. A couple of millimetres to the right and that bloody sniper would've accomplished his mission. We don't get to decide if it was fate or just good luck."

"Hmm . . . That's why we're going to Melbourne. To hide among the masses."

"Not only for that reason," Maggie put in. "But also for what Alice Springs cannot provide."

"Investment in private schooling?" I asked as though I was surprised. I wasn't surprised.

"It's expensive, yes. The agency's budget will cover all of it."

"Lucky girl," I said. "If only for the education." What would've been the case if Franco and Alisha were alive? Maybe she'd get to grow up like any normal kid.

"Don't make me regret my decisions, Nathan," Maggie said, as though cutting through my thoughts. "The facts are Franco turned. He played us all. He murdered his wife," she trailed off, pausing a beat. "Look. There's a special something with that girl. I saw it from day one. Her mother was also astonished by her abilities."

"Abilities? What are we talking about here?"

"I could tell you . . . but discover it for yourself. Call it part of getting to know her. I'm quite sure she'll amaze."

Then Maggie handed over the disk. At that moment, I thought I caught a glimpse of someone through the window behind Maggie's rear. I took the disk, eyed it for a second, and placed it into the folder.

"The disk and codes were in Angel's backpack," Maggie went on. "How it got there, I'll never know. But I assume Alisha put it in there. I assume it was an attempt by her to get it to me. What I found almost caused me an early death, Nathan. At your opportunity, take a look and see for yourself."

I placed a hand on my chin and eyed Maggie. Why was I not surprised this would jump up and bite me all over again? Operation Matchbook in Southern Iraq was a success, but with the cost of two lives. Two mates. I'd made a silent oath – nobody would die on my watch – but stepping down range, two fell. I will always have their blood on me. So, here it comes. It starts once more. "Let me guess. The Milestone theory?"

"The centrifuges in Southern Iraq were destroyed," Maggie said. "It turns out that was a small piece of a much larger picture. Iran was the culprit, and the one that got away."

"Milestone is alive?"

"Oh, Nathan. My dear boy, Nathan. So much more. The theory of Milestone is alive as you stand before me. Unfortunately for all of us it is now an inevitability rather than a theory. Milestone will be fully initialised within twenty years. Added to that, a secret project called Amber. Some of the documents have been heavily redacted, but we've managed to get an understanding of what could...*will* happen. With you in play, we can begin to formulate our counter operations, to this . . . so-called Amber project."

"Jesus."

"Yes. Jesus, as you say. Now you can understand how important Eagle Shield has become. Angel is the linchpin. Our hopes revolve around her. Even though you may not see it as I do just yet, you will in time. We cannot afford to fail. We are essentially humanity's last hope. We were under the radar with the Guardianship. That has changed. We *were* the only agency that has managed to stay dark to those players. It'll never be that way again. That girl in your charge is . . ."

"I can see where this is going. It's okay, Maggie. I've got this."

Maggie paused long enough to take a deep breath. At the window behind her, the curtains moved again. I thought I saw the shape of Angel's face peering through, but then she disappeared. Maggie continued. I listened. "It is imperative the decryption codes are secured in a separate location to the disk. See to it they are both well protected. You'll be coordinating with CIA Special Agent Don Bosco in due course."

"Bosco? No shit."

"Surprised?"

"We go back a way. Operation Matchbook."

Maggie smiled briefly, then her gaze hardened. I needn't have said anything. She knew everything.

"How is it possible Bosco is now CIA?" I asked. "I never would've guessed. He's a good man, but it fails to register how Bosco and CIA can exist in the same sentence."

"I'm curious. Why would you say that?"

"He's eager on the trigger. Bosco fires from the hip. He doesn't think about things. He takes no prisoners."

"And *that* is the reason the CIA recruited him. *That* is the reason we have him on board," Maggie said. "Bosco is your exact opposite. Honestly, I don't know where you go in your head sometimes, Nathan. You're good at what you do. Bloody good. But you tend to overthink things. Bosco is the man for the job when only the dirty option exists. The thing is it won't be easy for you *or* Angel. Better to have friends close by, huh? Friends in the same circle."

Just then, it occurred to me. "You made that happen?"

"Amazing, the ASIS machine," Maggie said. "I even surprise myself at times. After reading Bosco's records, I realised Delta operators are trained in the same way as the CIA Special Activities Division. It was a matter of a phone call to Langley. Next thing, Bosco was willing to oblige. Oh, and Nathan. You must understand by accepting this mission . . ."

"My private life is next to non-existent. It won't . . . *can't* get in the way."

Hmm . . . This is how my life plays out . . .

Again, cutting through my thoughts, "This is most probably for life. We can arrange for more time if you'd like to think further. But we'll have to kill you now, if you attempt to back out."

"Thanks for that. Let's get this started, shall we?"

I took all the documents in the yellow folder and thrust them into a leather zip-up briefcase Maggie handed me.

"A bit of cold war technology," she went on. "In the briefcase, you'll find a ballpoint pen. Do not take it out of the briefcase. It is a radio beacon and will activate if you and the briefcase are separated by more than fifty metres. Wear the ring I've given you. The ring closes the circuit to the radio beacon. It is not waterproof. When washing hands, take it off. I will *not* tolerate false alarms. Clear?"

I nodded.

"The bad news. If activated, the signal can be tracked by others. We've tuned a frequency that hopefully stays off radio scanners. Risky, I know. It's either that or a set of handcuffs. The best policy, I suggest you never leave the briefcase unattended. Keep it with you at *all* times. If the beacon never activates, that can only be a good thing."

"What'll happen if . . ."

"That's Bosco's job." Maggie cut in. "He's your actions-on. He'll be in the shadows, but always listening and never far away."

"Roger that."

That night was the last of my nights alone. At least up until Angel could manage her own life, I supposed. I slept in the Land Rover. For some reason I felt it better that way. Maybe I was savouring my own space for just a little while longer. Maybe being suddenly thrust into the position of being a parent was beginning to scare the shit out of me.

My mind dizzied with the taste of that awful rocket fuel at the back of my mouth. How I needed a good shot of bourbon. I sighed and put the paperwork away, thinking I could finally manage some shut eye.

CHAPTER TWO

William Creek

AT FIRST, I THOUGHT IT WAS THE rumble of another road train pushing past. At the edge of waking up nothing seemed real, and the motel room felt as though an earthquake was tossing everything about. It was no earthquake. And it was no road train. It was Angel, flailing in her bed as though struck by a seizure. She flew back and forth, hitting her head repeatedly with a god-awful crunch on the fake timber wall.

Alarm pumped through my veins. I didn't quite know what to do! I knew I had to do the dad thing. Step one: Don't panic. Step two: Panic. Wide-awake, I rushed over and cradled her head to prevent more damage. All I could do was wait until she awoke properly or went back to sleep. I held her as best I could. She whipped back and forth as though a demon had possessed her tiny body. Then she stopped abruptly. She sat upright, stiff as a nail. Her eyes red-rimmed and wide. "Nathan. Did I dream it?"

"You had a bad dream? You okay?"

She looked at me, ghostly pale with those big eyes. "They're here, Nathan."

"Who?"

"They're . . ."

She gulped back air. Her breathing laboured. Without a prosthetic limb on my stump, I flew awkwardly to her bag and got out her puffer. I gave the L-shaped device a shake and held it for her. "Breathe, Angel." She breathed back after a squirt. Then, she sat still and hung her head for a minute or two.

"Who's here?" I said, after I thought everything was over. I didn't know what I was dealing with. It could be epilepsy. Maybe it wasn't. I was no doctor. If it was, surely Maggie would've enlightened me about the condition.

She looked up. "The tall man with black skin. Did I dream it? Did I dream him?"

"You must've. Who's the man in your dream?"

"I don't know. Charlotte showed him to me. Charlotte, and Mum."

This can't be good . . .

Maybe it wasn't the right time, but I knew I had to get to the dream while it was still fresh in her mind. I sat at the edge of her bed, wiping the build-up of sweat from her distraught face.

I thought about Maggie telling me Angel was different. She didn't explain how. She said I'd find out. Was this it? I already knew my charge wasn't in any way ordinary. The dream. I must get to it. "What else can you tell me?" I asked.

"Mum and me. We were at the top of the hill where that big steel thing is."

I thought hard. Alice Springs. South. The MacDonnell Ranges. The telecommunications tower at the west peak of The Gap.

"What else?"

"Charlotte flew over me and I followed her."

"Who's Charlotte, Angel?"

"My eagle friend. Charlotte. Don't you know I called her that?"

She looked at me as though puzzled. I had no idea she'd given it a name. I had no idea she regarded it as a friend. How could that be? That eagle killed Franco. It mauled him. Franco's carotid artery was ripped out by a set of giant talons. A giant beak punctured his eyes and ears, and his tongue was torn from his neck as if the eagle had ripped a snake from a tree trunk. Franco's life was snuffed out before his body hit the ground. All this . . . and yet, a friend?

"I could feel the man standing behind me," Angel went on. "I thought it was dad. But then it wasn't dad. When I turned around, the man had black skin. He was really, really tall and he smiled at me with really, really big, white teeth. A smile like angry dogs get. He said something that scared me."

"What did he say? Can you remember?"

"Mmmm . . ."

She was thinking hard, I could tell. Her little eyes darted left and right. She hung her head. Her face became pink. The dream. It was getting away.

"What did he say, Angel?"

"He said . . . he said . . ."

"What?"

"Peace maker . . ."

It didn't make any sense. Dreams are like that. They never make sense.

"Then the tall black man reached out to gr . . ."

Angel sat still. Her little body froze into place. "What's that smell?" she said. "It's awful! What is it?"

"What smell?"

"Like that black stuff those men put on the road. I can taste it in my mouth. Make it stop, Nathan. Mak . . ."

Her body convulsed heavily. Her eyes rolled back and became white. She whipped back. Her back arched up and her head went into an awkward tuck. Her arms and legs wildly twitched and twisted. She foamed and grunted at the mouth. Holy shit! This *was* a grand mal seizure. All I could do was hold her and prevent any injury. She flailed on and on until finally her body relaxed and went limp.

* * *

I called Maggie at the first opportunity. Due to the isolation, the public phone from the street was the only line of communication available. The telephone number in the yellow folder came with a set of instructions. Someone answered immediately after two tones. "Hello." The voice of a man. American accent. Distant. "Do you have your laundry pick up number?"

"Docket number 774732," I said. "Make it quick."

"One moment please . . ." Click.

My mind numbed listening to the long ding-dongs at the other end of the line.

Click. "Your laundry will be available after two p.m. sir."

"That's not good enough. I need it now."

"One moment please . . ." Click.

Oh, my lord, I thought. More bloody ding-dongs. Fury rose in my veins.

Click.

"Canter?" Maggie said. "One moment please, patching a secured line."

Click.

Christ!

Click. "Go ahead, Canter."

"It's Angel. Not good!"

A long pause at the end of the line. "You know, Canter, I thought I wouldn't be getting a call so early into the mission. What's the matter?"

"You weren't forthcoming with her medical, Mag . . . err, Shilo."

"Canter. Protocols!"

"I apologise, Shilo. I'm a little flustered."

"Tell me what happened?"

"Epilepsy. She had a grand mal seizure. Twice actually. In the space of thirty minutes."

"You're kidding."

"I shit you not. Tell me you have the condition on record."

"I . . . we don't. She's never had one. You must get her medical assistance. ASAP."

"I don't have any of her medical records. Not even a Medicare card. You should've supplied it with the documents."

"I told those idiots in Canberra to include everything. Are you sure?"

"Would I be making this call if it were all there?"

I heard her huff at the end of the line. "Where are you?"

"On the Oodnadatta," I said. "William Creek."

"Bloody hell, Canter. What in god's name are you doing there? Why didn't you take the Stuart Highway!"

"I thought I had a tail and diverted."

The line went silent.

"Shilo. Are you there?"

"Let's get our heads back, shall we? Where is Angel now?"

"Sleeping," I said. "In a motel room."

"And what started this? Any ideas?"

"A bad dream. She said some black man tried to hurt her."

"She said that? A black man? Did she describe him?"

"Yeah. Tall. You sound as though you might have a clue."

"I do. Those black people she refers to are documented in the intelligence you have with you. However, I have no idea how she could have known. Have you managed to access the disk?"

"I have no computer."

"Canter. If you went on the Stuart . . . anyway . . . do you have access to facsimile where you are?"

"Not until Marree. A good day's drive."

"Get there. Immediately. And call me when you arrive. I'll facsimile her medical and Medicare details. Let's hope Canberra is forthcoming with what you need. Other than that, journal everything. Every small detail. We need to know what kicked this off. A bad dream is unlikely to cause epilepsy. Can you think of anything she did or said that is out of the ordinary?"

I thought about it. Then I remembered. "Peace maker. She said the person in her dream said it."

Another moment of silence.

"Shilo?"

"I'm here. I must admit, I'm very surprised. And shocked, I must say."

"You know about that? What she *means* by that?"

"It depends. Peace maker? Or Peacemaker, all one word?"

"That's unclear. What difference would it make?"

"It makes every bit of difference, Canter. Just get to Marree and call me. Out!"

Click.

I shuddered, standing there after hanging up the phone, and the recollection came. Black man. Tall. I'd seen one. Exactly as Angel described in her dream. It seemed so long ago.

On that first day of enlistment into the army, Franco was escorted into the recruitment office by someone matching Angel's description. He entered the hall where we were all to take our oaths to flag, Queen, and country. The lanky black man was wearing what I thought at the time was an American military uniform. He was so tall he bobbed down slightly, entering through those Tasmanian oak double doors.

And there was a connection somewhere else, but where? Franco wasn't alone. There were two from Alice Springs joining up on that day. And they were the only two that made their way down from the Northern Territory. The other guy had introduced himself as Scotty-Blue, as he sat down in the chair next to mine. It was from that moment I knew there was something sinister going on.

Franco and Scotty-Blue were never on any record. Their names were never called off on a roll. They were never issued dog tags, or the service numbers to go with them. It was as though Franco and Scotty-Blue were training as completely anonymous individuals.

CHAPTER THREE

Breakfast

MY HEAD STILL REELING FROM the phone call to Shilo, I went back into the motel room to find Angel fast asleep. Thank god for that. I wouldn't have known what to do if she had gone wandering on her own. I went straight for the kettle and switched it on. At the same time, I poured the rest of that wretched so-called rocket fuel down the toilet and flushed it away.

I reached for the overhead cupboard and opened it, looking for some coffee. No sooner had I opened it; the door came away. I was left standing there like an idiot, holding it in my hand with the hinges and screws hanging. But there was coffee in little sachets and others containing sugar. The kettle began to boil. I was only a moment away from getting a hot brew. I wasn't counting on the whistle. I held my hand over it in an attempt to stop the noise and burned my hand. Angel awoke from her sleep and sat up in bed. "Nathan?"

"Making a brew. Sorry for the noise."

"Coffee? Can I have some?"

"What? Not bloody likely. A cup of tea is better for you. Green tea, maybe. But there's none. Maybe just drink water. How are you feeling?"

"My head hurts. I'm getting a headache."

I thought about quizzing her further about the dream, but realised she'd need more rest. "We'll go out to the front for breakfast if you like. I'm sure they'll have something there. Don't expect miracles. Maybe they've got some pies."

"Eweee, gross," she said. "I don't think I'd like a meat pie for breakfast. What about chocolate?"

"Don't even think about it. That's not something to have first thing in the morning."

I checked my watch. It wasn't early. It was getting close to 1100. We'd have to get a move on if we were going to reach Marree before sundown.

"But Nathan. Chocolate makes my headaches go away. Same as coffee."

"Nice try. Not happening. Gonna make you a cup of tea. No sugar. No chocolate. Nothing. Got it? You need to get ready, Angel. We're out of here soon."

After getting up from her bed, Angel walked slowly toward the bathroom with her little shoulders hunched forward. "I don't feel good, Nathan," she said as she turned her head across her shoulder, walking past me as I poured hot water into two cups.

From the bathroom she called out, "How long does it take to get to Melbourne?"

"Two days from here."

"I don't want to go today. Can we stay here for another night?"

"No. We need to be in Marree before sundown."

"Oh, pleeeease."

"Nope."

"Oh, Nathaaaannn."

Here we go. I had no idea how to recover from an inbound tantrum. It left me wondering how I'd cope when her teen years finally hit. That was only three years away. I attempted to end the inbound sulk-fest by changing the subject altogether. "What if we make it a slow trip and do some sightseeing? We can stop at Lake Eyre and you can take some pictures with that snazzy Pentax of yours. You'd like that. I'd like it as well." It blew me away how Angel seemed to be so accomplished in using such a camera at her age. On the drive down from Alice Springs, I'd caught her muttering to herself as she made her selections with aperture and shutter speeds. So amazing. But then, there were eight-year-olds playing Mozart's symphony No. 14 on Steinways.

I remembered Maggie's instructions to get to Marree. Maybe it wasn't such a great idea to hang about. Angel didn't answer. I called out. "Angel, are you hearing me?" No answer. The words 'oh no' suddenly whipped through my head. I couldn't remember hearing a toilet flush. I certainly didn't remember any water flowing.

I went to the door and knocked. "Angel," I said. "Open the door."

I pushed the door, noticing a weight behind it. I pushed harder and caught a glimpse of her hair on the floor. "Angel!" I pushed the door further so I could get in and bent down at her side. Yellowish sputum was around her mouth. Another seizure. Good Christ!

This is not good!

I picked her up and carried her to the bed, grabbing a towel on the way. "Angel!"

Her eyes opened. "What happened?"

"You've been sick." I checked her over and wiped her clean. "You good?"

"Nathan, my head hurts."

I sat by her side and gazed down at her, cleaning her up a bit more. I pulled the covers up to her chin and tucked her in. "Rest a bit," I said. "Maybe we'll stay here for another day. Try and get some sleep, huh?" I was not looking forward to explaining this to Shilo.

She closed her eyes, at the same time smiling a little kid smile that said she was content and happy. I tucked her in and stayed by her side up until I heard the first sounds of her snoring. I lingered a bit more and for some reason, my mind drifted back to a much younger me. And to the time Angel's parents first met.

CHAPTER FOUR

Kapooka, 1980

BY WEEK THREE OF BASIC training, we were snapping together like a bunch of magnets. We'd been up to the barbers and had the humiliation of a crew cut. We'd been down at the Q-store to collect our uniforms.

Finding a uniform to fit me was an exercise and a half. It seemed either the length was right, but the width made it appear as if I was wearing parachute, or if I got something to fit my frame, the length was down around my knees. Eventually, something was found that would have to do. The rest of my uniform was destined to be tailor-made and would arrive by courier, so the Q master had said.

We'd been down to the armoury, issued our SLRs, and were trained with them. We'd set up and zeroed in sights. We'd even drilled with them.

I didn't know it then, but the rifle range was all the way up and over the top of a steep hill they called Heartbreak. Getting there in greens, boots, and kit was going to be a major pain in the arse.

On the roster for the day, however, was a trip to the Regimental Aid Post. Inoculations. Something to *really* look forward to.

We'd go in squads of four, then report back to continue with our training.

I was at the RAP with Scotty-Blue, Franco, and a stocky guy we called Beef. A civilian nurse was to do the honours. As she walked into the room, the whole place lit up with her presence. Something happened to Franco. It seemed he went away somewhere in his head. It was as though he was struck dumb. His mouth hung open. His eyes went wide. We all knew it was love at first sight. Bloody Franco. I've never seen anyone fall so hard.

The nurse introduced herself as Alisha Falkner. She gave us a good bit of background on her story as a kid growing up in the town of Wagga Wagga. After our shots had been administered, Franco was reluctant to leave without the prospect of seeing her again. He put the hard word on her and managed to get a telephone number. Smooth as a crooner. All the way back to our barracks, you couldn't take that smile off Franco, even if you wanted to.

* * *

It was just after midnight. The silence in our room was suddenly broken by a rustling sound, as though some idiot had decided to get out of his cot and get dressed. It was Franco.

I saw his shadow and heard a set of footfalls pad out of the room, down the hall, and then he was gone. His disappearance could be nothing but bad and meant the entire platoon now had to suffer the prospect of one of its members going AWOL. If Franco didn't get back before reveille, the dire consequences would be felt by all, and the lucrative Vasey Trophy our platoon was chasing would go to another. Worse, if he got caught, he'd be on the next call to back-squad. I wasn't about to let that happen.

Scotty-Blue was snoring like the bugle call that would get us up in a few hours.

"Blue. Get up," I whispered, at the same time giving him a hefty shake.

"Cripes, Franco. I was just 'avin . . .'"

"It's not Franco. It's me. Canter," I said in a low whisper. "Franco's gone."

"What?"

"Blue. You know where he went. We gotta get him back before it's too late."

Scotty-Blue sat up in his bed, looking as though he wasn't yet fully awake. Moments were getting away. I asked again, "Where do you reckon he's gone, mate?"

"That bird 'e met at the RAP," Scotty-Blue whispered. "I reckon he's gone to meet up. He rang 'er before, when we were up at the boozer. So, he's probly arranged to catch up somewhere, knowin' that bloody wanker."

"Where?"

Scotty-Blue appeared to think for a while, then answered, "The road 'ouse out on the 'ighway. 'E said somethin' about it. I didn't think 'e was serious though. Bloody 'ell. What a flamin' galah."

"Jesus. We need to get there and drag his arse back, Blue."

"Yeah . . ."

"I'll go wake up Beef. We'll need him," I said. "Get your kit, and let's get out of here." Then it struck me. We had no access to our civilian clothes, which were locked away in the security room at the end of the hall. We only had our greens. That meant Franco was in greens as well. He'd be lit up like a beacon out on civvie street. MPs were all over the place during the night, and they'd patrol places like the roadhouse out on the highway.

"We'll also need Lemon," I said. "I'll go get him up."

Getting Lemon out of his cot was an experience. The oldest in the platoon, Lemon had re-enlisted just for the money. He'd obviously learned the art of sleeping with his ears open during his time in Vietnam. I slunk into his room and crept up beside him. No sooner did I do that than his hand was squeezing around my throat. "It's Canter." I gagged. "Need your help."

"Canter? What in the . . ."

"You can let go if you wanna."

Releasing his death grip, he sat up and wiped the sleep from his eyes. I told him everything that transpired and saw his facial expression harden. "No. That can't happen," he whispered.

* * *

The four of us padded out of the barrack in greens, with camo cream that Lemon had painted in diagonal lines across our faces. It wasn't until we were a fair distance away from the Alfa Company barrack that we placed boots on our feet. Lemon suggested we take a bit of cash. Not to buy something, but to bribe the night picket if we got sprung. A few bills would easily persuade them, Lemon said. Who'd know if those so-called night picket duty recruits used the opportunity to get away for a while themselves?

By the time we got to the fence line, the lights of the roadhouse across the highway shone through the early morning fog with an eerie glow. A slight breeze was pushing in from the north, enough to prickle the skin on my forearms. The fence was no problem getting over. I expected to see a six-footer that was at least electrified. To my surprise, the fence was four-foot rural consisting of the usual four strands of wire. Not even barbs.

We climbed over and moved through the native shrubs and noxious gorse on the side of the road. We waited in the shadows, choosing a moment when no headlights could be seen in either direction to move again. No cars in sight, we slunk diagonally like black cats crossing a suburban street. Reaching the other side, we found shadows among the shrubbery and waited there for a bit.

From our position in the shadows, I could at last see through the window of the roadhouse. There was Franco, as suspected, in a cubicle with Alisha chatting her up. He wasn't wearing his green shirt – instead a white t-shirt, like the one we all wore at PT. Franco had thought this out. The real beacon was his haircut though, and he'd easily stick out to any patrolling MP.

We were about to make our move from the shadows when a set of headlights came over the rise. Lemon got us down as it approached. We'd have to wait a bit more. But as it drew nearer, it slowed down. The light from the half-moon hit it, and from the shape and sound of the vehicle I could tell it was a coach. Tourist coach probably. And heading straight for the roadhouse. It was going to make Franco's extraction even more difficult. Who knew if there were military staff on board inbound for Kapooka? If there were military on the coach, Franco was knee-deep in a hefty fine and back-squad. Perhaps even a dishonourable discharge.

From roughly a half kilometre away, I could see the coach had stopped. The odd thing was the absence of any sound of exhaust brakes, plus the fact the bus wasn't pulled over to the side. It was just stopped in the middle of the road. Stopped for no good reason. Just stopped.

"That's weird," I said to Lemon.

"Yeah," he agreed. "With those lights on, we've got no hope of getting to Franco."

"It's like it saw us," Scotty-Blue said.

"Bloody hope not," Beef said. "We're all fucked if it has."

"Roger that," Lemon said. "We don't have a choice. Until it leaves the area, we stay put. Got it?"

We all double-tapped Lemon's arm, and the waiting began. A few moments passed and I just happened to notice the headlights of a motorist in the distance heading our way. Another car sped past us going the opposite direction but it was too late. What I thought was certainly a head-on collision was only narrowly avoided.

"Holy crap! That was close," I said. "That can't be right. There's something wrong down there."

"Majorly," Scotty-Blue agreed. "I reckon we go take a bo-peep."

"Our prime mission is Franco," Lemon said. "We'll make the coach our secondary."

Something in my brain told me it had to be the other way around. "No," I said to Lemon. "I dunno what it is. Those lights down there need to be dowsed. Blue, you're on me. You two, when the lights go out, go get Franco."

Beef double-tapped my arm.

Lemon huffed. "Get down there fast and see what's going on. Then back here. We'll wait."

"Oscar Mike," I said, and moved through the shadows with Scotty-Blue behind me, toward the strangely stopped coach.

The pilot light in the cabin was on. From roughly forty metres, we could tell the engine was idling, but even more horrifying was the sight of the driver slumped over the wheel. My heart pounded hard at my breastbone. I instructed Scotty-Blue to run as fast as he could go back to the roadhouse and raise the alarm. The coach headlights drew long shadows on the road as he sprinted away.

Running toward the coach, I could see it was full of sleeping passengers. The air-conditioning unit on top was silent. That was one thing that should never be shut down. Then, it hit me between the eyes like a live 7.62mm full metal jacket. Carbon monoxide. Those people in there needed fresh air and fast.

I tried to pry the door open, but it wouldn't budge. I considered my options. I could break a window or two, so I could get in. But if I did that, maybe I'd cop a whiff of the deadly gas, and that wouldn't do. It hit me with the speed of light that the breeze was coming from the north. I'd need to smash the front windscreen and then the rear. The carbon monoxide would flush out.

But how could I smash it? There were rocks around the place, but none big enough to do the job. Nonetheless, I tried it. The biggest rock I found was about the size of my fist. I threw it a couple of times. No good. The rock bounced off. My mind was on the edge of panic; I worked hard at keeping my logical brain in check.

Reaching into my pocket, I pulled out a dummy 7.62mm round I kept as a lucky charm. The tip wasn't as hard as diamond, so scratching at the glass was no good. Instead, I positioned myself at the front of the windscreen and placed the tip of the round up to the glass. Using the rock I'd found, I hit the back of the round with a good solid whack. SMASH!

Glass everywhere. All over the place and all over me in small fragments. I immediately raced around to the rear and did the same there. SMASH!

Being so tall and agile meant getting inside was just a short climb from the rear bumper. I cut my hands getting in. The oozy sensation I put to the back of my mind. Adrenalin pumped inside me and made me lightheaded. Either that or it was the carbon monoxide making me feel as though I was about to tip over.

From the rear, I moved down the aisle, checking for vitals on seated individuals as I went. Unfortunately, a few sitting toward the rear had none. A few more were faint. I needed to think fast.

A slight breeze was pushing through, but not enough to flush the gases from inside. I tucked my mouth and nose under my shirt collar and raced to the driver's seat.

Had the bus been manual, I wouldn't have known what to do. As luck would have it, it was auto, which meant I could get it going. Hauling the driver from his seat took a little effort. Then it was a matter of climbing in and driving. The wind coming through would flush out any trace.

Pulling up at the roadhouse on a section of concrete big enough to handle an evacuation, I flipped the switch for the door and screamed out. "Need help in here!" Then I immediately went to the first person I saw to my rear.

By the time I hauled out half a dozen or so, Scotty-Blue, Beef, Franco, and Lemon had a few more down on the driveway. Alicia was pounding on someone's chest, trying to bring him back. We were all giving CPR when several ambulances and police cars turned up. Two MP Land Rovers screeched to a stop and the occupants scattered and went to work on those lying on the ground.

The guy I was working on had a familiar face. That he was dressed up in civvies was probably the reason I couldn't place him. I changed from giving him breaths of life to jumping on his chest with the heels of my hands, giving it heavy thrusts.

Soon, I heard the thumping blades of choppers, and after a few moments of tricky manoeuvring, it landed nearby. Paramedics jumped out from the choppers and scurried like mad hens around the place. At that instant, civilian police cars arrived and their V8 engines screamed past the location. I watched them skidding broadside, red and blue lights flashing through the fog, blocking off both directions of traffic. And there I was, with striped diagonal lines of camo cream over my face, getting down to the task of bringing life back to the familiar guy at my knees. As I thumped and pushed at his chest, his body shook like jelly. Then back to the breath of life, over and over again.

More thumping. More pushing. Pinch the nose. Tilt the head. Breathe and check. Do it again. I didn't stop. Then the horror of who he was suddenly struck me. The guy started to breathe and colour came back to his lips.

Lying before me, he slowly came back from wherever he'd gone. He looked up at me. He recognised me. I was sure of it. Camo cream and all. He closed his eyes again. A slight curl at his lips. He squeezed my hand and gave it a bit of a shake. I was now deep in the shit with our platoon sergeant, Sergeant Sheen.

Out of the forty-odd people on the coach, we rescued eighteen. Out of those eighteen, six were critical and airlifted away. Six more were transported by ambulance to Wagga Wagga Base Hospital. And the last six came around as though they'd just been asleep.

There was more military on the coach than I realised. I later learned they'd spent the day in Albury for business, along with military personnel up from Puckapunyal. The army had lost two officers and two NCOs that night. But among the survivors was the Battalion Commanding Officer, the eccentric Lieutenant Colonel Willie White, who two weeks later pinned the Distinguished Service Medal to my chest.

CHAPTER FIVE

Lies and Secrets

IT WAS A LOT COLDER AFTER the adrenalin wore off. A cell in a 'place of brief incarceration for petty crimes', they'd called it. Not jail. Not even military jail. But that's what it was so far as I was concerned.

A washbasin and a toilet. A roll of toilet paper hung from a bit of wire. Two bunks. A couple of blankets and the same green-grey painted walls that were everywhere else. A single light bulb in the centre, hanging, swinging slightly on a long cord. Sitting opposite on his bunk was Scotty-Blue, eyeing me intensely.

The others were elsewhere. Most probably in another cell, I thought.

Out at the roadhouse, before we were chucked into the back of the MP Land Rovers, the media arrived. A journo thrust a microphone into my face. Someone standing beside the journo snapped off a couple of pictures that dazed my eyeballs for more than a few seconds.

I was about to answer the journo who'd asked me to describe what happened when an MP came between us, then manhandled me away, my mouth still hanging half open. Manhandled all of us away. Franco, Beef, Lemon, and for all I knew, maybe even Alicia. I don't know what happened after that.

I assumed there'd be a shit fight to deal with. I assumed the coroner would've been flown down from Sydney. The place would've been shut up tight until the scene was cleared by the coroner's office. After that, I could only speculate.

Families had lost someone. A mother, father, brother, or sister. Perhaps I could've done more, but I failed. I rewound the whole scenario in my mind and played it back, looking for the critical moments I could've used to do more.

As I sat there, Scotty-Blue sat up and got himself to my side. I felt Scotty-Blue's arm about my shoulder. "Ya did good, mate," he said. "No point beating yourself up."

"Can I ask you a question?"

"Yeah, of course, mate. Go for it."

"What if Franco didn't go AWOL? All those people, all the military . . ."

"Yeah mate, dead as a doorknob."

"Nail," I said, correcting him.

"Canter. Sometimes things just 'appen," he said. "Sometimes things get served up for us and we deal with it. It's just 'ow it is. Shit 'appens, eh? Just like what we're in right now."

"What do you think will happen from here?"

Scotty-Blue sat back and appeared to think it over. "I reckon we might get a bit of a fine."

"Then back-squad?"

"Yeah. Probly, mate. Confined to barracks. Who'd know? We just 'ave to sit it out and see what eventuates, eh? In the meantime, try an' cheer up a bit. That was intense, but fun. Don't ya reckon?"

"Fun?"

"Yeah well, probly not the best choice o' words. But now we're 'ere, let's just see, eh?"

It must've been close to reveille. The darkness outside of the miniscule window was starting to get lighter. I'd expected the call to rally, but it didn't come. Instead, a set of keys jingled outside and the lock was unlatched. An NCO appeared wearing a red beret. "You blokes need something to eat. I've been instructed to get something for yas. Anything you want, apparently. We'll make it happen."

"Shit, eh?" Scotty-Blue said. "In that case, I'll 'ave some lobster. Never 'ad that before. Maybe some oysters too."

"Within reason, recruit," the MP smiled wryly. "But go for it. What else do you blokes want?"

"I'll pass," I said.

The MP nodded, then looked at Scotty-Blue. "You?"

"Bangers and scramble will do just fine, eh?"

* * *

Footsteps stopped at the door and it was again unlocked.

The big steel door squealed open. I thought it was food. It wasn't. In marched our platoon CO, 2nd Lieutenant Gustafson, dressed in full parade uniform including a sword at his hip.

"Stand fast," I yelled, snapping to attention. Scotty-Blue also stood fast.

"Thank you, men. As you were," Gustafson said after a snappy salute and removing his hat. An MP turned up, balancing a steel tray containing a decent serving of sausages and scrambled eggs.

"It appears you men have gotten yourselves knee-deep," Gustafson said. "Sorry for having you locked up in here. Rules are rules, and you were, after all, AWOL. That said, some of the circumstances are in your favour. After you mess, get yourselves a hot brew and back to lines. Clear?"

"Yes sir," we both barked.

"Both you lads will report to the RAP for counselling at 1800. Understood?"

"Yes sir."

"Good! Carry on then." And then he was gone as quick as he came in, while leaving the cell door open.

* * *

Gustafson was dressed up in his shiny boots and brass for a reason. It all made sense after we'd made our way up Heartbreak Hill after leaving our cells. Me, Scotty-Blue, Franco, Lemon and Beef approached our platoon who were lined up in full parade uniform and standing at attention. Gustafson bellowed out the order to present arms. They all responded, slamming boots into bitumen. Gustafson quick marched to the head of the platoon, about-faced, then presented his sword. I held my head up. The very first day pride burst up and through my body. Pride. I never knew it could feel so good. But Scotty-Blue milked the moment, shouting 'eyes-right' as we marched past them and beyond.

* * *

After 1700 up at the boozer, it was tradition to break your belt and remove your hat before stepping in. I didn't know where the tradition came from and how many times I'd screwed up before I got the message. Pubs weren't my thing, and as a seventeen-year-old I only spent a handful of hours in such places. If it wasn't for Lemon and Beef, Scotty-Blue and Franco, I don't think I'd have ever considered going there.

I was sitting at the table in the corner, glass of beer in my grip, when a green clad recruit I never knew put a newspaper over my shoulder. The coach tragedy had made the front page. However, there was no mention of any military involvement with the rescue. I was relieved, and at the same time baffled at how our involvement managed to stay out.

Scotty-Blue, sitting opposite, took the newspaper and scanned it. He huffed and laughed before passing it to Lemon, who made a crack comment, then placed it back on the table upside down, placing his beer on it as a coaster.

"Welcome to the world of lies an' secrets," Scotty-Blue said.

There was always something about Scotty-Blue. From day one, he and Franco were whispering to each other like they were hiding something. Me being me, I took the moment and seized it. "Now's a good time to tell us about the lies and secrets *you're* keeping, Blue."

To be honest, I didn't expect a response. I thought Scotty-Blue would shove my question aside and deflect like he always did.

"You 'aven't worked it out yet, have ya, Canter?" Scotty-Blue said.

Lemon looked up from his beer with a set of birdlike eyes. Maybe I should've waited to get Scotty-Blue by himself. However, I knew with a few beers under his belt, Scotty-Blue would be more likely to go with the moment. What he said next took me *completely* by surprise.

"Haven't ya noticed me an' Franco aren't on any rolls," Scotty-Blue went on. "We're not on any records. We don't exist 'ere. We don't even get to march out with you blokes. When we're done doing what needs doin', we'll just be gone. Without any warnin'. You'll wake up with two empty cots beside ya. An' there won't be no talk about it, neither."

Scotty-Blue lifted his glass of beer and took a big swig, not taking his eyes off me. After giving his mouth a wipe with his shirtsleeve, his gaze hardened. "Look, if I 'fess up to it, one: You probly think I'm a nutcase. Two: Once you know, there's no coming back. Believe me when I tell ya, it's a big weight to bear. But before I begin, I have ta ask yas to make me a promise that can't ever be broken. Can I trust yas?"

I nodded, the same as Lemon who was looking as though he'd already decided Scotty-Blue was a nutcase. "What promise?" I asked.

"You need to swear that you'll never claim to 'ave known me."

"What do you mean?" I said, sitting back, thinking how stupid this conversation was turning.

"What I'm sayin' is, no matter what, I'll always be a stranger. You've never known me, ever. Even from after we leave this place. Should we ever meet up again, you don't know me and I don't know you. Get it?"

I nodded, but half-heartedly.

"Well, I'm glad we've reached that understandin'. You don't realise the stuff I 'ave in me 'ead. It ain't nice. An' I live with it every day. Me an' Franco both do. This is serious, Canter. Bloody serious. This shit will make your skin feel like leather when I'm finished. You blokes ready for this?"

I was beginning to feel the same as Lemon. Maybe I was wasting my time. But one thing Scotty-Blue said couldn't be ignored. Scotty-Blue and Franco were never on any records. From the moment we arrived at Kapooka, their names were never read off anything. They had no pay book. They didn't even have dog tags or the service numbers embossed on them. They'd been training alongside us as anonymous individuals that were never there.

Lemon and I leaned in as Scotty-Blue started with his story.

"It's about the Guardianship. The Guardianship of Milestone. An' some kind of a secret project they've got going, which is the reason why me an' Franco are 'ere in the first place."

Lemon chose the wrong moment to take a swig of beer. He sprayed it all over the table and tried not to choke. But there it was. Lies and secrets. I wondered where this was going. I didn't know whether to laugh out loud or not.

Scotty-Blue leaned in. "You know about Jimmy Carter's nukes. An' you know about them Ruskies an' what they're up to, don't yas?"

I nodded, as did Lemon. But at the same time, I wasn't completely up to date with American politics.

"The thing is this," Scotty-Blue went on. "There's been big loads of enriched uranium goin' someplace. Someone's been buyin' it up from the Russians. There's keyhole intelligence showin' the uranium is leaving Russia, but from there no one knows where it's been endin' up."

"Keyhole intelligence?" I asked.

"Bloody hell, Canter. That's a term used to describe intelligence that ain't all there. What we've got is just a small snippet of something much larger."

"Okay . . ." I felt a yawn coming on. I even snuck a peek at my wristwatch.

"Anyway. Our government fellas 'ave been trainin' up blokes like me an' Franco, so we can lead the way to gettin' the bigger picture of what's been goin' on, from up there in Pine Gap."

"So, what's the Milestone thing about?"

"The Guardianship of Milestone we reckon are the blokes who's been getting hold of the uranium. Again, it's keyhole stuff. We think it's been endin' up in underground gismos called centrifuges and gettin' turned into weapons-grade plutonium."

"So, what?" I said. "Carter's got nukes. So has Brezhnev . . ."

"Mate, where's ya head at?" Scotty-Blue said. "Haven't you ever 'eard of M.A.D. theory?"

"No. But something tells me you're about to tell us."

Lemon laughed. He didn't say much. It appeared he was happy just to listen as things went on.

"M.A.D. Mutually Assured Destruction," Scotty-Blue said. "Nations that bear nukes are to 'ave no advantage over any other, so no nukes can ever be used. The theory is this: Say someone gets to launch nukes on another country, with early warnin' stations dotted around the world, the aggressor ends up gettin' pummelled as well, so the need to be an aggressor goes away. No advantage."

"Makes sense."

"Yeah but say someone has more fire power than others. The advantage swings in their favour. M.A.D. is out of the question. Now that arsehole gets to be a world dictator. Imagine it, if that ever 'appens."

"So, whoever is stockpiling the uranium is making a move to world domination?"

"Exactamundo," Scotty-Blue said. "We need the bigger picture, mate. So we can stop it from 'appening. That's where Pine Gap comes in. We intercept what's goin' around on the airwaves. Get the bigger picture. Find out where this uranium is goin'. Oversee and coordinate operations to shut that shit down."

"Pine Gap is American territory," I said. "Prime Minister Gough Whitlam tried to close it down."

Scotty-Blue stopped and glazed over. I saw his facial expression harden.

"Canter," he said. "Where in the fuck did ya 'ear that?"

I was about to answer. I remembered back to the time I was a kid, watching the World Heavyweight Wrestling. Killer Carl Cox was about to wallop Mario Milano for the last time when the doorbell rang. Father was at the table, tucking into his black bread with caraway seeds, stinky cheese, cabanossi, and pickles. Mother ran to the door, and Uncle Lennie rushed in urgently, his hands visibly shaking.

"It's on the ABC. They've gone and sacked the bastard," Uncle Lennie said, loud enough to get father up from the table. I saw father swallow his food with force and, at the same time, reach and twist the selector to channel two.

On the TV, Prime Minister Gough Whitlam stood on the front porch of Parliament House in Canberra. "Well, may we say God save the Queen . . . because nothing will save the Governor-General . . ."

I saw the look on father's face. He drew white as paper and his jaw swung open. Mother went still, shocked the same as father.

"Told ya, didn't I?" said Uncle Lennie, breaking the moment. "Those CIA blokes would get their way in the end. And now Whitlam's got the arse."

"The Gap?" Father said.

"Yeah. That bloody Pine Gap stuff . . ."

"Shoosh. The both of ya!" Mother shouted. "You won't say those things in my house!"

Lemon's ears pricked up the moment I got my headspace back. He looked incredibly surprised. Lemon was no fool. I already knew his bullshit tap didn't even have a handle. He placed his beer down and leaned in with a slight smile on his lips.

"My father and his brother talked about Pine Gap all the time when I was a kid," I put in.

"You gotta be kiddin'," Scotty-Blue responded, then sat back in his chair with a hand up to his chin, glaring at me with eyes squeezed into slits. He seemed gone for more than a few moments. I sipped at my beer, waiting for Scotty-Blue's next words.

Scotty-Blue smiled before finally coming back with his response. "Don't tell me. Don't fucken tell me your old man was Eric Masters. An' his brother. That crazy nutcase, Lennie."

A voice in my head kept telling me, 'get him to repeat that, in case you didn't hear it.' I went over Scotty-Blue's last words almost in slow motion. I rewound it in my head. Played it back. Rewound it again. Then, it was like someone lit a firecracker under my arse. It hit home.

Holy crap! If there was an earthquake, I felt it. I shook in my seat. I said nothing. My mouth went dry. I needed to go for a run. Anywhere. Just to get away. Away from what I was hearing. I commanded my legs to work and lift me from my chair. But they weren't there - a couple of jelly sticks attached to my torso. I said the only words I could think of. "How . . . did you know them?"

I shot a glare at Lemon. He looked just as shocked as I felt. His mouth open and swinging. Blowflies could've settled on his tongue and I doubt he would've noticed. His glass, empty. If Lemon sat there with an empty glass in front of him, there was a reason for it. The reason for him to stay seated now must've belted him in the head.

Scotty-Blue leaned forward and eyed me harder than ever. "Your old man oversaw a repeater station in the Blue Mountains. A place called Linden. The repeater station bounced signals from Pine Gap across the Tasman. But that repeater station is due to be scrapped. There's a new networkin' technology comin' up that's gonna replace all repeater stations. Internet, they're gonna call it. Everything goes down telephone lines. No need for them bloody humongous radio towers anymore."

"My father died not long ago," I said.

"Yeah, I know, mate. That was unfortunate. We 'ad 'im pegged to go off and do other stuff."

"You *are* a fucken nutcase, Blue!" I shouted. Heads turned.

"Hey, quieten down, Canter. All I'm doin' is giving you what you need to know."

"So, you're saying my father was a player?"

"That's the long and short of it," Scotty-Blue said. "Not just a player. But your old man made it possible for us to get some of the keyhole intelligence I was speakin' about. He was a soldier. In the true sense of the term."

"No. He had his own business. He was never a soldier."

"Cover story. Ever figure out how he could afford all that kit he owned?"

Can't be true . . . it's impossible . . .

"Cripes!" Lemon finally said something.

"Then what about my Uncle Lennie?" I said.

"Mad as a hatchet, your uncle. He got 'imself chucked from intelligence. The bloody idiot. Couldn't keep 'is mouth shut. Gobbin' off classified crap to everyone 'e knew. So, 'e was put into a home for the mentally ill."

"Yeah. I remember it," I said. "I thought he had a nervous breakdown."

"He did in a sense. He was pushed into it."

Before I could add anything further, Franco made his way over to the table, through crowds of recruits, with a big grin on his face. When he reached us, he didn't bother to sit. He stood there with a hand on Scotty-Blue's shoulder, smiling that big cheesy grin.

"Gawd, strike me, Charlie," Scotty-Blue said. "You look like you're ready to go for a root."

"It's gotta be love, mate. Gonna marry that woman."

Franco was about to step away when Scotty-Blue grabbed his arm. "Hey. You're not gonna believe this, mate. Canter's old man was Eric Masters."

Franco paused and stood there, biting his bottom lip. He put his hand down hard on Scotty-Blue's shoulder. I saw the tips of his fingers squeeze and disappear around Scotty-Blue's collar-bone. "Blue. Pow-wow, mate."

"Cripes. I'm in the shit now, eh?" Scotty-Blue said, wincing with obvious pain before getting up and stepping away.

I sat there watching Franco and Scotty-Blue as they exchanged words. I knew it was serious when Franco ground a finger into Scotty-Blue's chest. Scotty-Blue's face went as red as his hair. Lemon, in the chair opposite, took the opportunity to get another schooner. "You look like you need one too," he said.

"Make it a bourbon. No ice. Straight up."

"Like that, huh?"

"This is doing my head in, Lemon. What the fuck is going on?"

He slapped a hand on my shoulder. "Can't believe it myself. And I've been around for a long time. Anyway, we'll sort it. Take a breath, mate. Something tells me this is far from over."

I should've left it alone. I should've left things with Scotty-Blue where they were and not gone there. Regrets. I hated them. But now it was out, there was no turning back. Scotty-Blue was right. It was a weight I had to bear on my shoulders. Lies and secrets. I was left wondering how things would be different if I just *never* went to the boozer in the first damn place.

I continued to scan Franco and Scotty-Blue from where I sat. Their talking broke into shouts, then Scotty-Blue swung one at Franco, connecting with his chin. He fell backward into a few recruits having a drink. Then, the whole place lit up. Things went crazy.

A brawl broke out and stuff went flying. Chairs flew. Tables turned over. Glass smashed everywhere. Just as I thought it was time to get the hell out, someone aimed one at me. I managed to block it and send one back. That's when the MPs ran in, shouting and yelling to break it up.

CHAPTER SIX

Codan

ANGEL'S VITALS WERE ALL OKAY. I checked them over and over and over again – I had to be sure. I had to be certain. I felt her forehead and cheeks, which were cold to the touch. Too cold. Stuck in the middle of the desert with no hope for medical assistance, I wasn't sure what to do next. Raising the alarm was out of the question, and I couldn't stomach the idea of another call to Shilo. That would play out just as bad as having a sabre-toothed cat latch itself around my throat.

Angel's eyes opened slightly. "Nathan?"

"I'm here. Try to relax."

"That water you put in the jar wasn't nice. It burned my throat."

Every cell in my body went still. I tossed that stuff down the toilet. I didn't notice how much had been drunk. I thought it was me who'd taken at least half of it. Maybe a bit more than half, not sure.

"Angel, couldn't you smell it?"

"My nose is blocked."

Figures. The dust in the place also blocked mine.

"Why didn't you spit it out?"

"I was thirsty. I took a big drink. I don't like the water from the tap. It tastes funny and it's brown."

Crap!

"Angel, open your eyes. Can you see me?"

"I can see you. Why are you so scared?"

"Stay here and don't move a muscle. I'll get some clean water from the front."

I ran from the motel room, half limping around the corner. After punching the door open and leaping inside, I saw the lady with no front teeth busy with another customer. I didn't care. "Need the flying doctor," I yelled.

Heads spun and eyed me. "What for?" the toothless lady said.

"That stuff you sold me. My kid drunk some of it."

Instantly, she echoed my terror. She pointed with a finger. "The airstrip across the road," she said. "The tin shack with the red cross on it. That's the clinic."

My mind was in overdrive. Who'd know if the flying doctor was moments or hours away? Hours, I didn't have. That stuff in Angel's system needed flushing out and I had a job on my hands.

Springing through the motel room door, I saw Angel was mid-flight with another seizure. I raced over in time to save her head from colliding with the bedpost. At the end of the fit, she projectile-vomited onto the wall. Traces of blood. Angel was teetering on the edge of something catastrophic. I held her in my arms. Blood vomit dripped from the corner of her mouth. I opened her airway and checked her vitals. The tips of her fingers, lips, and tongue were tinged blue.

I raced with Angel's body being nothing more than dead weight in my arms across the stony street to the clinic with the paint-peeled red cross. Busting through the door, I yelled "Help!"

Two Aboriginal male nurses erupted from a cards game. I put Angel down gently on the nearest gurney. One nurse spoke in native tongue to the other while checking her over. He pointed to something and the other nurse went blurring away, sidestepping equipment with the prowess of a rugby player.

"The flying doctor," I said.

The nurse said some words in broken English that I thought contained the word 'Codan'.

"Where is it!" I yelled.

"Know how to use it?" one of the nurses asked, at the same time checking equipment.

I nodded and ran to the corner, where on a table sat a Codan HF Radio. "What's the call sign?" I yelled over my left shoulder, then I noticed it written on a Dymo label attached to the radio's hard case. I reached down to the Codan and activated the emergency request button for at least ninety seconds as per protocol.

A voice crackled over the speaker. "Victor zulu eight victor juliet bravo. Please state the nature of the emergency."

I picked up the mic and pressed a button. "Ethanol poisoning!"

"Roger. Inbound to your location, ten mikes. You guys are the luckiest arseholes alive. Patient delivery heading your way."

I couldn't help but roll my eyes. "Is the MO on board?"

A moment of silence, filled with radio background static. "Who is this? Identify yourself," the voice crackled.

"It doesn't matter. Get here. Out."

Back through the plastic curtain, Angel lay on the gurney with an IV already attached and an oxygen mask over her face. The two nurses regarded me, then went about their business with Angel.

It was at that moment a muffled bang rang from somewhere outside. The nurses looked up, regarding each other with a smile.

"When is 'e gonna get that truck fixed, eh?" one said. A backfire I thought and put it out of my mind.

Angel's IV drip was changed the moment the aircraft touched down. Stepping into the clinic, the doctor was followed by three others, including a woman in a wheelchair. The doctor ignored me and went to Angel to begin emergency care. An Aboriginal nurse instructed me to take a seat out in the foyer, and the awful waiting began.

Roughly twenty minutes—that felt more like hours—passed before the doctor came out of the room and into the foyer, almost nonchalant to the emergency. Finally locking eyes, he asked, "You're military?"

"That obvious, huh?"

"Takes one to know one," he said, then stuck out his hand. "Captain Will Bryant, 6RAR. That was then. Now, this. Not that I mind so much. The isolation suits me better. And I'm away from the bullshit grunt mentality."

"Shit," I said and shook his hand. "Nathan Masters."

"Where from? Or don't say. It's totally fine by me."

"152 Signals Squadron SAS," I said after a split second of weighing it up.

"152 Sigs? Impressive. That explains your knowledge around the Codan HF," he said, before stepping away slightly. Over his left shoulder, he asked, "Which group?"

"Special Sigs Intel." Maybe I shouldn't have said it. But I did. I was flustered with all that was going on.

"Intelligence man!" he said as though genuinely surprised. "You blokes are still out chasing down mobile scuds. But you're here."

"Slightly injured down range," I said, then lifted my jeans leg to show him.

He eyed me intensely over the top of his spectacles. "I see. That's unfortunate. But it also means you must be home soil deployed. Intelligence doesn't get to retire if you can still eat and defecate."

I said nothing. His probing was getting too personal. I shut up shop from that point on, telling him any further words would mean his death, to which he lightly laughed. I was absolutely serious.

"Your girl is lucky," he said. "She'll not need a medivac and will be fine after twenty-four hours on a saline drip. However, the question remains about her eyesight. We'll know more as she begins to rehydrate."

"What about the seizures?"

"A reaction to ethanol poisoning. They won't reoccur."

"Thank god for that."

"We're not out of the bush yet, Nathan Masters," he said, while checking his clipboard. "Two things. One: How did she get ethanol in her system? Two: Who is she to you? If you're home soil deployed, I find it hard to comprehend how a child her age is in your company." He lifted his gaze from the charts, scrutinizing me with a set of eyes that told me I needed a good answer, or he'd shut me down.

What could I say? "I'm her legal guardian."

"If that's the case, you'd have her Medicare and official papers showing you are who you say you are."

I paused. He looked back at his clipboard as though waiting for a response. I had the papers. Everything was in the briefcase.

Shit! The fucking briefcase! Was I more than fifty metres away from it?

The bloody radio beacon . . .!

The doctor went on. "Unless you can come up with the documentation to explain how she's in your care, I can't release her to you. Do you have anything? Birth certificate, passport, whatever?"

"Yeah, I do. But . . ."

"But? You're either her legal guardian or not. What aren't you telling me, Nathan Masters?"

"I'll be back shortly," I said, then made for the exit; at the same time someone busted through the door in a mad flap. "Doc Bryant! Where is 'e?"

Doc Bryant eyed the panicked local from across his medical charts. "What is it?"

"It's Lilly. She's got 'erself shot!"

* * *

Stepping across the stony road toward the hotel, Doc Bryant and the local guy strode quickly over. On entering the hotel, I realised the backfire I'd heard moments before was no backfire at all. Lying in a pool of blood, with two hotel patrons standing over her, the woman with no front teeth stared up with eyes fogged over. A shotgun blast to the chest had opened her dirty pinafore with red. A neat hole in the forehead said nine-millimetre projectile. An execution, gangland style.

Leaving them there to handle the situation, I retraced my steps to the motel room. The sight of everything turned over was something that I had only lived out in the worst of nightmares. The horror of the situation struck me. The radio beacon had activated. Someone had tracked it. Someone had zeroed in on it. Even worse, Shilo would know.

I searched for the briefcase and yellow folder. It didn't matter how hard I looked, nor for how long. Whoever had ransacked the place got what they came for. The briefcase and yellow folder, with all its contents – the documents, the disk, everything had been stolen.

Getting my head together, I began the process of looking for clues. Outside the motel room door were tyre tracks in the dirt. By the tread pattern, I knew it could only be BF Goodrich off-road tyres, and that said four-wheel drive. It didn't say *what* kind of four-wheel drive. It could've been any number of makes and models, and there were more than a few around these parts.

I also noticed more tyre tracks. The dirt between the tread pattern lifted and was sharper than the BFGs, indicating more recent activity. I guesstimated it had to be an SUV. I followed the tracks to the road and found both sets were headed south.

To the front of the hotel, Doc Bryant and the locals stood in a circle, discussing how to proceed. The woman with no front teeth called Lilly was still on the floor with a blanket tossed over her body. I had moments to react. Precious time was playing against me.

I needed to get into the air and head in the direction of the tyre tracks. Immediately. But Angel. Could I leave her? I'd have to forget about being her dad for a short time. I struggled trying to decide which way to go. I needed the briefcase. And I needed Angel to be safe. I needed to be there for her as she recovered. But without the briefcase, there was no Eagle Shield. The dire consequences and the repercussions of the disk falling into the wrong hands were too horrifying to imagine.

"Doc," I said urgently. "I need to get into the air. And I need a weapon. The guy who did this is heading south on the track."

"You can't use the RFDS aircraft, Nathan Masters. And I can't help with a weapon. But I can get you into the air with our helo."

"It needs to happen right now." I looked away as thoughts of how this would play out went whipping around in my head. "Angel. I need to know she'll be safe!"

"Of course, she'll be safe," the doctor said. His words reassured me. Somehow, I knew I could trust him. I'd only be away for a short while. An hour at the most. I'd be back. We'd be making our way south by the end of the day. Shilo wouldn't need to know the finer details. I'd have something worked out. I'd have something ready to report and everything would proceed as planned.

The local guy spun towards me, then said, "I 'ave a single shot bolt action 303 if that's any good. You can take it and kill that mongrel who's done this to poor Lilly."

"Get it for me!"

* * *

Stepping into the hangar, I was expecting a Black Hawk. It wasn't a Black Hawk. It wasn't even a Huey. It was a tiny Robinsons that would struggle in the effort of chasing down a four-wheel drive doing top speed on the track.

Up in the air, I pointed the barrel of an ancient 303 from the helo's open window. No scope. A single round chambered and ready to fire. As the helo reached its top speed, I was surprised how quickly we picked up the tail end of a long dust trail. I felt a rush of adrenalin to my head, as we got closer to a black SUV racing south. "Take us down," I said to the pilot over coms.

The black SUV raced on the track, I assumed as fast as it could go, as the pilot positioned the helo within range. I aimed my weapon at a tyre, then I noticed the driver's hand signals from out of his open window. Military hand signals. "Do we have Citizens Band UHF?" I said to the pilot, to which he gave thumbs up, then switched to channel eleven.

"The driver in the black SUV. Identify yourself," I shouted into the mic.

"Canter? Could that be *you* up there, big hoss?"

"Bosco!"

"Hey, Canter. Got yourself into a bit of a pickle?"

"Bosco? What the . . .?"

"Yeah. Thought you might say that. It seems I picked up the radio beacon, but a little too late, isn't it? Didn't you even know you *had* a tail? I've been tracking the bastard. Slimy sucker, this one. Slippery as cod in soap water. Time to get him shit-canned. What do you think?"

"Roger that," I responded. "What's the vehicle?"

"He's in an F100 Bronco. V8 probably. You've got your work cut out. Reckon he's making a run for the airstrip at Marree."

I thought about it. It was unlikely he'd use a civilian airstrip to get away. My mind ran through all the options he'd have.

Bosco came back. "You still got ears on, Canter?"

"A civilian airstrip is out of the question," I said over the CB. "I know these guys. He'll have an aircraft waiting somewhere. Somewhere an aircraft can land."

"What're you thinking, Canter?"

I thought hard. Where could an aircraft, most likely a Lear jet, land in the desert? Then it came to me.

"Bosco. Hang a left and make for Lake Eyre."

"Good thinking. I'll catch up with you there. Stay on the coms, Canter."

"Copy that."

Without any prompting, the pilot tilted the control stick, rolling the helo left. I instructed him to stay low and hug the terrain toward Lake Eyre. As the helo snuck up from behind the huge herds of cattle that were lazily grazing, they scattered in all directions as though their lives depended on it. In the distance, the white open space of Lake Eyre came into view—and there was the dust trail we'd been chasing down. As if reading my mind, the pilot flew down lower and positioned the helo behind the racing Bronco. We'd spring from the dust and take him down with the one and only round I had. Or I had another tactic to work with. "Take us up and straight on," I yelled. The pilot gave thumbs up.

The moment we blasted over the top of the Bronco; I could see the aircraft standing stationary on the white salt pan. Lear Jet, just as I thought. My one shot, I decided, would have to be at an engine to disable it. From there, I could only imagine what we'd do next. At least with the aircraft out of action, the documents and disk had no hope of getting away.

Moving in closer to the Lear Jet, I aimed the 303 at an engine. On the ground, two guys in black suits scurried and launched themselves up a set of stairs and lept inside. Waiting for a shot, the pilot slowed the helo. "No!" I yelled over the noise of the rotors. "Keep the forward momentum. We don't know if they have us painted. Assume it to be the case."

The pilot gave a thumbs up and increased speed.

"On my mark, roll left and I'll take the shot," I shouted. I trained my eye down the weapon, holding it steady as much as I could. "Ready . . . Mark!"

The helo rolled left. I breathed in and held. I pulled the trigger and immediately the recoil shoved the stock hard into my shoulder. Looking on, the one shot I had chambered missed the engine, but it must've pierced the fuel tank; the Lear Jet promptly erupted into a fireball and exploded, spitting a visible shockwave across the salt pan.

"I was *not* expecting that," yelled the pilot.

"It wasn't the plan," I yelled back, realising I had no chance to gather any usable intelligence. Maybe it was a good thing. Who'd know what would've occurred had those guys in black suits put up a fight. Without any firepower to give the bastards something to think about, the situation could've turned out worse than anything I could imagine. Briefcase or no briefcase.

After the pilot swung the helo back around toward the west, the incoming Bronco broadsided on the salt pan, stopped briefly, then sped off with wheels spinning back in the direction it came.

"Bosco. Got your ears on?" I yelled into the mic.

"I'm here. What's your status?"

"The aircraft has been destroyed. Tango heading your way."

"Roger that. Oscar Mike."

CHAPTER SEVEN

Lake Eyre

UP IN THE AIR, THE PILOT AGAIN leaned on the control stick. The helo changed direction and followed the Bronco's dust trail toward Bosco's SUV. Bosco had already broadsided his vehicle in the dirt and had jumped out, using it as cover. I saw the repeated flashes of the muzzle as Bosco began peppering shots at the Bronco, the moment it came into his range. The Bronco steered out of control, veered off the road, and turned over.

"Get us down there!" I yelled to the pilot.

As soon as the helo hit the dirt, I sprang from the door. I sprinted, limping toward Bosco as fast as I could go.

Bosco pulled the G-man to his feet, then raised his handgun, pointing the muzzle at the G-man's head.

I screamed out, "No! Bosco. No!"

When the shot rang out across the silent desert, the hope I had for gleaning intel was dashed for good. I moved over to Bosco, feeling my shoulders hunch forward with the disappointment. I stood there, looking down at the dead guy with the words 'yet another stuff-up' racing through my brain.

After a pause, Bosco casually turned and walked past me to the pilot somewhere at my rear. Bosco moved without any bother, as though it was of no consequence, raised his weapon, and K-POP! – put a bullet into the pilot's head.

"Bosco! Are you fucking serious!" I yelled.

"Can't risk it, big hoss. What option do we have?" Bosco said, as he took a red bandana from his jacket pocket. Using the bandana, he began wiping his prints clean from the handgun. Stepping back to the deceased G-man, Bosco placed his handgun into the hand of the dead guy on the ground. "Dumbass just took the easy exit," he said, while at the same time reaching and retrieving what I thought was a Glock pistol from the dead G-man's holster.

"Here, you take this one," Bosco said, passing me the Glock. "Something tells me this ain't over, and you're gonna need it."

I stood there stunned, not knowing how I'd report this one to Shilo. I took the Glock from Bosco without a second thought. I checked for rounds, then tucked it at the small of my back. Bosco rifled around in the Bronco wreckage. "Oh. Here it is." Bosco grabbed the briefcase from within the wreck.

He took it, walked to me, then slapped the briefcase hard on my chest. "Don't lose it this time. I ain't doing this shit again. I'll organise the clean-up crew with Shilo. Reckon that sits a little unsavoury with you."

"Let's just glean as much as we can, Bosco."

"There won't be much. These G-men don't carry anything of use. Exactly for that reason."

I sat in the passenger seat of Bosco's SUV while he drove at an easy pace, north toward William Creek. The briefcase containing the yellow folder, disk, and documents was safe in my possession. I placed the briefcase on my lap and ran my hands over the textured leather, thinking how I'd report back to Shilo.

I thought about Angel and somehow knew she'd be okay. However, the guilt over abandoning her played heavily on my mind. I needed to be there for her. But I also needed the briefcase. How I wanted to be two people at the same time.

I glimpsed sideways at Bosco. His dawdling was really starting to piss me off. Something told me that until I got back there, Angel was in danger. Maybe I should've stayed with her and let Bosco handle everything on his own. But then, there was the Lear Jet. I'd hate to think what would've occurred had I *not* been there. It made me shudder thinking about it. How frustrating it all was with Bosco, driving with an elbow hitched out of his window, cruising along like he was on some kind of Sunday drive.

C'mon, Bosco. Step on it. Fa Christ's sake . . .

But then there was another thought. A question to which I needed an answer.

"The woman at the hotel," I said. "Was that you?"

"What! No! Of course not! I don't do innocents. That was the G-man looking for you. That woman probably didn't give him anything."

"Oh, and the pilot wasn't an innocent?"

"Heck, Nathan. Told ya before there's no choice. It had to play that way."

Hmm . . .

I went back to being silent, weighing things in my head. Bosco was right, I conceded. There could be no leak. No loose ends. Had the pilot spoken of anything, even a slight hint, it would blow everything and there'd be a price to pay.

I caught Bosco eyeing me as he drove. He had that look on his face. I knew what he was thinking. I had thought this time he might let it rest, but Bosco being Bosco, there was no chance of that. How did I know he was going to bring it up all over again?

"What!" I finally said.

"How's that leg of yours going?"

That's how the conversation normally started. He'd bring the goat thing up and rub my nose in it all over again. "Operation Matchbook was a shit fight. How many times do I need to say it? Don't you think we need to move beyond what happened down range?"

Operation Matchbook. How could I forget it? How could I put it behind me? Once the smell of death gets up the nose, it never leaves. Burned and charred bodies only sometimes were aired in the media – and even then, briefly.

Looking at those articles, I wondered what kind of life they'd left behind. Their lives didn't make the papers. The details didn't reach civvie street or get viewed by the average Joe on CNN.

The movies tried to reproduce incidents like theirs. But how could Hollywood replicate something they'd not witnessed? How could they know about boiled-up, expanding brain matter that punched its way out of eyes, ears, and noses? Some of those guy's heads literally exploded from the immense pressure of a rapidly expanding organ. The average Joe will never see it. Never know of it. It was better that way.

Bosco sighed openly and then said, "You're right, Canter. Let's forget all that stuff and put it away for good. But tell me something. Where in the heck is your package?"

"That's a story for another day. But I'll give you the short. Angel is at the medical clinic. What a stuff-up I've made of it so far."

How could I explain all the things that led to Angel being taken into medical care? It *was* a stuff-up. The dad thing again. Why didn't I have it in me to be a father? It should've never happened.

I should've never left that awful so-called rocket fuel within the reach of a minor. It made me think about those labels printed on things that were bad for kids. 'Keep out of reach of children.' But there was no label on that jar. There wasn't even a childproof cap, for god's sake.

"Just tell me she's safe and I'll leave it," Bosco said, drilling into my thoughts.

"She's safe . . . I stuffed up. That's all I'm saying."

The way he eyed me and gave me *the look* told me he wasn't impressed. But to his credit, he didn't say another word.

Bosco stopped the SUV south of William Creek. I grabbed a jean leg, tossed my prosthetic limb to the side, and got out. In my hands was the briefcase and the local guy's 303. Walking back to William Creek, there would be at least three kilometres of thinking to do.

"You know they're gonna ask about the pilot," I said, peering back through an open window.

"You'll think of something. I've already given you the clues. I'll make it easy for you, Canter. Whatever you report back to Shilo, I'll back it up."

Then he was gone.

I was left there in the silence. I forced my steps forward and broke into a light jog, all the while thinking about Angel. I hoped the trust I'd put in Doc Bryant wasn't betrayed.

CHAPTER EIGHT

Matchbook

AT LAST, WE FOUND OURSELVES where we should've ended up in the first damn place. No more dead ends. No more wrong turns. No more getting into a trajectory away from the target. I stood agape at the colossal concrete structure housing the centrifuges we were about to destroy.

I wondered how we'd manage it. A few slabs of plastic explosive. A handful of detonators. That's it. How in the heck could a half-dozen blocks of C4 even scratch it? Even make a dent in it? There were thousands of the cylindrical uranium-enriching devices, as far as my eyes could reach. Trailing off into the distance, they didn't seem to end.

"Well, Canter," Bosco said. "We'll go looking for a weak spot. Everything's got one."

"Yeah. And where do you suppose we start?"

"Easy, mate," Scotty-Blue said. "At the beginning."

"You fucking idiot, Blue," Franco put in. "This isn't the time for clichés."

"Fan out," I said. "Look for anything that will make for a chain reaction."

Scotty-Blue said words that stopped everyone. "You don't wanna say those words chain reaction 'round 'ere, mate. Bloody unlucky in a place where they make nukes, don't ya reckon?"

I nodded. Bad choice by me. "Move out," I ordered. "Stay on coms."

Moving forward with my M-4 trained down range, I kept walking in a straight line. Franco and Scotty-Blue ducked left. Bosco and Granger ducked right. Smic went off in another direction altogether. As I traced the edges of the centrifuges, I was already getting a picture of the weak spot Bosco suggested.

"Bosco. You seeing what I'm seeing?"

"That depends, Canter. I'm not psychic. I don't have a crystal ball either."

"Smart-arse. Take a look. The centrifuges are arranged into banks."

"Yeah, I noticed. The banks are channelled into what looks like a main supply conduit?"

"Correct," I said. "I'll follow an MSC to see where it leads. Oscar Mike."

"Roger that."

I counted them just for good measure. Sixty centrifuges connected to a bank. Each bank on an MSC. I followed the nearest MSC to what appeared to be a tiny control room. A shack, small enough to house as least one individual. No one in sight, which was odd. Moving silently to the door I peeked inside. A column of switches in there.

It was no good. Planting explosives on a single control room would only dispatch roughly five hundred banks. I did the math. Our available C4 would never cover it. There had to be another option.

"Canter. Smic."

"What have you got?" I responded.

"Green gooey shit all over the floor. Rad counter off the bell."

"Step away for Christ's sake!"

"It's too late, mate. I'm afraid I've taken a big punch."

"Fa shit sake, Smic!"

"Sorry, Canter. But I think I've found that weak spot. The trouble is, you'll all get lit up and glowing by the time you get down here. I recommend yous all stay back and let me handle it. I have an idea that just might work. Copy?"

"Make it quick," I said. "And Smic. Maximum dial, okay? Rendezvous at checkpoint kilo."

"Roger that."

"Everyone but Smic. Fall back to checkpoint kilo."

Maximum dial was only two hours. Two hours to get far enough away. I hoped it was enough. Maybe it wasn't. We'd be dead either way. Each way I looked at it, the same result. A quick death, or a slow one. We weren't coming out of it alive and that's all there was to it. But then, from somewhere outside, the crackle of AKs opened up.

* * *

"Hardball! Come in, Hardball! This is Matchbook! Over!"

Surrounded. Boxed in. They were all over us, at every hour of the clock. It didn't matter which way we faced. We somehow found a wadi and tracked the edges, finding cover. Granger pushed on in front. A step too far. The earth opened up as an IED was triggered. Granger's body was left shattered into a horror I was not able to describe.

We hunkered down in the IED crater with AK fire zipping past. I screamed into the mic again. "Hardball! Come in, Hardball! This is Matchbook! We are a ground call sign, and in the shit! How copy! Over!"

Silence from the radio. I tore it off my back and noticed a hole big enough for my fist. The radio was as useless as a rubber beak on a magpie. I threw it down hard.

"Bosco!" I screamed. "TACTBE!"

Bosco immediately grabbed the tactical beacon from his chest pack and tossed it, at the same time firing from his hip.

The TACTBE in my grip, I brought the mic up to my face. "Turbo! Turbo! Turbo! This is Matchbook! We are a ground call sign! Over!"

A ping-zip over my right shoulder. I shot a stare back at Bosco and shook my head. A sharp shot ricocheted across the top of his kevlar helmet. I caught his smile, and he was back to what had to be done. I yelled again into the TACTBE. "Turbo! Turbo! Turbo! This is Matchbook! We are a ground call sign…In shit-state-fubar! Over!"

Within seconds, a voice crackled over the speaker, "Matchbook. AWACS . . . Reading you two by three . . . Send . . . Over."

"AWACS. This is Matchbook . . . Request immediate air support. Grid to follow. Flash . . . Lima. Golf. Oscar. Danger close. Wait! Out!"

"Roger Matchbook. Flash . . . Lima. Golf. Oscar. Danger close. Grid to follow. Wait. Out."

Bosco scooted over to my side, slapping a hand on my back then pointing his gloved hand. "Get the incendiary LGO on that ridge. Eleven o'clock, Canter. Clear it. Then let's get the hell out." He was gone. Back to six.

I immediately read off the grid under night scope. "AWACS. Matchbook. Grid. Over."

"Matchbook. AWACS. Send. Over."

"AWACS. Ten-digit grid . . . November. Echo. Six. Seven. Three. One. Two. Zero. Niner. Four. One. Five. Tangos in the open. Flash. Lima. Golf. Oscar. Danger close. How copy. Over!"

"Solid, Matchbook. Flash . . . Lima. Golf. Oscar. Five mikes. Out."

My heart dropped. Five minutes. We were dead in three. The crackle of AKs from the top of the ridge. A zip cracked past the side of my face. Another shrill of a projectile past my shoulder. That was close. Too close. Death was a moment away. Pinned down, running out of ammo. I was at eleven. Bosco at six. Franco at three. Scotty-Blue at nine.

We closed ranks on the two KIAs at our feet. Smic and Granger. Granger bled out. Nothing we could do. Smic was there, minus the top of his head. Bosco peppered shots to his front and flank. The same as Franco. The same as Scotty-Blue. Franco called out for another mag, to which there were none.

"Canter!" Bosco screamed over his shoulder. "Where is that Flash LGO!"

"Two mikes," I screamed back.

Over the noise of battle, the tinkling sound of a bell. A goat bolted down into the wadi. Down into the IED crater. It pushed up to my side, looking for cover. Its slitted pupils were wide. Its mouth hung open. It was silent and shivering. The look of shock in its eyes.

"I'm out!" Franco screamed.

On my last mag. Bosco at six, I knew he'd run out in a few. We could no longer afford rapid fire in bursts. Every shot fired would have to mean a kill. Then the sound. Angels on our shoulders.

"Incoming!" I screamed.

"Incoming!" screamed Franco and Scotty-Blue.

The ear-splitting scream of F-16 Fighting Falcons punched overhead. Fire support had arrived not a split second too soon, dropping their laser-guided incendiary ordnance exactly on the grid. The ridge at eleven. The night sky lit up with incredible explosions, raging with fire and flames. A hole had been punched through the line of fire. But down in the open wadi, down in the IED crater, we were still pinned at six, three, and nine.

"Bosco! Smoke flanks and let's get the fuck out!" I screamed at the same time as I saw Scotty-Blue picking up Granger's remains and doing his level best getting him across his shoulder. A full mag was under Granger's body. My eyes focussed. There were two. I kicked one across to Bosco. He picked it up and slapped it into his M-4 in a precision movement. I kicked the other to Franco.

"Smoke out!" Bosco screamed. His voice was drowned out by the noise of peppering automatic weapons in the distance, and the shrill of projectiles passing, cracking by.

"Leave the KIAs!" Bosco screamed. "We have to move now!"

Franco picked up Smic's body. "We don't leave 'em, mate. They don't get to be haji propaganda bullshit!"

"Fuck!" Bosco screamed, at the same time hurling a few more smokers.

I slung my M-4, picked up the horrified goat, and pulled it into my chest.

"Are you serious!" Franco called out.

"Hearts and minds, brother," I yelled. "Hearts and minds."

We moved out of the IED crater and tracked the edge of the wadi. Up over the ridge, we began to leapfrog in an echelon formation. The goat under my arm, I fired from the hip when it was my turn. Then, dead trigger. I thought it was a failure to eject, but no. There were no rounds left in my magazine.

Dropping my weapon, I grabbed my sidearm and opened up until Bosco, Franco, and Scotty-Blue made their way past. They settled and began firing shots. That's when I knew it was my turn to leapfrog. That's how it went for the next kilometre or so. Drop down. Turn and fire. Wait for them to pass. Then leapfrog again. All the while, the goat I had tucked under my arm had no argument. The shocked creature was still and silent, not so much as a bleat.

By the time we reached the same rammed earth huts we passed on the way in, the imminent danger was over. Every round we had at our disposal was spent. There was nothing left to answer a fight apart from the blade I kept in my chest pack. The handle was within easy reach and I was ready to do the job if it ever came down to it. We tabbed on, hoping to Christ haji wasn't around the next corner. The thought of getting into shit all over again wasn't far from my mind.

With the goat slung over my shoulder, we passed the familiar rammed earth huts and headed toward our designated extraction point, where I'd use the tactical beacon and call in. We'd get out pretty much quick smart.

A voice called from somewhere behind, and the goat all of a sudden wanted to get away. It was the herder, and his happiness at the sight of his goat coming home was everything I'd been working toward. The goat kicked and bleated. I let the thing go.

The herder beckoned us closer. I thought he just wanted to show his appreciation. Then there was a massive thump at my side. That's all there was.

* * *

I opened my eyes. A woman in desert fatigues was standing at my side. As my eyes focussed, I saw she was with someone else; they were talking in Arabic. The woman checked off things on equipment that clicked and beeped.

I felt stuff over my face. Tape. A mask. And something down my throat. I tried to speak but gagged. The woman appeared startled and looked down at me. She bent over and pulled something out. I saw it. A long plastic tube. I felt it rip up from my guts as she pulled it away.

I tried again with more words. "Water." All I could manage. It came out raspy and garbled. It probably didn't make sense, but somehow, I knew the woman understood what the word was. Even though I felt incredibly thirsty, she moved away without giving me any and my eyes closed again.

* * *

Someone shook me.

"I'm Teresa," the voice said. "Hello, Nathan. Wake up. Good boy. Wake up."

My eyes opened. The woman I'd seen before.

"Nathan. I'm Teresa. Your doctor."

The pain in my left foot was intense. I moved my toes and the pain went away for a second or two. Then the pain came back more intensely than ever. I moved my toes again and relaxed as I flexed them forward and back. Forward and back. The fiery pain left again, but then erupted in my left knee. Penetrating. Forceful. Fierce. A fire under my body. I placed my hand down on my knee to give it a rub.

A horrible realisation struck me: There was no knee there. Not even the toes I flexed a moment ago. Everything gone. A stump… A stump wrapped up in bandages. And a firestorm of pain racing up my back and through my head.

I felt a cooling sensation rip up my arm. Then into my shoulder. The pain left. I closed my eyes.

CHAPTER NINE

Marree

THE GOAT THING WAS ALWAYS the subject of banter. Catching up with Bosco again, I thought he might let it be. As I walked the dusty road back to William Creek with the local guy's 303 tucked under my arm and the briefcase pulled to my chest in the same way I'd taken that goat away from danger, I caught myself smiling briefly with the memory. Smiling, but with a certain amount of embarrassment, I supposed.

Getting my head together, I thought about what was next: To continue the journey south to Melbourne. I thought about what had recently transpired and it suddenly occurred to me. The weapon I had tucked at the small of my back was the one used on Lilly, the lady with no front teeth. The G-man's murder weapon. I reached around and pulled it out. I scanned it and thought about tossing it. The moment I thought it, a Police Landcruiser belted over the rise toward me with blue lights flashing and siren blaring. My next urge was to toss the handgun as far away as I could get it. Too late. I couldn't do it without being noticed. I thrust it back behind my back, hoping they'd drive on past.

The Police Landcruiser belted past me. Rising dust got up my nose, causing an inbound sneeze attack. But my sense of relief was short-lived. I spun on my heel to see the taillights of the Land-cruiser light up. I heard the rush of its tyres locking up in the gravel. I saw the silhouette of the vehicle in the late afternoon sun as it slowed and did a long U-turn. I heard the engine accelerate toward me, siren still blaring. Lights still flashing. Panic swept up my body and I stood rock still. The Landcruiser rushed to a halt, ten feet away from where I stood. I dropped the rifle. I dropped the briefcase and automatically put my hands in the air.

The door of the Landcruiser opened. "Get on the ground!" one cop yelled; gun drawn. The other bowled me over and pushed the side of my face into the dirt. I felt my hands being forced up my back. I heard the click and zip of handcuffs. I felt hands pat me down. Then one of the cops retrieved the handgun.

Fuck!

"Stop. Stop. Stop!" I said as loud as I could, under the immense pressure of someone with a knee between my shoulder blades. The words I said appeared not to be heard. No words were exchanged between the cops, even though I shouted STOP once more. "I can explain everything." The moment I said it, I realised any explanation needed to be far from the truth.

"Plenty of time for that, sunshine," one cop said while dropping the handgun in a plastic evidence bag, his pinkie finger delicately stuck up in the air. The situation was *bad*. If they dropped their eyes to the contents of the briefcase, Eagle Shield would become compromised. There could be no explanation. None at all.

In the back of the Police Landcruiser paddy wagon, being tossed about as it thundered south down the Oodnadatta Track, I thought about getting the ring off my finger. I needed to do something – anything – to activate the beacon. Water. I needed water. Water would do the trick. But what choices did I have? My hands were cuffed. At my back. I felt the smoothness of the ring on my finger and played with it a little. My mind twisted with the options. I could get the ring off. Easy. Then what?

I reached with my fingers and the ring came off in my hand. I sat sideways and tossed it onto the steel bed of the Landcruiser paddy wagon. It bounced with the bumps and the forward momentum. From there, I just had to get it wet. But how? Piss on it, my mind thought, then tossed out the idea. How could I manage it with cuffed hands? I manoeuvred over to the bouncing ring. I knelt down and the side of my face hit the cold steel floor. The ring bounced up and landed between my teeth. Immediately, the ring started to burn in my mouth. The beacon had activated.

I put up with the burning pain in my mouth for more than a couple of hours. The sun had long slunk under the horizon, and stars like jewels danced in the sky. My mind went back to Angel. I wondered where she was and hoped she was being cared for. Maybe Bosco was with her right now. I hoped that to be the case, seeing as he wasn't responding to the activated radio beacon. All I could do was wait and hope for any signs of change. Looking through the window of the Landcruiser paddy wagon, I saw the streetlights in the distance and I knew it had to be Marree.

* * *

The two cops reached in and grabbed me by the upper arms. I was desperately waiting for an opportunity to spit out the ring from the back of my mouth. That opportunity came. A few moments later, I was manhandled away. They chucked me into a small cubicle behind paint-peeled metal bars with more than enough graffiti etched into cold, grey walls. I kept thinking that maybe Bosco would be around somewhere. Maggie's words sprang to mind. '*He'll be in the shadows, always listening, but never far away.*'

Maybe Bosco was dragging this out intentionally. His sense of humour was something I struggled with most of the time. It wouldn't have surprised me if his stalling was meant to be funny. It wasn't funny, not even if it was supposed to be sarcastic. But as the hours dragged on, no sign of Bosco. No sign of anything. I called out down a lonely and empty corridor a couple of times. My words went ignored.

With the first signs of the sun's rays peeking through the miniscule window just above my head, at last a cop, who I'd not previously met, appeared at the cubicle with a set of jingling keys. He smiled down at me, at the same time twisting the key in the lock. "Toilet break, sunshine," he said dryly. As he reached through the bars and locked my hands around my back, I wondered how in the heck I'd manage it.

"You're gonna have to either take the cuffs off, or hold it for me," I said. As soon as I said it, he reached into his pocket and got out a set of blue latex gloves. I knew it was the latter. I rolled my eyes.

"The joys, huh? This job really sucks sometimes. Just make sure you aim it straight and we won't have any issues."

"Don't look at me. You're the one who gets to aim it."

After I emptied my bladder, the cop ushered me into an interview room and locked my cuffs around a metal loop on a plain old table that was etched with the same graffiti I'd seen everywhere else. The cop, without so much as an acknowledgment, closed the door and left. I sat there and ran my eyes over the place. No cameras I could see, but I knew they'd be there. No two-way mirror. Just a plain old table. A bin thrust in the corner, overflowing with empty paper cups. A couple of chairs.

I sat and wondered why nobody bothered to put fresh paint on the walls. Grey as a storm cloud. Plain as ever. A clock on the wall sat askew. It wasn't a happy place. Maybe it was that way for a reason.

Within a minute, the door opened. A fat guy came in, wearing a grey suit two sizes too small and a necktie that should've been kept solely for the Melbourne Cup races. Dragging out a chair that squealed across the dirty lino floor, he plopped himself down. The button on his blazer struggled to break free. I wanted to cover my face in case it did. He eyed me with a turned down brow and said, "I'm Detective Senior Sergeant Falconbridge. At a minimum, you'll be charged with being in possession of an unregistered firearm. It goes up from there. Talk, and let's get this thing sorted out."

"What about my phone call?"

He laughed. "This isn't the movies, sunshine. Start talking and we can see about where this will go. One: Make me happy, and I'll let you have that phone call. Two: Don't make me happy, and it means going back to one."

"Where's my stuff," I said.

"I assume you're talking about the briefcase?"

"Yeah. Where is it? Give it back," I said. My gut clenched at the thought that they'd already seen what was in it. That being what it was, it spelled out nothing but bad.

"That's where things get a bit twisty," he said. "Imagine my surprise at what we found in there. Lots of things. Weird things. But if it were all above board, all those documents should've been accompanied with a 'law enforcement on hold' order issued by the Federal Police and the High Court of Australia, which there wasn't. Your explanation?"

I said nothing.

"So, you're some kind of flashy government fella. You'd expect a guy like you would be issued with the order. But make no mistake. It's not a licence to kill. You're either kosher or a nutter. I've seen many things in my time. I've heard and seen everything. Maybe start by telling me what I should believe. I reckon that's a pretty good place to start. Don't you think?"

"Easy. I'm kosher. And the order is pending through the High Court. Now, get me out of these cuffs so I can go about my business."

The detective looked down and laughed as though his mind was already made up and that I was the nutter. Why was I not surprised? The man had on a red necktie with dancing, hip-thrusting Elvis's. If I was the nutter he claimed, it forced me to believe I was in the company of an idiot.

"The grazier at William Creek gave us his statement," he went on. "From that, we have reason to believe you weren't involved in the murder of one, Lilly McPherson. From the information we received from a second witness, one Doctor William Bryant, it appears your alibi is rock solid. However, it still doesn't explain how the alleged murder weapon was found in your possession. My gut tells me ballistics will match the handgun to the bullet found at the crime scene. Should that happen, and by all assumptions it will, you'll have a whole lot of explaining to do. I suggest you cut the crap and get your head in it. As I keep saying, start talking. I'm all ears."

It occurred to me that the police had not travelled the road out to Lake Eyre. Had they been out there, the conversation would've turned out differently. Or perhaps they had. I knew any further words would dig me in deeper.

Bosco . . .

Where in the fuck are you? You son of a bitch. This isn't funny any longer . . .

"I need a phone call to my lawyer," I said.

The detective laughed the same as before. He laughed so hard his big round belly shook. I looked down and saw the stressed button on his blazer. That thing was going to shoot off, I was sure of it. I wanted to cover my face.

"Holy crap, sunshine. Did you think that one will work?"

"I know my rights. One is a phone call. Are you going to deny it after you've already given me my rights?"

"Actually, no. We haven't done that step. Where did you get that idea?"

"Well, you'd better let me have them. Because anything I've said to this point can't be used."

"What exactly did you say? I've heard nothing."

Hmm . . . playing for time . . .

"Am I not under arrest?"

"Detained for questioning."

"Then take the damn handcuffs off!" I shouted.

"Okay . . . okay . . . Easy, sunshine." The detective reached into his pocket and got something out that looked like a steel pin; with it he began unlocking my handcuffs. When my hands were free, I sat back and folded my arms, hoping my body language would tell him I was in no mood for bullshit. "Where's my briefcase? You have no right taking it!"

His eyes went to slits. Poker face, maybe. Now was the time for formalities if he was going to do it. Either return the briefcase, or I'd have a phone call. After a heavy sigh, he left his chair, closing the door quietly behind him. My mind went to Bosco. Now's the time.

I shit you not, Bosco . . .

The detective returned. No briefcase in his hand. I looked away, knowing how this was going to play out. A second fat, uni-formed cop with three stripes on the shoulder waddled in behind him, an A4-sized laminated yellow card in his grip. We were now going formal, I realised. But by the end, I'd get to make at least one phone call. The thing was, how in the heck could I explain all this to Shilo?

The detective sat down. The constable behind him read off a couple of words from the laminated card. A knock at the door. It opened with the face of yet another cop staring in. "Pardon Boss. Feds are here."

I knew in my heart the exit was near. The two immediately disappeared from the interview room and I was again by myself. I kept my eyes on the clock as the minutes ticked by slowly. It wasn't long before three uniformed Federal Police officers en-tered, appearing dazed from an emergency flight I assumed was out of Canberra. They were followed by another extremely young-looking guy wearing a black suit. Eyeing him from where I sat, I was hard-pressed to believe he was older than eighteen. Maybe he just looked that way. A baby face. He stuck his hand out for a shake.

"Nathan Masters?"

"Yeah. I'm him."

"I'm Andrew Mack. I'll be escorting you back to William Creek."

CHAPTER TEN

The Young Gun

A SIGH OF RELIEF LEFT ME THE MOMENT the RAAF Challenger 604 lifted gracefully off a lone Marree runway. I gazed out the window, thinking about how things got so bad and if there was a way I could ever get back on track. I wondered if Angel had fully recovered from the predicament I caused, and I imagined her smiling face after we reunited.

After getting it all together, there'd be the simple matter of the continued trip south. But would it be simple? As I gazed at the diagonal landscape and horizon out the window, I wondered if it would go smoothly from this point. I needed it to be so. Something in my gut told me it wouldn't. I readied myself for any possibility.

Sitting opposite me in his luxury leather seat – with the three federal police officers just out of earshot – the young ASIO officer sat staring out of the aircraft window. It was as though he was away in his own internal world. Studying his expression told me he'd much rather be elsewhere, as though to him, the escort back to William Creek was a pain in the arse. Maybe it was. I cast a critical eye across him. His face looked familiar. A younger version of someone else I knew in the dark recesses of my mind. I remembered his name. Andrew Mack. It can't be true, I thought. It didn't stop me from enquiring.

"You're a little young to be in the game," I said, getting him back from his contemplations. He smiled and nodded, locking eye contact. "I get that a lot. I *am* qualified. Just in case you were wondering."

"I make no judgments," I said. "So long as the man can do his job. The rest is bullshit."

Saying those words appeared to brighten him up. He smiled with genuine warmth. "I know what you're thinking," he said. "I'm nineteen. ASIO pulled me in at eighteen."

"ASIO player at nineteen, huh? Most your age are still at university…"

"I graduated from university at fourteen," he cut in, his expression suddenly hard. Why was he was getting all defensive? Maybe he'd had this conversation a thousand times. Okay. A bit touchy. Maybe I'd try something a little different.

"A prodigy?" I'd never met one. For some reason, Doogie Howser from the seventies television show came to mind.

"I don't do the pigeonhole thing," the young Andrew said. "I never wanted to be in the game. I always thought quantum physics and microbiology was my calling. Step-mother changed all that."

"Your step-mother?"

He smiled wryly. "Gimme a break, Nathan Masters. As if you don't know."

In truth, I didn't know at first. I made the connection only a minute later. Maggie's husband, Theo. Theo, the Alice Springs police officer who'd been taken down . . .

And then it went thundering through my mind as I made the link.

Theo was killed in the same way as Lilly McPherson. Gangland style. A shotgun blast to the chest. A small calibre projectile to the head. His murder was never resolved. Was his assailant the same man who'd killed the lady with no front teeth? Could there be a connection? The more I thought it over, the more the two incidents resembled each other.

No way could Lilly's murder be a copycat. Theo's demise was never put out publicly. And now, in both instances, Angel was the target. In Theo's case, his murder was the result of something he had in his possession. A bullet fragment. The bullet fired at Angel that almost took her life. It was Theo who found the fragment. It would've led to an investigation into finding Angel's attacker. It didn't get that far. Theo was killed, and the bullet fragment stolen from him. It was only after that event; Eagle Shield came into being.

Even more than before, I realised Angel *was* in danger. Until such a time as she got to the safe house in Melbourne, she would always have watchers on her tail. Her life would always be threatened. I should've never left her alone.

Sitting there, I ran my hand over the textured leather of the briefcase in my lap. Andrew was still eyeing me as though on the defensive. It was as though he knew my next words. It was as though he was almost daring me to speak them. So I spoke what was on my mind. "I'm assuming you know all about Eagle Shield?"

"I know everything, Nathan. I knew before you."

There it was. His prodigy nature beginning to show. How could he know about everything before me? Matchbook was in play while he was most likely in primary school. But going by his earlier statement, he'd have already left primary school and gone on at a much younger age. Did he even *go* through primary education?

"How is it you know everything?" I asked, knowing his answer would somehow surprise. But his next words went far beyond surprise; they revealed something completely unexpected.

"Matchbook, and now Eagle Shield, were first considered out of the collaboration between Shilo and me."

"You started this?" I felt my eyes bulge almost agog. I tried hard to keep my astonishment in check. I thought everything we started, even from years ago, was out of the thinking minds of the closed community of intelligence officials locked up somewhere in Canberra. I couldn't – no matter how hard I tried – imagine such a young soul as the top brain behind what we went through.

"Eagle Shield was . . . *is* always about Angel's safety. We need her to be safe. We need her with us," Andrew went on.

"You need her with you? What do you mean?" This was something Maggie never explained. Or perhaps she did. Maybe I missed it. Did I read about this in the mission brief? That bloody stuff in the jar. How I regretted it. Regrets. I hated them.

"When she's older," Andrew said matter-of-factly.

Then it dawned. Maggie *did* explain it. The wish for Angel to join ASIS as an adult. Now Andrew was making this point as urgently as Maggie. It made me think about the disk and what it contained. All over again. "You know about the disk?" I asked Andrew.

He nodded vigorously. "Yes, I know what's on it."

By now, I was no longer surprised. I checked my attitude at the door. Something I should've done in the first place. The young Andrew was gaining my respect. I found myself leaning in and believing the words coming from someone so young. "Do we have a laptop computer?"

"There's no need," he said. "I can explain it all. Only God himself knows the shit fight we're in. Thanks to the Guardianship."

"Guardianship of Milestone?" Here we go again. It appeared I'd never escape.

"Yeah." He sighed loudly. "That . . . and the Amber project."

"Maggie has given me some info on Amber. The intel is on the disk, which I haven't yet had a chance to scan. I know about the Milestone theory. I know about the enriched plutonium and assumed Matchbook shut it down. That was the plan. It's come to light that not all the centrifuges were destroyed. And now Milestone is a clear and present danger?"

"Not so much as an immediate threat. Intel suggest things will ramp up around 2016. Your Eagle Shield mission with Angel will become part of Milestone's undoing."

"Part?" Part. I thought I had the whole. I must've missed something. Maybe I was out of the loop for some reason. Another hate. Intelligence can be such a dog.

"There are other objectives that go on behind the scenes. Away from Eagle Shield. None you need to concern yourself with. Not yet, anyway. After Eagle Shield has been accomplished, all the pieces will be put together and we'll stop Milestone."

"Let me guess. By destroying the Amber project? Without Amber, there can be no Milestone. And Angel will lead the way to Amber?" That was the assumption I had in my head. Now, let's see how close I was.

Andrew nodded in agreement. "That's why Angel needs to get in the program. You don't realise the job you have, Nathan. But I think you're starting to get a picture."

Hmm . . . so everyone tells me . . .

"My guess? Angel won't go willingly," Andrew said. "She has a strong personality and a mind of her own. I think she'll be wanting to end up somewhere else. You'll need to change that. I suggest starting early. Give her some inspiration and desire. I don't know what you'll do. Maybe spark her interest by watching spy movies and reading books."

I thought about it. Bugger thinking about it. I bloody well came out and asked it.

"Just *what* makes Angel so special? She's a ten-year-old kid. She doesn't know anything. Why her? Why is she such a target? Why does she need to get with ASIS?"

Andrew paused before answering. When he *did* answer, it was without expression and was a statement that didn't seem to have any sign of a struggle. "Angel is part human. And part Oudarretian. That's the reason she's in danger. And that's the reason she needs all this protection."

Andrew reached into his pocket for a biro. He got a notepad from the side pocket of his seat. He scribbled something down. He held up the notepad with the word 'Oudarretian' written and double underlined.

I'd not heard the word Oudarretian before. After Andrew said it, I imagined it was some undiscovered race on Earth. A lost civilisation, I supposed. But Andrew had said the word human. As I put it together, I realised he was making a comparison. If it was a lost civilisation, would they not be referred to as human as well? Now, there was a division. An us and them. My mind twisted. He was speaking of these Oudarretians as otherworldly beings.

Andrew went on and confirmed it. "Not from this world," he said. "But they're human in appearance. It's hard to tell the difference. You must know what to look for to tell them apart. They all have one thing in common. They're black."

He passed the notepad over. I held it briefly in my hand before he leaned forward and snatched it away. Then, he scribbled something else down. "This is the interesting bit," he said before giving the notepad back. I looked down at the scribble. The word Oudarretian was written backward with the first few letters omitted. 'Terraduo.'

My eyes focussed. I couldn't believe what I was seeing. Out of what was written down, I saw 'Terra-Duo.' Then I realised the Latin translation. 'Earth-Two.'

"Are you bloody kidding me?"

"Not a bit," Andrew said, smiling. "Oudarret is their home planet. Earth Two. Black people from a world similar to ours. Ten light years away, to be exact. Their host star, or sun, is much closer to the surface of Oudarret in comparison to our sun to our Earth. They've evolved with a protective enzyme that they host in their skin. The Oudarretian black colour results from this. The enzyme absorbs white light. White light isn't reflected. This enzyme also protects them from cosmic radiation and therefore melanoma."

It erupted in my mind like a strobe light. The black person in Angel's dream. And the black person I'd seen on that first day I'd enlisted into the army. The black guy with the American uniform.

Tall as tall. I took a moment and pondered what Andrew had told me. Pieces were finally coming together.

"These Oudarretians are part of the Milestone theory?" I asked.

"One: It's no longer a theory. Two: Yes, they are. They instigated everything. They've been among the human race for decades. Perhaps centuries, who'd know? You have to wonder about the technologies humans have to this day, Nathan. On the disk, you'll find out what those technologies are. One is nuclear. There'd be no nuclear weapons if it wasn't for the Oudarretians."

"They gave us the technology to quite possibly destroy ourselves?" How shocked was I to hear this? I always thought it started with Einstein. Then Otto Hahn. Then Oppenheimer. Then Edward Teller. The list goes on. They weren't black. They weren't tall. I found it hard to believe these men were otherworldly beings. I must've missed something – but what?

Andrew punched through my thoughts with his answer. "They gave us that technology. Absolutely. The Oudarretians aided our best-known scientists in the race for weapons of mass destruction."

There it was. The bit I missed. It still didn't seem real. Andrew went on. "That's what Milestone is about. They'll destroy us all. Part of their plan."

". . . Why?" I had more words. They wouldn't come. It was as though they were lodged under the lump at the base of my throat.

Andrew held his breath briefly as though somewhere in his mind he was at odds with admitting the reasons why. As I sat back in my plush leather seat, I began to understand humanity's rise in technology and a marked acceleration in knowledge. Things were beginning to make sense in a way I never previously imagined.

Andrew finally answered why. "We've got our hands on a document that points the Oudarretian's motivation toward world oil reserves and the balance of power it brings. You have that intelligence with you. But there's also a glimpse of intelligence to suggest their need for helium-3. They want it. They need it to survive."

"Helium-3? I know about helium-3, Andrew. I also know helium-3 is dangerous in the wrong hands. What on earth would they be wanting the stuff for?" Helium-3 said nothing but huge explosion. I quickly thought back to the Oudarretian motive Andrew addressed. Where was the connection? What was I not seeing?

"What would they be wanting it for? That's easy to answer," Andrew went on. "Earth humans metabolise sugar and complex carbohydrate for energy. The Oudarretians metabolise helium-3 in the same way. Without it, they can't survive."

The explanation was simple and straightforward. But also, helium-3 on Earth was rare. On Earth, it could only be harvested out of radioactive decay. Knowing there was little if any radioactive decay on Earth, I wondered how the Oudarretians were getting it? And from where?

I asked Andrew what I was thinking.

"That's unknown," he said. "But it's obvious the Oudarretians are getting what they need to survive. We've been able to ascertain the enzyme in their skin is also dependant on helium-3. Otherwise the enzyme will degrade over years. They'll lose the protection it gives them. They'll also become vulnerable and lose their connection to time and space. Then, it'll be a slow death for every one of them."

"But what of the quantities?" I asked. "Surely, there'd not be enough found on Earth for their purposes. I mean, look at the amount of complex carbohydrates humans consume on average. That's a vast quantity, Andrew."

"It's all relative. In the plain old language, the amount of energy released in five tons of processed sugar is equal to a quarter of a teaspoon of helium-3. Not only that, relatively small amounts of helium-3 can be used to power cities for centuries and also be used for weapons far greater than anything imaginable. Then, and only then, bigger quantities are needed. They already know where those quantities exist. Make no mistake, Nathan. The Oudarretians have their sights set on getting it. Even as we sit here and talk about it."

"Where?"

"On the moon," Andrew said. "The Oudarretians see the human race as an infestation. An infestation to eradicate. They're evil fucks, every last one of them. The plan is to wipe humanity away using the technology they gave us during the mid-twentieth century."

"Nuclear war?" Holy shit. I remembered back to the conversation I once had with Scotty-Blue. The theory of M.A.D. This could be the one thing that threatened the balance of power, tipping it into the favour of a sole player. Scotty-Blue was right, even from all those years ago. How did I not see this? How did I not realise this even from the days of Matchbook?

. . . Iran is the culprit, and the one that got away . . .

Maggie's words. It all went spinning around. A cyclone. Spinning, making me feel lightheaded. The eye of the cyclone hit me. Something didn't add up. Surely if a nuclear war loomed and became reality, no life would survive. It just made things appear contradictory to what Andrew explained. "That doesn't make sense," I said. "If they are going down the road of nuclear annihilation, they'd be also wiping themselves out in the process."

"As I've already explained, the Oudarretians are not affected by radiation fallout. Unbelievable, isn't it?"

Now it made sense. It made *perfect* sense. The post apocalypse would never hinder them. Never distract them. They'd get on with doing what they came for. Without Earth humans, it would be easy. The moment I realised it, I came out and said it. "They're gonna kill us all so they can mine the moon?"

"It's a done deal if we can't stop it. We need Angel with us if there's ever gonna be a chance, Nathan. That's the short and long of it. And guess what? It's your job to make it so. You have the entire globe and humanity itself in the palm of your hand."

Was this supposed to make me feel important? This was making me feel extraordinarily small. The entire length and breadth of humanity sat with me. I wished I'd never heard it. My mind kept telling me, I'm no good for this. This was too big for me. I couldn't do this on my own. Whichever way I looked at it, it *was* going to be on my own.

Andrew busted through my horrible thoughts with one word. 'Guardianship.' I focussed on what he was telling me. "The Guardianship needs nullifying," he put in. "Without the Guardianship there's no Milestone. And the way to do that is through the destruction of the Amber Project."

Angel again. She'll lead the way to this so-called Amber Project. To destroy it. How, was the question. I tried to imagine the day she'd lead us there, but not knowing exactly what Amber physically was or what it would entail to nullify the threat. I failed trying to get my head around it. My mind went somewhere else.

I wanted to know about the Guardianship. Who were these guys? I knew Andrew was privy. I asked him.

Andrew sat back and smiled as though the subject was his own pet. "At the top, the Guardianship have retired political officials and former secret intelligence officers from a gathering of countries," he went on. "Down the bottom, a collection of thugs, as well as underworld and organised crime figures, who are rich enough to bankroll the Guardianship's activities."

Crime figures . . .

"Mafioso?"

"Bet your arse they're there," Andrew replied still with the grin. "Bonanno, Gambino, Genovese, to name a few. Lucchese, Colombo . . ."

"Jesus, Andrew! Are you shitting me!"

"Now you know what we're up against. The Guardianship gets around cloaked under the infrastructure of world intelligence organisations. They're so deep under, the legitimate world agencies don't know they're there. But with the help of the crime families who are financially involved with their activities, they have power far beyond our better understanding."

"But the Guardianship is dead with the rest of us, Andrew. They're human. They don't have the Oudarretian's enzyme thing."

"Glad you said it. That brings us back to the Amber project. We think it's the Guardianship exit strategy. The exit strategy for the so-called 'ticket holders'. If we don't destroy the Amber project, everything is lost."

"Tell me what we know about Amber?"

"Little is known. The intelligence we've intercepted hasn't given up much other than to tell us Amber is solely conducted within Australian shores. Amber is out there, somewhere in the desert. Where, we don't know. We've got a handful of years to find out everything. Why? Because of the time needed for the Guardianship to perfect their exit strategy. That says genome engineering to me. And that brings me to Angel and why she's so important. Angel is the result of an early experiment. Perhaps an early attempt at procuring an exit strategy. Perhaps Angel didn't turn out as expected. And that's why the Guardianship has a clear directive to capture or to kill her outright."

Stunned, I sat back. I placed a hand to my face, not believing. This was pure and unconceivable madness. Andrew went on, looking down as though he, himself, was at the edge of his better understanding. "The Guardianship had Franco's help in this." Then Andrew looked away. Probably out of disappointment and disgust, I assumed. But his next words confirmed it was disgust. "Franco was behind Alisha's abduction. Alisha was artificially inseminated against her will. Everything moral about this scenario goes out the door backward."

I put my hand up to my forehead and tried to hide from Andrew's words. I said nothing. I couldn't. I almost felt sick. Now I was fully aware why Franco needed the disk so desperately. Franco turned and crossed the line. However, I didn't know the circumstances of what led to his temptation. My guess, Franco knew what was in the future. He wanted a guarantee to be included in the Guardianship exit strategy. The same as the crime families. The same as those caught up in the temptation to get away, who were willing to sell their soul.

How dark was the man, Franco? How cold and calculating? Certainly, he was not the Franco I once knew. Now, all the intelligence Andrew brought to light lay digitally etched onto a magnetic plate no bigger than the palm of my hand. Someone had mysteriously called end game and downloaded everything. Who? I wondered. Who wanted to blow the whistle? Who wanted to leak the data? In the end, lives had been lost trying to recover the disk in an attempt to stop the leak.

The hard nature hit home, clear and direct. I now had a job on my hands. To Angel, I was both guardian and protector. Now and forever. Being away from her, I realised she was now vulnerable to any attack. If I could've increased the speed to get back to William Creek any faster, I would've made it possible. The urgency to get there couldn't have been more crucial. More vital. I found myself urging the momentum forward. Willing it onward. I leaned forward in my seat, trying to speed up the fabric of time.

"She's in danger right now!" I said loud enough to grab Andrew's immediate attention.

He shot me a hard look. "We can't get there any quicker. Let's hope all is okay when we arrive. Your road trip is done, Nathan. We'll be flying you and Angel down to the safe house in Melbourne."

CHAPTER ELEVEN

The Seven

I PUSHED MY FACE UP TO THE aircraft window the moment the RAAF Challenger 604 came to rest. The tarmac was empty of souls. I could see the tin shack with the paint-peeled red cross. Beyond that, the main dusty track. The hotel was sitting lonely in the distance with no patrons out on the veranda. My Land Rover was parked where I'd last left it, still standing alone on the dusty car park.

A flock of birds were perched on the roof, seemingly basking in the sun. Then horror hit me at the sight of Bosco's SUV parked next to mine. That couldn't be good. Everything I'd dreaded had become real. Looking further out from the window, Bosco was running toward the aircraft, running at top effort, waving his hands wildly in the air.

I shot a glare at Andrew. He locked eye contact and echoed my concern. I couldn't have said any words to take the truth away. Angel was gone, my mind said. Andrew got up from his seat and went for the exit; at that exact moment, I pushed up with my one good leg. I made urgently for the aircraft door, which swung down and became a set of stairs. At the foot of the stairs, Bosco was already there. Red faced. Ranting in his panic. "She's not here!" he shrieked.

Stunned, I managed some shouted words while stumbling down the stairs. "Have you got word back to Shilo?"

"I have," Bosco shouted at the edge of his breath.

"What did she say, Bosco!"

"She didn't. She hung up on me!"

Panic. I didn't know it could feel so bad. Out of all the times panic came to visit, I shunned it away. I pushed through it. I used the energy, turning it into something positive. But this time...This time it was as though panic was an ugly black dog biting at my calf muscle. It had sunk its teeth right in. I could not shake it away.

I turned to Andrew who was at the top of the aircraft stairs and appeared to be frozen in his own shock. "Get me the fucking satellite phone!" I screamed at him. He spun and disappeared into the aircraft, not a word said.

Bosco and I walked straight lines on the tarmac, back and forth, heads down, waiting for Andrew. When Andrew arrived after bouncing down the steps, I took the phone from Andrew's shaky, trembling hands. I tried to dial. My hands shook probably worse than Andrew's. My fingers quivered back and forth, not able to dial anything. Bosco snatched the phone from my grip. His fingers went to work, then passed the phone back to me. Placing the cumbersome phone to my ears, it toned twice and then answered.

"Hello. Do you have your laundry pickup number?"

"Just connect me to Shilo!" I screamed into the handset.

"One moment please, sir . . ."

Swear words and profanities that I couldn't verbalise swept around my brain. I thought I'd heard my inner voice speak vulgarly before. Now, I winced at the words I was thinking. Four letter words. Multiple four-letter words.

"Canter!" Maggie yelled from the other end of the line. "Sloppy, Canter! Sloppy, sloppy . . . Bloody sloppy!"

"Shilo . . . I'm . . ." Holy crap! I was lost for words. I thought I had them. They were gone!

"Are the federal police still with you!" Maggie shouted.

"Yes . . . I . . ."

"Pass the damn phone to them, will you please?"

I passed the phone to the higher-ranking federal cop. He took it and didn't speak. He appeared only to listen to Maggie's words, which I could just make out. She was screaming! Her penetrating voice erupted from the tiny speaker and I was at least five feet away. I saw the federal cop's expression harden. After a moment, he handed the phone back to me. I placed the phone to my ear, at the same time watching him sprint away with two others at his heel.

"Maggie . . ."

"Canter! Its bloody *Shilo* for god's sake!"

Good Christ! I was digging in deeper. How cold was this ground that swallowed me?

"I . . . I'm . . ."

"I suggest you get your backsides back here! All of you! FORTHWITH! Do you hear me!"

Click.

She was gone.

"Jesus," Bosco said in a low tone. "I reckon she's pissed."

"No shit, Bosco!" I gritted my teeth and said nothing further beyond a low growl. I stomped past Bosco; my hands curled into fists. I wanted to belt something. Anything!

"Give me something to hit!" I yelled.

Bosco grabbed Andrew by the shoulders. "Here! This one! Hit him!"

It would've been funny if it hadn't had been so serious. I even wound one up and aimed it squarely at Andrew. Andrew shrunk back. He didn't know what to do. Nor did I. I got myself together. Only just.

I moved past Andrew, who was still standing as though stunned, his complexion almost matching his auburn hair. I turned to get in the aircraft. At the top of the stairs, I looked toward the hotel. My attention turned to the birds sitting on the roof of my Land Rover. "Birds," I said out loud. "Out of everything, I now have a job cleaning my canvas roof!"

"The weirdest thing," Bosco said, staring up from the foot of the stairs. "They're eagles. They've been sitting there for hours. You'd think they'd be off doing things eagles do. But not them. I ain't never seen seven in a pack before. I thought eagles only got around in twos."

"You sure they're eagles? From where I stand, one is white. There's no eagle that's all white."

"I already told ya it's weird. You think maybe they're trying to tell us something?"

I thought going over and pushing them into flight was an option. At least I wouldn't have to spend an entire day scraping bird business off the canvas roof. But then, something else occurred to me. "Maybe you're not that far from the truth, Bosco."

I walked back down the few stairs, past Bosco, at the same time the aircraft engines began to spool. Bosco shouted something. I tried not to notice as I walked away. Bosco shouted again at my rear, "You're not serious, Canter? Hey...Big hoss? Remember Shilo? Oh, shoot! Canter! Get back here!"

I ignored him. I ignored the sounds of the engines. As I got closer to my parked Land Rover, I began to realise how big those eagles were. The pure white eagle had something in its beak.

Albino?

I pushed the silly thought away.

Walking a bit closer, I realised what that thing was. A bullet. The bullet caught the light of the sun and glinted. Another eagle had something else. My curiosity wanted to know.

A metre away, the seven eagles towered above where I stood. Huge and ominous. Staring with heads cocked sideways. Not flinching. Not moving. Rock steady and watching me, as though beckoning. The albino eagle with the bullet clasped in its beak hopped forward on a set of giant talons. They were huge, much larger than I'd expected from the distance. I'd never seen birds so big.

Reaching up, its massive head tipped forward and it dropped the bullet into the palm of my hand. I studied it. Clean. Undamaged, but with the usual markings suggesting the make of rifle it came from. Another eagle hopped forward, dropping something else. A lock of hair. Not Angel's hair. Hair the colour of ginger.

Its talons were encrusted in dried blood. Lots of blood. Lots of ribbons of flesh still clung to its spurs as though the eagle had made a clean kill. As soon as the lock of hair was delivered, the seven eagles took flight. I felt massive bursts of air pressure as they pushed away with their enormous wingspans.

It was a moment that couldn't be ignored. With the clues the eagles had given, I knew there'd be more. I turned and hop-sprinted back to the aircraft with the fresh evidence thrust deep in my pocket.

Reaching the foot of the aircraft stairs, I waved a hand to Bosco who was in his seat. He eyed me from the window with an expression of disbelief, and then got up. A moment later, the engines spooled down and Bosco came prancing down the stairs.

"C'mon, Canter. We're wasting time," he said, as though out of patience.

"There's something around here, Bosco. We can't leave without investigating."

"I saw you push those eagles away. Good! Now, let's go."

"I can't leave just yet. Don't ask me how I know. I just know." I took the bullet from my pocket and showed him. He took it from my hand and studied it. "Nine-millimetre. The markings look like Glock. You're thinking Glock?"

"Yeah."

"You know, nobody has them around here."

"No one but G-men."

Bosco ogled me with a set of enquiring eyes. "Where'd ya get it?"

"Don't ask. You wouldn't believe me anyhow."

"Oh, Christ . . . alright! Let's get to work."

I walked to the front of the aircraft and signalled a cut-throat to the pilot. Then I hand-signalled twenty minutes. I saw the pilot reach to his console, then lift the seatbelts from his shoulders. Twenty minutes. Any longer would not go down convincingly with Shilo. Passing the row of windows, I signalled to Andrew. I needed all hands. The more the better. Within a moment, he was stepping down the stairs and the three of us left the area. I noticed the federal police, who were busy pinning up crime scene tape around the tin shack. I kept thinking I should go there and look further for clues. But I relented and pushed on with my hunch.

"Where're we headed?" Bosco asked, as I kept the pace going forward, finally pushing past my Land Rover, which radiated the incoming desert heat.

"The eagles went in that direction," I pointed. "Let's keep going that way."

Bosco reached and grabbed my arm, spinning me around. "Now, wait just a goddamn second. We're chasing eagles now?"

"You said it yourself, Bosco. Maybe the eagles *were* trying to tell us something."

"I was kidding. You realise how ridiculous that is?"

"Ridiculous. Maybe. My gut tells me we keep walking this direction."

"Yeah. How did I know you were gonna say that?"

Then, another thought. "Bosco, you said you'd been here for how long?"

"A few hours. I can't remember exactly. Why?"

"Did you check out the clinic?"

"Yeah. Of course. A couple of dead Aboriginals. Killed the same way as that Lilly."

"Find anything unusual?"

"Lots of things. There was one heck of a firefight in there. Oh, that reminds me. I found this. I figured it would mean something." Bosco retrieved a compact disk player from the inside of his jacket. He passed it over, and I took it and scrutinized it. Walkman. Orange foam headphones hung from a wire. But Angel had left her compact disk player in her bag. I'd left everything in the motel room. How did she get it?

"Sorry, big hoss. I meant to give it to you straight away. But things got a little out of hand with Shilo going off her face."

"That's okay. But I wonder how Angel got hold of the thing when it was left in the motel room."

"Hey, that's not all, big hoss. Take a look inside."

I flipped the lid open. A compact disk. Metallica. The music Angel enjoyed the most. "Yeah, it's a compact disk," I said. "Something I missed?"

"Flip it over," Bosco said.

I took the disk out and flipped it over. I sucked back a gulp of air as I saw what was written in black marker pen. Angel had written those words. *'blue man not a nice man.'*

"Get over here, Bosco. I wanna kiss ya."

"Shit. No thanks. Now we'd better get out of here, like we were instructed by Shilo . . ."

"Not yet. I still have my hunch."

Andrew butted in. "Nathan. Bosco's right. We have to get going."

I ignored him and Bosco. I turned and walked away. Their footfalls behind me told me they were coming after all.

We headed in the general direction of where the eagles had gone and it wasn't long before Andrew crouched down with a knee in the dirt. "Tracks," he said looking down, poking around in the earth with a stick.

I moved closer to Andrew. A set of fresh footprints led off into the distance. I crouched down and inspected the tracks more closely. I could see at least four sets. One set of footprints were small. My instincts told me they belonged to Angel. I shuddered all over again. I felt bile rise in my throat.

We walked on, eyes dropped, and followed the tracks up a small rise. At the top of the rise, a body lay spreadeagled in the dirt. Getting closer, I realised it was the body of someone I knew. Dried blood and a portion of skull were missing from the back of the head. I knelt beside the already-bloated form and turned the body over, revealing a clean shot to the forehead. Through and through. "Oh, fa shit sake," I said as I swished the multitude of desert blow flies away.

Bosco knelt down beside me. For some reason, he put his hand to the dead guy's throat. Maybe he did it out of habit. But the guy was gone and gone for a long time. "You knew this guy?" Bosco asked.

"Yeah. He was the doctor treating Angel. He must've given chase. He was one of us, Bosco. A brother. 6RAR."

"6RAR, huh? Vietnam 6RAR?"

"He was a good man, Bosco. He didn't deserve this. Who knows what he saw during his time? Checking out like this just isn't right. Not for this guy"

"Especially if he was a Long Tan vet."

"Long Tan? Who knows. He was certainly in the age range. I didn't get the chance to be all chatty. Maybe he *was* at Long Tan. We'll never know now."

"That's a crying shame."

"He was the real deal in my opinion. And you're right. It's a shame regardless of the fact. Let's move. We're in the right area."

We didn't have to walk more than a hundred metres. The tracks led to a large pool of now-dried blood in the dirt with more than enough flies making a meal. Blood and remains were everywhere. Flesh remains. Skeletal remains. One of the eagles, I thought, looking down. The eagle with the blood and flesh stuck on its talons. I could only imagine what took place. My logical brain took over. "Fan out," I said. "We're close."

It wasn't long before Andrew called out. "Over here!"

CHAPTER TWELVE

The Grazier

I RAN OVER TO ANDREW, Bosco's footfalls and heavy breathing behind me. I looked down to a set of depressions in the dirt. I knew straight away what they were. Bosco confirmed it.

"Goddam-it! A helo!"

"Yeah. A helo," I agreed. "By the looks of the markings, probably a Black Hawk. That says money. And that says…"

"Guardianship," Andrew put in as he stood up and scanned the area, cuffing a hand above his eyes. I wasn't sure what he was looking for. The thing was, we were too late. They'd taken Angel. Judging by the foot impressions, several more individuals were involved in this now. Who knew how many. Somewhere in the back of my mind, I'd already decided how this was likely to play out. The horror of it all. I reached down and inspected the depressions further, thinking there wasn't much more to glean.

"Look guys. I think we've got as much as we're ever gonna get around here." I began to walk back to the large amount of blood spatter we'd found earlier. "Anyone got a plastic bag or something?" The blood samples would go a long way with forensics. Maybe they'd lead somewhere. Just as I thought it, Andrew offered his help. "Good idea. I'll get to work on the samples as soon as we get back."

Let's see how that young prodigy mind of his can sort this out, I thought. Bosco dug into his pocket and got out his prized red bandana. "Here, scoop some up and put it in this."

I took Bosco's red bandana and after tying the corners together, I filled it with samples of bloody dirt. Walking back, I thought about what must've happened in William Creek. The town was empty of the few people I'd seen wandering around earlier. Those people had all but disappeared, and William Creek itself resembled a ghost town, something similar to the town of Kingoonya after the British government nuked the shit out of Maralinga during the fifties and sixties.

As we approached the motel, the air drew silent with nothing but the whizzing sound of the outback breeze pushing past fly-screened doors and windows. The dust eddies kicked up on the track. The little whirl-winds brought back images of the Wild West movies I'd seen as a kid.

Getting closer to the aircraft, I stopped for a second and cast my eyes toward the blue and white-checked crime scene tape the federal police had pinned up. Bosco must've sensed my hesitation. He reached and grabbed me by my shoulder and steered me onward. But I had unfinished business. I needed to see for myself what had taken place in the tin shack with the paint-peeled red cross. "Not now, Bosco. There's more." I knew there had to be something else. I wasn't going anyplace without the complete picture, or other things I could use.

"Bullshit! Shilo will have you nailed on a plank." Bosco started going off. I ignored him and ran toward the clinic. I heard him at my rear. "Canter! Jesus H Christ!" Before I knew it, I had Andrew stepping up beside me, pacing out in front of Bosco, who continued to sound off. Then Bosco's steps caught up with us. We were lined abreast, bearing down on that checked blue and white crime scene tape.

Entering the place, the scent of hospital ammonia was thick in the air. The three federal cops were bent forward, going about their business, bagging and tagging anything useful they could find. Those cops eyed me momentarily, then without a word got back to what they were doing.

I only half-expected to see the two Aboriginal male nurses on the floor. Dead the same as Lilly, just as Bosco described. Dead the same as Theo, I realised. Both with a shotgun blast to the chest and a neat hole in the forehead. Blood pooled under their bodies as they lay there staring up, eyes fogged over, at some unknown point of interest in space. I was beginning to feel nobody had any hope in this town when it came to the Guardianship arseholes who'd caused all the bloodshed.

The first thing that came to mind was to go to the gurney Angel had been on. I placed a hand down on the empty bed sheets and tried to imagine what had taken place. From there, I scanned the area in a full three-sixty. I said to Andrew, who was standing at my side, "What is it about this place that doesn't make sense?"

He put a finger up to his lips in thought. But as he stood there thinking things over, something came to mind. The Aboriginal nurses on the floor. Both killed gangland style. As the thought came, it set off tiny shockwaves that went rippling through my head. Bosco turned up at my side. I turned to face him. "It's odd, Bosco. When I think about all this, it doesn't add up."

"What doesn't add up? Guardianship assholes came in. They executed the Aboriginals, then made off with Angel. What's odd? How about getting back to the aircraft like we're supposed to."

"Bosco. The nurses were executed gangland style."

"Yeah."

"Why wasn't the doctor?"

"I'm afraid *you're* not making sense. The doctor wasn't killed here. He was killed out there," Bosco pointed.

"That's right, Bosco. Why wasn't he killed the same as the Aboriginal nurses? If you can imagine what must've happened, how did the doctor get away? He'd have had no chance ordinarily, if the bad guys came through the door guns blazing. But he was way out there, where we found him. What does that tell you?"

"It means he was away from this place when shit went down."

"That's my point. Why wasn't he caring for Angel?"

"Maybe he went to the bathroom."

"Even if that was the case, there's a toilet here."

My mind went back to the compact disk player. Could it be that Angel was bored and asked the doctor to go and fetch the player from the motel room? It would explain the absence of the doctor when everything went bad. Coincidence? Or was there something more sinister to it than I imagined?

And why did Angel suggest a 'blue man' when we were all looking for black guys? I closed my eyes and thought hard. But as hard as I thought, nothing else came. Finally, I conceded. There was nothing more to be found and the feds would have gleaned anything else. "We're done here, guys. Let's go," I said, then left the federal cops to it.

Outside, I pulled out the compact disk player and discussed my thoughts with Bosco and Andrew. Both agreed there could be more, or less even, depending on what really happened. But one thing was for certain. From the moment Bosco found the compact disk player, the clock had started and would keep ticking until such a time that Angel was back in safe hands.

I shoved the compact disk player in my shirt, ignorant to Andrew's requests to let him have it as part of the evidence we'd recovered. I didn't know why I refused to give it up. Maybe it was as simple as wanting to be close to Angel, knowing it was one of the last things she touched.

Heading back to the waiting aircraft, I heard a voice call out from somewhere behind me.

"Oi . . . you there!"

I spun, the same as Andrew and Bosco. The local grazier I'd met a day before raced toward me. I knew straight away what he wanted. My mind snapped backward, remembering his 303 rifle the cops had taken and confiscated back at Marree. His words confirmed it when he got close enough.

"Bring me rifle back, did ya?"

The moment the grazier said it, I caught Bosco eyeing me sideways; he was ignorant to the grazier, who smiled, with his hand stuck out for his rifle, like a kid waiting for a treat.

"Sorry. The cops confiscated it," I said. "It wasn't registered to me."

"Shit. Now how am I ever gonna get rid of the rabbits? I got nothin' to control the pesky shits."

"Maybe the cops will ship it back if you contact them. Now, if you can excuse me, I have things on." I apologised again and turned to step away. But then stopped. Maybe he witnessed what had happened. But something else hit me and made me start slightly backward. I got myself up to Bosco's side and whispered, "See what I'm seeing?"

"Yeah . . . I see it."

. . .blue man not a nice man. . .

I turned to the grazier. "I never figured out why outback guys like you always wear a blue singlet and blue King Gee shorts," I said. "Must be some sort of code thing going on?"

"Mate, it's always been that way. Where've *you* been?"

I turned to Bosco and gave him a quick wink. I turned to Andrew. Andrew mouthed back silent words in the shape of 'code orange'. I winked a quick response.

I turned back to the grazier, keeping code orange protocols in my head. "Tell us what you saw? Did you see anything?"

I tried desperately to keep my composure. I tried desperately not to take him down right there and then. Code orange meant caution. Code orange meant be aware. Code orange meant interrogation, but he must be willing to submit. At first, at least. How I wanted the situation to be code red. I'd take the fucker down, no argument. No hesitation. But that had the side effect of shutting the door on Angel's whereabouts. We'd need to nab him. Code orange. I'd play this one with care.

"Seen it? I lived it!" the grazier said. "They took everyone, whoever the hell they were. They loaded them all on the helicopter and shot through. I hid in that wheelie-bin over there," he said and pointed with a fat, calloused finger.

Here we go. Bullshit . . .

I shot a glance to Bosco, then back to the grazier. "I apologise. I never got your name."

"Me? I'm Doug Walken. I run stock not all that far from 'ere. I came into town to collect supplies for me dogs, y'know?"

More bullshit. . .

"I'm Canter. This is Bosco and Andrew," I said with my hand out. Yeah. I was going to shake the man's hand. He took it and shook. I'd never met anyone with such heavily calloused hands. But I squeezed it. Hard. I wanted to break the fucker's fingers. He eyed me curiously without so much as a wince. "Canter, eh? That's not your real name, I take it? Not unless you were in a 'urry to get out into the world."

I ignored his comment. "Did you see if the helo had any markings?"

"Markings? Nah, mate. All black."

"No numbers or anything?"

He appeared to think for a while. Both hands on hips, head down. Yeah. What an actor. This guy was playing it up big time. He went on. "There were the usual alfa-numeric numbers you'd normally see but buggered if I can remember any now."

I faced Bosco. He looked down. I knew he was the same as me, trying to keep a level head. Trying to keep things in check.

I turned back to Doug, looking past Andrew's poker face as I went. "What else can you tell us?"

"I heard a couple of those blokes talking as they walked past me hidin' in that wheelie bin. One of 'em said somethin' about somethin'. Buggered if I can remember it though. I stuck me head up for a bit. They'd already got hold of a few locals and chucked them in that helicopter. Martha Birch from the general store. Garry Penrose from the bottle-o. Mick Kettle from the barber shop. They must've done somethin' to 'em cuz they were goin' in no struggle. That's the reason why I went and hid. But there they were. Those black blokes."

"Black?"

"Yeah, mate. I don't reckon they were Aboriginal. Too bloody tall. Never seen any Aboriginal as tall as that."

"What else?"

"That's when it happened. They were walkin' away with that little girl you brought in yesterday. The doc came beltin' across the street and the chase was on. Then there was the shot. I stuck me head up in time to see them eagles come out of the sky. Shoulda seen it. Like angels of death, those eagles. Anyways, dunno what happened after that. I heard some commotion and that. A bit after, the helicopter took off. That's all I know."

"Did you get a good look at those guys?"

"Too bloody right I did, mate. Put me in a line-up. I'll peg 'em."

This guy wanted a line-up. The only way to do that was to take him with us. Maybe there was an ulterior motive. My guess, this guy was set up as an infiltrator. That gave me an idea.

"You need to come with us. We'll make sure you can have that line-up. Of course, we'll get you sorted with accommodation." I felt Bosco's protests. I ignored him.

"I dunno about that, mate. Got me herds to attend. And me dogs need their tucka."

"I'm sure your herds will be there when we get you back. Let's go," I said. As soon as he was in the aircraft, we'd have him and code orange would play out. Maybe it would get me back on board with Shilo. Or maybe not. I had to try.

"But me dogs . . ."

Now I was at odds. Maybe it was a better option to just grab him and bail him up. I shot a quick glance at Andrew. He shook his head slightly. It wasn't going to go my way. The grazier had to be willing. That's all there was to it. Law shit. Civil rights shit. How I wished those feds were close by. But then he'd belong to the feds. And that would shut the door on everything. I put my head down and walked a few paces closer to Doug. I locked eyes with him, hoping to give him something to think about. I was no longer in the mood for his bullshit. "Doug. We've got cops all over this place," I pointed to the tin shack.

"Yeah. What's with the clobber they're wearin'? Cops wear khaki. Are they interstate?"

"They're federal cops," I said. As if he didn't know. He was playing. "You have the choice of coming with us or going with them. Either way, you won't get back to your herds in a hurry."

"Who *are* you blokes?"

"We're with the government." Again. As if he didn't know. "I strongly urge you to come with us. The feds won't go easy on you. As soon as they see you're around, you'll be hauled in for questioning. Is that what you want? Now, you can come with us and we'll help you get back to your herds. Or go with them to Canberra. Who knows what after that."

It was no good. The grazier wasn't about to get in the aircraft. My options were none. I turned to Bosco and Andrew. "You two get on the aircraft and go. I'll drive up after we get sorted with the man's dogs," I lied.

Bosco and Andrew nodded in unison. Bosco got out his car keys and tossed them. I reached out and caught them. "Don't take your Land Rover, big hoss. Look after my Chev, won't ya?" Bosco hand-signalled. 'Firearm in the compartment.'

I pulled the items of evidence out of my pocket. The bullet and the lock of hair. I passed them to Bosco, hoping it was enough to get me back on board with Maggie. Holy shit! Where *was* I with her? The evidence we gathered might just save my arse. It might not. Maybe my new package would change things. I hoped it to be the case.

"You'd better give me that thing on your finger, big hoss," Bosco said, at the same time holding out his hand.

I almost forgot about the ring. I took the ring off my finger and passed it over. "Take care of the documents and everything else."

"Canter, you know how this is gonna play out?" Bosco whispered so lightly I struggled to hear him.

"Don't even go there. She's just a ten-year-old kid," I whispered back.

"Yeah, but there are three other civilians in this now. My guess, one will be executed before they even *come* to the table."

"Not if we liberate them first."

"Yeah," Bosco said, heaving a loud sigh. "How did I know you were gonna say that. See you back on the grid."

CHAPTER THIRTEEN

Ingress

I DROVE BOSCO'S BLACK CHEVY SUBURBAN north on the Oodnadatta Track, having a hell of a time getting used to the left-hand drive. Every now and again, the grazier gave me a shove if I got too close to the centre of the road. I hated him shoving me. I hated him touching me. Added to that, Angel's compact disk player tucked inside my shirt was quite uncomfortable. I ignored it as I drove. Regardless of everything, we were already two hours into the trip heading north.

"I thought you said your property wasn't far away."

"It's not. We got about an hour to go before we turn off at Oodnadatta. Then to Coober Pedy."

"Coober-bloody-Pedy! We won't get there until after sunset. Are you bonkers?"

"Not all the way to Coober Pedy. Just after the turn off, about half an hour south east of Oodnadatta."

I knew somewhere in my mind he was taking me to some bull-shit location. That being what it was, I began to prepare for any eventuality. I sighed, thinking about whether to keep going or not. The RAAF Challenger would've long since touched down in Alice Springs. Maybe this wasn't such a good idea after all. I could only imagine Maggie's reaction when I didn't turn up. But the prospect of a live code orange would change it. I pushed the thought from my mind.

The grazier gave me a good bit of his story as we travelled. The last of the knuckle men, he boasted. He supposedly grew up on the knuckle, bare fisting at shearing sheds from Paratoo to Roxby Downs. Nose jobs were many, so he said. His teeth had been broken and some were missing, much the same as Lilly McPherson back at William Creek. A sideways glance revealed a nose bridge shaped like that of a seasoned Wallabies player. He'd told me everything, but already I'd heard enough.

I switched on the radio, hoping to drown out any further gas-bagging. The only station to pick up a signal was the local country ABC. It had to do. But he went on with the gasbagging and I tried not to listen. My mind was elsewhere. He droned on. I smiled occasionally, not fully knowing what about. I figured I needed to give him some input to keep him happy, even though my attention was in a different place.

He stopped talking at the exact moment a tone erupted from the centre console at my right elbow. I lifted the arm rest. Bosco's satellite phone. It toned on as I pulled it out and answered.

"Canter? It's Shilo."

I gulped back. "Shilo?" I said, pausing a beat. I was stuck for words just like before. Maggie must've sensed it.

"Let's put it away for another time. We'll discuss it later, Canter. More important things on. Well done getting the blood and hair samples. I don't know how you managed it, but it doesn't surprise me in the least. The bullet fragment, I'll send to Interpol. Somehow, I get a feeling the rifling won't match anything on a national databank. I've got T working on the blood and hair."

"T?"

"The prodigy, you referred to him as."

"Oh. Roger that."

Maggie went on after a short pause. "Moments ago, our friends from Detachment 421 in Swartz Crescent picked up a seismological event. A small one. But enough to spark their interest. Having tracked where it was, they forwarded the GPS coordinates to me and requested an urgent investigation. I have a strange feeling about this, Canter. After everything that has recently transpired, this can't be ignored. In my opinion, it's got Guardianship all over it."

"You want me to get to the coordinates?"

"Have you got anything else on?"

An awkward pause. Not sure how to answer. "I'm transporting a witness . . ." I said out loud just for the sake of Doug hearing me.

"Yes, I know. Bosco has brought me up to date on your code orange. I hope I don't have to remind you he needs to be a willing party all the way to our front door?"

"Understood."

"Take extra precautions with him, Canter. Play it by the book and we won't have anything further to discuss later."

Jesus. I hoped the grazier didn't hear that. I glanced sideways. He was none the wiser.

"I suggest getting to the coordinates and waiting for Detachment 421 to arrive," Maggie went on. "Bosco will deploy with them."

"Roger that. What do we know about the location?"

"It could be anything. It may even be the location of a Guardianship base of operations, for all we know. Oh, and one more thing. Stay back from the area until Detachment 421 arrives. Am I making myself clear?"

"Copy that, Shilo."

"Good. I've sent the coordinates to Bosco's GPS receiver, which he has told me is in the floor compartment. Check it now, will you please?"

"One moment, Shilo."

After pulling up on the side of the track, I lifted the carpet away from under my feet and reached into the compartment. I grabbed the receiver. The monochrome monitor blinked with the announcement of a set of new coordinates. I noticed the weapon Bosco had left there. A suppressed nine-millimetre Beretta. I left the Beretta where it was and closed the compartment, knowing this one was going to be by the book as Maggie had stressed. No more stuff-ups.

"I can confirm I have the coordinates."

"Where are you now?"

"Ten clicks south of Oodnadatta."

"Use the receiver to work out your ETA, will you please?"

"Already on it," I said while requesting a search. The ETA came back. "Jesus. Eleven hours at an average speed of a hundred kilometres per hour. ETA 0217."

"Better get a move on then. I suggest a brief stop at Oodnadatta. Get a full tank and supplies. Lay up until daylight a kilometre back from your ingress. I'll instruct Detachment 421 to rendezvous at your location. You'll need to transmit your standing position when you stop. And Canter, after the Chinook arrives, it is technically correct to assume the helo *is* our front door. Get your code orange willingly on board. Then he's ours. Clear?"

"Roger that. Understood."

"Good. Who knows what's out there. Be careful, Canter. Out."

I positioned the GPS receiver on the dashboard above the steering wheel. Already, I felt my passenger's eyes scanning me. I needed a moment. Just a moment to get my head together. Everything that needed doing was swirling around in my head. What was at the coordinates? What caused the seismological disturbance that got the attention of those dark souls in Detachment 421?

"Anyhow," Doug said. "That look on your face says we're not goin' to my joint."

"No. You're a witness and now in protective custody."

Right there and then, I wanted to grab the gun and blow his bloody head away.

"And you're my bloody bodyguard, eh? Sheesus!"

"Don't make me regret it," I said. "Whatever happens, stay close and keep your head down. Do as I tell you and we'll do fine.

If you don't, you might just get yourself a neat little hole some-where on your person for your trouble. Got it?" *That* might happen anyway. I kept that thought well to myself.

He said nothing. Doug sighed at the same time as he reached into the pocket of his faded blue King Gee shorts, pulling out a bag of tobacco. With a cigarette paper hanging from his lip, he began to mould a wad of tobacco in his hand. "Wanna rollie?"

"Yeah. May as well." I didn't smoke. But what the heck. I needed something. Anything. I didn't have any bourbon. Maybe a rollie would help settle my mind.

"What's the thing you stuck on the dash?" he asked while lick-ing the edge of the paper and completing a work of art. I thought about not telling him anything. But what the heck. In my mind he was dead anyway. One way or another. I'd get my chance after we'd finished pulling intel out of him. I'd make sure I'd be the one to dispose of him. However, when answering his question, I played it up for my own amusement.

"It's a global positioning system receiver." I grabbed the de-vice from the dashboard and brought it closer. Time to nerd out. "You input your longitude and latitude and it will guide you to the location. The four lights on the handset get you there. The green means you're heading in the right direction. The red means you're heading away. The ambers on the left and right mean the location is either side. The idea is to keep the light green. Maybe one day, there'll be a set of maps to make it easier and more user-friendly. It's for military use only for now."

"Holy shit! Never seen one o' them gismos before."

"Yeah. And expensive. It also has GSM and CDMA recep-tion."

"What in the heck is that?"

"Mobile network coverage. It's new tech. One day, everyone will have a mobile phone. Maybe one day everyone will have a GPS."

He passed me a lit rollie and I sat back, took a drag, and coughed up a lung. Now I knew why I didn't smoke in the first bloody place. The stuff was vile. I immediately tossed the cigarette out of the window.

"Better get out and put ya foot on it," he said. "You don't wanna start fires, mate. It'll end up being a firestorm and we don't need that 'round here."

After putting out the cigarette, my mind returned to the objectives my mind ran briefly away from. Now it was time to get back into the game. My code orange eyed me as I climbed back into the vehicle and dragged the seat belt over my shoulder. "Better git," he said as though not caring where we were going.

"I'm Nathan. That's my real name," I said, at the same time twisting the key in the ignition.

"Nathan, huh? That's better than Canter. Since when does a verb get to be someone's name?"

I killed the ignition and eyed him, wondering if I should go there. That was so long ago. The memory came back and I momentarily decided I'd give him a throwaway line for the hell of it. But I sat back in my seat and folded my arms with the memory. "When I was a kid before I enlisted, the name Canter was given to me by a guy who lived next door. Billy Butcher. Fat Fuck Billy I used to call him. I'd go out for a morning run knowing enlistment wasn't far away. I wanted to get into shape, I guess."

"So you were . . . cantering?" Doug smiled, then started to laugh. But his laughter didn't last. I shot a stare at him that shut him up. I went on. He listened.

"That's what Billy Butcher yelled out to me as I ran past his house. Canter! Yeah. Exactly that. But the name stuck and I have it as a handle or call sign. It reminds me how close I got to killing the prick. That bastard wore a knife in a scabbard on his belt. A big letter B was embossed into the leather; he was such a show-off. He dared me once. A game of stabscotch. Damn he was good at it. But when he gave the knife to me, I showed him I was in no mood for his bullshit."

"What'd ya do?"

"Another time, Doug. But I'll just say Fat Fuck Billy came off second best." Again, I reached forward and turned on the engine. "Will your dogs be okay?" I asked, hamming it up for his benefit.

"Nah, dun worry about it, mate. They're off the chain. I wouldn't pass up an adventure if ya paid me. So, what in the heck are ya waiting for? Let's git!"

CHAPTER FOURTEEN

Sometimes They Come Back

THE MOMENT AFTER I SWITCHED OFF the engine and dowsed the headlights, I leaned forward and peered out of the windscreen to the wonderful night sky. Jewels of stars and galaxies sat there on a deep black canvas, twinkling and dancing. It'd been a long drive through the vast empty outback, avoiding roos and emus that bounced out in front without any warning. Even the odd camel crossed the track, which made for a speedy correction and a skilled touch of the brake pedal.

I slowed to avoid the many rutted patches and sped up with four-wheel drive engaged to escape the claws of muddy bogs. Doug was fast asleep and slept for most of the way. Thank god for that. I was in no mood for the chatter. Had I been a passenger, I don't think I could've slept for a second. My mind was live wired with the imaginings of what we were up against, not including the added responsibility of being Doug's so-called bodyguard.

Reaching down and lifting the carpet away from the compartment at my feet, I retrieved the Beretta. After checking for rounds, I sat back and rested the suppressed handgun in my lap. I fought the urge. I fought it hard. A bullet through the brain, he'd be shit-canned. Then my thoughts went to Angel. A bit of finesse was required here. Every step was crucial.

Grabbing the GPS handset, I requested my standing position and transmitted the data, knowing it would arrive within a second back at Alice Springs. Then the waiting began.

I checked the time on my wristwatch again and settled into place. Four hours until first light. It was cold out there. I put my finger up to the glass just to check. I rubbed my hands together then tightly folded my arms, knowing the cold from outside would enter in a few moments. I glanced sideways at Doug; the cold didn't seem to make any difference to him. King Gee shorts and faded blue singlet. Why was it outback guys seemed to wear nothing else?

0322.

I got out to stretch a leg. I had a piss by a tree while studying the edge of the Milky Way. Awesome. Back in the car.

0341.

It seemed like hours since I last checked.

0357.

0412.

I got out. Vapour shot away from my breath. Back to the tree. Maybe I shouldn't have drunk so much water. Back in the car. I looked at Doug while thumping the door closed. He didn't move. Out cold, so it seemed.

0432.

This time I took my wristwatch off and threw it on the floor. Within what seemed like thirty minutes I checked the time again. 0441.

I pulled Angel's compact disk player from my shirt. Metallica. Not my thing, but better than nothing. I placed the headphones over my head and pressed play.

I pressed play . . .

I checked the battery. All good. Pressed play . . .

Shit . . .

No disk would ever work with black marker pen scrawled over the data surface. I took the headphones off and placed the player in the glove box.

Doug, next to me, was fast asleep. I'll kill the bastard right here and now. I grabbed the handgun and brought it up point blank to his temple. That's when I heard it. And at the exact same time, Doug woke up. I lowered the handgun as Doug eyed me curiously. But the noise. A low thumping. The noise of turbofans. The sound of rotors in the distance, cutting through the silence.

Doug stretched forward, busting a yawn. Was he none the wiser? I didn't know. I imagined my hands around his throat. I imagined my fingers piercing all the way through his flesh and ripping out his voice box.

"What's the noise, mate?"

I didn't feel as though I could answer. Somehow, I did. "Choppers."

Chinooks. Our Chinooks. They're early . . .

"Didn't you say they'd be coming in after sunup?"

"Yeah."

"Then, they're early," Doug said.

"Yeah."

As the noise got closer, I realised the sound was no Chinook. It came in low over the terrain then punched past overhead doing top speed, kicking up dust as it shot over.

"Shit!" Doug said. "That can't be your blokes."

That changed my tune. I immediately grabbed the car keys and twisted them in the ignition. The V8 engine sprang to life.

"Did they see us?" Doug said. The look of horror in his eyes. Oh, he was such a player.

"I dunno. We're in the open. Now's the time to get to cover," I yelled.

The GPS data transmission must have been intercepted and we were nothing more than a ground target. No point getting to cover. With the gearshift in neutral, I put my foot down hard on the throttle. The tacho needle pushed past the red zone. The V8 engine screamed.

"What are you doing! Let's get going!" Doug shouted.

"It's too late. Time to run!" I yelled, at the same time grabbing the Beretta and GPS receiver.

The helo was coming closer for a second pass. Maybe the SUV's engine was hot enough. Any heat-seeking AGM would go straight to it.

"Doug!"

"What!"

"Get out and run! NOW!"

Getting out, I wished hard I had two good legs. I did the best I could getting away. I half ran, half hopped as fast as I could go. Doug paced out in front, occasionally looking over his shoulder.

"Find cover and get down," I yelled. The noise of the rotors was fast coming back. Closing in on Bosco's precious SUV.

I found a tree with huge roots sticking out of the desert ground and got down. Where in the heck was that grazier! I looked to my left and saw him getting behind some bloodwoods, just in time for an AGM to fire from the helo. It hit the side of Bosco's SUV and it erupted in an enormous explosion that lit up the night sky, trailing off in a huge fireball.

"Doug! Get on the ground and roll in the dirt. Roll. Roll. Roll!

"What for!" he yelled back.

"Just do it! Get that dirt over you as much as you can. Roll. Roll. Roll!"

I got down and rolled around, getting as much dirt, dust, and grime over me as I could. All over my clothes. All through my hair. All over my face. Up my nose. In my mouth. Doug was rolling around like a wild boar just shot. "Keep rolling around and don't stop! Roll. Roll. Roll!"

Die. Die. Die, I kept thinking. I should've left him in the SUV.

"Okay, I'm rolling. Dunno why. But you're the boss!"

"Your body heat! The helo can't see us if we're cold. Keep rolling around and don't stop. You gotta get cold, Doug. Make sure that dirt is all over you!"

The helo hovered over the wrecked SUV momentarily and slowly turned as though scanning the immediate area. A bright search light lit up and the scanning began all over again. It turned again while hovering. Dust kicked up, reaching up to it. The searchlight bounced around through the rising dust and reflected off native trees and bush.

"When I say go prone . . . go prone!" I yelled.

"Prone? What's that mean?"

"Just get down flat as you can! Do it now!"

I went prone, flat as my body would allow, and wiped more dust over my face for good measure. The search light hit, stopped for a split second, then went in another direction.

"Don't move, Doug! Not even a muscle!"

I held my breath. If I could've stopped my heart, I'd have done it. Then, without warning, the searchlight came back. I lifted the Beretta and emptied the magazine in rapid fire at the searchlight, which immediately shattered and went black. Projectiles ricocheted, pinging off the helo. More than a few bullets zipped past my body and hit the ground. I heard a yelp to my left. One of my shots had impacted Doug. I wanted to believe he was still alive if only for the opportunity to torture the bastard.

From where I lay cloaked in desert dust, I watched as the helo lifted up, turned, and shot off in the direction it came. I pushed up to the side of Doug's body and checked for signs of life, of which there were none. Prick.

* * *

I spent the rest of the night hunkered in a dried-up creek bed. My decision to fire on the helo still ripped through my mind. Had I not fired; Doug would still be alive. It was an awful price to pay. No intel. Now, what about Angel? I could only imagine what had died with Doug.

First light dawned with the steady thump of rotor blades in the distance. I relaxed, knowing a Chinook had a sound all of its own. Getting up and dusting down my desert-soiled jeans, I slowly headed back to the LZ carrying a shit load of guilt to deal with. More guilt to add to what I'd already stuffed down there in that dark pit where all my other bad shit lived.

The RAAF CH-47F Chinook landed on the road just next to the wreck of Bosco's SUV. Several armed figures dressed in black with faces covered by red bandanas and dark sunglasses climbed out of the rear, followed by one who could only be Bosco. He stood beside the wreck of his SUV and immediately spun his blue baseball cap backward, then put his hands on his hips in obvious disgust.

Tracing the shoulder of the dirt road, I walked with speed toward them. Bosco spun and faced me, raising his arms. "What have you done!" he called out. "Man, what have you done to my Chev!"

After approaching, it took a bit of explaining. I saw Bosco's jaw drop as I described what had happened. All the while, the men of Detachment 421 stood silent. No one would ever know their reaction up until the time they all checked weapons. Still no words were exchanged – it was as though they weren't human at all. Maybe they were all fucking cyborgs, who'd know? After checking the body of the grazier laying in the open desert dust, one of the black-clad guys said with words as blunt as a hammer to get in the Chinook. Which I did. Without any hesitation.

Climbing into the Chinook, I reached up and grabbed a headset. As I put it on, staring back at me were a set of sparkling ebony eyes I'd not seen since the hurt locker, south of Basra.

"Teresa?" I said it to myself at first. I locked eyes with her. She locked hers with mine. She smiled brightly. Her face. Her raven hair. She hadn't changed a bit.

"I would kiss you hello, Nathan. But you been out dirt wrestling again," she said in her most exquisite Israeli accent. Now, I realised, we had the company of MOSSAD along for the ride.

"Teresa . . ." I was about to ask what does MOSSAD have in this? But I was stumped for words. She kept smiling. Those ebony eyes kept sparkling. The same as always.

"Teresa . . . What are you *doing* here?" I finally asked.

"You need trauma doctor," she answered plainly. "But also, will put my talents to these Milestone."

Of course, I realised. Not only was she a fine surgeon, she was also adept and respected in the field of cyber counter-terrorism. Her English still needed a polish. That hadn't changed. She glanced to Bosco. Bosco winked back. I felt the blood rush to my face. My composure left. But somehow, out of my surprise, I managed to echo her smile.

As the engines spooled and the Chinook rose slowly, Teresa reached over and placed a hand on my knee. "How is it been going with you, this past years?"

"Teresa . . . I . . . I'm . . ."

"Stunned?" she said, still beaming.

"Yeah." I placed my hand on hers. "Why you? Why now?"

Bosco sat back and folded his arms as though pretending he wasn't there. He had something to do with it. Now, I was sure of it.

"Nathan," she said, grinning. "When you leave, I say to Bosco, if there is need he should call. I say myself, one day Bosco will call. And I wait until such time. Now, Bosco call. I get first plane. So now here to help with making the Milestone dead. You need trauma doctor. You need countermeasures. I shrug my shoulder. Who else but me, huh?"

"Teresa. I never meant . . ."

"Is okay, Nathan," she said. "I live. You have work. I have work. I understand."

The Chinook turned high in the air and headed to the coordinates of the seismological disturbance. I couldn't take my eyes away from Teresa's gaze. When I did, I saw Bosco sitting back and grinning. Had the others not worn their facial coverings, my guess is they'd be grinning the same. They all heard the words I said over coms. Even the pilot and co-pilot, I assumed.

CHAPTER FIFTEEN

First Blood

AS I WAS GETTING OUT OF THE CHINOOK, Teresa's words sprang to mind.

Trauma doctor . . . countermeasures . . .

It made me wonder what may be out there waiting. We were already prepared for anything. But MOSSAD? There was a connection, but where? It whipped around in my head. Then it came. The centrifuges in Iran. The one that got away, as Maggie had said. Without our MOSSAD allies, the intelligence of the Iranian centrifuges might not have come to light. Maybe one day, there'd be another seek and destroy mission to look forward to.

The highly armed men of Detachment 421 took point and led the way through the bush. I kept an eye on the GPS coordinates, sidestepping Bosco who was in formation, occasionally covering our six. Teresa paced beside me. Within a few moments we arrived at a clearing.

We all halted and half crouched. There was nothing at the location apart from the usual desolate isolation. "Ground zero," I called out at the same time weapons were relaxed. One of the black-clad guys called out, "What the fuck?" But after scanning a full three-sixty, I saw a depression in the dirt not far from where we'd stopped.

"Over there," I called out, pointing. We made our way across.

Arriving at the depression in the dirt, I glimpsed the edge of what seemed like a metal container. The majority was deep under and hidden in the soft earth, as if the container had been dropped from an aircraft. Maybe from a Black Hawk. I bent down to touch it.

Bosco slapped my hand away. "Out of everything, you're gonna go and blow yourself up again?" he snapped. I'd slipped up for a moment. I was a little distracted and Bosco, doing what he did, shoved me back into the real world.

The 421 crew knelt down close to the metal container, appearing to scan it. "Anyone with electronic devices, switch them off. Now!" one of them said from under a red bandana. I hit the button to the GPS receiver and it went dead in my hand.

"What do you think it is?" I said out loud.

Bosco came up beside me. "From where I stand, it looks like your average military footlocker. It's badly busted up. You reckon it was dropped?"

"The seismological disturbance," I replied through my teeth.

Before I knew it, one of the 421 crew began to sweep the red desert sands away. I felt a hand on my shoulder. Teresa urged me to get back. As I got back, the circle of black-clad men around it retreated while one was left alone with the sole job of making the object known. After thirty minutes of careful manipulation, he stood up and confirmed Bosco's belief. "Foot locker," he said. "Need the ordnance disposal bot from the helo."

* * *

We made for a safe zone while the remote bot went about its task. By this time, the sun was biting down and it was getting seriously hot. Who knew how it felt for those guys dressed in black with their faces covered. They kept their faces covered no matter what. Their words were few. Nods were plenty and no names or call signs were ever mentioned. They communicated among themselves using hand signals unique to them.

I saw Bosco quite a few times reacting to their signals, and at times commenting on their processes as though he was part of the team. If their hand signalling was unique, how did *Bosco* know? Then it occurred to me. The bandana those guys wore. Red. The same as the one Bosco kept with him. I eyed him for a second while he oversaw what they were doing. He was deep in the action even though he was standing right next to me. My enquiring mind went to work.

"Bosco. Your bandana is the same as theirs," I said. "Care to tell me why that is?"

Bosco stopped what he was doing. He placed his hands on his hips and put his head down as though there was nowhere for him to go. Then he looked up with a smirk. The same smirk that said 'you gotta be kidding.' He didn't need to speak it. I already knew it.

"Hey relax, will ya?" Bosco finally said after sucking back a long breath. "So, it's a red bandana. You gonna hold that against me?"

I turned away, held a hand to my chin, and calculated in my head. The numbers told me if Bosco was in Detachment 421, he was in play at the same time as that idiotic Candy programme. The CIA's programme at Pine Gap. Now I needed answers. He'd better have the right things to say.

"Normally I'd let it go, Bosco. But you know too much about those guys. What *aren't* you telling me? Were *you* 421?"

He said nothing. He avoided my enquiry. I asked it again.

"Bosco, now's the time to convince me you weren't 421. Just saying."

"So what if I was? What difference does it make?"

"It makes every bit of difference. It means you were in on that Candy programme."

"Canter. What in the heck are you talking about?"

Immediately, my hands curled into fists. Bosco's Adams apple dipped. I remembered Candy for the massive CIA botch up that it was. Without Candy, maybe Franco would still be alive. Maybe Franco wouldn't have turned. Maybe Angel would still have her parents.

I ran over it in my mind. The drug based on $C_6H_{12}N_4$. Methamphetamine that was supposed to be modified. The CIA claimed it was the drug of choice to subdue operatives who had access to sensitive material while being stationed at Pine Gap. It was the CIA's answer to protect their interests and assets. Whatever happened to trust and commitment? Was it ever considered?

It was Detachment 421 that administered the drug. Maybe even Bosco himself. In Franco's case, the drug was beyond anything toxic. It changed him. It turned him. He became volatile. Explosive. Had Franco not had it in his system, he wouldn't have bludgeoned his wife to death.

But then, there was something else. The disk had something to do with it. The disk, with all of the implicating intelligence that now rested in the hands of Firebird Station. Maggie expressed it was found in the possession of Angel, in her backpack. Who could have put it there and why? It could've only been someone close to Angel. It could've only been someone who wanted to leak the contents. Alisha. It made me wonder if she knew what was on it. Was it a forewarning? Was it an attempt to bring the agencies up to speed?

Had Alisha known about the Milestone mission and objectives? Had Alisha known about the Oudarretian motivations? Their need for helium-3? Their plan to eradicate humanity? Their plan to mine the moon? It was a war hammer between my eyes. Alisha. Angel's mother put that disk in her backpack. But where did *she* get it? I closed my eyes. My brain worked hard.

Think . . . It's what you're good at. Think. Think hard . . .

I turned away from Bosco's gaze and placed a palm to my forehead. I almost had it worked out. It was coming. I almost had everything put into place.

Welcome to the world of lies and secrets . . .

The words I heard so long ago. Who else could it have been but someone close to Franco? Who else but someone needing to blow everything wide open? I had my hunch. I needed proof. I needed concrete evidence. A hunch wasn't good enough.

"You don't wanna start this, Canter. Believe me. Just leave it." Bosco's words punched through my train of thought, wrecking everything I'd worked out.

"You *were* 421!" I shouted. "And you *were* in on the Candy programme!"

"Hey, big hoss. Hold it together. We can discuss it another time."

Fuming, I wanted to grab him around the throat and squeeze. "Why, Bosco. Why!"

Teresa's hand fell on my forearm. "Nathan, it is history, no?"

Just where in the heck was I? As I stood there and gazed into Teresa's eyes, I wondered with even more curiosity at her sudden appearance. The whole picture was there just a second ago. Something as simple as a phone call from Bosco, she'd told me. Was there more? Something told me I still wasn't completely in the loop, that I was more out of it than I should be. My mind tumbled and spun.

"Nathan. Where are you?" Teresa said, lightly placing a hand up to my face.

I wasn't happy. I was far from it. Out of everything that'd been said, everything that had been made known, it didn't seem to end. Answers. I needed them. Bosco and his story. Nothing but lies. Teresa with hers. Andrew with his. The disk I'd not yet seen. Eagle Shield . . .

"Nathan. Relax, no?" Teresa said. Again, with a hand up to my face.

Maggie's words came.

Sometimes you overthink . . .

My mind. My thoughts. My worries. Sometimes, I hated it. How could I turn this off?

* * *

"Clear!" someone yelled.

"You guys can open it now," someone else said.

I spun to Bosco, holding it together the best I could. My hands clenched at my sides. "This isn't over, Bosco. Not in a long way is this thing over. You'd better have something good for later. Just saying."

"Whatever, big hoss. But remember we had jobs to do. We might not have liked it. Orders are orders. Who are we to second guess that shit coming down from the top?"

No choice in the matter, I had to put everything away and keep it for another time. That time would come soon enough. For now, we had to get back to what needed to be done. With every moment that ticked by, Angel was spending more time in danger. I pulled my head out and got on with it.

When the footlocker was properly unearthed and the threat of any possible explosive jettisoned, I pushed past the crew of black-clad guys, claiming it was my job to open it. I crouched down and manhandled the mangled door. After a few hefty heaves, it finally opened.

The first sign something was off was Bosco suddenly pushing his head sideways with a hand up to his face. The next was when the 421 crew moved backward a pace, almost in an involuntary movement. It didn't register what was in there. In the first instant, I thought some mad bastard had slaughtered a pig and stuffed it in there. But as the stink erupted, I knew it was no pig at all. The mad bastard had dismembered a human body with the same kind of intricacy as packing a meat tray.

I mumbled my horror under my breath, stepping back with my hand to my nose and mouth. Bosco was beside me as though no cross words had ever been exchanged.

"Well, big hoss," Bosco said. "You were right. Looks like they *did* execute one of the civilians. And *before* coming to the table, just as you thought."

"Angel . . ." I said with urgency, looking down, trying desperately not to believe it.

"It's not Angel." Bosco kneeled and lifted something grisly and awful. "Check this out."

Bosco retrieved a note that was heavily stained in red mess. He stood back and eyed it before passing the note to me. I was hard-pressed to make out what was written in what must've been thick black marker. My eyes focused through the muck. One word only. 'Quinlan.'

My mind drew back. It wasn't one of the names of the locals from back at William Creek. I examined the note and held it to the sunlight in the hope of revealing any further clues.

"Now we have a contact," Bosco said. "Quinlan is the guy who's gonna do all the talking."

"Yeah. And this is the guy's calling card. Elaborate, don't you think?"

"He's obviously in no mood for bullshit, Canter. This guy is psycho. I reckon there'll be more dead guys turning up before we even get started."

* * *

After photos were taken of the grisly scene, Bosco and I, and one other from Detachment 421 did the best we could. Retrieving most of the body parts and placing them into the black body bag, we soon realised there was not a lot that could be recovered.

Apart from the head and limbs and a section of torso, the rest was a mush that I tried hard to ignore. A few personal items were left on the body. Left there with a purpose I assumed. They would aid in discovering the identity of this poor innocent individual. I was relieved it wasn't Angel. However, Angel was still missing and time was playing out of our hands. If it was urgent before, now it was even more so.

The Guardianship had just showed their muscle to us all, and what they were capable of doing. They weren't going to make things easy. The negotiations would start. What would it take for Angel's release? And when, exactly would we be contacted by the person who went by the name of Quinlan?

With a roll of 35mm film in my grip, the flight back to Alice Springs was silent of any chatter other than the words used by the pilot and co-pilot to control the Chinook. After touch-down at Alice Springs airport, a vehicle was waiting for those black-clad dark souls. They got out of the Chinook, got into the vehicle, and left without any bother.

Bosco and I ferried the two body bags to an awaiting Ford Transit van. One of the bodies was the civilian found in the foot-locker, the other, my code orange failure. I wasn't sure how this would play out with Maggie. But now he was dead, it could only spell disaster. And Angel . . . she was further away than I could ever care to imagine. It made me feel incredibly heavy, but more determined than ever. Quinlan. The day we'd come face to face, I'd take my pleasure slowly.

Moments after delivering the body bags and watching the Transit van drive away, all that was left was the trip back to Fire-bird Station. I knew in my heart things would instantly ramp up.

* * *

We arrived there disheartened from what we'd seen out in the arid outback. Maggie opened the door quietly and we all slipped through. Her displeasure deepened and turned into anger at the news of the deceased code orange. I'd waited until I was face to face with her before I gave her the news. I don't know why I chose to go that way. It would've been much easier to let her know over coms. At least by doing that, she'd have time to digest it.

Me being me, I chose to avoid telling her until I had to. Maggie turned away, saying nothing. I gave her a few moments to herself. She quietly sat down at her desk. It was as though she went away somewhere momentarily. When she finally came back, it was all heads back in the game.

The person who went by the name Quinlan had played a card in the inexcusable bloodletting of an innocent individual. The purpose, however, wasn't clear. Was it nothing more than the act itself? Was it a message? If it was a message, there was nothing more in it than to let us know he was indeed the psychopath Bosco claimed.

Maybe Quinlan was showing his muscle. Maybe he was showing how much power he wielded. Maybe he was playing for the disk. If he wanted the disk in exchange for Angel, it didn't matter which way I looked at the situation, it was never going to be as simple as that.

The ramping up of events I'd expected didn't happen. There was no sign of any attempt to communicate by this Quinlan. The day turned into two. Then into three. By the end of the fourth day, with no word of anything, my determination for Angel's safety intensified and supercharged. But somewhere in the back of my mind, I knew it was always Quinlan's intention to keep us hanging. To keep us guessing. To keep us on edge. That's how he was playing it. He showed his hand in the beginning. Now, not knowing was sheer and absolute terror.

During the nights, the lights were left on. Sleep came, but only for an hour or two. Maggie's meeting room became more like a command post. Someone was always there, forever manning all the communication devices we had. At the same time, Andrew sat at the computer and never left. He'd fall asleep still sitting in the same position as he was when last awake. As the time dragged on, we became nothing more than weary ghosts, walking the hallways, clinging to the expectation that something, *anything*, would begin.

CHAPTER SIXTEEN

Seed

DAY SIX. A CERTAIN BUZZ WAS IN THE AIR.
Things were stirring. From the coffee machine, I heard voices emanating from Maggie's ad hoc command centre. As I rubbed my weary eyes, Maggie sprang up from behind. She startled me enough to cause my coffee mug to hit the floor.

"We have something to go on, Nathan. My meeting room when you're ready." She looked down at the shattered coffee mug, then looked back up. "Mop and bucket in the laundry cupboard." Then she walked away.

When I arrived in the meeting room, Maggie gestured for me to take a seat. An awkward silence hung in the air, interrupted by Bosco's cough and Teresa saying something about the furniture. But Maggie went about her business without any delay at the whiteboard. "This is intelligence just in from Canberra," Maggie said as she started to write. In big bold letters, she wrote on the whiteboard. 'McMurdo Organic Seed Stores Antarctica Division.' Then placed her marker down.

I scanned the words not once, but twice. I narrowed my eyes, squinting a little. What stuck out was the acronym. MOSSAD. Was I seeing things? Surely not?

I stuck my hand up like some school kid in a lecture room. "Have you noticed the acronym?"

Maggie smiled back at me. "How did I know you were going to say that, Nathan. Yes, I'm aware. It has nothing to do with MOSSAD other than pure coincidence. But I was equally as alert as you when I was first given this information."

"What's this about then?" I asked.

"We'll get to it in a bit. But first, I want you all to know we're not leaving here today until we have no white space left on this whiteboard. I want ideas. Every idea, no matter how small. So, let's start people. Let's put our heads together and get something down."

I sprung up and asked the obvious. "What do we have on this Quinlan?"

"Nothing yet," Maggie said, almost despondently. "But make no mistake about it, Nathan. Whoever this fellow is, he will make contact soon enough. He has played this for far too long. You're right in suggesting Quinlan's tactic is to drag this out and keep us on the defensive. But now we have something that will bring him out of the shadows. No longer the deadlock. Time to smoke the bastard."

I knew what had to be done next. And I knew how it was going to get done.

"We can start by finding the Guardianship base of operations."

"That's not gonna be easy, big hoss," Bosco said. "The Guardianship don't have a base of operations. They're all integrated."

"You know as well as anyone here," Maggie added, eyeing me. "The Guardianship don't fly colours. They don't wear a uniform. Much the same as terrorists, the Guardianship could be here, there, or anywhere. You could walk right past one in the street and you'd never know. How can one find a base of operations when they appear to operate out of cells? One, we don't have any idea where those cells are, and two, we'll never know when the next Guardianship sleepers become activated. It's exactly as Bosco says. They are integrated into the very fabric of our lives. Invisible until activated. The worst kind of warfare."

I put my idea forward. "They have a Black Hawk."

"And that's not unusual," Maggie replied. "We already know they have access to top military spec equipment. And top military spec ordnance, I might add."

"What about the fuel?" I put in.

Maggie spun and wrote the word 'fuel' on the whiteboard next to what had already been written.

"Go on," she said. "What are your thoughts on fuel?"

"A Black Hawk has a range of 373 nautical miles," I said. "Which converts to around 700 kilometres."

I got up from my seat and walked over to the whiteboard. I picked up a marker and placed a mark. "Assuming this is where we were. Bosco's wrecked Chevy. Let's call it point A. It's just a matter of searching within a 700-kilometre radius of that point."

I penned out a circle on the whiteboard, calling it point B. Everyone locked eyes and listened. I continued. "We can assume a certain amount of fuel was consumed getting to point A. If the Black Hawk was at bingo fuel, then the radius of the search zone point B is smaller by half. Just 350 kilometres. We can also assume if the base we're looking for is outside of the zone point B, then we're looking for fuel dumps point C.

"If we find fuel dumps, then we can estimate a base of operations in the general direction between Points A and C. I believe the Black Hawk was either approaching, or at bingo fuel. Those guys were in too much of a hurry to get away. It would've been an easy search and kill. I was right there in their sights. But they didn't bother to put any effort into searching further. They were at bingo fuel. They needed to expedite their return. Trust me on this."

Maggie immediately spun and faced Andrew who was sitting at the computer. "Get us a list of abandoned military installations or anything else of interest within a 350-kilometre range of Bosco's wreck."

Andrew nodded and went to work.

"You see, Nathan," Maggie said. "It's all in the detail. You've earned your money today. Thank you for this."

As I sat back down, Maggie spoke loudly. "Anything else we can work on?"

"Any word back on the samples recovered from William Creek?" Bosco asked.

"Yes, actually. And I was getting to that. We have a match on the blood sample that points to this fellow." Maggie approached her desk and held up an eight by ten-inch photo, then passed it to Bosco. He scanned it and passed it Teresa who then passed it to me.

Maggie went on. "This man, a Columbian expat by the name of Alfredo Sanchez, was on the FBI blacklist after serving a prison sentence for cocaine trafficking in 1989. However, after he was released from prison, there was no record of him leaving the United States for Australia. Immigration have nothing on him at all. Unfortunately, there is no further intelligence on his movements. By this information, we can therefore assume this man was a Guardianship soldier."

"A dead end," I said.

"Not exactly, Nathan," Maggie said. "I have to say I wasn't prepared for what I found next. After digging further into Alfredo

Sanchez's activities prior to his conviction, I learned this man was also in the business of importing coffee into America. By all accounts, a legitimate venture, or so it seemed. He made the mistake of using the coffee as the vehicle for his illicit drug activities, which led to his arrest.

"Who could've guessed the cocaine was just a sideline for this fellow? For raising a bit of extra cash. It was the coffee itself that was of importance. Not the cocaine. As a matter of fact, had there been no cocaine at all, we might not have discovered the importance of the coffee shipment. I can only speculate the cocaine trafficking was off his own back and never part of the Guardianship operation. A clear cock-up on his part, I'd say. Wouldn't you agree?"

"That depends," Bosco said. "What's with the coffee?"

"Thank you, Bosco. I was getting to that. But first, let me sidetrack a little. It's all relative. Trust me." Maggie took a breath and looked down at something on her desk. "Canberra got in touch only hours ago with leaked intelligence from someone who chooses to go by the name 'Blue'. It was quite a surprise and completely unexpected. I have no idea how or why this Blue leaked to Canberra. I speculate my enquiries with the FBI sparked it, but who'd know? That being what it is, Blue's intelligence points directly back to this Alfredo Sanchez in ways that will astound."

Maggie then moved over to the whiteboard and double underlined the words 'McMurdo Organic Seed Stores Antarctica Division.'

She went on. "The leaked intelligence from Blue suggests somewhere in close proximity to McMurdo Station in Antarctica there exists a vault containing seeds of all known plant species, held in deep freeze. Having this intelligence can only lead to one speculation of why the vault is there."

"A doomsday vault?" Bosco said slowly.

Maggie nodded and winked. "Your deduction is correct, Bosco. That's exactly what it is. And there's more. Coffee plant seeds. Coffea Arabica to be precise. The intelligence Blue has given up suggests the Coffea Arabica seeds that are held in deep freeze in Antarctica have been genetically altered."

"How genetically altered?" Teresa asked.

Maggie paused then rubbed her eyes. It appeared she was as tired as I was. As tired as we all were. "This is complicated and there's much to get through. I think we should all take a break before we continue."

Nobody wanted the break. No one rose from their chairs. Maggie grabbed a wad of papers and tapped the edge of her desk lightly with her fingertips, casting her eyes over us.

"No break?"

"Give it to us straight," Bosco said.

"We don't have the time," I put in. "Every moment is crucial."

Teresa nodded vigorously.

Maggie put her papers down on her desk and paused. "Alright. I hope you've all got your heads in the right space before I start. This is not going to be easy to swallow. You must all take it for what it's worth. This intelligence is all confirmed by our top analysists at Ben Chifley." Maggie put her papers down and spread them out on her desk.

"Coffea Arabica genetically altered," she began. "These seeds, when germinated and planted, grow as ordinary plants. However, these plants have something extraordinary. These plants release helium-3. The coffee beans from the plant also contain the helium-3 element. And that's not all. The FBI managed to track down shipments of these Coffea Arabica seeds going into the United States from Columbia. This is the connection with Alfredo

Sanchez. From there, the FBI were able to intercept shipping manifestos showing the seeds and coffee beans being shipped out of America."

"McMurdo Station," I said.

"You're spot on, Nathan. But let me say this. Not only Coffea Arabica, but the intercepted manifest also records seeds of other plant species. *Thousands* of species. All originating from the Columbian source. All connecting back to Sanchez. But Sanchez was not alone in this. After further inquiries, we established a vast network of individuals exporting seeds out of Columbia. Perhaps these other seeds haven't been genetically modified in the same way as the coffee plant seeds. There's no intelligence to suggest otherwise. However, one can assume *why* they were listed in the same shipping manifest. My guess is they've used other seeds to mask the export activities of the Coffea Arabica. Either way, we've got a job to find out."

"What you're suggesting is too unbelievable," Bosco cut in. "And to be honest, coffee plant seeds? I mean, c'mon guys. This is a little odd and farfetched, don't you think? Why not turnips or tomatoes? Why not goddamn horse radish? I can't see it. It's all codswallop. This is a clever hoax to distract us from this Quinlan guy."

"I see and understand your scepticism, Bosco," Maggie said. "Let me put a little perspective on this. I'll ask you a simple question. How much coffee do *you* consume every day? How much coffee does the *average* person consume every day? I can tell you now, coffee is consumed in much higher quantities than turnips or radishes. Added to that, we can't ignore what has been virtually placed in our lap by this Blue."

Maggie trailed off. After pausing a beat she went on, ignoring Bosco's apprehension. "The intelligence shows the vault in Antarctica is a collaboration of the United States and other Western Hemisphere nations. Top secret due to the nature of the business. We can therefore assume it is, by all standards, an archive of seeds kept in storage for any future cataclysmic event. Whatever that may be. Manmade or natural. That day will come in humanity's future. That being the way it is, it seems the Guardianship have actively used the McMurdo facility for their own means. It gives us an idea of how cloaked the Guardianship actually is. The vault near McMurdo Station known as Vault Vitae-G is overseen by a detachment of CIA Special Activities Division operatives. By that, we can clearly assume the Guardianship has infiltrated the CIA and is somehow working with them shoulder to shoulder, unbeknownst to those in the genuine task force."

I wondered what was to be done next. Could Scotty-Blue be the 'Blue' who leaked the intelligence to Canberra? The more I thought about it, the more it began to fall into place.

Welcome to the world of lies and secrets. . .

"Questions?" Maggie asked.

"Who's Blue?" I already had my suspicions. I needed confirmation.

Maggie positioned herself for what I thought was going to be a lengthy discussion, only to be interrupted by Andrew at the computer. Andrew passed Maggie a printout. She took it from him and after reading the note smiled wryly.

"Maralinga," Maggie said with new enthusiasm. "Maralinga is where we start our search for Angel." She faced Andrew. "Get us in touch with CIA Director McKinnon. I think we might have enough to requisition that U2 aircraft of theirs."

CHAPTER SEVENTEEN

Coffea Arabica

BY THE TIME THE DAY WAS OVER, the whiteboard was completely covered in coloured marker and no white space was left. We'd nutted out all the intelligence we had. Unfortunately, no word yet from this Quinlan. It appeared whoever Quinlan was; he was out there somewhere biding his time. I only hoped Angel was okay. We *all* hoped.

It was only a matter of time before he made contact. From there, the negotiations would start. I already knew the policy. Negotiations with terrorists never went well. In the past, most instances never made it to the table. What made this case any different? It was a most discomforting realisation.

Maggie had disappeared from the meeting room the moment Andrew connected the coms to Langley. They'd been gone for almost an hour. Even so, their absence seemed to span just moments. Maggie walked back into the meeting room with facsimiles in her grip. "We have our U2," Maggie said. "Nathan and Teresa, pack a bag. You're both travelling with me to Canberra. Andrew will coordinate from here." Maggie faced Bosco. "We'll need you abroad, Bosco."

"Let me guess. Antarctica?"

"First to Langley for a mission brief," Maggie answered. "You'll be inserted into the next CIA rotation to Antarctica. This is a recon mission, Bosco. Not sabotage. We do not want to disturb any legitimate business down there. Find the Coffea Arabica seeds. Report back with your findings. That's all. Unfortunately, you'll be there until the following CIA rotation. I suggest you pack some extra woollies."

"Yeah," Bosco said, then put his head in his hands. "How did I know that was coming?"

"Anything further?" Maggie asked.

"Will you be doing the negotiations?" I asked.

"Absolutely not. We are all far too emotionally invested. A negotiator has been appointed. That's the reason for the trip to Canberra. Added to that, Canberra has more up-to-date electronic equipment to handle the situation than we have here. The negotiator is . . ." Maggie held her hand out to Andrew, who was standing as though he'd just had his hand on a dodgy electrical cord. With a hand visibly shaking, he passed a facsimile to Maggie.

"The negotiator is an experienced . . ." Maggie looked down at the facsimile. Her face paled. "The negotiator is . . . Mathew Malloy. ASIO counterintelligence." The paper she had in her grip slipped from her fingers to the table.

Bosco looked up. "No shit. The same Malloy as . . ."

"The same Malloy who did the Sydney Opera House botch up?" I said.

"How can this be?" Teresa put in.

"How did we get *stuck* with this guy," I said disbelieving. "Malloy is no good for this."

It was Malloy in control of the seven hostages held at the foot of the Opera House stairs in 1995. It was Malloy who called the bluff of the jihadist standing with them, armed with a chest full of explosives and deadly packets of ball bearings while chanting the words Allahu Akbar. It was Malloy who moved the SRG into place, ordering them to take the fucker down. Out in the open, in the middle of the day, an SRG sniper took the shot. After the dust had settled, all hostages were lost, along with another twenty-two dead and injured. Malloy's intelligence of the man carrying fake explosives was incorrect. He called the bluff. He went in on a hunch. The lives of many were lost as a result.

Maggie passed the facsimile back to Andrew. "I want clarification on this," Maggie said. "Get on the blower and get me the Director-General. If he's unavailable, then the Minister for Defence. Failing that, the Prime Minister, for God's sake. I want clarification, Andrew. Make it happen."

Clearly stunned, Andrew went back to his computer and sat down. He mumbled something under his breath.

Maggie went to her desk chair and slid down into it. "Obviously now, if Malloy takes this on we have our hands full. Let us all hope cool heads will prevail."

* * *

Andrew put his headset down at the side of his computer keyboard. "Prime Minister Keating on the blower."

"We'll take it on speaker, Andrew," Maggie said, then waited for the pilot light on the speaker to show up red.

As I waited for the voice of the Prime Minister, I thought back. The conversation I'd had with him amounted to a few short, sharp statements. It was the last time I wore the khaki pollies with sergeant stripes and the sand-coloured beret bearing the winged dagger. I knew I was due to be stood down. I'd already checked the paperwork and the date was drawing near. Although I had my suspicions, I wasn't fully aware why I was summoned to the Prime Minister's Sydney residence, Kirribilli House. The whole thing was lightning fast. No notification of anything until that exact same morning.

Getting there in my shiny kit, I found myself in the company of other military personnel and civilians who were in the process of being interviewed by the media. Then my suspicions were confirmed and I wrestled with the urge to get up and run from the place.

During that day, I hovered in the background as individuals were given their awards for certain occasions of heroism and good deeds done. I watched on as the number of awardees dispersed. There I was, the last to leave. On my left was the Minister for Defence Gary Punch. Next to him, Chief of Army Lieutenant General John Sanderson. On my right, The Governor-General Sir William Deane.

PM Paul Keating hovered in front of me. Immediately, the media were given firm instructions to cut airtime and pack up their equipment. Keating's eyes scanned me up and down. "Sergeant Masters," he said, eyeing me with a set of birdlike eyes down his long nose. "We owe you our gratitude. You've done your country proud."

After awarding and pinning the Medal for Gallantry to my uniform, he said in words almost at a whisper. "Walk with me. Walk and talk."

I found myself on the front porch of Kirribilli House alone with Paul Keating. His officials and minders were out of earshot as he positioned himself for words I was not expecting. Keating regarded me before speaking in the same volume as before, whispering down low, "I have something that might interest you." In a single breath, he went on and confirmed everything Scotty-Blue had said about Pine Gap and Prime Minister Whitlam's undoing. The rest of the conversation was pretty much a blur but ended with him convinced I could contribute with time spent among the elite of Australian Intelligence. ASIS.

That was then. Now, as I sat waiting for Paul Keating's voice to arrive out of the speaker, I wondered how this would begin.

"Good afternoon, Colonel Mack," Paul Keating said. "I don't need to remind you it's an election year. I'm afraid bloody Howard's campaign has got legs longer than mine this time. My arse is in the wind. Make it quick."

"Good afternoon, sir," Maggie responded. "I understand about your election commitments. But I must insist you give us your attention in this matter."

"And what matter are we talking about, Colonel?"

"The matter regarding Eagle Shield. I take it you've been brought up to date?"

"I have. And I also have a missive on my desk from the Director-General. Also, the photographs taken by Detachment 421. I have to say, what a bloody mess."

Keating chuckled lightly. Maggie rolled her eyes. I couldn't believe our PM's statement. He made light of the situation, expressing it with irony. Something he was good at, I supposed. It was the same arrogance the media had tagged and bagged him with. Either way, in that moment, my vote to Howard and the Liberals was a done decision.

Maggie went on. "I'm opposed to the negotiator appointed by ASIO, sir. I need you to intervene and get us someone more adept than this Mathew Malloy."

"Malloy," Keating sounded staggered. "You're kidding."

"We need to change this, sir."

"The last I heard, Malloy wasn't on the payroll, Colonel. But I . . ."

The room fell instantly silent. Maggie eyed the speaker. The red pilot light was no longer glowing red. She tapped the device lightly, then a bit harder. "Did we just lose the Prime Minister?"

Andrew, from his chair at the computer, spun and eyed his stepmother. Shock sitting there in his eyes.

"Andrew. What the bloody-hell is going on?" Maggie said.

Andrew responded with a slight stutter to his voice. "Q-Quinlan on the blower."

Maggie took a breath. She marched out from behind her desk with both hands on her hips. "Put Quinlan through to speaker, will you please?"

Maggie flicked her blond-grey hair to one side, and eyed the speaker on the table again, as though willing Quinlan's voice to punch through. The pilot light glowed red. No one spoke for a moment or two. The silence was deafening. We waited.

A voice jutted from the speaker. A voice digitally cloaked, generated from some electronic device. "We have your girl. We want the disk . . ."

I shot a stare at Bosco and Teresa, both of whom appeared to be struck silent. Their facial expressions were long in disbelief.

Maggie raised her hand, locking eye contact with Andrew. "With whom am I speaking?" she said, then paused.

A moment passed. I checked the pilot light. Still red. Still connected.

"Quinlan."

Maggie walked, measuring her steps closer to the meeting table. "Proof of life, Quinlan," she said calmly. "You and I both know this can't go anywhere without proof of life."

Another tense moment passed. A crackle. A bit of static on the line. The sound of footsteps erupted from the speaker. Hard footsteps, then more footsteps. The footsteps of a child. Another crackle. The urgent voice of a ten-year-old girl. "Nathan? Maggie?"

I was about to scream out her name. It took every ounce of will to hold it back. Maggie shot me a stare that said everything I had in my head must be silent. I bit my bottom lip hard enough to draw blood. The coppery taste filled my mouth and I swallowed it down.

"Nathan . . .!" Then Angel screamed a most blood-curdling squeal. A rustle. Commotion from wherever she was. I imagined what she was going through. I pictured in my mind how she was trapped and held captive. Maybe she was tied. Maybe not. Who'd know? I stood from my chair. I placed both palms down on the meeting room table and bent my head forward. I saw my own reflection in the highly polished table. My face, twisted. Snarled in anguish. I closed my eyes and bit down harder. Teresa reached and placed a hand on my back. Unwillingly, I sat back down.

The low, manipulated voice came back. "You have your proof of life," he said. "Now. We want that disk."

Maggie held up her hand. Her instruction was clear. No one was to speak. If it were possible, not even to breathe. Everyone was to hold. The room was silent enough to hear things not ordinarily heard. A car from outside. The tick from the clock in the hall. A drip from the tap in the bathroom. A moment passed. Then another.

"We want the disk!" the voice said again, louder.

My breathing shortened. A mere short sharpness just able to sustain life. Maggie was holding back. Why was Maggie holding back?

Maggie. What are you doing?

"What of the others?" Maggie asked, cutting through the silence. "No one else will die today, Quinlan."

No words. More footsteps. Rushing footsteps. More commotion.

Within the time it took for a human heart to push blood, the voice of a male somewhere in the background. "No . . . NO, NO!"

BLAT!

Then another. BLAT!

A metallic sound clinked on a hard floor. I heard Angel cry out. My heart shuddered. Yet another hostage was killed.

Quinlan's footsteps rushed back to his phone. "Now . . . do I have your attention."

It wasn't a question. It was a statement!

"And what makes you think we haven't made a copy of the disk?" Maggie said.

He laughed. A most evil, sardonic laugh. I'd heard that laugh, digitally cloaked or not. But where did I hear that laugh? Where?

Quinlan cut back in. "You cannot copy the disk. You will destroy it! But you know that already. If you destroy it. E-v-er-y-one-will-die."

Then Quinlan laughed. Again. The evil fuck that he was. I knew it. I knew that laugh. Where?

Maggie's look of sheer shock drilled into my head. Her stare hardened. She immediately spun and signalled a cutthroat to Andrew. Andrew disconnected the line.

I wanted to get up and object. Where was she going? What was she doing?

"Relax, everyone," Maggie said, at the edge of a sigh. "We'll no longer be on the back foot of anything."

The policy I'd dreaded arrived as expected. No negotiations with terrorists. But it was Angel's life in Maggie's hands.

"Quinlan needs the disk and he's played his highest card," Maggie said to everyone there, even though she regarded me, looking down into my eyes. "Angel *will* be safe, there's no doubt. There's too much in it for Quinlan. He knows how to get in touch. Next time, we'll be ready."

CHAPTER EIGHTEEN

Game On

TWO WEEKS PASSED WITH NO WORD of anything. Two weeks, equivalent to fourteen days. Equivalent to 336 hours. Equivalent to 20,160 minutes. Equivalent to 1,209,600 seconds. I counted every one of them. And the counting went on.

We'd not made our way to Canberra. However, Bosco's mission to Antarctica, codenamed Crossbow, was underway. I'd not noticed him leave, only that one morning he didn't appear in his usual manner. Bosco had crept away during the night. I thought for a brief second his clandestine departure was to avoid any further discussion of his involvement with Detachment 421. Then I realised it was normal for Bosco to just up and disappear. Something he was good at.

Where in the heck was this Quinlan? We hung around, sleeping little. Eating just enough to keep upright. I wondered at times if it was the other way around, that Angel would no doubt be hanging on for me. I hung on for her. I clung to every ounce of hope. I stuck to courage as best I could. And the time dragged on.

There on the whiteboard, several photographs clung to its edges, taken from the edge of space via the CIA U2 over Maralinga. Zoomed in shots confirmed everything we'd expected.

We'd found the base of operations we were looking for. The photographs revealed not one, but three Black Hawk helos on the ground, positioned around what appeared to be a set of old dilapidated, concrete buildings and shipping containers that were scattered around as though they'd been dropped. The question was what to do about it? Moving in on the target had its own set of consequences.

Angel's extraction was critical and without any further communication from Quinlan, any mission on Maralinga became locked in a standoff. As well as Angel, there was at least one other hostage to consider. And after all, we had no intelligence to suggest Angel and the hostages were even at Maralinga. In the end, it came down to nothing more than mere assumption.

* * *

Another white board was delivered into the meeting room and butted up against the other. One blank. One full of coloured scribbles and blue-tacked photographs stuck around the edges. I sat at the meeting table feeling heavy and malnourished, Teresa at my side. Her eyes no longer sparkled but were red-rimmed due to lack of sleep.

Maggie and Andrew walked in, carrying folders and wads of paper, placing them on Maggie's desk as though they were much heavier than they truly were. I scanned the meeting room. Without Bosco, the room felt empty. I couldn't help but smile while considering the fact Bosco made his presence known wherever he was. He was a pain in the arse, I thought. Oddly, without him I realised I'd lost a mate, no matter how much of a pain in the arse he was.

On the table in front of me, a mug of coffee had already gone cold. Considering Bosco's task, I was reluctant to drink it even with the dash of Wild Turkey I'd added out of habit. Teresa sat silently beside me with her fingers locked tightly together. Andrew was at the fresh whiteboard, taking the protective plastic layer off with a set of long zips. Maggie was behind her desk, looking down and shuffling papers. Her avoidance in making eye contact was already building up questions in my mind. Something was about to go down. This day was different than the last days and weeks. Something appeared to be in the air. It was game on. Finally.

Maggie raised her head and locked eye contact. "Righto . . ."

When Maggie said 'righto,' it was the same as 'Stand-to' being shouted by a commanding officer to his troops. There it was. 'Righto.' Teresa, at my side, sat with her back straight. Her body language changed. She knew the same as me, I supposed. My spirits lifted and I ended up taking a swig of that spiked cold coffee.

Maggie began. "We're not sitting idle any longer. The waiting has gone on long enough."

Andrew was writing on the fresh whiteboard. A single word in big red letters in the top left-hand corner. 'Barras.'

Maggie left her desk and moved toward the big red letters, picking up a marker and double underlining the words. "While we wait for word back on Crossbow, Barras is our mission for the rescue of Angel and any other hostages the Guardianship might have. We know of one other hostage. We have to prepare for the possibility there might be more."

Andrew made his way from the whiteboard to the meeting table and placed mission briefs in front of Teresa and me. I took up a document stamped with the Australian coat of arms in the top left-hand corner, Barras printed in bold. Objectives underneath. 'Insertion into enemy base, Maralinga' below that.

Maggie continued. "Nathan and Teresa. Your mission is insertion into the enemy base at Maralinga under the cover of German tourists gone astray. You are to be captured and held captive by whoever is holding Angel and the hostages. We hope you will find yourself in the company of this Quinlan fellow, and then work out what is necessary to evacuate Angel and the hostages. Your primary objective is the release and the safe return of those held captive. Your secondary is the capture of Quinlan. Your tertiary is the destruction of any infrastructure, adopting scorched earth policy to any Guardianship-controlled edifices."

"I'm not overjoyed with secondary," I said.

"You'll do your best, I'm sure," Maggie responded. "Think of the intel we can pull from this fellow after we capture him."

I wondered how Barras would succeed, knowing it was inevitable I would come face to face with Quinlan. I'd need to fight the urge to put a bullet into his head. Maybe I'd default to the tertiary, leaving the bastard tied. I held my breath thinking it over and scanning the pages. Maggie cut through my thoughts.

"Before you say anything, Nathan and Teresa, we can draw an assumption about Quinlan. Firstly, this man appears to have access to classified material. How this is possible is still being worked over in Canberra. However, that being the case, it is probable you both may be a known entity to him. We'll get your undercover worked out to take this unfortunate set of circumstances out of the equation. You'll not be compromised by the time we're finished. We'll have all of your documentation ready and you'll be as German as any German citizen."

"I don't know German," I said.

"I realise this. We're not about to drop you in without the proper coaching. Both you and Teresa will be dispatched to Swan Island for intensive training and tutoring. You'll have time to explore your objectives and formulate your actions-on. But time is of the essence."

"How much time?" I asked.

"You'll deploy in two weeks from today."

* * *

Two weeks slipped past at Swan Island. My head was shaved. My fake beard looked real and as long as ZZ Top's Dusty Hill. A tattoo at the back of my head, done by a guy who'd turned up suddenly and unannounced. He etched India ink deep into my skin. Not so much as a recoil in his eyes from the sharp and penetrating pain he inflicted. This guy, white. Hair pure white. His eyes. Those piercing blue-pink eyes. I watched him in the mirror as he went about his task. I was drawn to his appearance and couldn't look away.

"Relax," he said in a low and slow tone, while staring back at my reflection. "I'm an albino. Get over it."

"I never knew one. Never seen one," I said awkwardly.

"You have now."

He walked slightly away and grabbed more ink from a hard case. Like a barber, he came back at me with the tattoo gun buzzing and bent my head forward. I sat still, putting my trust in a guy I'd not previously met. The choice of tattoo wasn't my call. He'd already worked it out. The things we do, I kept thinking. With my head tilted forward in the reflection, I noticed the guy didn't have any tattoos on his body. Since when do tattoo artists have no tattoos?

I asked.

"I already told you I'm albino. I don't get to do this stuff on me. The ink won't take and it'll end up getting blotchy. Perhaps doing this job is my way of compensating." That voice. Every time he spoke, it was enough to chill my bones.

After he'd finished and I got control of my headache, he held up a hand-held mirror to the back of my head. I saw for the first time what he'd put there. A tattoo of a white eagle. The best I'd ever seen. With the white eagle in flight, wings flared, the image wanted to jump out in 3D. The intricacy and attention to detail was masterful. Almost photo-realistic. There was something else there. A sword gripped in an eagle talon.

"I'm amazed," I said, focusing on the sword. "I've never seen any tattoo of a white eagle with a sword." The tattoo by itself was far from any cliché. I was thankful for that, knowing it was going to be there until the day I took my last breath.

"The sword of destiny," he said across a shoulder, while placing his kit back into the hard case. "Everyone has a path, Nathan Masters. Most have several. Wisdom will help you choose. The sword of destiny will give you focus."

Post mission, my hair would grow back and cover it. Maybe I'd now keep my head shaved.

The tattooist continued to pack up his equipment with as much precision as it was unpacked. I was about to ask, but I could draw my own conclusions about the message in that tattoo. By the time I was convinced about the message, the tattooist was already making for the door.

"Wait!"

He turned.

"Thanks for the tatt. And thanks for the pain," I said. "I just let you get all intimate with the tattoo. The least you can do is offer your name."

"I'm Gabriel. But you already knew that, Nathan Masters."

Knew it? No. I had no idea. Gabriel who? Was it a puzzle I was supposed to solve?

"Gabriel who?"

He didn't respond. Like his low and slow voice, he'd already gone, almost melting away.

* * *

A passport bearing my new name, Karl Muller, was thrust into my hand on the day we left Swan Island. I was quietly confident with my new ability to speak German. I'd changed so much it was possible to be frightened by it. Along with my new persona, my cumbersome fake leg was replaced by a more modern equivalent. Titanium, with a knee joint that operated so smoothly the limp was now only slight. After they'd placed it on my stump, I couldn't help fist pumping the air. But Teresa – she was transformed into something quite extraordinary.

No longer the raven hair. No longer the Arabic accent. Teresa was a German blonde beauty in every sense of the term. Her name had become Adeline. Adeline Muller.

The mission clock was activated the moment our rental car arrived at the facility gate. A late model Jeep Cherokee kitted out for touring and with all the extras. It was no Land Rover, but it would do.

The Jeep smelled of a mix of leather and plastic and that new car smell. Two large suitcases were stowed on the rear seat. Inspecting the contents of the suitcases revealed clothes that said tourist, and a folder containing wedding cards and best wishes written in German by individuals we'd never know. A red velvet hard case containing matching gold wedding bands and a marriage certificate dated two weeks prior from somewhere in Las Vegas. My passport also reflected the recent visit to America out of Stuttgart and then on to Australia. Everything was put into place with much delicacy and finesse.

Just before I twisted the key in the ignition, I felt a warm kiss on my cheek. "Ich liebe dich," Adeline said with her beaming smile. She placed her hand on my fake leg. In that moment I wished I had my real limb. Even though there was no physical touch I could feel blood pushed to places that had recently only been used for the necessities of life. I returned her smile.

Before I had words, Adeline's mouth was locked over mine. I was in trouble for the first time in recent memory. Perhaps longer than that. I returned Adeline's passionate kiss with my hand on the back of her head, pulling her in with obsessive force. Like teenagers, our tongues wrestled together and I didn't care where we were. We were married after all. Newlyweds. In my wildest imagination, I never expected it. It was going to be a good mission, I thought. Different, but good. Our first night would see us pulled up somewhere in Adelaide and I was already in a hurry to get there.

CHAPTER NINETEEN

Distractions

WE'D STOPPED A HALF A DOZEN times along the way to the city of Adelaide. At times to fill the tank. Other times to go at it like a couple of eager bushy-tailed creatures hell bent on the task of procreation; we went at it at every opportunity we could find.

With the weather cold and rainy, and the Jeep parked at the side of the highway, we made good use of the back seat. The windows fogged. Moisture dribbled on both sides of the glass. Our bodies intertwined in a honeymoon dance, ignorant to the world outside. And nothing. Utterly nothing could take me further away from the reality of why we were here.

It was as though my lungs breathed new air. It was as though my life found new meaning. Getting into the driver's seat, I found my cheeks cramped with muscles I'd not previously known.

Just before sunset, we reached the traditional German-speaking town of Hahndorf. Another opportunity to get out for a stretch. An opportunity to mix with the locals and test our skills as German tourists, speaking nothing but what we'd learned. To my surprise, we held up well enough to pass off as the couple who'd made their way from Stuttgart to Australia. Finding a German beer hall, we feasted on weisswurst with spicy cabbage and mash, while drinking ale from insanely huge steins big enough to break a forearm. Leaving that place with a belly full of beer and sausage was much harder than I anticipated. After reaching the Jeep parked out the front, I tossed Adeline the keys. I was in no shape to drive.

With Hahndorf in the rear-view mirror, we motored down the mountain on the duel carriage expressway with Adelaide city and its beautiful lights soon coming into view.

"Es ist hubsch," said Adeline, pointing to the lights on the horizon.

"Ja. Es ist sehr hubsch," I replied, smiling. I wondered how on earth such a pretty sight could make its way into my awareness when in a matter of days, things would change drastically. Who knew what was waiting at Maralinga. Who knew the conditions and circumstances. We were, for all instances, detached from any safety net. We were on our own with no chance of any contact back to Firebird Station. No tap-out button. No rewind knob. Nothing but our cover story, which we hoped was good enough to fool. Considering our objectives, was it enough? We had no weapons. We had no tools of trade. Our mission was clear. Get to Maralinga and be captured. From there, one could only guess.

* * *

We made Port Augusta by 1200 hours the next day and travelled west on the Eyre Highway out of Poochera, Wirrulla, and Ceduna before pulling up for the night at Penong. The next sunrise saw us taking a sharp right turn at Nullarbor and heading due north into the wilderness, the desert hot enough to reach fifty-plus degrees.

Hot enough to cook a meal on a rock. Dead straight dirt roads stretched to the horizon and caught the unwary with their own death. No one sound of mind would attempt to travel the Trans Access Track without water and a vehicle that could hack it. It wasn't uncommon for unwary tourists to perish out here. So many had died or gone missing with no trace.

* * *

Dawn in the middle of nowhere was cold and amazingly dry. Packing up camp, Adeline said few words. Maralinga was a few short hours further north. In my mind, I rehearsed actions-on, then realised Adeline was away with her thoughts too. As Adeline stowed the tent back in its bag, I filled the tank with diesel from a yellow jerry can, making sure every drop of the slimy, stinky stuff was emptied.

"Karl . . . Up there . . . Look." Adeline said in German while pointing.

I put the empty jerry can back in its holder, then walked to Adeline's side and saw what she was seeing.

"What are they?" she said.

"Eagles," I told her after searching in my mind for the German translation. On the updraft, they were hovering in a line abreast appearing to have us caught in their sights. I realised I'd seen them before. They were the same seven eagles I'd seen back at William Creek.

"What are they doing?" Adeline asked, while swishing away flies. "Are they hunting?"

"No. They're showing the way. We'll follow. Let's get going."

There was no hesitation about it. After selecting four-wheel drive with the mere touch of a button, I steered the Jeep off the track and headed inland. The Jeep bounced hard over the rough surface that for all I knew had never previously been in contact with humans. The stony red surface, strewn with quartz and sand-stone rocks, rushed and scattered. I slowed down and sped up, pushing past trees that seemed to be screaming urgently for rain. And the heat . . . By ten in the morning, even the air conditioning struggled to keep the cabin within a range of twenty-eight and thirty degrees.

We drove down gullies and craggy creek beds. We pushed up sand dunes, sending frill necked lizards into a mad scramble. All the while those eagles were never far away. This was so surreal. I was chasing eagles across the desert. Was I mad? At times, we'd get close enough to see their eyes sparkling in the sunlight, then they'd move on again and I'd follow. They *were* taking us some-where. Showing us the way. The question was where? And to what?

In the distance, the eagles set themselves down on the ground. Getting closer, I could see the dirt around them darkened by what appeared to be . . . moisture? At first, I thought it was a billabong full of water. Logically, I already knew how rare that was and with the heat, how unlikely. Just before we reached the darkened patch in the middle of empty nothing, the eagles took flight and pushed away, disappearing into the remoteness.

"Stay here and I'll go . . ." I said to Adeline. "Better still, get behind the wheel. We don't know what we're dealing with."

Adeline nodded sharply and slid across to the driver seat as I hopped out. Walking to the depression in the dirt, I was horrified to find the darkness in the dirt was blood. Body parts and bone were haphazardly strewn about as though nothing else mattered. I was hard-pressed making out how many bodies. Two or three maybe. The few limbs sitting out in the open were stripped of flesh. Sections of torso had entrails hanging out in the sun.

As I got closer, the stink rose to my nose and punched me in the face. I covered my nose and mouth, but it didn't seem to help. I noticed something small and plastic in the shape of an L on the ground. I looked at the object awhile before it struck me. I knew what it was. I picked it up. Angel's puffer. She was here. My brain thumped. This was a place Quinlan was setting up for Angel's exchange. But what had gone wrong? The eagles, I wondered. Did they do this? It's no wonder Quinlan never got back in touch. No wonder so much time passed with no word of anything.

With Angel's puffer in my grip, I spun around. Before my legs led me away, I noticed something else. On the ground lay an electronic device partly covered by red dirt. I knelt down and studied it for a moment, then swept the dirt away. At first I thought 'booby trap.' But looking down at the object, I realised what it was. A tactical beacon. The exact same device I'd used down range in Iraq.

Getting back to the Jeep, I showed the items to Adeline. I explained about the puffer, telling her it could have only belonged to Angel. And that meant she was at one time in the vicinity.

"How do you know this belongs to Angel?" Adeline asked.

"Because it has no label on it. While we were driving down from Alice Springs, I saw her use it. I saw her peel the label off. Maybe it was a habit of hers. But this is Angel's asthma medication. So now she has none. If she has a bout of asthma without this, she's in serious danger."

Adeline took the item and studied it. Then I gave her the TACTBE.

"Communication device?"

"It's a tactical beacon," I said, struggling with the translation. "The tactical beacon is pre-tuned to the AWACS frequency."

"So, why is such a device here?"

"Hard to say. Maybe they've hacked it and are now using it for communication between them," I said. "The only way to find out is to…"

"Open a channel?" Adeline cut in, then held her breath. "Karl. This is very dangerous . . ."

"Yeah, I know. But the reason why we're here is to get compromised, remember? I can't think of a better way right now."

Adeline passed the TACTBE back to me with eyes wide and alert.

"You ready for this?" I said.

Adeline nodded slowly. "Yes, let's do this."

I took the device in my hand and switched it on. It lit up and there was a burst of static. My first instinct was to start talking, but I thought I'd tease it a little. I pressed the button on the side a few times to see if it grabbed anyone's attention. Nothing. I did it again, this time dropping a series of five carriers. Within a moment, a carrier came back. A series of two. I smiled. I'd just pinged the bastards. Whoever they were, they were listening.

I shot a sideways glance to Adeline who was looking extremely uncomfortable. I let it rest there for another moment, listening to the static. From out of nowhere, a series of five carriers came back. Four short. One long. Morse code, probably.

So I began.

Two short, one long, one short – the letter F.

Two short, one long – the letter U.

I let it rest and waited for a reply.

A moment later, a voice crackled and said, "Who is this?"

I knew I'd sparked their interest. Now let's drive this home.

I depressed the handset button. "Break . . . Break . . ." I said in German.

The voice came back. "Hey . . . who the hell is this?"

"Break-Break-Break . . ." I said again.

"Okay. Whoever you are . . ."

"Your mother sucks donkey dicks," I said in German.

Adeline rolled her eyes, but it didn't stop her from laughing. While she was laughing, I pressed the button for one long carrier, figuring it was a good bit of something to send.

"Stay right there, asshole!"

"Come get me. Mongrel." I yelled into the handset, then immediately switched it off.

I looked at Adeline. "So now's the time to get going, don't you think? Just for the exercise, let's give them something to chase."

Without a word, Adeline twisted the key in the ignition and planted her foot down hard on the accelerator. The little Jeep surged forward and swung north. No longer than forty minutes later, a Black Hawk came over the rise from behind, bearing down.

"What do we do now!" Adeline yelled.

"Now we stop and get out . . ."

CHAPTER TWENTY

Collapse

I STOOD BY THE SIDE OF THE JEEP and raised my hands in the air. Adeline was standing the same as me. From the door of the Black Hawk, which had hit the ground in a hurry, and several dark figures rushed toward us, springing from the dust. One aimed the butt of a rifle at my face. I felt the thud. I felt my brain pin-ball around in my skull. Then lights out.

* * *

It took me a second or two to realise my eyes were open. I could see nothing. Everything was black. The smell of hessian hit my senses. My head was covered with a sack. I tried to move my hands, but that was no good. My wrists burned with whatever they had used to tie them. I focused my hearing on the steady dripping of water into a bucket. I was in the same kind of horror story I'd not been in since SAS training back in '85.

I listened hard for any other sounds while I pushed my tongue hard up against my teeth. About three front teeth loosened and threatened to come out. The pain was an immense tug of war between the steady throb and the drilling headache. Nothing I couldn't handle. Another round of dental bills at some point, I thought. Listening with the full strength of my hearing revealed nothing but the sound of the water and someone, somewhere, listening to music I could barely make out. Every now and then I could make out a note. A guitar. An electric guitar. Where did I hear that before?

I stretched my hearing out as far as it could go. I sat not moving a muscle and concentrated on the sound. The music. What was it? I focussed my hearing and what I heard could be nothing else but a song by Metallica. I smiled. Angel. She loved Metallica. That meant one thing. Angel was being looked after. I felt my spirits lift and I knew I was not far from her company. But Adeline? Where had they taken her?

"Adeline?" I said softly from under the hessian hood. No response. No sound other than that constant dripping.

With my hands tied behind my back, I couldn't clap a hand to get a feel of any echo. It would've said a lot about where I was. Instead, I raised a foot and stamped it down. The echo told me concrete walls and floor. A splash also said water at my feet. My mind went to work. Bunker room. Putting it together, I guessed I'd been taken to the abandoned bunker complex at Maralinga, the same place they'd used for shelter from the nuclear weapons testing in the late fifties and sixties. Now, I had to work out what to do next.

Reaching down slightly, my fingers touched the metal frame of the chair. I wondered how long I'd been seated. Judging by my discomfort, it would've easily been a couple of hours. Curling my fingers revealed what was keeping me tied. If it was rope, there'd be a chance. Any knot could be undone. But I felt with outstretched fingertips nylon zip ties. I could break them, but not like this. Whoever had tied me had thought this one out. I was daisy tied. My breath left me as I realised there wasn't any hope of breaking free. My once raised hopes bled away. It was now a waiting game.

I listened, focusing on the music, wherever it was coming from. I concentrated on filtering out the steady dripping of water. *Enter Sandman.* That's what it was. It finished and I caught the edge of the next song. I heard the sudden eruption of footsteps from down there. Rustling and some muted voices. Then a scream. A scream that stopped the blood in my veins. Adeline!

"NIEN!" I yelled out.

From under the hessian sack, I screamed Adeline's name.

I rocked back and forth in my chair, hoping for something to give. I tried to force my bounds to break. "NIEN!" I screamed again. "FICK . . . DICH! FICK . . . DICH!"

A set of fleshy thuds bounced to my ears. Adeline cried out again. But then there were someone else's protests. The protests of a girl. Angel!

"NOOO! Leave her alone!" Angel cried out. I wanted to scream out to Angel. It took every bit of will to hold it back, but I had to keep things in play. I was German. A German tourist. It must stay that way. The game had begun and I had to hold it together or everything was lost.

From back there, wherever it was, I heard someone scream out, "Who the fuck are you! Who sent you!"

Adeline's cries went silent after a horrible fleshy sound told me she'd been knocked out. I heard Angel sobbing loudly. I felt useless and powerless. How I needed to be untied. How I wanted to let fly. But all those things I was feeling, all those emotions and reactions going on inside me, weren't doing me or anybody any good. It was time to suck it up. It was time to hold it down. It was time to get into the hard work and get going with what needed to be done. I was next. I readied myself.

* * *

With the hessian sack over my head, I wasn't sure how many there were. Two or three, maybe. I felt arms about my shoulders lift me from my chair. My body was dragged across the room and I found myself on my knees. The hessian sack was swiftly taken off my head. My eyes focused. Two muscle-bound freaks stood in front of me. Without knowing one way or another, I felt the presence of someone else from behind.

The first blow came down without any words. It felt as though I'd been hit by a train. My mouth instantly filled with blood. I spat it away. Number two wound himself up and he came down. If he'd used a bag of bricks, maybe it'd feel the same. I felt the ooze of more blood in my mouth. My tongue was mostly numb; I tried to get it safely away from my broken teeth.

"Who are you!" the big guy shouted down as he was winding up another blow.

"Nien Englisch . . . Nien Englisch . . ." I screamed, keeping things together, at the same time expecting more. He let me have it. I flung backward, reeling from the shock of a god-awful punch to the chin.

I brought my head up, shaking it a little. But that did nothing. Nothing at all. I saw them look at each other. One shrugged his shoulder. The other looked down at me. His eyes glistened with fury.

"Talk," he said. Then he wound up another and let it fly down. My head snapped sideways and I spat out some teeth with clots of blood. My mouth lock-jawed open. Blackness came to my left eye. My head screamed. Screamed out with pain! I fought it hard. I gave them nothing. I denied them all.

"Talk." Another explosion on my jaw. The same as the last, and the one before that.

"Ich bin verloren . . . verloren . . ." God knows how I got it out. My jaw was either broken or dislocated. It hurt more than I was willing to admit. I switched it off. I swallowed the pain. I gave them nothing.

"Talk." Another blow and my jaw was free and swinging. At the corner of my vision, something glinted in the dim light. I knew what it was. Knuckle duster. I held my breath, shut my eyes and braced for it. It didn't come. No more train wreck.

"No," the guy from behind said. "You'll kill him. And we need the fucker alive."

Before I knew it, the hessian bag was thrust over my head and I was lifted up off my knees. The metal chair squealed across the floor and I was sat down. For a brief second, I thought the bad was done. Reality checked back in. The chair was kicked over. I fell backward, my head connecting with the wet concrete floor. On my back, I knew what was coming. Still, I felt as though I could hold my breath for long enough.

As the water poured through the hessian sack, I pushed through the involuntary need for air. I held on until my mind said I could take no more.

Maybe a boot to my ribs caused me to break. I gasped and the putrid water entered, running down my throat. I tried not to swallow. I tried not to breath. The urge to cough came and I thought I might drown. I sputtered. Right at the edge. I could see something black coming. The very next second, they sat me back up.

A voice in front of me. "*Who* are you? *Who* sent you?"

"Nien Englisch," I said through my broken and blood-engorged mouth. I never knew saying words could hurt so much. But I still gave them nothing.

"Karl Muller . . . Ich bin Karl Muller . . ."

Silence. The dripping water. I heard one of them sigh.

"Quinlan wants to check this fucker's identity."

Footsteps splashing through water and a sudden draft told me at least two of them had gone. One was still there. I heard him pick something up. Something metallic. A snipping sound. The sound of metal on metal. He was coming at me with his implement and he was going to use it! I felt my eyes bulge from my injuries. I felt the cold metal on my hand. Then the sudden punch of pain exploded up my arm. The bastard had taken a finger. Now, along with the dripping of water into a bucket, there was the dripping of blood from my hand.

* * *

The door swung open. More were coming. Footfalls splashed on the floor toward me. I steadied. I braced. I tried not to breath. I wanted blackness. Maybe he'd get me there. I heard his footfalls step up behind me. I felt him grab my hand and swivel it around. Maybe he was going to squeeze it. I felt burning pain. I smelt alcohol. Then I put things together in my head.

"Joseph, Mary an' Jesus," a voice said. "Mongrel bastards did a good job on ya, didn't they, eh?"

I knew that voice from somewhere. The pitch. The tone. Everything about it sparked a memory from somewhere. I went to say something but stopped myself short. Maybe my mouth was in no shape to say anything. Who'd know if German was part of the guy's education. But one word I knew was universal across most languages.

"Wasser . . ." I was right out at the ragged edge of my alertness. I was on the verge of collapse. Blackness. It was there and I could almost touch it. Taste it. I wanted it. How dare it cheat me.

"Water? Yeah righto, mate. I'll get ya some, eh?"

That voice. How could I mistake it? I knew the guy. But what was he doing here? I must shut my mouth and not say anything. In the next moment, the hessian sack over my head was slightly raised and a steel mug found the corner of my mouth. I took a small sip, then coughed up blood clots that turned the water a cloudy red.

"Shit! Dun worry about it, mate. I'll get ya a fresh lot, eh?"

The guy I knew from years past took the sack off my head, then turned his back without looking at me. How could I hide? I looked to the side as much as I could. There was no hiding and nowhere to go.

With a fresh mug of water in his grip, he turned and met my gaze. The steel mug dropped from his grip. It hit the floor, loud. "Oh shit! You've gotta be bloody jokin', mate."

I mouthed words. It hurt like a bugger. "That obvious, huh?"

"Canter? What the fuck? What are you *doing* here?" he whispered. "An' that beard. Anyone can see it ain't real. It's hangin' off ya face all wonky."

Scotty-Blue reached over and peeled off my beard. "See? It's bloody worse than the hair of the dog. Reckon you should 'ave a go at ya wardrobe guy, eh?"

I put my head down. I smiled a bit, even through the agony. Despite everything, it was good to see Scotty-Blue. "Why're you here, Blue? You're not G? Tell me you're not."

Scotty-Blue looked down at me and winked. "Wish you knew the whole bit of it, mate. Lies and secrets, remember? And what's with the getup, anyhow?" He stepped back a pace, hand to his chin. "Oh shit. It's you who's got the disk, 'aven't ya? And you're 'ere for Angel?"

I nodded, but said, "No disk."

"Crap . . . Ya know they're gonna kill ya if they find out who ya are?"

I nodded again. I attempted to speak, but instead coughed up more blood. I looked up and Scotty-Blue had some kind of sad expression going on. In that moment, I knew he wasn't Guardianship.

"Well, we better not let it 'appen, eh?" Scotty-Blue said. "But that might be a bit 'ard right now. They took ya finger off so they can get at the print. They're scannin' records right now. You'd better 'ope that ya cover has been sorted. Cos if the prints don't match, they're gonna come down on ya harder than ya know."

"How much time have I got, Blue?"

"Mate, those blokes 'ave got kit that'll make ya eyes boggle. It's not gonna take long."

I said nothing. How could such an easy mission end up going so badly?

"Dun worry about Angel, Canter. I got 'er back. She's in me care," Scotty-Blue said as though reading my thoughts.

"Good on ya, Blue. But do you think you can get something to Angel? Her asthma medication is in my pocket. Can you get it to her?"

"Of course, mate. But I 'ave to ask, who's the sheila who came in with ya?"

"She's one of us."

"Already knew that bit. I'm askin' ya *who* is she? I'm privy to players. I know most of 'em. But in my book, she's unknown."

"Outsourced intelligence. MOSSAD," I said after thinking it over. "She's not to be harmed."

"Too late, mate. They bashed 'er up a bit, y'know? But she's alive, that's the main thing. They took her finger off too. They're doin' the same thing to her as they're doin' to you. I'd 'elp her a bit if I could. I can only push it so far. I got me own bizzo to get through, y'know?"

"What're you talking about? What bizzo. Are you G or not?"

"Look, Canter. Remember back in boot camp where I said to ya should we ever meet up again, you don't know me and I don't know you?"

"Yeah. I remember."

"That shit still stands, mate. I'll patch ya up best as I can. But ya gotta trust me on this. I got Angel's back. Nothin's gonna 'appen to 'er, if I can 'elp it. But you and your sheila? I dunno about that. I'll do me best. You've got an ally in this. That's somethin' at least."

Scotty-Blue patched up my hand with few words, then went to work on my broken face. He swabbed a bit here and there, obviously trying his best. His hardened expression told me there wasn't a lot he could do. While he swabbed at my bruises, I wondered what he was thinking about. He had that look on his face. He was away somewhere.

"I'll get ya a cup of coffee," he said.

How odd, I thought. He offered me coffee as though I was a visitor. Then it struck me. Maybe it wasn't as simple as that. Maybe he was probing me to see how much I was in the loop. It made sense. It made more sense than to simply offer me coffee. I tested the thought.

"I'm in the loop with Crossbow," I said. His brows dropped in a V.

"Thought so," he whispered. "But I 'ad to make sure."

"Did you leak to Canberra?"

"Hey, quieten down, Canter. There's ears 'round 'ere," he whispered down low. "An' yeah, mate. That was me. The word is Crossbow has isolated and contained the parent genome. That's good news, and stuff we can use."

"What parent genome? What are you on about?" I whispered, at the same time wincing from the sting of my facial injuries.

Scotty-Blue studied me with a serious expression on his face. He glanced to the door, then back to me. "Tell me you know about the O's," he said.

"The Oudarretians?"

Scotty-Blue immediately pushed a finger up to his lips. "Okay. Enough said. If you know the word, that tells me you're already in the loop. It's like this, Canter. Without the parent genome, the O's can't grow any more plants. When the source runs out, that's all there is."

"The Columbian source?"

"Yeah, mate. Columbia was the initial setup. To make it work and to get enough 'elium-3 for their needs, the O's need more crop. That can't 'appen without the parent genome. It was kept in the Antarctica vault for safe keeping."

I thought about what he was saying. Something wasn't adding up. Surely finding the parent genome was just a matter of looking for it elsewhere. "Where did this parent genome come from, Blue?"

"Mate. Do I have to spell it out for ya? Oudarret, of course. It's called Hadgitol. Alien vegetable. Why did ya think it's so closely guarded? There's only one parent genome. Should anything 'appen to it, the O's are most definitely up the Birdsville Track without a camel."

"And if it's destroyed?"

"It ain't gonna stop 'em from getting the 'elium-3. But it will slow things a pace. It'll put 'em back a few years. A decade, maybe. Like I said. Stuff we can use to our advantage."

"Are you in contact with Crossbow?"

"Me? Nah, mate. Firebird Station is. I intercepted the intel from there."

"Jesus, Blue. How in the heck . . ."

"You dun wanna know, Canter. I 'ave me ways. By the way, I'll get word back to your blokes so they can get a picture on ya status. Then we can work out what to do next. Like I said, I can only push it so far. Just . . . follow me lead an' she'll be apples, eh?"

After he'd finished, Scotty-Blue replaced the sack over my head. Then he was gone as quickly as he came. I was left wondering what next. Where to from here? I figured I'd find out soon enough.

CHAPTER TWENTY-ONE

Presence

IT WASN'T ANY LONGER THAN A COUPLE of moments after Scotty-Blue left that cold, dark place when I heard the door punch open. From beneath the sack over my head, I both heard and felt feet rushing toward me. I began to struggle as hands grasped me about the shoulders. At first I thought it was another shot of waterboarding. The sack partially lifted and a wad of material was pushed up to my face. I pushed back in my chair at the scent. Chloroform. Then there was nothing.

* * *

"Nathan Masters!" the voice yelled.

I heard it, but my eyelids still had the weight of a barbell.

"Nathan Masters!" Something suddenly connected with my right shin. I shrieked out with the sudden blast of agony. My eyes. I tried to open them. It was as though they'd been stitched closed.

"Wake the fuck up, Nathan Masters!" Then a rush of something cold, wet, and stinking over my head. I knew the ammonia smell. The urine smell. I pushed it from my mind. I shook my head wildly, side to side, and opened my heavy eyes.

In a chair opposite, Adeline was tied and gagged, horror sitting there in her eyes. In a chair next to Adeline, a civilian most probably from William Creek appeared equally as terrified. A G-man with black nylon tights over his head paced back and forth holding a knife in his grip. In my heart, I knew it was about to get bad, worse than before.

The guy with the black nylons moved up behind me, and with the knife he cut my hands free. Instantly I swung back with an elbow. It met air. I tried to get up from my seat. The horror, I'd been tied down.

Laughter from the G-man. "Holy shit. You're a live one, ain't ya?"

The voice. That fucking voice! Where had I heard it before?

He left the room, closing and locking the door with a few heavy, loud clunks.

On a table in the corner, I noticed a closed-circuit TV. The blank screen lit up. First graininess, then Angel in a seated position somewhere else, also tied down. The guy I'd seen a moment before appeared behind Angel with the knife. She shook her head, her eyes full of terror and tears.

"NOOO! NOOO!" I yelled out, rocking back and forth in my chair, trying desperately to escape.

The voice of the man with the black nylons from a speaker in a corner, "Nathan Masters. Where is that disk! What happens here today is about you, Nathan Masters!"

How did he know my name, for fucksake!

I reached down with shaking hands and began to untie myself from the chair. Quinlan, on the monitor, laughed. "It doesn't matter, Nathan Masters. Feel free to move around. Go ahead. Make like a free man."

"You bastard!" I screamed. "Touch the kid and I'll be the last one you see!"

"You're right, Nathan Masters. Someone *will* die. And guess what? You get to choose."

My mind buzzed with the punch of adrenalin. Removing the last piece of rope, I leaned forward and released Adeline, then the civilian. I immediately made for the door and tried to force it open. No good.

"There's a gun under the chair, Nathan Masters!"

I spun and looked, catching a glimpse of the metal lying there on the floor. I immediately moved and picked it up, then checked for rounds. One shot in the chamber. That's all there was. I sat down in the metal chair. Teresa and the civilian both stared, terrified, facing me. It suddenly struck me how this would play out.

"The clock on the wall, Nathan Masters. You have . . . I was gonna say twenty minutes. Let's call it ten. Choose wisely!" On the monitor, he placed the blade to the base of Angel's throat.

"Let's talk about this!" I screamed.

He laughed. A sardonic chuckle, most evil. That laugh again! "The disk, Nathan Masters," he said. "The disk. Until I have it, someone will die. *You* will choose."

I put my head down and thought hard. "I have it in my pocket," I lied, grasping at anything to turn the situation around. The only thing I could come up with. But the bastard ignored me.

Before I knew it, Angel's gag was swiftly taken off. She screamed out. "NATHAN!"

"Angel! I've got this!"

"NATHAN! HELP! ME!" she screamed.

"Tick-fucking-tock, Nathan Masters!"

I noticed a small amount of blood trailing down from where Quinlan had the blade to Angel. Where was Scotty-Blue? Didn't he say he had her back?

"Tick tock! Time is all you have, Nathan Masters. Someone will die. You must choose!"

I put my head down. Yeah, I thought it for a brief second. One round I could use on me. A selfish thought. I didn't know where it came from. Something human, I supposed. I eyed the clock. Time. It was getting away. My mind ran through the possibilities. How could I make something appear that I didn't have? It was impossible. Quinlan wanted blood, maybe just for his amusement and nothing more. I took the handgun and studied it. What was I to do!

Angel must live . . . Angel must live . . .!

Everything went spinning around.

My choice was none. Time. I felt like throwing the gun at the monitor. Somehow, I'd have to live with my conscience after making a choice. For the rest of my days. Collateral damage. My logical brain was trying to cut in. Trying to give me the answers. Out of everything, there was simply too much at stake.

My eyes met the civilian sitting there, visibly trembling.

But then.

I took a breath.

I closed my eyes.

I calmed myself down.

I eyed the civilian. "What's your name?"

"G-Garry Penrose," he said. "I've got the bottle shop in William Creek."

"Family?"

"Yeah. A wife and two kids. Seven and ten. My girl looks like the one on the telly right there. Here . . . Look . . ." He reached for his back pocket and went fumbling around for something. Maybe a wallet. His hands shook trying to grab it. He failed.

"It's okay, Garry Penrose."

But he went on, almost begging me not to kill him.

"I've got two horses, two dogs, five alpacas, seven chooks."

I held up my hand. "It's okay."

Adeline cut in. "You must do what must be done, no?" she said. Sadness twinkled in her eyes. She was no longer Adeline. She was Teresa. My Teresa. She was speaking with the same calm voice I knew and adored. I gazed into her eyes. I saw something in there that said forgiveness. I saw her expression change and she gave me a short nod.

It was then that I realised how much I loved her. In my mind, just for a second, I pictured what kind of life we'd have shared together had we not wound up here. She had my heart and now it was clear. She gave me forgiveness. She gave me permission. I must take it all away.

As I looked at Teresa with the weapon pointed directly at her forehead, she simply closed her eyes. A teardrop rolled down her cheek and fell away. My eyes fogged over. My tears welled up. My breathing shortened, and I felt helpless and vulnerable. I put the weapon down at my feet and sighed. Frustrated. Angry. Sad. Everything.

Teresa stared back at me in surprise. Or shock. I didn't know which. "Nathan," she said. "Do it. Please. You must do it."

My eyes went to the civilian who was shaking his head. He pushed back in his chair. No words left him. All the training I ever had told me civilian lives must come first. Teresa was a soldier. It must be her. I picked up the weapon and held the weight in my hand. I flung my eyes to the clock.

"Nathan Masters! Time's a wasting!"

Quinlan brought his knife in harder on Angel. More blood trickled. She screamed, "NATHAN!"

I felt the coolness of the gun metal. My mind shuddered. How I wished for more than one round. I winced. A sharp thump at my forehead pounded and threatened an aneurism. I picked up my weapon. I mouthed the words to Teresa, 'I love you.' She looked down. She knew.

Another glance to the monitor. Something had changed. Angel had dropped her head slightly. Her pupils skipped side to side. Her lips compressed. Something was happening. Something was going to happen.

"Angel! No! Hold on!" I yelled and dropped the weapon at my feet.

"Tick tock, Masters!" He brought his knife in on her harder still.

I felt a presence behind me. A presence, creeping up silently, collapsing around me. My ears pinged with a high-pitched squelch. Ambient sound melted away. So magnetic, the presence. Coming from behind and encapsulating my body, closing in around me. I felt a touch on my shoulders. I wanted to swing around and see. I couldn't. I couldn't manage it. The touch reached from my shoulders and drifted down to my arms. I picked up the weapon. I levelled it in front of me.

A voice. A slow, low tone I'd heard somewhere before was now in my head. "Give me your burden," the voice said, low and slow. "Give your burden to Gabriel . . ."

I found my hands were no longer my own. The barrel of the gun no longer shook. Steady and precise, my hand raised. My finger on the trigger. Pressure. Not mine. I wrestled. I fought. I looked at Teresa. Her eyes closed. Another tear.

"Teresa!"

The shot came.

BLAT!

Teresa's head snapped back. The weapon fell from my grip and hit the floor.

CHAPTER TWENTY-TWO

Fallen

WITH THE VIDEO MONITOR IN THE CORNER
showing nothing but graininess, I sat forward in my chair, my
head in my hands, wondering what the FUCK I'd just done. Looking at Teresa, I found myself absolutely horrified. I fought
through the overwhelming sadness that encapsulated my body
and trapped me, holding me there just as hard as being physically
daisy tied to my seat.

The shock of everything. The shame and the sorrow. The disgrace of my actions. The humiliation Quinlan led me to. There
was no changing anything. But all those feelings I fought hard,
knowing much more was in store and much more needed doing.
I did something I knew I was good at. I swallowed everything and
forced it down. Down, all the way down. I pushed it all to the
place where everything else bad in my life lived. I bottled the energy of my anger and sorrow away. Saved it up for a purpose
attached to the name of Quinlan.

I left my chair, my body heavy, and looked around the room
for the camera that looked over me and the civilian. With the lens
still trained down, whoever was behind the camera could see everything. I had to take it out and get them dark. I already knew the

camera must've been a keyhole device. I began to look for any crack or crevice where it could be found.

Garry Penrose appeared to know what I was doing. He pointed. I slapped his hand down. "Don't point," I whispered. "Don't even look at it. It'll make it obvious." I moved closer to him and down low I whispered, "You know where it is?"

"Yeah," he whispered. "I saw a red light before. It's in the crack in the corner to your right."

"Good." I sat back down in my seat, reaching down for the handgun that I'd dropped a few moments ago. I leaned forward and whispered, "You sure?"

"Yeah."

Doing what was required needed speed and I had but one chance to make it happen. I reversed the handgun in my grip. The barrel in my palm. Rushing up from my seat, I raced to the corner, then using the gun as a hammer, I belted the concrete crack open to finally expose the keyhole camera. "Son-of-a-bitch," I uttered, ripping the camera from the wall, thrusting it on the floor, and smashing it to pieces with the handle of the handgun.

It would only take a moment or two, I thought. They'd rush in through the door and I'd be waiting. I got myself there with the handgun, still holding it to use as a hammer. I waited with an ear pushed up to the wall just short of the opening. I gestured with a hand for Garry to get up and get behind me. He left his chair. "Ready for this," I whispered.

"No," he said.

"Just get behind me and stay out of the way. Got it?"

"Yeah, righto."

My ear pushed to the wall. I readied myself for what was about to happen.

C'mon Quinlan. You freaking son-of-a-bitch . . .

It wasn't all that long before rushed footsteps padded down what sounded like a long hallway. The footsteps stopped at the door, just as expected. I held the gun up above my head, ready to bring it down on the first person who came through. The door opened slightly, but before I could pistol-whip someone's head, something was pushed through the aperture and the door snapped closed.

I spun, wondering what the thing was. It hit the floor with a metallic clunk. My eyes focused on the cylindrical black object just in time for my heart to jump in my mouth.

"FLASH BANG! COV . . .!"

My ears went deaf. My eyes went white. Blackness came.

* * *

In front of me, a badly beaten up Scotty-Blue was seated and tied. Garry Penrose was tied in the chair next to him. Fortunately for the civilian, not a scratch on him I could see. I was in the same busted metal chair as before. Daisy tied all over again. But no hessian bag. No gags. No water that said waterboarding. Scotty-Blue was grinning about something. I put my head down, not believing how bad this was turning out. I'd spent too much time on the defence. Now it was time to turn things around.

My eyes went to Scotty-Blue. "What happened to you?"

"The G's don't like smartarses," Scotty-Blue said. "I hammed it up so they'd freak out and put me back 'ere. Guess I did a good job at it, eh?"

"Why, Blue?"

"Why? I saw what was goin' down. 'ad to think of somethin'. One thing I learned, spendin' time around this place, you don't mess about with that Quinlan. The man's a fucken lunatic."

"That tells me you know the guy."

Scotty-Blue nodded. "Quinlan isn't the guy's real name. He got it from somewhere. Dunno where. He was a pimp who 'ad a few prostitution rings goin' on. Got 'imself into trouble, stepping on toes up around Kings Cross with some of them underworld blokes. He's got a temper that goes off at the snap of a stockwhip. Him and that knife of 'is. Crazy bastard, y'know?" Scotty-Blue trailed off. Then added. "Ya know what, Canter? This Quinlan came out of the western suburbs of Sydney. I remember that's your stompin' place."

"A long shot," I said. "How many millions in Sydney? And we don't even know his real name."

"You don't, but I do. Billy Butcher."

FUCK!

No. It couldn't be. It just wasn't possible.

My mind went back to the time Quinlan contacted Firebird Station. He laughed. He had that laugh. I recognised it even though his voice had been altered. Fat Fuck Billy. Could it be possible? It wasn't *impossible*. It wasn't even *implausible*. Just hearing the shape of the words from Scotty-Blue took me back to that place. Then my logical brain checked in. How many Billy Butchers lived in Sydney? How many lived in the western suburbs? How many in the western suburbs during the seventies?

It didn't matter how hard I threw it around in my head, there was no running away from it. Fat Fuck Billy. Billy Butcher. The guy with the knife. But why? Why all this, Billy?

Scotty-Blue regarded me as my mind ticked over. "You know 'im! I know you do! You got a dog face!"

That brought me back.

"What're you on about!"

"Dog face. Y'know? Grrr."

I went over everything. The laugh. The knife. Quinlan's body language as he walked around the place. The stooped shoulder. It was him. I put a hand up to my face and lightly touched the bruising. The injuries. The swelling. The pain. I squinted my eyes and forced my mind back. There had to be a reason for all this. Now, it was personal. I needed answers and I needed them fast.

"So, what's this place about?" I asked Scotty-Blue who was still eyeing me with his piercing blue eyes. His gaze immediately hardened. He was thinking about it. Just doing that told me he wasn't going to admit anything. I asked it again. I noticed Scotty-Blue's hesitation as he lifted his gaze then sheepishly looked back down.

"Sorry. I can't 'fess it up to ya, mate. It's for ya own good. Trust me."

"Blue . . ."

"Canter, If I told ya, you'd be dodging blow-back for the rest of ya life. Better to just get ya head into getting Angel out of here. Forget about this place. It's no good knowin' too much. The G's 'ave a death squad set up for blokes like that. You dun wanna go there. An' I'm not gonna be the bastard who caused ya to disappear, neither."

How did I know he was going to say that? Figured. He kept banging on about lies and secrets. Another one to add to the list. I'd find out soon enough. He was right about one thing. My mission was about Angel and getting her to safety.

"Okay," I said. "Got any ideas about getting out of here? Now's a good time."

Scotty-Blue lit up. Almost like a kid who'd been told there're biscuits in a tin on top of the fridge. "Yeah, of course. I got just the ticket; I reckon. I know where they're hidin' Angel. An' that's just a start."

"They'd have moved her by now."

"Probly. But they can only take her so far. They'd have a fair bit of walkin' to do," Scotty-Blue grinned. "While the G's were busy with you lot, I snuck out and unplugged the start-up circuit breakers in the helos. I hid the circuit breakers where they'll never be found. I put them under Angel's bunk. If they try to jump away, they'll get no joy with gettin' those engines to spool. That's them pretty much stuffed, don't ya reckon?"

Shit. Scotty-Blue would be made to answer. And what would happen if they found the circuit breakers under Angel's bunk? Each way I looked at it, the same end result. More would die and most likely the red-headed guy with the piercing blue eyes sitting in front of me. It didn't take long to realise Scotty-Blue had dug his own grave. And it didn't take long to realise the need to get going.

"We have seconds to get mobile, Blue. We need to get away from here or we're done."

"Yeah. Don't I know it. Get up and swing your chair over here so ya can get something out of me pocket."

"What about cameras?"

"Mate. Nothing a bit of juicy fruit chewy gum can't fix. Check out me handy work, eh? Left corner to ya rear."

I swung around, saw what he did, then smiled. I got up and swung into a position to reach his pocket. I dug in and felt something metallic and pulled it out.

"Holy shit." I was stunned. But I managed a light chuckle. I swung back around and faced Scotty-Blue. "A cigarette lighter?"

"Not just any old cigarette lighter," Scotty-Blue winked. "A zippo, mate. Just the thing to melt cable ties, don't ya reckon? Dumbarses never bothered to check," he said, then laughed.

Within a moment, I was free. The moment after that, Scotty-Blue and Garry Penrose were rubbing their wrists.

"The door," I said. "How do we get out? It's locked."

"Ave ya tried it? Why not try it and see?"

"You've gotta be shitting me . . ." I said, quietly stepping up to the door and applying pressure to the handle. Sure enough, it wasn't locked.

Scotty-Blue's grin widened. "I rigged it. When you turn a key in the lock, the bloody tumbler just spins. It feels like it's been locked. But whadoyano? It ain't."

"I'd kiss you if you didn't have balls, Blue."

"Mate. It takes balls to do what I did, eh? No need for the slobber. C'mon. Let's git."

"You know the place. You get point."

"Roger that, Canter. Get outta me way."

I felt much lighter than a moment ago. Before the door was opened, we swapped to communicating with hand signals only. Scotty-Blue signalled 'control room to the left. Armoury to the right.' We'd need to clear a line of sight before leaving our confinement. I double tapped Scotty-Blue's arm and made sure the civilian was in close proximity to my rear. To the civilian I signalled a zipper across my mouth, which he understood with a nod.

Scotty-Blue knelt down at the doorway and used the shiny zippo lighter as a mirror to check the line of sight. He gave a sharp nod and we were on the move, slinking down the hallway to arrive at another steel door. Scotty-Blue pushed his ear up to it and listened for any sign of movement. Another nod and we were through.

Another set of hand signals told me 'trap door in the floor, bunker below.' I double tapped my response and moved silently to the location. Scotty-Blue gripped the handle and lifted the heavy trap door. "Go. Go. Go," he whispered, and we went down the ladder to an opening stretching out. Doors left and right. One door on the left was open. We swung left and leapt inside.

"Hang on a sec," Scotty-Blue whispered. He moved over to a large array of switches at the wall. One by one, he switched them off. "We got seconds now. I just switched off the cameras and security. They'll be blastin' down 'ere when they notice." He reached in and grabbed a set of keys from the drawer of an old steel desk, thrusting them into his pocket. "Now to the armoury. Quick. Don't just stand there, mate."

Scotty-Blue scurried away. I ran after him with the civilian in front of me. A hand on his back urged him forward. "This way! This way! C'mon!" Scotty-Blue yelled over his shoulder. A moment later we were at a door with Scotty-Blue pushing a key into the lock.

A large steel door opposite had big orange letters.

'Bunker M. S. Lvl 10 beyond this point. Intruders shot on sight.'

A strange-looking locking device was at the side of the door with a fingerprint scanner. Had there been more time, I might've gotten Scotty-Blue to 'fess up the info. He was already in the armoury, switching on the light. Stepping in, I couldn't believe what I was seeing. Racks of military weapons of all descriptions lined the walls. A double-sided rack went straight down the middle.

I grabbed the first weapon from the rack to my right. A scoped SA-80. Just the thing. At last I had the power to punch. The power to hit back. We'd need to get going and pretty much right now, but where? Scotty-Blue passed me a full magazine. Grabbing it, I locked and loaded. Garry Penrose held something in his hand. He awkwardly fumbled with it. It occurred to me he knew next to zilch about firearms. I took it from him and grabbed something else more user-friendly. "It's a Magnum revolver. Just aim and pull the trigger. Both hands, okay? Or you'll wear it on your face." He nodded in response, looking nervous.

"What are you waiting for, Blue?" I said. "Show us the way."

"Mate. Already told ya. They're comin' and it'll be from down there," he pointed. "But we got the guns and ammo. We hold 'em from 'ere."

The word fuck whipped around in my head. Ammo at our backs, yes. And about a tonne of TNT. Being boxed in was bad enough but add in a well-placed grenade and it was all over.

"Blue, this is no good. We're boxed in."

"No time for it. By the time we reach the manhole they'll be on top of us."

"Jesus!"

"There's only fourteen of the bastards," Scotty-Blue said. "They'll be funnelled from the far end and we can take them down one by one."

Yeah, I thought. Fourteen, but how many had grenades or anything else that went bang? It was the things that went bang I was worried about. Then I had an idea. I spun and eyed the racks of weapons, but it wasn't more guns I was looking for. I needed something else. If there were racks of guns and ammo in there, there must be something more. I went looking for stuff in a box, but I couldn't see any.

"Blue. Stuff in a box. Got some of that here somewhere?"

"Stuff in a box? Yeah mate. Right at the back. Under the RPG launchers."

"RPG launchers? Why didn't you say that before?"

"Ya already 'ad ya SA. Figured that's all ya wanted."

I left Scotty-Blue and ran toward the back, looking for RPG launchers. Just as he said, boxes of stuff were underneath. I dragged a box out and opened it. M18 Claymores. Curved directional charges. Just what I needed. I grabbed a couple out of the box and ran down to the end of the hall. At the end, I turned right to the foot of the ladder. I set up the Claymores. There would be a nasty surprise and maybe enough of an explosion to get more than a few dispatched at once.

After running back and taking up position, we were left in a waiting game. It appeared they weren't in a hurry as Scotty-Blue first thought. The fact was we were still at stand-to as time ticked away. Some thirty minutes passed and nothing. It left Scotty-Blue in a state of bewilderment.

"What do you suppose?" I said. "No one's coming."

"Beats the heck out of me. Thought this shit would've gone down by now."

I glanced at Garry Penrose who appeared to be relieved, then to Scotty-Blue who looked more befuddled than ever. The next moment, I heard a voice coming from down the end. Angel's voice! "Nathan. I'm coming down."

My mind erupted in panic. The Claymores at the foot of the ladder!

"NOOO! NO, ANGEL!"

"Nathan. They told me it's okay. I'm coming down to be with you."

I launched into a hopping sprint.

Scotty-Blue's voice from behind. "Canter! It's a trap! For fuck's sake!"

I managed a few metres, then Scotty-Blue crash-tackled me from behind.

"Fa gawd's sake, Canter. It's a bloody trap!"

"It's not a trap! That's Angel's voice. She's gonna . . . she's gonna . . ."

I got up and ran again. Scotty-Blue crash-tackled me again. "It's a bloody voice pitch modulator, Canter. It's not Angel!"

"How do you know this!"

"Because, mate, it's the same voice pitch modulator Quinlan used when he contacted ya the first time. Remember? I was there. I seen it with me own eyes!"

CHAPTER TWENTY-THREE

Stand To

STANDING AT THE ARMOURY DOOR, weapons trained. My heart was in my mouth. *Boxed in, boxed in . . .*

"Nathan," Angel's voice said from somewhere down there. "Why won't you let me come down? I want to be with you again, Nathan."

Hearing her voice was doing my head in. I fought it. I fought it hard. Every now and again, I glanced at Scotty-Blue. His weapon and red dot sight also trained down range. He was more in the game than I was. In the back of my mind, there was still doubt about Angel's voice. What if Scotty-Blue was wrong? Psychological warfare at its best.

Silent moments passed. I noticed Scotty-Blue double check his weapon before he went prone just at the edge of the armoury doorway. One eye firmly on his scope. Something had to give. The stalemate would finish. It would end in a bloodbath.

"Nathan, are you hearing me?" Angel's voice again. A slight pause. Then, "Prepare to bleed, Nathan."

Scotty-Blue looked up at me and winked. "Told ya, didn't I?"

The doubt gone from my mind, I scoped and red dotted my weapon on the wall at the far end. Footsteps came down the ladder. I heard them. I winced and held my breath. An almighty explosion erupted, sending a shockwave down the hall. My cheeks flapped like flags. My head rocked back. My body almost flew backward off my feet.

Soon after the dust had settled and my ears stopped pinging white noise, the sound of something metal hit the floor and danced down the hall toward us, clicking and clacking as it went. I watched it getting closer. I thought for a split-second it was a grenade. But then it rolled. Grenades don't roll, they bounce. They skip. Especially on hard surfaces. Then horror.

"Gas. Gas. Gas," I yelled.

"Gas. Gas. Gas," Scotty-Blue yelled the same.

We flew inside the armoury and shut the door. Now we were more boxed in than ever. "Lock it!"

Scotty-Blue thrust the key into the lock. "Dunno if it's the only key. Maybe it is. Maybe it ain't."

"It'll buy us time. That's something."

"You know they're gonna breach," Scotty-Blue said, shooting me a death stare.

"If they do, this place will go up like an atom bomb."

"They'll still do it. They're all mad fuckers."

With no weapons covering the hallway, it was easy enough for the guys in gas masks to give us one hell of a showdown. This was going to be up close and personal. Going toe to toe in an armoury spelled out nothing but bad. A stray shot. A bit of shrapnel. I forced myself not to think about it.

I eyed Scotty-Blue. "More stuff in a box. NVGs. Gas masks. Grenades if you've got any."

He spun and ran to the back. From the back he yelled, "Empty on M33s. No gas masks neither. But C4 we got. A bloody ton of the stuff, mate."

"Detonators?"

"Yeah. Not only that, wind-ups. Just the ticket, eh?"

Putting my SA back on the rack, knowing it was useless up close, I grabbed a nine-millimetre handgun and loaded a full mag. "It's gonna be one-by-one as you say, Blue." But then I noticed the sprinkler system on the ceiling.

I met Scotty-Blue down the back to get an eyeball on how much plastic explosive there was. Three crates. Roughly sixty kilos. In another box, five wind-ups. The box under that, detonation cord. I eyed the detonation cord for a second or two. I had a purpose for it in mind. I retrieved the spool of explosive rope and put it around my shoulder, knowing at the same time if I got hit, the detonation cord would explode and I'd be truly sliced and diced.

Two hours max on the timed detonators, I thought. A good round number. Could I pull it off? Grabbing large chunks of the green/grey stinky, sweaty plastic explosive, Scotty-Blue helped set up the charges at each corner. The rest was heaped in the centre and everything was wired for a co-ordinated explosion. We worked the plan. Scotty-Blue went on without words, knowing exactly what to do. Twisting the timers over to the maximum two-hour time limit and pressing a button, and at the same time synchronising my wristwatch, I knew the next stage was to get out of the place.

"NVG, Blue. Grab one and put it on. Time to take the fight back to the bastards."

I gave one of the NVGs to the civilian and gave him brief instructions. He put it on with a set of visibly shaking hands. I helped him with his grip around the Magnum revolver. "Stay close and you're okay. See a bad guy, put a bullet into his brain. Two hands, remember? Now's not the time for getting a broken nose."

It was as though Scotty-Blue knew what I was thinking the moment I set an empty crate on the floor directly under the sprinkler system. He reached into his pocket and passed me the zippo. Activating the sprinklers meant any trace of gas outside would get washed away. I flicked the lighter open, got my naked flame, and held it up.

A couple of seconds was all it took before the place was awash. Using the butt of my handgun, I destroyed the light switch and everything went dark. Under the green glow of NVG, we moved out of the armoury. Detonation cord coiled over one shoulder, SA-80 slung over the other, I closed the door, locked it, then slid the key back under. There was no turning back. Two hours until the place was turned into a five-hundred-foot crater. And we hadn't secured the primary objective.

I slunk up close to one wall, Scotty-Blue and the civilian right behind me. The barrel of my supressed Glock pointed downrange, I popped out lights as I went.

I expected heads to be protruding around corners. I expected contact. We reached the foot of the ladder, with the body parts of at least four tangos strewn about, and the only way left to go was up. We had no grenades to clear up top should anyone be waiting, and in the back of my mind those timers were counting down. I stood at the base of the ladder and peered up. I briefly hesitated and took a breath. Hanging around was doing us no good.

My first thought was to get the place dark, but there were no light bulbs up top within easy picking. I lifted my NVG the same as Scotty-Blue and I looked at him for a split second. In the next split second, the civilian mounted the ladder and was gone. I didn't know what the hell he was thinking. If he'd yelled out the word 'banzai' it wouldn't have surprised me. Then I realised it was the old adage. The quiet ones. They're all unpredictable and this one was no different. Penrose said nothing the whole time he was with us. It was as though he wasn't there. Now this. Before any profanity left my mouth, and no sooner did the civilian reach the top, gunfire sounded and his body fell back down with a heavy, meaty thud.

I had no time to think about what to do next. I had no time to get my head around what just happened. The sound of a click, then another. Almost in slow motion, two M33 grenades were dropped down to rest at my feet. I picked them up at the same time Scotty-Blue went scattering away down the hall.

I grabbed the grenades. One in each hand.

Three . . . four . . . five . . . six . . .

I threw the grenades back up the manhole and ducked for cover. The explosion rocked the bunker, bringing my ears white noise. The resulting smoke that came down was mixed with a pinkish cloud of what could only be the blood of the dead.

I scaled the ladder and poked my head through the manhole, scanning the place. It was as though the walls had been freshly painted.

"Blue," I yelled. "Clear up top!"

He ran back toward me. It was almost a scene out of Mack and Myer for Hire getting to the ladder. He got himself sorted and climbed, meeting me at ground floor. There were six bodies that I could make out, laying splayed open like old cans of sardines. Out of the fourteen, that meant there were four left. And those timers back there wouldn't stop for anybody.

Rushing feet headed toward us. I sat back on my haunches and waited. One came through the door. BLAT! He was down. Another came after. BLAT-BLAT! He was down. Now there were two.

We moved out of the recent bloodshed to arrive in the hall going off to the control room. Scotty-Blue took point. I nodded as he went past, knowing he knew the way. I checked my watch. Twenty minutes had gotten away. I could've sworn it was only five. Already, panic began to rise. There was still much to get done. Maybe the C4 wasn't such a great idea. Second thoughts. I hated them. But still much to get done.

Quinlan. I'm gonna break your spine . . .

CHAPTER TWENTY-FOUR

Quinlan

FLASHBANGS. AGAIN. NO DOUBT IN MY MIND.
I'd been tied yet again to another chair. What in the fuck happened? Scotty-Blue was beside me out cold, tied the same as me. I scanned around. The amount of electrical equipment around told me 'control room.' I noticed the banks of switches and the glowing red and green lights. Green-grey metal panelling shot off from one side of the cold and cracked concrete room to the other. I shook my head, trying to get the pinging white noise out of my ears.

Realising where I was almost made me shudder. A 'cold war' control room. A room that said, 'this is the button I push to end the world.' My eyes focused on those buttons. Red with dropdown plastic coverings. Key holes on either side. Two of them. I assumed one for the shot man, the other for the station chief. The paint-peeled and grimy walls still smelling of stale cigars and cheap scotch was the final clue. The Maralinga testing range control room. And that, over there, was the main desk where that button was pushed.

In the centre of the control room sat an aged steel desk with a computer terminal and a large CRT monitor. Grainy images flashed to someone wearing black nylons over his head. As he stood by the keyboard with his back turned, doing whatever it was that he was doing, I focused on the knife in a scabbard he wore on his belt. I squinted a little. I focussed on the scabbard. The leather. The shape. The big letter 'B' that was embossed into the sheath. And I knew . . . I knew where my fate was about to take me. There could be no mistake. Billy the Fat Fuck Butcher.

Finally, the moment had arrived. I narrowed my eyes, with anger and revenge cutting a short course through my mind, chased by the images of Teresa's final moments as though some kind of silent movie. Images of the knife Quinlan held to Angel's throat. Images of the death this bastard left wherever he went. I felt the bashings and the beatings as fresh as when it happened. My eyes narrowed further. I felt my nostrils flare. My breathing shallowed. Quinlan was standing there with his back turned, still standing alive. I was going to change all that.

I focused on the opposite wall and formulated a plan. The SAs leaned up neatly and stood in a row. The ammo we'd taken from the armoury rested in a heap on the floor. On the floor a few centimetres from the SAs was the detonation cord I'd once looped over my shoulder.

I quickly glanced sideways to Scotty-Blue who'd not yet come back from unconsciousness. Blood trailed down his neck from his ears . . .

Let's play . . .

One: Get untied. Two: Keep Quinlan talking. Three: Kill the fucker. Four: Get to Angel. Five: Get the fuck out.

Simple.

In my back pocket, the zippo lighter was still there. I smiled to myself. If these guys had a brain, I'd have been dead days ago. Dumbarses. Just as Scotty-Blue said.

One: Get untied.

I put my head down and closed my eyes. I reached into my back pocket and grabbed the zippo. But how could I use it without making a noise? My mind answered. Swap One with Two.

"You can take those lady's pantyhose off your head," I said, low and slow, much the same as Gabriel. "I know who you are, Billy."

Billy Butcher immediately spun from the monitor and faced me. With a hand, he reached up and took his black nylon stockings off his head. He eyed me as though surprised, but I knew there was no shock there. "Well, well," he said. "If it isn't Nathan Masters? AKA Canter. Who knew we'd ever meet up again."

"Why you, Billy? Why are *you* here? Of all the people in the world . . ."

"It wasn't my idea," Billy cut in. "Let's call it fate. Huh?"

While he spoke, I chose my moment and used a naked flame at my wrist. I felt the burn and pushed it away. I felt the squeeze of the zip ties release. Number One was done. Now to finish with Two.

"I've got time. You've got time. Give us your story, Billy." In reality, time I didn't have. Those timers down below kept on ticking, and still there was no Angel. I wasn't aware of how much time had gotten away. I needed to check my watch. Even though my hands were free, I had to play this one as though they weren't. Time. I had a feeling there was much less than I thought.

Billy tilted back and laughed hard. The same conceited, egotistical, narcissistic laugh from years ago. "You're such an arrogant prick, Masters," he said. "You think this is personal between you and me? This is so far from anything personal, it's pathetic. You're not even on the radar. But there you are. Nathan Masters. The big-headed, arrogant Nathan Masters!"

"I thought you said this wasn't personal. You're sounding like a jealous schoolgirl."

"Jealous! Of what! It was always about the disk. I was doing my job. The fact you're playing means nothing. I didn't know you were in this until, lo-and-behold, you showed up. Like I said. Fate. Go figure. But you're here and now I get to have a little fun. You never fooled me. Not even for a second. Not even with that poor excuse of a cover story you and your crew came up with."

"Then why did you need my fingerprint? And why take my damn finger off to get it!"

"Fingerprint? Whatever gave you that idea? Taking your finger off was a bit of amusement. To see you squirm. To see you feel pain. I wanted to see that pain in your eyes. I could've done more than a finger. So much more."

"It was never gonna go your way, Billy."

"There you are again. You're the same arrogant prick you always were. Go ahead and flatter yourself, Masters. You arrogant piece of shit."

"Then dazzle me, Billy. Tell me how this plays out."

"You want my story? Okay. Like you say. Time is what we have. But it'll make no difference. I've got your girl and you've got my disk. Then, what's a little chat between friends, huh?"

Billy walked a little closer. I was now within striking range, but my curiosity kept me seated. I toyed with the idea of stepping up and taking him down. It would've been finished right there and then.

Another quick glance sideways. Scotty-Blue was still out. Dribble from the corner of his mouth.

C'mon, Blue . . .

"I was making a bloody good living. I was rolling in cash up to my fucking chin. But those arseholes from up the Cross blocked any chance for washing my hard-earned money. I was making so much money but couldn't use it. It kept piling up. What was I supposed to do? What the fuck was I supposed to do, Masters!"

He came at me, his hands closed into fists. His face centimetres away from my nose. It was a moment coated in gold. But I held.

Timers . . . Tick tock . . .

He went on. I listened.

"From out of nowhere this guy gets up in my face. He tells me there's a way I can get to use all my cash. All he wanted was a tiny fee of three per cent. But it didn't stop there. This guy tells me shit about the end of the world. He tells me to give up pushing the hookers. There's a way to get in with a crowd who's set up to escape what's coming, he says."

"Let me guess. A black guy. And let me guess again. This crowd he tells you about is The Guardianship."

Billy eyed me sternly. "The Guardianship of Milestone!"

"I know all about it, Billy. That's why we can't let you have the disk."

"Fuck you, Masters!"

"I bet this black guy didn't tell you where he was from, hey Billy?"

"What the fuck are you talking about?"

"Looks like you've only got half the story. You wanna know what's *not* been said?"

"I have all I need to know. I have a ticket away from this place when that day comes."

"You think? Let me tell you what'll happen, Billy. Before you get to use that ticket you've got, you'll be nothing more than a slave to the Guardianship. Twenty years spent doing shit with no guarantee at all. Think about it. Reckon you can handle dirty work for twenty years, Billy? What if during the twenty years you're doing your dirty shit, murdering, stealing, and whatever else they get you to do, you get unlucky and get done by those same guys who've given you your so-called ticket?

"Don't believe me? Check it out. Project Amber, Billy. Go ahead and check on your gismos over there. Project Amber and your exit strategy doesn't exist. It will never exist. Why? Because we're going to destroy it. You'll never get that ticket. All that you're doing is a waste of your time. Go back to your prostitutes. Forget about the disk. Hand over the girl and I might just save your arse."

"You're wrong!"

"We've got the parent genome, Billy. Forget about everything. Do as I ask and you'll live. I can get you out of here. But you need to get Angel right now."

"You're wrong about Amber. And you're wrong about the Hadgitol."

"As I said. Go ahead. Check if you want. I'm sure your computer can patch you into Vault Vitae-G in Antarctica."

That rattled him. He immediately spun and went to his computer. While he was busy at the keyboard, I gave Scotty-Blue a shake.

C'mon, Blue . . . wake the fuck up . . .

Using the zippo, I melted Scotty-Blue's zip ties. At the same time, I took the opportunity to check the time. To my horror, only twenty minutes were left before things got ugly. I did what I had to do. With the heel of my boot, I slammed Scotty-Blue's toe. That worked. Scotty-Blue erupted in a horrible yelp. But that had the side effect of Billy spinning around.

Billy took the knife from his scabbard and launched himself toward me. With the knife held out in front of him, he came at me with speed. I dodged, getting up with such energy I left my prosthetic limb behind. Hopping sideways, balancing as best I could, I stood there. My eyes locked onto Billy's gaze of death. He held out his blade and lunged at me, the knife swiping sideways and just missing my face. Another thrust from Billy. I blocked it. I grabbed his wrist and using the energy of his forward momentum, I pulled him in toward me. I put a cracking head-butt to the bridge of his nose. Billy was gone. Lights out. He went backward, losing the grip on his knife, and he hit the floor.

I reached down for my prosthetic limb at the exact same time I saw Scotty-Blue kick Billy in the head. Billy instantly came back from unconsciousness and cried out loudly. The time had come. I grabbed my prosthetic limb from the floor.

Titanium . . .

Using the limb as a baseball bat, I swung out and struck Billy. He blacked out again and became spreadeagled, faced down. While he was on the floor, I brought my fake limb hard down between Billy's shoulder blades.

CRACK.

I'd broken his spine.

"Holy cripes, Canter. Did ya hear that?"

"Yeah. But I need to finish the bastard."

I picked up Billy's knife and eyed it for a second. Standing over him, I thrust the blade deep into his back, twisting it for good measure. Now I knew I'd cut his spinal cord.

I stood back up. Scotty-Blue eyed me with amazement. "I reckon ya done 'im."

"He's not dead yet. Just paralysed. Now we wake him up."

"Oh. Righto then. It'll be me pleasure," Scotty-Blue said. Before I knew it, Scotty-Blue stepped over Billy.

"Blue! What are you doing!"

"I'm wakin' 'im up. Plus, I'm bustin' for a leak."

I rolled my eyes. Yeah. It'd work. Then Billy *did* wake up.

Billy started with profanities, but he didn't move. He was totally paralysed, from the neck down. But bad news. That meant he couldn't feel pain. And I wanted him to feel every pinprick. After I'd slid back into my leg, Scotty-Blue helped me lift Billy Butcher's limp body into the chair.

"Grab that detonation cord over there, Blue." I said, pointing.

Within a moment, Billy's paralysed body was coiled up in detonation cord in the same chair I'd been tied in a few moments before. I wound a decent amount of detonation cord around Billy's neck; all the while, he was wide-awake and obviously fully aware of how he'd end up. He ranted and raved like a lunatic, not able to do anything. "Fuck you, Masters! Fuck you, Masters!"

"No thanks, Billy."

I ignored him at first. But what the heck. I wound one up and let him have it. Billy went lights out again. No more ranting.

Scotty-Blue finished with the detonation cord on Billy. "Ya reckon he'll lose 'is 'ead over this?"

"I reckon he just might, Blue. You know where Angel is?"

"Yeah . . . But . . ."

"What?"

"Sentry at 'er door. But no biggie with the SAs, though," Scotty-Blue said, while slinging an SA80 over his shoulder and then checking for rounds.

"Go get it done," I said. "I'll get this guy set up with a timer."

I checked my watch. Shit. Twelve minutes. It was going to be close. Under pressure, I was somehow relaxed enough to keep a level head. Just for good measure, I gave Billy the same kick in the shin he gave me, even though I knew he'd never feel it. I could've done so much more to Billy. Looking down at him, I thought about Teresa and desired retribution. But I held back from anything further. It was never going to be enough. Not even close. But Billy's days would be over soon. And much too quickly.

I placed a timer to the detonation cord, as I heard the eruption of gunfire coming from somewhere else. Somehow, I knew Scotty-Blue had things covered. After setting the timer to detonate in three minutes, Billy Butcher, the kid from next door, would most certainly lose his head and a bit more. That itself was payback enough. Payback for everything he'd caused. And for me, I had mere moments to get the hell out.

It wasn't long after the gunfire had stopped that I heard little feet running at top speed up the corridor behind me. In the next moment, I heard Angel's voice and found myself overjoyed. "Nathan!" I spun and picked Angel up in my arms. Nobody could take the smile from my face, no matter how much it hurt. But the smile lasted only seconds. It was now more urgent than ever to get away.

Without any delay, we ran. Down the corridors we ran. Outside, where real sunlight burst down on my skin for the first time in I didn't know how long. But no cars were in sight for the breakneck getaway we so desperately needed.

"To the helos!" Scotty-Blue shouted. "I 'ave a pocket full of circuit breakers an' we can get into the air."

"You fly?"

"Who did ya think got to fly drones into Iraq? We did that shit from up in Pine Gap!"

The moment Scotty-Blue said it, a deep thudding detonation from behind told me Billy Butcher was gone. I caught a glimpse of my watch. Four minutes and the place would go up in a massive explosion. Arriving at the helo, I placed Angel inside. How I would've loved to start consoling her. No time for pleasantries. Time to get away and fast.

"Blue! Two minutes. Get us in the air!"

"I'm bloody trying, mate. These things take a bit to get going. It ain't no car!"

"Blue. Hurry!"

The first sign was a series of loud clicks overhead. Then engines spooling up. Starting in a low hum, the Black Hawk began to whirr into life, building up in pitch.

"BLUE!"

Up top, the rotor began to move. Jesus! It was slow. I wanted to get out and give it a spin.

"BLUE!"

The helo shuddered. The rotors spun up faster. Dust erupted from the ground. But still no lift. I wanted to get out and lift the thing in the air.

"One minute! BLUE!"

"Hang on tight, you lot back there. It's gonna get a bit bumpy."

I checked my watch. "Thirty seconds! Get us up! Get us UP!"

"Nathan!" Angel squeezed up to my shoulder and buried her face.

"Hold on!" I screamed.

"Hold on, you two!" Scotty-Blue screamed.

The engine was now at full spool. The rotors thumping and vibrating the airframe. All I could do was hold Angel in tight while counting the last few seconds. The helo lifted. Scotty-Blue angled the airframe away from the blast zone. We rose up higher.

Four . . .

"Brace for impact!"

Three . . .

"Holy shit, Canter!"

Two . . .

"Grab on to something!"

One . . .

CHAPTER TWENTY-FIVE

Fallen Angel

NO EXPLOSION. I GOT IT WRONG SOMEHOW.
But as soon as I thought it, the earth below heaved up in a dome,
then collapsed back down into a crater. I was expecting the same
explosion as a World War I trench warfare catastrophe. The same
as beneath hill sixty, the infamous explosion known as the largest
non-nuclear detonation in earth's history.

From out of the helo's window, I watched as the dome sank
back down into a giant dish. It was everything I expected and
more. It was as though someone had taken a high-speed film and
hit playback in slow motion. After the eruption settled, a visible
shockwave spat itself across the desert plane. A low rumbling vibration erupted, audible even from the helo. Then fiery fingers
reached up from the explosion, licking the sky with deadly debris.
The earth screamed her fury.

Suddenly and without warning, the helo skipped sideways. On
my left, the cloudless blue sky. On my right, the brown-red dusty
desert. Warning tones erupted in the cockpit. The steady electronic drone of chimes and alerts accompanied by an electronic
human voice.

Woop-Woop. Rotor. Vortex. Woop-Woop. Rotor. Vortex. Woop-Woop. Rotor. Vortex.

"Blue! Get . . ."

"I've got it, Canter! Hold on."

"BLUE!"

"Gimme a sec! Jesus!"

The helo tilted further right. The alarms and warning tones from the cockpit screamed out in pain. Scotty-Blue fought with the controls. Somewhere deep inside, I knew he had it. But did he? It felt as though I was upside down. Thumped and bumped. Rocked and jostled. But Angel. Out of all the urgency. Out of all the panic to get away, I never strapped her in.

As soon as I thought it, I looked sideways. Angel was at the open door. Her feet were sticking out and thrashing like flags in a cyclone. She was clinging on for dear life. Her red-rimmed eyes big as hubcaps, full of fear, gazed back at me. Her mouth was compressed into a slit, her black hair flinging and whipping wildly. She closed her eyes and put her head down. I reached out. I was too late. She was gone!

"NOOO!"

She was gone!

". . . FUUUCKKK!"

She was gone! Gone! Just gone!

"Canter. Hold on!" Scotty-Blue screamed.

"Blue! Angel!"

"I'm getting it!"

"Blue . . .! Man down!"

"What!"

"Angel . . .! She's out the door!"

Scotty-Blue yelled out. I heard him thump his window hard a few times. He had a job on his hands. Momentarily after, by some miracle, one by one, alarms and warnings tones settled into silence. The airframe levelled out. Rattles and jostles stabilised. Rotors were rhythmical, thumping away without stress. Turbofan engines spooled down into what I supposed were safe parameters. I got myself to the edge of the doorway and looked out, hoping for any sign of Angel. My heart wanted it to be so. But there was no sign. Angel had been flung out. Flung out an easy one thousand feet above the ground.

I wanted to get down there. To the ground, as fast as possible. The second I thought it, another warning tone. My mind snapped to attention. I knew the tone. Missile lock. No denying it. Scotty-Blue confirmed it with a series of loud profanities. Then, flares punched out from the sides of the helo. I looked left, just in time to see the sidewinder explode not fifty feet away. The helo was thrust violently sideways and I was instantly taken to my arse.

"Canter! Bogey!" Scotty-Blue yelled back. "Recommend you grab onto something! And close the bloody door!"

I tasted my own heart in my mouth, getting to the edge and leaning into the wind. I stuck my head out. "Bogey, five o'clock!" I screamed.

"I know it, Canter! Close the bloody door!"

My mind was racing. Somehow, I managed to put everything aside. I closed the door and grabbed a restraint. Missile lock again. The warning tone screamed out. The flares and chaff punched out. Another explosion. Shrapnel penetrated the helo and came whizzing past my shoulder. That was close. Too close. I held my breath. The helo began to lose control. Flat spin. More electronic warning sounds from the cockpit. Black smoke filled the insides as the flat spin increased. Spinning and spinning. Going down and down.

Scotty-Blue yelled out, "We're goin' down, Canter! Goin' down!"

He needn't have said it. I already knew it. I jumped into a seat, fighting Gs all the way. I dragged the restraints over my shoulders, then shoved the buckles home. I put my head down and held on tight. Scotty-Blue fought on in the cockpit. Black smoke. Warning tones. Spinning and spinning. The engines' high-pitched shriek increased. They were about to explode.

I pushed my head sideways and caught sight of another missile screaming past. A miss. But they were going to finish us good. The spiral. The spinning. Down and down. I closed my eyes and braced for impact.

The helo tilted sideways. The rotors hit the dirt hard. Crunching and grinding. Pieces splitting off. Clattering and thumping. Dust erupting into the cabin. I put a hand up to my face. Then a sudden thud almost broke my back. I found myself upside down. Then right side up. Then tumbled again, finally coming to a rest. Dust and smoke, with the scent of jet fuel thick in the air. Everything was going to get worse.

* * *

How long was I out? I had no idea.

"Blue! You okay!"

"I'm good. This ain't over, Canter. Get out and find cover!"

Getting myself unclasped in a hurry, I reached up and gave the door an almighty tug. The thing wouldn't slide open.

"Fuck sake! Blue! The door!"

Then I heard it. Chopper closing in. I struggled, wrestling with the door, trying to pry it open. Scotty-Blue was gone. He was out of his seat to somewhere. "Blue!"

I heard him up top, bashing at the door with something heavy. "Give it a shove, mate!"

I grabbed the handle and put my weight behind it.

Two seconds later I climbed up and out in time to see the chopper bearing down. Rounds fired, strafing the ground, kicking up dust. I jumped sideways. Scotty-Blue jumped in the exact same second. The metallic clinkering of rounds hitting the helo. The chopper punched overhead with speed.

"Fucking RUN, CANTER!"

I did my best. Run hop. All I could manage. Scotty-Blue sprinted in front, then got down behind a tree. I saw him waving his hand. Beckoning me over. Run hop. The helo exploded at my rear. I felt a massive burst of pressure and I was off the ground. I was in the air and flying. The tree. I caught a branch with both hands and gripped on tight. My leg flung off.

Scotty-Blue laughed his head off. What was so funny?

"Shoulda seen it, Canter. That leg coming off was the stuff of funny 'ome videos. I'd be a rich man if I 'ad a movie camera."

"Idiot. This isn't the time! Help me out of this bloody tree!"

Things got serious. The chopper was again coming in. I heard a sharp thumping change pitch and tone in the distance. An indication of a change of direction.

"Jump!" Scotty-Blue shouted. "You're only up by eight feet."

Minus the leg, I jumped. We found cover behind the tree and got down. The chopper came in low from the east. I knew by the sound of the engines and rotors; it wouldn't be strafing this time. It was configured for a landing. This one was going to be hand to hand. Up close and personal. Eye to eye. I readied myself. Without any weapons. I wished I hadn't left them behind. If they had firearms with them, we'd be done. We had nothing to answer a fire fight. We both went prone behind the tree, as flat as we could get.

Silent, we lay there as the chopper landed. The dust settled and engines spooled down. The all-black chopper sat noiseless in the dirt, no occupants exiting from the doors as the rotors slowed and became still. My first thought was to get up and break from the area. Minus the leg, it was a tough ask. I'd not get away fast enough. Moments passed. Silence ensued with nothing but the sound of desert flies at my face and Scotty-Blue breathing heavily at my left.

"What do you suppose?" I whispered.

"They've got us, Canter. No point cryin' over it. They've got us. Time to meet the boss, eh?"

"You're giving up?"

"Nah, mate. I'm savin' me life. So, we get to make another escape. That's gotta be better than a 50cal through the head, don't ya reckon?"

The moment he said it, my thoughts went to Angel. I sighed heavily. Her body was out there somewhere. She couldn't have survived such a fall. She was lost. The mission was lost. I had failed so dismally. Now it came down to this. My own death or another attempt to escape. Escape where? That was the hard choice. Maybe Scotty-Blue was right. Maybe it was for the best to just give in. Temporarily, at least. But who'd know what they'd do to us on the next round. They'd be harsher. Perhaps unforgiving. Perhaps they'd take us to a slow demise.

The right door of the chopper swung out and then opened. For the first time, my eyes met the black guy I'd heard so much about. Then there were two, then three. Tall. Just as I'd heard. Just as I'd seen all those years ago. And armed with what I thought were scoped weapons. Sniper rifles. M107s. 50cals, just as Scotty-Blue assumed. It dawned on me they were going to take us down as though we were nothing but a couple of feral boars.

My suspicion was confirmed when one went prone next to the helo and expanded the feet on the barrel of his weapon. The other two moved further away and after going prone in the red dirt, did the same. The first shot fired sounded like a cannon. The projectile struck the tree and went straight through it, sending bark and woodchips flying.

That was the moment I agreed with everything Scotty-Blue said. No sooner I had the thought, Scotty-Blue went up on his knees, putting his hands behind his head. That was it. Job over. Everything shot to shit. I went down on a knee and placed my hands behind my head, the same as Scotty-Blue.

While I had my hands up behind my head as though a white flag was put out, I caught sight of several figures high up on the winds, circling. I narrowed my eyes and witnessed the figures getting closer. One by one, the wings on the figures tucked in and became missiles. A shriek and a cry told me what they were and confirmed my suspicions.

CHAPTER TWENTY-SIX

Hell for Leather

THE BLOODBATH THAT FOLLOWED WAS sudden and swift. I'd not previously heard flesh ripping. It had a sound all to its own. It was a sight never to be forgotten.

The seven eagles, of which one was all white, came in on the wind from the south. A series of piercing shrieks swept through the sky. They came in low, wings tucked with talons poised for a strike. Swooping down, they attached themselves to the three men, then went to work with precision. I watched on as the eyes and ears of those on the ground were punctured one by one with giant beaks. Tongues were ripped out. Flesh was stripped away. Blood sprayed and gushed high in fountains amidst their chilling cries of agony.

When all was silent, the ripping and tearing continued with large chunks of red flesh being tossed about and scattered into the distance. They were dead, but it went on. It went on until the white bone was prominent against the red blood-stained ground. It went on until entrails shook and hung like long lines of sausages from the eagle's beaks.

By the end, three skeletons remained. Red dirt and chunks of stuff hard to describe littered the place. The eagles left the scene just as quickly as they came. They took flight and circled, shrieking out before dispersing into the southern sky. Gone, as though no one else was ever there. As though nothing else mattered.

It took a few moments of reflection to come to terms with what I'd witnessed. I knew Scotty-Blue was the same. He was empty of words. If ever Scotty-Blue had nothing to say, it was a complete phenomenon. It seemed Scotty-Blue's inner larrikin was never at rest. This time there was nothing. I had nothing. He had nothing.

I broke the silence by getting up and hopping away. At my back, I heard Scotty-Blue say the first words in roughly twenty minutes. "Did that just 'appen? I didn't just dream it, did I?"

"No, you didn't dream it, Blue. It happened. And we're still breathing."

I heard a thud. I turned around to see Scotty-Blue smacking himself around the head.

"Blue, what're you doing?"

"I'm tryin' to wake up."

"I already said you weren't dreaming. Can you get over here and give us a hand?"

"With what?"

"I'm trying to look for my frigging leg."

Scotty-Blue got up and ran over. Then, he tripped on his own foot and face planted into the dirt. I couldn't help it. I laughed. The moment of laughter was oddly refreshing. I laughed so hard my eyes watered. Then I felt my emotional tide collapse around me. I went the other direction. Everything I had kept bottled in escaped. Just momentarily. I sucked back a sigh, got a hold of it, and put it away. Now wasn't the time. With a heart as heavy as a blacksmith's anvil, I continued the search for my fake leg. Finally, I found what I was looking for. A bit of expensive titanium glinted and stuck out of the soft earth. I picked it up and slid back into it, the same as I'd done thousands of times.

"What now?" Scotty-Blue asked.

"Now? We go back and find Angel's body. We need it before."

"Before what?" he said.

It occurred to me that I'd seen something quite extraordinary with the eagles. Not once, but a few times. My mind went back to the presence I'd felt at Maralinga. The albino, Gabriel. As I put it together, I realised it for the first time. The white eagle. I put my hand on the back of my head and thought about the tattoo Gabriel had put there. A white eagle with a sword. The sword of destiny.

I tried not to believe it. I don't know why that was. Maybe what I was thinking was just too weird. Or too hard to understand. But having those thoughts took me to another conclusion. Somehow, in my heart, I knew Angel was alive. I didn't know how. I couldn't imagine how this was at all possible. But the feeling was most overpowering.

"Angel is alive," I said to Scotty-Blue, who was busy dusting himself down.

"Nah, mate. We were too 'igh up. She couldn't 'ave survived such a fall."

"Don't ask me how I know. I just know."

Scotty-Blue cast his blue eyes on me. "You're serious, ain't ya?"

"Like I said, Blue. She's alive and we have to find her. Fast."

"I guess we take that chopper then?"

"Yeah," I said. "We'll grab the weapons from the dead guys too. Something tells me we're gonna need them."

Stepping over the grisly remains and climbing into the chopper, I wondered about the search area. As Scotty-Blue lifted the chopper off the ground, I thought about how it was not the recovery mission I first assumed. My feelings grew stronger as I became even more certain it was to be a rescue mission. Once again, I didn't have a clue why I felt it so strongly. As Scotty-Blue leaned on the flight control stick, I willed him onward. We had a vast area to search for Angel.

Scotty-Blue piloted away and pointed the airframe into the general direction we came.

"Head bearing 180 degrees, Blue," I said over coms.

"Roger that." Scotty-Blue gave thumbs up.

The seven eagles came in from the south. If they originated from Angel's location, we were heading the right way.

From an open door, I peered out, looking toward the ground for any sign of her. After forty minutes of travelling in a southerly direction with nothing on the ground other than clumps of malnourished trees, dry and dusty planes, and the odd bit of wild life, I began to wonder. The thought of dingoes lit my mind like a strobe light. But I managed to push those thoughts away.

Then.

"Three o'clock low, Canter," Scotty-Blue said over coms.

Scotty-Blue tilted right and I saw for the first time what he'd seen. Down there, a lone individual was seated in the shade of a rather large sandstone boulder. My heart thumped as I looked down. As my eyes focused further, the individual looked up. I saw her face peering up as we got down closer and there could be no doubt.

"Angel!"

"Maybe it is, maybe it ain't," Scotty-Blue said. "My common sense tells me it ain't. Don't get ya 'opes up is all I'm sayin'."

"Yeah, you're right Blue. Get us down there." But in my mind, I was already down there with her. I kept my eyes on her as the chopper came closer. Just before the dust raised from the thrusting rotors, she waved her hands into the air, and I knew . . . I knew Angel was safe. How? I had a suspicion, but the thoughts in my head didn't make sense. I grappled with the logic. She was alive, and that's all there was to it.

After landing and spooling down, I got out and saw Angel standing next to a huge sandstone boulder with her arms raised.

"Angel!" I called out.

Angel came running over, completely unharmed. Then she stopped ten feet away. Scotty-Blue came to my side. I glanced at him sideways. Shock was in his eyes. Angel ran to him. "Uncle Scotty!" she squealed. Scotty-Blue knelt and caught her in his arms. My heart melted right there. She looked up at me in wonder. "Nathan? Is it you? You have no hair. Why did you shave it?" In her next breath, without any pause. "Your face. You're hurt. How did you get hurt?

I shot a stare at Scotty-Blue. He eyed me back as though muddled.

Amnesia?

"Angel. What can you remember?" I asked.

She didn't answer. Her little eyes scanned me. She looked down at my ugly swollen hand. She reached over and put my hand in hers and straight away I felt a cool sensation sweep up my arm. Morphine. I was no stranger to it. As Angel took my hand, she looked at me with sadness in her eyes. The punch of something cool swept over my body. When it reached my head, the kick in the brain cut off any trace of pain.

. . . I could tell you, but discover it for yourself . . .

Maggie's words. I remembered them. The pain was gone. Morphine. Wonderful, magnificent, sublime morphine. But no head throb. No dizzy attack. Nothing to bowl me over.

"You were going to take me for photos at that place you said. But why am I here?"

After a bit of confusion, I realised Angel was answering my question. I bet she didn't even realise she'd taken my pain away. It was all so innocent. So unknowing. "Was that the last thing you can remember?" I asked her.

"I remember my headache. But Nathan, you told me we were going to Melbourne and you said we could go and take some pictures."

"And that's all you can remember?"

"Yeah. That's all. Why? Is there something else?"

I bent forward and put a knee in the sand in front of her. "Well, let's go there and take some pictures, huh? But first, what about a trip to go and see Maggie."

Angel nodded vigorously. "But what am I doing here?"

What could I tell her? There was the long story or the short one. I figured the long story would come one day. Maybe she'd remember it in time all by herself. I opted for the short one. "You were stolen by some bad men. We came to find you."

"Bad men? I don't remember. What bad men?"

I got up and looked at Scotty-Blue who was scratching his head. Disbelief, maybe. But I was good with it. To someone else it would've been weird. Maybe far-fetched. Angel was safe and that's all I cared about. "It's okay," I said, feeling a smile rip through the bruises on my face. "Let's get going before it gets too hot."

Chapter Twenty-Seven

North by South

SCOTTY-BLUE SET THE CHOPPER DOWN ON the airstrip at William Creek. I looked across the road. My Land Rover was still there waiting like an old friend. The hotel still stood lonely. The paint-peeled shack with the red cross still had crime scene tape wrapped around it. For a moment, I thought Scotty-Blue was going to join us for the trip north back to Alice Springs. He didn't climb out of his seat. He stayed there, watching me with a set of eyes that said goodbye. "Ya still got ya keys?"

"No keys. I have no idea what happened to them. But nothing I can't handle. I take it you're not coming?"

"I can't, mate. You know it's not possible."

"Why?"

"Lies and secrets, my friend. Lies and secrets."

I smiled and felt relief for the first time in how long? How did I know he was going to say something like that?

"Nothin's changed, Canter. I don't know you. And you don't know me. Always remember it."

I nodded, smiling a bit more. "I don't know you, should we ever meet up again. Like you always said."

"It 'as to be that way. Make no mistake. It's all important, Nathan Masters."

"You just called me by name. I can't remember a time you'd ever . . ."

"You gettin' all gushy on me? Bloody hell, Canter. Better get ya hard arse back on. It don't suit ya," Scotty-Blue said. "You need a weapon? There's the M107s."

"I'll pass. I think I'll be fine from here."

"Nah, mate. You won't. Take this one then." Scotty-Blue handed a Glock through the window. I took it. "It was on the floor. Take it and you'll be fine. Gonna sleep tonight. I reckon you might too."

Scotty-Blue gave a quick wink, then pressed a few buttons and twisted a lever. The engines' RPM increased and the rotors began to spin. "Lies and secrets, Canter. Remember it. Oh, an' your job's not finished. Remember the Hadgitol? Gotta get it sorted, mate. Stop those pricks who's got it!"

I stepped back, holding Angel's hand. She waved her Uncle Scotty-Blue goodbye as he slowly lifted away, turned the chopper, and moved away on a north-westerly heading. I stood there wondering if we'd catch up again. Should that happen, it'd be as though complete strangers, I realised. He had his reasons. Who was I to second-guess it. But I knew there was more to Scotty-Blue. It brought up a whole new set of questions.

* * *

Stepping up to the Land Rover, I eyed it for a second and smiled. I placed a hand on the canvas roof, amazed there was no cleaning to do. Having no keys, it was just a matter of attaching a couple of wires and we were on our way. Gotta love the little non-turbo diesels. Everything so simple. Just the way I liked it. This time, we'd head north back to where the trip started.

"What about my bag, Nathan? I need my camera."

I looked down at Angel's beaming face and couldn't help but wonder what she'd been through. It was a relief to know she had no memory. How traumatic for such a young soul. "No problem. Wait here and I'll go get it."

Thank god the door wasn't locked. Inside and saw the mess with everything tipped over. It didn't take long to find our bags. I took them and left that room forever. Stepping outside, I saw the hotel windows were boarded up. A big 'for sale' sign sat on a post out the front. The entire place was a ghost town. I eyed the phone box on the street and wondered if I should check in with Shilo. Placing the bags in the back of the Land Rover, I decided against it. Maybe it was better to turn up and face whatever needed facing.

I got myself under the dash and looked for those two wires. Having found them, I touched them together and the little diesel motor turned over and idled without any argument.

I wasn't ready to head north. One more job to get done. The promise I made to Angel a couple of months ago. I steered south and headed out to Lake Eyre. It also meant I could get an eyeball on the calamity Bosco had left behind. I had to be sure. I needed to know the scene had been cleaned and nothing was left over. Arriving there, nothing to tell the story. No Robinsons helicopter. No dead pilot. No turned-over Bronco and dead G-man on the ground. Everything was gone, as though it hadn't happened. Not even tracks in the dirt. I wondered who cleaned the site. Was it the cops or the clean-up squad Bosco had arranged? I'd never know.

At the edge of the vast white open space, Angel hopped out of the Land Rover, camera in her grip. She giggled at the beautiful sight she held in her viewfinder while she went to work shooting the landscape. In the distance, high in the bright, cloudless sky, eagles were up on the wing. Only two that I could see. I knew in my gut they were ordinary wedge tails and not those of the seven. How could I explain it to Angel? How could I tell her the long story? How could I tell her once she was ready to hear it? I sighed with the thought. That day would come. I'd have to work on it from this moment. When that day came, I'd have something ready for her mind to digest.

We stopped there for a little more than an hour, taking in the scene, enjoying the space and silence. Breathing the air. It gave me much-needed respite. It gave Angel a great amount of joy watching the eagles up there on the wing, circling. When it was over and her film was spent, she pushed up to my side. "I had an eagle friend once," she said.

"I know. You told me about Charlotte."

"I did? When?"

"In the motel room when you were sick."

"I was sick? I don't remember."

"I know. Maybe a good thing, huh? C'mon. Let's go. It's gonna be late by the time we get back to Maggie's house."

* * *

The landscape whizzing past the window was now all too familiar. Heading north on the Oodnadatta Track, my mind went to Doug the grazier. I remembered the early stages of the darkest times of my life. Had Angel known the complete story, I don't know if she'd be sitting next to me right now. Maybe she would.

Her camera, even though she was out of film, seemed to keep her busy and I was thankful for that.

I took the trip slow. I was in no hurry. Angel was as silent in her seat as she had been while driving down. I wondered what she was thinking. I wondered how she was feeling. I was about to open up and tell her at least some of the story. Maybe it would help the amnesia. I glanced sideways and sure enough, she was busy with the landscape out of her window; her eyes pointed to something in the sky. "Nathan. Do you think those birds up there are following us?"

"What birds?" I asked.

"Those ones up there. See?" She pointed and tapped the window lightly. "I've been watching them. It's like they know where we're going."

I bobbed my head down to see better. "I can't see them. You want me to stop?"

"Yeah," she said. "But I don't have any film left."

I stopped, pulling up on the side of the track. As I got out, Angel was already out of her seat and walked a few paces away. "They're beautiful, Nathan. Come see."

They circled high up. The seven I'd seen and already thought of as friends. "Eagles," I said. "And yeah, kiddo. They are beautiful."

Angel turned and stared back at me. Her eyes had a little pain in them. "You called me kiddo," she said, and I noticed a tear sitting lonely at the edge of an eyelid.

"Sorry, Angel. Is it something I shouldn't have said?"

"Mum used to call me kiddo. My dad did something horrible to her. Please don't say that anymore. It reminds me of what my dad did."

"I'm so sorry . . . I wish I could've changed it."

"What do you mean?"

Collecting my thoughts, I wondered how to answer. One of my weaknesses, I supposed. I was never any good at matters of the heart. When it came to feelings, I had no idea. Maybe Angel was about to change all that. Maybe being with her was part of my path. To show me the way out of emotional emptiness.

I'd spent the best part of my life training in the art of killing. Through the process, I'd learned to empty my soul. Nothing lived in there. I could take a life without any bother. I could look down on the dead guy at my feet and not feel anything. It was a job and nothing more. At that moment, I realised why I never got close to anyone. I felt sad that I lived my days emotionally dry and had not welcomed relationships into my life. But Teresa changed that in me. We'd see where this new path lead. But I made no promises. I am what I am. I chose the life willingly. Next life, I'd do it much differently.

I gazed down at Angel, who was standing and waiting patiently for an answer. I felt my eyes quickly fogging over. I constructed a sentence in my mind and I thought it may be the one to offer. "I knew your mother and father long ago," I said. "Angel. They were two people very much in love with each other back then. Sometimes, I wish I could go back in time and change things. Put things right. If I knew your father was going to do those horrible things when I first knew him, I'd have done everything I could to keep those two apart. But you know what? If I'd come between them, there'd be no Angel. And we'd not be standing here right now. And you'd not be looking at those beautiful eagles up there. Those eagles now showing us the way. They're your guiding light. They're here for *you*. And something deep inside me tells me they'll never leave you. They'll be with you for life, forever guiding, forever protecting."

"They're my eagles?"

"More than you know, Angel. More than you know."

"And if I wish for them like I wished for Charlotte, they'll come?"

I smiled a little before answering. "If they don't come, they're always in your heart. Look for them there. Trust them to show you the way and they will. You may not understand what I'm saying just yet. You will in time."

Angel looked up as though what I'd said didn't make sense. Her little face was trying hard to understand something profound. Then, her eyes dropped slightly. "I'm tired, Nathan. I think I can go to sleep now."

She wrapped her arms around me as little kids do. Before I said anything further, she was in her seat, waiting for me to get behind the wheel. We left and continued our trip north. As we drove, the eagles left and disappeared into the horizon. Angel closed her eyes and sleep came.

CHAPTER TWENTY-EIGHT

Return to Base

ANGEL HAD SLEPT THE ENTIRE WAY TO Alice Springs. We arrived close to midnight. I stopped the Land Rover out front of Firebird Station, killed the engine, and just sat for a moment or two. A perfect time to reflect a little. The lights shone brightly through the tattered curtains. People were up and about and I wondered all over again what was next. I remembered Scotty-Blue's words before he up and left in the chopper at William Creek.

It ain't over, Canter. Remember the Hadgitol?

Already, I was preparing for whatever that may be. At the very least, Angel was safe and in the care of not only me, but others who had a vested interest in her security. Mission accomplished, I thought. I relaxed, knowing the final play was at hand. But what would that entail? And how would it be accomplished?

At the heavy front door, I knocked in the code known only to those in the game. Angel was fast asleep in my arms. I held my breath. The door opened. Bosco's face came out of the darkness and he made himself known. He smiled and went to say words. I put a hand up to my mouth and signalled a shoosh. "She's asleep,

Bosco." I whispered. I carried Angel's sleeping body to the bunk-room at the end of the hall.

For some reason, I envisioned Teresa sleeping in there. My heart plummeted. The hard nature of her demise hit me. Teresa was never coming back. She was never going to hold her warm body against me again. She was never going to hand me coffee with a kiss. Those times were gone. Ripped from my heart. And it was *me* who pulled the trigger. It was *me* who took her life. If there was anyone to blame, all I needed was a mirror.

Teresa's death came with such a high price. I would take that regret with me like a black dog, whenever I heard her name. But through it all, I would always ask myself if I could've done more so that she didn't have to die. And I would ask it every single day until I took my last breath.

Placing Angel down in the bunk, I covered her to her chin, switched off the light, and closed the door. In the hall, Bosco watched with an expression of surprise.

"Thought you were still down range," I said in a whisper.

"I was, and I'm back, big hoss. You turned up just in time. Fireworks about to start."

"Oh? And what fireworks are we talking about?"

"I'll let Maggie do the honours. Grab a hot brew, do the for-malities, and come downstairs. I think you'll be amazed."

"Formalities? What formalities?"

He didn't answer. Bosco spun and left, disappearing down to the control room. I took a sharp left-turn and headed straight for the coffee machine. It had been one hell of a time and my little luxury was only a moment away. That's when I heard someone to my rear. I turned to face Maggie. The moment I dreaded and had somewhat avoided arrived.

I was expecting much sharper words. Maggie regarded me in the way only she knew how. "How did you end up?"

There it was. Simple. Direct. Straight to the point. No 'Hello, Nathan.' No 'How's Angel?' No 'Where's Teresa?' Nothing.

How did you end up . . .?

What could I say?

"Mission accomplished, Maggie."

Maggie stepped back a pace and folded her arms. I was no expert at body language, but how could anyone mistake such an action for anything positive?

"I see you've accomplished the primary objective," she said. "What say you of the secondary and tertiary?"

"As I said. Mission accomplished. All is destroyed. But Quinlan – there was no way he was gonna be brought in."

"That's a shame. But good work. We'll debrief in the morning. For now, however, more important things are on. Normally, I'd say go get some rest. But believe me, Nathan, you won't want to miss this. There's some paperwork in the meeting room for you to sign."

"Paperwork?"

"Regulations, really. *Official Secrets Act* Form Ten-B. Your intelligence security level has been raised to level eight. I need a signature before you're eligible to come downstairs. Level eight eyes only for what you're about to witness. Are we clear?"

"Sure. What's going on?"

Maggie laughed, stepping back another pace. I was tired and it was a bad choice of words. I realised she couldn't have answered without my signature. "Sorry. I'll get the paperwork out of the way."

"Good. Come on down when you're ready. Oh, and by the way," Maggie said over her shoulder while stepping away. "A letter for you from Teresa. She left it in the bunkroom before you both left for Swan Island."

* * *

Coffee in my hand, I sat slowly down at the table and eyed the envelope Teresa had left behind. On the envelope, the words, 'My Dearest Nathan.' I sighed and tears sprang to my eyes. I knew what was in there. Somehow, I even knew what she'd written.

It'd start with a greeting. Her words in broken English. I smiled a little knowing just that. I loved the way she spoke. None other could speak as she did. Her accent was one of the things about her I found so attractive. I hung on every word she ever told me. I often laughed to myself. The struggles she had. The corrections I made. It was all so lovable and enjoyable listening to her talk.

After a greeting, she'd let me know that I'd only ever read such a letter in the case of her death. She'd go on by saying how sorry she was for how she passed. She'd even tell me how much she loved me. She'd remind me of all the good times we shared. She'd tell me not to mourn her in death, but to treasure the moments we had together. The love we shared. The laugher. The tears. The disagreements and the shouting that came with it. She'd remind me of all those things.

Then she'd end her letter in forgiveness. She'd remind me that she was always and forever looking down from wherever she was. She'd say to not give up on love, but to open my heart should it arrive again. She'd tell me it wasn't our time, but our time would come again.

After I finished the letter and put it away, I realised all those things were written in there. Almost word for word, just as I felt.

CHAPTER TWENTY-NINE

A Different Perspective

THE PLACE WAS LIT UP WITH BLUISH lights, down there. New electronic equipment had been installed since the last time I visited. New banks of computers along the far-right wall. Two huge flat panel screens screwed into place. New tech, I thought. Plasma screens. Probably more expensive than a Mercedes-Benz SL500. I was beginning to see firsthand how much money was splashed this way.

Maggie turned and regarded me with her hands firmly on her hips. Bosco was standing beside her with his blue baseball cap spun backwards, chewing on what was probably gum. Andrew was at one of the several computers, bent over a keyboard, tapping madly.

Maggie beckoned me over. "Come," she said. "Take a seat, Nathan. We're waiting for the satellite connections at this time."

"We'll have the Daydreamer uplink in a few moments. Minotaur shortly after," Andrew said. He got up from his chair and came toward me, taking the trouble to reach out and shake my hand.

I repeated my original question to Maggie, sitting down in the chair at the long Tasmanian Oak table.

How in the heck did they get it down here . . .?

"Mind telling me what all this is about?" I asked.

"Yes. Of course. I apologise, Nathan. My mind is firmly else-where, so it seems. Welcome to Operation Cobalt Blue. Mission brief on the desk over there if you'd like, but I'll give you the rundown. We are conducting a coordinated drone strike. Our tar-gets are Vault Vitae-G; McMurdo Station; Antarctica; and Halifax Winthrop Engineering in North Eastern Iran, approxi-mately six hundred kilometres south of Mashhad. We are going to obliterate The Guardianship capability. It all comes down to this."

"Maggie. Vault Vitae-G is blast-proof. We've already estab-lished it can't be compromised with AGMs. That was the reason for Crossbow, wasn't it?"

"Crossbow was reconnaissance, as you know, Nathan. This is about the destruction of assets."

"Then why can't we lead a sabotage mission old school?"

I said it. Maybe I should've left it. Maggie flicked her hair to one side as she did when she started to get annoyed. She took a breath, then said, "It's much too late for that, Nathan. Black ops are out of the question. Cobalt Blue has CIA and Presidential ap-proval. We're going ahead as planned."

If the mission had Presidential approval, it could only mean one thing. The thought spat cold ice through my mind. Many in-nocent people were going to lose their lives. How many were stationed at McMurdo, I wondered. A hundred? Maybe a thou-sand?

"You're going to nuke the place?" I asked, still not believing it for a second.

Bosco strode over and got up in my face. He was on a hair-trigger, I thought. I wondered what it was about. Maybe he'd heard enough arguments over the mission's pros and cons. "Canter, there's just no option," he said. "What I saw down there was *not* just a couple of coffee plants and a handful of seeds. The bastards are stockpiling fuel cells. Antimatter fuel cells."

"You're shitting me," I said. "Antimatter is theoretical."

"Not anymore, big hoss. It's as real as that damn fake leg of yours."

"So you think nukes are gonna finish it? Nukes are airburst weapons. They won't make a dent in a blast-proof bunker."

"Ahem," Andrew butted in. "You might be a bit wrong there. This one we're using is a little different to the airburst variety. This one is a ground-penetrating bunker buster nuke. 3.5 megatons. Two warheads. One for penetration, the other for the destructive yield. Just in case you wanted to know."

Holy shit. They were going to do it! And not only that, it was planned well in advance. While I was down range. I wondered about that timing. Was it done this way with a purpose? I, for one, wouldn't have given it my endorsement. Not this. Not the death of innocent civilians. I said it aloud. "And what of the people down there? There's at least a thousand innocent civilian scientists who have nothing in this. You're gonna go ahead and murder them? Cold and calculating? Are we not as bad as the bloody Guardianship?"

"Collateral damage," Maggie said matter-of-factly, sighing heavily. Her complexion reddened as though she was losing her patience. "The stakes are much too high to consider a mass evacuation of McMurdo, Nathan. The Guardianship will be alerted and we're back to where we started."

"Are you people shitting me!" I shouted.

"Canter!" Maggie snapped. "I'm reminding you of where we are! Yes, people are going to lose their lives. Yes, those people are innocents. We CANNOT conduct this operation without making the Guardianship cognisant. All bases have been covered. This has Presidential approval. Are you going to sit there and second-guess the leader of the free world? Do you *not* think the President of the United States has taken the trouble to calculate the outcome? We are talking about the human race, Nathan. The stakes are just too. Bloody. High."

Maggie trailed off long enough to take a deep breath. Then added, "I wish it didn't come down to this. But with the Hadgitol and now the antimatter fuel cells? We must stop it. There *is* no other way. Andrew! Get some fresh coffee down here for god's sake!"

Andrew left his seat and shot up the stairs. After he'd gone there was a silence in the control room thick enough for a chainsaw to hack through.

"Everyone take a breather," Maggie said. "Clearly, with a certain amount of opposition to Cobalt Blue, this is not going to be an easy mission."

"And what about Halifax Winthrop?" I asked without pause. "Are we to nuke that place too?"

"They're the centrifuges," Maggie said. "A present from Teresa, if you will. The same weapon will be used. The casualties, however, will be at a minimum."

"How many?"

"There are employees there. Intel suggests they're all Guardianship working for the same cause. Halifax Winthrop Engineering will procure enough enriched plutonium for the manufacture of a super-bomb in a few short years. The Peacemaker."

Peacemaker. Where did I hear that term before? It was a memory, but from where? I got up from my seat and walked back and forth with a hand to my chin. Then it came to me. Angel's dream. The one she had with the black guy. Peacemaker. All one word as Maggie had said. There it was.

"What of this Peacemaker," I asked.

"Little is known," Maggie said. "The intelligence we have on the Peacemaker doesn't lead us anywhere other than to an intention for it to be used. Even on that score, there is grey. We know Peacemaker is proposed as a super-bomb. A super-bomb with enough destructive yield to dwarf anything this planet has ever witnessed."

"What kind of destructive yield are we talking about?"

"One-gigaton. MOSSAD infiltrated Halifax Winthrop for a short time before becoming compromised. The plutonium required for such a device will no doubt come from there. Other than that, zip. And that is the reason why this facility needs to be shut down. We can't let such vast quantities of weapons-grade plutonium fall into the hands of the Guardianship. I can't imagine there'll be a safe place on earth should that happen."

"Okay, so nuke the place. But leave Antarctica and McMurdo intact," I said. "There is another way we can accomplish the task without taking lives."

"And what do you propose, Nathan. Go on. I'm happy to hear it." She wasn't happy. I could tell. She stood bolt upright with arms firmly folded, her eyes like blades of fine Tamahagane steel cutting through me. Now was my opportunity to come up with something. Anything. I thought hard. I walked back and forth. Head down with a hand to my chin. I had my opportunity. And it was fading away. *C'mon, Nathan . . . Think, for Christ's sake . . .*

"What about non-nuclear bunker busters?"

"Already considered that," Bosco said. "They don't have enough reach and yield to do the job. I'd know. I was there. We'd have to use more than a dozen. That would mean a number of drones, which we don't have."

"A full-frontal invasion with special forces," I said. "We'd have that place shit-canned in a minute."

"Nathan. You know that's not possible," Maggie put in. "We'd have to wait another six months for the weather. We don't have that time on our side."

"There has to be something. Anything but a nuke!"

Bosco walked to my side and put a hand on my shoulder. I pushed it away.

"C'mon, Nathan. I know you don't like it. We all don't like what's gonna happen. There's simply no choice."

I looked at Bosco and frowned. Anger built up inside me. It took an almighty will not to reach out and squeeze his throat. Him and his days in Detachment 421. No, I hadn't forgotten it. But this wasn't the time.

"Think about it," I said to everyone there. "Thermonuclear and antimatter. What does that sound like to you? Can you *not* imagine the cost? Not only to innocent bystanders, which is bad enough. What about the marine ecosystem and wildlife you'll be destroying for a hundred thousand years into the future? Species forced into extinction. Doesn't it sound like stupidity knocking at your door?"

"I've had enough!" Maggie shouted. "Enough! Do you hear me!"

Maggie slammed something down on the table. I wasn't sure what it was.

"Leave, Nathan! Leave and don't return until you have something productive to offer. This mission goes ahead. As planned!"

CHAPTER THIRTY

Cobalt Blue

MY MIND TWISTED WITH EVERYTHING I'd heard. Seated at the dining room table, I added a decent amount of Wild Turkey to my coffee. Maybe it would help. Maybe it wouldn't. Everything spun in my head. Was this really happening?

I got up from my chair and decided to check in on Angel. I opened the door softly and peered in. Thank god she was still asleep. The amount of shouting and yelling could've woken anybody. For some reason I couldn't work out, I reached down and placed a hand on her forehead. She was hot to the touch. Too hot. Maybe she was coming down with something. Another seizure. I pushed the thought from my mind and went looking for some aspirin. Maybe it would bring her temperature down.

Stepping into the bathroom and opening the box with the red cross that was positioned near the door, I reached in and grabbed the aspirin. An empty glass was by the sink. I grabbed it and filled it halfway with water.

My hand instinctively went to the Glock handgun I had tucked at my back. Before leaving, I caught a glimpse of my own reflection in the mirror. The reflection staring back wasn't me. I didn't know who that guy was. But now, with a handgun, maybe I could stop this madness.

I moved fast toward the hallway, then to the stairs. By the time I got below, the uplink to the Daydreamer and Minotaur satellites were underway. Andrew was seated at the computer. Maggie stood with her full attention on the monitors. Bosco was standing beside Maggie, still with his baseball cap turned backward.

Maggie turned and eyed me. Then she beckoned for me to take a seat. Bosco didn't react. His eyes were firmly fixed to what was going on.

On the left monitor was a daytime vision high above the earth, looking over a vast desert in Iran. On the right, a night-time image under infrared. Both drones getting into position, I thought. How much time did I have left?

"Agent Blue," Maggie said. "ETA to ingress?"

"Ingress to target ten mikes, ma'am," the voice said over the speaker. That voice. I knew the voice. No. It couldn't be.

"Agent Grey?" Maggie said.

"ETA thirty mikes. Diversion due to weather."

"Agent Blue. Possible to go around to meet up with an ingress on thirty mikes?"

"Negative, ma'am. Bingo fuel."

That was it. It was going ahead. Nothing I could do to change anything. Or was there? I slowly rose from my seat and walked over toward Maggie. She turned and smiled briefly, then she went back to the monitor.

"Abort the mission," I said at Maggie's rear. Maggie immediately spun and eyed me. "Belay that last statement Agents Blue and Grey!" Maggie shouted.

"Ma'am? Still a go on the target?"

"Affirmative. Carry on," Maggie said, watching me intensely.

I pulled the gun out and pointed it directly at Maggie's head. "Abort the mission! For Christ's sake! Abort!"

"Belay it!" Maggie yelled.

Bosco turned and stood as though in shock. "Fuck sake, Canter! You idiot! What're you doing!"

Andrew got up from his chair, tipping it over, then pointed a handgun directly at me. "Drop it!" he shouted with intense resolve.

Maggie raised a hand, then let it relax. She took a breath. "This is how you want to play this, Nathan? Are you sure? It comes down to this?"

"Maggie. You can't let this happen. Please. If you murder these people . . ."

"Murder, is it? The exact same murder as you yourself are party to? How many lives, Nathan? Can you count them? Give me the gun and we'll discuss it."

"No. You'll abort this mission. You'll . . ."

"Nathan?" A voice from the top of the stairs. Angel.

"Angel, go back. Please!"

Then a voice in my head. Deep from within. Not my voice. Not my inner voice.

"Nathan, this not how I wish it to be. Let it go, my darling. Let it go."

Teresa . . . ?

"Let it go," Teresa's voice repeated in my head. "It must be these way. Let it go, Nathan. A price will be paid, no? You and I have other work. In much years from now. Let it go . . . ."

Teresa . . . !

I relaxed my weapon. My arm dropped to my side as though it was much heavier than it truly was. The gun fell from my grip and clacked, hitting the floor. My leg quivered from under my body and I fell. I spun to see Angel teetering at the top of the stairs. She was going to tip. "Angel!" I yelled. I scurried madly to her side just in time to stop her fall. She was still burning up. I held her in my arms at the foot of the stairs. Nothing I could do but watch on in terror. I had no power to stop anything!

"Ma'am. Agent Blue. Ingress to target. Proceed as planned?"

"Affirmative, Agent Blue. Proceed," Maggie said, showing the professional she was. I realised what I had just done. Maybe there was no way back. But Maggie carried on regardless. "Agent Grey, proceed to target."

"Copy that, Colonel. Proceed to target."

Maggie spun and faced me. Her expression told me there'd be a price to pay for my insubordination. I knew it. I felt it. And thousands of souls were about to meet their end.

The monitor on the right showed a row of lights under infra-red. The drone was almost within range. "One mike, ma'am."

"Agent Blue. I authorise you to engage your target at your ready."

"Roger that, ma'am. Thirty seconds before rifle."

I climbed up from the floor with Angel in my arms and found an empty chair. She was fast asleep again. Her temperature was quickly coming down. I was relieved, but at the same time on edge with what was about to occur. My eyes fixed to the monitor on the right, I held my breath.

"Rifle, rifle, rifle. Weapon away. Countdown begins. Sixty seconds to impact."

Maggie then took a seat and buried her head in her hands for just a second before looking back up to the monitor. Regret maybe. I saw it. She was human. It occurred to me that Maggie was doing her job. She was a Colonel. She was answering the orders from those above her. She had no choice. I knew, watching her, that she opposed this too. Her own feelings. Her own reservations. The same as me. But she'd never admit it. She'd check that at the door. The true professional she was.

"Thirty seconds . . ."

Bosco moved closer to the monitor. It was as though he was willing it on. Maybe he was getting some enjoyment, I supposed. It wouldn't have surprised me.

"Ten seconds to impact . . ."

My eyes grew large. Holy hell. Please God!

"Five . . . four . . . three . . . two . . . Impact."

The screen under infrared immediately lit up bright blue-white. Blue-white! For a long time, blue-white. I wondered about the immense explosion down there. I wondered about the lives lost. All souls instantly vaporised. I hung my head for a second. It was done. Looking up again, still blue-white.

"Something wrong with the monitor?" Bosco asked.

Then the voice of the drone pilot from the speaker. "Woo hoo! Woo hoo! Fucken boom, mate. Lies and secrets can go an' kiss my lily arse!"

Bosco and Andrew laughed. It wasn't funny. Not at all.

"Agent Blue!" Maggie shouted. "You're still on audio! Check your words, thank you very much!"

"Ah, sorry ma'am. Thought I 'ad that bit sorted. Forgot I 'ad to press the bloody button, eh?"

"Thank you, Agent Blue. You may recall your drone. That is all. Out."

Maggie signalled a cutthroat to Andrew, who disconnected from the Daydreamer satellite. The monitor went blank without sound.

"Agent Grey?"

"Ingress to target, two mikes, ma'am."

"I authorise you . . ." Maggie broke off. Her voice became hoarse. Her words quivered slightly. Then she took a breath and regained her composure. "I authorise you to engage your target at your ready, thank you."

"Roger that, Colonel."

The camera from the Minotaur satellite showed the Halifax Winthrop structure from high in space.

"Thirty seconds to rifle, ma'am."

"What's that?" Maggie said, moving closer to the monitor, as though seeing something for the first time.

"What?" Bosco said.

"That!" Maggie repeated.

Maggie put her finger on the screen. I noticed what she was viewing. I hadn't seen anything like it before, but there it was. After Maggie lifted her finger away from the monitor, I had a better view. Something out of the ordinary, sitting lonely on the desert flat. Something that began to glow.

"Rifle, rifle, rifle. Weapon away. Sixty seconds to impact."

The glowing object intensified, then lifted off the ground slightly. Instantly, it shot away as if it was never there.

"Ten sec . . . what the . . . Hang on . . ."

"What is it, Agent Grey?" Maggie said, holding her breath.

"Ma'am? It appears we've lost the weapon. The weapon has been compromised. It's been destroyed."

CHAPTER THIRTY-ONE

What Now

MAGGIE SAT BEHIND HER DESK, avoiding eye contact. Her avoidance cut deep. I knew I'd stuffed up severely. I knew answering my mutiny was here and now. In the shit again. I'd been here before, but never so deep. I sat nervously bobbing a knee up and down.

Maggie kept her eyes down, shuffling papers. Shuffling photographs and everything else. Angel was away with Andrew for an appointment with the GP. Bosco was out on an errand, Maggie had said. I sat there, still and silent. The emptiness and avoidance was murder.

"Do you have anything to add before we start?" Maggie finally said, not bothering to look up from her desk.

"No," I said. "Just put it out there, straight up with no bullshit."

Maggie smiled, but not out of happiness. Exactly the opposite, I thought. She placed her papers down, locked her fingers, and eyed me. "You know this will have to go down to Canberra, Nathan. I can't avoid it. What you did is completely inexcusable. Not only do your actions warrant a court-martial, but you were on the verge of ruining everything. And nobody gets to put a gun to my head. I have given this a lot of thought and you give me no option."

Her undertone was one of sadness. Disappointment. She held up a document with her own handwriting scribbled down the full length. "This is my Form-T describing your insubordination. It discloses everything that has happened. I suggest you read it to yourself before we go any further."

Maggie slid the document across her desk. I picked it up and read what was written. A blow by blow account of everything that transpired two nights before. After reading it, I gave a nod and slid it back over Maggie's desk. She picked it up from her desk and held it up before ripping it to shreds.

"Maggie. I'm guilty as charged."

"There's method in my decision," Maggie said, at the same time raising her hand. "You might think you've got off lightly. You'd be wrong in that assumption. I'll get to this a little later. But I know you, Nathan. This was *not* you. I want to know *how* you managed to get yourself down to such a place. I'm thinking there was a lot that went on to cloud your judgment. Talk to me. Tell me everything."

I settled back into my chair and thought things over. There was much to explain. By the time I'd finished, I'd given Maggie an account of everything in detail. I watched her expression change from hard to something more empathetic. She leaned forward in her chair, locking her hands and listening intently to the finer specifics.

I saw compassion twinkle in her eyes for a second, but then her professionalism cut back in, hardening her facial lines. I'd told her everything but left out one aspect. The time Angel fell from the helo. No matter which way I looked at it, I wasn't able to describe the event leading to Angel's amnesia. I made something up to put in its place. Maybe it was more palatable and easier to swallow.

"So, you're telling me Angel has no recollection whatsoever?" Maggie said.

"None."

"Have you tested it?"

"Yes, I have. A number of times I put questions to her to see if any memory would come back to her. She really has no memory of the ordeal."

"Hmm . . ." Maggie put a hand to the side of her face and sat back. I could tell from her cutting-ice gaze the whole scenario had her confused "Stay here," she said. "I need a moment." She got up and left.

I sat there with my knee still bobbing, the unfortunate set of consequences twirling and whirling in my head. I was ready. The real prospect of being stood down and sent to prison for attempted treason was starting to sink in. It was now a reality and not just a fleeting thought. The hard call would be announced the moment Maggie came back. She'd be back with a couple of federal cops in tow. My hands would again be cuffed behind my back and I'd be on my way.

When Maggie finally entered and sat down in her high-back office chair, there were no federal cops behind her. She simply sat and took a heavy breath, then began with her hands locked together on her desk. "It's clear you'll need counselling, Nathan. Before you object, let me say this is non-negotiable. I will set it up for you."

"Sure," I nodded. "But what now?" Here it comes, I thought. Let's get to the big crunch.

"What now?" she said, as though surprised. "Have you forgotten? You still have your Eagle Shield mission. You *have* to get Angel into play. It's more important now than previously."

"We killed the Hadgitol. That makes Eagle Shield void, doesn't it?"

"We've taken the Hadgitol out of the equation, yes. But Halifax Winthrop is still standing. We don't get another go at it, unfortunately. We've lost the element of surprise to sneak up and destroy that threat. Without the parent genome, the Guardianship capability has been slowed, but not absolutely nullified. Perhaps they won't come out of dry-dock in a hurry. But make no mistake about it. They'll be back."

"Eagle Shield original objectives still stand, I take it."

"To the letter," Maggie said plainly. "But I'm still cross with you. I'm human, after all. I feel disappointment just the same as anybody. It will take some time, I'm afraid. Just appease me by going to the counselling sessions. We'll work it out, I'm quite sure."

"I dunno how that will work out, Maggie. Everything I'll need to talk about is classified."

"Exactly why we have our own. And he's in Melbourne. He's name is Xenon. Xe for short."

"Xe? That doesn't sound like an ordinary name."

"He's not an ordinary man. You'll see what I mean after you meet up."

"Okay. Done."

"Now. Other business," Maggie said. I could see some relief in her expression. She went on. "I need to bring you up to date on a few items. Do you feel like taking a look at some happy snaps? I'll understand if you don't."

I thought it over. Was I in the mood to look at images of destruction? I already knew McMurdo was no longer, and probably a good portion of Antarctica didn't exist. My mind again went to all the carnage. All those lives lost. I had no choice but to get over it and carry on. "Sure," I said. "I'll take a look."

Maggie passed a couple of photographs across her desk without any delay. The images weren't of Antarctica as I'd suspected. Instead, the photographs were of the infrastructure of Halifax Winthrop. Maggie reached across her desk and placed a finger on an object in one of the photos, the object that was believed to have destroyed the incoming weapon. "Any thoughts on what that might be?"

After scanning the photographs, I passed them back across Maggie's desk. "I have no idea. I've never seen any object like it before. But why do I get the feeling it has something to do with the antimatter fuel cells we found?"

"My deductions as well. We'll need to investigate it. We don't need anything like that in our way on the day Milestone finally comes."

"I still can't get my head around a theoretical antimatter becoming reality."

"I hear you. Anyway. I'll pitch this one to Canberra for a priority follow-up with Andrew," Maggie said, then placed the photograph back in her drawer. "Now, here is something that will surprise you." Reaching into her desk drawer, Maggie took something out. Small. Metal. She passed it over. I held the tiny object in my hand. I'd seen it before.

"The projectile from the William Creek crime scene?"

Maggie nodded vigorously and smiled. Not a happy smile. Maggie gave me the impression she was slightly perplexed, and the smile reflected her frustration, I supposed. "Interpol came up with a match a couple of weeks ago. The bullet was dispatched from Canberra just yesterday and it arrived this morning."

I took the bullet sample and eyed it. Immediately the image of the seven eagles came to mind. Gabriel, who'd dropped it into my hand. "Do we have a trace? Do we know who?"

"We have a trace. Doug Walken."

"The grazier guy?"

"He was a player."

My god. Maggie was right. I leaned forward in my chair. "But surely if he was Guardianship, the bullet could *not* be traced back to him."

"The man used his own weapon. Why? Because he was a sleeper. And he himself must've known just how temporary he was."

"Temporary?"

"Oh, absolutely. While you were away on Barras, we initiated a full autopsy on this fellow. What we found was something absolutely extraordinary."

Maggie reached into her drawer and retrieved something small in a plastic evidence bag. She passed it over. The strange object was obviously damaged, but I knew straight away what it was. "A bloody homing beacon? That explains the helo knowing where to find us. I assumed the Gs tracked the GPS upload after I transmitted the data back to you. But now this? It explains a lot."

"The beacon was surgically implanted just below his left armpit," Maggie went on. "However, that's not the extraordinary part. The man had another implant. A high explosive device. The man was literally wired from the inside. A kidney had been removed and the device was implanted into the cavity. When we found the device, the entire mortuary was locked down. In the end, the bomb disposal squad was called in and the only safe way out of the situation was to relocate the body and detonate the device in a controlled environment."

"Hmm . . . Hence the beacon being so damaged. How did you recover it?"

"Metal detector, and a lot of man hours."

I sat back and placed a hand on my forehead in disbelief. During the journey up from William Creek, I was literally sitting right next to a bomb. It made me wonder how things would've turned out had I bailed the guy up in the beginning. It also made me wonder how he was supposed to detonate it. He had no trigger device on him. None that I knew of. Certainly nothing obvious on his person.

Maggie cut into my thoughts as I was going over everything. "The device and the beacon were set up to be used as a coordinated attack, Nathan. Make no mistake about it. This fellow's mission was *never* about Angel or Eagle Shield. *His* mission was us. I speculate as soon as he came into the range of his objective, whomever was behind tracking the beacon would've remotely detonated the charge. Had you brought him here, things would've turned out much differently. I'd hate to think.

"Now you can let go of the guilt. He was a soldier. A Guardianship soldier. This goes much deeper than we first assumed. It means even seemingly ordinary people are intertwined into Guardianship ranks. We are at war, Nathan. We are at war, and with this new threat, we have no alternative but to consider the fact there're more of these so-called wired sleepers. Now we have our work cut out for us, wouldn't you agree?"

"I can't believe it. The man had me fooled. He had herds . . . and dogs."

"We did some research into his background. He lived alone in a shack on a property located not far north from Roxby Downs, which was burnt to the ground after we got there to investigate. It makes you wonder, doesn't it? He must've had a cover that was worked out far in advance. So far, in fact, the local populous at William Creek were none the wiser and indeed knew him well. Can you imagine the catastrophe had his mission played out? Perhaps we'd not be sitting here now and discussing it."

I shuddered in my seat, realising how close I came. How close we *all* came. The fact that I'd gotten him killed was nothing more than dumb luck. But was it more than that? How had Angel managed to send her warning? No matter how hard I thought it over, with Angel's amnesia I'd never connect those dots. Now, the whole scenario was nothing more than hindsight. Or was it?

"No, Maggie. I don't believe it for a second. It's too farfetched. How in the hell could a sleeper be in close proximity to where we were at the time? The entire length and breadth of this country. This guy was in the middle of nowhere waiting for us to arrive? It just doesn't sound plausible."

Maggie looked at me as I sat back folding my arms. Considering everything, my head was in a spin. "That's what I am getting at, Nathan. One: There're more of these fellows out there than you care to think about. Two . . ."

Then it hit me. "A mole?" Holy shit. Now it was coming together, and I hated seeing it in this new light.

"A mole," Maggie agreed. "Mathew Mallow. ASIO counter-intelligence."

"The guy who was set up to be the negotiator with Quinlan!"

Maggie nodded vigorously and explained, "Mallow was recruited by the Guardianship after he got his nose all out of joint with that Sydney Opera House botch up. He was actively tracking you and Angel. When you arrived within range, this sleeper was activated. But it doesn't stop there. After the Federal Police arrested Mathew Mallow, we looked into his activities. At his place of residence, we found the intelligence of literally thousands of sleepers. All of them geared up and aimed toward our assets and infrastructures. There are ongoing operations right now to nullify the threat. It is with great sadness we expect things to worsen before this danger has been quashed for good. You can expect side missions coming your way. You have your Eagle Shield mission and there will be no rest for you, Nathan."

I heard what Maggie was saying and I accepted it for what it was worth. But something stuck out and I wasn't sure if it had already been addressed. "Firebird Station is compromised," I said. "We can no longer continue to conduct operations from here."

"I know. Sad, isn't it? I've sent Bosco away to investigate the prospect for a new location. Everything will have to be uprooted and moved, unfortunately."

Bosco. The mention of his name brought to mind older issues that needed to be sorted. I thought back to his involvement with Detachment 421. Maybe now was the right time to bring it up. I came right out with it. "Maggie. I'm afraid I don't have full trust with Bosco in Eagle Shield."

Maggie looked up and appeared stunned by my abruptness. "What on earth are you saying? Bosco is absolutely crucial to Eagle Shield. He is your wingman, for God's sake. Are you telling me my decision to have him in play is wrong?"

"It's not that at all. I'm sure your decision is sound. There's history with Bosco I can't get my head around. I'm certain he was at some time involved with Detachment 421."

There it was. I'd finally spilled my suspicions about Bosco. Maybe I should've left it. Already, regret for saying the words was sinking in. I hated my mind sometimes. Maggie sat back and folded her arms, eyes cold ice. "I'm not confirming it!" she snapped. "But what of it?"

"The CIA's Candy programme."

"That's classified," Maggie said plainly. "It's not open for discussion."

I saw her eyes leave me and go off in another direction. She stared at the window behind me before finally adding, "Let me put it this way, Nathan. I will not tell you that Bosco was an operative with Detachment 421. I will not tell you Bosco was inserted with the sole purpose of bringing the Candy programme down. I will go on by not telling you if it wasn't for Bosco, more lives may have been lost due to this CIA stupidity. I *never* told you those things. I never *discussed* them with you or anybody else. How you discovered this information is beyond my comprehension. And it stays that way. Clear?"

I nodded, not saying anything further. But I couldn't just leave it there. I was about to push this thing right out on the ragged edge.

"Agent Blue," I asked. "Who is this guy?"

"Classified." Maggie's word was dry as water crackers. She looked down and avoided eye contact.

"And where was Agent Blue's drone piloted from?"

"That's classified, Nathan. Bloody hell!" Maggie huffed. "Please do not push down this road again. Get to Melbourne. Go to your counselling sessions with Xe. Keep a clear head for your side missions as they come about. I'll be in touch in due course. That is all."

CHAPTER THIRTY-TWO

Melbourne 1996

ANGEL COULDN'T WAIT TO GET THROUGH the front door. No sooner did I have the key in the lock, she busted through into a very well-appointed apartment. The first thing I noticed was the television set on an expensive-looking table. Flat screen plasma. It took me by surprise.

Everything was new and the place smelled of new carpeting and furniture. There was even a large array of books on a bookcase. On the left, a balcony overlooking Port Melbourne. Angel wasted no time getting out there. I met her on the balcony. I imagined what it must look like at night as the city lit up with its colourful landscape. I wondered how all this was made possible. So much money. Where did it come from?

"Wow, Nathan. Wow!" Angel giggled. "Is this really ours?"

"Yeah. It is," I said, not believing it. Only the richest of the rich had a place like this. Maybe it wasn't so bad, this mission. Maybe I'd get to enjoy it. Things like this don't ever come for free. There's a price to be paid somewhere. Perhaps one day I'd find out what.

For now, a bit of respite away from all the bloodshed and killing was what I needed. Away from the stress of everything. I left

Angel by herself and went back inside. I felt almost childlike exploring our new home.

"You hungry?" I shouted from the kitchen. I opened the fridge and nothing, I mean nothing, was left out. An entire grocery store in a metal box. Then to the pantry. My mouth watered. The shelves were stacked high. Every need catered for.

"Am I hungry? Like . . . yeah!" Angel answered from wherever she was now exploring. The bedroom I think. I went to see.

Angel's bedroom was a ten-year-old's dream come true. A comfortable bed. A bookcase with rows upon rows of books. A desk in the corner. On the desk, a laptop computer. How in the heck was a laptop computer made available? Those things had just hit the market and were so expensive nobody could afford them. My mind whirled with amazement.

Which room next? My room.

I opened the door, walked inside, and placed the leather briefcase containing Eagle Shield objectives and that disk on the side table. A luxury bed. A desk and another laptop computer. All the trimmings I could imagine. It was such a delight. Things were looking up. Finally.

"Nathan . . ." Angel called from her room.

"Coming . . ." I said, like a real dad.

Walking into Angel's room, I found her sitting on her bed with books from the shelf sprawled out in front of her. "Look what I found," she said, holding up a couple of books. "These are about taking pictures!"

"Photography books," I said. "Nice."

"Look, Nathan. This one says how I can make some money from taking lots of pictures."

Hmm . . . Now this is not how it's supposed to go . . .

My first urge was to go looking for anything spy-related. Get there, I thought. Nothing like a beginning. But maybe I wouldn't push things too hard. Little by little, I'd get there in the end.

Angel sprang from her bed and blurred past me. I heard her call out with an echo. "Nathan. Oh my god! Two sinks! One for me and one for you!"

I got myself in there. The first thing I noticed was a luxury bath. Deep. With jets. I didn't know how long it was. I hadn't had the luxury of a spa in recent memory. Maybe longer. A shower cubicle to one side. Two shower heads in there. Then my eyes went to the door and I hoped it had a lock.

A lock . . . Good . . .

Stepping out, a sweet scent in the air. An arrangement of flowers on a small table. A note under a vase. I picked up the envelope and found something written by hand. 'Welcome home, big hoss.'

Bosco . . . ?

I opened the note.

Welcome to your pad. You've got everything to make yourself at home. You deserve it, Buddy. Check out the Nintendo. Every goddamn shoot-em-up game to keep your skills fresh. Keep that girl on course and we won't have a problem. I'm in the shadows as I always was. Just call. Phone in your desk drawer. See ya!

Bosco's errand, I thought. He was gone for how long? The bastard. I smiled, knowing he'd sorted everything. Now my head was clear, Maggie's explanation of Bosco's time in Detachment 421 made sense and I was able to rediscover the trust I once had with Bosco. Now, it was like I knew him as an old friend. And all this? Only friends and comrades got to do this for each other. Time to get on with it.

In the desk in my room I found a Motorola mobile phone the size of a small house brick. How in the heck could I ever carry that thing around? Another note under. A series of numbers and a short missive to suggest a safe. Stepping over to my wardrobe, I slid the big glass mirror door sideways. Suits. My size. Armani. Black. Seven of them. A safe at the floor with a dial and handle.

I dialled up the combination that was on the note and opened the steel door. A suppressed nine-millimetre Beretta with boxes of ammo. A big wad of cash. Hundred-dollar notes. Picking up the wad of cash, I guesstimated a couple of hundred grand. I felt the weight in my hand and juggled it a little, just because I could. Placing the cash back in, I closed the steel door and spun the combination lock. Next to the safe on the floor, shoes. Seven pairs. Gucci or similar. Shiny and black. Sneakers. Two pairs. Reebok.

A set of drawers to one side. I slid one open. Tracksuits. Grey. Australian coat of arms. Nike. Just what had I gotten into? I couldn't remember the last time I went for a jog.

Bosco, you idiot . . .

"Nathan! Come see! Come see!"

I dashed into the living room to see what Angel sounded so excited about. She pointed. "Look," she said, giggling.

On a shelf, figurines of eagles. About a dozen of them. Different poses and postures. Another note under. I passed the note to Angel and she read it out loud.

Dear Angel, something for you to enjoy. Love, Maggie. XX

"I'm so happy, Nathan. This is a really nice place, isn't it?"

"It is," I agreed. "Now, let's see about getting us some KFC."

CHAPTER THIRTY-THREE

Of All Things

ANGEL TURNED SIXTEEN YEARS OLD TODAY.
Where did that time go? As I finished setting the table, I reflected briefly on old memories. All the memories once hard like crystal had softened with time. My mission was going not exactly as scheduled, but it had its moments and I was optimistic. There were times when I thought I could never accomplish it. Angel, as I'd been told by several people, had a mind all of her own. Her school grades were exceptional. The top of the crop, her teachers said. No issues there. I couldn't have asked for any better. But how could I get her into the field of play when she was so passionate about her camera?

There were moments I'd even considered hiding her camera to make it a little hard for her. But every time she used it; her photographs were spectacular. Angel was indeed a master in the craft. How could I take that away? I didn't have the heart. She enjoyed it so much. Nobody in their right mind could ever do such a thing, knowing her talent and the pleasure she got out of it.

I'd even set up the laundry as an ad hoc darkroom. I'd covered the windows with black plastic so no light could get in. On a bench I made out of scraps of pine sat an old photographic enlarger. In a drawer, boxes of unexposed multigrade sheets of paper. Trays to the left contained developer, fixer, and stop bath. Those chemicals smelt like vinegar and probably were. But I never had the guts to taste it just to see. Who'd know if vinegar and water were the only things necessary to make prints.

On so many occasions, I attempted to guide and direct Angel into a position to build a desire toward spy craft. There seemed little interest there. So, no choice but to go with it. To see where it led. Maybe she'd change and become curious. I kept the hope going forward. Everything would fall into place, I kept thinking.

The table looked like a sixteen-year-old's party table by the time I'd finished with it. Everything I could come up with to make the occasion just right. Sweets and savouries. A balance of healthy and not so healthy. A birthday cake I'd made myself. Something I was proud of. Not perfect, but there was a lot of love in there, even though it sat crooked and wasn't flat on the top. Sixteen candles, ready to light. I stood back and sighed. My girl was growing up.

A present from me sat at the edge of the table. I couldn't wait to give it to her. It took an awful lot of will not to give it to her early. But now it was there, it was only a little while longer to wait.

"Angel," I said loudly from the table. No response. I bet I knew why. Opening her bedroom door, I found her with her headphones on. I bet I knew what she was listening to. I walked over and lifted an earpiece away. Just as expected, Metallica screamed from her headphones. Angel looked at me up as though annoyed. "Hey. Now I have to start the same song over," she said.

Figures, I thought. I lifted the earpiece away again. "Time to get yourself ready, Angel. They'll be knocking on the door in half an hour."

"I'll be there in a sec, Nate."

Nate . . . ?

At least it was better than, mate.

I smiled briefly with the memory of that first day while traveling from Alice Springs.

Back to the kitchen. Stuff still needed to be done. Was there time?

I heard the shower starting and relaxed a little.

The doorbell rang. Here they come, I thought. Too late for the final touches.

Opening the door was the one person I knew wouldn't be late. "Hello, Jenny."

"Hey, Nathan. Am I too early?"

"You're never early for Angel, so it seems. How goes it today?"

"I'm great," Jenny said. "I have a present for Angel. Where shall I put it?

I pointed to the table where I'd left mine. "I guess that spot will do nicely." I couldn't help it. I told Jenny what I got Angel. "It's a camera," I said. "Not just any camera. It's a digital. No more messy chemicals, huh? And two tickets for the Metallica concert."

I didn't tell Jenny there were also two backstage passes to meet James Hetfield and the boys. I also didn't tell her they'd be invited to the after-concert party where Mr Hetfield would have his signed guitar ready to give to Angel. That was a moment I'd have to do my best to imagine. I tried desperately to put aside my imaginings of the party.

Amazing, the ASIS machine, Maggie once told me. If it wasn't for Bosco's help with Angel's birthday, I'd never have managed to accomplish as much.

Jenny beamed. "That's so cool, Nathan. She'll love that. Are you taking her?"

"Me? I don't think so. Not my thing. The other ticket is for you. But don't tell her before she opens her present or you're history. Get it?"

"You're such a kidder," Jenny laughed. If only she knew, I reflected. I also imagined Jenny becoming jealous after Angel got her guitar. Maybe I went too far.

At the same time Jenny set her gift on the table, the doorbell rang again. More sixteen-year-olds filed through the door, some giving me high-fives as they stepped past me. It didn't take long before there was no space at all. The place was a mad scramble of sixteen-year-old school friends. The atmosphere was electrified with the shouting and laughing, and I was already feeling the headache coming on. However, I was happy. Happier than I could imagine. The life of being a dad brought about such a big shift in my lifestyle, and I was thankful.

* * *

It was time for the ritual. At the table, everyone crowded around for the candles to be lit. I lit them up one by one. The doorbell rang again. Angel, getting ready to blow them out with a beaming smile, looked up from her sixteen candles as though wondering who it could be.

Answering the front door I knew who the final visitor was. I also knew Angel didn't know and how much of a surprise she'd have.

I opened the door. Maggie was smiling widely. I'd not seen her for so long. "Hello, Nathan."

"You made it," I said, smiling.

"A bastard of a trip. I'll never do it again."

"I appreciate the trouble, Maggie. She'll be a very happy birthday girl."

Angel ran to Maggie as she walked in. It was something so heart-warming to see. Although, with all the laughter and high-pitched gasbagging going on it was hard to hear anything. After all the formalities, the candles were blown out and Angel's gifts unwrapped. The camera was a great gift, but the tickets to see Metallica brought her to tears. The backstage passes, however, brought her to the kind of happiness that ripped my heart from my chest. I always thought it would've been the other way around. How wrong was I?

Then I found some peace out on the balcony. Finally, a bit of a breather. Just me and a hot brew with a dash of Wild Turkey. Life's little treasure. As I stood on the balcony that day and looked out at the city skyline, I thought of all those times way back when. The friends I made. The friends I'd lost along the way. The pain of losing Teresa. There wouldn't be a time without pain for her loss. Rather, a coping strategy to cover the suffering. I reflected on Matchbook, Crossbow, Barras, and the ultra-stuff-up I made in Cobalt Blue, which would never stop haunting me. It was but a reminder of how close I came to the edge and looked over. I glimpsed – for just a second – the darkness over there.

"You okay, Nathan?" Maggie said, joining me on the balcony.

"Yeah. Just having a moment."

"Sounds heavy."

"Yeah. Old memories. I often think back to old times when I'm out here."

"You think too much, Nathan. When are you ever going to learn to just go with the moment?" Maggie paused, then added, "How goes it with the counselling?"

"I'm holding my own, apparently. But I never thought I'd be still doing the counselling sessions after all these years."

"Call it maintenance. That way, if you have to spend a good amount of your life with the sessions, it's validated."

"You said Xe was no ordinary man. You didn't tell me he was one of them."

"Oh," Maggie said ironically. "One of who?"

I smiled with the same dryness as Maggie. "Don't think I don't get it. Xe is Oudarretian. Tell me I'm wrong."

Maggie opened a metal cigarette case and took out a cigarette, tapping it on the back of her hand before lighting up.

"You smoke?"

"So many things you don't know. Yes. But casually. I keep promising myself to give them up. But I only ever partake when things feel right and are going smoothly. Are they going smoothly?"

"You're changing the subject."

"Maybe." Maggie shrugged. "Let me put it like this. Xe is our biggest ally. He's deep undercover. His security clearance is higher than yours and mine combined."

"And yet he's my counsellor."

"A man of many talents, Nathan. But back to Angel. Tell me you've got her safely on schedule."

"Not exactly. Angel is a great photographer. But now she's showing interest in journalism. That's where she sees herself. I have to admit, she's so damn good at her art."

"And yet, that talent she possesses will inevitably take her to the realm of the tabloid press? I can't see her lasting in it. Too much of a dog-eat-dog world for our Angel." Maggie sighed audibly. "Perhaps that's partly my error. I encouraged her photography. When Angel was so young, Alisha was forever turning up with Angel's film cartridges. I too saw Angel's capability. Such an amazing young soul. But don't stress too much. Plenty of time."

"Two years isn't plenty of time. By the time she's eighteen, everything we've worked toward will be for nothing. I've tried so hard. Everything I could think of. I'm sorry, Maggie."

"I don't believe it for a second. Just keep going. We'll get there in the end, I'm sure."

"There's something else," I said. "I don't know how to tackle this one."

"That sounds awfully serious."

"Well, it depends on which way you look at it. I know how I feel about it. But I don't know if you'd be the same."

"Go on."

"Jenny. Angel and Jenny . . . they're more than best friends. I caught them together. What I saw didn't say just best friends to me. And they're too young. They're just little kids. They should never be . . ."

Maggie laughed wholeheartedly.

"Something funny I said?"

"You're more of a dad than you realise, Nathan. Angel is sixteen. She's a young adult. Has no one ever told you about female hormones? Girls grow up much faster than boys. However, I agree with you to some extent. But you'll have a challenge on your hands if this is something that's meant to happen."

"Angel being gay is of no nuisance to me."

"And so it shouldn't be. That's not what I'm getting at."

"Then what do you suggest I do?"

"Talk to her. Let her know that you're approachable but don't overdo it. You can push her away just as easily as having her come to you for your support. Young adult minds are very sensitive. Use care and caution."

How many opportunities over the years had come and gone? I never had 'the chat' with her. That part of me had failed dismally. I always assumed school would take care of it. I avoided it. I let it go.

"I assumed . . ."

"Don't assume anything," Maggie cut in. "You're in control."

I thought things over while Maggie enjoyed the view over the city. I don't know why, but after that moment, *nothing else mattered.*

BOOK TWO

Project

AMBER

THE MILESTONE INCIDENT

CHAPTER ONE

Alice Springs, Central Australia 1996

MY MOTHER HAD SWITCHED OFF everything that used electricity. The fridge. The dishwasher. The radio that she loved so much on Sunday afternoons while she sat in her easy chair and spun Merino wool into long curly skeins. The tall clock that demanded attention at the end of the hall stood proud but no longer ticked. There was no whirring of the Whirlpool from the laundry. There was no scent of freshly baked lamingtons or vanilla slices from the kitchen. There were no songs by Hi-Five from the television in the living room. There was no laughter. There was no happiness. There was nothing. And everything was dark.

After pulling down all the blinds, my mother scurried around the place, and with her hands visibly shaking, she reached with her trembling fingers, clawing at power points and switches. She raced methodically from one switch to another, muttering to herself as though somewhere in her mind there was a method in the things she was doing. But I could see it on her face. Her skin was sweaty. I was just old enough to recognise panic. I was old enough to feel brewing terror that made my skin feel incredibly hot. I remember as my mother scampered around the place; I kept telling myself it was just a game. It was, of course, no game at all. "Quickly, Angelique. We have to hide," my mother said with a voice that crackled and quivered.

My mother's eyes darted here and there. Was she trying to decide the best place in the house for us to hide? We had no basement or attic. There was only one place inside the house which had a lock behind the door — the bathroom. I recall as a child; there were so many times I got into trouble if I stayed in the shower for too long. The door was locked. Nobody could do anything about it. My mother decided to hide in there as soon as she grabbed me tightly by the top of my arm. She pulled me forcefully into the cold darkness behind the shower curtain. In the bathtub, we both quietly sat down facing each other. My mother's facial expression was steady as she appeared to listen for signs of movement from the outside of our house.

"Mum?"

"Shhh. We'll be safe in here," my mother told me while she held her finger up to her lips.

"But Mum, Dad will know we're home. Our car is at the end of the driveway. He'll come looking for us as soon as he gets inside."

"He can't get in. He doesn't have a key. I've changed all the locks. And he'll think we're at Maggie's house."

If my father knew we were at Maggie's house, he'd never go looking there. Maggie's husband was an Alice Springs police officer. And not only that, he was a sergeant, I recall thinking. My father and Theo were always at each other. Theo sometimes brought my drunken father home late at night and dumped him near our front door. My young mind began to put things together. What my mother was trying to achieve was to give my father a decoy. He'd turn up at our house and find he wasn't able to enter.

He'd put his ear up to the door and listen for anything inside. My father would then most likely choose to meet with his mates at the pub. Or maybe an afternoon betting on horse races at the TAB. That's how my mother had explained it. She said it to me in plain words and sentences like I was already an adult. Then after she was done, she began to cry.

"Mum, you're scaring me."

My mother pulled me into her chest and wrapped her arms around me. I remember feeling nothing could ever hurt us. Any ten-year-old would be comforted. But I was also cautious. I was also vigilant. Why did Uncle Scotty have to show up and ruin everything?

* * *

As I sat in the cold and darkened bathroom with my mother, who seemed to be thinking of ways to get us out of danger, I reflected briefly on the horrible things that had happened. I remembered the blue, square, object that Uncle Scotty had given her after he arrived so urgently on our front porch. My uncle's tone of voice said he was hopelessly in a mad flap. "You need to get this to Maggie," I heard him say. "I'd do it, but I can't, love. You know I'm on the grid. If I approach Maggie, I'll blow my cover."

I recall as I stood and peered through the living room window, my Uncle Scotty gave my mother something else. It was something that looked like a handkerchief—a piece of cloth with something printed on it. He took it from his pocket and thrust it into my mother's hand. "These are the decryption codes for the computer disk," he said.

"So, what am I supposed to do with them?"

"Alisha. Get them to Maggie. Find a way. She'll know what to do next."

"And Franco? Any ideas where he is right now?"

Scotty immediately answered without a breath. "He's most likely down the pub gettin' plastered. Maybe . . . I'm not sure."

"You can't be sure? This place is so much better when you're both away on work. The two of you should've stayed at Pine Gap!" My mother sucked back a big gulp of air and paused a beat. "How much time do we have before he shows up?"

"You've got as much time as it takes to grab a few things and get out, I reckon. Grab your kit and go. Right-bloody-now."

After Scotty launched himself from the porch, ran to his car and drove away, my mother slowly closed the front door. She turned and looked down at me. I'll never forget her face. Her skin was paper white. Her eyes had become glassy like they were full of fear and sadness. I knew she tried her best to hide her true feelings from me. I could see straight through her. I knew what was *really* going on.

"Angelique, we have to pack a bag and get ready to go. Quickly now, kiddo."

I sprinted into my room, thinking about the things I needed to pack. I slid open my wardrobe door and grabbed my rucksack from the hanger. My mind immediately thought about my camera and photos. They were up on a high shelf. I often wondered why my mother had placed them up so high that it was difficult for me to get to them. My toes almost broke with my weight as I reached up to grab them. I jumped and missed. I jumped and missed again. It was no good. Then, I used the bed as a trampoline. That worked amazingly well, and I had my camera and all my photo albums, all at once.

After ramming my most precious items into my rucksack, I grabbed some of my clothes from my dresser and quickly formed them into a tight ball, shoving them in so hard I swore they were going to burst through the bottom. My mother stepped inside my room as I was finishing up. She brought the objects in that Scotty gave her. She showed them to me. "If anything bad happens, make sure Maggie gets these things." My mother then slipped the blue computer disk and codes into the top pocket of the rucksack. As soon as she was done tightening the straps, she held out her hand to me. "Let's go," she said. "Fuck this place."

We were only five footsteps from my bedroom door when that sound of someone pushing a key into a keyhole, punched through the silence. My mother instantly crouched and pushed me down next to her. She put a finger up to her lips. I knew what it meant. Not a sound. Not a movement. Just like the game we used to play called 'quiet as a mouse.'

As we both crouched, whoever it was at the front door continued to scratch away at the lock. Then, the Mad Man made himself known.

"Alisha!"

My mother looked at me with terror sitting in her red-rimmed eyes. She again pushed her finger up to her lips. When she removed her finger, she tried to give me a comforting smile. But the corners of her mouth refused to cooperate.

"Alisha! Open the bloody door!" My father bashed the door a couple of times.

"Don't say anything," my mother said to me in a whisper so low, it was difficult to hear. But then she physically turned me around and gave me a gentle push toward my bedroom. "Go. Quietly," she whispered.

"Alisha. Open the door. My key won't fit the bloody lock!"

I couldn't be sure how many times my father had yelled out and demanded to be let inside. Each time he yelled out, his voice raised in obvious frustration. His bashing at the door became louder and heavier. Then, there was no sound at all. He was gone. And my mother immediately began shutting things down and switching things off.

* * *

In the darkness of the bathroom from behind the shower curtain, we both waited in the cold silence. I could feel the steady beat of my mother's heart through her chest as she held me tightly in her arms. Sometimes her heartbeat picked up and raced race as soon as she heard sounds from outside. But through it all, it occurred to me; we could've easily used the time to exit through the back door and get far away. It might've worked out better than being boxed in. We could've already arrived at Maggie's house. And after having arrived there, we could've been safe from the rage of my drunken father. Things and events could have been drastically different than they turned out. It was a moment in time that has stayed with me for my entire life. I keep asking myself the same question. Why didn't we go? In that precise moment? Why? All through my twenties. All through my thirties. Even to this very minute, it still causes me heartache. It still causes nightmares and chills me awake. Why can't I go back and change anything? Why?

It was as though my mother had the same thought as me, and at the same time. She let go of me and looked down into my eyes. She seemed so much better without any panic. I was even able to breathe long breaths again. "Time to go, eh kiddo?"

I nodded my happiness, but my moment of joy shattered with the sound of someone scraping at the lock in the back door. My father was back from wherever he'd gone. He was angry. I could hear it in his tone. "Alisha! You've bloody-well changed the back-door lock too? What have you done? Are you doing this to make me angry? Alisha, this is my house too. Let-me-in!"

I shrunk from my father's rage. "Mum!"

My mother pulled me into her arms again. "It's okay kiddo. But I want you to understand something. Whatever happens, run. Run as fast as you can. Take the rucksack and run to Maggie's. Don't look back. Don't worry about me. Just run. Do you hear me? Just run."

I nodded, hoping my mother could feel my answer on her chest.

"That's good. You know what you need to do. That's good." It was as though my mother had said those final words to herself rather than to me. It was after she'd said it, I noticed for the first time how badly she was trembling.

But then, silence ensued once again. We both waited. We both listened out for the slightest of sounds. It was as though my father had finally left. Each moment felt more like hours, and we waited.

SMASH!

I heard a window somewhere near the back of the house, cave in and shatter.

"MUM!"

My mother pulled me in tighter. Much tighter than before.

I heard my father stomping with heavy footsteps around the house. "Alisha! Where are you? Are you home? Angelique?"

My mother immediately got out of the bathtub and went to the window. She used both her hands to push the ages-old window up, but it wouldn't budge. She put her entire weight behind it. It was no good.

"Smash it, Mum. Just smash it."

"No good, kiddo. The glass has got wire inside it."

Then, my father's footsteps stopped at the bathroom door. I could hear him breathing as though he'd pushed his face up close to the door jamb. My mother put her hand over my mouth. She placed her lips right next to my left ear and whispered, "Not a word, kiddo. Shhh."

"C'mon Alisha, I know you're in there. Angelique. I know you're both there. The car's outside, remember? I'm tired, and I need a lie-down. C'mon out and we'll chat a while. Maybe, I'll put a few snags on the barbie. What do ya reckon?"

For some reason, my mother took her hand away from my mouth. Perhaps it was a moment of weakness. Maybe she was about to get up and let my father inside. I couldn't let her do that. I had to stop her. I seized the opportunity, and I shouted, "Just go away and leave us alone!"

"Kiddo! What have you done? Didn't I say not a word?"

"Ya see? I knew you were both at home. Now, c'mon out, the two of ya. This is being silly; don't ya reckon?"

"Go away, Franco. Take the car keys; they're on the kitchen bench. Go away and leave us in peace."

"Peace? Do'ya want peace? I'll show ya fucking peace!" It was like my father's rage came rushing up from wherever he'd put it last. This time, he beat heavily on the door. "Don't make me break this door in, Alisha. I will break it if I need to. Come out! Come out now!"

I screamed as loud as I could. I hoped my high pitch squeal was enough to grab anybody's attention who might be in range. Perhaps the people from next door would hear. Maybe they'd call

Theo Mack, and he'd rush down here with his siren blaring and his lights flashing. But even for someone as young as I was at the time, I knew it wasn't likely.

Then it was like a miracle. Suddenly, my father's footsteps walked away. I heard him walk through the kitchen, grabbing at the keys that my mother had told him were on the bench. I heard him a couple of minutes later start the car. The car reversed up the driveway, and my father was gone.

It was like a weight had lifted from my spirits. Even my mother looked happier than she was only a moment ago. We both cautiously exited the bathroom. I ran straight for my bedroom and picked up my rucksack. "Come on Mum; we need to get going to Maggie's. Let's go." I was happy that I could make a suggestion. My mother even laughed a little under her breath. "Oh, I see. You're making all the calls now, huh?"

"Let's go, Mum, let's go."

We were about to leave.

We were both about to exit our house of horrors, and I couldn't have cared less if it was for the last time in my young life. I was happy to be away and to be safe. But just as we were at the back door, my mother suddenly stopped her forward momentum. I grabbed her arm and pulled her. "What's wrong? C'mon Mum. We're running out of time."

"No, kiddo. We'll stay here. Your father already knows where we're going, and he'll be waiting for us somewhere."

I watched in dismay as my mother closed the back door, then grabbed a chair from the dining room. She brought the chair back with her and wedged the chair under the doorknob. "I'll make a phone call to Theo Mack, and he can sort this out; once and for all."

I couldn't believe what I was seeing. We had the chance to get away, and it was gone. Even if it were only to the house next door, even if that were the case, we'd still be away. But now . . . We were again trapped. There was only one thing left for me to do. And that was to get under my bed as far as I could get and hide. I ran there. I ran to my bedroom while my mother picked up the phone. I heard her jiggle the hanger a couple of times. "Hello?" Another jiggle. Another jiggle. "Hello!" I heard my mother draw an annoyed sigh before she banged the handset hard down. "Shit!"

As I lay hidden under my bed, my eyes began to fill with tears. I was now more scared than I can ever remember. I only hoped the chair at the back door was strong enough to keep my father out. Just as I had that thought, the back door exploded into what I thought must be more than a thousand pieces.

I hurried out from under my bed and raced to the back door to where my father was standing in the aperture; a gigantic sledgehammer dangled ominously from his grip. It occurred to me then that this was his solution to the locked bathroom door. I realised much later in life, had my mother and I still been in there; we would've been much more boxed in and vulnerable than we already were. Maybe my father would've killed us both.

As I stood, shocked, seeing my father with his face that told of nothing but hatred and anger, I managed to catch sight of my mother as she suddenly burst past me. "Get out! Get out! Get out!" my mother screamed with words that still chill me after all this time. She tried with all her weight to push my father back through the door. He grabbed my mother and spun her around. He locked his elbow around the base of her throat and squeezed. "Now, none of that," my father said in cold tone. "You don't have to be all pushy. I'll go. But you know what I want don't ya? I want those things my mate Scotty-Blue gave ya. I know you have the disk and codes. Give them to me, and I'm gone, Alisha."

My mother managed some words through her squeezed neck. "Franco . . . What're you talking about?"

"Don't play games with me. Don't-you-fucking-play-games-with-me!"

I picked up my rucksack and threw it at my father with all the strength I had in my body. "Leave my mother ALONE!"

"Angelique . . . run. Run, Angelique. RUN!"

My father laughed at me. He laughed hard, and sardonically like he'd seen something so very funny. He let my mother go. But only for a second. It was like he had all the power. He quickly gathered her up and choked her all over again.

"Angelique! RUN!"

"No Mum. I can't leave you!"

"Just . . . run . . . Kiddo!"

My father squeezed his elbow around my mother's throat harder than before. Her face immediately went cherry red. Her eyes bulged, and I saw blood at the corners of her eyelids. She tried to say something, but it never came out. Her body went limp, and after my father let go of her, she slid slowly to the floor. Then, my father turned his attention on me. He reached and grabbed a handful of my hair. I remember the hot pain on my scalp as he picked me up and swung me. I floated only inches above the floor. "You're going in your bloody room, and you're gonna STAY THERE!"

After my father had thrown me through the doorway, I again slid under my bed as far as I could get. My cheeks felt raw and wet as I cried uncontrollably. But my father paused, laughing at me like my sobbing was one of the funniest things he'd ever seen.

Before slamming my door closed, he shouted, "And don't come out!"

* * *

While I lay there, I listened as my father stomped around the house. I heard him rummage through drawers then slam them closed. I heard cupboard doors open, and I imagined the contents thrown across the room. I heard clanging of pots and pans. I heard the smashing of glass. I heard my father racing around the house. "Where is it? What have you done with it?"

"I don't know what you're talking about, Franco. You must be out of your mind. Go back to your mates at the pub. Maybe they know where it is what you're looking for."

I was glad I heard my mother's voice, but I was also terribly afraid for her. I heard my father's heavy footsteps rush across the floor. Then, the ugly sound of his fist connecting with flesh.

"NOOO!" I scampered madly from under my bed and ran out of my room. I saw my father standing over my mother. I launched myself onto my father's back, I began beating him as hard as I could.

My mother pleaded with me; her voice so dry. "Angelique. Stop. Please stop. I'm okay."

Before I had the opportunity to do more damage, my father peeled me off his back. He again lifted me by my hair and carried me to my bedroom. He tossed me like a pendulum with such force, I flew through the air and landed heavily on my bed. I grabbed my pillow and buried my face as I cried harder than I'd ever known.

Outside my room, I heard them arguing. The bickering went on and on and on. He wanted whatever he wanted, and she wasn't about to let him have it. Back and forth, they fought. Sometimes it was physical with the awful sounds of fleshy beatings. If I knew my mother, she'd give back just as much as what she was given. Maybe that would make things worse. She screamed at him. He yelled back at her. Hurtful and spiteful. Cruel and cutting. Words and sounds a child should never have to endure.

But suddenly, everything stopped.

I felt an urge rip up through my body. I felt as though there were eyes upon me. There was something outside of my bedroom window; I just knew it. Looking out, I saw an eagle had settled and had found a perch on the back fence. The moment the eagle's eyes made contact with mine, I knew it was not just any eagle, but it had to be *my* eagle. It was Charlotte.

It was at that moment that all my sadness and hurt had melted away. I felt strength take over the weakness in my body. I sprinted from my room and out through the back door. I cut a short distance across the back yard toward where Charlotte was busy, happily preening her feathers as though she was making herself beautiful just for me. I couldn't have been happier than in that moment. It was one of the most delightful times of my life. As I approached Charlotte, it was as though she beckoned me closer, and when I got there, she put her head down and flared out her huge wings in a warm gesture of hello.

I don't know how long I was there in Charlotte's company. It seemed like only minutes. But after Charlotte had lifted her head again, she appeared to become startled. She turned away from me and put her head down. She looked over her shoulder one last time before she launched into the sky; her huge wingspan compressing the air as she lifted herself into the sky.

I stood back and watched Charlotte disappear into the afternoon sun. And after she'd gone, my thoughts returned to the horrors of which I was given just a small amount of respite. Remembering my father's words to 'not come out of my room,' I slowly turned to get back into the house, but instantly, my legs stopped carrying me forward.

"Time to come in, love. It's gonna be tea-time soon," my father said as he stood there on the back veranda, watching me.

But in my mind, a warning sounded, and somehow, I knew not to go to him. As he repeated the same sentence over, I noticed the sledgehammer in my father's grip. I noticed the thick dark coloured blood that dripped in steady drops from the shiny metal. I noticed the red stains on his white singlet. I noticed the blood spatter all over his face and arms. He repeated his words slowly. "Come inside, Angelique. Tea-time."

My legs were like pins that held me into place. Not forward. Not backward. I was frozen still. I felt coldness sweep up and over me, giving me goosebumps on my arms and neck as my father appeared to grow angrier with each passing second. "Get inside you little bitch!"

I moved one foot in front of the other. Then the other in front of that. Slowly, I gained speed, and in the next crucial second, I began sprinting across the back yard toward the gate. As I moved as fast as I could go, I caught sight of my father as he hitched the sledgehammer over his shoulder and launched himself off the veranda. "Get back here!" he screamed. I ran. I ran hard.

At the back gate, I jumped and cleared it with my father only inches behind me. I felt the breeze of his sledgehammer swish past me. I could hear his hard breathing as he struggled to get over. I ran on and paced away. Breathing. Running. Breathing. Running.

Out in the street, I turned and sprinted down the middle of the bitumen. If a car was coming, I could put up my arms and scream.

Maybe whoever was driving might stop. As I ran, I saw a shadow on the road. The shadow of an eagle raced on ahead in front of me, and then suddenly, it disappeared. From behind, I heard an eagle screech with an ear-piercing cry and echoed through the suburbs. I stopped and spun around in time to see Charlotte's silhouette in the late afternoon sun. Her outline became backlit from the bright sunlight, as she tumbled and turned over high in the sky. I saw Charlotte as she tucked in her wings and became a bullet, head down, screeching her cry through the air as my father ran almost out of breath, panting, and still trying to shut me down.

With no warning, Charlotte came down from behind him and attached her giant talons around my father's neck. Screeching and squealing, she flared out her wings, and I saw her talons disappear deep into his flesh. Long red ribbons ripped away from my father's neck as Charlotte again took to the skies. My father screamed out then gurgled chillingly in a way I'd never heard before. He placed both his hands over his gaping open wounds but to no avail. The fountains of his blood reached high above him. Then, his body seemed to collapse from under his weight. I knew from that moment; there was no life left in him. The Mad Man was dead.

From a distance, I heard the sounds of sirens. Theo Mack would arrive, but by the time he reached the scene where blood was everywhere, the mandatory police 'guns drawn' approach was of no use. Theo exited his police vehicle exactly as I thought. "Get on the ground!" he shouted; pistol pointed at my lifeless father. When he got close enough, I saw his shoulders droop, and he put his gun away.

As I turned away from what I was seeing, Maggie was there, standing in front of me with her arms held out. "Come with me, love," she said, gathering me up and pulling me into her arms.

Maggie smelled of lavender. After that moment, lavender took on a new meaning for me. Whenever I smell lavender, it transports me back to the time I was orphaned and left without my parents. My Angel saved me from the Mad Man, but now, I must somehow live with the memory.

CHAPTER TWO

Melbourne Present Day

OUT ON PORT PHILLIP BAY, the *Spirit of Tasmania* clung to her moorings. From where I stood, I saw people lined up, resembling a trail of ants on a mission, as they'd begun boarding via long gangways. I saw vehicles of all descriptions nose to tail that were all making a line to get going.

HMAS Canberra, with her strange upturned bow, sat in the water, up close and personal, to the Bass Strait Ferry. I assumed *Canberra* had cut her way silently through the heads during the night, while most of Melbourne slept. And berthed behind *Canberra* was the Nimitz-class nuclear-powered super-carrier, the *USS John Steinbeck.* She was a monster of a warship – a city to herself. It wouldn't have surprised me in the least if *Steinbeck* had her own weather patterns that followed her wherever she went, and she towered ominously out of the water, dwarfing all other ships in close proximity, making them appear to be nothing more than bath toys.

From the balcony of my apartment in Port Melbourne, I couldn't help but cast a critical eye over the US Flagship. I wasn't as happy to see her as most citizens of Melbourne, and I had valid reasons for my concerns. The Americans were either remaining silent or lying.

I'd spent hours digging and searching, utilising all the sources I had available. Every little possibility of the answer I was looking for, in the end . . . led me nowhere. Then it hit me. After I realised it, I knew in my heart that I'd found the Americans' achilles heel. As I played it around in my head, what I discovered had the potential to wreck relationships. America was a friend and ally to Australia. What could happen to our alliance if I choose to speak my mind?

From my balcony, and looking out over the bay, I tapped the tip of my cigarette on the back of my hand. After lighting up, I hoped the rush of nicotine would help settle my mind. I drew back smoke and held it in my lungs, wishing it had the same effect as something else that wasn't quite legal. My mind thumped hard. It was going to be one hell of a day.

I felt a hand land gently on my shoulder. Those horrible thoughts about *Steinbeck* melted away to the back of my mind as I turned around to meet Jenny's sweet gaze.

"Coffee for the birthday girl?" Jenny smiled, handing me my favourite mug of coffee that smelt so heavenly. Only God knew how much I needed the caffeine. I needed anything to help make this day easier.

"Thanks . . . Another birthday. I forgot. How about that?"

"Oh, I think you remembered, all right. You just choose to ignore."

"You know I don't like birthdays. It's my right to forget. And why you keep insisting I have them is beyond my better understanding."

Jenny laughed. Then I watched her eyes regard my smoking habit. "Better enjoy them while you have them. Who knows how many of them you have left?"

"Ouch!" I immediately stubbed out the cigarette.

"Seriously, Angel. The handrail?"

"It needs paint anyway."

I smiled, then I turned to avoid Jenny's scorn. I peered back toward the *Steinbeck*. My mind drifted to that bloody subject all over again.

"How do you think you'll go?" Jenny asked me from behind.

"I really don't know. But I reckon it's no big deal." Yeah. I lied.

"No big deal? You've just turned thirty. You're the youngest journalist in history who's managed to score an interview, one-on-one, with the US Secretary of State. Who else could do that?"

"Sometimes, Jen, I just wish I could get back behind the lens where I used to be."

"Why on earth would you want to do that?" Jenny said while taking a seat on the metal chair and placing her mug noisily down. I wondered if she did that on purpose just to gee me up. Gosh, where's my head? This business with *Steinbeck* is getting to me.

"The tabloid press is no place for you, Angel. They're all a bunch of dogs biting each other to get to a bone."

"Yeah, I know. But I think it'd be nice just to have a break for a while. I miss my camera. And I miss the action down on the streets."

While I gazed once again out at the *Steinbeck*, my thoughts returned to the documents I'd received as an email attachment. The dossier included all the interview questions I was expected to share with Madam Secretary and listed with those questions were her prepared responses. Protocol, I kept thinking. It all amounted to rules, regulations and the need to keep things tight. But my interview questions were at best described as lacklustre. I knew it was my job to break the protocol. I knew I had to bring up the *Steinbeck* debacle and bloody-well throw it at her!

Nathan Masters. If it wasn't for him, I wouldn't be in this mess right now. Nathan had discovered that *Steinbeck's* arrival was unauthorised. The United States Chief of Naval Operations had informed Australian officials, and the Australian Nuclear Safety Commission—dubbed 'Nuke Patrol'—of the US impending arrival. Things went bad for them after the Americans chose to button their lips and keep quiet about their planned manoeuvres. However, because of their non-disclosure of operations, Nuke Patrol flat out rejected the *Steinbeck's* entry into Port Phillip Bay. The super-carrier arrived anyway, blatantly ignorant to the instructions of the Australian nuclear watchdog.

Now, I had a choice.

One – Play it safe and go with the interview down to the letter. Two – Take a risk and give air to something that will never go down well. But I'd already decided. I'm all about risk. Safe is for wussbags. But how could I manage it? And was it at all possible? My mind began to twist with trying to find an answer, and then, I was most rudely interrupted from my train of thought with the vibration of my mobile phone in my pocket.

Jenny's eyes were full of words.

"What is it, Jen?"

"Nothing. Go ahead and read your messages."

Messages received.

Nathan: "Angel. Congrats on your birthday. Big 3—0 today, huh? I remember it well."

That made me smile.

Delete. Next message.

Chief: "Congrats Angel. Have a great birthday."

Hmmm.

Delete. Next message.

Melanie: "Hey Angel. Happy Birthday. Hugs."
She'd better have my coffee ready when I get there. Just saying.
Delete. Next message.

Eddie: "Angel. H.B. Enjoy."
I'll be needing your expertise later today, Eddie.
Delete. Next message.

Sender unknown: "Happy birthday Angelique."

I don't know what I must've looked like from the outside. Everything inside me went still. I hadn't used the name 'Angelique' in . . . how long?

I fingered and swiped the screen and then flipped to my contacts. Nothing. The number didn't match anything in my address book either. Was this some kind of sick joke? Was this supposed to rattle me? Get me all out of whack for my interview?

"Something wrong?" Jenny asked.

"Nothing . . ." I quickly tapped out a reply.

Angel: "Who is this?"
Send.

But it seemed like minutes before the message actually left my phone.

Message failed, Retry?

"*What* . . . is going on?"

I heard Jenny leave her seat and she appeared behind me. "Hon? What is it?"

"Somebody sent me a message. I don't know who. It's weird."

"A random prankster?"

"Maybe. But how does this person know my name?"

"You're on the telly. That's not hard."

"My old name. Angelique. It's been twenty years since . . ."

Without looking up from the screen I was about to dial the number but then I held back. What if it was a scam? I shut the phone down and stuck it deep in my pocket.

* * *

I tried to let things slide as I met Jenny in the kitchen. I was protective of her, and probably a little too much. Jenny didn't need the worry, and I guessed for her to be living with a *'celebrity'* must've been at times difficult to cope with. But she was also master at hiding her true feelings if she knew it would be to my detriment. It was as though Jenny was also protective of me.

Jenny smiled warmly as I approached her. "You might've forgotten your birthday, but I haven't. There's a small package for you on the table," Jenny said as she pointed with suds that dripped from the tips of her fingers.

Still distracted by that strange message, I regarded the package Jenny had left on the dining table. The package was wrapped in silver paper and tied with a red bow. I noticed a birthday card was tucked underneath. "Jenny, you've gone to so much trouble." I unwrapped the package, noticing the scent of my favourite perfume. Obsession. That just made everything even more wonderful. My eyes went to Jenny who was smiling like I'd never seen her smile before. From a very expensive-looking polished timber box, I retrieved a figurine of an eagle which I knew must've been delicately crafted from rock crystal. Holding it up to the light, I suddenly found myself overwhelmed. "Oh, Jen, it's beautiful. How on earth . . . where on earth . . .?"

"I saw it at Federation Square. It's just you, isn't it?"

I held it up and spun it around. The rock crystal figurine also had a gold inclusion running diagonally through the base, stopping at the tip of one flared out wing.

"I don't know what to say." My eyes went all watery as I held the figurine up a final time and looked at it with awe. I placed it on the bookshelf, giving it pride of place, setting it among the other figurines, statuettes, and dioramas of eagles which were set in various poses and postures. "I think I'll call this one Charlotte."

* * *

I burst out of the elevator checking my watch at the same time. 10:42am. Late again. I juggled my briefcase and dossiers as I cut my way across the newsroom floor. The chatter. The sounds of telephones ringing. The sounds of live and breaking news echoed around from several strategically mounted LCDs above workstations. Normal as ever. I almost made it to my office door unscathed. Unchallenged. The relief at just that. My PA met me as I strode, carrying a cardboard tray with large paper cups containing black and unsweetened coffee. My hand fell on the door handle and I entered my office with Melanie at my heel.

My Desk . . . I must get there.

I pulled my chair out and sat heavily down. Time to breathe. Melanie closed the door quietly behind her and placed my coffee down on my desk. "Wow . . . Angel, ready to do this?"

I could've given Melanie a straight answer. Umm-no. But I decided a quick change of subject would do. "Melanie. Where're my missives for this morning?"

"Nothing yet."

"Thank goodness. Bloody traffic, Mel. It does my head in."

"There's the tram. Why not give it a try?"

"Yes, and get a cold. No thanks."

I couldn't help it. My eyes were already on my coffee. The aroma of Colombian legal crop reached my senses. Breathe, and something delightful to enjoy. "Is she in Melbourne yet?"

"Her PR sent a memo. The US Secretary of State will be on time. Are you looking forward to it?"

Melanie giggled.

I sighed. "Yes . . . and no."

I thumbed through the dossier pages over again. I flipped to the back page, then back to the front. "This interview isn't how I would've preferred it to go. These questions suck big time, Mel. I'll look like an idiot in front of the US Secretary of State if I stick to this bullshit." I closed the file and slammed it down.

It was the first time I saw Melanie without her smile. I realised it then how a smile-less face didn't suit her. I almost wanted to kick my own arse.

"So . . . Chief tells me Madam Secretary has insisted on a delayed telecast. Why am I not surprised? I wonder what kind of feed buffer she's requested?"

"Chief didn't tell you?"

"He managed to get side-tracked when we spoke. He said there was going to be a delay. He didn't tell me how much of a buffer."

"I'm not sure. Eddie would know more. As a matter of fact, I think I overheard someone saying there's a twenty second buffer for tonight's scheduled program."

"Twenty seconds? bloody hell! This won't do."

"It's there for her security, Angel."

"It's there so she can't stuff up. Nothing more. Do you realise, the *Steinbeck* is here without formal authorisation?"

"No. I didn't know. How is it possible?"

"The Americans just muscled their way in. Ignorant to anything. Know what that means?"

Melanie finally sat down. After she sat, she placed a hand to her chin. Now, I was worried. "No Nuke Patrol security measures?"

"There're no nuclear protocols set up," I replied. "But worse than that, Mel. Non-disclosure of operations. They shut up shop. There must be a reason for doing that. I mean, what a risk to take. Are we supposed to let it slide? This is serious. This is the kind of news that has my name on it and I can't break this if there's a twenty second feed delay. No, it won't do. Tonight needs to be live as it happens."

"I'll get Eddie up here pronto," Melanie said as she quickly got out of her chair. "Was there anything else I can get you?"

"That's it for now. Oh, and by the way, I love your outfit. You know you're going to have to tell me where you got those boots."

"Thanks, Angel." Melanie beamed brightly. She was Melanie again. "Don't forget. Makeup and wardrobe at 3:00pm sharp."

* * *

Just as I thought I was finally getting my head around things, my desk phone suddenly rang, slicing the silence, causing me to startle. I glanced down thinking perhaps I should let it ring out. My voicemail could have this one. But my mind went back to that message again. The phone kept ringing. I put a hand on the handset. Crap, it wasn't going to voicemail.

"Hello, newsroom."

"Angel," Nathan Masters said urgently. Why did he always sound like he was calling from the Moon?

"Oh . . . thank god, Nathan. Why don't you ever reply to my emails in a timely manner? Have you read the interview dossier?"

"Canter," Nathan said. "You're on a desk line. It's Canter."

"Sorry . . . Canter."

"Yeah, I've read the dossier."

"And?"

"At first, I thought—it is what it is. Nothing anyone can do about it. But then I thought... if it were me? I'd be bloody upset right now. So, I reckon you'd be wanting to break the protocol. Am I right?"

"I'm stuffed, Nathan . . ."

"Canter."

"I somehow have to bring up the rejection order on live TV. But Madam Secretary, in all her wisdom, has requested a twenty second buffer on the broadcast."

"Did she request the delay? Or did her PR request it?"

"Does it matter?"

"It matters because if it were her public relations, there'd be room for negotiation."

"And if *she* requested it?"

"Then she'll kick your arse around the studio if you break her protocol. Besides, what we've found out is too hot for you to handle by yourself. If you spill it, your life will never be the same. They'll shred your reputation, and you'll never have another interview opportunity like this again. How about lifting the drama? Spin it a little."

How did I know this would happen?

"You know, Canter . . . I thought you were with me on this. What's happened to you?"

"Just thinking about your safety. You're important to me. The Americans flouting the rejection order is never gonna go down well. If you wanna play, you've picked a dangerous opponent.

They can do you serious damage. They'll get you. And I mean literally."

"There's simply no choice in the matter. This is serious. It makes you wonder what the American motive really is. We can't pretend this never happened. Our public has the right to know."

"Angel. People have been known to simply disappear over finding out too much. Stick with the script . . . and play nice."

"I think about it time and time again. Something in my DNA is telling me *Steinbeck* has a secret agenda. This agenda that needs to be explained. How dare they . . ."

Silence.

"You gonna give me an answer?"

"It wasn't a question."

"Okay. Let's make it one. So, answer me!"

"Yeah, I will. Gimme a sec."

I reclined back in my chair and waited. Then, it occurred to me Nathan knew something he was not about to let go of easily. "You bloody-well know, don't you?"

"About what?"

"Don't give me the shits. You're keeping something from me. What is it?"

"Look. This not for airing on live TV. Throwing mud at the US Secretary of State is asking for trouble. Don't make me beg you. Please."

"Beg? That doesn't look good on you, Nathan."

"It's Canter! So, you've made up your mind? You're going through with it?"

"Yes. We should take this opportunity now that we have it. But I need to know the whole story. So, spill."

Silence. White noise. I waited patiently.

"Jesus," Nathan finally said. "I can't believe this. You're scaring the shit out of me. It seems I don't have a choice, do I?"

"None."

This was getting to be like a bloody tooth extraction. "Canter, your silence is deafening. Please. Time is a luxury, and I don't have any."

"Okay, here's what I can do. I'll pull the video delay with a local area patch-in. But I need to know the LAN address."

"So, you'll fix it for me?"

"Yeah . . . anything for my rock star. But it'll cost you. Make sure your IT guy gets back to you with the LAN details. Without that, there's no live, as it happens, broadcast."

"But *why* is that damn warship here? Can't you give me that?"

"Just bring up the *Steinbeck*. Madam Secretary will either deflect, trip up or shut down. Either way, it isn't gonna be pretty. That's all I can give you right now."

"I'll get on to it. My treat at Busby's this Saturday night." Then I realised Nathan might not show up at all. Even if it was an invitation to a steak dinner at his favourite.

Before I hung up there was the subject of that strange message. Perhaps Nathan might know what to do. "I received a strange text message on my phone this morning. The number it came in on was unknown to me. There was also no matching number in my address book."

"Were you on Wi-Fi or 4G when the message came through?"

"Wi-Fi. I'm sure it was Wi-Fi."

"Did you dial the number?"

"No. But I messaged back. It came up message failed."

"You should've left it alone, Angel. In that case, I'll need your phone. First, manually disable Wi-Fi and Bluetooth and remove the Sim. Wrap the phone and Sim card in foil. Tonight before you go to air, leave the phone at your desk in a padded bag. I'll take care of the rest. Maybe there's nothing to worry about, but we'll take precautions."

CHAPTER THREE

Enter Sandman

EDDIE BURST THROUGH THE DOOR and into my office, dressed in his usual casual attire, still wearing his studio headset with attached microphone that dangled a little awkwardly from the corner of his mouth. I gestured with an outstretched hand for Eddie to take a seat. He looked oddly anxious as he pulled out a chair and sat down. I met Eddie's gaze as he took his headset off. Then . . . Eddie just stared and said nothing.

"I need you to give me the LAN address for tonight's program," I asked, as Eddie let his head drop and he audibly groaned.

"Why, Angel. Why're you asking this of me?

"We're going to delete the feed delay."

"Yeah. I'm not a dumb-arse. I knew that's what you wanted. It can't be done. It's protocol. If we break protocol, the studio can be prosecuted and guess what? I'll lose my job. The same goes with you."

"Trust me, Eddie. This needs to happen."

"I don't think you understand. It's just not possible," Eddie went on. With an elbow on my desk, I listened as Eddie went on with his protests. Finally, I raised a hand and Eddie stopped his ranting. As Eddie sat silent and staring at some point in space, I went about doing as suggested by Nathan—prepping my mobile phone exactly as he'd instructed.

"Can I at least ask why we're about to delete the feed delay?" Eddie said, breaking the silence.

"Of course, you can ask."

"Oh, and you're not about to say, are you?"

"The less you know, the better. We'll leave it at that. Besides, you'll be in the know after I go to air."

"Now, you're making me nervous."

"No time for nerves, Eddie. Let's make this happen. Give me the LAN address, please."

Eddie didn't reply. I looked up and regarded him as I placed my mobile phone into a padded bag. "Tick-tock."

Finally, Eddie reached for a Post-it note. "The LAN address is static. I can give you the address now." Eddie scrawled the details and stuck the Post-it on the back of my laptop monitor. "After the remote patch-in, you'll hear a tone in your headset. I'm not even gonna ask where the remote location is. I reckon you've got that part all sorted out and you're right. The less I know, the better. After you hear the tone, you've got a live as it happens feed. You need to keep me out of this, Angel. I have a mortgage."

"Don't worry. You'll be fine. I promise."

After Eddie repositioned his headset, gave a sharp nod and left my office as quickly as he arrived. As soon as my office door was closed, I hurried an email back to Nathan containing the LAN address. Almost immediately, I had Nathan's reply.

canter@bya.com
GTG.

* * *

"Fifteen minutes to air, Angel." Eddie said as he opened the door to the Green Room and peered inside. "Your chair is ready when you are."

I *was* ready.

I'd specifically instructed makeup to give me the best damn smoky eyes they'd ever created. Getting into the mood, I left the green room with my favourite high-powered earbuds slammed into my ears. Metallica played loud. Full volume. The way I liked it. I entered the studio from the rear door. I don't know *what* I must've looked like to others. I strutted, giving an extra swish to my hips with enough energy to throw anybody. I moved across the studio floor, dressed to destroy in that executive-styled, figure-hugging black business suit I loved so much. I walked between hot halogen pillar lights with black barn doors that swung out on a wide arch. My black patent leather stiletto pumps clicked on the hardwood floor as I strode. Eddie noticed as I walked past him. He ogled and mouthed words in the shape of *'Oh my god,'* and I was happy. I smiled briefly, then put it away. I was convinced, heads would be severed.

Seconds later, I was at my anchor with a background that looked surprisingly realistic – a view, high over the city of Melbourne across the Yarra. I removed my earbuds and with a defiant smile, I gave my hair a huge flick to one side. I stepped up and shook the hand of Madam Secretary. I exchanged a few brief, polite words, then took my seat while straightening my skirt with the palms of my hands. No one knew how I was truly feeling. In reality, my insides were nothing but mush. My lips were parched. My throat was dry. My inner voice was telling me not to do it. Not to go through with it. To get out of the chair and walk away. My true feelings; I hid them as best I could. The time had come.

It was too late to back out. It was too late do anything. Let the chips fall where they may. Time to play. Let's do it.

To my left was the second-most powerful person in the world, who was encircled by her entourage of security men and makeup artists. They fussed over her, dusting her cheeks, repositioning her hair and making final adjustments to her audio equipment.

"Five minutes to air, Angel." Eddie snapped a clapperboard in front of me, then he disappeared seeming to be as nervous as how I was feeling deep inside. I took a deep breath and placed a tiny earphone into my left ear.

"One minute to air."

I reached for a glass of water and took a quick sip. I cleared my voice, checked my papers, everything was ready. Another sigh. Another adjustment to my skirt.

"Stand by . . . in five . . . four . . . three . . ."

After two long seconds, the light shone green and lenses zoomed in. I opened the interview in my normal way—the way I'd done so many times. My nervous tension left me as soon as I began. The expected small talk, to begin with. It went off well and without fuss.

I'd memorised the bullshit questions I was supposed to ask. There was no further use for the bunch of papers I had which were attached to an aged and well graffitied clipboard. I chose to disregard them all. There was no further use for the autocue that shone through the studio darkness which scrolled steadily with text. I started to ask Madam Secretary some of the scripted questions, and as predicted, I received her well-rehearsed replies.

The US Secretary of State was looking much too comfortable for my liking. She was smiling with the smugness of a seasoned politician. Then, a low tone sounded in my earpiece. Nathan had patched in. Now, there was no delay in the broadcast. The feed was wrenched off the twenty seconds delay. From this moment, every word said would be transmitted around the world without the possibility of wind back – without the possibility of a censor.

I took my moment and locked my eyes with hers. I hardened my gaze and shoved the politeness to one side. "Madam Secretary, Let's talk about the *USS John Steinbeck*."

And there it was.

As soon as I'd said it, I noticed her eyelid twitch. Not that anyone would notice a split second of discomposure. It was, nonetheless, a small victory. My small victory. I'd rattled the second most powerful person on earth and now, there was no coming back.

The US Secretary of State glanced fleetingly sideways, perhaps for her microphone. Then she leaned in and hardened. The game had begun. "Isn't she wonderful, Angel? Have you had the chance to visit her? I'm sure you'd be impressed. Our flagship is the pinnacle of technology and engineering."

Madam Secretary continued on about *Steinbeck* as though it was the show pony of the United States fleet.

She's hiding, my inner voice told me. She's running and hiding. I had to find a break in her dialog and finally drive this one home.

"Madam Secretary!" I blurted out, and I found myself surprised that I actually *did* stop her monologuing. I was also surprised by the studio crew's shock. Now was the time. Let's do this. "The *USS John Steinbeck,* being a nuclear-powered super-carrier, requires the authorisation from the Australian Nuclear Safety Commission before she can enter our waters. But I have it on good authority that the ANSC, *and* the Australian Federal Government, rejected the *Steinbeck*'s entry into Port Phillip Bay."

"Wind-Back!" I heard someone yell from somewhere in the studio background. Madam Secretary's response to my probe was professional and she held her own. She was uncomfortable. I knew it. But no one would ever guess it. "Are you asking me a question, Angel?"

"I'm asking you why the *Steinbeck* is here? Seeing she was disallowed entry into our waters due to non-disclosure of operations, that says to me that *Steinbeck's* ignorance of the rejection order was a risk the US Navy was willing to take. What, I wonder, could be behind all that risk?"

"Wind-back. Wind-back for god's sake!"

The producers in the studio background went wild. I imagined them attempting to rewind precious seconds in time. I imagined their horror when they found out no feed buffer existed. Even if the producers tried to cut to a commercial, I guessed that wouldn't have worked either. Nathan had fixed it. Nathan had fixed everything.

I held up a set of documents I'd kept secretly and in safe keeping for this exact moment. "These are your rejection orders issued by the Australian Federal Government and the ANSC, dated four weeks prior to the *Steinbeck*'s arrival. You ignored it. You took the risk that perhaps Australia wouldn't do anything about it. Yet here we both are. Would you care to explain why that is?"

"Wind-Back! Wind-Back, damn it!"

The damage was done. I sat back and waited patiently for her reply. I wondered at the same time what that reply might be.

The US Secretary of State reached for a glass of water and then cleared her voice. She was about to speak. She opened her mouth and it was as though her mind went elsewhere. I noticed she'd snuck a murmur into her coat sleeve. Going live as it happened, I wondered if viewers from around the world caught the same glimpse I'd seen. I almost felt sorry. It didn't matter. People ran back and forth beyond the studio lights. Things got knocked over.

There were clatters and bangs. Voices erupted into shouts. Finally, Madam Secretary's minders sprung from out of the darkness, scooped her up, and immediately whisked her away.

* * *

I arrived at my office at 9:00am sharp the next day. There was no buzz in the air. Everyone was silent and seated at their workstations. I cut my way across the newsroom floor. LCDs positioned on poles and pillars high above workstations showed the *Steinbeck* out to sea. Breaking news of the scandal scrolled across the lower portions of the screens. Headline title—US WARSHIP SHUNS AUSTRALIAN DO NOT ENTER ORDER.

I made it to my office door. At my desk, I discovered two Post-it notes attached to my laptop monitor. The first note from Nathan said, 'Call me on this number, landline only. Canter.' The second note was from Chief. There were two words. 'My office.' Which were double underlined.

Just as I thought my head would explode, Melanie appeared, coffee in hand. "Good morning, Angel. It's extra strong. I think you'll probably need it today."

"That bad, huh?"

"That depends on which way you look at it. There's already talk about everything that went down."

"No one's saying anything out *there*. It's like a funeral parlour." As soon as I said it, I wondered what my funeral would be like. Then it dawned. They were *all* avoiding me. Maybe everyone was embarrassed to be working here.

"Well, I think they're all in shock," Melanie said, breaking my train of thought. "Chief isn't happy and that's to be expected. Rumour has it he came a cropper with the Prime Minister's office. I recommend you go there now and get that all sorted out."

"Yeah. I expected the blowback. I'll get up there after my coffee."

"Oh, any preferences on your new phone?"

"New phone? What new phone?"

"There was a missive on your desk requesting a new phone. I assumed it was from you."

I noticed the padded bag I'd left was gone. Nathan had already taken it. "Yes, new phone. Anything will do, Melanie. Thanks."

* * *

By the time I got to the elevator and pressed the call button, I thought I could taste my own heart. Getting out of the elevator on the top floor felt as though I was trapped in a sort of slow motion. I walked, measuring my steps, toward the Chief Editor's office. As I approached, I heard him in there, ranting and raving and I knew this was going to be a long day. I stood briefly to take a breath, then I walked on.

I knocked, opened the door and entered. Chief, still on his phone, spun and eyed me, gesturing with a hand for me to take a seat. I sat and crossed my legs, folding my cold, shaking hands in my lap, but at the same time, I'd never show Chief how I was feeling inside. I called upon all my energy to change my outward appearance and remain steadfast.

Chief finished his phone call, placing the mobile phone upside-down on his desk. He reached across and drank from a glass of water. Wiping the corners of his mouth with a tissue, he patted away beads of sweat from his brow. "That was the Director-General of Security. He wants your source. I told him in no uncertain terms—we will *not* divulge our sources. Not even to ASIO. Who knows how this will play out, Angel?" Chief paused long enough to take a deep breath, then continued. "I was going to fire your arse. I was going to put you out on a spike. That was before I took the call from Canberra. It appears there's more to this we don't know about. Or, it's as simple as they're not likely to 'fess up any sensitive info to guys like us. Probably the latter. I feel it."

"Guys like us?"

"C'mon Angel, we'll never be privy to what goes on behind closed doors at ASIO HQ. And because of your blatant public exposition of *Steinbeck* with the US Secretary of State, you've managed to cause an uproar, and there's a monumental shit storm heading our way. The PM's office had this whole situation in hand. What you put out publicly was being handled in Canberra, away from the public domain. Throwing it up and giving it air served no purpose other than to cause an outrage. One—You've managed to cause an untold amount of damage between allies. Two—You've achieved a public upheaval to which, now, the entire population of Australia will demand answers. I don't know if there's a way back from this. Maybe there just isn't."

I braced myself for a continued verbal onslaught, but instead, the dressing down melted away and there was something else. Chief sat quietly in his chair and began to rub his hands together as though he didn't quite know how to proceed. He avoided eye contact momentarily while breathing heavily. "The late-night news crew called me at 3:00am about the Chinooks," Chief went on.

"What Chinooks?" I asked him. "I'm afraid I don't know what you're talking about."

"Angel. A dozen or so Chinooks left the *Steinbeck*'s flight deck and headed inland. North-westerly direction by all reports. Here, have a look for yourself." Chief reached to his laptop and spun it around. A video played that was shot by onlookers from the street at precisely 3.00am. "Any ideas on this?"

"No."

"You live so close to the water, Angel. How is it that you didn't hear anything?"

"How is it that I wasn't contacted about this?"

Chief cleared his throat as though he had no direct answer. "Breaking the story of the Chinooks was expressly cut short by the Australian Secret Intelligence Service."

"Holy crap! ASIS is in this now?"

"Yeah. How about that, huh? Anyway. I don't like it. This entire sorry mess should've been left up to the politicians."

"They'd have botched it. You know they would have."

"Maybe. But we don't get to decide that, do we, Angel."

I leaned in, "Boss, the *Steinbeck* was here for a purpose. That purpose appears to be shrouded in secrecy or the Americans wouldn't have ignored the formal rejection order."

Chief held up his hand. "I know, Angel. We don't know what we're dealing with. Clearly, there's motivation for the Americans to take all that risk. The question is why? And I have an ugly feeling the Chinooks have something to do with it. Something is going on that defies our better understanding. And now it's out? I have no idea *where* this will go.

"So, considering ASIO and the PM were already in the loop, I have to ask, how is it *you* knew about everything?"

"You said it yourself, Boss. And I can't divulge my source."

Chief paused, rolling his eyes. He got up from his chair and went back to the office window. He gazed out anxiously as though expecting to see something out of the ordinary. "I might've known. You're behind removing the feed buffer. You disappoint me, Angel. That's a rule not to be broken. It's against all the laws and procedures we exist by."

"I'm not entirely happy about this, Boss. But I might not have succeeded at all with a twenty second feed delay."

"My oath you wouldn't. That's what the delay is for. I expect the United States won't let this one slide. There'll be blowback. But the PM's office is grateful you've managed to get *Steinbeck,* the fuck out of here. Not so with ASIO. The entire agency is on the warpath. The repercussions are anyone's guess. We'll wait and see what happens. That's all we can do."

"I can chase down some American Chinooks. That's a start."

"Absolutely. Take all the time you need. Get us something but do it quietly. No heroics this time. By the book. Okay?"

"Sure. By the book. As you say, Boss."

I left Chief's office realising nothing was going to be by the book. Since when has Nathan ever done that?

* * *

The buzz had returned by the time I got back to the newsroom. The US Secretary of State was on breaking news. Crews from all available networks jostled her as they flung all manner of questions in her direction. Security men jostled with cameras and people bearing microphones, getting Madam Secretary safely into an awaiting SUV. She made no attempt to comment. The heavy SUV door closed, and with her eyes darkened by sunglasses, she faced directly forward as she and her entourage sped away.

As I continued to cut my way across the floor to my office, hoping to go unnoticed, everyone turned and arose from behind their workstations. An eruption in applause left me standing in my own surprise. It was in that moment, I realised I'd accomplished the impossible. I looked into the eyes of the world's most powerful nation and did something that no other had previously dared. With the super-carrier out to sea, I'd given the Americans something to think about. But also, it was time to get over it. What came out of everything was much darker than I at first understood.

Much more disturbing than ever. I'd have a job to discover the secrecy behind the Chinooks. There was only one who I knew would have answers and he was just a phone call away.

As I sat down at my desk, I again pondered Nathan's Post-it note. I grabbed it from my laptop screen, and using the desk phone as instructed, I dialled the number.

The phoned toned twice and Nathan answered immediately. "Angel."

"Yes, it's me. I need to discuss something. And you'd better tell me what you know this time."

The line went silent. Nathan baulked as though he knew what I was about to ask, but he changed the subject altogether. "I located the source of the message you received on your phone. I apologise in advance for destroying it. It was for your own safety."

"You're changing the subject!"

"This is important, listen to me. The message originated from a location close to Alice Springs Airport."

"That doesn't make sense. Who'd send a message from there?"

"Can you think of anything on your phone that could compromise you?"

"I keep everything on my phone. You know that."

"This isn't a joke. I hope you're calling from a landline. Not an internet connection?"

"Yes. It's my office line."

"Good."

"You're scaring me."

"I apologise. But it is what it is. They hacked your phone. They took your data."

I thought about it. Horrible, the realisation. "No . . . Oh, no. All my contacts? All my call history? Everything?"

"Angel, they're gonna make a meal of you! Didn't I tell you to leave it alone?"

"The Americans knew I was going to break the story?"

"The CIA knew."

"SHIT!"

"I had your phone connected to my laptop. I used ROVER protocol to ping the IP originator of the message."

"And?"

"A CIA hack appeared at the ROVER back door and locked everything down. That's when I unplugged your phone and cooked it in the microwave. Scratch one mobile phone. And scratch one bloody microwave. Whether they got most or all of your data is impossible to say. But it's clear with a CIA hack, there's more to this than we know."

"I need you to tell me everything, Nathan. I don't like where this is going."

Silence again.

"Nathan?"

"It's Canter! Jesus, Angel!"

"Sorry."

"Now, we need to be careful."

"I did what I had to do. Don't even think about giving me that guilt trip."

"Yeah. I get it. But we need to think about what to do next."

"So, what do you suggest?"

"Let's get up to Alice Springs and look around. I think we should start up there."

CHAPTER FOUR

Secrets

TWO-THIRTY AM. MY LAPTOP COMPUTER awoke from sleep mode and chimed loudly, announcing the arrival of an email. I chose to ignore. I chose sleep. But that lasted only seconds.

"Another email for you. I hate it when you keep your laptop in sleep mode," Jenny said groggily as she nudged me hard in the middle of my back.

"There's no choice. Important things are happening with work. You know that."

I sat up and rubbed my eyes awake. I managed to push my legs to the side and dangled them from the edge of the mattress. The polished floorboards were cold at night. In the darkness, I hoped my slippers were in the right position to make contact with my bare feet.

The laptop chimed again.

"Just leave it, hon," Jenny said as she turned over and pulled up the covers.

"Go back to sleep. I'll handle this. It'll keep chiming until I see what the fuss is about. It'd better be worth it."

Grabbing my robe and flinging it over my shoulders, I cut my way through the darkness. My laptop chimed once more before I lifted the lid and peered into the bright screen. After my eyes adjusted and the screen became clear, I opened the email from Nathan.

* * *

I arrived at Busby's at roughly 4.00am. I entered through the large rotating door, and I was welcomed by a brightly lit array of bain-maries that had more than enough breakfast offerings. A lone figure of jet-black skin colour worked frantically behind the window to the kitchen. The glass displays with fresh offerings for the coming morning rush were always Busby's priority.

Nathan was seated in his normal booth and most probably tucking into his usual Canadian-style pancakes. I ordered coffee at the counter, then cut across the polished black-and-white tiles, taking a seat opposite him. "This had better be good. I take it this is on the record?" I said at the same time as I grabbed my brand-new smart phone and placed it on the table at exactly the same distance between us. I glared at Nathan. I wasn't happy. I needed a cigarette.

"No." Nathan put his hand out and stopped me from starting the recorder. "This is not on the record. This is between us, and it stays that way."

Most annoyed, I put my phone back into my handbag, secretly activating the recorder as I placed it inside. Risky. But I had a job to do. "It's pitch black outside. Have you noticed?"

"I wouldn't have got you out so early if this wasn't important. If we're going up to Alice Springs today, you need to know."

"What about?"

I couldn't help it. I reached into my bag and grabbed a cigarette. Of course, I couldn't light up. But smelling the tobacco would have to do.

"About everything," Nathan laughed nervously. "It's your lucky day. I've decided to break my OSA contract and give you something that every journo dreams about."

"Really . . . But I can't use it, seeing what you're about to spill is off the record. How is it the stuff of dreams?"

Nathan didn't answer, only to put his head down with an almost child-like pout. I almost felt sorry for him but I quickly put that aside. "Start by telling me about this OSA."

"*The Official Secrets Act 1989*. I'm about to tell you everything. The things I've seen. The things I've done. You'd better prepare." Nathan rubbed his palms together as if he was cold as he dropped his eyes and scanned the area around us.

Nathan faced me directly. He opened his mouth to say something, then he closed it again. His expression caught me off guard. It seemed as though he had a bout of having second thoughts. He was about to change his mind and say nothing. He pushed his plate to the side, looked away and scanned the area again.

"Nathan?" Now, I was concerned. I'd never seen him seem so uneasy. This wasn't the Nathan I'd known all my life. This was somebody else. "What is it?" I asked. "For god's sake, say something. Anything."

Nathan finally spoke, but the words quivered as they came out. I didn't understand them. I didn't know what he was talking about. He shook his head and looked away; once again, scanning the area and slowly checking if anyone was close by.

I put my cigarette away and reached out to him. I was no longer the journo he'd called out so early in the morning. I was his friend. I was the little girl he'd taken from Alice Springs and raised on his own. The moment I put my hand on his, Nathan became Nathan again. He was again the steadfast, resolute and committed man I'd grown up with.

"Nathan, did you write it down?"

"If I wrote it down, it would end up being a book."

Busby's was absent of souls. Nathan checked around us again. It was as though he needed to be absolutely sure. Finally, he took a long breath and leaned forward. In a soft whisper, he said, "Jesus. This is major. I hope you're up for it."

I was now concerned for Nathan. I lightly squeezed his hand. "Just start from the beginning."

"Roswell, New Mexico. 1947. That's a good place to start. But it's not the beginning."

I immediately released myself of any worry. I wasn't sure what to make of it. At first, I wanted to laugh. However, Nathan's expression told me it was nothing funny. I knew about the incident in New Mexico. I remembered what I'd heard about what happened at Roswell, which in the end became a cult for millions of believers. I considered what happened at Roswell the stuff of great fiction stories; far away from anything that resembled hard facts. It was either aliens and UFOs or the Project Bluebook version. I pushed back in my chair and folded my arms, wondering if Nathan was all right; or if he was just being Nathan. I almost reached into my bag to turn off the recorder. But that would do more harm than good. Best never let Nathan know I'd switched it on. I'll get rid of the recording later.

"Yeah. I know about the crashed weather balloon. What about it?" My god, I wished I was outside so I could at least smoke and let that wonderful nicotine settle my mind.

"Weather balloon my arse," Nathan said. "Project Bluebook concluded that was the case, but it wasn't. Project Bluebook was a scam. It was an attempt to debunk. But the thing is, it worked.

Project Bluebook instilled doubt and confusion. It caused deflection. Exactly how *they* wanted it to go down."

I thought about what Nathan might say next. I wanted to close my ears. But it came out exactly as I imagined.

"It *was* a crashed spacecraft," Nathan said plainly.

"Okay . . . I'm leaving."

I'd already had enough. I could've used my time more productively elsewhere. I got up from my chair. Nathan grabbed my arm and pulled me back down. "Hear me out. Please. There's more to this than you realise. It's where Milestone begins."

As I sat down, I realised I'd heard the word before. A memory from somewhere. My mind reacted with the recognition but no matter how hard I tried to force the memory, it wouldn't come. As I sat, I asked Nathan about Milestone. I wasn't as prepared to hear Nathan's explanation as I thought.

"Milestone was conceived in 1948 by a secret organisation called The Guardianship of Milestone. A collaboration of former and retired top political officials from a coalition of countries. They work autonomously, deeply shrouded in secrecy using the infrastructure of several intelligence agencies. The Guardianship of Milestone flies so far under the radar, the legitimate intelligence agencies themselves don't even know they're there. The CIA, MI6. Even MOSSAD, FSB and BND. The Guardianship is dark to them all. But they lurk. They operate. They plan and execute. They are, by all standards, invisible and deadly. They have but one objective; the mission called Milestone."

Nathan went silent for a while. He looked around then gestured for me to move in closer. In a whisper, he said, "Milestone is an operation to bring about calamity on Earth. Milestone is an operation to destroy humanity. That's the aim of The Guardianship. That's their mission."

"Okay. Stop."

I tried hard to stem my laughter but I only marginally succeeded. I giggled. "I don't know what to tell you. Do you seriously want me to believe you when you say there's a bunch of guys walking around out there who are planning to . . . what? Blow up the planet?"

But Nathan sat there quietly facing me with an expression that told me he was not amused.

"I'm going outside for a cigarette," I said, still giggling. "Back in a sec. Okay?"

"Sure. Go ahead."

* * *

It took a certain amount of effort to go back inside Busby's. If Nathan wasn't such a dear friend, perhaps I might've got the next tram home. But as I returned to my chair, Nathan eyed me critically as though he knew what I was thinking. The thing was, did I have the stomach to hear more of this trumped-up nonsense that Nathan so clearly believed in.

"I need to know something right here and now, Nathan. I want a yes or no answer."

To my surprise, Nathan nodded his response.

"I need to know why those Chinooks are here. The Chinooks that left *Steinbeck's* hard deck. Do you know why they're here?"

Nathan looked down and shook his head. Why didn't I believe him?

"I suspect the Chinooks have something to do with Milestone."

"How do you know?"

"A hunch. And that's why I'm telling you everything now. I feel like Milestone will begin sooner than we both realise."

I didn't know if I was ready to hear it or not. I forced my mind to be the professional me this time around. I owed Nathan that much at least. I will sit and listen. After that, I will decide what I must do.

"I have the hard proof to back-up what I'm telling you. I know this is hard for you to believe."

"Hard to believe is putting it mildly. What you're suggesting is seriously insane, Nathan. I'm surprised at you."

"Just . . . hear me out."

"Go on. Give it to me. I'm ready. You can start about your thoughts on what actually happened at Roswell. What exactly was it that crashed? And don't even think of telling me it was aliens, because if you do . . ."

"It wasn't aliens," Nathan cut in. "It was worse than that. They were humans."

Nathan immediately retrieved a blue plastic 3.5-inch floppy disk from his back pocket and placed it on the table. I instantly recognised it. "That belonged to my mother. I was supposed to give it to Maggie. I thought I'd lost it."

"It never belonged to your mother. But you're right, it was to go to Maggie. You never knew about it after Maggie took you in. She found it in your backpack."

"I was ten years old but it's one of the things I remember clearly. My mother put it in my backpack. Uncle Scotty gave it to her. I remember how scared my mother was."

"Scotty-Blue was mates with your father," Nathan said. "And he was working with him at Pine Gap. It means he was the one who downloaded the intelligence. Without him, we wouldn't have gotten a head start on Milestone. Perhaps we'd never know. Maybe, we'd all . . ."

"All what? Perish?"

"Maybe. But Scotty-Blue changed that inevitability the moment Maggie found out what was downloaded."

I reached out and picked the disk up from the table. I finally settled into my chair and ran my eyes over it. I spun it around in my hand. "We'll need an old computer to look at this."

"There's no need. I keep the disk just to remind myself where the human race is headed if we don't change it. If we don't intervene. If we don't get there in time."

After hearing those words, I found myself softening a little. I placed the floppy disk back down on the table and pushed back in my chair. "All right. Go for it. Tell me what we have that's on this disk."

It was as though Nathan wasn't Nathan anymore. He was someone else. His face lit up, almost like a child. And as he explained what needed explaining, I found myself starting to believe.

"They *were* humans who crashed at Roswell. Humans, not from Earth but somewhere else."

"Human aliens."

"Yeah. If you insist. And they're still here, Angel. It *was* a spacecraft they were testing. A spacecraft meant to be capable of interstellar travel. However, one can only guess why it failed. But out of what was learned by testing the technology, they later used it in the Oxcart Program, at Area 51 in Nevada."

"Oxcart?"

"You and I know it as the SR-71 Blackbird. Oxcart was the CIA version and is still classified to this day."

Nathan leaned forward and took a deep breath. He was about to speak when a young couple entered Busby's and took a seat in a booth to our rear. Nathan gestured for me to lean in closer.

"These other worldly humans are known as Oudarretians. They've been here for centuries, living among us. We didn't know of their existence until 1935."

As soon as Nathan said those words, I couldn't help but draw a correlation between what he mentioned and something else which I considered to be much darker. "The rise of the Nazi Party?"

"Correct." Nathan smiled for the first time in what seemed hours.

"So, something major must've happened during those times."

"Something did happen, Angel. It was the time of new science and new discoveries. The splitting of the uranium atom in 1938 by Otto Hahn. You see, Otto Hahn had an assistant who was close to him at the time. In 1941, Otto Hahn's assistant was captured by the Gestapo and he was never heard from again. He was taken prisoner; we suspect purely because of his black skin colour. But, out of the ground-breaking discovery of nuclear fission, the Manhattan Project was born. As a result, the Americans had what they needed to end the second world war."

"So, what? Are you saying Otto Hahn was an alien?"

"Angel. It wasn't Hahn. It was his assistant. It was the guy with the black skin. The assistant taught the teacher."

"And?"

"They're all black. The Oudarretians. The other-worldly beings. They all have the same skin." Nathan sat back and tapped lightly on the floppy disk. "It's all there, Angel. Everything is on the disk."

I had another foggy memory of the word, Oudarretian. I didn't quite know from where. Just a strange feeling that was enough to tell me that Nathan was truthful in what he was saying.

"That's who you call them? Oudarretians?"

"That's who they're known as. Yes."

"And you're saying if not for these Oudarretians, we might not have had nuclear weapons in the first place?"

"Exactly. During World War II, American intelligence revealed Germany was coming close to a super weapon. If they had the weapon, Hitler would use it. But the fall of Germany in 1945 tells us they didn't get there in time. Who knows what the world would look like today if they did get the bomb and use it? After Germany fell, Truman decided to use nuclear devices on Japan. The rest is what we learn in school."

I thought about it for a while. Something just didn't sit well no matter which way I looked at it. "Why would an advanced race show us the way to our destruction?"

"It's all part of the plan. Otto Hahn's Oudarretian assistant wanted to give the Germans the war, only, it never eventuated because of the unforeseen circumstances. A close call, wouldn't you say?"

CHAPTER FIVE

Terra Duo

I SAT QUIETLY AND THOUGHT ABOUT WHAT Nathan had told me, taking a few sips of coffee—if only to lubricate my desert-dry lips. I locked eye contact. "Nathan, why now? Why destroy the Earth, if that's the motivation behind this . . . Milestone of yours?"

"I'm getting to that. But first let me explain something." Nathan paused long enough to take a heavy breath and sat back, scanning the area before leaning forward. "Edward Teller. Do you know about him?"

"Vaguely. The name sounds familiar. But I'm not sure."

"Edward Teller was the man responsible for the thermonuclear version of the Manhattan Project. The hydrogen bomb. The explosive yield of Little Boy and Fat Man, which were dropped on Japan, pales into insignificance in comparison to the massive destructive capabilities of a thermonuclear device."

"And your point is?"

"Edward Teller also had many assistants working with him during his early research. My point is this—One of his assistants was black."

"The same person who assisted Otto Hahn?"

"No, not the same person, but the same race."

"So let me guess. Another Oudarretian?"

Nathan smiled. "Now you're seeing the picture." Nathan tapped lightly on the floppy disk again if only to draw my attention to it. I realised for the first time how everything was beginning to fall into place. I wanted . . . needed to remain sceptical, until I had the evidence to prove the things Nathan had told me were true. But my enquiring mind began to release me of my scepticism. Now I wanted to know more. I leaned forward towards him. I asked him, "These Oudarretians. Tell me about where they come from. Do you know?"

"They're our galactic neighbours. They're from the vicinity of the Perseus Arm in our galaxy. I'm not privy to the exact location. That information isn't on the disk, I suspect because it's classified beyond the reach of all but a few."

I took the disk and eyed it momentarily. "I take it a copy of this has been made?"

"Oh absolutely. All of the information has been downloaded and is in the hands of the people who need it. But that doesn't change the inevitability of the things which are going to occur."

The significance of Nathan's words passed over me. My curiosity speared off into another direction. I wanted to know more about these so-called Oudarretians. "Perseus Arm? I can't begin to imagine where that is."

"Pass me your pen and I'll show you."

I immediately rifled around in my handbag. I also realised it was an opportunity to turn off the recorder. At the crucial second, however, I decided to keep it recording. Who knew where this was going to lead? It was my job, and if it screws up my relationship with Nathan, so be it. He'd have a tizzy for a bit. Nothing major. Finally, I found what I was looking for. I retrieved a gold Parker ballpoint that matched my cigarette case. I handed the pen to Nathan. He took a napkin from the holder, unfolded and straightened it out with the palm of his hand and began to sketch.

Nathan drew out long spirals that looked like the shape of a galaxy. I recognised what he was doing.

"Andromeda?" I asked.

"You wish. Andromeda is much too far away. I imagine it's too far away even for the Oudarretians. No, this is our galaxy—the Milky Way."

When Nathan completed the sketch, he placed a dot out on one of the spiral arms. "This here is where we live," he pointed out. "Our solar system on the Orion Arm is here. The Perseus Arm is here, the next spiral arm in parallel. Roughly ten thousand light years away."

I thought about it but it didn't make any sense. "It's not possible. Ten thousand light years equals ten thousand years spent travelling at the speed of light. Even I know that."

"I know. But they're here. What does that tell you?"

"They have technology beyond our known physics?"

"Yeah. It's hard to imagine that Einstein's theories have been shot to shit, huh?"

"And the connection with Milestone?"

"Hang on a sec. It's all relative, Angel. Trust me."

Nathan sat back in his chair. Without making Nathan aware, I managed a sideways glance to my wristwatch and saw it was getting close to five-thirty. I thought about how much more time was needed to get ready for the trip to Alice Springs. Time was getting away. It was going to be a tight squeeze. But I needed to get the full story for my record. "Human, you say?"

"They are indeed."

"And do they look like us? I mean have you . . ."

"Met one? I think we all could've come into contact with them. And they absolutely resemble us. No doubt about it. They're human in every way you can imagine except for their deep black skin."

"So, it would be impossible to tell them apart?"

"It's possible. But it's a process. Not an easy one. It just so happens that I knew our conversation would go this way. Believe it or not, I've come prepared. I'll demonstrate to you now."

Nathan eyed me curiously. He had a look in his eyes that for a second scared me. In all the time I'd known him, I'd never seen that expression on him. It almost made me start. He appeared to go away somewhere in his head. Then after a lengthy silence, he dropped his gaze.

"You okay?" I asked.

"I'm okay, Angel. There's much to process. I said to you before—you needed to hear some details. It all relates to this. I've had it in my head for many years. In all those years I tried to find a way to tell you in a way you'd understand. I failed finding the right words. So, I'll tell you how it is, and hope for the best."

"This all sounds serious."

"Serious? Angel, it's very serious. This is the cross I've had to bear for twenty years. You're a very strong personality. I know you can handle it. All I'm saying is . . . now's a good time to prepare. So, prepare hard. Always know I'm here for you. I always have been. And I always will be."

"Should I be scared?"

"That's hard to answer."

"Nathan!"

"Prepare, Angel. Just . . . go with it. In any case, it's of no consequence now."

Without any further delay, Nathan began by pricking the tip of a finger with his fork and squeezed until he drew a drop of blood.

He then smeared the blood from his finger onto his forearm. In that second, everything seemed so surreal. I couldn't think of a single reason why Nathan would do such a thing. My eyes opened wider. I felt the moisture rise to my eyelids and pool there. Nathan took some liquid from a small plastic container which he'd kept in his pocket. He drew some out and lightly smeared it over the patch of blood on his forearm. Under a hand-held UV light, Nathan momentarily made the patch of blood glow a light blue before it faded away.

I blinked, sort of relieved it was something that I was already familiar with. Nothing strange there. "Crime scene investigators do that. But what's your point exactly?"

"My point is this. If you did that to an Oudarretian, there'd be no glow. The Oudarretians' skin hosts an enzyme that absorbs white light, ultraviolet and gamma radiation. Their skin has zero light reflectivity. They've evolved this way because their 'home Sun' is closer to the surface of their planet in comparison to ours."

"So, you need cut them and make them bleed. Then hit them with the luminol to find out if they're Oudarretian?"

"There's no other way of knowing."

Nathan sat back and eyed me with the exact expression he had on his face as before. Once again, I became concerned and wondered at the same time where Nathan was going to go next.

"I want you to do the same test."

And then, the relief washed over me. "Oh, haha. I don't have black skin. I don't have an enzyme thing. Why on earth . . .?"

"Please—just do it. There's a reason why I ask. The details I have to tell you will be a lot easier for me to explain after you have the test."

I pricked my skin and bled for Nathan. But there was no blue glow on my skin. None at all. Nathan sat back in his chair and breathed heavily. I watched the colour in his complexion drain. I burned into him. "No! This is complete bullshit, Nathan. I'm not one of them." I stood tall from my chair. I wanted to get away from the place but no matter what I thought, I realised, walking away from Nathan was never going to do any good.

"Angel, please. This is not aimed at anything other than to put you in the right picture."

I put both hands up to my face. I felt like screaming. Nathan got up and grabbed both my hands. I slowly sat back down. "I'm . . . I'm . . . I'm an alien?"

"No, Angel. You're not one of them."

"But I don't understand. What's all this about? My father? He wasn't my father? Is that what you're trying to tell me? My whole life? Was it all a lie? Now you? What am I supposed to think, Nathan? What the *fuck* am I supposed to think?"

The urge to get up and run ripped up through my body and pounded at the back of my forehead. Nathan hadn't let go of my hands. If he had, perhaps I would've left Busby's with a great amount of speed. But Nathan held on tight, catching me as I fell; I fell rather hard.

"How?" I finally managed to ask.

"Your mother was taken by the Guardianship."

"My mother . . .? Did they rape her, Nathan?"

"No. It was never like that. Your mother was artificially inseminated."

"And did my father know about this?"

Nathan put his head down and slowly nodded as though he was ashamed to give me any further detail. "Your father was party to the unfortunate scenario. Your father turned and became a member of the Guardianship."

"Shit!"

"I'm sorry."

"And so you bloody-well should be sorry! Why, Nathan? Why did you keep this from me?"

"I . . . I don't have that answer. Over the years I've looked for an opportunity that never came."

"So, why now. You could've kept it, and never said anything at all. Why now?"

"Because, Angel, you're humanity's only hope."

* * *

After a while of sitting and breathing, I managed to settle. But my mind still twirled after what had been said. But somehow there was a place within me that wanted to know more. Confusion and anger –and maybe a bit of sadness had melted away and my number one emotion rose to the surface to greet me again. Curiosity. "Okay. You may continue with this horrible shit. But I'm still angry with you."

"You *will* get over it. You're strong. I'd never consider giving this to you if I knew for a second you couldn't handle it."

"You'd be right, Nathan. I'm stronger that you think I am. Start by telling me more about these black-skinned people."

"Are you sure?"

"Well, they're *my* people, are they not?"

Nathan chose to ignore my sarcastic remark and continued to scribble on the napkin. He wrote the word 'Oudarret' and held it up. "That's the name of their home-world. That's not hard to work out why. But what's most interesting is this." Nathan then re-wrote the word. But he wrote it out backward, then held it up.

I looked at it, which took more than a few seconds to sink in. "Terra Duo?" When the realisation hit me, I became genuinely shocked. "Are you kidding me?"

Nathan smiled and nodded. "In Latin, it means what?"

I was about to answer. My voice almost left my lips. I wanted to say, 'Earth Two,' as perhaps Nathan might've expected, but instead . . . "I need a moment," and I promptly got up and left the table.

As I moved toward the restroom, it felt as though the door shrank further and further away. I pushed the heavy door open and entered, virtually throwing myself at the wash basin. My heartbeat raced, and I could feel the thumping at my chest bone. Sweat broke through and prickled my face. I felt my breath slow to a shallow, asthmatic rhythm. I reached into my handbag for my puffer. I flicked off the lid and gave it a shake, then squirted life back into my lungs.

I must give up the damn smokes . . .

I reached down and turned on the tap, then splashed cool water over my face, stopping momentarily just to breathe again. My hands rested on the sink as I leant forward supporting my weight. I looked down.

Breathe . . . Just breathe . . .

Finally, I was able to stand tall again. My reflection in the mirror showed a woman under stress. Real stress. There was a part of me who wanted to believe Nathan. I felt an overwhelming rip at my logic and common-sense. It wasn't easy to swallow. Then, looking at my reflection in the mirror, I flicked my hair around my left ear and studied it. I placed a hand up to my earlobe and ran my fingers over the empty space. It was as if some small creature had taken a bite from my ear. An ear with an upturned U shape in the place of an earlobe. How I wished I had the chance to wear matching earrings for once. It was no tiny creature—it was a bullet. A near miss. Someone had wanted me dead. Why would anyone want to kill a child only ten years old?

Then the realisation came. Whoever wanted me dead was of no importance. It was all about what was on the disk. If Nathan was right, things would happen. Bad things. Massively bad things. What did Nathan mean by telling me I was humanity's last hope?

I cast my mind back. Nathan had taken me away from Alice Springs. At Maggie's specific request? This brought up a whole new set of questions. Who the hell are you, Nathan Masters? What were you doing in Alice Springs all those years ago?

Now I find Nathan had protected me and kept me out of harm's way. I thought about the floppy disk and how my mother had slid it into the pocket of my rucksack. The disk Scotty-Blue had given to her with a direct request to get it to Maggie. But why Maggie? Was Nathan right? Was Scotty-Blue trying to leak its contents? What has Maggie got in this? Why leak to her? The owner of a photography shop? It didn't make any sense. And now the scenario that Nathan claims will happen. The fall of humanity.

It all spun around in my mind. I opened the cold water tap and splashed more water on my face. I regarded my own reflection. Another breath, another lungful. I decided then—I'd need to suck things up and take them all in my stride from this moment on.

The recorder. It was in my handbag and still recording audio. I grabbed it out of my bag and looked at it. I hovered my thumb lightly over the stop button. How could I use what was recorded? Who would ever believe my story? How would it go down with Chief? There was no evidence, just words. Just innuendos. Nothing concrete. If I was going to use it, I needed hard evidence to back it up. Could I get that evidence? And what would be the consequences if I *did* break the story? Almost certainly, it would ruin my relationship with Nathan. Almost certainly, it would go viral around the world. With absolute inevitability, it would cause an upheaval. Perhaps even world-wide panic. I'd already caused an untold amount of damage with the *Steinbeck* debacle. Could I risk anymore? Did I have what it took? My hand trembled lightly as my thumb hovered over the stop button. I didn't stop the recording. I placed my phone neatly into the side pocket of my handbag and left.

* * *

I returned to the table just in time to see the manager of Busby's talking to Nathan. He was a man as tall as a professional basketball player, jet-black skin that was black as onyx. The man had his notepad out, jotting something down. He nodded to Nathan and left as soon as I approached. I sat slowly and stared at Nathan sitting there. "Did you manage to get him with your luminol trick, Nathan?"

"Funny."

"Well, how would you know?"

"That guy's been here forever. He's not one of them."

"Are you sure? I mean, every black person in the world is now potentially an alien."

Nathan said nothing, choosing only to stare out of the window.

"Anyway, you were going to tell me how this is all connected."

I asked the question with the sole purpose of getting it on the record one way or another.

Nathan came back from the window, eyeing me intensely as he picked up the plastic floppy disk from the table. At first I thought he was going to break it and toss it away. But instead, Nathan took a deep breath while shoving it back in his pocket. "It's all on the disk but there are some pieces missing. It forces me to draw my own conclusions about what's to come."

"So, what're your conclusions? And don't bother telling me the Chinooks have nothing to do with it, because I know they are. You can't hide from that."

"Nobody can hide from them, Angel."

It was the first time Nathan admitted the Chinooks were all part of what was about to happen. To get the complete picture on the record, I only needed one more thing. What is it exactly that threatens to topple the human race? I looked at Nathan with my best stern expression and asked.

"Something *is* about to happen. Something major," Nathan trailed off and paused. I saw it in his eyes which became red with concern. That told me one thing. Whatever it was, he could do nothing about it.

"Milestone is here," Nathan continued. "It's no longer a theory." Nathan looked away then back. Moving in closer and leaning forward, he whispered. "I've been tracking increasing activity at Pine Gap. I seriously believe The Guardianship have activated Milestone."

Nathan retrieved a hundred dollar note from his wallet, folded it in half and thrust it beneath the menu holder. "Now that you know everything I know, believe me—this is just the very start. There's more I'm certain we all don't know about and won't find out until we see for ourselves. We need to take extra precautions. The Guardianship is everywhere. Furthermore, I think a Guardianship soldier sent that message to your phone. The question is why? It's obvious they're making a play. We must now make this stop before it's too late."

"We?"

Nathan seemed not to hear me. He ignored me while he got up from his chair and threw his coat over his shoulders.

"Wait a minute. We?"

But this time Nathan wouldn't have answered. He was already making for the door. I noticed he'd left the napkin with the sketch on the table. I was about to pick it up, but something inside me told me it was of no importance compared to where we were about to head.

CHAPTER SIX

Spies Like Us

I WOKE UP. THE AIRCRAFT shook wildly, dropping suddenly, then came the inevitable seat-planting upward thrust. A tone came through the overhead speakers, and the fasten seatbelts warning light flashed on. I shot a sideways glance at Nathan. He appeared oblivious to the rattling and jostling, sitting there comfortably with a novel in his lap. The aircraft bounced hard again. I flung back in my seat. I dug my fingernails deep into the armrests.

Oh, god . . . It's the Oodnadatta Track all over again.

My mind went back to Nathan's ex-army Land Rover. Why did he love that beast so much? I remembered back to the time I was violently bounced and shoved around as Nathan drove the Land Rover down the Oodnadatta Track, with the little diesel engine running at its maximum revs. The flight to Alice Springs felt the same. I braced for more.

Nathan looked up from the pages he was reading. "Relax, Angel . . . Just a little turbulence." Nathan lingered for a second and smiled empathically before dropping his eyes back to the pages he was reading.

I stared out of the aircraft window. The aircraft cruised high above the outback desert. There were no clouds. The Sun was low on the horizon. I reflected briefly on the flight we'd missed in Melbourne. We'd spent nearly an entire day at the airport, and I was tired. I was tired and miserable. I just wanted to get this finished and back on the ground.

Sprawling out to the horizon below was a vast, open desert, abstractly patterned by red dust, trees and rocks. I looked out on squarish spaces of different earthy hues as far as my eyes could reach. The view briefly made me feel better.

The Lake Eyre Basin came into view with its massive plane of white salt which could only be appreciated from a high vantage. I felt Nathan gently place a hand on my elbow. "Lake Eyre is the lowest point in Australia. It's thirteen metres below sea level, did you know that?"

I viewed Lake Eyre with a sense of nostalgia. "I remember. It seems so long ago."

"It *was* long ago. Twenty years since we stopped down there. You were only ten."

"I never asked you why we took the Oodnadatta Track instead of the Stuart Highway. I've wondered about that over the years."

"Do you regret it?"

"I remember how rough the road was. That old Land Rover of yours wasn't all that good in the suspension department. And I remember we stopped at William Creek."

Nathan laughed. "It was a rough ride, but there's nothing like the simplicity of basic engineering in the desert. That's why I loved that Land Rover. Hardly anything to go wrong."

"Oh? How many times did we stop because the engine overheated?"

That was enough to cease Nathan's nostalgia. It made me smile for the first time in hours. "So, why did we go down the track? Surely the highway would've been better?"

"It seemed like a good idea at the time. The Stuart is boring. Flat, straight nothing. There were lots of things to see on the track, didn't you think?"

"Yeah. Roos and snakes. Ruts and potholes. A sore arse and a mouth full of red dust. It was a blast."

I surprised myself by saying those words. Nathan seemed to start and sat upright. "Hey . . . are you okay?"

"A headache," I said, reaching for my handbag. I took out my absolute favourite thing that was ever invented. A peppermint Migrastick. I dabbed the essential oils about my temples and at the nape of my neck. The scent of peppermint hung in the air and it was powerful enough to turn the heads of a few fellow travellers.

The flight smoothed out a little. I reclined my chair and settled back. I wondered what might be waiting at Alice Springs after we arrived. I thought about the event of Milestone that Nathan had told me about and I wondered what it might entail. But even considering everything, I still wasn't totally convinced it could be as bad as Nathan described.

Glancing sideways at Nathan, I was surprised to see he still seemed engrossed in what he was reading. He looked up as though felt my eyes on him.

"How's it going? Is that peppermint stuff working yet?"

"I like the smell. I forgot to bring some meds, so I'm in for it, unfortunately."

"I'll get you something to drink," Nathan said while reaching up and pressing the call button.

"What're you reading?" I asked.

"You wouldn't like this one. But I find it interesting the way it was written. *Gerald's Game* by Stephen King."

"And what makes you so sure I wouldn't like it?"

"It's seriously dark, Angel. I've never known you to read this kind of stuff."

"I've read a couple of Stephen King's novels."

I placed a hand up to my forehead and massaged my temples. Sometimes massaging worked. Sometimes it didn't. I did it anyway, hoping glean some relief.

"Really? Which ones?" Nathan asked.

"*The Stand*. Another one called *Needful Things*."

"You're kidding."

"Why so surprised?"

"I dunno. *Needful Things* is a great book. But I can't picture you reading *The Stand*."

"I read it when I started Uni. Come to think of it—*The Stand* is kind of like what you've told me about Milestone. And I reckon your Milestone thing is the reason for this damn headache."

Nathan dog-eared a page as a bookmark and neatly tucked the book away in the seat pocket in front of him. "It's gonna be fine. We'll be on the ground in a couple of hours."

"You know, I really don't know why you decided to put me in the loop."

"It's as I've already explained, Angel."

"But what am I supposed to do with it? As if I can make a difference. As if I could change anything. I thought I was on this journey to find out who sent me the message, and to find out about the Chinooks. But no. You go and put all this shit in my head. Look at me. I'm a mess. I think my head's about to explode."

In my mind, I was only a second away from a confession about the audio recording that was on my phone. I opened my mouth. To stop words flying out, I tried to think of something else. But no matter what I thought about, I knew I had one thing to do. I had to get rid of that bloody recording. Then, nausea. It came in a wave, and I lunged forward, and grabbed an airsick bag.

Nathan reached up to the overhead and tapped the call button again. "I'm sorry, Angel. The hostess is taking her time." He promptly got out of his chair and made for the rear of the aircraft.

* * *

Nathan was gone for more than several minutes. I wondered what was taking so much time. Water. I needed water. I was tired and miserable with a migraine that had made me sick to the stomach. How I wanted just to fall asleep.

Finally, Nathan returned to his seat and sat down quietly. I locked eyes with him as he refastened his seat-belt. "The message sent to my phone was from Maggie, wasn't it?" I don't know why I had that in my head. But Nathan's reaction surprised me a little which also told me there was an element to all of this that involved Maggie in some way. Somehow, I now felt more confused than ever. I should've kept my thoughts to myself.

Nathan kept reacting by saying nothing at all. The warning sounded in my inner voice as I noticed Nathan biting lightly on his bottom lip.

"Well, was it from Maggie?"

Nathan shook his head. "Why would you think that?"

I leaned over and pushed up the sleeve of Nathan's leather jacket. "This is why." I ran my hand over the tattoo on Nathan's forearm that bore the winged and bannered dagger. *Who dares wins.* The mark of the Special Air Service. The tattoo was old and slightly blurred, but I could still make out the words in the banner. "One night when I was at Maggie's, I saw someone talking with her from my bunk-room window. He had the same tattoo as this. It was you, wasn't it? You were talking with Maggie outside. I saw her give you that floppy disk. I remember it now. So, what other bullshit are you feeding me?"

Nathan was about to answer . . .

"Hello, sir. Glass of water?" the air hostess said.

"Thank you so much," Nathan said as he unclipped and took his tray down. I heard him sigh and I knew it was out of relief. The air hostess passed him a bottle of Evian and a long plastic cup filled halfway with ice.

"Miss?" I'd noticed the air hostess's accent, and it was as though she was from two continents at least. "Yes, please." I politely took the bottle of Evian. The air hostess beamed while passing me some Panadol in a small plastic cup. My eyes met her then. Her eyes of sparkling green. Maybe they're coloured contacts. It seemed everyone had them these days. But I couldn't get my eyes away from her hair. The silkiest bright auburn I'd ever seen accentuated her pale complexion with a light sporadic dusting of freckles. And the thing was, her face was familiar.

"How did you know I wasn't well?" I asked the hostess while studying the shape of her face. How did I know her and from where? I could've been a memory from somewhere in recesses of my mind.

"Your partner asked for some headache medicine. I'm afraid Panadol is all we have. I hope it does the trick and you're feeling better soon."

The hostess turned to walk away. I guessed Nathan had already been acquainted and called her by name. "Natalie-Jade, before you go . . ."

Natalie-Jade stopped and faced Nathan, beaming at him with a set of expensive white pins.

"Thank you so much," Nathan said. "But do I detect an accent?"

"Born in the US; Lincoln, Nebraska," she replied.

"And what brings you out here?"

"Family. I live in Alice Springs. We all packed up and moved down here after I finished up with college. My Dad works at the copper mines not far from Alice Springs."

"Copper mines? My Fa . . ." Then it hit me. The copper mine where my father worked was a complete lie. Perhaps there was no copper mine at all. Perhaps the cover story my father was issued with was as generic to him as it was to others. That being the case, the word 'danger' appeared in the mind like a beacon.

Just then, the fasten seat-belts warning light illuminated in the overhead, which was accompanied by the all familiar tone.

Natalie-Jade's smiling face drained slightly. "There's more turbulence I'm afraid. I'm so sorry. Please be sure to stay seated and keep your seat-belts securely fastened," she said, with a small amount of concern in her voice, as she turned and stepped away.

"I don't know what to make of it, Angel. She resembles someone I knew from long ago. Her face is almost the same."

"I was thinking the same thing."

"And she wasn't part of the crew before our flight left Melbourne. Something isn't right," Nathan said, taking me away from my thoughts. He pushed his bottle of water away. Suddenly, the aircraft shuddered, and the bottle of water I was holding fell away from my grip and tipped over. "Shit."

Nathan looked at me sideways with the same sort of expression he had after Natalie-Jade had left us. "When you opened your bottle, did you feel it click?"

"Ah . . . As a matter of fact . . ."

"Lucky it tipped over. Mine didn't click either."

"What're you saying?"

Nathan didn't answer.

The turbulence hit the aircraft like a hammer. The engines spooled to a high pitched scream. I was thrown back into my seat as we suddenly yawed left and then violently pitched up. The captain announced a diversion over the speaker which to me just spelled more delay into Alice Springs. I gripped my armrests and held on tighter.

Cold Steel and the Odd Explosion

AT ALICE SPRINGS AIRPORT, Nathan placed a hand under my elbow and moved me with urgency toward the airport locker array. We arrived at a locker marked 2157. He scanned the area before opening the locker and retrieving a small amount of cash and a handgun. After pushing the handgun under his jacket and behind his belt, he scanned the area one last time.

I stopped in front of him and folded my arms. "Are you going to tell me why you're carrying?"

"Not now. No time. Let's go."

Nathan put his hand under my elbow and moved me away.

Trolley bags in our grip, we pushed our way through the crowd of tired and dazed travellers who'd arrived on the bumpy flight up from Melbourne. As I looked outside the airport front window, I couldn't help but notice how dark it was out there. We'd have made it to Alice Springs several hours before if we hadn't missed the flight, and perhaps we'd have had some time to take in some of the scenery.

We stepped through the main terminal exit to the footpath outside, and I attempted to hail a taxi. Nathan stepped in front of me and pushed my arm back down to my side. "Not that one, Angel. The one over there."

Nathan pointed in the direction of a parked black car, and its engine turned while the headlights illuminated. After the black car rushed over and stopped abruptly, Nathan opened the rear door and pushed me unceremoniously through.

"Jesus, Nathan!"

Nathan stepped quickly to the rear of the vehicle and stowed our baggage, then rushed to the opposite side of the SUV and flung himself inside, thudding the door closed.

Nathan quickly introduced me to the driver. "Angel, this is Bosco . . . Bosco, this is Angel."

"Hey, Canter. Glad you could make it," Bosco said in what I thought was an American drawl. His driving position on the left-hand side of the vehicle confirmed it. Bosco's eyes studied me from the rear-view mirror. "Nice to meet you, Angel."

What else could I say? "Nice to meet you, too." I politely shook his hand and winced as he almost broke it with his grip. It took an amount of effort not to show him how much it hurt.

Bosco studied me again in the mirror. Then he shot his eyes to Nathan. "You didn't tell her, did ya, Canter?"

Tell me about what?

"My bad. I was in the shit deep enough. Get going, Bosco, will you please?"

"Roger that. Oscar Mike."

The SUV responded after Bosco put his foot on the throttle, pushing me back into my seat. Moments later, we were accelerating away from the airport and motored north along the Stuart Highway, headed for Alice Springs town centre. I stared out of the dark tinted windows to an empty highway that was devoid of any traffic and couldn't help but wonder why that was the case. So, I spoke up. "There's no traffic."

Bosco and Nathan exchanged glances in the mirror. Nathan checked his wristwatch. I was able to make out that Bosco checked his. They exchanged glances again. "A little weird for 21:42, wouldn't you say, Canter?"

"Probably nothing. Maybe it's punter's night at the local."

"Yeah, you Aussies are big on that shit. I keep forgetting."

I smiled to myself as the possible explanation was at least plausible enough. It suddenly occurred to me that soon I'd have a good opportunity to erase the recording that was on my phone. But then there was another thought. Welcome to the world of spycraft. Is that what I am now? A spy? Like my father? Do I need to swear in somewhere? Do I need to take an oath to Queen, God, and country? The thought of it played on my mind. I rewound moments in time. I played back everything Nathan had told me while back at Busby's. I was starting to believe every word. Now, where was I headed? What was this journey about? I thought about everything from the time of my interview. But something was missing to all this. The Chinooks. The reasons why they're here still eluded me, and nobody was saying anything. Why?

I turned to Nathan, who seemed preoccupied as we drove. "I want a gun, Nathan. If I'm now in this with you, I want a gun."

"That's not how this is gonna play out. You're out of the equation."

"No, she's not out of the equation," Bosco interrupted. "The lady needs a firearm. We *all* need them where we're going." Bosco laughed to himself. I saw that Nathan wasn't amused. But what was even scarier was the fact that Nathan didn't say anything else. He sighed and pinch rubbed his eyes as though he needed sleep.

On the other side of a small rise, red and blue lights flashed through the outback darkness. Bosco announced it just as I thought it. "Oh, nice timing. Random breath testing ahead."

The police random breath testing station was set up on the side of the road just before town.

Bosco slowed and followed the orange and white reflective cones into the RBT waiting area. Several cars had stopped in front. Bosco pulled up and reefed the gearshift into park, cranking the handbrake up with force. He then reached into his glove box and retrieved a handgun. "You better pass yours over, Canter."

Nathan said nothing at all while he passed his weapon the Bosco as though he'd done it several times before. I noticed there was a section cut away on the floor of the SUV. Bosco pushed the weapons down into the compartment without any trouble. He closed the lid and covered the flap of carpet back over it. After catching my gaze in the rear-view as Bosco sat up straight and cleared his voice. "Yeah, I know. We might be on government business, but we still need to hide this shit from the cops. It saves the paperwork if they start kicking up a stink."

"And Maggie hates the paperwork," Nathan added.

The night was lit up with the dancing of red and blue flashing lights. Bosco's headlights illuminated three cops out front, and out of the darkness, a cop appeared at Bosco's window. The cop tapped lightly on the glass with his knuckle. Bosco tapped a button in the center console, and his window whirred down. The cop bent down slightly. "Good evening, driver. Random breath testing. Can I have your license, please?"

After the cop walked away with Bosco's license, somehow, I started to feel uneasy. Something wasn't right. I felt it. And Bosco appeared to have doubts. I saw his expression of concern in the rear-view mirror as he and Nathan shared something that was like a code. Bosco suddenly stopped chewing on his gum and eyed Nathan again. I shot a sideways glance to Nathan. His expression told me his apprehension. But then Nathan came out and said what he was thinking. "That guy's not the real deal, Bosco."

"That's what I was thinking."

"Wait until those cars are gone then get us out of here."

"Copy that."

I wound my window slightly down, and a soft breeze pushed past my face, making my headache feel a little better. After Bosco had his license back and they'd finished with his breath test, I watched as more cops waved away the cars in front. I thought, at the same time, we were also good to go.

Suddenly, from behind me, someone reefed open my door and grabbed my hair. Another cop had Nathan's door open and pulled him out and to the ground. Bosco jumped out of his seat but was taken to the ground by cop number three. I instinctively pulled back and away, but it was no good. I was dragged by my hair away from the car at a furious pace.

"Angel!" I heard Nathan yell from behind me. Then, after loud fleshy punch, his voice was sharply cut off. Through the pain of being dragged by my hair, I managed to spin my body, and I was able to make out the cops who were laying blows with batons into Nathan and Bosco.

I screamed, kicking out as he dragged me. "Fuck you! You arsehole! What the fuck are you doing?" I fought the cop as much as I could.

"Shut the fuck up, bitch."

The cop threw me into a chair within the RBT bus, and I realised for the first time how deep I was in it. I managed to notice the RBT bus was not what it was supposed to be. It was as though we were all caught by an elaborately planned ambush. Then the cop swung a decent punch to my face.

After I came back from semi-unconsciousness, I found myself zip-tied and bound. My head hurt. I felt congealed blood stiffen the skin below my lips. And, two cops were standing before me who were smiling as though they'd achieved the impossible.

One of the cops stepped closer to me and announced that he'd beat the shit out of me if I screamed. He took off my gag. But all I was interested in was what happened to Nathan and Bosco. "Where are they and what have you done with them?"

"That's none of your concern, girly-girl."

"Why are you doing this? What do you want?"

As soon as I asked the question, I heard the popping noises of gunfire from somewhere outside. Both cops exchanged glances, and in my mind, I knew they'd killed Nathan and Bosco. I screamed out. "NOOO! You fucking arsehole!"

One of the cops lurched forward and bare-fisted my face again. I felt the earth beneath me shatter and begin to spin. Blackness was coming to take me away, and for the first time I welcomed it.

"I said don't fucking scream, didn't I?" Then the cop swung another bone rattler to my left eye socket. My head spun to the side, and I was sure an amount of blood spurted from my face. I heard the cop walk a few paces away and pick something up. Then I felt cold water over me, and I again was brought back from the brink of blacking out.

"What do you want?" I repeated with words that were enveloped in my burning pain.

"We want you, little Angel. All we have to do now is wait for the bird to come and pick us up, and we're outta here."

"Bird?"

"Oh, fuck. You're a journalist. You're supposed to be smart. Can't you figure it out?"

After he said it, he and the guy with him started to laugh. Then I concluded. They planned to fly me away to somewhere, but how? Then it struck me hard. *Chinook.*

They were both standing in front of me, eyeing me intensely, scrutinizing me as though they'd won a most precious prize in some sick and twisted competition. I reached down into the pit of my soul and pulled out the courage to ask the question I needed answering. I needed to know one way or another. "You're going to take me somewhere. But I need to know about the Chin . . ."

Instantly, the head of one of the cops exploded, and then the other. Blood and gore showered me. Through the cloud of red, I saw Nathan and Bosco standing there checking their weapons. They both rushed forward and scooped me up by my elbows.

* * *

We'd left that grizzly scene behind us, and through the eyes of my injured face, I gazed out of the window and stared up at the night sky. The lights of Alice Springs town centre cut through the darkness as we entered through The Gap.

"Can someone tell me what the fuck just happened?" Bosco yelled, cutting through the silence.

Nathan leaned a little forward in his seat. "We've been made, Bosco. Everything is dead in the water."

I wanted to add something meaningful, but all I could think about were those cops. "Slow down, Bosco. The last thing we need right now is a frigging speeding ticket."

I was surprised that Bosco eased off the throttle, bringing his vehicle back down to a much more legal speed. Nathan eyed Bosco in his rear-view mirror and shook his head. "Hollow points. Seriously, Bosco, you loaded our weapons with hollow points?"

"It did the trick, and we're Oscar Mike."

"You okay?" Nathan turned and asked me.

I tried to speak, but I couldn't manage anything. Nathan put his hand on mine. It made me feel better for a few moments until my enquiring mind, ignorant to the pain I was feeling, started to work all over again. "They said they were going to take me away."

"Angel. Those guys weren't real cops."

"Yes, and I knew that pretty much straight away. But why me? What did they want with me?"

"Remember what I said back at Busby's? You're our last hope. You're humanity's last hope. Do you believe me now?"

Nathan's words burned deep into my mind. Why now did I feel so small? I felt as though the entire world now rested with me. It was an awful responsibility, and I didn't want it. I preferred not to have it at all. I was nervous as to where everything I'd learned was about to lead me. Lead us. "You need to head straight through town and keep going," I said.

Bosco replied, "And why's that?"

"We need to get rid of the evidence."

I don't know why I thought of it. But Nathan agreed. "Do it, Bosco. We'll need to trash everything. Find a place where we can put a match to your lovely Chevvy."

"Aww heck. That makes two, Canter."

"A worthy cause, Bosco. A worthy cause.'

"Yeah, I get it."

Everything familiar to my early years in Alice Springs went whizzing past the window as Bosco drove. The township was familiar, but oddly smaller compared to how it lived in my memory. Shops and structures started sparsely, then concentrated, then got sparse again as Bosco followed the Stuart Highway north.

Again, there was no traffic on the roads. As we passed through the town, rural machinery yards replaced the car yards. Bosco pulled over roughly thirty kilometres north of Alice Springs. He parked his vehicle almost with seasoned ability down in a ditch, somewhere in the middle of the open desert. Nathan got out of the vehicle and limped around while tapping a message out on his phone. Within a moment, he had his reply. "Shilo will be here shortly," Nathan said as he placed his phone back into his back pocket.

I walked over to Nathan, and my inner voice told me to see if I could help him in any way. From his beatings, he looked incredibly injured. He looked at me with a bloodied smile as he took my hand. "What is it?" I asked. "You haven't finished telling me all there is, have you?"

This was the moment. Nathan was about to tell more all there was to know about the Chinooks. I could feel it.

"Do you remember when you were ten years old, and those men took you away?"

It wasn't about the Chinooks. But it was about an early memory that still lived with me. "Yeah, I do. Those guys. Do you think it's them again?"

"There's no doubt in my mind. We're in their killing zone this time. We need to take the fight back to them. But Angel, you also did something for me when you were so young. Can you remember?"

I tried to cast my mind back to the time, but most of those early memories refused to resurface. "I'm sorry, Nathan. All the memories I have are so distant. I don't seem to be able to recollect them."

"I'm about to show you for the first time what you did for me back then."

Nathan grabbed both my hands and took them into his. "You're a healer, Angel. You have this gift. The only way to prove it to you is for *you* to try it out on your own. Look at me. I'm injured as you can see. They broke my face. You've done this before."

"You're scaring me."

"No, Angel. I want you to see for yourself. Don't be scared. I know you can do this."

I closed my eyes and concentrated thoughts. Immediately, I saw Charlotte again. I had her picture in my mind as she flew high above the MacDonnell Ranges. I drew the memory back to the surface. I saw Charlotte had joined other eagles; there were seven of them, high up on an updraft circling, then all of a sudden, they all seemed to hover line abreast. They all seemed to be looking down on me. I wondered what they wanted. Then, I felt an immense amount of energy wash over my body. Pure energy. It flowed over me and through me. Through me and out of me. I opened my eyes to see that Nathan was fixed into position and not moving as though he was simply switched off. But as I looked closer, I saw with my own eyes that his wounds slowly began to heal. The dry patches of blood on his face disappeared. His complexion began to glow. And as I looked down at his hands, the finger that had been missing for so many years had remarkably returned.

Almost in shock at what I'd done, I let Nathan's hands go and he came back to the present, stepping back a pace. I sucked back a huge gulp of air and immediately felt giddy to my stomach. The world around me spun and forced me to sit on the ground, if only to catch my breath once again.

It felt as though an hour had passed. Nathan placed his hand under my elbow and helped me up to my feet. I noticed Bosco was standing right next to him. I wouldn't have believed it if someone had told me. But what made everything even more surreal was the fact that I had also, somehow, healed Bosco.

"No. I don't believe this. I . . . I can't . . ."

"It's always been your gift," Nathan told me. "You just didn't realise you had it."

"They're after me because of my gift?"

Nathan nodded slowly. "That. And many other things.

"You're our top priority number one," Bosco added in a military kind of intonation. "Now we need to think about *how* to bring all this up when Shilo gets here."

"Shilo? Who is this Shilo?" I asked.

"It's Maggie," Nathan answered.

"Nathan is Canter. Maggie is Shilo," Bosco put in.

"But why is Maggie, this Shilo? She owns a shop in Alice Springs. She's a retail shop owner. She's not one of you. Is she?"

Nathan coughed lightly in his hand and turned away. I saw Bosco smile a little as he pitched stones into the distance. Both of them didn't answer my question and chose to avoid.

"What do you think, Canter? It's time to go off the grid for a spell, huh?"

Nathan nodded, then answered. "Going dark isn't as it used to be. We'll need to dump everything. Phones, devices, hard drives—we need to trash everything."

Trying desperately to get my head back, as soon as Nathan had said it, I realised my phone still had the recording. If I had to dump my phone, the recording would go with it. It was like someone had lifted a heavy weight off me. The realisation made me relax a little, but I also felt some regret that I'd failed in breaking the story. Nonetheless, it was a relief, and I no longer had that burden. It was at that moment I realised how the importance of breaking this story now paled into insignificance. I needed to get rid of the evidence. That's all that mattered.

Bosco walked up close to Nathan and eyed him. "You know, Canter, I can't for the life of me figure out how those Guardianship assholes got the jump on us."

"They must've intercepted Angel's phone. The CIA pinged it and locked it down."

"Serious? And you didn't think to bring this up with Shilo?"

"I was about to. Things happened so quickly."

"That's mighty unprofessional of you, big hoss."

"Maybe. Let's see if *you* could do better."

"Well, we're all screwed now," Bosco said while pitching another stone harder than before. "And not only that. Firebird Station is screwed."

Nathan added something else into the mix. "Something else happened on our way up. I'm sure an air hostess on our flight into Alice Springs was a Guardianship soldier. Don't ask how I know. I just know."

"Aww no! Are you shitting me? I mean look where we are now, big hoss. It's not good. We're compromised. There're five dead G-men on the ground with gunshot wounds to their heads, and we're no closer to our target. The mission has officially gone to shit. It's over."

"It could've been much worse, Bosco. They could've captured Bunjil."

"Bunjil?" I asked. It seems now everyone has a handle or callsign.

"Oh, that's your codename, Angel."

But I wasn't expecting my own designated codename. "Wait a minute. That's me now? And when were you going to tell me that part of the story, Nathan?"

I felt as though Nathan was about to confess everything this time. But as usual, he was interrupted by something else. In the distance, a set of headlights pierced the darkness. A Landcruiser with a broken muffler and rusty old bull bar parked close to where we were standing. The motor was killed with a loud pop from the exhaust. Out of all the emotions and everything I'd gone through; I somehow became thrilled and overjoyed to see a familiar face when Maggie wound her window down.

* * *

Before leaving the area, Maggie had handed Nathan a large canister of petrol. He and Bosco liberally dowsed the Chevvy. All the evidence we had, including my phone, was left on the back seat. From the window of the Landcruiser, Nathan aimed his suppressed handgun and fired a volley of shots in quick succession. The Chevvy burst into flames, and after a few moments, exploded, casting debris far into the desert wilderness.

CHAPTER EIGHT

Welcome to Firebird Station

IT WAS THE SAME SMALL, fibro-clad cottage as I always remembered. After twenty years, nothing had changed. The typical Alice Springs landscape still surrounded the house. There was no lawn and only a few native trees that were still the same as ever. Even though it was dark, I knew I'd returned to the place where Maggie had taken me in all those years ago.

Bosco left the driver's seat of the Landcruiser and ran around to open the door for Maggie. Nathan and I followed Maggie up the driveway to the front door, where Bosco was already at the doorstep. Bosco waited momentarily before turning and knocking on the door in a sort of code. The door opened, and a face greeted him. "Guten abend," the young woman said, then she quickly corrected with, "Oh, hallo Bosco." The door widened, and Bosco nodded to the young woman while he stepped inside. Nathan and I followed Maggie into the small but well-decorated hallway which was adorned with all the trimmings of a house that sat frozen in time during the late 1980s.

The scent was exactly as I remembered. I recalled the musty old house smell that seemed to arise from the foundations and work into the walls where it would stay until the house gets knocked down in some distant future. The furniture was the same as I remembered. Maggie never updated or replaced anything, and I was somehow thankful for that. Maggie only got new things when old things broke down or completely busted. I remembered Maggie once saying, "If it ain't broke, why get rid of it?" That was Maggie. That's just how she was.

The first port of call was to the bathroom if only to wash off thousands of kilometres of travel and stress. While there, Maggie came in, reached into the shower, and turned on the taps. "You'll feel better soon, love. I'll get Nathan to get your bag, and I'll bring you some fresh clothes." Maggie left and returned a little while later with fresh, lavender-infused towels and a brand new fluffy white bathrobe. I lingered long enough in the shower for the water to run cold. It seemed like only minutes.

I heard a polite knock on the door, and Maggie peered into the bathroom just as I was finishing up.

"Are you okay, love?"

"I feel like I've been hit by a train," I said, holding a towel up to the side of my face and staring at my bruises in the mirror. I wondered briefly why I was able to heal Nathan and Bosco but not myself. My left eye was almost completely closed over. My lips were thick and engorged with blood. But the smell of lavender in the towels was gorgeous. The softness of the towels was something Maggie was expert at. They made me feel instantly better. "I've missed your towels," I said, smiling.

"I only ever did the lavender thing for you. I never liked it much myself."

"So, you must've known I was coming to the Alice?"

"Nathan said so, yes."

"Oh." I was surprised. "Nathan keeps in touch with you?"

"He has to. It's his job."

I wondered why it was Nathan's job. But before I could ask, Maggie had already left.

With my fluffy bathrobe on, and my wet hair wrapped up and twirled high, I walked slowly into the living room expecting to see only Maggie. But they were all there standing in a circle discussing things in low voices. Everyone stopped speaking abruptly, making me feel as though I was an outsider. I did a sharp about-turn and was about to step away, but Maggie's words invited me in. "Oh, don't be silly, love. We're all in this together. You're among friends now. Come."

I stepped past the smiling face of a woman in her mid-twenties. She was frightfully thin, as though verging on anorexia, yet at the same time, she was stunningly beautiful. I stopped momentarily and put my hand out. "I don't know you—I'm Angel."

Maggie then apologised profusely. "Oh, where's my head these days? Angel . . . This is Christina Schumacher. Christina is our IT specialist. We managed to steal her away from German Counterintelligence. The Bundesnachrichtendienst. I challenge anyone to say it correctly for the first time. It took me literally months of practice."

Christina nodded and smiled brightly. However, I was a little confused. Maggie must've noticed. "Oh, we call it BND for short. It's much, much easier."

"Yeah, I understand." I smiled and received Christina's handshake. Her greeting was as strong as a set of vice grips and went longer than was comfortable. It must be a German custom of some kind. "I've heard of BND," I said. "I've also heard that German Counterintelligence is supposed to be the duck's nuts."

Christina looked a little confused. Maggie giggled lightly. "Duck's nuts is slang and means that something is outstanding, Christina." Maggie smiled warmly, then instructed Christina. "We'll need eyes on the area south of The Gap, Christina. See if you can requisition the Keyhole Satellite from our friends in Chantilly." Christina nodded and left to go downstairs.

"I guess sleep is out of the question?" Bosco asked while hovering in the background.

"Go and get yourself a couple of hours of rest. But be sure to be up and running no later than 07:00, Bosco. That goes for you as well, Nathan."

Bosco and Nathan left the living room without so much as a good night. I half expected Nathan to give me a peck on the cheek as he'd done for almost twenty years. But this time it was as though his personality had changed. Nathan seemed harder. He seemed almost like a soldier around Maggie. I wondered why that was the case.

Maggie turned and faced me. "We've got ourselves a huge day after the sun comes up. Get some rest, love. The bunk-room has been kept the same as it ever was. You may need some earplugs, however. Bosco . . . he's louder asleep than he is standing up."

"I'm on all pistons now. Any coffee?"

"Oh, that sounds like the Angel I know. There'll be some brewing if I know Christina. She's like you. She loves her caffeine." Maggie paused, and her expression hardened a little. With one brow raised, she asked the one question I was most dreading. "You're off the fags, then?"

How could I answer? I didn't. I looked away to the Norman Lindsay etchings, which still hung above the mantelpiece after all these years.

"Smoking is bad, Angel. It'll be the death of you. Asthmatics who smoke won't do." Maggie winced and turned slightly. "But I'm not going to harp on it. I've said my piece. Now, let's relax a little before we work out what to do about this trouble Nathan and Bosco have managed to get us into. We'll also discuss your future with Firebird Station," Maggie smiled. "Now that you're here with us, you can consider yourself as an inductee to intelligence."

The word spiralled around in my mind. Intelligence. I was still thinking about it as Maggie sat me on the sofa.

"I have to tell you a few things. You may not fully understand, considering what's happened. But I'm afraid there's not much time. So, what I have to tell you may come as a shock."

"Maggie?"

"There *is* no good time for this," Maggie said, looking slightly away. "And it starts with Eagle Shield."

Talk about a sudden slap and wake me up call. Intelligence? Now Eagle Shield? I had no idea what Maggie was talking about. But I didn't have to ask. Maggie began to explain in her next breath. "Nathan's mission," Maggie said. "Eagle Shield was funded by ASIO. The mission was all about your safety and up-bringing from when you left here as a child. Up until *this* day, as it turns out. Now that you're with us, Nathan can rest easy, and Eagle Shield is concluded."

"That's why the change of my name?"

Maggie nodded. "We changed everything so they couldn't get their hands on you."

"They almost did."

"So, Bosco tells me. That would be the second time, Angel."

"The second?"

"You still can't remember, can you?"

"Nathan has always told me about those men when I was ten, but no, I can't remember anything after that. So, you're telling me that those guys are the same guys as back then. Nathan thinks exactly the same. I wish I could remember those things instead of having people telling me everything all the time. It can get so frustrating."

Maggie grabbed my hand and held it. "There's a reason why you can't remember. And I think it's to do with you being so young at the time. What you went through was traumatic, and young minds have a safety net which tends to shut out traumatic experiences."

"I'm not a child now. Why hasn't Nathan said anything?"

"He sees you as his daughter. He's still very protective of you. Perhaps in Nathan's mind, you're still the ten-year-old he'd risked his life to protect. And that's why he's never said anything in great detail."

"I'm not an idiot. I can put things together."

"I'm sure you can. But there has always been one thing that in my mind at least, has scared Nathan half to death, although he's not willing to admit it. He's had counselling for several years over this one issue, and he's never been able to shake it, Angel. Imagine his pain."

"What issue."

"The day you fell from the helicopter."

I didn't know exactly how to take it. It was the first time I heard anybody tell me of such an incident. As I thought about it, if it was true, I became thankful that I *couldn't* remember.

Maggie went on. "Nathan rescued you from the hands of The Guardianship, but in the process of getting you away to safety, the helicopter you were in came under attack. You were thrown out. But later, Nathan found you on the ground, unharmed. How you were unharmed remains a mystery and can't be reasonably explained. And this is something that Nathan still struggles with. He loves you like a father with all of his heart, and he has *never* forgiven himself."

"But I survived."

"Yes. But you have to imagine what Nathan went through before he actually found you. He had to struggle with the fact you couldn't have survived from a fall at such a height. He prepared himself to find you dead. He's a soldier. He's seen and done many things. But nothing could've prepared him for that."

As Maggie explained it, I teared up, and all I wanted to do was run to Nathan and throw my arms around him. I wanted to tell him that everything was alright and he could finally let it go. Maybe this was something I could heal so he could finally have peace in his life. I decided there, and then; I would use all my power to heal Nathan if it was the last meaningful thing that I did in my life.

Maggie held my hand for a few moments of peace as I thought everything over. But my train of thought stopped abruptly at something I just couldn't get past.

"Do you mind if I ask a question?"

"Go ahead, Angel. What is it?"

"Just who are you, Maggie? I thought you owned a retail shop. But you're among these . . . spies and it's as though you're boss to these people."

Maggie let go of my hand and stood up. She folded her arms, and she instantly became somebody else. "Okay, love, I'll be brief. ASIS runs Firebird Station. Everyone here is an ASIS operative. Do you remember Andrew?"

"Yes. I remember. He's your stepson."

"That's right. Andrew is with ASIO. He's been with ASIO even from when you were so young. Andrew is currently away on a mission but will join us again soon."

Maggie relaxed a little and sat down next to me again, not saying anything, but at the same time, she appeared to brace for more of my questions. She seemed still and rock-steady, but at the same time, she appeared less hard like a soldier.

"And your photography shop?"

"The shop is a legitimate business owned and run by ASIO. Profits from the shop are back-channelled into both ASIO and ASIS assignments. Eagle Shield was one of those assignments."

"So, what's the deal with this Firebird Station?"

Maggie laughed at my abruptness. I wanted to get to the answers quickly. "Of course," said Maggie, clearing her voice. "We're in the business of counterintelligence. But we're a little different from most of ASIO operations and task forces. You see, we sit much deeper as an undercover task force with one sole objective to carry out. You'll no doubt learn more about what we do, but for now, you must rest. Now you're part of the team; you'll get to learn more after a bit of rest." Maggie patted my hand as she stood slowly up.

"Maggie. What makes you think I'm part of this?"

"It was always planned that way."

"Planned? How? This so-called Eagle Shield thing?"

"Well, yes. As I've already explained."

"You're not hearing me. I have a life. I can't run away from everything. My job. My home. Jenny . . ."

Maggie walked away. She left me there to wonder. Then Maggie turned and eyed me. She had an expression that suddenly seemed hard again. She appeared much harder than I've ever known her. "I was going to save this for another time. Okay. Perhaps now is the time for you to hear it."

I held my breath, wondering at the same time what was about to be said. But it was without any delay and with next to no emotion at all. "This will be hard on you. You need to hear it and, before saying anything, you need to think about it. Do I have your understanding?"

I nodded. "This is serious, right?"

"More serious than you could ever guess, unfortunately. But here it is. You're now aware you have a natural gift. But this natural gift has been given to you not *solely* by birthright. The gift was bestowed upon you by external events. And it's because of this gift you are a target, my dear. This is the reason they made an attempt on your life. Not once but three times now. What I'm trying to say is this . . . Your father . . ."

I put up my hand and stopped Maggie. "Nathan has told me everything."

"He did? Well, I'll be bloody-well damned. That one was meant for me. I'm most annoyed, Angel. I'm most annoyed, indeed."

"Don't be. Nathan was looking out for me. As he always does."

"What else did he divvy up?" Maggie snapped.

"Everything on that was on the disk, I assume."

"Milestone?"

"That too."

"Hmm . . ." Maggie pushed a finger to her lips. "So much for the Official Secrets Act. There'll be backlash over this I'm afraid."

"He had no choice. I probed him, and I wouldn't stop."

"You'd think a man of his calibre would know how to deflect. I'm a little disappointed, Angel. I'll have words when he's up. But anyway," Maggie changed her tone. "You must know your mother was an innocent party in this. She was always your mother. In every way."

"Any ideas about my . . . *real* father?"

"We don't know." Maggie hung her head and went silent for a while. She began to walk around in tiny circles while studying the pattern in her worn carpet. "But, Angel, perhaps we'll find out in due course. Perhaps we'll all find out. Consider your past concluded. You're one of us now."

"And Jenny?"

Maggie said nothing. She appeared as though my relationship with Jenny wasn't important. The Maggie I once knew wasn't hardened in this way. It was as though I was in the company of a complete stranger. The Maggie I once knew was gone!

"No," I said. "Maggie, I can't be part of this."

"Your old life is OVER, Angel. The quicker you come to terms with it, the better. We must now think about what's coming and get our heads back in the game! Is that understood!"

"Ah . . ."

"That's yes, Colonel."

"Maggie?"

"Look, I've got Christina working on getting us over the area where they ambushed you. From what I've learned so far, it sounds like The Guardianship was prepared for you long in advance."

I immediately thought about the air hostess. "Nathan felt odd about an air hostess while we were on our flight up from Melbourne. I thought Nathan was just paranoid."

"Nathan never gets paranoid. He sees and hears everything. If he's flagged something, it'd be for a damn good reason. Do you know if this air hostess was still on the plane when you left?"

"Of course, she was. She couldn't have jumped."

Maggie laughed to herself. It was at that moment she became human again. "I'm sorry, love. I'm a little tired. What I meant to imply is the possibility of her being a Guardianship soldier. She might have dumped her disguise and melted away into the masses. Guardianship soldiers happen to be good at that."

"Come to think of it, I can't remember seeing her again," I said. "You'd think if she *was* kosher, she'd be one of the crew at the end of the flight, but I can't recall."

"It sounds like she's a soldier. She'd most likely sent the tipoff even before you left Melbourne." Maggie held her breath for a beat. "Come. We'll see if Christina has managed to get eyes over The Gap."

"What? In my bathrobe?"

Maggie blinked, shaking her head almost apologetically. "Of course. If you're up for it, go and get changed. Feel free to come down to the ops room. Come down when you're ready. Okay?"

* * *

As I followed the stairs down into the ops room, the place was illuminated only by cool, bluish lighting. The smells of hot electronic devices and computer equipment hung in the air. Several large LCDs were hung on walls which displayed scenery high over Australia. Christina was seated and looking at her computer screen while Maggie stood behind her. I noticed the surprise in Christina and Maggie as I came down. Maggie smiled warmly and gestured for me to come closer. Christina looked up from the computer screen as though she'd accomplished the impossible. "Sehr gut . . . ist sehr gut!"

As I walked across the floor past several computer terminals—one of which appeared to be an ancient, ragged old box that they should've scrapped—I saw first-hand what the fuss was about.

On the screen was a bird's-eye view of the area just south of The Gap. Christina had managed to hijack one of the most hacker proof satellites in space. *The Keyhole Three Satellite.* "A genius, isn't she?" Maggie beamed. "All we have to do now is wait and see what happens next."

After approximately thirty minutes of eyeing a monitor with nothing of interest, several vehicles suddenly appeared out of the early morning darkness with red and blue lights flashing. Figures in police uniforms sprang from the vehicles. They scurried around the scene at a frantic pace before they then appeared to become more organised.

"They're not real cops. They're more of the guys who ambushed us."

Maggie nodded. "I think you're right."

From the back of one the vehicles, two figures retrieved stretchers. They ran and knelt beside the bodies Nathan and Bosco had put to death. While unravelling what appeared to be white body bags, the figures went to work packing up the bodies and getting them ready. But the question was, getting them ready for what?

"I'd have thought the real Alice Springs police would be on the scene by now."

"It's weird, isn't it?" Maggie replied. "Yet there's been no police chatter at all. Another thing—there's been absolutely no traffic past the location. None."

I remembered as we drove up from the airport that there was no traffic. Maybe I was about to find out why this was so. "Can we look further down the road to the south?"

Christina nodded and tapped on the keyboard, commanding the satellite to a new location. After a few moments, the camera slowly moved away and followed the Stuart Highway to the south.

"There. Look." Maggie pointed. "They've set up a roadblock with a diversion across the river. That's why there's no traffic." I saw Maggie's eyes sparkling with excitement. "They're bloody good at what they do. See what we're up against? Okay, Christina, move us back to ground zero again, will you please?"

Christina nodded again. She tapped on the keyboard. The camera changed position back to The Gap. After the camera arrived, I felt both my legs almost give away under my weight. A Chinook helicopter had already landed just metres away from the RBT bus.

"Maggie?"

"I hear you, love." Maggie seemed as equally stunned.

"What're they doing?"

"It looks like they're clearing the scene of evidence. Hence the traffic diversion. Oh, they're cunning pieces of shit, aren't they? They'll have the entire scene cleared before sunrise."

"So it seems."

Christina noticed something. She pointed to the screen, where from under several floodlights, sparks were flying from some kind of cutting device.

Maggie peered a bit closer at the screen. "What the hell are they doing now? Is that what I think it is?"

"I know what they're up to. They're grinding the identification numbers from the chassis. I think they're going to leave the bus where it is."

"That makes sense. It's not the genuine article. Chances are the bus is stolen anyway. It'll be interesting to see what happens next. This is all so elaborate, isn't it?"

"But how is it that there's no police at the scene?" I asked.

"They look like the police. No one will ever bother reporting if they think the police are already there. The Guardianship is literally calling the bluff of everyone. That said, it can only last for so long. Hence their need to hurry things up."

The Guardianship soldiers picked up the pace. The Chinook helicopter now contained the five dead bodies, along with crucial parts of the bus that could most likely lead back to them. Then their activity slowed, and the figures hurled themselves into the fake police vehicles. The rotors of the Chinook started to spin.

After a couple of moments, it lifted into the air, swung around and took off in a westerly direction. There was one lone figure left standing at the side of the bus.

"Christina, can you zoom in a little closer on that man please?"

Christina punched a few keys, and the camera moved in.

"What do you suppose he's doing?" I asked.

"I'm not sure," Maggie said. "But it looks like he might be planting explosives. You know what? I reckon he's got Semtex all over that thing."

Maggie's words were confirmed the moment the lone figure raced back to a waiting vehicle which took off with its wheels spinning. A blinding flash erupted, and the bus disappeared into a cloud, exploding into fragments. The very thing that would get the real police urgently on the scene.

"We'll need to find that Chinook," Maggie said. "That's now our utmost priority."

In the back of my mind, I wondered if the Chinook was one of the six that left *Steinbeck*. The notion of my concern caused me to shiver on the spot. Were they Guardianship who left *Steinbeck?* If they were, this now brought *new* questions into the mix. I decided to keep that question to myself and leave it unanswered for now.

CHAPTER NINE

Going Dark

NATHAN STEPPED THROUGH THE DOOR AS I was at the coffee machine. Wiping the sleep from his eyes, Nathan busted a yawn, and gave me the same good morning as he'd always done; a peck on the check and warm glowing smile. He stepped up to the glass jug on the counter containing hot black get up and go. Glancing sideways at his wristwatch, he grabbed a mug down from the cupboard. "07:00," Nathan said. "Any sign of Bosco?"

"Hear that sound? That drilling sound?"

"Yeah. What the hell is that?"

"Bosco. Snoring." I rolled my eyes.

"Figures. Is there a bucket around here anywhere?"

"Well, I think there's one in the laundry. Why?"

Nathan didn't answer me. He stepped past me and into the laundry. I heard unmistakable sound of running water filling a bucket. I smiled to myself as Nathan again stepped past me, armed with a bucket of cold Alice Springs bore water. I knew what he was about to do as I sat down at the dining table. I waited for the inevitability with both hands wrapped around my hot mug of coffee. After a few moments, I heard Bosco's yelling emanate from somewhere down the end of the hall. Bosco was up and alive. No more drilling snoring.

Christina bounced through the door wearing her flannel PJs. I felt my heartbeat pick up as I saw the outline of her figure at the coffee machine. At first, I thought she wasn't going to say anything. But as she turned and faced the dining table, she greeted me in German. "Guten morgen."

"Hello, Christina. The coffee is fresh. I hope you enjoy."

"Danke." Christina smiled warmly as she pulled out a chair and sat down. "Wurden sie ein fruhstuck mochten?"

I didn't know how to speak German and I let Christina know with a few universal hand signals.

Christina tried again. "Es tut mir leid . . . umm . . . sorry." She tried again. "Vood du like some breakfast?"

"Oh, breakfast? No thanks, Christina. I have my coffee, and I'm about to step out back for a cigarette. It's a Journo's breakfast, don't you know. But that doesn't appear the be the case any longer, does it?"

Christina shook her head again. I looked down at my mug and smiled to myself. I then gestured the sign language of having a smoke. Christina responded. "Ja . . . bitte. Smoke . . . yes?"

I waved my hand toward the back door. "Okay. Come with me."

The early morning sun floated; peeking just above the fence line, which drew long shadows on the dusty red ground. It was cold for an Alice Springs morning. Dry and cold. No vapour from my breath, only the bluish cigarette smoke as I exhaled letting the nicotine do its duty.

As I found a place and slouched up against fibro cladding, I realised nothing outside had changed. It was the same backyard I remembered but seemed smaller. As I scanned the area, it was as though time had frozen, and I was again a ten-year-old. Over toward the shed was the swinging bench seat that I'd sat on as a child every morning before heading off to school. The dry earth was absent of grass. Beyond the bench seat, was the Hills Hoist, which was still kinked and stood slightly askew. The aluminium fence needed some paint but it was still the same as ever. And there . . . I pointed. "See that?"

Christina looked over to where I'd pointed. She shrugged her confusion, then looked at me curiously with her big beautiful blue eyes.

"Come with me. I'll show you."

I walked toward the back fence; Christina padded lightly behind. A small spear of light poked through a hole in the fence. I bent down slightly and placed my finger over it, remembering how close I came. Christina looked at it momentarily. It appeared now that she was more confused than ever.

I lifted my hair around my ear and showed Christina what was missing. Christina looked up again and reacted with a hand toward me. "Sie habe geschossen?" She was surprised, but at the same time struggled with her English. "Err . . . shoot. There?"

I nodded. How could I answer in words?

"Mein Gott!" Christina placed a hand over her mouth and ogled me. She raised her hand and placed it gently on my face next to my ear. In that moment I felt a warmth. I felt a genuine caring from someone I didn't know. It surprised me and caused me to sharply look away. But also in the moment, I didn't notice Bosco who was standing at the back door. "Hey, you two. 07:30." Bosco tapped the face of his wristwatch. "Time to get to work."

After returning inside, I found Nathan already seated at the table, cradling a mug of coffee as though he was cold. To Nathan's left sat a man with a face that was familiar; and I knew who this man was. "Andrew? Is it you?"

"Angel, it's good to see you again." Andrew smiled and I knew it was out of genuine affection. I stepped around the table and I took Andrew's hand. His grip was strong but welcoming. Not forceful like Christina's. Andrew's hand was warm, and he withdrew it with satisfactory timing. He kept smiled brightly, just the same as he did way back then . . .

"T," Andrew said, breaking my train of thought. "You're one of us now, so it's T."

I'd forgotten where I was. I'd forgotten that all these people are players and they have their own callsigns.

"Short for Teflon," Nathan looked up from his coffee and offered.

"Huh?"

"T is for Teflon." This time Nathan took a swig of his coffee in a nonchalant way and I suddenly realised he was different. How different? I couldn't say.

"I hate that name, Canter," said Andrew. "And we don't *all* get to choose our own call signs, do we? You'd know!"

Nathan smiled a big cheesy grin. "Well T, it was you who implied that nothing sticks. The fact you became Teflon was inevitable."

I finally pushed past the banter and offered my own to Andrew. "It's been such a long time," I said. "And I never realised you were ASIO."

Andrew laughed. Nathan almost choked on his coffee.

"I don't normally admit it to anyone if they ask me," Andrew replied. "And your question has never been asked so casually, by the way."

I couldn't help but feel rookie small at their laughter. Where was the nearest corner small enough for me to hide in?

Andrew grinned in a way that told me I shouldn't worry. I remembered he'd done that a few times when I was a child.

"It's okay, you'll get the hang of it. Just . . . try not to say anything in public and we'll do just fine."

Shrugging it off, head down, I immediately bee-lined for the caffeine. While pouring coffee into the mug that was a favourite when I was a child, I said to Andrew, "Maggie tells me you were on assignment." Andrew said nothing. It then occurred to me that perhaps he couldn't answer. Not even if he was amongst other players. I realised then, that even under the one roof, there're many layers. This was something that I now had to somehow come to grips with.

I snuck back to my chair and silently joined them all at the table. To my left, Nathan was grinning and sharing jokes. Opposite him, Christina was smiling brightly, but hid her lack of understanding well enough. Bosco sat beside her, also joking, wearing his baseball cap tilted back while chewing on gum. And there was Andrew, seated exactly on my right.

I didn't know what it was about Andrew. He had a certain magnetism, almost pulling me in with his charm and charisma, and somehow, I found that I adored it. Andrew even took the trouble to stop mid-sentence and give me an expression that I knew in my heart was just for me. I melted. I felt things I shouldn't have. I wanted to stay in that moment forever. But then Maggie's voice drilled through the delicious moment and shattered it into fragments. "You people get your backsides down here. It's time to get to work."

* * *

Down into the bluish, electrically charged ops room, Bosco and Christina stood behind the main computer with their arms folded. Maggie tapped madly at the keyboard, then replayed a video recording that was captured by the *Keyhole Satellite Three* over The

Gap, south of Alice Springs. When it was over, no one said anything, and the silence was deafening.

Finally, Bosco was the first to break the silence. "That's it; it's all over. Our best choice is to go dark."

"For once I think Bosco's right," Nathan added. "We need to break away from whatever it is that they know about us."

Maggie acknowledged Nathan and then turned to Andrew. "Your thoughts?"

Andrew shrugged then replied, "It is what it is. I agree. There's no option for us but to go off the grid."

Maggie turned and asked for Christina's opinion. She was about to speak when Bosco cut her off. "This isn't for BND to decide," Bosco said sharply then stomped away.

Maggie stepped forward and grabbed Bosco by the upper arm. "What in god's name is wrong with you? Get a grip. We all have a job to do. Christina is part of the team. Do I make myself clear?"

Bosco said nothing.

"Is that clear! And don't make me pull rank Bosco. We've survived without the formalities for so long!"

"Yes . . . Colonel," Bosco huffed as he sat heavily in his chair.

Christina then began to speak. "If ve must go dark, ve must destroy our netverk, vich includes hard drives and surveillance. Ve cannot hold any recovered data. Everything must be destroyed."

Maggie nodded in agreement. "It'll be expensive. No doubt about it. Angel? Your thoughts?"

Still feeling the perfect rookie in their company, I never expected to contribute. I took a breath before I said, "The photography lab for starters. Won't that need to be shut down also?"

"Good point, Angel. The shop will have to go. No more funding for us. The problem is how? We can't even sell it as a legitimate business. It'll draw too much attention."

"Is there a way for the shop to stay operational?" Nathan asked.

"Too risky, big hoss," Bosco put in. "I say we put a match to it. The place is full of chemicals. It won't seem suspicious."

Maggie put her finger up to her lips. She was actually considering Bosco's proposal. But then, Maggie again turned to Christina. "Anything further to add before I decide?"

"I think Bosco's idea ist sehr gut. But ve don't vant to cause damash to ze shops next doors."

"That's true," I added. "We can't cause undue stress to innocent parties. We don't even know if they *have* the appropriate insurance."

"I disagree," Bosco put in. "If we go down this road, it'll have to look realistic. If it's done surgically, it *will* be suspicious. I say burn, baby, burn. If the other shops get lit up in the process, then that's how it is."

I'd had enough of Bosco's attitude. "I've not known you for long, Bosco. But already I can see how much you're a complete arsehole."

Nathan laughed. Christina laughed. Maggie was most annoyed. "Enough! You're like little school kids! Bloody-well get your heads back in the game!"

There was a certain awkwardness after Maggie silenced everyone. She turned slowly, walked to her chair and sat down.
"Okay. I take it we're all in agreement then?" One by one, Maggie made eye contact with everyone in the ops room. We all nodded including myself. I wasn't happy knowing innocents would be part of the collateral damage. But what Maggie said next was completely unexpected.

"Andrew and I have discussed your next assignment, Nathan. Now that Eagle Shield is concluded, we'll be needing you abroad."

It was to be the first time in twenty years that Nathan and I would be separated. I wondered how things could change so drastically in so little time. Nathan was going to leave me and I had no control over it. My eyes filled with tears.

"Okay then people. The ayes have it." Maggie looked away, seeming to be a little upset. "Sad, isn't it? All the work we've done. Everything we've achieved. It just gets destroyed. We were so close."

"I'll get a report back to Canberra, and I'll request our redeployments," Andrew said almost under his breath as he stepped past me.

Maggie agreed with her stepson. "We'll start with the hard drives after our meeting concludes. I'll get a clean-up detail from HQ to deal with the photo lab. Angel, I'll need you here with me this morning. We'll have a chat about getting you some training at Swan Island."

As soon as I heard the words from Maggie, it was like everything became set in stone. Nobody goes to Swan Island without the one sole purpose of becoming a spook. Secretly, I'd always wondered about that place. I was almost excited to go there just to see what existed behind all those doors. The excitement, however, melted away as I realised after graduation, I was almost certainly destined to do time behind a desk. It wasn't how I saw myself.

"How do you feel about going straight into ASIS?" Maggie asked me. After she asked it, I realised that maybe the desk job I thought about was never on the agenda. Maybe this was all intricately planned from the time I was so young.

* * *

It was easy to say goodbye to Bosco. It was a little harder with Christina. It was especially difficult to say goodbye to Maggie and Nathan. But after Andrew dropped me off at Alice Springs Airport, he unexpectedly kissed me softly on my cheek. It was no ordinary peck, however. It wasn't one of those things that was done with the speed of light, as though it never really happened in the first place. Andrew had left me with a kiss that had a special something that can't be pulled from the air. I felt myself fall to a place I'd never visited. There was something about Andrew, I kept thinking. It was so strange; I'd never felt an attraction to men. Andrew was different. But he had the same effect on all women, apparently. Even with young thin women who struggled to speak English. I saw it as though he had his own force of gravity. But I was in love with Jenny. I like girls. I might like boys too . . .

Andrew left me on the footpath with my luggage outside the Airport main entrance. I waved to him as the white government limousine pulled away. I never waved to anyone in that romantic way. But this time, it was something that I couldn't have helped if I tried.

CHAPTER TEN

Graduate

THE OLD BITUMEN TRACK THAT SPIRALLED its way around the Swan Island facility never seemed empty of young candidate joggers. They ran dressed in their official grey Swan Island tracksuits, most of them were firmly plugged into their music devices. I ran hard. I made a habit of putting everything I had into it. I ran on. I ran to forget.

After doing laps around the facility, I slowed, and walked it out as I sucked huge gulps of air down into my lungs. I sat down on the edge of a jetty that overlooked Port Phillip bay to the north. I could just make out the tall Melbourne skyscrapers that pierced the horizon. I thought about Jenny. She was there, somewhere. I couldn't help but wonder what Jenny would be doing right now.

I drew my knees up and I wrapped my arms tightly around my legs. I sat there enjoying the cooling breeze as it pushed past the sweat on my back. As I looked out across the water, a lone figure stood on a nearby boat, tossing out burley, while flocks of noisy seagulls fought over the spoils. In that moment whilst looking out across the water, I felt peace. I felt peace even though I missed Jenny and my heart broke every time I thought of her.

As I sat there, my thoughts were rudely interrupted by some-one's sudden appearance. I glanced sideways to the person who sat heavily down beside me. "Nice job," I said.

"Even if you *do* say so yourself."

"Sorry."

"No. Don't be. Now I know we've trained you well."

"It looks that way, doesn't it?" I said smiling a little.

My instructor briefly echoed my expression, then he lifted his hand to his broken face. "Normally I'd say you deserve a few shots tonight, but somehow . . . I don't think I'm able to partake."

"I don't like tequila that much. It gives me reflux. Besides, I'd much rather be elsewhere right now. My old life. My old home. My old job . . ."

"You know that's not an option."

"So you keep saying. What? Am I in some kind of a jail?"

"Candidate . . . this is a seriously important institution. Of the hundreds that apply for intelligence each year, only six get to graduate. You're one of the six. And not only that, you've leap-frogged them all. They'd all kill you for the chance you've got."

"And that's supposed to make me feel special."

"Check your attitude, candidate. You've got small arms as-sessment to get through, at 14:00. After that, you're officially on stand-down, awaiting deployment."

"Then what? No one's said anything. Just gossip. I don't do gossip."

"You'll know soon enough. HQ will let you know. Just do me one favour. When you're out in the field, do as you're instructed. Don't go on gut. That way you won't get your own arse handed to you. ASIS *will* kick your arse severely if you stuff up. Make sure it doesn't happen. Number one above everything; back up your players. Got it?"

I shook my head and looked away. "You're all the same. You're all on the need to know. I seriously doubt if I'll spend the rest of my days as a player."

"You will. That's the way it is. Now you're with us—you're with us for life. We're your family now. You'd better get used to it." I heard my instructor breathe deeply before looking away. "Okay, Angel. Here it is and you didn't hear it from me. What I'm about to tell you is rumour. It's innuendo. It's speculation. Get what I'm saying? There's no graduation for you. There's no ceremony, or anything like it. Not like the others. Those guys are bound for that desk job at Ben Chifley you've been worried about. But you know what? This one comes from the top. From the boss himself. Make no mistake about it; you've already been assigned and deployed. And I'll repeat it, in case you didn't hear me. It's rumour and speculation."

I took notice of my instructor's serious tone and when I did, all the memories of the time at Busby's with Nathan bounced back. Just *what* was I getting into?

"You'll deploy from 07:00."

"Deploy to where?"

"Forward ops. But it's rumour and speculation, remember. You'd better get your head in the game, Angel. I shit you not."

I thought about it momentarily. It just didn't sit well in my mind. "I don't believe you. It'd be suicide for everyone if Firebird Station came back out of the shadows."

"It's no longer Firebird. That's finished with. Firebird Station is dead in the water. Colonel Mack requested your reassignment. You belong to her as of 07:00 tomorrow. I will not disclose the location of your ops post. It's for everyone's security including mine. Report to the range before 14:00. That's all I have to say."

My instructor slowly heaved himself up, wincing in the pain from the injuries that I bestowed upon him. Without anything further to add, he walked with a slight limp toward HQ.

"Wait!" I shouted after him. "I need something!"

"What is it?"

As I walked toward my instructor I wondered that it may not even be possible. But I asked it anyway. "I need something before I deploy. I need a new look. Some new clothes. A new hairdo. Can you get me out of here for a while?"

My instructor scrutinised me up and down as though he was looking at some object that was far from human. "Don't change your look too much. Canberra has sent new travel documents including your new passport. Rumour has it, you're going to Langley after you deploy to forward ops."

"Langley? Why?"

"You're going to help the CIA locate the whereabouts of a stolen Chinook. Apparently. Rumour and innuendo, kiddo. Remember? I'll get Andrea to take you into Geelong. I need to go there myself. Nose straightening sucks big time. And not only; you've made my testicles feel like they're the size of St Clement's bells. I hate this job sometimes, just saying."

"Sorry."

"Don't be. But your ops post needs a name. Colonel Mack tells me you have an idea."

I *did* have an idea,

"Charlotte," I shouted as my instructor turned and walked away. "We'll call it Charlotte Station."

CHAPTER ELEVEN

Jenny

I'D SPENT THE MORING SHOPPING FOR CLOTHES. It wasn't an easy choice—there're so many options. With only two hours at my disposal, I scampered around the main areas of the Westfield Shopping Centre in Geelong. I hurried along at a frantic pace, almost running, while at the same time checking for time on my brand-new smartphone number three.

In and out of the dozens of boutiques I blurred, stopping occasionally for a few moments before moving on to the next. My PA for the day, Andrea, followed closely behind me. "Hey. Slow down, Angel. We've still got time."

It was the smell of leather that caught my attention. The smell of a saddlery. It reminded me of home. The scent brought back images of a much younger me, who grew up in Alice Springs. I pushed on toward the scent and stepped through open glass doors into a large area of an RM Williams retail outlet. At last I could choose. At last, poor Andrea was likely to rest and catch her breath. I took several garments from hangers and stepped into the change rooms to try them out for size, then rushed to the checkout, knowing my hairdressing appointment was just moments away. Out of the shop, I lugged several large orange plastic bags with big RM Williams longhorns printed on the sides. Andrea followed closely, and it was in that moment I wondered why she was along in the first place. I didn't need a PA. I knew Geelong quite well. It didn't matter. I strode on, loaded up to the chin with bags upon bags.

After I'd finished with the hairdresser, I asked if I could use the back room of the salon to change into my new outfit. I needed the final picture immediately. The salon manager agreed, and I stepped through into the back.

I stared into the mirror, and I was happy with my new me. But I wondered about my passport photo—I'd changed so much. My long, flowing raven hair was now dead straight, cut, shaped and styled into a short bob and glistened blue-black under the salon lights. I smiled as I ran my eyes up and down my reflection. I loved the way my new white blouse – which was open-necked and buttoned low – accentuated my complexion. I loved the hint of my pink lingerie under my blouse. Everything was masterly measured and properly fitted. My nails were freshly polished with a neutral tone and manicured to just beyond the tips of my fingers. A chocolate leather waist jacket which was tailored in the classic Australian rural style, and a pair of figure-hugging beige jodhpurs that clung to my curves. My new look was finished off with a pair of leather, knee-high RM Williams boots. I was no longer the city slicker of my former self. I was no longer the journalist everybody knew on evening television. I was no longer the conservative chick that lived high up over Melbourne's skyline. My look returned me to my rural origins, and I was happy.

* * *

Returning to the range at exactly 14:00, I wondered what would be waiting for me tomorrow. As I placed my ear protection over my ears, and a set of amber safety shields over my eyes, I stood there and waited for the command to check weapons, aim and fire. I knew what I had to do. The question was, was I capable of doing it? With all that training behind me, it now came down to this moment.

"Candidates! Welcome to your final objective! Fail this test and it's a handshake before you return to civvie street. Take your time and make every round count. Remember. This is for MPI, and not the perfect bullseye. Ready . . . At your own time, begin!"

I was still thinking about Jenny as I squeezed off my first round. Miss this shot, my inner voice kept telling me. Miss it and you can go home. I didn't know the reason why I opted in. Perhaps I felt as though I was now duty bound to my country. Nathan was right. Something dreadful was about to happen to everyone on this Planet Earth. And now, it would happen over my dead body.

After I fired five rounds, the paper targets came whizzing back via overhead snatch rails. I smiled to myself at the outcome. My mean point of impact was small enough to pass my exam. I was on my way.

* * *

07:00 the next morning was heavily overcast and with driving rain. The rain came in horizontal sheets that was carried in on gale-force winds. As I stood alone at the facility guard house, my umbrella offered only momentary cover before the howling southerly wind turned it inside out. Dressed in my new full-length black trench coat, I bobbed up and down on one spot with my arms tightly wrapped around my body. I tried desperately to keep out the cold. But suddenly, a set of headlights speared through the gloom.

A white government Holden Statesman with black licence plates embellished with the State Crown of Victoria slowly motored over and stopped by my side. The dark tinted windows prevented me from seeing inside. I waited momentarily for someone to step out and give me a hand with my luggage. It never happened, but just as I thought about it, I heard a click and the boot lid rose slightly up. After putting my luggage in the back I jumped inside and shut the door. The government vehicle then moved off slowly and did a wide U-turn, and I left that lonely place forever.

There wasn't much in the way of conversation on the way to Tullamarine. The traffic was heavy on the Princes Freeway, up from Geelong. It was even heavier approaching the West Gate Bridge. And by the time the government car made a left turn and headed for the *Bolte Bridge*, the traffic was almost at a standstill.

I finally got up some gumption and seized the moment. "How about a small diversion to Port Melbourne," I asked my driver.

My driver flatly refused my request in a cold, formal tone. I said nothing else for the rest of the journey to Melbourne Airport.

On arrival at the domestic terminal, I grabbed my baggage from the boot of the government car – all by my bloody self. Head down and bent forward, I fought my way through the rain and the wind.

New electronic technology made check in a breeze. With my luggage checked, I decided to take a seat and rest before doing battle with airport security.

The scent of freshly brewed, real coffee hung in the air. How could I *not* have a Starbuck's. After I grabbed a large paper mug of unsweetened black coffee, I made my way back to my very uncomfortable chair. Glancing down at the screen of my phone, I realised it was an hour before my flight was due to board and we could've easily accommodated a diversion to my apartment. But now there was no hope of seeing Jenny for one last time. There was no hope of collecting some of my belongings. And there was no hope for closing the book on a chapter of my life, once and forever.

Countless times I'd tried to contact Jenny. After dialling home, there was no answer. The phone rang a couple of times and then went directly to voicemail. I'd left dozens of messages, but it was impossible to leave a phone number for Jenny to return my call. I made inquiries using the techniques that were not readily available to the masses. Everything I tried came up empty. The line was disconnected the last time I called home. Later, I'd discovered Jenny had deleted her social media. It was as though she'd already moved on.

But then, there was the title of our Port Melbourne apartment. That was something that could never be taken away. It was a purchase we'd both made. I instantly checked my bag for my apartment keys and they were there. If only my driver diverted after I asked him. Now, it was too late.

Coffee finished, I decided to get one more before boarding. On the way to the Starbuck's kiosk, I passed by the notice board and checked for boarding in the hope of an early departure to Darwin. To my horror, the flight was delayed due to weather. Three hours. But maybe it wasn't a bad thing after all.

I quickly did the sums in my head. Leaving the airport to go to Port Melbourne then getting back before boarding was going to be a tight squeeze but not impossible. I'd need to get going right now. I picked up my belongings and sprinted for the exit.

Outside, thunder and lightning cracked through the greyness as I hailed a taxi. It took more than a few goes, before eventually, a yellow Melbourne taxi stopped and I launched myself into the back seat.

* * *

The first thing I noticed after I placed my key into the lock was how easily it slid in. It never did that before. But also, the door wasn't locked at all. It was slightly ajar. My brain thumped hard. Something was wrong.

"Jenny?"

I pushed the door open and stepped inside. Somebody had ransacked our apartment. Stuff was strewn all over. Things that stood up right now lay on its side. Bookcases, shelving, chests of drawers, kitchen bureau, everything. The floor was littered with broken and smashed debris.

"Jenny!" The horror of it all. There was no reply.

"Oh god. Jenny!"

I stepped through the mess on the floor and headed into the kitchen. Cupboards were open. Plates were smashed. Things were strewn and thrown from one corner of the kitchen to the next. Even our outdoor furniture on the balcony was upturned and tossed about.

I tiptoed over debris from the kitchen and stepped into the bedroom. Everything was a mess. Everything was everywhere. Even our mattress stripped and ripped up and upturned.

On the floor, in the rubble, there was something that caught the corner of my eye. It glimmered for a second. I tiptoed over to it and picked it up. My rock crystal figurine—the one Jenny had given to me as a birthday present. I retrieved it, wrapping it up in tissue before putting it deep into my trench coat pocket.

Getting my head back took a few moments. I fought through the urge to start cleaning the place up. But now, time was getting away. Reluctantly, I stepped back through the front door, closing it behind me. Out on the street, the taxi waited just as instructed. Dodging the downpour, I flew into the back, and departed for Tullamarine with a great amount of speed.

TWO

Stand-To

CHAPTER TWELVE

Red Bandana

AFTER LANDING IN DARWIN, I was still feeling the stress with what I'd discovered back in Melbourne. I remained seated whilst passengers got up and prepared to leave. I was still sitting, daydreaming out of the window after all passengers had completely vacated the aircraft. I held the figurine Jenny had given me in my hand. I twirled it around, eyeing it, running my fingers over it. My mind ran like a silent movie over the memories I'd shared with Jenny. Happy memories. It was Jenny who'd kept me grounded. It was Jenny who'd listen—often late at night—to the stories of my stressful days. At times, I caught Jenny at the edge of falling asleep, but she never did. She was all ears. Jenny my rock. Jenny my sounding board. Jenny my soul mate. Jenny my lover . . .

At that moment, I was brought back from my thoughts by a polite touch on my shoulder. "I'm sorry, Angel. It's time to leave the aircraft now," the flight attendant said. I looked up and nodded. "Thank you. And thank you again for listening to my worries. I was a bit of a mess, wasn't I?"

"It was no trouble. But I'll let you in on a secret. It's all part of our job." The flight attendant smiled warmly before disappearing down the aisle toward the business class bulkhead.

I pulled myself up from my seat. It felt as though my heart was heavier than the rest of my body. I got up slowly. I collected my things from the overhead locker and stepped forward toward the exit.

In contrast to the weather in Melbourne, Darwin was stiflingly hot and sticky. I was overwhelmed by the humidity as I stepped out of the aircraft door. With my trench coat dangling around my forearm, the first thing I thought of was, what to do with it? Darwin was no place for a trench coat. No one in Darwin would ever need one—much less own one.

Arriving at the baggage carousel, I waited patiently for it to start moving around, indicating bags were on their way. I held back from the crowd that gathered there. I was in no hurry and I couldn't have cared less if I was the last to leave. I was sluggish to react and I felt as though some kind of invisible force was weighing me down. Head down and sad—I waited by the carousel.

My bags passed by. I knew they'd already passed by several times. I'd collect them the next time around. Then they passed again. And again. After a while, the carousel was empty with my two bags floating on the conveyor, passing me by—lonely, as I was alone. They passed by another time. I made no attempt to retrieve them. I stood motionless, still, like some porcelain statue. And then suddenly, my breath left my lungs.

Dizziness attacked me. I spun from the carousel and headed to an empty seat at the edge of the large open space. My mind wound and twirled. I felt inner heat rise. My skin prickled and I gasped for air. I felt tiny beads of sweat break out over my arms. With the back of a hand, I wiped perspiration from my face. Then the tears came. I tried to control it. I tried hard. I failed. I bent forward with my head almost touching my knees.

I tried to breathe. I wanted to scream. Wave after wave, it came. I buried my face in my hands. I screamed out. As hard as I could. Uncontrollable. Overpowering. Overwhelming. I was so sad. So angry. So heartbroken. Alone at an airport, devoid of souls. Souls that had long since left and returned to their lives.

Bent forward in my chair, I did my best to hide. But then, I felt a comforting hand on my back. I imagined a stranger had come to comfort me. Someone who took the trouble to console me. I was such a blubbering mess. Wiping my eyes, I grabbed some composure before looked up and I recognised him straight away.

"Bosco?"

Bosco said nothing but only nodded slowly. Perhaps even empathetically. Something I couldn't imagine coming from Bosco.

"I was expecting Maggie," I said.

"Maggie's got things on. I'm here to pick you up," Bosco said, gazing down at me. He patted his pockets then took something out. "It's not a tissue, but it's clean, and you can have it," he said as he sat down next to me. Bosco passed me what I thought was a red bandana. I took it with thanks and used it to dab at my tears.

"I don't leave home without it," Bosco said. "And Maggie keeps making sure it's clean."

"And why do you have a red bandana in your pocket?"

"A long story. But it's a lucky charm, I guess. I think knowing what's coming, maybe I don't need that lucky charm no more."

"Oh? I never saw you as the superstitious type."

"We all have something. Canter has his dummy round. Maggie has her Norman Lindsay etchings. Andrew has his father's police badge. And I had my bandana. A story for another time. You good?"

"Getting there. I just had a moment . . ."

It was roughly thirty minutes before I had the strength to stand up. During that time, Bosco sat next to me, silent, not a word said as I explained what had happened to Jenny. It was as though he wasn't there at all, but somehow, I knew he was listening. He put a hand on my shoulder occasionally. It was somehow odd to find comfort Bosco's company. But certainly, it was better than nothing at all.

"Your bag," Bosco said, pointing, breaking the silence. "A guy just got it off the carousel. You'd better go get it before these guys start jumping around."

"Shit. I forgot."

"Yeah. You can thank 9/11 for that. But don't worry, I'll get it."

Bosco sprinted away, and after collecting my baggage he strolled back with a big smile on his face. He looked kind of goofy. A big muscular military type trailing a very feminine looking bag behind him. It made me return his smile and for the first time I found myself warming to Bosco. I stood from the chair, still feeling heavy as he approached me. After passing over my bag, he stepped back. Bosco's eyes scanned me up and down and he smiled again. A very different kind of smile.

"It's just a haircut," I said, handing him back his bandana. But he took my hand and closed it. "I said you can keep it. It's yours. I know you're not into guys. But you're a fine-looking woman, Angel."

* * *

There wasn't much in the way of conversation out from Darwin domestic. Much the same as the ride up to Melbourne from Swan Island. I tried to hide my sadness as it attacked me in waves. There were a few moments where I thought I'd succumb to tears all over again. And then there was Bosco's lucky charm which he gave to me. The scent of wonderful lavender in the bandana helped me immensely. I had to wonder. Maggie did the lavender thing for me, she'd told me. Now Bosco? Maybe it was Maggie's way with everyone.

Bosco glanced at me sideways occasionally as he drove. I knew he avoided the chit-chat, and I was quietly thankful. On the other hand, Bosco seemed almost glad about something. I caught him smiling—then he'd snap his head forward, eyes back on the road.

"Not long now," Bosco said. "It's just up ahead."

"Are all original Firebird players deployed?"

Bosco nodded. "We've got a newbie with us this time."

"Really? Who?"

Bosco glanced sideways again. "I think I'll let Maggie do the intros."

"And Nathan?"

I caught Bosco's expression drain a fraction. Something was wrong.

"Canter is about to jump on a flight from Seoul International. He's due into Darwin at 23:00."

* * *

The white Holden Commodore drew to a halt out the front of an inconspicuous, timber clad cottage that was raised off the ground on stilts. I noticed a shipping container that was out the back. I wondered what it was used for. The place was new. Perhaps the container was for supplies or for storage. But I also noticed a light that was set up on a pole in front of the container door. Even more strange was some kind of antenna on top of the container.

Bosco reefed the handbrake lever and killed the engine. "Welcome to Charlotte Station," he said. "I heard it was you who'd given the station the callsign."

I nodded as I looked from the window. The obviously newly built cottage had no lawns or gardens and sat raised on a patch of bare earth. I left the vehicle, still feeling heavy as I followed Bosco up wooden stairs that smelt of new cut pine and fresh paint.

Bosco stepped forward and knocked on the bare wooden door. After a moment Maggie's smiling face appeared as the door opened.

"Shilo," Bosco said. "Mission accomplished."

Maggie beamed and stood to one side. The smell of home-style cooking wafted through and was instantly spoiled by the awful smell of freshly painted walls. I couldn't help myself. I flew into Maggie's open arms. "Goodness, love," Maggie said as she wrapped her arms around me. "Whatever is the matter?"

I could say no words as my tears erupted and I'd succumbed to my sadness all over again.

"You didn't tell her, did you?" Maggie said to Bosco. Bosco shook his head and quickly disappeared down the hall.

"Told me what?" I asked.

"Come inside, love. We can't stay out here any longer."

Again, Maggie asked as I stood in the warm light of the foyer. "What is it, Angel. Whatever is the matter?"

As the words came out of my mouth, it seemed as though it was no longer a thought in my head. It was real, and there was nothing I could do about it. "It's Jenny. She's missing."

"But Angel . . ."

"I thought it might be an idea to catch up with her before leaving Melbourne. My apartment is a mess. Everything is ruined, and Jenny's gone!"

"And when, may I ask did you go there? Did your driver take you there? Damn it. I specifically requested for that *not* to happen."

I was amazed at Maggie's choice of words. My sadness left me and shock took over. "You knew Jenny was missing?"

"We know all about what happened at your apartment. That's why you were not to go there. Under *any* circumstances."

"My flight was delayed due to bad weather. I had the time to go there, so I did."

"God no! I'm so sorry Angel. That was something I was not expecting."

"Maggie . . . How could you *not* tell me what happened? And now Jenny . . ."

"We couldn't tell you, love. You were training. If we'd contacted you even on a secure line, we might've been compromised yet again. It was much too risky, you must understand. We're all far too deep in the game, and there's no room for risks. Not now."

"But Jenny . . . she's missing."

Maggie took a step back and folded her arms. "That Bosco. I'll kill him. He was supposed to tell you about Jenny the moment he saw you. Jenny is here, Angel. She's safe."

CHAPTER THIRTEEN

Canter

MY SPRITS LIFTED IMMENSELY at the sight of Jenny. Jenny padded quickly to the front door. She reached for me the exact moment I pushed past Maggie. The embrace was a long one. Tears again. Happy tears. I witnessed, for the first time, Maggie with red-rimmed eyes. Her hardness disappeared and she was again the Maggie I'd known all those years ago.

An old-fashioned lamb roast, cooked old-school, was my favourite. Around the table, hoeing into plates piled high, were all the familiar faces. Christina, the lovely polite German girl who'd been smuggled from the BND for her obvious talents. Maggie's stepson, Andrew. 'The ASIO guy,' I'd once called him. I winced slightly at my own recollection. Even among operatives, the mere mention of the word was deemed taboo. Bosco sat beside Andrew with his baseball hat that he never, ever took off. Maggie was sitting opposite, beaming with her chin resting on the back of her hands, watching on proudly. And Jenny right beside me. Thank god Jenny was safe.

Nathan, of course, was more than a few hours away, on a flight out from Seoul International. When he finally arrived, all originals would be reunited. But there was one other seated at the table.

The newbie Bosco had mentioned. A man with skin the colour of ebony. A man who was as tall as an NBA major league player and a grin that lit up the room. The introduction to this man was one of my biggest surprises. I recognised him before any words were exchanged. "I know you. I know you from Busby's. You're the manager. You were there when Nathan and I were there." It all started to sink in. He nodded and began to belly laugh. A very weird sense of humour, I thought.

This man's real name was non-existent, as was his history. He was known only under the codename of Xenon, and all referred to him simply as Xe. It wasn't clear what Xe's mission entailed. However, Maggie explained everything I needed to know. Somehow, I knew there was much more to what she let on. Xe was ops forward. Black ops, mostly. But the biggest shock of all came after Maggie went on with the details. There were many layers to the operations of ASIS. Xe was deep below the layers of secrecy. He'd been assigned a security level equal to that of the Director-General himself. He moved among the world silently, unknown to all but a few and answered only to the Prime Minister. His cover was cleverly cloaked, and his whereabouts at any point in time was classified. Xe had the luxury of autonomy. He could plug in and unplug as he saw fit. And Maggie explained it in words that now seem like slow motion. He's Oudarretian. The realisation was an explosive moment in my mind.

Around the dinner table, with Jenny's help, Bosco began clearing up plates and taking them back to the kitchen. Wine, beer, spirits, everything, cluttered the table with half-full, half-empty glasses. The was the chatter about this and that. Small talk and shared jokes, to which bouts of laughter rang out. But among all the chatter, I decided to change the subject. My words stopped everyone and a silk sheet of silence fell down around us.

"So, what's in the shipping container out the back?" I asked. Everyone held their voices, and quickly glanced at one another. I thought their reaction was guilt. But why?

"Don't tell me," I said trying to make light of the situation. "You've got someone stashed in there, right?"

If it was taken as a joke; it was a bad one. No one laughed.

Maggie looked across and eyed me directly. "Well, love, that's for you. Consider it your dessert. Now's the time you get to use some of your training," Maggie said, smiling.

"High priority, huh? Who do we have in there? A G-man?" I laughed a little under my breath.

Maggie smiled wryly before winking at Xe. "That's right, Angel. We have ourselves a Guardianship soldier. How about that, huh?"

"You're kidding."

"It's true. However, we've already extracted all the intel we're ever going to get out of the man. Xe was tacking him. He got hold of him as he was making a play on your apartment. The Gs thought there was intelligence at your place and they went there quite obviously looking for it. But Jenny walked in on him. The rest is history."

Jenny placed her hand on my knee and she gave me that expression that told me not to worry. But now, I was angry. I thought about what the G-man did to my home. I thought about how Jenny must've felt when she walked in. I was angry. I tried to keep it in check. "Did you manage to extract any intel on the CIA's stolen Chinook?"

"Xe had a go at it. So did Andrew. There's nothing else forthcoming from him, unfortunately."

"I bet I can drag it out of him."

"If Xe can't, then I'm afraid we're at our wits' end. However, you may interrogate him as part of your growing experience.

Show us what Swan Island has taught you. But I want you to do it constructively and by the book. Am I clear?"

I was about to answer Maggie. Suddenly Christina bounced through the dining room door. "An email received from Canter. Schnell! Schnell!"

* * *

The email from Nathan was only one line. It was something I never wanted to read. Nathan words were by using the code known only to those in our tight intelligence community.

canter@bya.net; Airline has lost baggage.

Maggie stepped back from the laptop and half turned away. Others scrutinised the screen in horror as Christina began the various stages of verification. After it was complete, she turned away from the screen with her wide eyes.

"Jesus," Maggie said. "We don't need this right now."

As I realised what was happening, I felt my heart plummet. "Nathan has a watcher? Who?"

"We need more code," Bosco said. "Maybe it's Gs. But maybe it's Norks. If it's Norks, god help him."

"Norks?"

"North Korean spooks," Maggie answered almost under her breath. "We can only speculate as to how this has happened. Can't we, Andrew!"

Andrew said nothing but his expression of embarrassment said everything. Nathan was in danger. Surely there were friendlies who could help.

Everyone crowded around the laptop, except Andrew who began to pace around with his hands stuck in his pockets.

Maggie asked, "Christina, can you verify a secured SMTP server back to Nathan's emails?"

Christina tapped out a string of commands, then nodded. "IP encryption enabled."

"Reply to Canter's email to disengage, will you please."

Christina opened a new email with the new encryption settings locked in.

charlotte@bya.net; Check airport lost and found.

"No, wait," I said just before Christina had the opportunity to press send. "If I know Nathan, he would've already long ditched his countermeasures procedure."

"That's true, Angel." Maggie said after thinking it over. "It would've been his number one. We have to think more like Canter. What would he do instead of the standard ops?"

I leaned over the laptop and typed.

charlotte@bya.net; Check your travel insurance.

I hit send.

"Good work. If he says, 'no insurance,' at least we'll know where we stand, and we can use Alfa Two Bravo for his extraction."

It only took only a minute for the reply.

canter@bya.net; Airline will on-send baggage.

"Log Canter's IP will you please, Christina?" Maggie asked sternly after stepping back from the screen.

Christina responded and typed out a string of commands. "Hess connected to Vi-Fi via Seoul International."

"That means no Nork watchers," Bosco said.

"Not necessarily, Bosco. Norks are all over the southern peninsular. I wouldn't rule it out just yet." Maggie went back to the laptop. "Christina, see if you can access the passenger manifest of his flight out from Seoul."

Everyone went silent as Christina worked her magic. Nathan was in serious trouble. If he failed to board his flight from Seoul International, it could only be for one reason. He was trying to tag his watchers. To my horror, I realised Nathan was not about to disengage.

After Christina accessed the passenger manifest, she looked up from the screen and shook her head. "He's not on ze list."

"He's not disengaging, damn it! Christina, we need to get him to safety. Initiate Alfa Two Bravo. Extraction priority."

Maggie started pacing the floor then she turned and scorned into her stepson. "Andrew, what the fuck have you done! Didn't I tell you *not* to break his cover! Didn't I tell you to bring him home under code black!"

"Another email received," Christina said loudly over Maggie's shouting.

canter@bya.net; Baggage recovered at Lost and Found.

I looked at the email. "What does that mean? It's not part of our cypher."

"Canter is trying to tell us the Norks have disengaged," Bosco put in. "But I don't like it. They never disengage from an active target. And Canter knows that."

"Christina! Initiate Alfa Two Bravo! Immediately!"

"It's too late for Seoul friendlies," Bosco said. "They won't get there in time."

We stood around the computer. My eyes never left the screen. We waited for updates. I held my breath. My heart thumped in my mouth. Moments ticked by. A blinking lone cursor against a white computer screen. I hoped for the confirmation of Nathan's departure out from Seoul International. The clock showed thirty minutes had passed since the flight had left the ground. Nothing. No confirmation of anything. It was as though Nathan had stepped off the edge of the world and vanished.

CHAPTER FOURTEEN

Mea Culpa

AT 03:44 HOURS, I LINGERED ALONE by the tactical laptop. I sat and stared at the blank screen, at the same time clinging to any hope I had left. A lonely cursor blinked in steady rhythm on a white background. I stared at it, willing it to make letters and words but nothing changed.

Padded footfalls were loud enough to take my mind away from the computer. Jenny appeared at the open door and peered at me through eyes that were hardly awake. She stood there in her new nightclothes and her new fluffy slippers. Her skin glistened from the humidity. "Coming to bed?" she asked as her eyes struggled to adjust in the darkness.

"A few more moments, please Jen. Don't be angry. I need to know if Nathan's . . ." Then the tears.

Jenny came to my side and placed an arm around my shoulder. "C'mon, hon. You need to sleep," she said. "How would it be if Nathan resurfaced and you were too tired to do anything? Put the laptop in sleep mode. The chime will wake you if he sends another email."

I nodded. "Okay. You're right. I'll be there in a bit."

"Besides," Jenny added. "We have some catching up to do if you think sleep won't come." Jenny's face lit up with a wicked smile. She kissed me softly and left, almost skipping with cheeky intention. It made me smile. But how could I get in the mood knowing what'd happened?

* * *

I was still at the laptop as the first signs of a new day began to lighten the night sky. I hadn't moved from the chair. Every muscle in my body hurt but I didn't care. I was determined to be the first set of eyes on Nathan's next email and I'd stay seated there for however long was required.

07:22. The first up for the morning was Andrew.

"Morning," Andrew said as he strutted past me, wiping the sleep from his eyes. "I'm about to make a brew. Can I get you one?"

"I need a cigarette. Got any of those?"

"I can do coffee. Smokes, I don't have. And Maggie . . ."

"Don't give a shit about Maggie! I want a fucking cigarette!"

"Hey . . . You okay?"

I didn't answer Andrew. He had the ability to read my body language. If he couldn't do that, too bad. My thoughts of Nathan began to fade. My hopes diminished, and by that time, I didn't quite know what it was that held me there. I slowly put my hand out for the shutdown key and hovered.

Andrew stepped up beside me, and took my hand, helping me to shut down the computer.

"We'll get those fuckers," Andrew said. But there was no comfort in his words. None. Somewhere deep inside, I could no longer keep my anger from growing into something of a monster. It rose silently like the black, evil thing that it was. I needed retribution.

I needed it, and I was going to get it. The shipping container. That's where I'd go and get my revenge. I desired it like something delicious; something delectable. Payback. Something I could taste, swallow, and enjoy. That evil thing inside me. It lay down swishing its tail, looking up at me with dog eyes, baring its teeth. I gave the thing a pat; said sit, good dog. Now, it's calling me. I'd take the leash out and go for a walk. Meet my evil twin sibling; that horrible dark me that stayed mute at the back of my mind. Not any more! They say hell hath no fury. I scoff. I say, my fury hath no hell!

I got up from the chair and faced Andrew. He stood there smiling as though Nathan's demise no longer mattered. I placed a hand softly and calmly on Andrew's cheek. I echoed his smile. I felt his smooth skin beneath the tips of my fingers.

"What?" Andrew asked me while smiling his sexy smile.

"Your skin is so smooth. You've shaved." I looked at him closer and continued to run my fingers softly over his face, tracing my fingers along his cheekbones and neck. He smiled again. "You're flirting with me?"

"I don't know, am I? But I do want something of yours."

I noticed Andrew's Adams apple bob up and down and I knew I had him where I wanted him.

"What is it, Angel. What?"

"I want your straight razor. I know you have one; I've seen it. Go and get it for me."

Andrew turned and disappeared upstairs without adding another word. Spinning around, I grabbed the pump-action sawn-off shotgun from the rack inside the steel locker. I cracked it open and checked for rounds in the chamber. Two brass eyes stared back at me; a welcoming sight. I was loaded and ready to spit death. I slammed the twin barrels shut at the same time as I saw it. Just what the doctor ordered, I told myself. A nine-millimetre

Beretta in a holster was slung over the door of the locker. I grabbed that too.

Andrew bounced down the stairs as I shoved more shotgun cartridges into my pockets. He eyed me curiously, pausing momentarily, looking more confused than ever. "Angel?"

I stepped forward and took the straight razor from Andrew's grip. I turned without any hesitation and made directly for the back door.

I bounced down a set of wooden steps to where the large paint-peeled and dented shipping container stood. Andrew called out after me. I heard him. I didn't respond. My head was elsewhere. I turned sharply just to give Andrew a wink. Why? I had no idea.

"Don't do it, Angel." Andrew called out from behind me. I ignored it.

I ducked around the edge of the container, oblivious to Andrew's words. I felt my heart pumping madly at my breastbone. I grasped the handle of the shipping container and wrenched it up. The large container door creaked open and I stepped inside.

The inside of the shipping container was *not* as I'd expected. There was a concrete floor and a stairwell going down into the earth. A pole stood next to the stairwell. An electrical box and a set of light switches were positioned on the pole. I threw all the switches one by one and lights revealed my way down.

Below the cold, cold, earth I heard muffled cries coming from behind a main door at the end of a small corridor. I paced myself forward, opened the door and entered.

He was in there; the son-of-a-bitch. He was seated and tied with nylon zip ties into place. I stepped up closer and leaned forward, peering into his blackened eyes. As he made eye contact with mine through his contusions, I noticed he shuddered in his chair.

"Hello there, little man. Know who I am?"

His eyes immediately widened and bulged but he shook his head.

"Oh? Well let's make it a little easier for you to remember, shall we?"

I leaned forward a little closer and flicked my hair around my left ear. "Surely you'd remember that?"

He *did* remember. The guy shouted something from behind the gaffer tape that trapped his voice. I laughed most heartily. I enjoyed my retribution. I ran my eyes over him, smiling at him up and down. I reached out. The tips of my fingers just hovered above the backs of his hands.

I studied his injuries. The bruises on his face. The nose that sat crooked. The cuts beneath his eyes. I could do better. So much better. "No real damage done that I can tell. Let's see if I can change all that, huh?"

Getting out Andrew's straight razor from my pocket, I unfolded the blade in front of his eyes. He immediately flinched back in his chair.

"Let's call it an ear for an ear then, shall we?"

I reached forward and grabbed his ear, pulling it forward. With the razor in my grip, I cut through the gristle and sawed the thing clean off. The son-of-a-bitch screamed so hard, the gaffer tape flew from his face. I laughed at the same time placing his severed ear in his shirt pocket, giving it a pat just for good measure. I stood back and eyed him. Tears streamed from his contused and closed over eyes.

"Uh oh. That looks a little odd to me. I'll probably need to even it up a bit, don't you think?"

The yelling and screaming stopped me from taking his other ear. A moment of weakness.

"What the fuck, lady! You fucking crazy bitch!"

I wiped the razor blade clean on his shirt, choosing to ignore his cries. I brought the razor to the side of his face. I could've finished him right there. But I relented. He flinched back. I decided it was moment of pity. I was human, after all.

"Let's have the location of the Chinook," I asked him. "We both know you're privy to its location. So, be a good little man and tell me where it is. Then all this will go away."

"BITCH! You fucking crazy bitch."

I got my mouth up close to the hole in the side of his head that was once an ear. "THE CHINOOK! WHERE IS IT!"

"Bitch! You'll never end what's gonna happen. Kill me now; just do it!"

"Oh, I will. You can count on it," I replied calmly. "It's up to you, though. Slow or fast? Which way will you have it? Killing you will be easy. Quick, and painless, or . . . you can die with a great amount of pain. Isn't it lovely how you get to choose?"

I stepped away to the corner of the concrete room and dragged a chair over. I sat down in the chair and eyed him; patiently eyed him until his breathing started to slow.

"Tick-tock," I said. "Fast or slow? Which way will it go?"

He looked up almost empty of soul.

"Oh well, this was fun." I shrugged as I got up from the chair, making sure he would see me. I reached into my pocket and got out a set of iPod earbuds and plugged the cord into my device. "Oh. It's for my benefit. Shotguns are unbelievably loud. In a room like this? I could go deaf. That isn't happening."

I pressed play. 'Sad But True.' by Metallica played loud. The bastard sat there wincing up at me. I brought the shotgun over and aimed at his left kneecap point blank. I pulled the trigger. His patella exploded into a thousand bloody shards that scattered, clinking around the room.

I laughed. "Fuck . . . that was loud, huh? And guess what? There's another one of those."

His screams began to chill me. But I pushed on.

It seemed he was about to black out. "This won't do. I'm not done with you yet!" I gripped the warm barrel of the shotgun with both my hands. I held it up like a baseball bat. With a decent wind-up, I stepped up and belted him across the face. His teeth flew from his mouth. "THE CHINOOK! WHERE IS IT!"

He hesitated answering me. Big mistake. An instant later, another kneecap exploded. A bone fragment landed on my lips and I spat it away.

"TELL ME WHERE IT IS!" I screamed and cracked open the weapon, ejecting the spent cartridges. I reloaded the shotgun and pointed the muzzle at his left hand. "TELL ME!" He hesitated and winced again. I pulled the trigger. His hand blew away in an ugly red cloud. I held the shotgun to his other hand, knowing he was moments from death. Time was running out.

"ALL RIGHT!" he finally choked. "Okay, I'll fucking tell you what you want to know!" The muthafucker had the audacity to eyeball me. "Nurrungar. You'll find it there . . . Nurrungar."

I looked down at him. A wave of pity washed over me. I pushed it back and away. I stepped forward and clutched his hair, tilting his head back. He opened his eyes for a second or two and closed them again.

From my holster, I retrieved the nine-millimetre handgun. I placed the muzzle to his temple. I held it there. But I did not pull the trigger. "No," I said. "No neat hole for you."

One last shot in the shotgun chamber. I held the shotgun barrel up to the side of his head, but far enough away for maximum damage. Bosco and Andrew burst through the door. Too late.

"This is for Nathan," I said and squeezed the trigger. His head exploded and disappeared in a cloud of blood and bone.

CHAPTER FIFTEEN

Unity

I HAD NO IDEA WHY I RESORTED TO SUCH measures. What was it that overcame me? It was as though a dark force had taken over and invaded my body, pushing me forward, taking control, getting me to do things I never imagined it was ever possible for me to do. I was never the monster who made violent choices. But now, I cannot undo what's already been done. I must somehow accept the fact that I'm capable of doing such evil, just as easily as I can do things for the good. Just *what* have I become?

The disappointment in Maggie's eyes was something I couldn't ignore. It was the mere act of her turning her back on me that made me feel ashamed. Maggie said nothing. After she was informed about my bloodshed, she simply retreated to her quarters and closed the door quietly behind her. But my shaming didn't stop there.

Xe shunned me big time. His shunning disappointed me, no end. He avoided eye contact and chose silence, much the same as Maggie. Bosco openly belittled me, choosing the words, 'rookie cluster fuck' to describe his disapproval of my actions. Under the circumstances, however, Andrew and Christina seemed to evince some empathy. They looked beyond my act of carnage to see the person behind the choices I'd made.

The truth of the matter was clear. I'd succeeded in extracting the valuable intel from that Guardianship arsehole. Pending confirmation, and eyes on target, I realised the mission to assist the CIA in the US for their stolen Chinook was likely to be scrapped.

Maggie announced that all operations were on hold pending updates from Charlotte Station's parent ASIS Task Force known as Crossfire. As time slipped by, she continued to spend her days locked away in the solitude of her quarters. She came out briefly for the necessities of life, only to wordlessly retreat again. And also during the days that dragged on, Andrew and Bosco spent a large chunk of their time either on their iPads, or on the Xbox. But their laughter and chatter fell silent whenever I approached. Xe, however, came and went as he saw fit, with no questions asked.

During the backlash that never seemed to end, I kept my promise to Christina. I did my best helping her come to grips with perfecting her English skills. Then after a while, I began to long for my former life.

I was tempted to just walk out and leave them all to it. If it wasn't for Jenny, I most likely would've walked out; no matter the politics; no matter the logistics. But in the end, it was Jenny who reminded me of my position and the oath I'd taken to protect and serve my country. I was at odds. Just as I was to decide to stay with it or run, Maggie again changed all my plans.

"News in from Task Force Crossfire. My ops room at 1200."

CHAPTER SIXTEEN

Gloves Off and into the Muck

CHARLOTTE STATION'S OPS ROOM WAS much larger than the ops room I remembered at old Firebird. I entered through a big double door that looked as though it was made from Tasmanian Oak. The command post was filled with cutting edge, state-of-the-art electronic equipment, computers, LCDs, and communication equipment. There were several high-back leather chairs positioned around a large dark timber boardroom table in the centre. A large LCD was positioned on the wall at one end of the table which showed a green background displaying the Kangaroo and Emu of the Australian Coat of Arms. It was obvious Canberra had splashed a truckload of money, with no expense spared.

Maggie was present, shuffling through papers as I looked on. Other members of Charlotte Station filed through the double door and casually made their way to their chairs. No one spoke, not even Maggie. Her expression was serious, I noticed. It was time to get into the game. No more fucking around—In my heart, I knew it was gloves off and into the muck.

Bosco nudged me gently with his elbow as he sat down next to me. He pointed to the LCD and whispered, "That's direct optical link back to Ben Chifley. It's the only way to guarantee a secured connection. You can imagine the labour and cost to install."

By the time we were all seated and waiting, Maggie held up the blue plastic computer disk which I instantly recognised. It was the same disk from Scotty-Blue, who'd expressed such urgency for it to arrive in Maggie's safe hands all those years ago. It was the same disk my mother had slid into my rucksack. It was the same disk which had blood all over it. My mother's. My father's. Even Charlotte's. And also, the blood of all the dead Guardianship soldiers who'd tried to take it back. I wondered briefly how Maggie obtained the disk from Nathan. Back at Busby's, Nathan was always adamant that it was his property, and served only as a reminder of his early years protecting it. I wondered what I was missing.

Maggie then stepped to the whiteboard and wiped it down, then turned and faced everyone. "Some of you know, and some of you don't. So we'll start from the beginning to bring everyone up to speed." Maggie then gestured for Christina to take a seat at an antique Pentium 386 computer. Christina took the disk from Maggie and plugged it into the drive. Maggie passed Christina a yellow folder. Christina opened it, then began tapping commands on the old and aged looking keyboard.

After several moments, the contents of the disk appeared on the overhead LCD. The first page showed an emblem that appeared to be the same as the seal of the US Central Intelligence Agency—a blue circle bearing a star-encrusted shield with an American bald eagle above it and looking left. Underneath was the yellow banner with the text 'United States of America.' In block print above the shield was, 'THE GUARDIANSHIP OF MILE-STONE.'

"Hey, that seal belongs to us," Bosco blurted out. "The Guardianship just can't grab it and make use of it!"

"That depends on which way you look at it, Bosco." Maggie went on to explain that among Guardianship ranks, there existed retired top American officials and more alarmingly, a former US President sat at the top of the Guardianship tree. "Clearly, these former American officials see it as their right to use the seal of the CIA. The only thing that's changed is the text as we see here."

Maggie reached to her console and made a few clicks with the mouse. A portrait appeared on the monitor. I was stunned, straight away recognising who the former US President was. I was almost about to shout out his name. Maggie raised her hand and instantly silenced me. "Don't even think about it, Angel. This man no longer has the right to his former title. To us, he's just one more of those pricks who mean to do us harm. Sad, isn't it? And, he now controls all of Milestone operations. I know what you're all thinking. I'll make it absolutely clear right here and now; decapitating this man from his position in the Guardianship is *not* on our agenda. We'll leave that to our overseas counterpart. Our mission takes us elsewhere." Maggie faced Xe and nodded before returning to her chair.

Xe stepped over to the main LCD and plugged a USB stick drive into the side. On the screen, several yellow folders appeared. With the tip of his finger he double tapped and opened a folder which contained several digital images. "These photos of *Peacemaker* were taken by Canter during his close target reconnaissance mission, while he was embedded with the South Korean 707th."

Immediately, my head screamed the word back to me. *Peacemaker*. Where had I heard it before? Where? Then it erupted in my mind, spewing my memory back at me. The dream I had as a child. Nathan was with me in William Creek when I was sick. I had that dream then. The black man with the white teeth grinning back at me. He'd screamed the word *Peacemaker* and scared the bejesus out of me.

"*Peacemaker* is well secured within the city of Pyongyang," Xe continued on. "Intercepted intelligence suggests *Peacemaker* is essentially an Atlas Five vertical launch vehicle with a modified guidance system."

"That means any continent on Earth is within range," Bosco said.

Xe nodded to Bosco. "Correct."

From the images on the screen, I could tell the Atlas Five rocket towered upward roughly twenty stories high. There were zoomed shots and wide-angled shots. My mind reeled with shock as Xe flicked through the images on the screen. Then it dawned on me. The words Nathan told me back at Busby's were true. Realising it almost took my breath away.

Xe continued, "*Peacemaker* is a thermonuclear hybrid superbomb. The explosive yield of *Peacemaker* is speculated to be within the vicinity of 1.1 gigatons of destructive force."

I was about to react. Bosco butted in "Hybrid? Hybrid to what?"

"Thank you, Bosco. That was my next point. On *Peacemaker*, the deuterium shell has an outer layer to magnify the explosive yield by three-hundred-fold. Helium-3. How the Guardianship have managed to procure the large requirement of helium-3 isn't clear. However, our intelligence suggests helium-3 in a crystallised state is encasing the entire deuterium outer shell. This is something horrifying to say the least. To get our heads around this, let me give you some comparisons.

"Imagine one ton of high explosive. It would be enough to fill a small truck, measuring five metres in length and three metres wide. Imagine the damage one ton of high explosive is capable of doing. To give you an idea, it was estimated as one ton of high explosive that was used by the Oklahoma City bomber. Now multiply that picture in your head by a thousand. Imagine a fleet of trucks that now stretches five kilometres long. We've just arrived at one-kiloton of destructive force. Now imagine a multiple of that by twenty, and we get one hundred kilometres of high explosive. We've arrived at the twenty kilotons, which was the destructive force that destroyed Hiroshima. We move up through the range of kilotons and then through megatons to reach one-gigaton. We now have the equivalent of one *billion* trucks, loaded with TNT. Your fleet of trucks now stretches five-*million* kilometres; the same distance from the Earth to the moon and back by seven times. It's hard to imagine, but here's another perspective. There is now a truck full of high explosive for every one square kilometre of land on Earth. A 1.1 gigaton detonation has enough destructive power to dwarf the asteroid strike of the K-T extinction, sixty-five million years ago. That said, if *Peacemaker* is ever deployed and used, it alone will be the end of all life on Earth. The debris in the Earth's atmosphere will cause a darkness lasting long enough to push into another ice age, and perhaps, even into the theoretical Snowball Earth."

Xe clicked the folder closed, then stood back. "Questions?"

"Yeah," Bosco said. "Seems odd if *Peacemaker* was ever used, the senders of the package would be toast along with everybody else."

Xe immediately responded to Bosco. "It makes you wonder about their motivation, doesn't it? I'll address this in a short while."

Christina raised her hand and added, "This is madness, how can the destruction of life ever be considered as some means to what end?"

"It *is* madness," Xe agreed. "And we'll stop it from happening. That's our objective."

"So, what's the Guardianship's motivation?" I asked. "There must be something behind all this insanity."

"Good question, Angel. Here's what we know. The early intelligence we managed to procure suggests this. It's about oil. Or, on the other hand, it's about not having enough to meet world supply and demand. It's also about world financial collapse. Overpopulation. Also, the never-ending war on terror. Added to this, the runaway cycle of global warming. The Guardianship see all these issues as a situation that requires a means to an end, as Christina suggested. In other words, they think humanity cannot return from the damage humans have done to the Earth; directly, indirectly, or otherwise."

Xe paused, taking the opportunity to sip at a glass of water before continuing. "Let's start with the world oil reserves. It's finite, and as world supply recedes, the addiction to oil will intensify. China currently possesses more than ninety percent of world manufacturing infrastructure. Without oil, China's manufacturing capability will fail, and their economy will collapse. The knock-on effect will resonate around the globe, directly causing other economies to fall. If China collapses imagine the logistics that's required to bring manufactured goods back to the consumer. It wouldn't be possible. Why? Because there are simply not enough alternative manufacturing infrastructures set up to meet world demand. With an end to China's manufacturing capability, world stock markets will crash. So, then what? It's frightening to contemplate. How can a world population survive without ability to manufacture the missing ninety percent of consumer products? What will happen if no-one has access to the items we all take for granted? Shops and supermarkets will literally empty in days. Businesses will close. Transport industries will grind to a halt. People will begin to starve. The list goes on. The result is mayhem and anarchy on the streets. Rioting and looting. The entire world is thrown into a chaos never previously imagined. And all this is just the very start of a very dark picture.

"Now consider the direct effects on the oil-producing nations just by themselves. If they had no more oil to sell it would mean there'd be no income for them to purchase food, supplies, and commodities for their people. Terrorism will strike back. Islamic fundamentalists and radicalised jihadists will put the blame squarely on the capitalism of the western world. We all see the effects of terrorism every single day. Terrorism by itself is a war without an end. As jihadists die for their cause, babies are born into Islamic State and are radicalised from early childhood. It's a never-ending cycle with fresh soldiers to replace those who've died and entered their so-called paradise."

Bosco raised his hand. "That's not a dark picture. That's a god-damn black picture you're painting, Xe."

"You'll certainly think it's a black picture when I'm done, Bosco. What about global warming? This is now accelerating at a pace where there is little chance humanity can change anything. We—humans—have released a billion years of carbon into the atmosphere through burning fossil fuels. A billion years of carbon released in just shy of a hundred and fifty years. Fifty to a hundred years from now, the Earth will have a climate that is out of control. Crops will die. Food will run out. People will fight and die over something as simple as a can of fresh water. The fine balance of Earth's ecosystems as we know it will be annihilated. Added to that, as the world's oceans warm and expand, the waters will swallow most of humanity's coastal cities. All these issues are now considered unstoppable. A snowball effect, running away after each and every day. It needn't have come to this. Clean and renewable energy has been available, and viable, for many decades. It was never exploited nor embraced. With the many trillions of dollars tied up in oil, clean energy was left behind and never truly included. Now, before I go on, let me add that everything I've covered so far was our first school of thought. Our early intercepted intelligence lead us to believe all these issues stopped there. But there's more to this. And it goes much deeper than all of the items I've touched on so far."

Xe stepped to the LCD and double tapped a folder. A folder named, '*The Blue Enquiry*.' He went on.

"The Blue Enquiry began with leaked intelligence in 1996 suggesting a need for helium-3. It sparked interest concerning a genetically modified plant that released helium-3 into the atmosphere. The plant seeds also contained the helium-3 element. Our investigations led us to the location of where the seeds were stored. McMurdo Station in Antarctica. Operation Cobalt Blue, launched in 1996, destroying the seed vault known as Vitae-G. Along with the seeds—the sole parent genome codenamed Hadgitol was destroyed, so no further genetic modification of the Coffea Arabica plant was possible."

"And your point?" I asked.

Xe took a breath. "Thank you, Angel. I was getting there. You all must know how hard this is for me. You all know my origin, and due to that, some of these things are quite uncomfortable to share. As an Oudarretian, and as all Oudarretians are, we require a certain amount of helium-3 to survive. We metabolise helium-3 in the same way Earth humans metabolise complex carbohydrates. Although the required amount of helium-3 is vastly less in comparison, it is, still, a necessity for our existence."

"And what'll happen if you guys don't get the helium-3?" Bosco asked.

"We die slowly. There's no other way to say it. First, our protection to Ultraviolet and Gamma radiation will diminish. Cancer will be the end of us all."

"How much time?" Christina asked.

"Years. Sometimes it may stretch to a decade or two."

"And that tells me you guys already had access to helium-3," I said. "Or you wouldn't have been here as a race for so long."

Xe nodded. "That's true, Angel."

"So, where'd ya get it?" Bosco asked. "Helium-3 is rare on Earth. It's much too rare for you guys to procure in the quantities you'd need."

Before he continued, Xe began to appear a little ashamed. He struggled bringing his words to the surface. "We've had access to the modified version of Coffea Arabica for many decades. Simply put, coffee with helium-3. The Hadgitol, or parent genome I described previously. That by itself has kept us alive. Now, and from the time Cobalt Blue destroyed the seed stores in McMurdo; all Oudarretians are on time they no longer own."

Then it erupted in my mind like a strobe light. "This has got something to do with the *Peacemaker*," I said. "The Oudarretians are going to destroy Earth for the helium-3? The helium-3 harvested from the radioactive decay?"

Xe winked. "We're not going to let it happen. Now, that may seem odd coming from me."

"You're right, Xe," Bosco said. "Coming from you, it's just weird."

"But there's more." Xe put his head down and sucked back a heavy breath. "This is most uncomfortable as you can appreciate. Helium-3 exists in vast quantities elsewhere. I'm talking about Earth's Moon. Everything is geared toward that end. Mining the

Moon of its helium-3 remains the prime Oudarretian objective. The destruction of life on Earth is their number one mission only because they could never accomplish mining tasks with . . ."

"With a living human race," I said out loud.

Xe made eye contact with me and for the first time, I saw tears welling in his eyes. I couldn't believe what I was hearing. The things Nathan had told me back at Busby's were all true. But now, this was worse than ever. I sat there nursing the tiny shockwaves that rippled through my mind. But I also had a question that needed an immediate answer. I stood from my chair. "You people travelled ten thousand light years to mine Earth's moon of its resources? That's hard to believe, Xe. You could've found Helium-3 closer to your home world. So now, that tells me something else. That tells me our tiny Moon must be one of many. So, assuming that's the case, Xe . . ."

Xe immediately deflected. "You need not worry, Angel. We won't let any of this happen. You're exactly right with what you're thinking. The subject of the Helium-3 wasn't on today's agenda. But it seems now, I owe you all an explanation, so here it is.

"In 1961, Frank Drake, an American astrophysicist theorised the possibility of intelligent life within our galaxy. His famous equation leads to the speculation that at least fifty thousand *intelligent* lifeforms exist somewhere in the Milky Way. But the Oudarretians were already aware of this fact before Drake even penned out his formula. Like you, we have become explorers. As we traverse the vastness of space, we rely on the resources we find to get us from one place to another."

"Helium-3?"

"Got it in one, Angel. But, through our journey, all of the lifeforms we'd encountered on other Earth-like planets inhabiting a Goldie-lox zone around a star, were nothing more than what you'd refer to as 'extremophiles.' That's to say, life has evolved in its early stages, *before* becoming the free-thinking intelligent individuals as we, ourselves are. We look for the Earth-like planets that have a moon, or moons, such as Earth. We harvest the resources, and then on to the next. That's how it's been for countless millennia. Until we have the required resources to move on, we cannot continue to explore. Earth's Moon is the Oudarretian target and also their objective."

By the time I had the right words in my head, Bosco cut in. "But what about the Guardianship?" he asked. "They're not the same as you guys. They'll die from the *Peacemaker* like anybody else. Why would they even *want* to be party to this?"

"My next point," Xe put in. "Milestone will begin with the deployment of *Peacemaker*. Then the exit strategy. The Guardianship plans to escape Earth and come back at a time in Earth's future. It will then be the time for the Oudarretians to carry on with their moon mining objective."

"But escape to where?" I asked. I shot a look to Maggie, who appeared equally surprised. My eyes darted back to Xe. I realised for the first time the predicament he was in. Who'd know what the case would've been if we didn't have him on our side.

Xe gave a sharp nod and went back to the LCD. He double tapped a folder on the LCD labelled '*Exit Strategy.*' He began by describing the dark earth after *Peacemaker*. He also explained how post *Peacemaker;* mother nature would begin her fight back. It would take many millennia, Xe went on to explain. And he described the passing of thousands of real time Earth years using the Oudarretian exit strategy; a neutrino particle cannon that was set up to strip organic matter down into subatomic particles and blast them into deep space. On their return, Earth would be theoretically habitable again. "To a degree," Xe then added. "After Milestone, Earth will certainly need more than twenty thousand years to heal. However, after some time has passed, there will be locations that will allow for repopulation more readily."

"Vhere?" Christina asked.

"Antarctica for one. Parts of Alaska and Northern Canada. Also some parts of Southern Australia."

"How many years," I asked.

"Re-inhabitation in the areas I've described may begin after a hundred and fifty years, give or take."

"How in the hell can the Guardianship expect to repopulate with only a handful of individuals?" I had to ask. "I'm sorry. It doesn't sound possible. And didn't you just explain the need to move on? Why even *consider* re-inhabitation?"

Xe smiled avoiding my question. Perhaps he'd had enough of the embarrassment. "I'll hand over to Maggie for this one."

Xe gazed down as he went back to his chair. I wasn't happy about his body language. But I understood, knowing he couldn't be pleased about his origin. Then it settled heavily in my mind. All of the issues Xe touched on a moment ago—the addiction to oil, the threatened collapse of world economies, the runaway global warming, the never ending war against terror. And now, the threat of a nuclear war that loomed and was a real possibility. All of it, cleverly put into place over the last two centuries. I collapsed in my chair, numb to the realisation it would take nothing short of a miracle to turn anything around.

"You have a right to your scepticism, Angel," Maggie said while stepping up and taking over from Xe. "And you're right. The whole idea of Milestone is extraordinary, and yes, I'm aware of my understatement. When I first came to this operation, it took me a long time to come to grips with the data we'd found. I didn't want to believe it at first. That was until we retrieved the disk your mother gave to you as a child. Without that disk, we wouldn't be sitting here now. We'd all be unaware, and there'd be nothing in place to counter the entire situation. We have a chance, and we're going after the Guardianship's Achilles heel," Maggie said while stepping up to the LCD and double tapping a folder labelled *Project Amber*. Maggie eyed us individually, with intense resolve. Her eyes locked on with a sternness that hardened her facial lines. "This, my people, is the Guardianship's highest playing card. It's also their weakest link. Our mission? Find and destroy Project Amber. What is it you might ask? We know of it so far as an immense gene ark. Amber carries all the required DNA for human repopulation. We know the DNA profiles contained in Project Amber are engineered specifically for the purposes. So, Project Amber encapsulates the hopes and dreams for starting a new a new world order. With Amber destroyed, Milestone is effectively, and immediately nullified."

Maggie briefly smiled and nodded to Andrew. She stepped to one side, allowing Andrew room on the floor.

"Project Amber is our target," Andrew began. "Find it. Destroy it. It's as simple as that. But it'll be anything else other than simple. Our intelligence so far suggests Project Amber is located somewhere within the Pine Gap facility. The precise location, however, is unknown."

"What are we physically looking for?" I asked.

Andrew replied while staring back at the LCD. "It's an unknown quantity, unfortunately. As you can see for yourselves, our intelligence has been heavily redacted. So now we can only speculate about Project Amber's size, shape, colour, smell, taste, whatever. We won't know what Project Amber *is* until we actually get our eyes on it. We'll begin by leading close target reconnaissance on Pine Gap. After that, we can begin to formulate our objectives."

Bosco raised his hand. "Yeah, but without further intel, it's gonna be like trying to find a blowfly in a dust storm."

"And that's why we need the Chinook, Bosco. There're at least five Guardianship bodies that we know of, possibly more. We speculate the Guardianship is using digital security to access Pine Gap. Therefore, recovering the digital security devices will increase the chances of finding our target."

"What if the bodies have been cleaned?" I said. "And that's assuming the bodies are still there."

Andrew nodded and coughed lightly in his hand. He took a sip of water then answered. "We just don't know, Angel. We have to play this one up against the odds. We also know there're other security devices the Guardianship is using. Fingerprint scanners. Retina scanners. This is our plan B. Xe has this one covered and it's Xe's responsibility should the plan B become a necessary diversion. At this moment, we have a US Delta team on the ground at Nurrungar. We'll patch in with them shortly. We must not forget; the Chinook is US property. They have the right to recover it."

"And the bodies?" I asked.

"That's why we're patching in. The bodies are ours if they're there." Andrew then nodded to Maggie and stepped aside.

Maggie stepped back in and gazed directly into my eyes. "I'm not going to stand here and lecture you, Angel. You know exactly how this intelligence was recovered. But you also got us closer to Project, so thank you."

Bosco then stuck up his hand. "When do we start kicking Guardianship asses?"

"Immediately," Maggie said. "We're patching into Canberra as we speak."

"Almost there," Christina said, while working at the main computer. After a couple of moments, the LCD went blank and then sprung back into life showing a background with an empty executive chair and bookshelves stacked with books. A steady tone sounded. Then, the smiling face of the Director-General appeared on the screen. He took his seat then said, "Colonel Mack. Everyone is up to speed, I take it?"

"Everyone has been briefed. We're ready to proceed."

"Excellent. We're still waiting to go live with Langley. There appears to be a minor technical problem with the satellite uplink. Our techs are working on it. I'm sure we'll have the situation in hand soon. A moment ago, we had received confirmation of boots on the ground at Nurrungar. At this time, operation Clean Skin is on standby awaiting a go."

"Very well, Sir," Maggie responded.

A female voice erupted from the Director-General's phone, announcing the successful satellite uplink. Christina worked feverishly at the computer. "Ve've established za link to Nurrungar. Ve're live with Ghost Recon. Patching us through."

The LCD flashed. An image appeared showing the dusty surrounds of Nurrungar with the various outbuildings in the background. The video moved around with the motion of the Delta operator's helmet. A few more clicks and the LCD came back in split-screen mode. A second later, the large main screen divided into three, with the arrival of the CIA uplink. Dressed in casuals, CIA Director Petersen stared almost devoid of expression from his office location in Langley, Virginia.

"G'day George," the Australian Director-General said with a very Aussie grin.

"It's fucking 0300 here, Phillip. Let's get this over with, shall we?"

"Do you want the honours? Or shall I do it?"

Director Petersen laughed. "You Aussies are all the same. Just patch the audio through. I'll get this shit started, if you don't mind."

Maggie nodded to Christina. Christina patched Ghost Recon's audio through to Langley. From across the Pacific, the audio arrived without any delay.

"Hardball. Ghost Recon . . . Radio check. How copy?"

"Ghost Recon. Hardball. Five by five. You are go for Operation Clean Skin. Repeat. Go."

"Copy that, Hardball. We are go."

A set of gloved hands signalled the advance of troops. The helmet camera video feed moved forward. The team of Deltas cleared their way across and around abandoned outbuildings, bunkers, and concrete structures. Then the feed stopped suddenly in forward momentum as the Deltas' advance halted. The helmet camera showed several figures lurking. Then the feed slowly backed up as the Deltas retraced their steps, finding cover behind a pile of rusty steel diesel fuel drums.

"Hardball, Ghost Recon. Tangos twelve o'clock, ROE, how copy?"

Director Petersen replied, "Stand by for ROE, Ghost Recon." He suddenly broke off.

I stood tall from my chair. I placed my finger lightly on my lower lip as I stared at the LCD. The Australian Director-General placed his head in his hands, then looked up red-faced.

The video feed lowered as the Deltas went prone behind cover.

"Hardball, Ghost recon? ROE?" The Delta operator spoke with experienced resolve.

"Ghost Recon, Hardball. We need numbers to decide your ROE."

The video moved slowly forward and showed three figures standing almost motionless at the doorway of a large aircraft hangar. Three more figures walked slowly back and forth from a position roughly twenty metres south of the hangar door. The video moved back again behind cover.

"Hardball, Ghost Recon. Tangos six. Maybe seven."

"Roger that, Ghost Recon. Please stand by."

Director Petersen stepped away from his desk, leaving his Delta team in limbo. He came back and sat down again with a glass of water. I noticed our ASIO boss biting down on his bottom lip. "George? What's your game plan, mate? Your guys need your ROE."

"We weren't counting on any enemy contacts, Phil. Rules of engagement weren't specified."

"Are you telling me you sent in special forces with no actions-on? George, you can't be serious."

Director Petersen didn't reply, only his expression told me he'd really fucked up.

Again the Delta operator demanded. "Hardball! Ghost Recon! ROE. How copy?"

"Stand by . . ."

"George! Get in the game or get out, will ya mate!"

I stepped closer to the LCD with an incredible sinking feeling. I glared at Maggie. Maggie echoed it back.

"George. In or out? Don't leave your guys hanging."

A most urgent voice from the Delta operator broke through. "Hardball. Ghost Recon. ROE."

"Ghost Recon, Hardball. Engage the target. Critical stealth; I say again, critical stealth."

After a long pause, the Delta operator responded. "Copy that, Hardball. Critical stealth."

I held my breath but I had enough air in my lungs to whisper, "Maggie, I don't like it."

Maggie ignored me and said nothing.

"Maggie . . . this isn't how it's supposed to go," I pleaded.

The video streamed the Delta's gloved hands signalling to move forward. A lone operator went prone behind a concrete pylon and peered downrange through the scope of a suppressed M107.

"They need to fall back," I whispered. Maggie again didn't respond.

"Maggie. Please."

After a moment, a voice crackled over the speaker. "Hardball. Ghost Recon. Eyes on target, ready to engage."

"Roger Ghost Recon. You're go to engage."

I stepped back from the LCD and looked away, expecting to hear an exchange in gunfire. But there was nothing. I held my breath. I briefly closed my eyes but something else inside me kicked in. I looked back to the screen. I couldn't believe what I saw. The same Delta operator's voice I'd heard a moment ago crackled over the speaker and confirmed what I'd seen. "Hardball. Ghost Recon. Tangos bugging out."

CIA Director Petersen drew a long breath with a hand to his face as he watched the live feed. "Roger that, Ghost Recon. We see it."

I watched on as the figures in the foreground scurried away then jumped into several Humvees and sped off in a cloud of red dust and black smoke.

"Hardball, Ghost Recon. No fubar. I say again. No fubar."

Director Petersen sighed and appeared to relax a little. But our ASIO boss seemed exactly the opposite. I noticed how he bit down harder on his lip. That was a bad sign and I reacted while I remained glued to the LCD. The bastards had left in a hurry. The question was why?

"It's not over, Maggie. Something just doesn't add up."

Maggie eyed me curiously and finally, she reacted. "Get your men to fall back, Hardball. The mission is compromised."

"Negative, Colonel Mack. We're moving ahead as planned." In the same breath, Director Petersen ordered his team of Deltas to advance toward the hangar.

"Copy that, Hardball. Advance on the hangar."

The video showed the Delta operator wave his team past. Moving out from behind cover they advanced with speed. They cut across the dry dusty plane, weapons hot, clearing the area as they went. Moments later, they arrived at the aircraft hangar's towering sliding doors.

"They need to fall back. Get them to fall back," I said urgently.

Maggie nodded and repeated her words more sternly than before. "Tell your men to fall back, Hardball! Abort the mission!"

"Negative, Colonel. We'll have our Chinook momentarily."

I stood rock still with both hands up to my face. My heart thumped from beneath my chest cavity. "Maggie!"

Maggie gave another sideways glance, then looked back at the LCD. "Director Petersen! Stand your men down! Immediately!"

"I outrank you, Colonel. The mission goes forward as planned."

I thought our ASIO boss might use his powers to force Petersen to back down. He said nothing, only watching with stun in his eyes.

The Deltas continued plastering Semtex around strategic positions on the hangar doors. When they were done, they sprinted back behind cover. "Stand by for breach . . . BREACH!"

THUD

The main hangar door came clean off and landed several metres away with a loud metallic clang. The Deltas moved forward through the dust and the smoke. They sprinted into the hangar. As the dust and smoke settled, the video streamed the Deltas silhouetted against the sunlight in a large open area inside the hangar. It became apparent the moment the Delta announced it. "Hardball, Ghost Recon. No package. I say again. No package."

The mission was over. The mission had failed. I knew it in my heart the worst was yet to come. "Maggie you have to do something!"

"It's over! Damn it, Director Petersen . . ."

But if not listening to anything at all, Director Petersen instantly yelled to his men. "Fall back! Fall back! Abort, goddamn it. Abort!"

"Copy that, Hardball. Getting the fuck ou . . ."

A blinding flash bright enough to dazzle my eyes lit up the LCD screen, then, the video feed cut to grain.

CHAPTER SEVENTEEN

Eyes of The Reaper

THE VIDEO LINK BACK TO LANGLEY ended. Maggie stood fixed as though hypnotised by the grey static on the LCD. Andrew stepped up behind her. He placed a hand on her shoulder. Maggie shrugged him away and turned slowly to face us all. "Well. Isn't this a fine piece of shit we're in now?" Without another word, Maggie turned and disappeared from the ops room.

I got up from my chair. Andrew raised a hand, gesturing for me to remain seated. "Give her a moment, Angel. It's been a bugger of a day."

In the same breath, Andrew asked Christina if she could get the *Keyhole Satellite Three* up and running. Christina nodded vigorously and made for the keyboard.

Bosco got up from his chair and made for the door. "You can have this shit. I'm done with it!"

The next to leave was Xe, following Bosco without saying a word.

"Sohn einer hundin!" Christina yelled as she thumped the tabletop with the heel of a closed fist. But after a pause, she went back to typing out strings of commands. Her fingers moved so fast, they became a blur of movement until finally, she sat back clearly delighted with her accomplishment. "It vill be up soon. I promise it."

We waited, not moving, eyes fixed on the screen. The screen flickered into an image above the area of Nurrungar.

"Danke Gott!" Christina clapped her hands and blew a kiss to her computer.

Andrew leaned in and inspected the scenery. He pointed to a section of land that had his interest. "Move the camera there, Christina."

Christina went to work on the keyboard. The camera zoomed down. After a few minutes we realised we were looking in the wrong location.

"Take us back up," Andrew said. "We might get a better view."

Christina tapped keys, and the camera responded, lifting up higher.

I fought the urge for a cigarette, as I viewed what was going on at the computer. But something caught my attention. As I moved in closer to the computer screen, I noticed an area that didn't seem quite right. I leaned forward and trained my eyes while looking over Christina's shoulder.

Andrew came in closer and I felt his presence up behind me. I could feel his breath on my neck as he spoke softly about the situation. Oddly enough, knowing full well the state of affairs we had on our hands, all I wanted to do was push back toward him. My head ran away for a second. There was work to be done, but something else had surprised me. It was all about Andrew's magnetism. How I wanted him, and I was sure, Andrew knew it.

Dragging my head back, I forced myself to re-focus. My eyes went back to the one thing that looked out of place. Another outbuilding, but the colour was all wrong. What I'd seen was much darker than the others areas. "There. Move the camera down on that spot," I asked Christina.

A few taps on the keyboard and Christina had the camera zoomed down. It was horrible to see what had happened to the hangar. "That's what's left of it? Ghost Recon had no chance. What could have caused all that damage?"

Andrew peered in closer, pausing, I could almost hear his magnificent mind ticking over. "I know what happened. The bastards used AGM 114s. Probably more than one."

"What are they?"

"Hellfires, Angel. Air-to-ground missiles."

Andrew stepped back from the computer, thrust his hands in his pockets and walked away. "If that's the case, this thing has just become a whole lot worse than we can ever imagine. If I'm right in what I'm thinking, the 114s came from a Predator. That means only one thing. The Guardianship has access to top military spec weapons. If the Guardianship has access to a Predator, our momentum to Project Amber has just hit a huge roadblock."

"We need the Chinook. If it's not in the hangar, it has to be somewhere."

"Yes, Angel, I know. It's all about that, isn't it? But where is it? We now know it was never at Nurrungar. We're back to square one."

I thought about what Andrew said but somehow, I couldn't have believed it. I saw it in the eyes of the Guardianship soldier before I executed him. He wasn't lying. The Chinook was there. But perhaps not as we'd expect. "You know, Andrew, what if it *was* there but not as we'd imagine."

"What do you mean?"

"Well think about it. If you were trying to hide something the size of a Chinook, how would you do it?"

Andrew shook his head. "It's a bloody big piece of kit, Angel. I can't see it being anywhere else other than in a hangar or out in the open. Both options are no longer."

"Chinook equals hangar, we both know that. Don't you think that's a bit obvious? I reckon it's not even close to any *sort* of hangar."

I had Andrew's attention. He stood there staring at me with a hand to his chin. "So, what're you thinking?"

"I think the Chinook is no longer a Chinook. I think it's in pieces somewhere. I think we may be looking for something in all the wrong places purely because of its size. Maybe it's not about size anymore."

Andrew began to smile. "Okay. Let's assume they've dismantled it. That's not implausible."

"Implausibility isn't what we go on. We work with probabilities that lead to facts. It's possible they've cut it up into pieces, so I reckon we go looking with that in mind. Let's look for something smaller and out of place."

Christina heard and pre-empted what to do next. She moved the camera to different locations above the Nurrungar site. She zoomed the camera in and then out.

"There. Look," I smiled and pointed to what appeared to be a series of shipping containers which were lined up side by side. At first glance, the containers didn't appear to be out of place. There were various objects and debris scattered around Nurrungar that sat out in the open. But now, with a different perspective, the containers were exactly what we were looking for.

"Zoom down, Christina," Andrew asked.

A closer inspection of the containers revealed the absence of desert dust, indicating they'd recently been positioned into place. I also noticed fresh tyre tracks running up to the sides of the containers.

"A little closer please, Christina." Andrew asked and the camera zoomed in.

"There. Look." I pointed. "There's footprints around the area. And that means . . ."

"That means recent activity," Andrew smiled. "And the idiots left an oxy kit behind. Can you believe it?"

"Yeah. That's what they've used to cut the bloody thing up."

"Holy crap, Angel. Holy crap. We need to get this up to Langley, Angel. Most pronto."

"No. We do this ourselves this time."

* * *

It was as though Maggie had a new life to her step as she appeared in the ops room.

We were all seated and expecting good news after what we'd discovered at Nurrungar. I looked around and felt an enormous boost in morale, noticing at the same time, Bosco slouching in his chair while chewing on gum. Bosco's demeanour had changed. This time Bosco wore his baseball cap backward. I wasn't used to it, and it looked odd for Bosco.

"Bosco only wears his cap backward when he knows something's about to happen," Andrew whispered as he sat himself down next to me.

At the time, Andrew's words registered but they weren't important enough to take my mind away from other thoughts. My mind was elsewhere. I felt as though I wanted to ask Andrew how he slept, and did he have a nice breakfast. It was surprising how all of a sudden, I wanted to know more about him. How I wanted to be closer to him. But Jenny! Why was I doing this to myself?

I'd spent part of the night with Jenny. Our lovemaking became rushed and somehow inconsiderate. It wasn't slow and delicate as it used to be. It wasn't romantic and not even erotic. It was over shortly after it started. And then sleep came for Jenny. I lay wide awake, staring up, fighting the urge. It was almost a primal need that was just as much confusing as it was exciting. So I left Jenny's side.

Dressed in nothing more than my white undergarments and a smile, I stepped with speed toward Andrew's door. There, I'd discovered Andrew awake as I quietly entered his bunk room, silently closing the door behind me. Soundless by word, I went to Andrew, and he immediately drew me in, taking my body close to his, feeling his steamy skin next to mine. My body spoke to Andrew, and he spoke back. We entered a new chapter with all the words, sentences and paragraphs until, by the end, a new book had been written in my life. As we climaxed together, I noticed tears in Andrew's eyes. Then his smile. How could I help not loving him? I knew in my heart something had changed, and as I left him and closed the door, my thoughts returned to Jenny. My god, what had I done? What had I just done to my Jenny?

Now, here was Andrew, sitting, sending out his magnetic charisma all over again. An internal battle over Andrew and Jenny began to overwhelm me. But . . . his eyes, his smile. That smile. That chin. The irresistible profile of his face. His hands and fingers, strong and slender, soft—not calloused. I had no idea how I was ever going to recover and come back to being normal again.

Then, Xe bounced into the ops room. His sudden appearance brought me back from wherever I'd gone. Getting my head back, I noticed Xe had brought a large green canvas bag draped over his shoulder. He dropped the bag in the centre of the room, then settled in his chair at the meeting table. Something was in the air. Bosco's demeanour was exactly spot on.

I scanned their faces, sitting there, staring up like a bunch of eager school kids who were bright eyed and bushy tailed. I stopped at Xe, and I remembered the *Star Trek* series that I watched all those years ago. Xe reminded me of Mr Spock. Xe was devoid of any emotion. He said little. His eyes said more than words. And when he did speak, it was worthwhile and to the point. I even wondered if he had *the grip*. I smiled a little to myself at the thought.

There was Christina. She danced around the place as though in preparation for something. She moved quickly between terminals and keyboards, shuffling things, picking things up and placing them back down. She was also smiling and had a new something to her step. Christina, the lovely German girl. Too skinny. Much too skinny. She never ate much; just like a sparrow. She was the only member of Charlotte Station who smoked all day and probably well into the night. Her English was improving, and her intellect was breathtaking.

Sitting there, I wondered about Nathan. Where are you, Nathan Masters? What's happened to you?

After I thought about Nathan, I noticed a bottle of tequila on the meeting table surrounded by shot glasses. On a tray to one side were slices of lime and salt. It was customary to toast to absent friends before deployment. I felt saddened, and my eyes became unfocused as my tears once again rose to the surface. I missed Nathan so terribly.

Maggie came to the centre of the floor and took away my sadness over Nathan "Welcome to day one of Operation Mogul, my people," Maggie said as she smiled brightly. It was such a long time since I'd seen her looking so eager. "Our first mission won't be easy. But it appears we have a leg up, and every bit counts." She then turned and nodded to Christina.

Christina bounced an image onto the main LCD. Everyone sat silent and stared.

"This is an image of an MQ-9 Reaper," Maggie went on. "It's the deadliest UAV of them all. It's equipped with the AGM-114 Hellfire air-to-ground missile and has enough capacity to carry the same firepower as an F-16 fighting falcon."

There was an almost overbearing silence in the room as the news settled on everyone.

"So, our mission is to shut down the Reaper?" Bosco then asked.

"No. Unfortunately we don't have the intelligence to suggest where it may be piloted from. It could be anywhere, even a location outside of our shores. So, shutting it down is not an option. We'll have to accept the Reaper is always looking down. The Reaper is equipped with one forward-looking and two ground-trained IRCs. What makes matters worse, of course, is the heat-seeking hardware. It will pick up the heat signatures of anyone on the ground. If the Reaper locks onto body heat, our operation is finished."

"That sounds like a suicide mission to me," Bosco said.

"You're in good hands." Maggie smiled briefly then nodded to Xe.

Xe stood up and stepped to the centre of the room. He upturned the large green canvas bag that he'd brought earlier. The contents spilled onto the floor. He held up what I thought at first was a full-length wetsuit.

Bosco laughed out loud. "Wetsuits? You gotta be kidding."

"Not wetsuits," Xe explained. "These are thermal evasion suits and will mask any heat signature, making us invisible to the Reaper. But there's a disadvantage. The suits trap body heat. We'll be uncomfortable. We'll sweat inside them. Wear them too long, and it'll be inevitable to succumb to heat stroke. So, therefore, we must be well hydrated before deployment. And we must stay hydrated while using them. Added to that, carrying extra water will slow us down. So, we must develop actions-on strategy to cope."

Andrew was smiling, rubbing his hands together. Maggie was smiling. Bosco appeared determined as ever. Xe was his normal, devoid of any emotion.

"That's a big ask," I said. "Considering the heat down there, we wouldn't last very long—hydrated or not."

"We'll infiltrate at night when it's cooler," Xe said. "But there's a complication. At night, the Reaper will pick up the slightest heat signature. These suits are not one hundred percent protection. They will leak. The Reaper will know soon enough. So, speed and timing is crucial. We'll get to the target, and get out with the package, whatever that package may be."

"We'll need the NVGs," Bosco added.

"Night vision goggles we'll have. Luck is something only the gods can provide. Make no mistake; it's going to be tough. We don't have the intel to suggest if there's Guardianship combatants on the ground. And that's something else to consider."

"So, we can assume the Reaper is in the air at all times?" Bosco asked.

"It may or may not be the case. There'd be downtime. The problem is, we don't know when that downtime is likely to occur. Therefore, we must assume as you suggest."

Bosco adjusted his baseball cap. "Weapons and ROE?"

"We'll have our silenced SA-80s. Rules of engagement have been authorised as echo-charlie engage the enemy at will. We're not about to make the same mistake as Langley. After we find the Chinook, our primary objective is to get us anything we can use to access Pine Gap. Anything we can use to get us closer to Project Amber. The Guardianship bodies. Let's find them. That's the start. We'll infiltrate from the drop-off point, forty-five kilometres south at the position of Pimba and Stuart blacktop. From there, we'll tab to the Nurrungar facility. We'll be issued GPS coordinates before deployment."

Bosco shook his head and stood up. "Tab a total of ninety clicks dressed up in these thermal evasion suits? Now, you know that's not gonna be easy. The amount of water we'll need to carry goes beyond our human capability."

Andrew then added, "It's probably not an issue getting in. We can tab in with the suits in our bergens. Getting out, though, we'll need to dump the suits before we tab back to exfil. But then the Reaper will target our heat signatures."

Xe nodded in agreement, "Yes, it will. I suggest we wear them for as long as possible. Let's do what's possible to get acquainted with the symptoms of heat exhaustion. That way we'll know how far to push ourselves."

Xe then turned and nodded to Maggie.

"Anything further?" Maggie asked, stepping up again.

"God help us," Bosco said. "God help us all."

CHAPTER EIGHTEEN

Eve of War

BEFORE LEAVING DARWIN FOR Alice Springs, I'd spent time with Maggie and Christina in the ops room, as Bosco, Xe, and Andrew continued formulating actions-on strategy. Christina made use of Chantilly's *Keyhole Satellite Three* system, tracking an increased amount of activity at Pine Gap. Various vehicles came and left the facility. Some of the vehicles appeared civilian, others very obviously military, seeming to be mostly American. We speculated among ourselves why this was so, then learned the American vehicles arrived in Alice Springs aboard the C-5 Galaxy Star-Lifters that were always coming and going. But then, almost as suddenly as the activity increased, it slowed down until there was no movement left at all. Now, the place seemed empty. Christina zoomed the camera down to near ground level. She shifted the lens around. From the outside of the facility at least, Pine Gap seemed to be abandoned.

"The place is deserted," I said to Maggie as she stepped back from the computer and folded her arms. "That's to our advantage. I think we should go there now and look for Project Amber."

"That's called complacency, Angel. Don't be lulled into a false sense of security. They're there all right. The question is, where?"

* * *

The absence of humidity at Alice Springs was a welcome change. At last, I could move around without constantly feeling the need for a shower.

After we arrived on the tarmac, my mind began stepping through the entire exercise, completing all the possible actions-on we'd formulated earlier that day. It was as though I was working out an internal puzzle. What to do if this happens? What to do if that? What to do if things went seriously bad? Every possible scenario was thoroughly thought through, played out, formulated and fixed down. If Nathan was with me, I wondered if our final actions-on scenarios would be similar—or would they be completely different? Either way, it had taken five entire weeks of drilling, thinking, sorting, formulating, and speculating, which had brought me closer to the required confidence I needed to get the job done.

And there was something else. I was late. I was *never* late.

At the time, I didn't know whether to laugh or cry, and letting Andrew know he was going to become a father was a subject I jostled with internally. And then there was Jenny.

I'd hurt Jenny immensely even though she didn't show it. After I confessed to her, she seemed to take things on board. Her only reply was to tell me of my need to be a woman, and of the primal urge to procreate which came at a time of weakness. She forgave me. She never had to, but she did. I fell in love with Jenny all over again, and even though Jenny gave me her understanding, I will spend the rest of my days doing penance for my feebleness.

Outside the airport terminal, our black bergens were heaped in a single pile on the footpath. Bosco, Andrew, and Xe stood together in a semicircle, chatting lightly about anything other than the mission. I wondered about having a cigarette. But now being pregnant, I had even more motivation to never again experience the rush of nicotine.

Almost involuntarily, I found myself pushed up to Andrew's side which confused me even more than Jenny's forgiveness. Could it be that I was in love with two people at the same time? Could it be that I'm now officially bisexual? My head reeled thinking about it, and I made a conscience effort to step away from Andrew's side. Then, more confusion set in and I began to feel a hole in my heart. Suddenly, from out of nowhere, a minibus appeared, rushing to a halt, pulling up just where we all stood on the pavement.

Xe eyeballed, then nodded to the driver. The driver got out, then shimmied around the minibus. Without making eye contact, the driver briefly scanned the area before lifting the rear door. Without any hesitation, he then made his way back to the driver's seat.

We picked up our bergens and threw them into the back of the minivan and I straight away noticed something that was hidden under a dark canvas tarpaulin. My curiosity got the better of me. Under the tarp was a shiny olive-green metal trunk with the stencilled words, *CART H K SA-80 5.56 RNR 6*

As I stood there looking under the tarp and trying to imagine the firepower that was left to our disposal, the others had already climbed inside the minivan. Bosco eyed me with an expression of impatience. "Are you coming?"

I was about to get in, but something grabbed my attention. I looked up and saw a group of eagles circling high above us. There were seven of them that I could make out, one of which was all white, and I momentarily thought back to Charlotte and her demise. Then, the ear-splitting noise of turbofan engines landing on the runway dragged my thoughts away.

"Are you coming?" Bosco asked again.

"Hang on, Bosco. Give me a second." I cranked my head towards the Lear jet after it touched down and taxied out from view. I turned to Andrew and asked him, "A Lear jet. Is that strange? For around here, I mean?"

"It's not entirely strange. It could be just some rich guy coming for a round of golf, for all I know. But then it could be just about anyone rich or famous, Angel. Why?"

"I have a feeling. Can we see who gets off and where they go?"

"If we had the time I'd say let's do it. But time is what we don't have. We need to get . . ."

I sprinted back to the terminal entrance, without the chance to hear the end of Andrew's last sentence. By the time I got through security and appeared at the window to look out over the airport, the Lear jet was in the process of taxiing and heading toward the main terminal. It taxied and docked with the nose of the aircraft disappearing just out from view.

The aircraft door swung down and became a set of stairs. Whoever he was—he stepped out dressed in a shiny black suit, the same suit Nathan wore when he was on the Prime Minister's security detail. The stranger walked away from the aircraft and then disappeared under where I stood watching.

I raced over to the other side of the viewing area, hoping to catch a glimpse of the stranger after he reappeared. He stood at a steel door near the entrance to the main hangar. He scanned the area before holding something shiny and metallic up to a device at the side of the door. The door swung open, and he stepped through.

Returning to the minibus, I imagined Bosco's usual sarcasm. But, after I arrived, Bosco was quiet. They were *all* quiet. They all appeared stunned into silence not able to move.

"What wrong? What's happened?" I asked as I jumped into the back of the minibus.

"We've had coms with Darwin," Xe said.

"And?"

"It's started." Bosco blurted out. "This Milestone shit's going down."

"What? How?"

Then Andrew replied slowly. "Detachment 421 reported a subterranean nuclear shot in North Korea. But there's worse news. The US Embassy in Tokyo has been breached and the US Ambassador, with his family . . . they've been captured."

The words pin-balled around my brain before the reality started to sink in. At first, I thought it was another of Bosco's not very funny pranks. I almost expected him to come clean at any second. Now, I felt slow and in a place of limbo. Was Bosco going to 'fess up or not? After everything we've prepared and trained for. This *can't* be real.

"Shit!" It was all I could manage. "By who?"

"Norks!" Bosco put in. "Bet your ass it's Norks"

"What now?"

"The mission goes ahead as planned, but our drop off point is now by Black Hawk," Xe told me. "We're waiting for confirmation back from Canberra, and the details of when a Black Hawk will become available. Time was against us before, but now? We need to destroy Project Amber before things escalate. And it *will* escalate. The capture of the US Ambassador is an act of war, Angel. The Americans are expected to retaliate. *How* they decide to retaliate is the question."

Xe was about to go on when the tactical laptop sounded. He looked down at it momentarily before lifting the lid. Maggie's sullen face appeared via a secure satellite feed from Darwin.

"It seems things have turned for the worse, unfortunately," Maggie said with sadness. "Canberra has informed us that United States Strategic Air Command has lifted defence condition to DEFCON 2!"

I noticed Christina was in the background, smashing her fingers into a keyboard. Maggie's voice then lowered into a sombreness that I hadn't heard before. "Xe, I'm afraid you simply *must* find a way to Project Amber. There are no second chances. We're sending a Chinook from RAAF base Edinburgh in Adelaide. A Black Hawke won't have the range before it goes bingo, so it's the best we can do on short notice. Stay put until the Chinook arrives."

"How much time do we have?" Xe asked Maggie.

"I think a week. Two at the most. The *USS John Steinbeck*, along with the *USS Minnesota,* and the *USS Dallas* have been deployed to the South China Sea. They're pulling out of Pearl Harbour at this time. If Project Amber is *not* destroyed by the time the fleet arrives, there's no way of coming out of this unscathed." Maggie looked down, then she held up something that looked like an official memo. "One more thing. Something a little positive out of this sad situation. The 707th in South Korea received a tip off from an unknown source. They mounted a rescue mission for an Australian citizen who was being held captive in the city of Kaesong. This all went down during the time the US Ambassador was captured in Tokyo."

Oh my god. I knew in my heart it had to be, "Nathan?"

Maggie nodded. "Yes. Canter is now on home soil. He is at The Royal Darwin Hospital as we speak. He has sustained some minor injuries but nothing he can't bounce back from. He'll be back on deck by the end of the day. Now, use this as positive energy to get the job done. Godspeed to you all."

The news was immensely uplifting. But I also thought about Jenny. Maggie cut off before I had the chance to ask after her. Strangely enough, I wondered briefly if it might've been the last chance to speak with her face to face.

Xe closed the lid and slid the tactical laptop back into the top of his bergen. I noticed his hands were trembling. If Xe's hands shook, something had him rattled and Xe never got rattled. I wondered how bad things had become.

"Are you okay?" I asked Xe.

He didn't answer. Like the logical being he was, he changed the subject altogether. "Did you see anyone get out of the Lear jet?"

I nodded. "Some guy with a very expensive suit."

"People who own Lear jets dress in expensive clothes. Nothing strange about that."

"Yeah, but you'd think even for that guy, he'd have to go through security before leaving the airport. Instead, he took out some kind of device and used it to open a steel door down in the main hangar. Who gets to do that?"

That got Xe's attention. "Show me."

When we got there, the Lear jet had already departed. Xe had his nose up to the glass checking out the steel door with the security locking device at its side.

"Do you know about the message that was sent to my phone?"

Xe nodded. "Yes, I know about the message. What's your assumption?"

"Nathan tracked the origin. The message was sent from Alice Springs Airport. You know what? I think it came from somewhere behind that door."

"We'll flag this one for later. We have a job to get done first. We need to put our efforts behind finding a way to the Project Amber. Let's go, Angel. We have little time . . ."

"But what if Project Amber is down there?"

"Unlikely. Our intelligence suggests Pine Gap. That's ten kilometres due west from here."

"I know. I studied the maps. Pine Gap is exactly west in a straight line. What does *that* tell you?"

"You're suggesting a tunnel?"

"It's possible, don't you think?"

"It's plausible," Xe replied. "We'll still need the digital security to access it. Perhaps you've got us a bit closer, Angel. Perhaps you've saved us some valuable time. I'll inform Shilo while on mission. Let's go."

I went to follow Xe, but my attention was grabbed all over again. I looked up from the window. The same seven eagles I'd seen before circled as though they were trying to tell me something.

* * *

We infiltrated by Chinook roughly ten kilometres south of Nurrungar. Without the moon casting its glow, I struggled to see my own hand. I huddled down with the others in a tight circle, waiting for my eyes to adjust. After approximately twenty minutes, Andrew finally signalled weapons ready. The metallic clacking sounds cut through the silence, as we slapped magazines and cocked breaches. A quick coms check and everyone gave thumbs up.

Dressed in the black thermal evasion suits, weapons hot, we began the long tab under NVG to the target area. Almost immediately my suit began to drip from the inside. I pushed on, Andrew taking point, Bosco scanning from the rear. Soon, it was my turn to take over until someone else slunk up to take point. That's how it went. Every one thousand metres, down and scan. Drink more water. Change point. Swapping and changing and creeping through the darkness like a centipede on a mission. NVGs showed the path ahead as shades of green. We sneaked on into the night like a machine; silent and deadly.

Eventually, the sparse and irregular Nurrungar outbuildings came into view under a strange green monochrome. We moved silently toward the buildings, stopping only to check our flanks. Through my NVG, several beams from our laser-assisted optical sights danced around as they made contact with objects in my path. We snuck up behind the first building, then made tactical approaches to the next, and then to the next, and the next.

Xe was on point at the time he put his hand up, signalling a stop to our advance. Everyone halted behind him in single file, then we all went prone, at the same time trying to avoid the nasty spikes of the desert spinifex.

"Target ahead," Xe whispered over coms while giving the signal to approach under critical stealth. We crept on.

We were approximately thirty metres away from the first shipping container. The NVG gave me a false sense of security. I didn't realise how black it was until I flicked the device up from my face to chase away a huge outback moth.

By this time, my TES was seriously hot and uncomfortable. The amount sweating inside was incredible. Every time I made a move, the suit made squelching sucking noises as I moved forward.

Xe signalled to advance near a concrete pylon, and we all slunk across. "Fall back zone here," he whispered. Everyone nodded, giving thumbs up and dropping bergens. We drank more water, then lined our bergens up in a row to create a last resort barrier in case things went bad. So far, the place was empty. But I also knew that things can go to crap real fast.

We snuck up to the rear of the first container and it was an opportunity for everyone took catch their breath. The door lever on the container was held into place with a large heavy looking padlock. Andrew retrieved a bolt cutter from his chest pack and was about to go at it. Xe stopped him. "Wait, we need to secure the area first."

Xe signalled for silence. We all dropped low. With his gloved hand, Xe signalled for Bosco to scout forward. Bosco crept past Xe with experienced precision. He was gone for a brief time before he returned. "Contacts. Six of the assholes in one Humvee," he whispered over coms. But then without any notice, Bosco disappeared again.

My mind went back to my training at Swan Island.

"Fear," my instructor said to all of us in lecture-one. "Fear is good. Fear is healthy. Fear . . . keeps you sharp. Use your fear. Use the energy it provides. If you're down range and fearless, do not stand next to me. I'd rather not have you on my team. Fearless means you're a loose cannon. And we do not do loose cannons on my watch."

Then, the sound of gunfire broke through my thoughts as Bosco engaged our enemy. I was ready to take the fight to them. I was ready to use everything I'd learned. I waited for the command from Xe; he said nothing, only signalled for us to wait it out. Gunfire ceased and everything went silent. We waited in the darkness safe behind cover. My breath shortened as my heart pushed blood around my body. What was Xe waiting for?

"Tangos down," Bosco then whispered over coms.

CHAPTER NINETEEN

Drake Equation

ANDREW AND XE GOT DOWN ON ONE knee at the door of the first container. The head of the bolt cutter was poised, ready to do damage to padlock number one. I crouched down with them—green monochrome images, shining through the NVG. The head of the bolt cutter bit at the hardened steel padlock. Andrew and Xe grunted, putting their weight behind it. After several moments of trying, panting from exertion, they stood up to take a breather.

"Bloody hell," Andrew said. "This isn't gonna work."

"What about a crowbar?" Bosco said.

"We don't have a crowbar, Bosco. If we did have one, it'd need to be longer than the damn container to get enough leverage on it."

As Andrew and Xe got down again and went back to the task with the padlock, my mind returned to the bodies in the Humvee. The dead soldiers would certainly be cause for alarm if the Reaper was in the air. As I thought about it, the scenario went rocketing around my mind. We were all in danger from the Reaper as one by one, the soldiers' heat signature slowly went cold.

With the thought racing around in my brain I went down to Andrew. "We have to make this quick!"

Andrew looked up from what he was doing, breathing heavily. "It isn't gonna be quick or anything close to it, Angel. Why?"

"The Reaper," I whispered. "The Reaper knows about the dead guys."

"I doubt it."

I shook my head thinking Andrew misunderstood what I was getting at. "The dead soldiers. They're going cold. The Reaper will know something has happened to them."

Andrew dropped the bolt cutter and stood up. "Fuck!"

Xe looked up from what he was doing, "Bosco, get to the Humvee. When you get there, take your thermal evasion suit off, and start moving around like a guy that's not dead."

"Serious?"

"Do it. Don't run. Just walk over there."

"Roger. Why do I always get the shit jobs?"

"I think that might buy us some time," I said.

"It might. Who knows for sure? It's a start." Andrew picked up the bolt cutter again and went back to the business with the padlock. He tried harder to break it but it seemed it was no good. He and Xe fought on to no avail.

"Andrew . . ."

Andrew looked up to me from what he was doing. "What's on your mind, Angel?"

"Maybe if Bosco starts the Humvee and lets it idle, the heat from the engine won't raise any suspicions with the Reaper. They'll think everything's good on the ground."

"Good point."

Bosco heard the talk over coms. "Doing it," he responded. The Humvee engine turned over. The sing from the turbo cut through the desert air, and then the engine settled and idled. Andrew went back to the bolt cutter. He and Xe put a massive amount of weight behind it. The padlock was still looking like it was never going to break. "We need more leverage. Look around, Angel. Find something. Anything we can use to get more leverage on these damn handles."

I had an idea. I remembered the oxy kit they'd left behind and I wondered where it might be. But the flame from the oxy would certainly give away our position. I offered my idea anyway.

Andrew stopped trying to force the bolt cutter and stood up almost exhausted. "Okay. See if you can find the oxy. With a bit of luck, we'll be out of here before the Reaper gets eyes on us."

I spun and moved swiftly toward where I'd seen it on the computer screen via the *Keyhole Satellite Three*. It didn't take long before I found what I was looking for. Two gas cylinders sat atop a trolley with the brass burner. I began to drag the oxy toward the container we were working on. Then, I noticed the handles on the trolley were removable. The handles were held into place with simple locking pins. I undid the pins, and the handles slid off. I imagined they would get the extra leverage we needed on the bolt cutter. And it also meant we didn't need to worry about the heat.

Leaving the oxy kit where it was, I brought the handles back to Andrew.

"Good work," Andrew said. He placed the lengths of pipe over the bolt cutter handles. With the help of Xe, they worked the cutter and applied brute force.

With a loud snap, the padlock finally broke free. Xe stood up while Andrew stepped out of the way. The container handle creaked and groaned as Xe tugged at the lever. He pulled. The door squealed open. Andrew peered inside. Nothing. It was empty.

To the next container.

With the bolt cutter at the padlock. Andrew and Xe once again put their weight behind it. Another snap. The padlock shattered. Xe pulled the lever again. The door opened. "This one's empty again! Can someone tell me why they put these here if they're not gonna use the damned things?"

I felt my hopes drain. We had no Chinook and I realised it for the first time—everything might be a waste of our effort. And the Reaper will find us before long.

"Next container. Go," Xe ordered.

By the time we reached the next container, my hopes had all but diminished. Xe had the head of the bolt cutter poised at the padlock.

"Tap it first," I suggested. "If it sounds hollow, forget it and move on. There's still two more after this one."

Bosco came over coms. "Hey guys? It looks like we might have a situation."

"What is it, Bosco?" Andrew said at the same time tapping around the container. As he tapped the metal walls it sounded very hollow to me.

"Radio dude just checked in. Do ya want me to respond?"

"No," Xe said. "Don't do anything. Just make sure you move around. Get out of the Humvee if you have to. Walk around. Just do something so you don't raise their suspicions."

"Copy that."

Xe tapped the sides of the next container. Hollow. He looked up and shook his head, then signalled to move on. I stopped him. "It smells like somethings dead in there. Can't you smell it?"

Xe lifted the NVG away from his face. He put his nose up to the hinges. "You're right. This might be what we're looking for."

Bosco came over coms. "The radio guy keeps checking in. You're gonna have to pick this shit up a pace."

"Bosco. Search the bodies," Xe ordered. "If you can't find anything useful on them, dig out their eyes."

"I already searched them. I found some kind of shiny thing. It's got some seriously strange markings on it. I've never seen anything like it before. But why the eyes? Are you shitting me?"

"Just get it done. Make sure you get a good length of blood vessels. Don't damage them more than you have to. It's my Plan B if we need it."

"Roger that. Beats the shit out of me but I'll do it."

After Xe and Andrew shattered the lock with a bolt cutter that was fast approaching its use-by date, the door creaked open. Xe and Andrew stepped quickly inside. Just as they did so, a pungent stench punched me straight in the face. I covered my nose with my gloved hand as I stepped inside. Several ordinary looking caskets were lined up and stacked along one wall.

Bosco came back over coms. "I got one dead guy's eye out. Now what?"

"I have a cryo cylinder," Xe replied. "Stay where you are. I'm Oscar Mike." Xe sprang away and disappeared into the night.

"Hey! Can I at least ask *why* we need the dead guy's eyeballs?"

"We need the retinas." Xe said over coms. "They'll get us past scanners."

"Nice idea, Boss, but that ain't gonna work. May as well use potato mash. Just sayin'."

"Get the damn eyeballs, Bosco. I'll be there momentarily."

Andrew stepped up to a casket and kicked it over. The lid fell off. A grisly bath of maggots rolled out onto the floor. I turned away, trying to stem the rush of nausea that rose up my throat.

"Angel. Are you okay?" Andrew asked me at a most inappropriate time.

"I need a moment."

I sprinted out of the container and promptly threw up on the ground.

Stepping back in, I looked down at the corpse while holding my hand up to my nose.

"You could've spewed up in here," Andrew said, "This isn't my living room. I hope you kicked some dirt over it. Just so there's no heat signature."

Why didn't I think of that? I rushed back out and fixed up what needed fixing.

After I stepped back inside the container, Andrew leaned down closer to the casket and brushed away the handfuls of maggots. In the casket, under waves of heaving maggots, was the body of someone dressed in a dried-up, blood encrusted, Northern Territory police uniform. Andrew knelt to study the body more closely. At the same time, Xe returned, sprinting back into the container. Xe held up the strange device Bosco had found. "We have our plan A. Also, we have what we need for the plan B if it's required."

Then Bosco came back over coms. "Hey, Boss, I think I need to answer this damn radio. They're starting to freak out."

"Don't fuck it up," Xe responded.

"Roger that."

My attention was split between Xe with his device, Bosco answering his radio, and Andrew searching the dead body. "Found something!" Andrew said while shoving his hand deeper into the dead guy's trouser pocket. Something in my mind told me to stop him. I was about to yell it out, Stop, Stop, Stop! But it was far too late.

CLICK!

CHAPTER TWENTY

Singularity

ANDREW WENT IMMEDIATELY STILL AND QUIET. "Don't move, Andrew. Please don't move," I said as I pushed my hands out to stop him going any further.

"Do me a favour, guys? Get the fuck out of here," Andrew said in a tone I didn't recognise. "Get out, Angel. Go, go, go.

Bosco then came over coms. "The radio dude's freaking out. Suggest we get our asses into gear."

"Fuck!" Andrew shouted as if not hearing Bosco. "How was I so stupid?"

I couldn't believe what was happening. It was the worst of my nightmares. "Andrew. Just stay calm and don't move."

Xe, crouched down to Andrew's side. "Don't move. Don't even breathe," Xe told him as he began to gently probe around Andrew's hand. He lifted a small piece of blood encrusted fabric away from the dead body. A metallic object with a set of wires was well hidden within the folds of the dead body's clothing. "Pressure-sensitive trigger. Old school. But where's the charge?" Xe continued the search around the body, then found a long cylindrical object. He stood up slowly as though he already knew how bad the situation was. Xe then looked for other signs around the container.

It was in that moment I saw the same thing Xe was seeing. More improvised explosive devices were strategically placed around the inside of the container. It seemed the entire place was wired for a massive explosion. My mind whirled. This was now no more than yet another deadly ambush. There was no Chinook, nor was there ever going to be one. How did I get this so wrong?

"Get out. All of you get out!" Andrew said again.

Xe again got down beside Andrew and probed a bit more. "Bosco, we need your expertise on this. Get back into your TES and get over here. Move it."

"Oscar Mike . . ." Bosco immediately responded.

Andrew appeared to hold his breath as Xe probed around him. "Don't hold your breath, Andrew. Breathe or you'll faint. We don't need that at the moment."

I relaxed just a little as I saw Andrew begin to breathe again.

Xe put his nose up to one of the devices. He stood up and stepped back more urgently than before. "This isn't your average," Xe said directly to me. "I know what this is. The charges are rigged with helium-3 We've a job on our hands."

Before I had words to reply, Bosco entered the container. "Shit's about to go down if we don't extract digits from assholes. What've we got here?" Bosco stepped with speed toward an a clearly exhausted Andrew. He kneeled down beside him and pulled up sections of cloth, peering under in the same way Xe had already done. Bosco checked it with expert eyes, then stepped slowly away. "Triple loop jury-rigged. We need to find the power source."

As we looked around, I found the main wire we were looking for. A single black wire trailed away from the casket and through a hole in the container to the outside. I followed Bosco, picking up the wire from the exterior that led away from the container to a pile of rusty fuel drums. We all scratched frantically at the ground with our bare hands and after a while, we dug up a plastic box which contained a motor cycle battery as the power source. Bosco studied the battery for a moment then put it back in the plastic container.

"Aren't you going to do something? Please do something!"

"It's no good, Angel. See the circuit board? If any of the circuits become corrupt, the others will activate. It doesn't matter which way we look at it. Disconnecting the power source ain't gonna happen."

"So, what does that mean?"

"Option one—We'll need to maintain the down pressure on the trigger sensor. We'll need to replace the down pressure with something heavy enough to equal the down force. *Before* he can take his hand away. That's the only way we're ever gonna get him out."

Bosco continued to inspect the jury rig in the plastic box. "I've seen these things before. Damn pressure-sensitive triggers tend to activate even if you try to swap them out. I hate to say it. Fatigue is the biggest threat. It's a race against time."

"We can't give up."

"That brings us to option two, Angel. I ain't saying we give up. We can bungee Andrew away from the devices. It was always a last resort actions-on in cases like this. But even so, IEDs either killed, or they were duds. The chances are slim but we'll work with what we have."

"Great. If the blast doesn't kill him, we'll break his ribs, and he'll die from a collapsed lung?"

Bosco shook his head. "If you think he's gonna come out with a few broken ribs, think again. He'll lose something. A leg. Probably both. Who knows? The few broken ribs are a given, but the least of his worries. If he lives, we'll need to make sure he keeps *on* living. What we need to do is get ready for the bleeding. Shell dressings won't be enough. If we can't get it under control, he'll bleed out. Simple as that."

Xe walked away slightly. I knew he was hard at work thinking of a plan. It was as though Andrew heard all the chatter over coms, "It isn't gonna work! You won't do it quick enough. Save yourselves and go!"

"I'll go and get the Humvee to the container," Bosco said, ignoring Andrew's words. "Go grab your toggle ropes."

* * *

"I bloody-well told the lot of you lot to get out of here, didn't I? You've got what you came here for. Go and destroy Project Amber before it's too late."

I kneeled down to Andrew and gently placed my hand on his shoulder. "We're going to get you out, Andrew. Let us take care of things."

Andrew dropped his head and I knew exhaustion was catching up with him. Droplets of sweat fell away from his chin and the tip of his nose. "You're just wasting time, Angel. Forget about me."

I didn't respond. I began wrapping the fabric that we recovered from the dead soldiers uniforms around Andrew's waist. Bosco ripped more fabric into shreds and passed it to me. I took it and wrapped more around Andrew.

"It isn't gonna work, Angel."

"It'll work. We'll have you out of here soon; I promise."

Andrew looked at me and appeared to lighten a little. Finally, he had a huge amount of padding around his waist and I was satisfied that maybe we'd only break one or two of his ribs. Xe kneeled and helped tie one end of the toggle rope around his waist. Behind my NVG, my tears were already beginning to blur my vision. I was about to save Andrew's life, but at the same time, I was also going to cause him a massive amount of injury. The extent of his injury, I could only imagine. If Bosco was right in what he'd said earlier, Andrew would at best most likely spend the rest of his years in a wheelchair. I owed it to him to give him the news of his unborn child. Perhaps it would give him the strength to fight for his life.

"Andrew. I have to tell you something."

Andrew looked up at me and I could see it in his eyes how tired he'd become.

"Andrew . . ."

"What is it, Angel?"

"I . . ."

Bosco wrecked the moment as he brought the Humvee to the container, pushing the bumper up to the door, switching the engine off but keeping the lights on. For the first time, the headlights illuminated the grisly scene, and also for the first time Andrew appeared to be losing his will to endure.

"We need to hurry," I said.

Xe and I finished securing the toggle rope around Andrew's waist. I decided could tell Andrew of the news after we finally got him clear.

But then, Xe froze into one place. "Stop!"

Bosco did the same but stepped silently to the door of the container and cocking his head to the side.

Xe got up from Andrew and crept over to Bosco.

In that instant, my heart plummeted. The sound of helicopter blades thumped through the silence in the distance. I stood up from Andrew, not believing how bad the situation was getting.

"Stand-to! Stand-to!" Xe shouted, then spun to Bosco. "Tie the end of the toggle around the bumper, Bosco. Move your arse."

Bosco bounced back in and grabbed the rope out of my hands. The toggle rope unspooled as Bosco stepped back toward the Humvee, clutching his SA-80 with his free hand. He stopped just short of the bumper and dropped his weapon. "It's not fucking long enough!" Bosco yelled.

Bosco gripped the rope with both his hands. He was about to wrench the rope toward the Humvee.

"No! Don't pull on it!" I screamed at him. "If you pull Andrew over, the charges will detonate. Move the Humvee closer."

"STAND-TO!" Andrew yelled from behind me. "Stand-to, Angel. Go . . . just go."

"I can't get the Humvee closer!" Bosco screamed back at me. "It's already hard up on the container!"

I put my head down and felt so sick, I thought I would vomit again. I turned to Xe. "Do we have more ropes?"

"No. That's all we have."

"Then we'll have to slide the casket closer to the Humvee. Xe, help me, please."

"Get out before it's too late!" Andrew yelled again. "Take the device and fuck off!"

Bosco ran over and with the three of us at the casket, we began the slow process of sliding it forward toward the Humvee.

"Angel, it's no good." Andrew pleaded with me to stop. "The wire. It's not long enough."

I looked down to what Andrew was talking about. The sound of the helicopter was getting closer and closing in. There was no slack in the wire. Andrew was right. There was no room for any movement toward the Humvee. The wire leading away from the casket to the battery outside was already taut.

Bosco raced toward me and grabbed my arm. "We have to go. Now!"

I jerked Bosco's grip away from me. "I'm not leaving without Andrew. You can go if you want!"

"Now, Angel! There's no time," Xe said as he locked and loaded his weapon.

"We'll get to the battery and bring it closer," I said as I got up from Andrew and started for the door. "If we bring it closer to the container, we'll have room to slide the casket!"

Just as I appeared at the door of the container, the chopper came in hot, strafing shots down. The metallic pinging rang out across the top of the container. Shots pierced through just missing the IEDs. Xe stepped out and fired his weapon in a steady burst as the chopper punched overhead.

Andrew pleaded again but I ignored him. I was going to get him out or die trying. I spun and attempted to run back toward him. Xe gripped me by the top of my arm and dragged me back.

"NOOO! ANDREW!"

"No time for this," Xe shouted at me. "We have to move."

Bosco was behind the wheel of the Humvee, engine revving, waiting to go. "C'mon! Hurry the fuck up!" The engine revved. The turbo spooled. The heavy thumping of the chopper returned for a second strafing.

"Incoming!" Bosco screamed. Xe manhandled me into the back, then threw himself inside.

"Go! Go! Go!" Xe thumped the side of the Humvee.

Bosco stepped on the throttle. The Humvee leaped away in reverse. Dust kicked up as he jerked the wheel hard over, sending the Humvee into a controlled one-eighty. With a crunch, he fought for first gear, then stepped on the throttle again. The chopper came bearing down from behind.

THUD!

It was the sound I never wanted to hear. I spun in my seat. Then the shock wave from the explosion struck the Humvee, jolting it forward.

"ANDREW!"

"He's gone, Angel," Bosco yelled back to me. "He's gone."

"NOOO!"

The chopper came down from the rear, strafing more rounds. Xe immediately screamed out, "I'M HIT! I'M HIT!"

I spun around in time to see Xe buckled over, squirming, blood oozing from between his fingers. I noticed it then. A long green wooden crate on the back seat, jumping around as Bosco drove the Humvee at full speed down the rutted and potholed dirt track. Clouds of dust kicked up from the rear as he forced the Humvee forward. I reached out to grab at the crate. The bumping and jostling bounced my hand away.

"Bosco! There's a launcher!"

"I know. I'm trying to get us to cover. You've got one shot, Angel. It's already loaded and primed. It's not guided so make it count!"

"But you can't slow down if the Reaper . . .!"

"If the Reaper was up there, we'd all be shit-canned by now. I'll get us to cover. Then get the bastards. How copy!"

The chopper came back hot, peppering shots down as the Humvee drove at top speed. The Humvee engine began to gurgle and misfire. Black smoke erupted from both sides of the hood. "Hang on, Angel, I'm gonna go broadside. You'd better get ready with the launcher!"

I gripped tight and braced. Bosco reached to the handbrake lever and reefed it up while at the same time turning, spinning the steering wheel hard left. I felt two wheels leave the ground as the Humvee broadsided in the dirt and rushed to a stop. I reached around through the cloud of dust and grabbed at the crate. I lifted the lid away and grabbed the long, cylindrical weapon. Springing out of the Humvee with my heart pounding in my chest and almost out of breath, I sprinted away for several paces. Bending on one knee, I flipped open both ends of the optical sights. I held the weapon up, catching the chopper in my crosshairs and waited for the shot.

I fired. The rocket shot away from the launcher. I dropped the tube and watched on as the missile got closer to the target.

Without any warning, the chopper suddenly banked left. Chaff and flare countermeasures pumped with tiny explosions out from the sides. The rocket flew under the chopper making contact with a flare, exploding but leaving the chopper undamaged.

Out of breath and feeling the failure, I fell on both knees.

"We gotta get to cover!" Bosco screamed at me from behind. "C'mon, Angel. Suck it up and move your ass!"

Xe heaved himself from the rear of the Humvee, holding a blood-soaked hand to his shoulder. "Angel. Run . . . And leave me here. Go!"

I sprinted to Xe and tried to help him to his feet. Xe resisted.

"I said leave me. Get to cover with Bosco. They're heading back this way."

"You're coming with us, Xe."

"No, I'm not. Trust me. Just get to cover with Bosco."

Xe kneeled in the dirt and placed his both palms onto his temples.

"What're you doing?" I shouted at him.

Bosco ran up behind me and grabbed me by the wrist. "You finished? Get a move on!"

I left Xe and ran for cover, dropping down behind a clump of malnourished bloodwood trees. Spinning around, I saw Xe pushing his hands to his temples using force. He screamed out as though he was in extreme pain. The chopper strafed us again.

Rounds hit the dirt and kicking up dust all around us. Xe again screamed out more chillingly than before. Instantly, a bright blue glow appeared in the sky above him. I watched, not believing, as the glow began to move slowly across the sky, then began to chase the chopper down.

After the bright blue glow encapsulated the chopper, it immediately imploded and crunched down into something tiny. It disappeared from the sky. Somewhere out in the desert, the sound of something metallic hit the ground. I stood there both astonished and horrified as I watched Xe's body slump and fall to the ground.

The chopper was gone. The threat was gone. I moved out from behind cover and ran to Xe. Kneeling down in the dirt, Bosco took off his glove, placing his hand up to the side of Xe's neck. Shaking his head sadly, Bosco confirmed the horror of Xe's untimely death.

CHAPTER TWENTY-ONE

Fallen

WE'D BEEN SHELTERING BY THE DEAD HUMVEE for hours. The first light of dawn broke low over the desert horizon to the east. The stars slowly extinguished, and the blackness of space drew lighter into shades of blue. Another hot, cloudless, desert day was on the way. I sat in the bullet-ridden, pock-marked dust, hunched over Xe's body. At first, I wanted to mourn him. But tears evaded me as I sat silently in the arid, red earth. I placed a hand on Xe's chest to check for life one final time.

Bosco sat quietly close to my side, while doodling in the dirt with a stick. "We'll need to bury him," Bosco said sadly. It was the first time I heard Bosco speak with such sadness. I didn't know Bosco had it in him to be sad, but there he was.

Already, flies were doing steady work on Xe's body. I swished them away as best as I could. "It's not over, Bosco. There's a job to do. They might've thumped us this time. They won't get a second round."

"Yeah, I know," Bosco said, as he stared vacantly into the distance.

I eyed him, frowning a little. "You sound like you've given up."

"It's just me and you left in this. Without Canter, Andrew and now Xe, we have ourselves a shit of a job getting to Project Amber in time. I don't know where *Steinbeck* is right now. If she gets to the Sea of Japan, Angel. If she exchanges ordnance with North Korea . . ." Bosco shook his head, pausing a beat. "Anyway. I'm sure you know the consequences if that shit starts to go down."

"That shiny thing will get us there," I said, casting my eyes over the chrome metal object.

"Yeah. I'm not sure why we need those eyeballs, though. Using them for retina scanners seems too ridiculous for words."

"Xe's plan B?"

"Yeah. How in the heck would a plan like that work? You and I both know there needs to be blood supply to the retina before it can possibly be scanned."

Bosco got up and dusted himself down. "I wasn't in the loop with Xe's plan B. Only Andrew. But he's also gone."

I looked away to the horizon, thinking I'd heard something low and thudding. It was faint, and only just audible. Thinking it was just the wind somewhere out there, I put it to the back of my mind.

"We'll need to check in," Bosco said. "For that to happen, we'll need to tab back and get Xe's tactical laptop from his bergen."

The thought of going back was a hard prospect to consider. The first thing I thought about was Andrew. Going back there, I'd need to see him a final time. But I also knew his physical body was gone. What made matters worse was the thought of Andrew not knowing about becoming a father. It almost brought me tears. I caught myself involuntarily placing a hand on my belly thinking of him. Then, for some reason, I smiled at the thought of Andrew's DNA growing inside me. It confused me a little, having that feeling. But it was something I couldn't have helped even if I tried. A smile, when I should've felt nothing but loss and bereavement.

I gazed down at Xe's body while swishing more flies away. "What was that thing he did?"

"Oudarretians do it sometimes. It kills them, though. Xe didn't die from his wound. He didn't die from blood loss. He died giving his life up for us, Angel."

"What? Some kind of telekinesis or something?"

"No . . . Nothing like that. Oudarretians are connected to the universe in ways we only get to imagine."

"So, what did he do, exactly? That blue glow in the sky. And where did that chopper go? It looked like some kind of implosion."

"That's because that's exactly what it was. An implosion. Xe opened a time and space singularity. A point of condensed universe."

"An event horizon?"

"You've been reading science mags."

"I'm a journalist. I read everything."

"You *were* a journalist . . . And yeah, something like that. But it is what it is. The moment the chopper went into the singularity, the forces of the condensed universe destroyed it. I've only ever seen an Oudarretian singularity once before," Bosco said eyeing me with intense resolve. "C'mon. Let's get our asses into gear. It's a long way back, and these suits are gonna kill us if we have to spend daylight hours in them."

Bosco stepped toward the rear of the Humvee and retrieved a small spade. "We don't have the time to bury Xe's body. But we'll bury the shiny thing and the cryo cylinder for safe keeping. We'll grab it back after we make contact with Charlotte Station."

We walked to the edge of a clump of bloodwood trees. Bosco put the spade into the earth and grunted as it made little impact in the dry dirt. As he dug, that faint noise in the distance I'd heard earlier, cut louder through the desert silence. Now, I was sure about what the sound was. It was the steady thumping of rotors.

Bosco stood up, immediately cocking one ear in the direction of the sound. "We gotta move again. This shit ain't over! Quick. Back to the Humvee and get under it for cover."

"No, Bosco. If they decide to blow it up, we're done."

I got Bosco by the arm and pulled him down. We both went prone behind spidery arms of large tree roots that seemed to be screaming for water. I tasted the gritty dust between my teeth as I hit the ground.

Together we watched as the chopper came in closer. The thumping increased as dust blew up in the wind. It came in low, and hovered near the dead, bullet-riddled Humvee.

"Black Hawk," Bosco said loudly over the noise of rushing turbofan engines. "Maybe our exfil. Maybe friendlies. There's no aggression yet. That's something at least."

The wheels slowly padded the ground and the noise of the engines spooled down. The rotor slowed, and the dust began to settle.

"If not friendlies, we're prisoners, Bosco. There's no hiding from this. They'll find us soon enough."

"Yeah," Bosco smiled. "Let's pin our hopes up on exfil then, huh?"

The Black Hawk rotor blades finally stopped. The desert was silent again. The cockpit window slid open, and a voice called out. "Operation Mogul! Are you there?"

I wanted to sit up at the sound of his voice. I couldn't believe my ears and I fought through the urge to get up and run to him. The voice, I recognised. Unmistakable. Distinctive.

"Operation Mogul! Do you copy?" he called out again. "Are you gonna get your arses over here or what? Time's wasting."

Bosco shot me a sideways glance. He was about to get up. I dragged him back down.

"Hold on a second. We don't know exactly who they are just yet. It might be another trap."

Over at the Black Hawk, the door slid open, and someone stepped out onto the dirt. He walked around with a slight limp, the same as Nathan did. He was wearing dark sunglasses and a baseball hat, and he also had a full beard.

Nathan hated beards. He'd never grow one. He always said a beard got in the way of things. I remember I asked him once, what he meant. He just laughed. He said nothing else. So, I never asked him again.

The figure with the sunglasses, baseball hat, and full beard walked over to the Humvee. He poked around, while the pilot dressed in desert fatigues and aviator's helmet stepped out from the helo's cockpit door. The two had words out of earshot.

The figure that walked around and sounded like Nathan did a whirly sign above his head with the point of his finger. The pilot echoed the gesture in response, then went back to the Black Hawk. Moments later, the engines came to life and began to spool up.

"Angel, they're about to leave. Can't you see that's Canter over there?"

"Maybe it is, maybe it isn't. The beard tells me maybe it isn't."

"Are you shitting me? How would he know about Mogul if he ain't Canter?"

I wanted to believe Bosco. I wanted to believe it *was* Nathan. The sunglasses, hat, and beard made it difficult. If it was the enemy, there'd be no escaping. How would I know for sure without giving up our position? But my head wanted to know, one way or another.

I called out and immediately the unnamed man spun around and began to walk over toward us.

"Halt, stand still!" I yelled as he got closer. To my surprise, he stopped as instructed, and for some reason put up his hands.

"We're armed," I said. "Turn around."

He did what I asked without question.

"Get on your knees."

He began go down on his knees. He hesitated.

"On your knees!" I yelled again.

"I'm doing it, Angel. My leg, remember? And I know you don't have your weapons. We already retrieved them from where you left them. And your bergens. And the tactical laptop. Do you want me to go on?"

Bosco and I got up off the dirt in synchronicity to each other.

"Nathan Masters! As I live and breathe," Bosco called out with a big cheesy grin on his face. Nathan got up from his knees to face us. I cut my way past Bosco. I felt as though my face was on fire. I paced toward Nathan, fists clenched, gritting my teeth. Nathan held out his arms toward me with his usual smile on his face. A few seconds later, he was flat on his back, and I was shaking the hurt away from my hand. "Fucking do that to me again, I'll kill you myself," I screamed at him, then promptly burst into tears.

CHAPTER TWENTY-TWO

The Eyes Have it

"I CAN'T GET MY HEAD AROUND HOW you managed to find us out here," I said to Nathan.

Nathan pointed a finger in the air. "Look up and smile to Christina. She had your back. Pity Xe didn't check in. Things might've turned out differently. We also managed to kill the Reaper. We found where it was piloted and shut that shit down. The drone crashed somewhere in the desert. If we could've established communications with you, we would've. Xe stepped outside protocol. The reasons aren't clear—we'll never know now. Maybe he stuffed up. Maybe not. Maybe he decided it was too risky to check in. Now Andrew's gone. Maggie's beside herself," Nathan paused, then added, "Things are about to happen, and I'm talking about worldwide catastrophic events."

"There was so much coming down on us—there was no time to check in. Things got all out of shape. We had no actions-on for what happened back there."

"Nonetheless, you managed to do well under the circumstances. The shiny thing. And the eyeballs in the cryo cylinder. It's a major step in the right direction."

"You know what that thing is?"

"The shiny thing? Yeah. I know exactly what it is."

I waited for an explanation, but it wasn't going to come without applying additional pressure.

I gave Nathan my eyes.

He relented. "It's a microwave emitter," Nathan explained. "It's as simple as that. Nothing more. Nothing less."

"And?"

"They're used to disengage the locking mechanisms that are using the microwave wavelength." Nathan then flipped the shiny thing over and studied it. "The markings are the Drake equation. But they're just for the sake of decoration. It seems a little odd but I get it."

I looked at Nathan using my best blank stare expression. It made him chuckle.

"Xe said there was a plan. For the eyeballs, I mean. They're to be used to get past retina scanners. Bosco seems to think it's a waste of time. He says the eyeballs won't work without blood circulation. I can see what he's on about. They aren't going to work, are they?"

"One—There *is* a plan. Maggie briefed me before getting down here. Two—They *will* work."

"How?" I asked. "They need to be in someone's head to get blood circulation, don't they?"

"Absolutely," Nathan nodded, then grinned. "But . . ."

"You're not gonna tell me something crazy like transplant, are you?"

"A full eyeball transplant has never been done before. Not successfully anyway."

"That's good. I thought the idea was crazy."

Nathan then added something I wasn't expecting. "A full eyeball transplant has been attempted before, and full blood supply was successfully re-established. The problem is the reconnecting and regrowing the optic nerve. Medical science hasn't got that far."

It was enough for me to raise an eyebrow. "You're seriously thinking transplant?"

"Yeah. But not as you might think. The plan is to get them surgically implanted. But . . ."

"But what?"

"Not in your head."

I gave Nathan another of my blank stares. "What do you mean, not in your head? Is it a transplant or is it not?"

"As I said. Implant—not transplant. You get to keep the eyes you have, but we have to supply blood circulation to the implants so they work with retina scanners."

I couldn't help falling back slightly. My legs weakened beneath my weight and were threatening to collapse.

"Relax, Angel. It's temporary. They'll be removed at the first opportunity."

"Okay. So, where are we supposed to have these . . . implants?" I thought about trying to close my ears, so I didn't have to listen to anymore. My imagination ran away and there was nothing good in the pictures I had in my mind.

"On our wrists; like wearing a wristwatch."

"And who, may I ask, gets to get one of these bloody eyeball wristwatches?"

"Well that depends."

"On what?"

"It depends on how many good ones we have in the cryo cylinder. Knowing Bosco, he'd probably butchered some of them. If they're all good, then we all get to have one."

I looked away stemming the rush of bile in my throat. After a moment, Nathan added more to this grotesque set of circumstances. "It's for the . . ."

"Don't even go there with that 'greater good' crap. I'll do what has to be done. I don't have to like it, though. But if that's the plan, I'm assuming we need a surgeon?"

"Yeah. Soon enough."

"I bet Bosco doesn't get an eyeball wristwatch."

"Yeah, he will. We need to play this one up against the odds."

Nausea attacked me again. I leaned forward slightly with a hand on my abdomen, trying to get fresh air into my lungs.

"You good?" Nathan asked just as I felt I was going to be sick.

"Just the thought of someone's eyeball looking up at me. It seriously grosses me out."

Nathan nodded his reply, then turned away. I couldn't hold on to it any longer. I reached out and gripped Nathan's shoulder before I promptly threw up.

"You're *not* good. I wouldn't have thought this idea would make you sick to your stomach. Like I said, it's temporary." Nathan eyed me up and down. I hadn't seen his expression of compassion in so long. I was beginning to think Nathan wasn't Nathan anymore. "You need to get out of that TES and get some hydration back. There're some fatigues in the back of the helo. They may not fit you as you'd like, though."

* * *

Nathan looked down at the body of Xe before zipping up the body bag. "He was a good man, Angel. He was one of them, but in the end, we all considered him a brother. Such a shame he had to go this way."

I was angry. I tried hard to keep it in check. But there were things that needed to be said. "You know what? I'm sick of you keeping things from me. Why didn't you just tell the whole truth from the start, when we were back at Busby's?"

"I keep telling you, Angel. There're things I can say. And there are things I can't. What would you have done if I told you he was Oudarretian?"

"I wouldn't have believed you. I would've thought you were crazy."

"And you would've walked out on me, right there."

"Yes that's true."

"And you wouldn't have gotten yourself to Tullamarine."

"No."

"And you wouldn't be pregnant."

"How did you know?"

"Maggie told me."

"Maggie? I never said anything."

"Maggie knows everything. And congrats, Angel. I never would've thought . . ."

"Yeah, but Andrew . . . It's not fair."

I adjusted my desert fatigues that were three sizes too long for my limbs. But even so, I was glad to do away with the thermal evasion suit that was wet through with my perspiration.

With the help of Bosco, we heaved Xe's body into the Black Hawk and placed it gently down, next to another body bag that appeared to be much lighter, and much smaller.

"Andrew's remains," Nathan told me out of respect and empathy.

I stood over the body bags feeling extremely saddened. Reaching out with a trembling hand, I hovered lightly over Andrew's body bag and remembered all the good things that Andrew stood for. My mind also replayed all of the happy times I shared with him. I never knew him for very long. Now I wished I had spent my life with him. I did love Andrew. And it was with all my heart. It was exactly the same love as I have for my Jenny. I was sure of it now. It is indeed possible to be in love with two people at the same time. Looking down at Andrew, this was the proof.

Taking a seat, the Black Hawk's engines slowly came to life and began to spool up. Bosco looked at me with a glum expression that I'd never seen on him before. For a second, it wasn't Bosco at all. Just for a second, I thought I was sitting opposite a complete stranger. Then I realised that these hardened men of war have feelings like any human. Yes they're hardened from the things they've seen and done. Bosco was no exception. There was a place and time with combatants to let their true self come to the surface. Perhaps now, it was time for Bosco.

As the Black Hawk lifted away, Nathan grabbed a set of head-phones off the rack behind him and gestured for me to do the same. After we plugged in, it became easier to communicate over the noise of the Black Hawke. Bosco produced a packet of gum and offered it around. I waved it away with thanks. Nathan took some with a nod and placed them between his teeth before beginning to chew. Bosco bit the packet of gum and forced a few pieces into his mouth. He then reached into his bergen for his blue base-ball cap with 'NY' in white letters embossed across the front. But then, Bosco straight away placed it on his head backward. He eyed Nathan with a sort of expression that told of his frustration. The gum chewing, the hat turned backward, I knew that Bosco wanted to get back into the fight. He wanted blood. That was his sign.

"Bosco," I called out over coms, as the Black Hawk lifted higher into the air. "You're a good man, Bosco." Why I said it, I had no idea. But as I looked, Bosco's blush was something that only comes once in a lifetime. I smiled wider. He blushed more. Then we both broke out into fits of laughter. The laughter was something I needed. And I think it was something Bosco needed as well.

After a few moments, the Black Hawk veered left and headed south, high over the position that had seen bloodshed only hours previous. I looked out of the window and saw for the first time how much damage was done to the container. It was no longer the shape of a brick. It was warped up and domed at the top, the sides were twisted out of shape and distorted. Black soot was spattered all over the ground. It sat twisted and askew, like some kid had made it out of plasticine. I realised then that even if we could've pulled Andrew out of the container, he was already dead. The blast radius would most certainly have killed *all* of us. Andrew, at his final moment, had managed to save the lives of his comrades. With the thought, I found myself again involuntarily placing my hand over my abdomen. Then I realised, like Maggie, Andrew probably knew.

The Black Hawk pitched left again and headed exactly southeast. Within a few moments, we passed over the white, salty vastness of Lake Eyre. I looked out and sighed, then met Nathan's stare. He, too, now had an empathetic expression, with his head slightly tilted to the side. I wondered what he might be thinking about. Nathan was so complicated. And then, due to his stubborn secrecy issues, maybe I'd never know.

"Mind telling me where we're going?" I finally shouted, probably a bit too loud in the microphone. Both Bosco and Nathan simultaneously winced.

"We're first going to stop off at 4 Military Hospital," Nathan said. "Andrew and Xe will start their journey north from there.

After that, we'll make our way to Adelaide repat, where we have an appointment with an ophthalmologist."

I gulped at the hard lump that had formed my throat. Suddenly, it became real. I'm going to have some arseholes eye implanted somewhere on my body.

"I thought we were going to check in with Shilo." They were the only words I could come up with. I needed to know if Jenny was alright. I needed to urgently speak with her. I needed to . . .

Nathan responded by words that were way too loud. "You can if you want. It's a bit noisy, though. You might like to wait until we get on the ground."

I nodded my agreement but I didn't like it.

"When was the last time you guys ate something?" Nathan asked.

"Roughly eighteen hours."

"That's good. In that case, we should be able to go straight into surgery!"

CHAPTER TWENTY-THREE

Holiday

THE BLACK HAWK TOUCHED DOWN on the main helipad at Adelaide Repatriation Hospital. We were met there by a team of doctors who were dressed in the white garb all doctors get around in. But also, as we left the Black Hawk, we were treated as though we were all high-profile patients. After being whisked away on wheelchairs - which was quite odd considering our legs were capable of taking us anywhere we needed to go - we then found ourselves on gurneys, then taken down corridors, elevators, and more corridors, until we arrived at a darkened and empty ward.

Finally, an army officer bearing a peaked cap with the insignia of the snake going up a pole, stepped into the ward. He quickly introducing himself as Captain Bryan Holiday. Then, he stepped back slightly and appeared to hold his breath. After a few seconds, he relaxed a little.

"Are you okay?" I asked Doc Holiday.

"Yes, I'm fine thank you. Let's begin, shall we?"

There were the normal formalities and paperwork to sign, then we were off to pre-op. By the time we reached the operating theatre, I really couldn't have cared less about anything. The lights were so bright. Doc Holiday's face faded from my memory. Then came the dream.

* * *

I found myself drifting to another place. A place where I'd never been before.

Where am I?

While on my back, I looked up at a solid circle of bright orange light. The light pierced my skull and made my brain throb, forcing me to squint and to look away. I was forced to try and cover my eyes, but my arms . . . they didn't work. I tried again. My arms were . . . tunas that were floppy and dead. There was no feeling. They were just there.

Where am I?

I squinted, gazing into a cloudless deep blue sky. Deep blue, like nothing I'd seen before. Deep blue like the deepest oceans on Earth. I lifted my head. I managed only a couple of centimetres. I was just able to see the tops of my toes. I relaxed, knowing my body was all there. But the tunas! I still couldn't move those tunas. They were floppy, motionless, dead about my sides, heavy and lifeless.

What is this place?

The ground. Red. Dusty. Dry. Hot. The light beat down from a disk too bright to see. It hurt. I winced again. It wasn't enough. Then wind. Slight at first. A cooling breeze pushed up against my face. Then, the sound of something in the distance, racing up toward me. The galloping sound of hooves pounding the ground. With the sound, the laughter of a child echoed through the valley, as the hooves pounded closer. Suddenly, the sound stopped. I looked up with a squint. It was a horse, but no, it couldn't be. I focussed my eyes on the beast which was supported by one leg at the front; one leg at back.

"Mummy! Get up, Mummy. Poppet wants to play."

I tried to speak.

"Mummy. C'mon," the little girl with bright red flowing hair said, looking cheerful sitting on her strange beast thing. I tried again.

"Ada . . . Adakol."

It didn't make any sense.

"I know, Mummy. You gave me my Adakol. C'mon. Poppet wants to play!"

My arms . . . tunas hurt trying to move them.

Then, an eagle cried in the distance. The sound of it drilled through the sky. Instantly, the girl who called me Mummy galloped away. She giggled, riding off to the sound of belting twin hooves.

This place. Where am I?

The land, deep red in contrast to the dark blue at the far horizon. I managed to move. I got up on an... elbow. A fish spine. The fish spine bent. It hurt all over again with sharp spears of electricity that went straight through my left eye socket. The eagle cried and hovered and soared high above towering red craggy peaks—the shape of upturned cones. Then there were seven. Seven eagles, one of which was all white.

Where did I see those eagles before?

Then, the first white-hot shot of pain drilled deep into my forearm. White-hot and unbearable. The pain drilled. The tuna's head. Or was it tail? I lay back down, wincing away from that bright yellow glow beating down. The music started to play in my head. The whooshing. The beating. A helicopter's blades in slow motion, whooshing high above me. I'd heard that sound before.

The Movie. Apocalypse Now . . .

Whooshing in slow motion like a ghost helicopter flying over. The sound of a Fender electric guitar sprang to life. A sound, all of its own—unmistakable. Someone was looking down at me. A face, all I could see. I saw the outline of an old man with deep facial wrinkles. Black and white feathers dangled from the end of interwoven braids. Another white-hot spear of pain drilled into my tuna. The tuna alive, looked up and started to sing.

. . . this is the end . . . Beautiful friend . . .

* * *

I awoke with a serious feeling of vertigo, and with a big, puffy, white pad wrapped on my forearm. Nausea. Oh no. I placed a hand up over my mouth, fighting and uncontrollable sickness. My eyes were foggy and everything swam. As I gained focus, a nurse stood beside me swabbing my sickness away. Then, wordless, she stepped away and was gone.

A few hours into the day, with a small packet of Panadol Forte and repeat prescriptions of antibiotic, I finally met up with Nathan and Bosco, who were both wearing the same big white pads over their forearms. They also appeared groggy and suffered the same symptoms. I wondered oddly if I looked as bad as they did. The dark circles around their eyes. I stood there with Nathan and Bosco, bandages over our forearms, pondering what might be lurking beneath.

"No time to waste. Are we all good to go?" Nathan asked.

Bosco gave thumbs up. I went to acknowledge Nathan, but the nausea was intense and relentless. I was horrified and struggled for composure. Then I projectile vomited.

It was the 'oh no' look Nathan gave me that sent me into a panic. I needed to sit down and get things under control. Taking a seat, I held my hands up to my mouth in the hope of keeping things down.

"I feel terrible. I'm sick all the time."

Nathan grabbed a napkin from a hospital chest of drawers be-hind him and offered it. "Angel, I think you need this."

"Oh shit! You know, I rue the day you talked me into all this. What a mess I'm in right now."

I did my best cleaning myself up. A few moments later, Doc Holiday arrived in the ward. The doctor leaned forward looking down at me. He checked my pupil dilation and I wasn't sure why he did that. Then, he slightly lifted the bandage on my forearm and quickly glanced under. Grinning wide, Doc Holiday took a step back in time to avoid another sudden violent wave of nausea.

"Doc," Nathan said, "What's this all about?"

"It'll pass. It's a reaction to the anaesthesia. Nothing major."

If things weren't bad enough, a hypodermic needle into my shoulder was just what the doctor ordered.

"How long, Doc?" Nathan asked him. "How long will this go on for?"

I wanted to say something but I couldn't. I did the universal sign language for pen and paper. Nurse somebody understood and quickly got me something to write on. I took it and started scrawling. After I finished writing down what needed to be said, I held it up. "I want this fucking eyeball off me!"

Nathan ignored my message and cut me off. "Doc, how long?"

"Could be a couple of hours. A day at the most. It'll pass. I don't think there's cause for alarm. But it'd be different if she was pregnant."

I fainted.

* * *

I woke up again and found myself back in the ward, just as Nurse Somebody was speaking with Nathan. "I'm guessing by the nature of this operation you guys are in urgent need of being elsewhere?"

Nathan nodded his reply to Nurse Somebody. "Time is luxury and something we don't have."

"Take the pads off in the morning, not before. We don't want any bumps. And . . . you'll need to prepare before you see what you have on your arms. It's a medical miracle, if you want my opinion." Then she turned and disappeared from the ward.

* * *

"Nathan Masters, you might want to come and take a look."

We were in the C-130 Hercules transport out from RAAF Base Edinburgh, heading for Darwin when Nathan was given the message. He disappeared for several moments before returning to his seat, opposite Bosco and me. I knew something was wrong. I could see it in his complexion that had drained of colour. Bosco must've felt it as well. He immediately spun his baseball hat backward. Then, Bosco began jiggling his left leg up and down.

Nathan looked down at the floor and rubbed his hands together. Something had him rattled. If Nathan got rattled, it was serious. Now I wondered what in the heck was wrong.

Just as I was about to ask, Nathan spoke without any prompting. "The US Ambassador to Japan is dead. He and his family were executed this morning."

". . . Fuck!" Bosco shouted. He took his hat off and threw it to the floor. I felt glued to my seat, knowing what it all meant.

"And so, it begins." Nathan got up again and walked away before turning back. "Project Amber. We need to get there. We need to destroy this critical mass."

"Can we please check in with Shilo?" I shouted. By now, the pain in my arm was throbbing with every beat of my heart.

Nathan nodded and stepped toward the front of the aircraft, returning with Xe's tactical laptop. He sat down in between Bosco and me and flipped the lid open. After a few seconds, Christina answered the call. "Guten tag."

"Jenny," was my first word. Christina nodded and disappeared from the screen. Maggie appeared momentarily after. "I don't know if destroying Project Amber is going to make any difference with what's just happened."

"It's still worthwhile," Nathan replied. "In my opinion, we should proceed as planned."

"After you get back here, we'll discuss it. And Angel, I know what you're about to ask. I'm sorry, Jenny's gone."

"GONE. How? Why?"

"We don't know. She left a note. That's all I can say."

I was left reeling as Maggie expertly changed the subject and continued. "We need to regroup and discuss our options. The game has changed. This plays out differently with the Americans' imminent retaliation. How it plays out *now,* is the question. If we had our backs up against it before, consider yourself on borrowed time from this moment on." Maggie's expression hardened further before she disconnected from the server.

Nathan closed the lid and carried the laptop back to his bergen. He went over to the door and looked out of the window. I knew what he was doing. I knew he was contemplating. Then he turned slowly and made his way back. "How bad do you guys want Project Amber?" Nathan asked. "It seems the only way we're going to get a chance at destroying it is if we go outside Shilo's request."

"You're thinking of a HALO?" Bosco began to rub his hands together.

Nathan nodded with a wink. "I've already checked. There's enough gear down the back."

"HALO?" I asked. "What's HALO?"

"High altitude, low open," Bosco answered. "You've never jumped before, have ya?"

Nathan butted in. "Yeah but there won't be a low open this time, Bosco. Angel and I will jump tandem."

I was all of a sudden on the edge of freaking out. "Not happening!"

"Nothing to worry about," Nathan assured me.

"I say we do it." Bosco agreed. "I haven't had a good HALO in years."

"Roger that." Nathan got up and walked to the front.

As he came back to his chair, the aircraft yawed slightly left and straightened out again. "We'll be over Alice Springs in about thirty minutes. We should prepare and be ready for my go."

"Why can't we just land in Alice Springs?" I asked. "Its much easier if you want my opinion."

"Because, Angel, we're gonna drop right into Pine Gap. The lights are on but no-one's home."

CHAPTER TWENTY-FOUR

Jump

I FELT NATHAN PRESSED up behind me. I felt his lungs fill, then compress. I felt his heartbeat pumping in a steady rhythm. In the tandem harness, facing forward, I could only see his gloved hands pass my peripheral vision. Vulnerability washed over me as Nathan gave thumbs up to the Jump Master.

The rear door of the Hercules was locked down in the open position. Nothing beyond that, just the bitter cold I felt trying to invade my HALO jumpsuit. I had all the right gear for the job. My hastily modified jumpsuit, altered to allow for the new addition on my arm, consisting of a big plastic bag to cover the grotesqueness I hadn't yet seen. The breathing apparatus, the helmet and goggles. I felt Nathan behind me. His heartbeat picked up as he waddled, fully laden, closer to the ledge. I felt him hard up against me. Nathan had the life-saving parachute. Bergens attached to a line. SA-80s attached the bergens. Beyond that, luck. Nothing else. Just rabbits' feet, four-leaf clovers and rusty old horseshoes that were nailed to a fence.

Bosco stepped forward and faced the outside, then stepped further to the wide-open aperture. His form became silhouetted against the light. Nathan followed awkwardly with his attached human cargo at his front. He reached out and placed his hand on Bosco's shoulder. Bosco looked back and gave thumbs up again. Nathan's gloved hand passed my vision. Another thumbs up and maybe for the last time. Bosco waited for the Jump Master's hand signals. He stood motionless, poised and ready to go on command.

The Jump Master signalled 'jump ready.'

Bosco moved a little closer to the edge of the opening and looked down. I couldn't see, but I imagined the view from where Bosco was standing. There'd be no clouds. There'd be nothing but the wind and the cold. And the hard ground far below that would rush up and instantly kill. My heart rate picked up. Nathan's increased—I could feel him. I'd placed my life into his hands.

The Jump Master held up a hand. Fingers out. Four, then three, then two. Then the signal, and Bosco was gone, just like that. No second thought. No hesitation. Just gone, out into the never-never. Nathan pushed forward. I lifted my feet off the floor. Nathan now had my full weight in his harness. He waddled to the edge. I peered down then closed my eyes. The Jump Master must've signalled him off, and Nathan must've stepped out into mid-air. The tumble. My eyes still shut tight; I held my breath. I clenched my teeth. I was on my way to the ground. If I could scream, I would have. I was now head down as Nathan tilted forward and became a bullet, head first to catch up with Bosco.

At last, I dug up the courage to open my eyes. Bosco did something with his arms to slow himself down. He stretched them out like a bat. When Nathan caught up to Bosco, he did the same thing. The mad rushing wind pushed past my ears to the point of real pain shooting somewhere inside my head—we slowed down into a controlled free-fall.

It was mere moments of gliding and soaring. It seemed like forever. I was surprised with my loving it. I felt like an eagle. It was Charlotte's view on the world and it was awe-inspiring, breath-taking, wonderful.

Bosco repositioned himself and came in closer. I could almost reach out and grab him. He gave thumbs up again. This time, I answered him with my own gloved hand. He moved away far enough to perform a few manoeuvres in mid-air, just to show off. Bosco was doing the 'woo-hoos,' I just knew it. What a blast. If it were possible for Nathan to join in, perhaps he might have. But Nathan was a mid-air pack mule. He had no business with the manoeuvres Bosco was doing.

Nathan positioned his right arm to view his altimeter. The ground was rushing up fast. He swooped in toward Bosco and signalled to deploy chutes. They pulled on their ripcords almost in complete synchronicity. The parachutes blew out and opened, fluttered and arranged without effort. Then, a sharp jolt and an immense tug and we began to float.

Bosco pointed down below to a squarish patch of land the size of a postage stamp. If it was Pine Gap, I could only just make out the all-white radomes. In the next second, the circling and spiralling began. I wasn't sure why both Nathan and Bosco leaned into their cords, steering their chutes into a controlled spiral. We drifted down, spiralling, circling as we went. Then, it was perfectly clear why.

The first few projectiles zipped and cracked past, missing us by only centimetres. "They're shooting at us!" I screamed into my facemask, and I was horrified to realised that no one could hear me scream.

I felt Nathan's chest compress. He put a hand on my shoulder, pulling me in. More bullets cracked past. It was no longer fun. I felt panic and bile rise to my throat.

More shots cracked past. This time there were tracer rounds. I screamed again but this time with no words. My heart was in my throat and I could taste my own blood.

Down, we drifted and the spiralling intensified. I glanced at Bosco as a burst of shots cracked past us again. Bosco's helmet flicked back. A cloud of red vapour ejected into the atmosphere and Bosco's spiralling ceased.

Nathan immediately screamed from behind his mask; I felt his lungs compress and another scream to Bosco. Nathan pulled on the control cords and changed direction, following Bosco as he drifted out of control. All the while, I felt Nathan's lungs inflate and compress. Inflate and compress again.

We drifted down and away, somewhere to the east. Somewhere over the MacDonnell Ranges, where the tops of trees and sharp rocks rose up and craggy creek beds that were the colour of deep red earth. The ground was rushing up fast, getting close, almost close enough to my touch toes.

Bosco hit the ground first, narrowly missing a clump of ghost gums and the jagged edges of sandstone rocks. As he hit the ground, his legs collapsed from under him. I watched as the wind on the ground dragged his lifeless body along for a short distance. Finally, Bosco came to rest wedged between two large sandstone boulders.

"Legs up, Angel." Nathan yelled, then he pulled the control lines of his rig hard down. After we were steady on the ground, Nathan ripped off his helmet and tossed it away..

"BOSCO!" Nathan screamed out. "NO. BOSCO. NO!"

Nathan desperately and frantically wrenched the parachute cords and harness away from his body. "GOD! NO! BOSCO!"

Nathan wept openly as he cradled Bosco in his arms. It broke my heart to see it. I got down beside them and comforted Nathan as best as I could.

* * *

It was well into the evening before Nathan could finally let go of Bosco's body. I'd already tried several times to coax him away. But it was dangerous out in the open in the desert during the blackness of night; and we needed get back to home base. The question was how?

"Nathan, listen to me. No one knows we're here. How do we get out of this place? We have to think. I know it's hard. We have to think about getting out."

Nathan pointed to his bergen. "There's an emergency GPS beacon in the side pocket. Activate it, and we're out of here."

CHAPTER TWENTY-FIVE

War . . . War never changes.

—Ulysses S. Grant, 18th US President, 1869-77

THE DOOR OPENED, AND CHRISTINA stared back through her watery eyes. She stepped aside slowly. Nathan walked through. I followed, expecting to see Maggie somewhere—if only to start with the dressing down. But Maggie was nowhere in sight, not even in earshot. Christina had explained the circumstances of Maggie becoming ill. It happened so quickly, Christina explained in her best English, then Christina explained that Maggie's demeanour had totally changed. The light had gone out in her eyes, and it was as though Maggie had lost her will to endure.

We stepped past Christina. I wasn't prepared to see Maggie so different. It seemed only hours ago Maggie was the same hard, steadfast individual I'd always known. This Maggie was reduced to something I'd not at all expected. As Nathan and I approached Maggie in the ops room, she was seated at the head of the meeting table, staring vacantly, clutching at a bunch of old photographs. She looked up at me and smiled as I sat down next to her. The photos she was holding in her hands, I noticed, were photographs of a much younger Maggie with her husband, Theo. Maggie's smile then fell away after her eyes met Nathan. At first, it was as if Maggie wanted to say something. Her mouth opened slightly, and then closed.

"Maggie?" Nathan said as he approached her

Maggie then came back from where she'd gone. "What, may I ask, were you thinking, Nathan? Everything we've worked for. Did I *not* instruct you to return here? Look where we are now. We had a solid plan. We had options. We had a chance. Not any more, Nathan. None. Thanks to what you've done."

"Maggie . . . I'm sorry. Our intelligence suggested Pine Gap was empty. You know that. I had the opportunity on Project Amber, and I took it."

"You're sorry." Maggie's top lip curled slightly. "Is that it, Nathan? You're sorry?"

Maggie then coughed into her hand. She reached and grabbed some medication from the top drawer of the credenza to her rear. Before taking a tablet from the blister pack, she held it up. "Heart medication. I'm only alive because of these damn tablets. I've considered not taking them at all. Why bother?" She sighed then swallowed a handful of tablets, chasing them down with a long drink of water. "It's pointless now, Nathan." Maggie coughed again then pointed to the LCD on the wall. Christina stepped over and switched it on. Maggie sunk in her chair and became quiet as Christina replayed the live and breaking CNN broadcast from the streets of Tokyo.

I watched on as the video showed The Democratic People's Republic of Korea push the entire globe to the point of no return. Random shelling had begun on the city. I then understood this was less about war and more about mass murder on the citizens of Japan. People ran panic stricken in the streets. The camera moved down on a group of civilians who were hunkered down behind concrete road barriers. A flash, and an almighty explosion. They were instantly erased as though they were never there at all.

The shelling was relentless, causing collateral damage on a scale not seen since World War II.

From his high-rise apartment window, a CNN broadcaster's voice broke with sadness and dismay through the audio while attempting to cover the shelling from his view over the city. Below him was anarchy, bloodshed, rioting, and looting. Another flash, then a massive thud. Glass and debris were sent flying into the air, mixed with body parts, and only God knew what else.

"That was an hour ago, Nathan. These were the first shots fired in anger by the North Koreans," Maggie said. "Unfortunately, there has been no other forthcoming news broadcast from Tokyo. We don't know what's happening over there as of this moment. It seems all communications, in or out, have been cut off"

"And the *Steinbeck*?"

"*Steinbeck* is in the Sea of Japan, with *Minnesota* and *Dallas*. They were on the way to the South China Sea but diverted. China started amassing her forces, threatening the island of Taiwan. Now that the US Ambassador to Japan has been executed, things have escalated out of control."

"China is in on this?"

"Thick into it," Maggie replied. "Who would've thought? Diplomacy goes out the door backward, now everything's dark. But bet your arse, China is in cahoots with the bloody North Koreans. Our secured communication network back to Langley and the United States has been severed. I imagine the US President and his Joint Chiefs are already in the air, formulating joint war strategy from Airforce One and the E-4B. Had we managed to destroy the Project Amber in time, this mightn't have started. But now, there's no way back. It's a matter of time before North Korea ramps things up with their bloody Peacemaker. And Milestone? Nathan, our worst nightmare is unfolding before our very eyes."

"It's not over." I immediately produced the microwave emitter from my thigh pocket. "I bet this is what'll get us to Project Amber. And I know where to start looking."

"It's no good, Angel," Maggie chuckled lightly. "That thing you've got. *And* your Plan B, I might add, won't change anything now. Pine Gap isn't deserted, as our intelligence had us believe. Getting into Pine Gap would require nothing short of a full-frontal invasion. Even then, the Guardianship would be well dug in. And even if we *did* succeed, it'd make no difference now."

I described to Maggie what I'd seen from the window at the airport terminal. The door that led to somewhere. The door that required a certain security to pass through. I turned to Nathan. "The message sent to my phone. You said it came from Alice Springs Airport and the IP was via Airport Wi-Fi. My gut tells me it came from behind that door. I bet my life on it. We need to investigate, and I think this microwave emitter is our ticket to wherever that door leads."

My words got Nathan's attention. He placed a hand to his beard and rubbed it vigorously, at the same time I noticed Maggie's eyes sparkle. She sat up straight in her chair. Her body language changed. It was as though new purpose brought Maggie back to the here and now.

"What do you think, Maggie?" Nathan put in. "One last shot at this? No one's nuking yet. Maybe we stand a chance after all."

"Better get your arses into gear then," Maggie said, then turned to Christina. "Get us a government charter, Christina. Top priority, if you please."

Christina nodded and stepped out of the room.

* * *

Before getting ready for the trip south, I slowly opened the door to the bunk-room where I'd spent my last night with Jenny. I stood at the door momentarily before stepping through. The night lamp was left on. The bed had been neatly made. On the pillow where Jenny rested her head was my rock crystal figurine I'd given the name Charlotte. A note lay underneath it. And also, Bosco's red bandana. I couldn't help but wonder if Bosco would still be alive if he'd had it on him. His lucky charm.

I moved forward and placed a hand on Jenny's pillow. My chest felt tight, and my heart started to break. I sat on the edge of the bunk, knowing the note was still there, unopened. I didn't want to read it. I wanted a moment, and knowing what was in front of me, I decided a moment to remember Jenny wasn't too much to ask.

I picked up my figurine which Jenny surprised me with on my birthday and held it in my hands. I felt the weight, and smoothness which was cold to the touch. The note from Jenny had been infused with perfume, the kind Jenny knew I loved. Finally, I picked up the envelope and opened it. The paper inside was a matching pink. Jenny loved pink. I opened the letter.

Always remember who I am.

* * *

The government-staffed RAAF Challenger 604 left Darwin the day the United States airstrikes began on strategic targets around the city of Pyongyang. Nathan and I watched on from an overhead LCD as CNN covered the United States' answer to the shelling of

Tokyo—the destruction of five Democratic People's Republic of Korea warships which were in the Sea of Japan. During the flight out of Darwin, bound for Alice Springs, a secured feed via ASIO HQ showed live video that was earmarked *'not for general release.'* Live from the hard decks of the *Steinbeck*, among the flurry of activity, several F-117 Nighthawk stealth fighters shot across and up, with afterburners blasting them aloft. The United States flexing its muscles from the decks of the *Steinbeck* was a sobering sight. No sooner did the F-117s disappear into the distance, they were followed up with the deafening turbofan engine scream of F-16 Fighting Falcons and F-14 Tomcats, all of which dispersed into the distance under the parade of afterburners, armed to the max, ready to rain hell.

I pointed to the overhead display from my seat. Something got my attention. Several fighters stood parked at the rear of the *Steinbeck*'s flight deck. They were poised, but it wasn't clear which way they were facing. Of all things, they looked similar from the rear as they appeared from the front.

"Nathan, what are those things?"

After holding his breath a little, Nathan began to explain. "Remember you asked me about what else I knew about the *Steinbeck*?"

"Yeah, you knew about something, and you weren't going tell me."

"No. I couldn't at the time. But you're about to see," Nathan pointed. "These are the craft the Americans were testing at Roswell all those years ago. Now you know everything, Angel."

"You must be joking. Spaceships?"

"No. Not exactly. But Oudarretian technology nonetheless."

"Now I know why there was such an uproar when the *Steinbeck* was in Melbourne. Now I know why the Americans shunned nuke patrol. I can imagine the backlash if any of this stuff was leaked. So, I'm assuming these crafts are nuclear powered?"

"Not nuclear powered. Force Generational Antimatter-Electromagnetism. F-GAE." Then it was as though the nerd in Nathan *really* started to shine. "The LHC in Geneva. Heard of it?"

"The Large Hadron Collider? Sure. I think everyone knows about that."

"Without the LHC, there'd be no fuel for the F-GAEs. Why do you think there was so much money thrown at it? F-GAE technology warps space and time into an envelope. The crafts travel within the envelope through gravity. Mind-blazingly fast. They can stop and change direction instantly. There's no G-force inside them because they generate their own force of gravity, free from any other external force."

I paused, then said, "My head hurts thinking about all this."

"Don't think about it. We have other things to worry about. And only a handful of hours to get it done. I hope your gut feelings are right. This is our final push. If it doesn't work out, I hate to think . . ."

Five F-GAEs were standing line abreast at the rear of the *Steinbeck's* flight deck. Aerodynamically shaped, matt black, the same colour as the F-117 Nighthawks. One by one, they came to life, glowing blue. The same glow as the point of condensed universe Xe created. Nathan pointed to the overhead screen. "Look. The show's about to begin." He grinned at the sight of human/advanced human hybrid technology. The F-GAEs lifted off the flight deck vertically, and then suddenly shot away as if they'd never been there.

Whoever was behind the camera on deck followed the F-GAEs out to the horizon, where all five craft instantly burst into flames and exploded into fireballs.

"That wasn't supposed to happen!"

"I reckon!" Nathan said.

The video shook wildly, and voices of horror were heard in the background. The camera shifted up high. Another F-GAE, huge, much larger than the first five, hovered above the *Steinbeck*.

I was about to ask. The video suddenly went blank.

"NATHAN!"

"I know!"

"Did we just lose the connection?"

"Beats me. I hope it's as simple as that." Nathan got out of his seat and bobbed down slightly while pacing to the front of the aircraft. He was away for several moments. All the while the LCD above showed nothing but grain. Returning to his seat with a couple of bottles of water, he sat slowly down, devoid of emotion.

"Brace yourself," Nathan said, clasping his seat-belt. "Airborne early warning control reports the *Steinbeck* is lost."

"How?"

"We don't know yet. AWAC hailed all frequencies while I was up front. There's no response. Over five and a half thousand souls on board. They're also reporting *Air Force One* has turned back to Washington. The E-4B stays airborne and is now in the control of the Joint Chiefs. They're gonna lock down the Whitehouse. They're going to ground."

"What does that mean?"

"DEFCON One, Angel. 'Cocked pistol.' As soon as the President is safely below Andrews Air Force Base, he will authorise EMERGCON. We won't hear from him again. No one will. He'll emerge during peace; whatever that means. We're in unchartered waters from here."

"Jeeeesus Christ!" I was truly shocked. "Is this really happening?"

"I'm afraid so."

"Can we patch in with Shilo? Maybe she's up to date."

"I'm already on it. The ASIO guys up front will let us know if they can get a patch. The problem is with the internet. It's dark. Maybe it's temporary. Maybe there's too much traffic. We just don't know. I hope America hasn't been hit. If it has, it's more likely dark because of EMP."

"Electromagnetic pulse attack?"

"Yeah. It knocks out everything electronic. Computers, devices, you name it. Everything that uses a computer chip is dead. Even the computer management in car engines. You can imagine the result of . . ."

"Oh no, Nathan. All those people, driving on the highways. Their cars just stop?"

"Yeah. A catastrophe just in itself."

"Who would do this? How?"

"It only takes one high altitude nuke. The resulting EMP does the damage."

A man in a black suit appeared from the front of the aircraft. He leaned forward and whispered something into Nathan's ear. Nathan nodded, and the man stepped away in a hurry.

"They've managed to get Charlotte Station on the 5G network. They'll bring a handset down in a moment. It appears Australia isn't safe from EMP either. As a precaution, our national airspace is on lockdown, and our nation's airports are being evacuated as we speak. After we land at Alice Springs, there'll be no flights in or out until further notice. Until the EMP threat is over."

I suddenly realised. "Nathan. Aircraft in the sky?"

"I'd hate to think what America is going through at this moment."

"And *Air Force One*?"

"The US President's aircraft is shielded from EMP. Exactly for that reason. Civilian and commercial aircraft, on the other hand, is another story."

I paused for a second. "This aircraft?"

"I'd say so. Or we'd have been told to land by now."

As I had that horrible thought in my mind, the ASIO guy from up front brought the handset down the aisle, I guessed, with Maggie already on the other end. Nathan took the handset from him without any acknowledgment. The ASIO guy stepped away with a nod. Nathan then switched the handset to hands-free.

"Angel? Nathan?"

"We're here, Maggie."

"Oh, thank god. News from Canberra. The Prime Minister and his Chiefs of Staff have locked down Parliament House. They're in the War Room discussing strategy at this time. We have our entire available navy on its way to the conflict zone in the Sea of Japan."

"It'll be over before they get there."

"Sadly, I agree." Maggie sighed heavily. "But there is also a coalition of special forces on the ground in South Korea. The South Korean Army is preparing for an invasion to the north. They're going after the Peacemaker, Nathan. If anything, the ground invasion may get us a bit of time."

"Time—yes. Maybe. But they're . . ."

"Remember your objective. Just get to Project Amber and destroy it. I want us all to get through this madness. Do you hear me?"

CHAPTER TWENTY-SIX

Project Amber

REMEMBER, AS LONG AS IT'S DARK, we have the advantage. Let's keep things dark, Nathan told me, at the exact time he pushed his NVG over his forehead. I did the same. I got the device from my bergen and positioned it so I could flip the NVG down as soon as the lights went out. We stood at the door and prepared to move. I got the microwave emitter out and was about to place it up to the security device. "Wait," Nathan said. "Weapons check."

"I already did it."

"Do it again just to be sure."

I rechecked and re-cocked my suppressed nine-millimetre Beretta. I eyed Nathan with intense resolve, "Good to go." I held up the emitter again. Nathan put a hand on my sleeve. I stopped.

"Our first priority is to shoot out any light switches. If there are cameras in there, they'll go dark."

I nodded and held the emitter up again. This time there was an audible click. The door opened, and we stepped through. I crouched down and shot out four ceiling lights one after the other. The place went black. My NVG lit up the stairwell again, under a green monochrome glow.

Down the flight of stairs we tabbed. Our footfalls echoed around concrete walls. Another flight of stairs down to another door. Still dark. Now, it was starting to get cold. The scent of cold concrete hung in the air. The scent reminded me of exiting Coles through the back entrance. I held up the emitter. Another click and the door unlocked. I pulled the lever. Nathan reached out and placed a hand on my sleeve. "Slow," he whispered. "Slow and quiet." I opened the door very slightly and peered through. Then closed it again.

"What is it?" Nathan whispered.

"Fluorescent lights. Lots of them."

"Can you see a switch?"

I peered through again. I nodded.

"Lift your NVG and take out the light switch," he whispered.

I opened the door enough for the Beretta to poke through. I squeezed off a volley of shots, and the place went dark. Under NVG again, we walked through. A small corridor ran away. Another corridor shot off to the left and one to the right. More fluorescent lights went dead after we destroyed more switches.

"This place is already a rabbit hole, Nathan. Which way will we go?"

"Go straight on. We'll come back here if we get to a dead end."

The corridor led to another door marked N412. Another security device was attached to the side. I brought up the emitter. Immediately, electronic servos disengaged the locks with a series of loud clunks.

"Look, but don't go through. Tell me what you see."

"Why don't *you* bloody do it this time?"

Nathan said nothing. He gave me a small push from behind.

I opened the door slightly and peered through a tiny slit. I closed the door again. "More lights. Another corridor. I think an elevator at the end."

"Shit. We don't do elevators yet. We won't know what we're dropping in on. We'll go back and try the other corridors."

I double tapped Nathan's arm and retreated under NVG green.

We took a right turn and arrived at a door marked N526.

"Go ahead, your turn this time," I said, passing Nathan the emitter.

Nathan held it up to the security lock. Nothing happened. "Shit! Not to worry. We'll try the other way."

We about-faced and headed down the corridor past the entry door we'd trundled through, and into another corridor, arriving at a steel door marked N577.

"Retina scanner, this one," Nathan said reaching up touching the security device with two gloved fingers. "You need to place your eye implant up and press the sensor button at the same time."

I sighed, unfolding the flap of artificial skin on my arm. Someone else's dead eye looked up at me. I was about to hold it up to the locking device.

"Wait just a second." Nathan got something out of his breast pocket that looked like a suction cup attached to a wire. He placed the suction cup to the door and then placed an earplug into his ear. He listened for a few seconds before taking the device, winding it back up and putting it back in his pocket. "Ready for this?"

"Yeah. I hope it works."

I held up the implant to the sensor and pressed the button. A red laser started to scan across the surface of the eye and then, electronic servos gave way within the door's internal locking mechanism.

"Open it. Take a peek," Nathan whispered.

I double tapped him and peeked through. I closed the door again.

"Large open area. Incandescent lighting. A large amount of electronic equipment."

"Good. Don't destroy the light switch. Look for cameras and take them out first. We need to know what the equipment is used for. Take another peek and see if there are cameras around. Look at the ceilings for black domes or other obvious signs."

I peeked through. I scanned the area. I closed the door again.

"I can't see any cameras."

"Are you're sure?"

I peeked through again, then closed the door.

"No cameras."

"I don't like it," Nathan whispered. "There'd be some kind of security at least."

Nathan paused for a while then said, "Looks like we take the elevator after all."

"Too risky. What if we land well and truly in the shit? I think there must be an electronic control actuator for the other wing somewhere in there. It makes sense, don't you think?"

Nathan paused a beat then slowly nodded. "Okay. Make it quick. Look for security measures first."

I opened the door slightly again and peered through. A little further for a better view. A bit more, and it was open enough for a body roll to the desk in the centre of the room. We hunkered down behind the desk. I flipped up my NVG and looked around at the four corners of the ceiling, then back to above the door. "Nothing in here," I whispered. "No cameras."

"That's too ridiculous for words," Nathan replied.

We both stood up and stepped back to the door with our backs hard up to it. I looked around. There was an array of steel filing cabinets to the left. A steel locker stood next to the filing cabinets. A small desk was next to the locker with a computer terminal, switched off. Another computer to the right, also switched off. A desk in the centre with a laptop and other stationery items scattered around on the desktop. A large LCD monitor was mounted on the wall opposite and shut down. A rack roughly two metres high, full of electronics, all switched off and shut down.

"Looks like this place has been abandoned," I whispered.

"Okay. I think it's clear. Have a look around and see what you can find."

Then, the sound of an electric motor from down the end of the main corridor.

"What's that noise?" I whispered.

"It's the elevator. Someone's coming up."

"Shit!"

"Behind the door, quick."

We both snuck back behind the door and waited. The elevator arrived, and voices were heard.

"Hey . . . what happened to the lights?" someone said.

"Dunno. The light switch is broken. It looks like someone went to it with a hammer."

"Power surge?"

"Yeah. Maybe."

"I hate this place off the grid. Everything blows up, breaks down or goes to shit one way or another."

"I know . . ."

Voices and footfalls were coming closer. My heart leaped into my throat.

"Angel," Nathan whispered so lightly I struggled to hear, even though I was right next to him. "Stealth kill only. No weapons. Got it? We don't want any blood. Not yet."

I double tapped his arm, while trying to remember the silent, unarmed method I'd learned back at Swan Island.

The door swung open. Two men stepped through. Nathan lunged at the first guy, taking him to the floor. I struggled with the second guy who managed to spin around as I attempted to squeeze him up. He pushed me away, the same moment I heard a loud crack coming from the first guy's neck. The second guy swung a punch, connecting, sending me backward. Nathan was up behind him with the pit of his elbow pushed hard up to his throat. Nathan grunted, lifting the guy's chin to the ceiling.

CRACK!

His lifeless body, like a bag of fish, slumped to the floor.

"You good?" Nathan asked.

"Yeah. Sorry about that."

He shook his head. "No need. Let's get into their uniforms."

"That's not a good idea. We won't have our gear."

"Yeah, I know. The element of surprise, Angel. If we need to use the elevator, it might buy us a bit of time. Every second in our favour is crucial."

We dressed in the American desert fatigues and a baseball style cap. I rolled up the sleeves and adjusted the length of my trousers. "I'm a freaking beacon in this."

Nathan smiled. "It'll do. Don't forget your knife and sidearm," he said while putting a couple of flash-bangs in his pocket. "Before we go, let's have a look at the computers. Maybe there's something we can use."

"What about our Semtex?"

"Leave it. We'll improvise, depending on what we find."

Nathan lifted the lid of the laptop and appeared surprised when the screen came to life without any security login. He smiled and rubbed his hands together. I turned and went for the filing cabinets. I rifled through them, unsure of what I was looking for.

I opened and closed drawers, moving quickly to the next. And the next.

"I have something," Nathan said. "Finally." He lifted the laptop off the desk and brought it over to the filing cabinets.

"Look at this." He pointed to the screen.

I saw what he was seeing. An accessed Excel document revealed a list of archive numbers he ascertained to be relevant, corresponding to the filing cabinets in the room.

"A list of reference numbers. This one popped out at me," he said, smiling as he rubbed his beard. 'N526 Amber Sanctuary.'

"What's N526?"

"The door that wouldn't open. But there's more. Look. 10324-269. It's a reference to a file. I reckon a hard copy. We're getting close. Are there numbers on the cabinets somewhere?"

I looked. "They have a Dymo label on the top drawers. One to ten."

"Good. It's in the cabinet number ten, third drawer, twenty-fourth file. Dunno what 269 is yet, but we'll know soon enough. I can feel it."

"How'd you cross-reference that?"

"Old school, Angel. Sometimes you need to think old school."

I moved straight to the cabinet, to the third drawer, and grabbed out the documents from the numbered file. I brought the bundle of documents across to the desk and sprawled it all out. In among the pages were progress reports, but some pages that didn't make any sense. The pages that didn't make any sense, Nathan pored over. And a handful of colour photos. I held up the photos one by one and studied them.

"Oh fuck, Nathan!"

"What did you find?"

"This photo. It's my uncle Scotty-Blue."

Nathan took the photo, then looked at it. He then appeared to turn into stone.

"Yeah," I said. "I thought you might do that."

"Blue is part of this?"

"Seems so. This is so hard to believe, Nathan."

"And guess what else? I've found Project Amber," Nathan said. "Here."

The Excel document Nathan opened led to another, which led to more references to the cabinets behind us. On inspection, we found more photos in full colour of people. Records of people, of varying ages, ranging from young to old, both male and female. Records of births. Records of deaths. Records of health and medical status. Records of physical strengths and weaknesses. Records of marriages. Records of mental capabilities and IQ assessments. The more we dug, the more we found. It was never-ending. It was almost as if these people were the product of some scientific experiment. And they were all here, living somewhere in this rabbit warren. But there was something else we found that couldn't be ignored. Everyone—every single one of them had white skin with a decent sprinkling of freckles, and, everyone had auburn hair. Hair the colour of red. The colour of . . . Amber?

After reading through the dozens of dossier pages, the horror of Project Amber suddenly dawned. We both stood agog for a few moments. Nathan finally broke the silence. "We have ourselves a job kicking this one in the arse."

I stood back almost in shock. "Nathan, how do we do this? We were looking for something tangible. We were looking for a device of some description. Something we could pick up and hold in our hands. Something we could take away from this place and destroy. Now, this? Every one of them? Who knows how many. Hundreds? Thousands? They all have it? Project Amber is—are *them*? They're all down here somewhere. Somewhere among these walls. They're all genetically modified to resist radiation. And melanoma. This is seriously insane. And then, one has to think—if this is one bunker, are there any more? Then, how many bunkers?"

"It's been going on for decades," Nathan responded. "They've found a cure for cancer and are using it for their own purposes. To prepare for Milestone. Now it all falls into place. The DNA, or gene-ark we've been looking for is not a device as such. They're all *living* DNA. Modified over time. And Scotty-Blue? Many years ago, Scotty-Blue told me that under no circumstances was I to acknowledge him. In his words, 'you don't know me, and I don't know you.'"

"Now, where are we?" I said. "To destroy Project Amber means . . ."

"To kill them all," Nathan finished my sentence.

I stood back shaking my head, thinking it over. "I've only killed once and that guy needed to be dealt with. But this? This is mass murder, Nathan. This is genocide."

"N526 will give us a clue. We need to access that wing and find out how to get this done. 269. It's a clue. Look around."

I went back to the photos again. Some were old—some weren't. But they all had that one thing in common. I cast a quick glance at the dead guys on the floor. "They *ALL* have red hair."

"Amber. Project Amber. Now it's making sense."

"Red-headed, fair-skinned people who're normally more susceptible to melanoma?"

"Ordinarily, that would be case. Not with these Ambers. Their immunity has been specifically engineered. This is part of the exit strategy and the new world order."

"It's seriously fubar. So, there'd be breeders no doubt, women who do the breeding? Somewhere behind the door marked N526?"

"Maybe. But maybe not. What I do know is this. They've engineered an entire new community. Maybe the Ambers pair off, then have babies as do ordinary people. They'd keep their genetic code in a controlled closed circle."

I picked up the photo of Scotty-Blue and studied it more closely. I put it back on the desk, then picked it up again. I flipped it over. On the back, written in blue ink were some numbers at the very lower right edge. 14/2/69.

I remembered Scotty-Blue being the same age as my father. Now I knew about the 269 part of the equation. I took the information to Nathan and showed him. "That's the 269 you were looking for. It's a birth date. Maybe the computer terminal over there can tell us more."

"I've booted it but . . . it's old—It's Windows XP and requires a passcode."

"I think I know what the passcode might be. Try typing 'Scotty-Blue.'"

Nathan stepped back to the terminal. At the flashing cursor on the screen, he typed the passcode.

Access denied.

"No good."

"Try again. All lower case. XP is case sensitive."

Nathan retyped the passcode with a few repeated taps of the backspace key, then hit enter. The computer terminal came to life showing a graphical menu.

"How'd you know how to do that?"

"Old school, Nathan. Sometimes you gotta think old school. Is there a button there that will let us into Amber Sanctuary N526?"

"There is. But there's also another that says CCTV feed." Before I had the chance to stop him, Nathan moved the cursor over to CCTV feed and clicked. The screen flickered then split into several camera views.

"Holy crap! We've got a view of everything from here."

We hovered over the terminal trying to make out what everything meant. I pointed to the thumbnail that said, *'MCOC.'*

"Any ideas what that might be for?"

"Let's take a wild stab. Milestone Control Operations Centre?"

"Jesus, Nathan. You don't think . . ."

Too late. Nathan immediately clicked on the thumbnail. A full screen appeared complete with real time audio feed. We both stood back and watched the mad flurry of activity, with people running back and forth from computers screens and workstations. They spoke loudly and shouted to each other in a language I thought could be Chinese.

"It's not Chinese." Nathan said as though reading my mind. "It's Korean. But check out what they're doing! Can you see what's on their terminal screen?"

I saw it. I didn't want to believe it. But as it began to register, I knew, now, there was no turning back. "Shit Nathan. That's the *Peacemaker*?"

"Yeah."

"How are we getting a real time feed if there's no internet?"

"Satellite. That's not important right now. Look."

The Atlas Five rocket stood tall as explosions and fire raged in the background around the city of Pyongyang. People screamed in panic, racing around aimlessly, trying to hide and shelter from the shelling and bombing from US lead air strikes.

"You're about to witness the destruction of the *Peacemaker*, Angel. It looks like we got there in time after all."

"Destruction my arse. Even I can see it's being cycled for launch."

"They're almost on top of it . . ."

Just as Nathan said it, the real time video feed from *MCOC* showed the rocket's service gantries and beams collapse. Then the engines ignited and burst into billows of white-hot flames. Slowly, *Peacemaker* lifted from the ground.

Nathan screamed his fury at the sight of the rocket lifting into the sky. He thumped fists hard down on the table. "They're supposed to blow the fucker up, not let it escape!"

For the first time in my life, I had become genuinely lost for anything to say. The consequences of what I'd seen took its time to hit home. Then finally, I realised it. I thought about this unfolding scenario as the line in the sand which early humans once dragged across the beach. The line that one tribe had dared an enemy to come across and make war. The North Koreans had just stepped over that line. Now, the notion of a world living in the tranquillity of peace and harmony had just been tossed into the nearest rubbish bin. Peace . . . Peace will now become the stuff of legend handed down to the few who might survive the devastation of this approaching apocalypse.

We both stood there glued in horror at the sight of the 1.1 gigaton thermonuclear hybrid ICBM lifting higher into the sky, heading downrange, on its way to the designated target, complete with the audible applause from those in *MCOC*.

A metallic click from behind made me instantly spin around. The man stood there in the doorway with a handgun pointed directly at me. "Nathan!" I called out, and he instantly rotated to see what I was seeing.

"Don't fucken move," the man said. "Get on ya fucken knees. Put ya hands up there on ya 'eads." He stood there momentarily. He took a step closer, then stopped. His hand began to shake slightly. I could see him waver as his angry facial expression immediately faded. "Angelique?"

His eyes went to Nathan. I saw him, scrutinising Nathan up and down.

"Canter? Fuck-me, Canter is that you? Well, Jesus H bloody Christ, mate. You took ya time getting here, eh?"

CHAPTER TWENTY-SEVEN

Death from Above

I INSTANTLY RECOGNISED HIS BLUE EYES, which were the colour of glacial ice. His face was the same as I remembered, although now, his facial lines were much deeper. His hair was no longer the rich shade of red. Scotty-Blue's once bright carrot top was now replaced with the grey-whiteness of age. Through his smile and through his eyes, I could tell he was still my Uncle Scotty. I couldn't have helped it if I tried. I launched myself into his arms.

Scotty-Blue dropped his weapon with a 'clack' on the floor. I felt his arms squeeze me in. "Angelique. 'ow I've missed ya all these years, eh?"

After I was done, Scotty-Blue turned and vigorously took Nathan's hand and shook. "I still can't believe you're 'ere. Looks like what I did worked after all, eh?"

"You sent the message to my phone?"

"Ah, T'was I. Tadaah! Now, let's git our backsides out of 'ere, eh? Times a wasting."

"Wait, Blue. I think it's high time for an explanation. Wouldn't you agree?"

"Too bloody right, Canter. But now there's a shit storm you've never imagined comin' down on us. Now's not exactly the time to 'ang around gasbaggin'. Walk and talk, mate. Let's git to the tunnel. We gotta get there before they leave without us."

Nathan reached and grabbed Scotty-Blue, spinning him around. "No walk and talk! You owe me!"

"You wanna hear it? Okay here it is. You already know most of it so let's skip a few details. You already know that Project Amber is the preparation for a new world order after we all come back to this place. But this is what you don't know.

"We're Bunker N. And Bunker N Ambers are a resistance mob set up by the CIA. Partisans, if ya like. We call ourselves 'The Breakers.' We aim to fuck the Os over in another future. Stuff 'em up really bad, y'know? Remember them Chinooks you were looking for, Angelique? The ones from the *Steinbeck*?"

I nodded my response even though I was trying hard to close my ears. This was turning out to be much too hard for me to swallow for one day's work.

"Those Chinooks are all 'ere. They're waiting for us now. And as much as ya try to come to terms with it, the fact remains you're with us. It was always planned that way."

"The Americans are party to this? Everything that's here?"

"More than ya know, Angelique. When you broke that story on live telly, I thought more than twenty years of prep just got shit canned. It doesn't matter now. None of it matters any more. What matters now is you. It's time to realise your destiny."

"Destiny? What destiny?"

Scotty-Blue took a step closer toward me. "Bunjil. You're our Angel of Bunjil. You're the one who gets to lead the fight and take it back to the Os."

Before I had words, Nathan butted in. "No. This stops. We need to make it so."

Scotty-Blue laughed. "Stop it? ICBMs are rising up from American airspace right now. They've already answered the North Korean's launch of the *Peacemaker*. Not only that, mate, the Russians cycled their ICBMs. A few moments from now, they'll be risin' up too. A shit storm. It's all comin' down."

"What's the designated target for *Peacemaker*? Do you know?"

"Well, it was supposed to be DC. The North Koreans had the heart of the Yanks pegged right from the get-go. But there were some technical things that went wrong. Guidance system stuff-ups. Stuff they couldn't control. So, them Nork arsholes went for the secondary."

"Which is?"

"Frisco, mate. San Fran-bloody-cisco. They going for the soft target."

Nathan put his head down and began to pace around in circles with a hand to his beard. "The President is in his bunker. Maybe he'll ride out the storm."

"You gotta be fucken kiddin', mate. A 1.1-gigaton thermonu-clear super-bomb is a worldwide catastrophe. No-one survives."

"There has to be a way," Nathan said. "There has to be a way to put an end to this madness!"

"Mate, there ain't nothin' short of the 'and of God 'imself that can change anythin'."

"There must be a way to hack *Peacemaker's* guidance control system!"

"Ya can't stop it. Ya don't seem to be 'earing me. It's like you got some kind mushroom growin' in ya ears. Those up top are done and dusted. Why even think about it?"

"How much time have we got before *Peacemaker* goes critical mass?"

"A couple of hours at the most. Then . . . fucken boom, mate."

"I have an idea, Blue. Satellite phone. Have you got one?"

"Yeah. There's one in me drawer. Why?"

"We can use the satellite phone hooked up to the laptop and ping *Peacemaker's* override systems. We can at least disarm the warhead."

"You've got a slim chance at best, I reckon. Okay, if that's what ya want, let's get up top and get this shit done. Like the old days again, eh Canter?"

"Up top?" I said. "Have you two lost your minds?"

"We have to try, Angel It's worth it, don't you think?"

" 'ang on a sec, mate. Since we've decided, an' there's not a bloody thing I can do about it, there's something else you need to know first. The Russians. I know of at least one of their ICBMs, targeted 'ere. They've targeted Pine Gap. We need to move fast. Right bloody now."

* * *

I wasn't sure why I did it., but before heading up top, I reached into my bergen and retrieved my rock crystal figurine. I ran my eyes over it for a second before I thrust it down into my thigh pocket. The three of us bolted through doors, up flights of stairs, and finally reached the outside.

Nathan found a place out in the open and knelt down just outside the ghostly silent airport hangar. A strange orange glow hung in the air to the north, and the wind blew past, bringing with it the scent of something that smelt like a bushfire. The sound of the wind sang eerily as it pushed past the abandoned aircraft that sat silent and empty on the tarmac.

Nathan opened Scotty-Blue's laptop. I passed Nathan the satellite phone. "Nathan. I have a bad feeling about this. Please hurry."

Nathan didn't acknowledge and I was ignored as he grabbed the satellite phone and unfolded the large antenna. He held it up and waited for a connection . . .

"It's not happening!"

"Go out further, mate," Scotty-Blue said. "The buildin's are blockin' the signal."

I grabbed the laptop and followed Nathan as he moved away, holding the phone up for a signal as he strode. We came to rest on a small rise away from the main runway. "Here. We got reception. Blue! Get your arse over and give us a hand!"

Nathan connected the phone to the laptop and waited for the signal to transfer.

"Good stuff, mate" Scotty-Blue said. "Now we need to login. Get outta me way."

Scotty-Blue went at the keyboard and punched in strings of commands. The screen suddenly went blank. He clenched his fists and stood up. "Fuck-it!"

"What?"

"The laptop battery's dead!"

"You're kidding!"

"Nah, mate. Fucken serious! The bunker power supply is off the grid. Chargin' the laptop was one of the things we 'ad to do without, since we mainly used the terminals down there."

"Calm down and think, Blue. How do we get a charge on the laptop?"

Scotty-Blue pranced around like a spooked racehorse, then suddenly stopped as though an idea abruptly struck him.

"C'mon, Blue! Think!" Nathan yelled.

Without any warning, Scotty-Blue turned on his heel, and sprinted away.

"Where're ya going, Blue? BLUE!"

I watched as Scotty-Blue disappeared behind a parked aircraft. A few moments later, I heard a truck engine rev up and black smoke billowed from twin stacks. Scotty-Blue was behind the wheel of an airport support vehicle, and was driving it flat out, diesel engine screaming, chugging out black smoke. He screeched the vehicle to a halt just where we stood.

"Get in yous two!"

* * *

The airport support vehicle bounced and veered as Scotty-Blue drove it north along the Stuart Highway as fast as it could go.

"Blue? Where're we going?"

"We need a battery. I know where to get one," Scotty-Blue shouted over the diesel engine. "The old Camera Shop. It's still there."

As we drove, for most of the way into Alice Springs, there was silence. But Nathan cut the silence, "Tell me it's not true, Blue."

"It'd be good to know what you're on about first, mate." Scotty-Blue shouted over the diesel engine.

The Blue Enquiry. Was that you!"

"Ah, that Cobalt Blue thing. You've had that in your head all this time and couldn't work it out? That's surprises me, Canter. Yeah, that was me who leaked to the agencies. It was also me who flew the drone. Any more bloody questions? As if we have the time for this right now. The Camera Shop. That's our objective."

"I thought ASIO shut it down," I offered.

"Nah, Angelique. ASIO sold it to someone. They didn't have the heart to burn it, like you blokes were gonna do. So, they just sold it off and prob'ly at a discount rate, knowin' ASIO."

As we drove north, billows of smoke from the direction of Alice Springs blew up high into the atmosphere. As the support vehicle cut through The Gap, I saw almost the entire township was engulfed in fire. Crowds were rioting and looting on the streets. People were shooting and killing each other. Bodies were strewn all over the ground. Cars had stopped on the sides of the roads, their hoods up, some of them ablaze.

Closer into town, our momentum slowed to a crawl as more and more people gathered on the streets, shouting and screaming, killing with weapons ranging from sticks to automatic assault weapons. There wasn't a shop on the main street with a window intact. Fire was everywhere. The whole place was overwhelmed in upheaval and devastation.

"Why don't they just get in their cars and go?" I asked.

"They probably would, if they could. Notice all the cars on the sides of the roads? They're all late model. That says one thing. Their computer management systems are all dead. That says something else. An EMP attack."

Scotty-Blue put in, "Hence the need for this vehicle. No turbo and no engine management, mate! And we're also lucky, we were in the Faraday shelter when the EMP struck. Otherwise, no bloody laptop neither, eh?"

We finally stopped in front of the old photo shop that looked as though someone had thrown a grenade through the front door. Broken glass was everywhere. Not a speck of anything inside was left untouched. Debris was strewn all over and spewed out into the street.

Nathan got out of the vehicle; Scotty-Blue followed behind him. I was also about to step out.

"No," Nathan called out to me. "Stay with the damn vehicle. Get behind the wheel. Lock the doors. We'll be back in a few moments." Nathan and Scotty-Blue stepped away with the sound of crunching debris under their feet.

Then, people appeared at my window in the numbers, all begging me to take them away from the calamity. They stood at the door and screamed. Someone stepped up behind a woman that was wailing, screaming to please, please, let her in. Then her head exploded, sending blood and brain all over my window. The man who pulled the trigger pointed the shotgun directly at me. "Open the fucken door!" he screamed. "Open the fucken . . ."

CRUNCH!

Someone stepped up behind the man with the shotgun and belt him in the back of the head with a brick. The man with the brick then demanded to be let in, just the same as the dead man with the shotgun, and the woman who lost her head. The man grabbed at the door handle and tried to force it open. He put a boot on the door pillar for leverage. Then, after failing to force the door open, he started pounding on the glass with his fists. By some miracle, the glass didn't break. He kept beating on it. He stepped back, picked up his brick and was poised to throw it. Nathan stepped up behind him and smashed him to the ground.

"Open up, Angel!" Nathan screamed above the noise of the rioting.

My shaking hand went for the door lock and I unlatched it. Nathan and Scotty-Blue flew into the back. "Go! Go! Go!"

I stepped on the accelerator, and the airport support vehicle lurched away.

* * *

Back at Alice Springs airport, Nathan flipped the laptop open, then connected the laptop to the satellite. Scotty-Blue went at the keyboard again. "We're in," Scotty-Blue announced. "Just need to log in . . ."

Then.

It happened!

A blinding white flash—brighter than the sun—lit up the sky and everything was turned pure white. I screwed up my face, raised my hands and tried to hide from the heat. Radiant heat! It was all over my body. I felt the burn collapse over my skin. After the white blinding flash faded away, the ever-familiar, forever-threatening mushroom cloud from a nuclear explosion towered up high through the clouds in the distance.

"JESUS!" Nathan screamed. "Not good! Not good! We gotta run!"

"We're already dead, mate! Look!" Scotty-Blue pointed.

Out there on the horizon, the shockwave rolled across the desert plane. I could see the top of the shockwave mushrooming, pushing over trees as though they were mere toothpicks, picking up dust and debris, racing across the desert at a furious rate. Somehow, I knew, just behind the shockwave was the ear-splitting low roll of the blast that was coming toward us at three hundred and forty-three metres per second.

"NO! NATHAN!"

I ran to Nathan as he put his arms around me and pulled me in. "Angel . . . I'm sorry!" Nathan yelled out over an increasing low rumble that seemed to move my feet sideways in the dirt. I looked up. Already a wind had Nathan's hair dancing around as though a freight train had rushed past.

"Don't look!" Nathan yelled over the wind storm. The low rumble intensified. The earth then wanted to kick me over.

Then.

Another blinding white light fell down, once again drowning out all of my vision . . .

I scrunched up my face while trying to see through the pure whiteness. I saw her. How could I not notice her face. The outline of Jenny's face looked down at me.

"JENNY!"

"Get down," Jenny said.

Jenny pushed me onto the ground. The heavy pushing sensation over my body wasn't at all gentle.

In the next split second, the shockwave rolled in, carrying with it the ferocious energy of a thermonuclear blast. I didn't feel anything. I didn't hear anything. And yet, debris of everything, humanmade and natural, flew ferociously past me. It went on for minutes. In went on forever.

When it was over, the entire landscape had changed. Once there was an airport with large buildings and hangars. It all was gone, replaced by a blackened wasteland of debris and carnage. Once there were aircraft parked on the tarmac. They were all gone, replaced by upturned and shredded metal and aluminium. Everything that was once there had disintegrated. Fire had erupted and the radiant heat was intense.

I managed to get up on my feet. Jenny's smiling face was staring down at me. What was I seeing? Jenny appeared to float. Her feet were inches above the ground.

"Jenny?"

"Remember who I am," Jenny said softly. "Remember who I am, Angel."

I remembered the words she'd written on the note she left me. But what did it all mean?

Then, right in front of my eyes, Jenny was no longer Jenny. Jenny shifted her shape and became an eagle. She lifted into the sky with her wings stretched out. "Remember who I am," she said again as I felt the bursts of air pressure from under her enormous wings. "I am your Angel . . . I am Azrael."

The archangel Azrael lifted further up under her immense eagle wings, then she became one of seven eagles which were circling as though waiting for her; one of which I couldn't help but notice, was all white.

Nathan finally broke the silence.

"Need to get to cover. Now!"

Before running, I caught sight of Nathan's face. His complexion was burned. His face was a fiery red.

CHAPTER TWENTY-EIGHT

Hard Farewells

AFTER SPRINTING THROUGH SMOKE, FIRE and debris to get to a door that was no longer there, we stepped into the hole in the ground that was once a stairwell. The door at the bottom of the stairwell was lightly damaged, and after clearing a passage through minor rubble, it was easy to pass through.

Nathan placed his hand on Scotty-Blue's shoulder and I placed mine on Nathan's as we traversed the total blackness below.

"Blue, what now?" Nathan asked in the stale air of total darkness. "Get us outta here?"

"Mate, follow me. Destiny. All Ambers are at Pine Gap at this point."

"What do you mean, Scotty?" I said. "Pine Gap is gone. It doesn't exist."

"The surface has been wiped away—that's all. The connecting tunnel to the Pine Gap bunker is down 'ere. C'mon. No time to waste," Scotty-Blue said as he somehow managed to find the elevator call button and pressed it. The electric motor kicked over and whirred. The elevator was on the way up, then suddenly, it went dead. Scotty-Blue tapped the button a few more times. "I reckon the power for this wing just got shut down. Not to worry.

We'll 'ave ta take the stairs down. This way, you two. Follow me—an' please don't take ya 'and off me shoulder, eh?"

Scotty-Blue put his eye up to the device and opened the door marked N526—the door that earlier eluded us. Down the flight of stairs we stepped, then another, and another.

"I thought there was no power," Nathan said.

"The doors and scanners are on a different circuit. Just in the case of blackout situations."

We stepped through into a large open space, filled with the glow of amber light. It was good to be able to see again.

"What's this place?" Nathan looked around in obvious amazement, then coughed lightly into his hand.

"Welcome to the lab. Twenty years ago, this was the place where us Ambers got assigned our genetic code. Now, it's used for medical research. I reckon this was the place you blokes were gonna put an axe to, eh? I'd love to stay and chat a while, but youse can see we don't 'ave the time right now." Scotty-Blue paced off again, immediately headed down another corridor that was lit up with fluorescent lights. "C'mon people. Keep up, will ya? Sheesh! Times gettin' away."

Nathan reached out and grabbed Scotty-Blue's shoulder, stopping him in his tracks. He again coughed in his hand and cleared his voice.

"Are you okay, Nathan?" I reached up and placed a hand on his face. "My god, you're burning up."

"Was afraid of that," Scotty-Blue said. "You got some heat goin' on inside 'ave ya?"

Nathan nodded. "It's nothing but a cold coming. Nothing I can't handle." As soon as he finished his sentence, Nathan threw up. "Jesus!"

"Nah, mate, you're red as a fire truck. It's more than a cold."

It was as though Nathan knew what Scotty-Blue was talking about. "How much time do I have?"

"Mate, you've been kicked in the arse with more than a few thousand rems a second."

"That didn't answer my question, Blue."

I was dumbstruck. Nathan coughed again into his hand. As he pulled his hand away, he tried desperately to hide the blood. "Jesus!"

I raced to Nathan and took both of his hands.

"Not now, Angel. We don't have the time. You'll get another chance at the end of where we're going."

"You're not going to die from this. I'll make sure of it."

Nathan smiled, looking down at me. He had a certain look in his eyes that I didn't recognise. It was as though . . .

"C'mon people, we 'ave to keep movin'. You think this is over? It's only just started. Feel the tremors at your feet? That's Melbourne or Sydney or Brisbane going up like a firestorm you've never imagined. Maybe they've all been hit at the same time. These bunkers are blast-proof, but they're not waterproof. That's the real danger we're lookin' at."

"What do you mean water? We're in the middle of a desert."

Scotty-Blue stopped and stepped up closer with an urgent expression on his face. "Angelique. *Peacemaker* just carved a crater the size of a half-moon into the ground. Worse than that, the entire Pacific Ocean has been disrupted and a wave you've never imagined is heading this way. Frisco is gone. The catastrophe after that is what we're all trying to avoid. That, combined with all the other nukes going off, what do ya think's gonna 'appen? Roughly twenty-three hours. That's what our pre-modelling 'as foretold. That's all we've got 'til up top goes under the waters. Now, we gotta get goin', because the Gadget is our only chance to escape this hell hole."

"Go with him, Angel," Nathan said. "Leave me here. I'm just holding you two up."

"Nah, mate. You're comin' too. Our doc can do something for ya. Now, I ain't sayin' he can save ya, but he might be able to stem it long enough to get through to the other side."

"Other side? What other side?"

"Oudarret. That's where the Gadget's gonna take us. But time, people. We have to keep moving."

Nathan coughed again. "I've had a lethal dose, Blue, just like you say. This is it for me. Get going will you."

"Jesus, mate. Stop ya bloody whining. I'm not gonna tell ya you're sounding like a little schoolgirl. If we get ya through the Gadget, who knows what medicine will be available for ya. Maybe the Oudarretians can get ya better. So, stop with the martyr shit, and let's get a fucken move on, eh?"

I relaxed a little and placed a hand on Scotty-Blue's back, urging him on. Nathan coughed again in a fit, before picking up the pace.

Down more flights of stairs we traversed, then it levelled out through more corridors and small passageways. We walked on at route-march pace. Nathan fell behind and began limping badly. I ran back to him and raised his arm around my shoulder.

"I can fix you now, Nathan. Let me help you. Please."

"No time right now. You'll have your chance later. I promise."

As I helped him along, Nathan gripped his chest as though he was in pain. Lesions had already started to appear on his face, and the whites of his eyes yellowed to a dark shade, with the redness of burst capillaries.

I'd had enough. "No. Stop. We do this now."

As I stopped and helped Nathan balance, Scotty-Blue raced back toward us. "C'mon! They'll leave without us. Can't risk being left behind."

We trudged on but I was more worried than ever. Nathan was getting worse as every second went past. We needed a moment for me to tune in to my healing powers. I could fix him, right here and now. But it was precious moments we didn't have. We had to keep moving.

At last, we came to a large double door that was labelled J.D.F.P.G. We went through to an underground rail car network that sprawled out into the distance. The air was musty and smelled like coal. Scotty-Blue reached out and pressed a button that was raised on a steel post just short of the doorway. We waited a few moments. A few moments more. "Looks like the powers been cut down 'ere too," Scotty-Blue said. "Damn it. We'll need to walk down the line. I reckon our mob are already in the process of leaving for the Gadget. Gotta make this quick, people!"

I sucked back breath as I strutted along, angry at myself only because the moments we waited could have been used helping Nathan. I fumed from under my skin. Why didn't I do anything? It was an opportunity that was missed.

Scotty-Blue turned and got under Nathan's other arm.

"It's no good, Angel," Nathan grunted. His stride slowed to almost a crawl. "I'm just holding you up. Please. Get going. The both of you."

"Nah, mate. Not havin' it. Stop ya girlie shit and move your arse."

"Thanks, Scotty," I said. "He's a bit of a pain in the backside at times."

Nathan coughed again. Blood trailed from the corners of his mouth. He placed his hand to his mouth, and when he pulled it away, some of his teeth had come loose and fell out, landing in the palm of his hand. He flicked them away in disgust and they scattered against the tunnel wall, clicking and echoing as they fell. We trudged on.

Finally, under floodlight at the far distant end of the tunnel, I saw the silhouettes of figures walking around. "Hello!" I called out. "We need help!"

"Who's there?" a voice instantly demanded.

"Calm down," Scotty-Blue shouted back. "Amber N526-269, Scott Thomson, and company of two. And yeah, we need some bloody help down 'ere, mate."

The figure in the distance relaxed his weapon to his side and jogged down the tunnel toward us. Two other figures at his rear, ran to the sound of booted feet echoing around the tunnel. They held up their weapons again as they got closer, looking at us from down their sights.

"I said company of two! That means they're with me, you fucken dope."

One figure stepped a little closer and scanned us. The man was Oudarretian. There was doubt in my mind. "Not authorised," he said. "Scott Thompson, this way. You two . . . this is as far as you go."

"As I said, they're with me. The lady 'appens to be the daughter of Franco 269. That's authority enough, don't ya reckon?"

"Bunjil?" the man sounded genuinely surprised. He moved in a little closer, peering at me. "Are you sure?"

Scotty-Blue gestured for me to tuck my hair around my ear. "Go on. Show the man, Angelique."

As I sighed and flicked my hair around my ear, another tremor hit. It was enough to make me wonder if mother nature had begun her fightback. It was strong enough to loosen the dust from the tunnel walls, and a cloud of white powder sprinkled down on us.

At the same time, I was surprised by the Oudarretian stepping back in pure amazement. Then he stepped up closer squinting his eyes. He lifted a hand to my left ear and I instantly smacked it away.

As if reading my thoughts, Scotty-Blue intervened. "Don't worry. We have other Os on our side. Such are the ways of human nature," Scotty-Blue chuckled. "But now we 'ave our Angel of Bunjil—it's gonna lift the spirits of many a thousand."

"What makes you think I'm this so-called Angel of Bunjil? And what makes you think I even *want* to be this person?"

"It's destiny, Angelique. Destiny. C'mon then, there's not much time."

* * *

By the time Nathan found a gurney in the medical ward, I was at his side, gripping his fiery hand. A young Amber doctor by the name of Lang administered morphine to take the pain from his internal blaze. Nathan's once flowing hair was patchy, and most had fallen away. His eyes were seriously bloodshot and sunken. His face was covered in burns and lesions that oozed a strange orange/red sticky liquid. His lips were cracked, and most teeth were already missing. The sores had spread from his face to his body and limbs. Large boils had developed at the base of his neck and chest. I was incredibly sad, looking down at him. He tried to speak as soon as it appeared he found the strength. I don't know what I must've looked like to him. I did my level best to keep that in check. I knew he didn't need to know my sorrow.

It was only a moment before when Nathan objected to my helping him. He refused any healing I could give him. Sadly, he pushed me away with just one word that escaped him. The word, "Teresa". And as soon as he said, it I understood completely.

As he tried to speak again, I placed my hand softly on his lips. "Shhh. Don't speak." I passed him a glass of water and helped him to drink. He took a sip and coughed. The fit lasted much longer this time. He winced, as blood appeared, and I wiped it away. He looked up at me again through the eyes of someone who was at the very edge of his life.

"Angel," Nathan said hoarsely, as though trying to stem another fit of coughing.

I leaned slightly forward and peered down at him through my watery eyes. "Please don't speak," I whispered gently. "Save your strength, Nathan."

"I see her. I see my Teresa. She . . ."

Nathan smiled for a second, then he coughed again. More blood. I again dabbed at it with a moistened hand towel.

"Angel . . . We've had a wild ride, you and me."

It was as though he fought for every letter in the words he'd just told me. He smiled as though more for his success, than at getting the words out. He coughed hard again but this time there was a rattle in his chest I couldn't ignore. It made my tears flow in a stream. "Yeah. We did . . . didn't we."

Nathan's breathing heaved and the rattling sounds of liquid in his lungs got louder. I placed my hands on my face and tried desperately not to bawl like a baby.

Nathan raised a hand, reached up and placed the back of his blood engorged fingers on my cheek. "Don't be sad, Angel. One day, the entire world will step aside for you. And you'll be with me again. You'll be with me and Teresa."

I was surprised by his words. I wanted to show strength for Nathan. Somehow, I knew I'd not manage it much longer. But my internal desire wanted only for Nathan to be at peace, and without pain. I looked up to the doctor and nodded.

More morphine was delivered into Nathan's central line, and Nurse Rosemary Keane nodded and stepped away without a word. The beeps and chirps of equipment began to slow in the background. Nathan, I knew, was only moments away from his last breath.

I looked down at him lying there, his chest rising and falling. He went to say something again, but I relaxed him from his words with a soft touch to his lips. "It's okay. I'll be fine. You may go and find peace, my good friend."

Nathan's lips curled into a smile, and I recognised his grin. It took me back to happier times. Only Nathan could smile in that way. All of my memories with Nathan flooded back to my senses. All of the memories of those years together flashed past as I sat looking down at him. The battle had begun to keep my sadness in check. Another tear came. It sat at the edge of my eyelid and lingered. I blinked, and it fell away, landing on Nathan's fiery red and boiled skin. "It's okay. I'll be fine," I said again smiling down at him for the last time.

Nathan closed his eyes. His chest raised and fell slightly before his life quietly left him through a last rush of air.

Nathan, my lifelong friend, was gone.

CHAPTER TWENTY-NINE

Mother Nature Always Wins

DOCTOR LANG STOOD BEHIND me in the underground medical clinic. Behind the doctor, Rosemary Keane placed her hand on my shoulder and comforted me, as best she could, as I wailed openly for Nathan. The doctor had done all he could do, bringing comfort and taking pain away from Nathan, and I was thankful for his efforts. However, already, there was a sense of urgency in the air and it was something I tried hard to push aside.

"A few more moments, please," I asked, Rosemary Keane. She leaned forward over the body of Nathan and positioned his hands across his chest, in the same way an Egyptian pharaoh might be laid to rest in his sarcophagus. She glanced respectfully at her wristwatch. "Take as long as you need," Rosemary said. I placed my crystal eagle figurine down on Nathan's chest. I leaned over and kissed him lightly on his forehead before my sobs erupted all over again.

I made a silent promise before I left him. I promised that some day I would return. And when I do, I will find Nathan's remains and give him the burial he deserves. This was my vow. And it was written in stone.

* * *

I followed Scotty-Blue down the tunnel to another huge open space that was lit up under large fluorescent lighting. Ambers—both men and women, some with children—crowded around the base of six Chinook helicopters that were parked side by side. It all became clear at that moment. In big letters, down the sides of each Chinook were the letters, '*USS John Steinbeck.*' I realised I was standing among friends and a well thought out plan by the Americans that will come in to play many years from now.

The Chinooks stood in silence as the human cargo began to load from the rears. Oddly, escaping from this place was the last thing on my mind. If things were different, I wouldn't even consider it. But what was left for me now? The entire surface of the planet was under siege. The death of billions was at hand. Millions upon millions of lives had already passed. And my thoughts returned to Maggie and Christina. What had become of them? Were they alive or not? And after I gave it some thought, I knew without question they had to be among the dead.

There was no longer a reason for me to hang on to anything I used to be. I'm no longer Angel, the kick arse journalist. I'm no longer the girl who lives in Melbourne. As I got my head around it, I realised the importance of Breakers. Could I be the one to lead them all to their destiny? Am I the one who they should follow willingly into battle? No, there was no longer a reason to hang on to my past any longer. From this moment on, the Angel I once was . . . is gone.

As I stood among the hundreds of orange-haired humans making a queue to get on the Chinooks, already murmurs filled the space around the immense underground hangar. People turned and faced me as I walked to my calling. One by one, they placed their hands on their hearts. One by one, they stepped back a few paces, and space opened up for me to walk through.

Scotty-Blue gave me a sideways glance and smiled. "Destiny, Angelique. They're all realising your presence as you walk among us."

Suddenly, another earthquake hit that was much stronger than before. The Chinook helicopters danced sideways on their suspension. Dust came down in a cloud, and orange-headed people coughed as it sprinkled on top of them.

I took a few paces forward, and the crowd of Ambers responded by making a path clear, all the while holding hands on their hearts.

"What's the sign they're making?" I whispered. "Surely that's not because of me."

"It is," Scotty-Blue smiled. "It's their mark of respect, and honour for Bunjil."

"You make me sound like I'm some kind of chosen one. What if I'm not?"

"You'll know yourself soon enough. But we already know about The Angel of Bunjil. Now, they've made way for you. The least you can do now is respect their honour. Go Angelique. Walk through your followers."

Another earthquake hit the bunker which was strong enough to toss people off their feet. The scent of kerosene thickened in the air as the Chinooks were being fuelled. I walked the small distance to the first Chinook arriving at the rear door. People with bright orange hair reached out and touched me as I walked among them. "Bunjil . . . Bunjil . . ." they chanted softly to themselves.

Just before stepping aboard, I heard an urgent voice.

"Dad!"

After I spun around and saw the woman running up behind us, I immediately recognised her face. There was no doubt in my mind. It was the air hostess I'd met on the aircraft up from Melbourne.

"Angel. This is my daughter, Natalie-Jade," Scotty-Blue said.

I put my hand out and shook hers. Natalie-Jade smiled at me as though she knew me, intimately. "Glad you could make it along with us, Angel. I'm sorry about what went down after you left Melbourne. We did try to warn you. If it wasn't for the turbulence, we might've got you and Nathan out of harm's way. But I heard you had that sorted without too much trouble."

"You said you were from Nebraska."

"A throwaway line. I couldn't tell you the truth, could I? And if I told you I lived in a hole in the ground at Pine Gap, *what* would you have thought then?"

I thought about it and she was right. There wasn't anything in my mind that could've registered had she told me the truth.

"Nat," Scotty-Blue cut in. "I thought you'd got up top sorted out."

"Sorry, Dad. The blast-proof roof. It won't open."

"You've gotta to be kidding me, love. Why?"

"I think there's debris stopping the roof from sliding open. We've disengaged the clamps. Everything's jammed."

"Cripes!" Scotty-Blue shouted out loud and people stopped boarding the Chinooks. "And I'm guessin' by ya expression the escape shafts are also blocked?"

Natalie-Jade nodded. "There's no way up there to see what the problem is. The cameras up top have been knocked out, so there's just no way of knowing one way or another."

Scotty-Blue began to pace around. His white complexion drained even further. After everything that went on, now it's a real threat that everyone might drown.

I tapped Scotty-Blue on the shoulder. "I'll go up there and see what the problem is."

"How, Angelique? There's no way up. If the roof won't open, we're all trapped down 'ere."

"The airport end of the tunnel," I said. "Nathan and I brought explosives with us. It's in our bergens back at the other end. I can use it to clear the debris from up top."

"But there's no time."

"There *is* time if you divert power back to the rail car. I can take it back down there and get the Semtex."

Scotty-Blue stood there and thought it over. "Even if you could get to the Semtex, ya still can't go up top because the shafts are blocked."

"It's not blocked at the other end, Scotty. We'll walk cross-country to Pine Gap."

"That's ten bloody Ks."

"What choice do we have? I need to try." I turned to Natalie-Jade. "Open the blast-proof roof after I clear the debris away. You can pick me up from up there."

* * *

Scotty-Blue was with me, as we raced toward the Pine Gap bunker entrance. Stepping out in front of us was nurse Rosemary Keane. I called out to her as she ducked out of sight. She didn't look back.

"Where in the heck is she going?"

"I dunno, love. But we need to keep focused. Time is getting away."

Leaping from the entrance door, we emerged into a darkened underground rail car tunnel. The car was waiting for us with its internal red lamps glowing. We jumped aboard. Scotty-Blue went for the controls, pressed a few buttons, and wrenched at a lever.

The car lurched forward, slowly at first, then picked up speed as the wheels clacked and squealed on long steel rails.

"You'll need ya HAZMAT, Angelique," Scotty-Blue said, handing me a parcel from under the seat. "We'll be at the other end before you know it."

"I won't need it. I didn't need it before. Why would I need it now?"

"It's gonna be crazy hot up there. The HAZMAT will give ya some insulation."

I took it and opened up the package. "Can I ask you something, Scotty?"

"Yeah, what is it?"

"Can you please stop calling me that name? I'm Angel, not Angelique."

Scotty-Blue looked back at me with a half-smile. "Yeah. Okay then . . . Angel. It's kinda ironic, isn't it?"

"What is?"

"What 'appened up there? What we saw before."

"You're talking about Jenny?"

Scotty-Blue nodded. "Y'know, I wouldn't 'ave believed it if I didn't see it with me own eyes. Do ya think . . . Nah, forget it. That's for another time."

"Why Jenny didn't save Nathan from the radiation? Jenny saved us all from the nuclear blast. I think it was my job to heal Nathan from radiation sickness but he didn't let me do it."

"Yeah I know love. I reckon Nathan already knew he was a goner. So that being what it is, I reckon 'e was lookin' forward to peace with Teresa. That's why 'e never let you heal 'im."

"He spent his entire life alone. I'm just now learning why. I thought it was because of me."

"Oh? Nathan never talked about Teresa with ya?"

"Not even once. I don't know who she is. All I know is that she must've been part of Nathan's life somehow."

"That's a shame 'e never shared it with ya, Angel. Nathan and Teresa were very much in love with each other."

"What happened to her?"

"She died. Nathan shot her in the 'ead."

"WHAT?"

"It's a story for another time, love. But the fact Nathan spent the rest of 'is life alone tells of 'is love for her. It also tells of 'is guilt with the way 'e 'ad ta end 'er life. Shockin' as the truth is."

"I think perhaps Nathan's story isn't over," I added. "Don't ask me how I know. Intuition maybe. But I can't believe he could just end this way. It doesn't seem right." Then I thought about the figurine I left him. The figurine that was given to me by Jenny. By Azrael. It's not the end. He might be deceased in body but, something told me, Nathan's spirit will never die.

The car arrived at the end of the tunnel, coming to an abrupt halt. After we dressed in our HAZMAT suits, and under the green glow of NVGs with our trusty SA-80s, we travelled through the adjoining corridor and upstairs until, finally, we were at the location where Nathan and I had left our bergens. I was relieved to find the Semtex and detonators still there. On my travel down the tunnel, the horrible thought of someone coming into the airport bunker and stealing the explosives had played on my mind. We left the darkened room and began the journey to the surface.

CHAPTER THIRTY

Nuclear Winter, Acid Rain

WE STEPPED OUT OF THE BUNKER AND made our way up a flight of stairs, out into smouldering wasteland that smelled thickly of death and destruction.

"Hey. I thought you said it was gonna be hot up here. It's snowing."

"Not snow," Scotty-Blue said as he held out his hand. I did the same. The flakes floated down into my open palm. I closed my hand and the flakes fell away in fine particles of dust.

"Is it ash?"

"Yeah," Scotty-Blue said. "It's ash comin' down. And it's a lot cooler than I first thought. Prob'ly a good thing. We've got a bit of a hike in front of us. We can't stay out here too long, though. The nuclear winter is comin'. The temperature will drop below zero before too long."

"Which way is it?" I asked. "I can't see more than thirty metres out. It's like a blizzard."

"It *is* a blizzard in a sense. Instead of snowflakes, ash flakes. Boggles the mind, eh? C'mon. Let's get going. I reckon we'll head directly west of 'ere, and reach the road going into Pine Gap. Then it's just a matter of followin' the road in."

We trudged along the scorched earth that was absolutely littered with debris. We passed trees that were no longer trees, but blackened trunks that stuck out of the ground—some still smouldered, and smoke billowed straight up in the strange stillness. Some trees were still well alight with fire and crackled as we stepped past into the grey.

Finally, we found the road to Pine Gap. We followed the dirt track that disappeared into more ash fall. We walked on, following the edge of the track into the distance. Then another earthquake hit and was strong enough to knock me off my feet. The ground rolled and bumped and went sideways beneath me as I sat dazed from the force that had planted me square on my backside.

"You okay?" I yelled out Scotty-Blue. He responded with thumbs up as the earth beneath me settled again.

"We have to move," Scotty-Blue muffled back. "We're most definitely running out of time."

I got to my feet just in time to see a pack of angry, snarling dingoes racing towards us. "Watch out!" I yelled. I aimed my weapon and squeezing off shots that silenced the dingo's rushing attack.

"Jesus, Angel!" Scotty-Blue hopped backward, as a dead dingo skidded to a halt just short of where he stood.

I stepped toward the dead dingoes and looked down at them. They were severely burned. Their skin was covered in open red sores, and radiation burns. I kneeled down and placed a hand on each of them, stopping momentarily to show my dismay. "It's sad that wildlife has to suffer like this," I said before moving on again.

"Time, Angel," Scotty-Blue said.

Overhead in the distance, the thumping sounds of helicopters cut through the silence. I suffered an incredible sinking feeling.

The feeling that they'd succeeded getting the blast-proof roof open, and now they were headed away. I stopped and looked up toward the thumping rotor noises as they trailed off into the distance. Scotty-Blue raced back and gripped my arm, pulling me forward. "C'mon Angel. We have to move."

"They're leaving!"

"No. That's another bunker heading for the Gadget."

"There's another bunker around here?"

"Not here. Nurrungar. How I'd love to shoot those mongrels out of the sky. Now c'mon," Scotty-Blue muffled, grabbing me by the arm and pulling me forward.

The track ended at the entrance to Pine Gap. It was a sobering site. The ground at my feet crunched as I walked toward the debris field. I looked down and noticed the dirt was no longer dirt, but glass. It crunched as though walking in snow. However, there was no crater, as I was half-expecting to see. I wondered where the impact crater was. Then I realised, if the impact crater was at Pine Gap, there'd probably be no sign of any bunker below. And most likely, no debris field to deal with.

As we got closer, the debris thickened with steel girder work twisted up like plasticine scattered around. Large sheets of iron and glass fragments littered the place. Military vehicles, large and small, were tossed around and upended on their roofs. All of them smouldering, with black smoke rising up. Then, there were the body parts that was horrifying to see. It made me baulk in my place, only to be edged forward again by Scotty-Blue's tugging at my HAZMAT suit.

Another earthquake hit, and this time the ground cracked and opened. One part rose while the other part fell away. Dirt and dust went flying off as I once again was left planted on my rear.

"I don't like this," I muffled out after the ground settled once again.

"That's why we 'ave to get this done quickly, Angel. Gawdsake!"

We arrived at the blast-proof roof just as it started to rain. The rain fell with the cracking of overhead thunderclaps. Strange thick globs of black grossness fell on my yellow HAZMAT. Black liquid stuff that looked more like crude oil. The noise of the rainfall on my suit seemed to drown my voice short of yelling. At last, I could see what was preventing the roof from opening. The debris was heaped in a pile—almost as if it were purposefully placed there by some God of wrath. Steel pylons twisted and distorted, mixed with materials that were once large buildings, sat on top of a burned-out and wrecked semitrailer, all heaped in a pile of calamity and destruction. Somewhere below the rubble was the blast proof roof, and under that, a new chance at making things right in some distant future. It all had to be somehow cleared away with all but a few small slabs of Semtex.

We set about placing the charges under a grey sky that spat gritty black globs of ugliness back down.

"One chance at this," Scotty-Blue muffled over the increasing sound of the deadly black rain. "We have to make sure the charges are laid, so it pushes the debris clear. Not up in the air and straight back down."

The charges were laid strategically enough. Sufficiently for the job. We strutted awkwardly away, far enough away to seek protection from when it all goes bang.

Holding the detonation device in my grip, I wondered if it would do the job. "Get down," I yelled out to Scotty-Blue. As soon as I saw he was down, I twisted the knob.

An almighty explosion drilled through the ground and caused me to fall over backwards. Dust leaped up into the air and blocked out my vision. But with the sound of debris landing somewhere out there, it was welcoming to my ears.

Momentarily after everything settled, Scotty-Blue and I returned to the blast proof roof and waited.

* * *

The roof gave way and began to retract with metallic screeches ringing out as it slid. The first sign of success was the sound of applause erupting from way down there. The next sign was the sound of turbofan engines spooling up. But there was another sound not so welcoming. The sound of water. The sound of the sea. Out in the distance, it was rushing toward us.

CHAPTER THIRTY-ONE

The Plan

I LOOKED OUT TO HORIZON THE MOMENT the first Chinook lifted up through the blast proof roof, with its enormous twin props thumping. I could see to the north-east where the crest of a wave had formed and as I focused, I knew it would only be moments before this place is swamped; probably forever. It was coming just as Scotty-Blue predicted, raging along the desert plain. From my view, the wave seemed small. But somehow I knew, it was anything but.

"C'mon Angel," Scotty-Blue yelled with his HAZMAT undone from the top and now dangled from waist. "This way."

The Chinook promptly landed not far from where we stood waiting. The rear door opened slowly and I willed it on hoping to speed things along. After we were finally aboard, we had barely found a seat before I heard the engines scream and then I felt the Chinook virtually leap into the sky from a standing position. The twin rotors thumping hard and I was jostled as the aircraft rolled hard left.

As we climbed, all I could think about was all those people who'd died. For the first time in all of this, I began to feel a sense of anger. It wasn't fair at all that the human race had to end in such a way. In my mind, I saw myself for the very first time as a leader and I would indeed lead my people back to their right to have their redemption. If this was my calling, so be it. If this was the way to return our species to Earth in the distant future? Then *I* will be the one to lead them. This is my oath. This is my vow and I will make this happen, or I will die with my enemy on the field of battle.

Rotating to the south-west, the nose of the Chinook dipped before accelerating and climbing higher. As we tracked, the vision of the ocean rushing in was replaced by smoke, fire and debris. Destruction was everywhere and I just couldn't believe the carnage. As the Chinook reached higher altitudes, so did my wanting for revenge. The anger inside me, I knew, I had to channel into a positive energy and save it all for another day. But even so, rattles and vibrations with the scent of jet fumes filled the cabin space and invaded my thoughts of seeking retribution.

Scotty-Blue took his seat before grabbing a headset, while gesturing to me to grab for an identical pair. After I plugged it in and placed it over my ears, I was on the same channel as all the other voices on board.

Scotty-Blue reached and twisted a knob then did the same with mine. "It'll be a while," he said. "Let's 'ope we make it to the Gadget on time."

"What happens if we don't?"

After appearing to be away in his thoughts momentarily, he said, "In that case, we go due south."

"South? Where? Everything will go under the water, won't it?"

"Yep. But there's another place that's been set up for just in case. Somethin' that was worked out in case the Gadget gets to be out of the question. Kangaroo Island. The Breakers built a bunker system down there. It's big enough for all of us should things turn out shit. It's a fully decked out back-up plan with life support ready to take us on if the Gadget is compromised."

"But it'll be underwater for God knows how long."

"That's the thing, Angel. Pre-modelling didn't show any sign of water going up to it. That's why it was considered. Also, there's somethin' else."

"What?"

"Ambers are to settle there, on Kangaroo Island when we get back. We start there. It's set up, but the passin' of time is the problem. No one knows if the bunker system will still be viable after so many years. As it is now, it's fully decked out and ready, but nobody knows what'll 'appen over the next one 'undred and fifty years. The Earth will most likely start to reclaim everythin'. Also, there's the threat that it might become overrun by survivors. And it doesn't matter what anybody thinks. I still reckon that there might be people who've survived all of this shit. Y'know?"

I remembered Nathan's drawing and what he'd told me all that time ago. It came back slowly.

"Nathan told me, Oudarret is ten thousand light years away."

"Ya spot on, love."

"And yet humans will return in only one hundred and fifty years? That's not making any sense."

"Well, Angel. It depends on who's technology ya using. If using our technology, ya lookin' at a twenty thousand year return trip. And that's at the speed of light."

"I know that already. What I can't understand is the one hundred and fifty year return trip."

"That's because we're using the Os technology. The Gadget is a neutrino particle acceleration cannon. Or, N-PAC. It converts matter into subatomic particles and then shoots the particle stream into deep space way beyond the speed of light. That way, we get to span vast distances." Scotty-Blue went on, "But never forget,

Angel. The Os are our enemy. The Os, the As, and the Gs. We'll live among them because that's the plan with the Breakers. But there'll be the day when we bring the fuckers down. Every last one of the bastards."

"So, when we get to where we're going, we're all operating undercover?"

"We already *are* undercover. How do ya reckon we're passin' through the Gadget? We're all dinky-di Ambers to those blokes. Won't they get a big fucken surprise, eh?"

"But what about me? I don't look like an Amber."

Scotty-Blue nodded to his daughter, Natalie-Jade who was a few seats away and gave her a wink. It seemed Scotty-Blue had worked this problem out a long time ago. Natalie-Jade reached into her bag and got out a set of battery-powered clippers. I knew then, my hair would have to go.

"Dun worry, Angel. It'll grow back, and we'll make sure it's coloured proper. In the meantime, we've got ya sorted with a wig. It's bloody real 'uman hair too. Natalie-Jade went to so much trouble, y'know?" Scotty-Blue smiled.

CHAPTER THIRTY-TWO

The Gadget

THE PLACE JUST NORTH OF MUNDRABILLA, in Western Australia, came into view after several hours of travelling in a steady south-westerly direction.

By the time we arrived, my ears were ringing from the noise inside the cabin. I was feeling very giddy from the ever present scent of jet fumes. My backside was numb from the hard, uncomfortable seats. But even so, I'd made several new friends along the journey, all of whom were adorned with the shiny red, glowing hair, and white skin almost the colour of milk, dotted with an abstract pattern of freckles.

Scotty-Blue had introduced me to a handful of his associates who were senior members of the Partisan group known as The Breakers. Those souls were all hardened to the task of seeking revenge for the collapse of the Earth's human race. All through my introductions and conversations with these people, I felt our cause become more and more justified. I listened to their conversations through my headset, with an ever growing enthusiasm and an ever increasing will to do battle and put to them to death once and for all.

* * *

Out of all the people I met while traveling on the Chinook, one who interested me the most was an Amber woman. Natalie-Jade introduced me to Ruby Cross. Ruby was a science officer, and she was helpful giving me a heads-up as to what to expect when I finally made my way through the N-PAC, and into another world, another future, and another time that was so far away.

"How do you know it to be so?" I asked, after grabbing Ruby on a private channel. "Have you been through it?"

"No," Ruby said. "Of course not. But my position in science, and from what I've learned about Oudarretian technology, I'm more than sure that I'm spot on."

"So, it's the pulling sensation you feel? Nothing more than that?"

Ruby smiled. "Yep. Just a slight tug and that's it. Then you're spewed out the other end."

"Do you know what's on the other side?"

"Yes. I've been given detailed info."

"Let me guess, you're not gonna tell me, are you?"

"Nope. It's a surprise. And I'm not going to spoil your adventure."

Then, it was the laugh that immediately attracted me to Ruby. The laugh was exactly the same as Jenny's laugh.

"Tell me about you." Ruby asked me, smiling in the way I just happened to adore. "Tell me about who Angel is, and where she grew up. All that stuff."

I was about to answer Ruby's personal inquiry when I happened to look out of the window and noticed so many Chinook helicopters advancing toward the N-PAC, down there at Mundrabilla. "There's so many of them. I had no idea."

"Oh yes, you'll see how many when we arrive."

"Arrive down there?"

Ruby laughed and shook her head. "No, silly. I mean after we arrive at Perseus. At Oudarret."

"East Kandesh?"

Ruby's eyes widened. "You knew?"

"Scotty-Blue told me."

I didn't know why I asked it, let alone thought it, but when it came out, it surprised us both equally. "It won't . . . hurt, will it?"

Ruby smiled and placed a comforting hand on my knee. "No, Angel. It won't hurt a bit. I promise." Ruby then launched into her logical scientific tone. "The particle separation is exactly what it means. You'll have no memory of the event. So, there's no pain. And it'll seem instant just like a dream." She took her hand away from my knee. Something inside me gave me the willies. That feeling of butterflies. I felt giddy and sweaty. Exactly the same way I felt after Jenny . . . No, this is too soon. Way too soon.

But I couldn't ignore it. Could this be another first time? Could this be the start of something again? Out of all the sadness, and death, and destruction; something nice? Maybe it was something to feel happy about all over again. A new beginning. A new life, and a new adventure just over the edge of the horizon. All the options are just waiting, just over there. I could almost reach out and touch it. Then, I thought about the Ambers who considered me as their chosen one. The Bunjil. The Breakers wanted nothing short of vengeance for the global death and destruction of human-kind. I was now convinced I could lead them and become part of their vengeance. But now? when it appeared a happier life might be just dawning?

"Penny for your thoughts?" Ruby asked, eyeing me inquiringly.

"There's so much to do."

"What're you saying, Angel?"

"Being Bunjil. The responsibility of it all. Everything is happening so fast. I'm so exhausted. I . . ."

"It's okay," Ruby cut in. "Rest. You deserve the rest. There's a brand-new world for you. Welcome it into your heart and rest. Our people will understand."

As the Chinook began to descend, my breath began to shorten, and my heart rate picked up. The palms of my hands became clammy and sticky, my mouth suddenly went dry. I looked out the window again, and I saw for the first time what I'd heard about from Scotty-Blue. The N-PAC everybody talked about was down there.

Two towering radomes rose from the ground—the same radomes that once existed around a place that was once called Pine Gap. And between them was a steady, pulsing, glow of blue light. Below the radomes were a series of lights that lit up the twilight sky. Chinooks in the dozens had already arrived and landed— and their passengers with their shiny red hair and pale milky skin had already stepped through for the new world.

After our Chinook had landed in what I supposed was a predetermined position away from the N-PAC, the rear door opened and everyone stood. Some groaned audibly, as they stood for the first time in several hours. I stood and I realised my leg muscles refused to cooperate.

I left the Chinook in the same way as I left my home Earth. Ruby took me by my hand. We both stepped through the N-PAC together without looking back.

CHAPTER THIRTY-THREE

Greater Things

UNDER THE SHADE OF A TOWERING tree we all referred to as a Hadgitol, I sat among the thorny rough grasses on a hill overlooking the East Kandesh Citadel. I looked out across the thickly vegetated valley, to the snow-covered peaks in the distance. Just above the horizon, the huge fireball hung low and would stay there—not rise, nor fall.

On Oudarret, to see the stars, travel was required. To feel the cold, or the heat, or to see the numerous galaxies at night, travelling to other locations was the only way. Soon after I came to the place, I learned the rotation of Oudarret was locked in a dance where the same face of the planet faced the sun at all times. It was difficult to get used to in the beginning. Sleeping at night and waking in the morning was an Earth human biorhythm that wasn't easily changed.

But I *did* change.

Nadine was down at the bottom of the hill, about a hundred metres away. Nadine, my daughter, with her face the mirror of her father, Andrew, played and laughed with her pet Adakol she'd named Poppet. It warmed my heart to see her so happy. I smiled contentedly while smelling the sweet air as it drifted in from the mountains behind.

One day, Poppet will carry my daughter away. From where I sat viewing, Poppet was a creature resembling an old-Earth animal known as a dog. That will change. With one leg in front and one in back, it will grow to the size of a living being once known as a horse. Nadine will share most of her life with her Adakol. And, there'll be a time soon for Poppet to be trained in the way old-Earth humans once trained their beasts to carry them.

"Nadine's growing up, isn't she," Ruby said.

"Yeah, she is. Too fast. It's much too fast, Rubes. It seems like only yesterday when she was born."

"Eighty wind cycles. Where did that time go?"

"Nadine! Don't tease your Adakol! Play nice!" I shouted down the hill.

A young voice answered, "I'm not teasing her, Mummy. Poppet's not playing nice with me. That's all."

"You know we've got to get her into school soon," Ruby interrupted me. I glanced sideways to Ruby. "I thought we'd discussed this already."

"We did, but you seem to keep dodging the subject whenever I bring it up. There's no certain answer, yes, no or otherwise."

I said nothing. I realised I *was* dodging the subject. Living among our enemy wasn't too hard so long as I kept the colour in my hair. It seemed I was accepted and melted into the crowds of Non-Breakers easy enough. But if Nadine went to school, it would mean only one thing. I'd lose her for the rest of my life.

Then, my thoughts drifted back to Nathan and the oath I made. I knew I'd find him again but how? When all that land is now under the ocean.

"See? Your silence is deafening," Ruby said.

"I know. It's just . . ."

"What?"

"I made a promise. To Nathan. And to the Breakers. Ruby going to school seems to complicate things."

"I see. But you realise school isn't forever and your commitment with the Breakers doesn't have to be right away."

"I never wanted to be settled here, Rubes. Not in the beginning at least. I always thought going back was the priority with The Breakers. I thought you'd be with me on going back. I know you've changed your mind, being happy here and all. But Nadine going into school . . .? I'll miss her. If I go, I'll never see her again."

"Whatever gave you that idea? Of course, I'll go with you. *We'll* go with you. We're a family. I haven't talked about it as openly as you. And you're right. I do love it here. But I'll be glad to go back home again. Nadine will come with us."

"She can't, Rubes. You know she can't. We both know as soon as she steps onto the surface, she'll get radiation sickness."

"There's a way," Ruby said. "Even though Nadine isn't an Amber, we'll find a way. What was it that Nathan told you once?"

I nodded, then smiled. "Yeah. One day, the entire world will step aside for me."

BOOK THREE

The

LOST
ONES

NOTHING IS HOW IT SEEMS

CHAPTER ONE

The Marooned USS John Steinbeck

Ross Ice Shelf, Antarctica, 2157

THROUGH THE CUTTING GLARE THAT reflected off ice and snow, I could make out the line of individuals curling around Emert's Turn in a long S-shape. Trailing behind them, tied in a sled, was the body of that asshole, Chad Lucifer. Good riddance. The seal skins wrapped around his body were such a misuse of resources. They should've taken him away naked. Good seal skins. What a waste. Now he was getting something reserved for those who *deserved* a funeral. If it were up to me, I'd have had him dragged down to the coast; chained him on an ice floater and watched those killer whales out there rip him to pieces. But no. They decided to give him that funeral. I huffed my disgust and, head down, I walked on. Seeing that funeral procession was like seeing something filthy and not worth my trouble. Maybe I'd get to forget the bastard if I just kept walking.

My eyes followed the yellow line as I walked the metal and cracked bitumen surface of the flight deck. Trying hard to get Chad Lucifer's image out of my head, I cast my gaze around the place and focused, but no matter what I did, his memory infected my mind. How would I ever get over it?

After giving my face a good whack with my fur mitted hands, I began to wonder what it must've been like on the *USS John Steinbeck* during the Pre-Fall. I imagined it must've been buzzing with activity. Jet fighters everywhere. Maybe the smell of kerosene. Cold, salty sea spray. Shouting, yelling voices. Guys in colorful shirts sprinting here and there, each with their own job to get done. I imagined the deafening sound of the catapult shooting down the middle of the strip. The ear-splitting roar of afterburners. Orders bellowed over the PA. I imagined it must've been one heck of a show. But the visions I had in my head were, in reality, nothing more than a bunch of tattered and tarnished photographs that hung on walls where we all got together to mess.

After the bombs fell, they'd dumped all those aircraft over the sides. Sometimes we shared movies in cine-hall showing history as it was back then. But showing movies used up electricity. It was one of the luxuries that had to go.

"Hey, Ditch," my brother said over his shoulder as he clicked his big steel cleats past me. "Not surprised you wouldn't be part of Chad Lucifer's send-off, huh?"

Ditch. He'll never let me live it down. Not Richard. Not even Dick, even though I hated that name even more than Ditch.

"Hey . . . Quit calling me Ditch!" I said through my teeth.

"Well you did fall down that crevasse," Jason said eyeing me curiously. "Well, crevasse equals ditch . . . Ditch. Not to mention the major pain in the ass job it was to get you out. You're lucky. I'm just saying."

"Son-of-a-bitch!" I yelled after Jason as he turned and stepped away. But I had other things on my mind. "It seems you're the same as me or you wouldn't be here. You'd be part of that freaking waste-of-a-funeral they've got going for that asshole, Lucifer."

Jason spun and gave me that look again as I caught up with him. "Yeah, Ditch. I *am* like you. I'm just not so vocal about it. What Chad Lucifer did was horrible. If I had a hand in it, he wouldn't be taken off to no cemetery. I hate to think about his body being buried in the same ground as our clan. But he *has* the right to share the same ground as his, don't you think? Especially after the *good* stuff he's done. We remember the good, not the bad. And I have to keep reminding myself, all that's going on down there right now is, after all, his human right. Something you need to think about, Ditch. In the end it's *our* choice to pay, or not pay our last respects to a man who murdered his wife and kids then opted out by taking his own."

In my mind, I thought about what Chad Lucifer had done. We were *all* in danger of losing it. Losing grip on reality was as horrifying as just thinking about it. It made me shudder as I stood there. The fact was, the blackout was coming. Another stretch of months with nothing but the cold and the black. But this time it was different. This time, with *Steinbeck's* reactor dying out, the horror of the blackout was made worse. We'd not have enough electricity to see it through. Maybe Chad Lucifer's deed was done out of empathy for his family. Maybe he didn't want to be alive during the black nights and days, as one by one, people turned into psychopaths with an intent to murder anyone. How I hated this place. How I wanted to be away. How I wanted to get in a boat and get to Australia. It was a chance to start a new life. A chance to survive. A chance to have night after a day, and a day after night. No blackouts. No whiteouts. How would that feel? Everyone talked about it.

Jason dragged me back from my thoughts. "Where are you, Ditch?"

"Jase. We need to get away. Before the blackout. Before the reactor is dead and everyone is . . ."

Jason reached and pushed his hand up to my face. "Hey, quieten down," he whispered. "Haven't you noticed how Skipper didn't go to the funeral either? And that man's got ears all over this place. I agree. But how? Don't you think that's been worked over already? If it were possible, we'd *all* already be there."

Jason put his hand down and looked at me. I didn't know what it was that was sitting there behind his bluish-pink eyes. For a second, I thought it looked like sadness. Jason was never sad about anything. But as he blinked and looked down, it was there. For some reason, I felt a smile coming on. Maybe it was because

I'd seen him in a light I've never seen before. It told me Jason was human and he feels things. But, as I caught his gaze again, I put that smile away. Fast. Knowing Jason, he'd never admit to having feelings. Jason and feelings? That seemed so odd. But there was no denying it. It was the same hopelessness sitting there in his eyes that we all shared knowing, blackout was coming, and coming fast. After the reactor dies, there'd be no electricity for heating. There'd be none for lighting. There'd be no desalination, which meant no fresh water. And harvesting fresh-water-ice in blackout was a suicide mission. As soon as I thought about it, I realized it was going to be the last stretch of black months for everyone. Without the reactor, nobody on *Steinbeck* would ever emerge into the daylight again.

"Jason. Listen to me." I brought Jason back from wherever he went. As he looked up at me with a set of red-rimmed eyes, almost childlike, peering directly at me through his pure white fringe, I knew I only had a moment to confess everything. Jason the hard was gone. This Jason was somebody else. I came out and said it. "Chloe is pregnant." I took a half step back and held my breath. Jason didn't react. I expected him to swing a punch. I expected his abuse. But there was nothing. He turned his back. I thought for a second, he might step away and not respond at all. After a long pause, he spun and faced me again; his expression was much different than before. Harder. Nastier. Jason the hard was back. I stood and braced.

"How far along?" Jason said in his normal unforgiving tone. I looked down at his hands that seemed as though they'd be used at any second to put me on my ass.

"Not sure. Fourteen weeks, I think." By now, maybe covering my face with both fur mitten-clad hands was a great idea. I didn't. I just stood there waiting for the worst. My fault. I'd take whatever was coming.

"You idiot! How did this happen, Ditch?"

I shot my brother a stare, telling him with my eyes what was the obvious scenario.

"Skipper will know soon enough," Jason said after a couple of seconds. "You can't hide from this for too much longer."

"Chloe is going full term, Jase. Nobody's going to take our baby away. We need to get away from here and get to Australia. It's the only hope we have left."

I saw Jason's shoulders drop slightly. Then he stepped up and got into my face. "You need a plan, little brother."

"I've got one, but I need your help."

"You've already thought about this?" Jason was surprised. He stepped a pace back and looked at me, scanning me up and down as if he thought his little brother was all grown up. Of course, I was all grown up. Maybe older brothers never change.

"I've had nothing else in my head, Jase. I've thought about everything. But so far, I don't have all the things I need to make it work. Are you with me on this?"

I told Jason about what I had planned. It'd start with collecting enough ice to thaw for fresh drinking water. We'd stash blocks of ice at the edge of the coast. The next stage was to repair a lifeboat.

Jason's eyes compressed into slits, looking at me as though I'd already lost my mind. "Repair a lifeboat? Those boats have got holes in them the size of basketballs; put there to make sure no one will ever leave here. Guess what? That was a hundred and fifty years ago. No one's ever going to leave. Forget about everything."

As soon as he said it, I realized it for the first time. I often wondered why the Oudarretians sabotaged the lifeboats. They could've simply dropped them into the seas as they did with the entire squadron of returning aircraft. Maybe it was a visual reminder to our ancestors they'd become prisoners to the elements. Jason was right. But I was about to change his mind or die trying.

Just when Jason turned and clicked away, I managed to grab his arm and spin him around. "The boats can be repaired. Believe me. We have seal skins. We can mend the holes."

"Oh, you think no-one has thought of that? And if what you're thinking is plausible, how do we get to keep the seal skins in place? So that nothing leaks?"

There it was. Jason said the word 'we.' Now I knew he was on board. I smiled briefly before saying, "We'll paint the seal skins into place with glue."

Jason looked at me, his eyes wide open. In an instant, the surprise was sitting there glistening at the edge of his eyelids. But he didn't know I'd already done some playing around. The gelatin

I'd got from boiling seal' flippers. They always threw flippers away. There was no use for them. But I had other ideas. Then there was the glycerin I got from penguin fat. It took a while before I managed to extract the stuff. Once I had it down, I ended up with the glycerin I needed. The final piece to the puzzle was vinegar. I was vigilant, always watching for the opportunity to gather vegetable castoffs from ship's garden deck. I took little by little, sticking small bits of castoff into my pockets when nobody was looking. Once I had enough, I squished down the castoffs and waited for it to go off. In the subzero temperatures, it was a challenge. After I had all three things, I was able to come up with a glue that would do the job nicely.

Jason stood agog in front of me as I described my invention. It was the first time in my life I might've genuinely impressed him. But he'd never tell me. It was all in his expression, and that was good enough for me.

"How did you?"

"Ship's library," I cut him off. "I've read every book there is."

I saw the edge of a brief smile. I had him! "Okay. So, you've got glue," he said. "Now. Tell me how we're going to get the boat down to the water. And if they float, how're we ever going to stop from floating around in circles?"

"I haven't worked that part out yet. That's why I need your help. I can't do this on my own."

Jason eyed me intensely with a hand up to his chin. "We'll need to make sails."

"Not sails. We'll use the life boat's diesel engines."

Jason smiled, but this time it wasn't out of anything cheerful. He looked at me briefly, shaking his head, and then turned to step away. I grabbed him by the arm and spun him again. "C'mon, Jase. We can do this!"

"You know no-one has ever cranked those diesel motors. And even if they *did* crank, where's the fuel?"

"Biodiesel. All that seal and penguin fat we've used for cooking. It's all still there buried in drums out past Emert's Turn. If we don't do this, we'll die with the rest of them. All our clans. Lucifers, Michaels, Gabriels, Raphaels. The blackout is coming. We have a month at the most. Chloe *will* be showing. What do you think is going to happen to her?"

"You still haven't given me an answer about navigation," Jason said. But the fact he wasn't walking away in disgust meant he was more in the moment than I thought. "And, you haven't told me who you've got planned to join us." This time, Jason grabbed my arm and spun me around, while at the same time checking over his shoulder. We both sat at the edge of *Steinbeck's* flight deck with our legs dangling over the edge, both silent, looking out at the pure white snow from roughly eighty hands up. Several moments passed before Jason finally broke the silence. "Tell me who's in on this," he whispered, checking again over his shoulder, swinging his head around just to make sure no-one was around.

"So far it's just you and me who know. I'll be letting Chloe know later."

"Our mother will join us," Jason put in.

"Our mother? Jase. Our mother left us a long time ago. I don't know who she is now."

"She's still our mother."

"She won't make the journey. She's not strong enough." Yeah, I was going to say it out loud for the first time. The words sat at the edge of my tongue and lingered there as though the words themselves had tiny hooks that screamed, *'no . . . you're not gonna say it!'* But out they came. "She's already dead, Jase. Her body lives. That's all there is."

As I said it, I held my gaze and saw the glisten in Jason's eyes. Something told me he'd finally conceded with the topic of our mother's health. He put his head down and sighed.

After a couple of moments held in silence with nothing but the low howl of the cutting ice wind, I asked my brother, "Is she still doing that London Bridge thing?"

"Yeah." Jason's sniffles broke into light sobs he seemed desperate to hide. The very first time I'd seen him like that. He tried to say something. It came out garbled. Even though his words seemed to curl around his sadness, somehow, I knew what he was trying to say. Now, it was my turn to take this idea home. "Jase. I'm about to tell you something that's gonna be hard. But before we leave here, our mother will be at rest. We'll not leave her to the blackout. We'll not leave her to a slow and painful . . ." As I realized it, it went whizzing around in my brain. If I take my own mother's life, am I not as bad as Chad Lucifer? All the hate. All the anger I had for him. I'm now about to commit the same offense. It was an epiphany that went pinballing around inside my

head. There was no escaping it. I was going to murder my mother!
I was another Lucifer.

"How?" Jason cut into my thoughts, dragging me back. He
wasn't angry like I expected. He was exactly the opposite. It
seemed so surreal, and it was as though a stranger had stepped
into his body. Cautiously, I put my arm around my brother's
shoulder. "I've got sleeping meds stashed away. It's supposed to
be a most pleasant passing."

"How'd ya get it?" Jason pushed my arm away from his shoulder. "The sleeping meds. How'd ya get it?"

He was back to being Jason. *Jason the hard.* I paused a little,
then answered. "Moonie."

"MOONIE!"

"Hey, shut up, will you!"

"You've signed your death warrant, you idiot! Moonie's a Lucifer. Did you think you could trust him? One—our sleeping meds
are all we have in case somebody needs an appendix taken out.
Two—they'll float you when they find out. And they *will* find
out."

"We'll be gone."

"You hope!"

"Hey, drop your voice, Jason. Jeez . . ."

"I can't believe the risks you've taken!"

"I know, but I've thought everything out. Ever since Skipper
told us about the reactor." I didn't say anything else. I let my
brother sit there and mull things over. But I *did* have everything
planned in my mind. Who'd know if my escape strategy was

possible, much less plausible? We had to try. Or enter the darkness and perish in unspeakable ways. Everyone sound of mind would see their demise. And those already mad would be the last to die. Nobody could ever last months of blackout when the lights went out, and the cold entered, collapsing over everything with its icy claws of death. The only thing that lifted my spirits was the thought of one-day stepping onto dry land and doing away with the cleated boots. Doing away with the furs and feeling the sun burn my skin. But we're albinos. We'd need to learn coping strategies all over again.

Jason broke through my thoughts as we sat there at the edge of the flight deck, staring out toward the Ross Ice Shelf that held us captive. "You've had this in your head for how long?"

"Don't you listen? Since the time Skipper told us about the reactor. After that, I worked on coming up with a solution for fixing a lifeboat."

"And how are we ever going to repair it without being noticed?"

"I've thought of that too. We'll need to paste the skins over the holes from the inside."

Jason immediately shook his head and attempted to get up. I grabbed his arm and pulled him back down. "I know it's crazy. It's the only way."

"I dunno, little brother. Those skins will come off if you fix them from the inside. Imagine that happening while we're motoring, sailing, or even paddling halfway across the South Pacific!"

"Two things," I said. "If we fix them from the inside, we can do it without the fear of getting busted. And the glue will harden quicker because it's not open to the elements. But we need to paint the skin black so from the outside; the holes still look like holes."

"We need navigation equipment," Jason said, quickly changing the subject. "Charts and compass! A sextant as well!"

"For that, I have a plan."

CHAPTER TWO

Time to Go

THE PIPEWORK RUNNING STEINBECK'S lengthy corridors drew shimmering shadows on the walls as I stepped past a single lit oil lantern. Oddly, I wondered what might happen when *Steinbeck's* last lantern drew its last breath and went out. I'd be long gone. *We'd* be long gone. But it didn't stop me from wondering. Black. Not just black, but true black. Silent. Cold. That old ship smell; leather, grease, and fish oil filling the cold Antarctic air. And out of the cold and silence, the crying voices of those trapped would arise. The cackles and wallows of the insane. Then the happenings. The rampage. The random, indiscriminate slaying would begin. But it'd be much worse than anything I could imagine. So much worse. Death would come for every last being.

I shuddered in my spot as I thrust those horrible inevitabilities to the back of my mind. There was no point filling my brain with a weight I had no control over. Turning on my heel, I put my hand up and knocked on my mother's cold, steel stateroom hatch. The corridor around me echoed as I knocked. I smiled briefly, wondering why I bothered to knock at all. Old memories, probably. At a time long ago when my mother was lucid, she'd give me a mouthful of abuse if I didn't knock before entering. Old habits, I thought. Some things never change. I pushed the big steel hatch open and stepped inside. I could already hear her doing that London Bridge thing.

"London-bridge-is fall-ing-down . . ."

"London-bridge-is-fall-ing-down . . ."

She sang the first line, repeating it over after a slight pause. The same as she always did. Nothing had changed even though I hoped. From under a single dim light bulb that hung, slightly swinging from a long cord, she rocked herself forward and back while sitting at the edge of her bed. Singing. Rocking. Singing. The sight of her doing that brought me to the edge of tears, and it was as though someone had thrown a rock on my heart. There was a time this woman was one of the hardest individuals living among us. A true Gabriel. Hard, but at the same time compassionate. Caring. Considerate. Now, my mother was awake but gone. And she'd gone without telling anybody.

"London-bridge-is-fall-ing-down . . ."

I sat beside my mother; a bowl of warm broth made from the meat of emperor penguin resting in the palm of my hand. I swept her hair from her face, then; placed a spoonful of the broth next to the corner of her mouth. She wouldn't take it.

"London-bridge-is-fall-ing-down . . ."

"Mom. Please. You know you have to eat something."

"London-bridge-is-falli . . ."

"Mom!"

"London-Bridge . . ."

"MOM!"

I loved my mother, and it was so painful to see her trapped behind this thin membrane of insanity. At times I wished hard to be given the power to reach inside her body and pull her back to the surface. This thing that has taken her; it made me feel anger and frustration in a whole new way.

Just as I thought I could scream out my frustrations, my mother stopped with the singing. She rocked forward and back as though singing those words inside her mind. It occurred to me then; had she noticed my anger? Was she more lucid than I realized? If that was so, was she playing games? Maybe she wasn't insane at all. Maybe, just maybe, she was doing all these things as a means of escape. A way to hide from the others. A sort of evasion and deception. What if she had a plan to escape *Steinbeck* all to herself? What if she was playing us all, and at any second she might come clean, laugh her lungs out, and 'fess up? My mind began to spin knowing what I had stashed away. Nine vials of highly concentrated sleeping medication. Probably the last in existence. I'd locked them away in a place they were safe. They were ready whenever I was ready. But now this. Doubt. Uncertainty. It made me want to cancel all of my plans and start over.

"Mom? Are you faking this?"

There was no response. My mother kept up the same rocking tempo without so much as a slight change. Then I realized I was clinging to hope. And hope makes things appear to be what they are not. Hope is an emotion that can cloud logic and sensibility. I had no room for hope in my escape strategies. Then, as I realized it, I felt as though somebody dropped me from an awful height.

Again, I attempted to feed her. Now it was like I wasn't there at all. She didn't attempt taking her once favorite soup. "Mom, it's emp. You like it. Remember?" I placed a hand on her back, so she'd be still. I held up the spoon. There was no recognition that it was ever there. She'd retreated even further into her darkness than I realized. There was nothing further I could do.

* * *

My mother's stateroom hatch squealed opened, and Jason stepped inside. He went straight for the metal chair in the corner and dragged it over, sitting himself down heavily as if he'd spent the entire day harvesting blocks of ice and stowing them away in secrecy.

"Did you stash them with no trouble?" I said over my shoulder as I tried again with feeding my mother.

"Yeah. We've got enough freshwater ice in reserve for a couple of weeks. It's safe. I think it's stored close enough to the McMurdo ruins without it becoming radioactive. But you still haven't told me how we're gonna store it before we leave. You can't drink ice, Ditch."

"I've got it covered. We'll cut the blocks into sizable chunks first then tie seal skins around them. As the ice melts, they'll be like water inside skin canteens."

I'd already made seven canteens that were ready to go. But seven wasn't going to be enough. I estimated we'd need around thirty canteens to last us the trip safely across to Australia. And that was being conservative. Forty was a good round number with a buffer in case there was trouble. But fifty was the goal I had in my head. We'd not leave without having fifty canteens full of freshwater ice. Or as close to it as possible.

Jason suddenly seemed a little brighter. "You and your seal skins, huh? How's our mother doing?"

I handed my brother the bowl of emp broth. "Here. Your turn. See what you can do."

Immediately after he took the bowl off me, my mother again began to sing her tune, rocking back and forth as she'd previously done. "London-bridge-is-fall-ing-down . . ."

Before my blood had the opportunity to boil up all over again, there was a polite tap on the hatch. The hatch swung open, and Chloe delicately stepped inside. It never stopped amazing me how the Raphael clan were inherently light on their feet, and Chloe possessed the ability to slink around the place with the prowess of a puma. She stepped past Jason and me while grabbing the other metal chair, sliding it over. "Hope I'm not too late." Chloe sat slowly, eyeing my mother as she lowered herself into her chair. "How is she?"

"She's in la-la land," I said. "No change."

Then, all of a sudden,

"Chloe? Is that you? Come here, dear." My mother said it as though it was of no nuisance. No bother. Jason and I exchanged our shocked glances.

Lucid.

"Mom? It's Ricky. How're you feeling?"

"Richard? Richard? I . . . It's the bridge, Richard. It's the bridge."

"Mom?"

"It's falling . . ."

Shit!

"London-bridge-is . . ."

"MOM!"

"Leave her," Chloe took the bowl of broth from my brother and began the same task with which we'd had no success. I watched Chloe go through the same steps I'd worked with, and with the same result. No good. She turned and placed the bowl out of the way. Somehow, I knew the broth had already gotten cold, and emp broth that went cold always had a gritty texture with an aftertaste that wasn't pleasant. If I knew my mother, she would've complained bitterly had she been lucid.

The hatch opened. Immediately, Jason shot me a look that told me he wasn't impressed. Moonie stumbled, almost tripping through the opening. He was intoxicated again, but with all of his faults, we needed him. Jason would have to get over it.

Not able to grab a seat in time for gravity to take over, Moonie sat heavily on the floor with crossed legs as though a little kid at school time. He looked up with a grin as though he'd accomplished something impossible. Getting the meds that I needed *was* a feat by itself. Being a Lucifer, however, Moonie's greatest gift was at night. He saw things with the clarity of a nocturnal creature. The other reason he had to be with us was for the need of a sextant. Skipper had one locked away on the bridge. Moonie was Skipper's son. How simple could it be? Not only did we have access to a sextant, but we also had someone with us who could use it. Moonie was far too important. I knew he *had* to be part of the plan and now, I only hoped Jason knew it as well.

Convicts

THE RAPHAEL CLAN SHARED THE SAME auburn hair, blue eyes, and the same sporadic dusting of freckles as each other. But each time I looked into Chloe's crystal eyes that reflected the same blue as glacial ice, I never stopped enjoying the one thing I loved to do the most. I'd linger there in the reflection of her gaze where sometimes her eyes were so liquid, I swear I could swim in them. Trance-like, there'd be no words, and I'd stay there. Chloe seemed to know it was something that made me feel contented. She never looked away. She always smiled. "I love you," she'd say, breaking the silence by words louder in volume than they truly were. I'd look away from her smile. I'd rest my head on her chest and listen to her heart, feeling the muscles in my cheeks. I was happy.

Life's realities can invade even the happiest of thoughts and the most peaceful of moments. Earlier, I'd told Chloe about our plans to escape. At first, Chloe was like Jason. She was disbelieving of the whole affair. She couldn't picture in her mind how such an audacious plan could ever succeed. But after she'd had the time to think it over, she conceded. For the sake of our unborn child, it was the only option we had left. But I omitted one important detail. I held back on telling Chloe about my mother. I didn't tell her about the nine vials of sleeping meds I'd kept stashed away in my footlocker. I didn't know why I couldn't bring myself to say it. It appeared I was having a bout of indecision. I was having second thoughts.

Deep in my mind, the decision to end my mother's life was in utter turmoil. It was as though some dark force was throwing me in one direction, then back to the other. How could I sit there at my mother's side and watch her take her last breath? Was it evil of me to do such a thing, even if it were out of compassion? I kept repeating in my mind, the steps I needed to take. But it never made anything easier. I was still a murderer. It didn't matter which angle I looked at it. I was going to commit a murder, and not only that, I was going to commit an appalling crime; matricide.

"I can feel your brain ticking over." Chloe's words were loud through her chest as I laid my head there. At that moment I decided she must know everything.

"My mother . . ." I took a huge gulp of air. I was about to continue.

"You're going to euthanize her, aren't you?"

Chloe knew me so well; there wasn't a thing I could keep from her. She knew my unspoken words as plainly as any spoken words. It was another trait of the Raphaels. They all seemed to possess this strange ability. I'd gotten so used to it, it never surprised me, but this time it did.

"You've got meds to send her to sleep?"

Not able to answer her question outright, I nodded. I hoped Chloe could feel my nod on her breasts. It was then I felt her arms pull me in and I cried openly. Oddly at the same time, a voice inside told me there's no shame for a man to shed tears if he shares them with his wife. I'd never wept so hard. So uncontrollably. I don't think there was a time, ever, in my life where such sadness trapped me. I was overwhelmed and broken. The reality of what was to come hurt so bad; I felt every bit of it. With every pulse around my heart. With every breath of air in my lungs.

"Ricky, this sadness inside you is hard. But you'll take care of this."

After I was able to regain my composure, nothing more needed to be said, but at least now, I knew it in my heart, Chloe was right.

* * *

I opened my eyes to the sounds of commotion coming from somewhere at the end of the corridor. From down there, someone screamed out obscenities and other nonsense. I recognized it as Moonie. His outbursts instantly made me chill to the bone. My skin prickled on my forearms. I realized through his cries; they were beating him with terrible blows.

I responded, sitting upright in my hammock, cocking my head in the direction of the uproar. With the flat of my hand, I carefully attempted to awaken Chloe, taking extra care not to alarm her. As though reading my gesture, I felt her move in closer toward me. I was sending the wrong signal.

"Chloe," I whispered. "It's Moonie."

"What?" Chloe rolled over and raised herself on her elbow, listening with the same awareness as I'd done a moment before. "My goodness. What's happening?" At the same time, Moonie yelled out chillingly after another round of fleshy thuds. I flew from my hammock. Before I made it to the hatch, someone pounded at it with what I thought were bare fists. "Open up! Open-the-fuck-up. Now!"

The sound of his voice made me recoil on the spot. *Shit. It's Skipper!*

Somewhere in the back of my mind, I knew what was happening. All our plans. All our strategies. Everything. It was all over. Jason was right. They're going to float us.

I moved to open the hatch but stopped. I looked at Chloe. She pointed with a quivering finger to the footlocker. The vials of sleeping medicine. Panic went rocketing through my brain. Chloe knew where I'd stashed them. How? It didn't matter. But what was I supposed to do with them now? *Make them disappear.* My eyes went to the porthole. They'd land softly on the snow outside. Maybe nobody would notice them. And if there was no evidence, there'd be no floating. Maybe, just maybe, everything might not be lost after all. Maybe, after everything had died down, we could pick up where we left off.

I leaped across to the footlocker and opened it, at the same time signaling to Chloe. I whispered loud enough for her to hear, "Open the porthole, Chloe. Quickly." I rummaged through the footlocker and my fingers curled around the small metal box with the sleeping meds inside. Then I realized it for the first time. I might be able to get rid of the vials of death. But what about all the seal skins? What about the big containers of glue? What about the charts and compass Moonie had stolen from the ship's bridge? My head was about to explode in panic.

"Open the hatch, seaman Gabriel! That's an order!"

Chloe was at the porthole. She opened it just in time. I held the metal box up in the same way as I'd read in books about football. In my mind, I tried to work out how to make it spin after I hurled it.

"Seaman Gabriel! Open this hatch! Immediately!"

More footfalls arrived outside the bunkroom. Maybe there were seven sets!

I wound up my shot, aiming the box for the tiny opening that let in the daylight.

My life depended on it. *All* our lives depended on it. Getting busted with the seal skins and glue was bad enough. The stolen charts and compass was a long-term in the brig. If I didn't make the sleeping meds disappear, *holy shit* . . . It most certainly was death by floating. That small porthole wasn't much bigger than the metal box in my hands. Could I do it? From around thirty hands away?

I wound up my shot but before I threw it . . .

The hatch swung open. Skipper burst in and stood there with his master key dangling from his grip. His black as black pupils fixed on me. The word 'busted' whipped around my brain like a headless snake. I stood there and his pupils grew to cover the whites in his eyes. He looked as evil as ever. His voice lowered to some dark place, "Give-it-to-me!" He moved toward me with speed. I quickly glanced sideways to Chloe. She held her hands to her face and mouthed the word 'no,' but it was too late.

I got that metal box and raised it above my head. As soon as Skipper was within range, I brought the metal box down with my full weight, smashing it between his ebony-black eyes.

"No Ricky, NO!" Chloe screamed.

As Skipper collapsed to the floor, I caught sight of the heavily armed security detail who were with him. Two men moved swiftly toward me, metal batons extended. I gritted my teeth. Hard. As soon as one got close enough, I aimed and kicked. He spiraled away cupping his testicles, yelling out in pain, falling backward over Skipper's unconscious body.

In the next second, a loud *CRACK*, and the agonizing pain went straight to my head. Just as the horror of being kneecapped became real, my leg folded under my weight and I went down. Another crack on the collarbone and instantly, a wrecking ball of severe agony shot through my body.

Somewhere in the background, Chloe screamed out more chillingly than before, and I knew from that second, no amount of fighting and struggling could ever change anything. It was over. There was no hope and no chance of getting away to Australia. No hope to escape from the inevitable blackout. We'd all perish. And my execution would come sooner than lights out. There was no doubt in my mind that my fate was sealed. They'd have us chained on an ice floater, where I'd meet up with an orca, and my body would cease to exist.

* * *

A security guard yelled as I was dragged with speed down the corridor toward the ship's brig. "Make way! Make way!"

My feet skidded past Jason's bunkroom and I noticed his hatch was left open. The fear of it all struck me as I felt a hard lump form at the base of my throat. I was just able to fleetingly peer through the aperture of his hatch as they dragged my body past. Jason wasn't there. My mind tried to hide from the reality, but there was no hiding. They had Jason and had taken him away.

Betrayal settled heavy in my mind. And the worst part of the realization was Jason's words, telling me I'd signed my death warrant by letting Moonie in. I thought I had it sorted. I thought Moonie would be a valuable asset when it came to navigation. I knew the risks. I knew the dangers. And I always thought Moonie never had it in him to turn. I was wrong. I took it for granted. Now I was pulling everybody I ever cared about down into this pit of despair I'd created.

They threw me to the floor in the brig and the loud echo of the brig hatch clanged behind me. Jason eyed me from one corner of the big space with his gaze of death. As I lifted my head, still dazed and dizzy, I expected him to say something. Anything. But instead, Jason got up from his awkward crouched position, and within a couple of seconds, I was feeling myself reeling back from an immense thump to my left eye socket. As I shook away more daze and came to, I noticed we weren't alone. Sitting right behind me in the opposite corner was Moonie.

Chapter Four

Break Out

WE EXCHANGED NO WORDS. OUTSIDE the brig, the voices and footfalls of souls going about their business, padded up and down the corridor as though it was the same day as any other.

I sat on the edge of a metal sprung bunk bed, swallowing back biting pain in my shoulder and left knee. The amount of damage I'd received from the end of a metal baton was immense, and I wondered how in the heck I could ever recover from such injuries. Somehow, I knew from beneath my swollen knee that was the size of a small melon; the bone had shattered into a million tiny shards. I knew my collar bone would never heal normally if nobody put it right. Then I thought, why would anyone bother fixing it? Our execution was probably only a matter of days away.

Jason finally broke the silence. "Little brother. What's your plan now, Ditch?"

I would've *shrugged* my response if it was possible. The thing was, I had no clue. But Jason's folded arms and pushed down brow told me he was demanding an answer. Who was I to deny him? "There's no plan, Jase. You and I both know what'll happen next."

"Orca teeth." Jason said it not as a question but as a realization. He was thinking out loud. I nodded my response even though he didn't need it. But in my mind, I thought there must be a way to get out of this mess.

I looked around the place. Everything was solid metal and cracked green-grey paint with the same pattern of intricate rivet-work as everywhere else. I'd watched movies of prison escapes back when there was the electricity supply to show them. The first thing I did was to look up, and there it was. But the air ventilation system was minuscule, and it wasn't big enough for anybody to use as an escape route. To my left, there was the porthole to the outside. No good. It was too small for any human to get through and they'd covered it with metal bars. Maybe they put the bars there to make the place look like a brig. The only way we were ever going to leave was through the hatch. So that left only one option.

Leaving my bunk bed, I scooted sideways over to Jason's side, grimacing with pain. "We'll need to overwhelm and disarm any-one coming through," I said.

Jason looked over his shoulder toward me, not bothering to change his seated posture. His body language said everything.

"And judging by *your* condition, you'd be wanting *me* to take care of it."

"Who else? It's what you're good at. You're a natural born killer."

"You and your movies."

"Yeah, and I read too."

But just as I said it, I noticed something on the floor. I left Jason's side to go and take a closer look. I put my hand down and felt it to make sure I wasn't dreaming. Jason came over to my side in a hurry. "Well, will you look at that."

"Yeah. But how . . .?"

There was a metal plate on the floor that screws held into place. It wasn't riveted down. That said the plate was covering something that needed maintenance. The plate was roughly four hands by four hands.

"A crawl space?" Jason asked.

"The main electricity supply conduit," I answered him. "But maybe big enough to *use* as a crawl space. I think we can use it to get out of here."

"Only if we could undo the screws, Ditch."

Jason was right. How would it be possible to undo them? I sat back and thought it over. I wasn't satisfied leaving the morsel of hope alone. There must be a way, I kept telling myself. There must be a way, damn it! But even if we *did* escape the rusty steel confines of the brig, where could we go? We were on a ship. It didn't matter which way I looked at it; we were rats in a trap. In or out, it didn't matter. As soon as I thought it, my spirits melted away, and I was at the same place I started.

The big hand-screw on the hatch spun anticlockwise, and it swung open. We madly scurried to our bunks and made like a couple of guys who were up to nothing. Before the guard slammed the hatch closed and locked it into place, he'd hastily tossed another prisoner to the center of the brig. As I focused, it was as though my mind was playing tricks. Looking up from his half seated, half kneeling position in the middle of the floor was the ship's medical officer, Eli Raphael.

Jason put a hand up to his face. "You gotta be kidding,"

Out of my mouth came the obvious. "Why are *you* here?"

Eli looked up and his face contorted into something I thought was out of embarrassment. It was obvious he'd screwed up, but how?

"It seems a breach of security in the medical stores falls on my shoulders. The buck stops with me if things go missing, especially things like vials of sleeping medication." Eli shot a hard look to Moonie. He got up and raced toward him; hands clenched into fists. I grabbed Eli before he could do any damage to Moonie's physical appearance. "There'll be a time for that," I said as I somehow stopped him from getting any closer. "More important things need doing first. How would you like to come on a trip?"

"Ditch!" Jason yelled. But before Jason could protest further, Eli's mood appeared to brighten up. "Trip? Where?"

"Ditch, we have to get out of *here* first."

"So, what's your plan?" Jason asked again. Now I felt the pressure to come up with something. Anything. I began by looking around the place, taking stock of what we had available – things that could help us. We had a couple of steel sprung beds with cotton bedding. That was about it. I squinted my eyes and looked at those things closer. I looked beyond what they truly were and imagined what they could become. Parts. I needed items to; one – stop anybody from getting inside the brig, and two – to use as screwdrivers.

I closed my eyes.

I thought things over.

How could I get this done?

And then everything fell into place. I had all the pieces put together. And better than that, I knew it would work.

I said to Jason, "When was the last time you saw any metal cutting equipment on *Steinbeck*? I'll answer that for you. You haven't because there isn't any. Why? Because they'd destroyed all that stuff after The Fall."

Jason folded his arms tighter. "Your point?"

"If we block the hatch by jamming the hand-screw, nobody can get in. And even if they did find something to break in, it'd be too late. We'd be far away."

"And how do we block the hatch?" Eli asked.

"How? Like this." Managing to get to my feet, I cast my eyes on the steel frame bunk bed. I grabbed one of its steel legs and tugged. After a tug, I fell back to the wall and pain instantly shot up my spine and into my head.

"You'd better let me look at that," Eli said as he began to examine my injuries. My knee wasn't broken after all but severely bruised. My collarbone had broken, and from one of the bed sheets, Eli made a sling and placed my arm into it. After he'd set it up, the pain melted away and I could finally breathe.

Turning my attention to the job at hand, "I need one of those bed legs," I said and started pulling at it again, but the bastard wasn't coming off as easy as I thought. It was as though Jason caught on to my idea. He had his hands all over it, and I saw it was only a matter of time before he ripped the thing from the frame. With Eli stepping in to help, the steel leg made a snap, and it came away in one solid piece.

I pointed with my available hand, and Eli knew what to do. He took it and placed one end of the leg through the spokes in the hand-screw; the other end rested on the floor. Nobody was ever going to get in without cutting equipment. That's all there was to it.

"Now how do we get away?" Eli asked. I looked over to Jason who was again sitting on his bunk with his arms firmly locked in a fold. It was as though he was daring me to sort this out. He didn't know that I *had* it sorted out and I was almost thrilled to show him. I smiled as I reached and pulled a small spring from the side of the bunk frame. I got myself to the steel plate in the floor. The tip of the spring fitted snugly into the screw heads that were holding the plate down. I began undoing the screws.

Jason laughed as he got himself over to my side.

"Go and grab another spring, Jase. You can work on getting more screws out. The more, the better."

Eli grabbed another spring from the bunk frame. He came back to the plate and went at the screws with vigor. As several minutes slipped past and then turned into roughly twenty without so much as a single screw loosened, we all sat back out of breath.

I wiped the sweat from my face as I realized, all the screws were corroded and frozen into place and maybe frozen for over a hundred years. I wasn't prepared to give up that easily. I grabbed a sheet from the bed and stuck a corner of it in my mouth. With my good arm, I ripped off a strip. Eli, as though reading my mind, grabbed the sheet from me and ripped a strip away. "What do you want to do with it?"

"Put it around the spring so we can get more leverage."

Eli wound a strip of bed sheet around the spring and handed it over. At the same time, Jason ripped a strip of bed sheet and did the same. I placed the tip of the spring in the screw and put my weight behind it. Then something I didn't expect. The head of the screw snapped off.

"Shit!" Jason said.

"It's okay, Jase. If they break, we'll still be able to get the plate off."

Another screw head snapped off at the same time someone unlocked the hatch from the other side. The big hand-screw on the hatch moved a fraction and with the bed leg stuck in it; it became jammed into place.

Here we go.

We all held still and watched the hand-screw jiggle back and forth. Then it jiggled violently. We were only minutes from getting away to our new freedom.

"Open the hatch!" The voice yelled from the other side. The hand-screw jiggled back and forth more violently than before. "Open the hatch! Now!"

"Shit!" Jason said more urgently than before.

"Get your head into it, Jase. They can't get in. Concentrate. You too, Eli."

We bent down and went at the screws. Some screw heads broke off as expected. That was good. But others refused to break. And a couple of the screws just would not budge. If there was a time this needed to go smoothly, it was now. I counted them. Ten screws were busted. We'd loosened three. Two screws refused to do anything. Their heads became burred over. The slots were beginning to disappear. If the screws were located closer together, it wouldn't have mattered. But as Murphy's law would have it, they were far apart which meant levering up the plate to break them was impossible.

More booted feet came thumping down the corridor and stopped outside the hatch. Whoever it was this time worked the hand-screw over again. We watched as it jiggled back and forth. Then the voice spoke loudly on the other side, and I knew it was Skipper. "You have two minutes! That's all you've got! It's up to you!" There was an inaudible conversation between Skipper and others who were out there; then they sprinted away.

Jason shouted, "SHIT!"

"Jason. It's like I said. They can't get in. Just get that damn plate off!"

With only two screws to go, I tried hard to stem the rise in my frustration. I was beginning to feel sick. My hand ran around the edge of the plate, and I could almost get a finger under it. "We're almost there!" But something made me instantly stop. The breeze of someone rushing past me. Moonie scampered to the hatch and began tugging at the metal bar. I reached out and grabbed his jeans leg and tried to drag him back. Pain screamed into my head, and I couldn't move.

Just as I thought it, Jason sprang up and rushed past me. He grabbed Moonie and pulled him back. He pulled a sleeper hold on Moonie. Within a moment, Moonie went still and collapsed to the floor.

The danger was over. I went back to the screws.

Then, the sound of something rushing in. For some reason, my eyes went to the air vent above, and the horror struck me. "Eli. Can you rip off a couple more strips from that sheet?"

He nodded without question and went to it. After handing me a strip, I pointed to the vent. "Tear gas. The bastards are trying to gas us out!"

For the first time in my life, I saw terror in Jason's eyes. Eli handed him a piece of rag which he took and used to take cover from the rushing gas.

I pointed with a finger to the air vent and motioned to Eli. Without words, he took the rest of the bed sheet and pushed it up to the vent.

"SHIT!" Jason yelled.

"Jason get it together!"

Then, the last two screws gave way with an audible snap. I shot a stare at Jason and smiled as I lifted the plate away. The happiness of getting away was shortlived by mere seconds. What I thought would most certainly be a crawl space, turned out to be nothing more than a pit going down roughly five hands, filled with pipework and valve handles. We weren't going anywhere. We were done.

Jason stood and as though without thinking about it, took the bed leg away from the hand-screw. The hatch sprung open. In ran the booted feet of armed guys in gas masks. The butt of a rifle rushed at me. Blackness came.

Chapter Five

Ice Floater

I OPENED MY EYES, AND I WAS welcomed by the cold crispness of the Antarctic outdoors. Vapor shot from my breath, and somehow, I knew I was closer to the floating than I could ever realize. When they wanted to get rid of a prisoner condemned to death, these guys wasted no time. Why waste time on a guy who was about to commit murder by killing his own mother? Why waste time on a guy who was behind the theft of valuable medical resources? A guy who planned to initiate an audacious escape strategy? A guy who made his woman pregnant? I was fast-tracked. No fuss. No bother. I was on my way. I could almost feel a set of cold orca teeth puncture my body and rip me apart. And I'd be alive to feel every bit of the pain.

I tried to jiggle my wrists free and I realized with a heavy heart I wasn't alone. Eli's voice protested profusely at what was happening. Then there were Jason's words in his standard tone telling

Eli to *shut-the-fuck-up*. From behind me, someone was sprouting off garbled nonsense, and I knew it was Moonie.

"CHLOE!" I shouted.

"Ditch! It's no good, Ditch! They're floating us today, Ditch!"

"Richard . . ." Eli's voice from somewhere in the front. "Don't waste your breath, Richard. You'll need all your strength."

Is this really happening?

"CHLOE!"

"Ricky . . . Don't die, Ricky."

Chloe's voice was faint from somewhere far behind. I realized she was still on-board *Steinbeck*, probably the flight deck. She was probably being made to watch.

"CHLOE . . . I'LL COME FOR YOU!"

"Ricky . . . I love you . . ."

Some big guy stepped over me. Blackness came.

* * *

I opened my eyes to find myself chained on the ice right by the water's edge. From what I could tell, Eli, Jason, and Moonie were close by. They'd chained all of us within easy reach of the orcas that roamed the freezing Antarctic seas. There were no words between us as the bastards who put us there got busy with finishing things up. Skipper's words came slicing through the subzero stillness, sounding every bit as cold. He spoke as though reading aloud from some official paper, the numerous charges and a quick, emotionless verdict of guilty; then, he imposed the death sentence with the same blasé as making a morning brew. Our deaths would arrive through the teeth of an orca, or worse, through the gut pinching distress of dehydration.

In the next moment, a series of vibrations through the slab of ice confirmed they'd cut us from the ice shelf and cast us adrift. The cold Antarctic wind took over, and it wasn't long before we were well out to sea.

* * *

I had no idea how long we'd been out floating. The ice had already partly melted beneath us, and for the first time, I felt water splashing and lapping at my boots. I oddly thought how amazing it was that they'd tied us fully clothed. We were dead anyway. Why waste good clothing?

I jiggled my right wrist at the end of the chain and checked if the ice had melted around the poles that held us captive. The poles wiggled a little but not enough to make any difference. I no longer felt any sensation in my back, or pain in my knee and shoulder. I assumed the ice had anesthetized my body as I lay there.

"You guys okay?" I asked with my voice lightly crackling; my throat so dry.

No answer. I might as well have said it to the fish out there. But even so, how could I not be in awe of the scenery. The water so calm. The clouds hung low enough for me to reach out and grab them had I not been chained. Seabirds spiraled and cried out to each other. The sun cast visible rays of light across the water's reflection. If my head told me I was in a dream, I'd have believed it.

"Ditch! Wake up! Don't sleep or you'll die!"

What would it matter? I was dead anyway.

"Richard! Open your eyes, damn it!"

I immediately opened my eyes and pain racked my body. I just wanted to curl up and get away from it. Looking around the place, I was in exactly the same scene I'd been dreaming about. But this time I knew I was well in the stages of dehydration. I thought by the way I was feeling, I'd live another twelve hours. Maybe. Nausea came in waves, and if there was something in my gut to throw up, maybe I'd have done it. If an orca didn't take me soon, my eyeballs would become nothing but food for seabirds. We'd all end up that way. Then the ice would melt, and we'd become history.

As I lay there and listened to yet another bout of Moonie's nonsense, I attempted to get my head away and think of Chloe. I felt a big vibration strike the ice from underneath and my heart sank. Here we go.

Chloe . . .

In that split second, a killer whale breached the water right at my feet. All of a sudden, I was sweating needles. I wanted to kick it away. The orca stared, surveying the area with one huge eye before slowly sinking back into the water.

"Oh . . . This is it, guys," Eli said. But just as he said it, the huge mammal breached the water with its full length, then fell back down, causing a wave of salty sea to crash over us. For a few seconds, I became fully submerged. Not properly prepared, I swallowed back a big mouthful of seawater, and after breaking the surface again, I coughed hard before I could finally take another breath.

As though in a mad panic, Moonie started to sound off. The huge sea beast breached the water and came down belly first, wrapping its teeth around Moonie's abdomen. Moonie yelped, and before any other noise escaped him, a snap, a rip, a spray of blood, then Moonie was gone. I gazed out on the blue water where I'd last seen Moonie and the sea bubbled, became tinged with red, and I knew he could never survive.

"Hey, Ditch. Today is a good day to die. Die easy, my brother."

I closed my eyes. I always thought when death came, I'd meet it head on. But this was something else. I closed my eyes to concentrate. I wanted to know for sure. The sensation was no lie. We were moving; there was no denying it. I felt the unmistakable awareness of movement. Something was under the slab, pushing us through the waters. The question was what, and how? As I realized it, we were moving through the water and picking up speed. The entire slab tilted at a steep angle and a bow wave began to form. An orca's tail broke through the water's surface. Then there were two. Then another. And another orca of no color at all. White as an albino. The same as me. The same as Jason. The same as any Gabriel.

"Ditch . . . What's happening!"

"We're being rescued." I didn't know how I knew it. I just knew it.

"Rescued, my ass. We're going further out to sea!"

"And we're going north," Eli worked out. "North into warmer waters!"

"Warmer waters! The ice will melt!"

I wondered briefly why the pod of orcas seemed to be helping rather than killing. Jason was right; the ice would melt in in the warmer waters. Then what? Logic told me, the only way to go was down. There'd be no chance for survival at all. The weight of having the chains on our wrists and ankles would pull us under. Even as my logical brain expressed these thoughts, there was the gut. And my gut told me there was something else.

After what seemed hours, skipping over the crests of waves, being pushed north, all of a sudden, nothing. No more forward momentum. No more speed. Rushing to a stop, I was horrified to see that the ice under us was minuscule in dimension and the fact we remained above the water's surface was nothing less than a miracle. The poles that held us chained had completely fallen out of the ice and disappeared. And out there; there was nothing. There was nothing but the sea, horizon, and blue-blue sky.

Eli pointed into the distance. "Over there. Look."

I adjusted my gaze in the direction Eli pointed. Jason jiggled his chain and cupped a hand over his brow. At first, I was hard-pressed making out anything. But as I looked harder, a container surrounded with some old rags bobbed up and down with the motion of the sea. When the object finally got close enough, for some reason, all I wanted to do was kick it away. A person's skel-etal remains in bedraggled clothing floated with its arms outstretched; one boney hand still grasping a handle of what looked like an old military footlocker.

"There's a box," Jason said as he tried to reach for it. "A plastic box, I think."

"Yeah, military footlocker but don't touch it, Jason. If you bring it up on the ice, it might sink us."

"It appears we won't have to worry about drowning after all," Eli said from behind me. "There's a ship out there. See it?" He pointed. I gazed into the direction, and I saw a silhouette backlit from the sunlight. The silhouette of a tall ship.

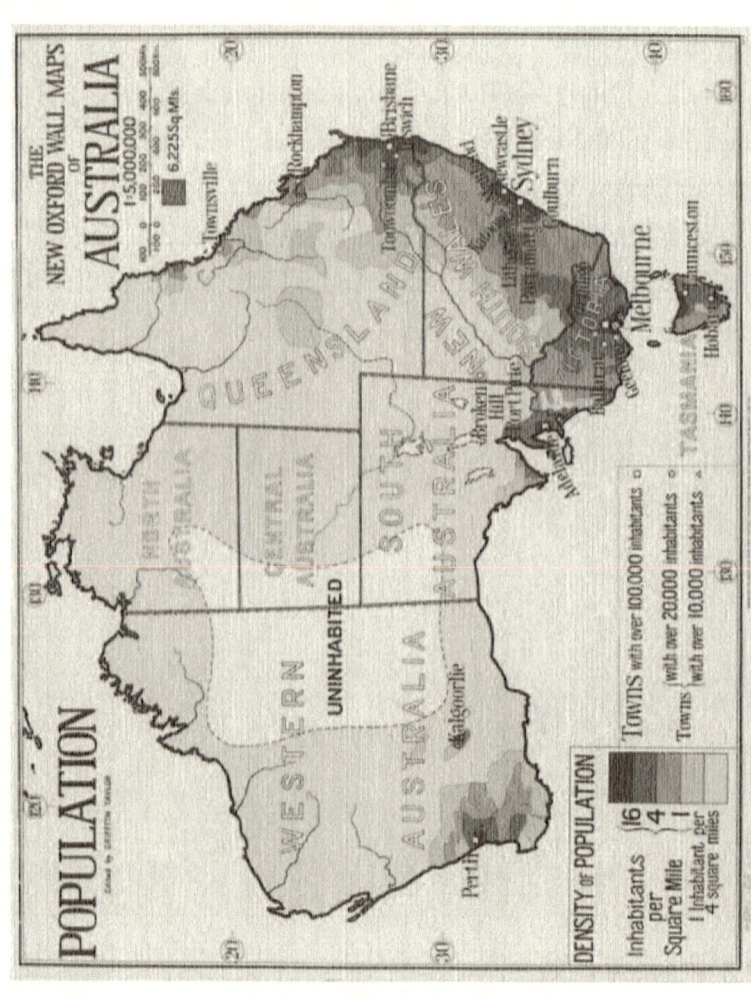

Chapter Six

Victory

THE ICE THREATENED TO SHATTER under our mass. If we fell into the water, having the extra burden of the chains on our wrists and ankles would certainly pull us down. But, as the unsavory fear of drowning settled heavily in my mind, the tall ship that had mysteriously appeared out of the blue, began to hoist her sails.

Men scurried about her yardarms in the processes of tying her sheets into place. I saw men hurrying to get into a longboat, and with their oars dipping into the water, they stroked in synchronicity toward us. It was a race against time. Even as our apparent rescue was near, the ice began to crack in protest. Any sharp or sudden movement was the end. I held my breath and waited, hoping the longboat might arrive in time.

When at last the longboat drew alongside us, the danger was still not completely over. Getting into the longboat was a three-way coordinated exercise. Tricky maneuvering and a whole lot of luck was required. My injuries made moving around difficult and even more dangerous. But in the end, all three of us managed to get to safety.

The last item to be dragged into the longboat was the foot-locker, which a sailor clad in tattered clothes immediately dubbed as 'dead man's chest.' "We'll take that dead man's chest wiv us. There might be treasures to be 'ad in there. We don't take dead blokes either, mate. Leave 'im in the water."

Finding a spot in the longboat, I quickly looked sideways to Jason. "This guy talks strange. What's a bloke?" I whispered.

Jason shrugged. "Maybe it's just another way of saying dead guy."

Approaching the tall ship, I could see the figurehead mounted below the tall ship's bowsprit. I rubbed my eyes a few times. I thought maybe smacking my face a few times would bring me back to reality because, of course, I was dreaming. I'd seen the figurehead before. I'd seen it in books. I'd read the history. I was well acquainted. As soon as I realized it, it was without a doubt. But how was it possible? With her colorful English coat of arms, embellished in gold leaf, being in her presence was just as much surreal as it was awe-inspiring.

The men in the longboat pulled up oars as we came to rest alongside the huge timber and wrought iron ship. I looked up and counted them. Three levels of portholes where I knew the barrels of cannon were only inches from the apertures — a host of deck guns above that. Oddly, I wondered if it was true what they claimed. I'd read that if they fired all her cannon at once, there might be enough energy to tip her on her side. I was humbled in her presence. I fought through the urge to jump out of the long-boat and swim to the stern if only to see her name in all its glory. Eli and Jason appeared just as much awestruck. At that moment, several ropes were flung down from the quarterdeck. The cumbersome climb aboard this both magical and infamous vessel had begun.

* * *

At last, we were relieved of our chains. A couple of young sailors not much older than twelve gave us fresh dry clothes, and for the first time in a long while, I felt as though there wasn't any immediate danger around the next corner. I found myself relaxing a little as I checked out the surroundings. Below decks was the same as I'd learned in *Steinbeck's* library. The place was dark and lit up with oil lanterns in much the same way as I'd already become accustomed. Long shadows danced around the place with the aroma of what I assumed was whale oil in the air. I wasn't familiar with the smell of old timbers, however. I found it pungent – smelling of a mix of mildew, animal waste and what I thought might be gunpowder, saltpeter, and charcoal. Maybe it was just a case of getting used to it. Every now and again, loud cracking sounds erupted from the timbers as the ship rocked in time with the motion of the seas. It was somewhat unsettling as though this ship was alive and breathing.

With my arm in a sling that Eli had made from what they called 'calico gone spare,' the ship's Master, by the name of William Fletcher, ushered the three of us to a series of hammocks they'd slung between huge, ominous looking cannon. They'd given us instructions, and we were to refer to these hammocks as our allotted spaces. "We all work for our keep 'round 'ere," Master William Fletcher told us in an accent I'd not heard before. "There ain't no free lunch on this lady. You blokes are on swabbin' detail after first light. 'Cept you," he pointed at me with a gnarled knuckled finger. "Dunno what cappy wants wiv you just yet. It'll be at 'is pleasure, I'm supposin'. Nigh-nigh, yous lot."

It took a bit of an effort climbing up and into my hammock. But once I got in, my thoughts returned to Chloe. I hoped she was safe. Deep in my heart, I knew I'd have the opportunity to embark upon her rescue. In the morning, I'd lobby the Captain for his help. But I was tired. My eyelids had the weight of a barbell, and they almost instantly slammed shut.

* * *

Early in the morning and after mess, the three of us were invited above decks to meet the captain for the first time. My heartbeat quickened in anticipation but after we were face to face, I was completely taken by surprise. Dressed in the navy-blue woolens of a bygone era, he looked eerily, almost the spitting image of the pictures I'd seen of Horatio Nelson. The same Nelson who died during the battle of Trafalgar. This captain standing in front of us wore the same hat and all.

I was about the exchange my first words.

We have to go back . . . Chloe . . .

The words I had in my head never got the chance to form in my mouth.

"Welcome aboard His Majesty's Ship of the Line, *Victory!* I'm Captain Henry Bass. At your service," the captain said, then stepped back a pace and did this odd bow thing. It was so surreal, and I felt as though I'd gone back in time by a few hundred years. It looked as though all these guys were stuck in some weird time warp. But I couldn't ignore what was in front of me. What I was seeing was authentic. Everything down to the last stitch. Was I dreaming? Was this all for real?

Still not quite sure, I caught myself laughing a little under my breath as I asked my question, and Captain Bass answered with refreshing vigor. "Is she the real *Victory?* That she is, young lad, to be sure. I've known this ship both man and boy. We found her adrift. Albeit without masts, mind you. We fitted her with new masts and new rigging. We brought her back to her former glory. But we also added a few little . . . err. . . modifications to make her the very fine ship she is today. There isn't a vessel out on the high seas which can put a scratch on her paint, truth be told."

"You certainly dress for the occasion," Eli put in.

Captain Bass appeared to shrug off the irony, instantly changing the subject. "On the morrow, we shall set sail for the colonies."

"Colonies?" I butted in. "We need to head south. Back to where we came from."

"You came from the south? Are you sure? There's nothing south beyond this point, young lad; nothing but the ice and the wind. If you came from there as you say, I find it hard to comprehend how any man could feasibly endure such bitter conditions. It's quite impossible."

Eli stepped forward with a hand outstretched. For some reason, Captain Bass took a step backward, and I saw him place a hand on his sword. Eli immediately raised his hands and stepped back. "I'm sorry. I never meant any harm. I'm a doctor and wanted to offer my services if there's a need."

"Good to have another doctor aboard, Mister Raphael," Captain Bass said almost without pause. "I will make haste and acquaint you with our surgeon Doctor Hamell. I run a tight ship, and good morale among my men is my utmost priority. However, there are always the temptations to mutiny among those who may become, for whatever reason, discontented. For that reason, we do not move around below decks with abruptness unless it's required to do so. Mind you take heed of those terms during your stay. That way you shall keep all of your limbs intact by the time we reach the colonies."

I couldn't stand it any longer. "What colonies? We need to head south to Antarctica."

"Why should we, Mister Gabriel? What could be so important that I must abandon my business with the colonies and go on this gallivant extraordinaire of yours? Hmm?"

"There're people there who are trapped. My wife is one of them."

"Trapped? How?"

"They're aboard the *USS John Steinbeck* which was wr . . ."

"*Steinbeck,* did you say? Do I hear you correctly? Did you say *Steinbeck*, Mister Gabriel?"

I nodded. "We don't have much time. Everyone there will perish if we . . ."

"Legend has it; *The USS John Steinbeck* was lost with all hands. In the Sea of Japan. Why, that was over a hundred years ago."

"One hundred and fifty years ago," I corrected the captain. "Those who still live there are the descendants of the original crew. *Steinbeck* was never lost at sea. She became marooned on the Ross Ice Shelf, near McMurdo."

Captain Bass immediately put a hand to his chin as though I had him puzzled. Maybe I succeeded in my lobby. He turned his back slightly, then looking over his left shoulder, he asked, "How many souls, Mister Gabriel?"

In my mind, I didn't know how to answer. Only now I realized things might be different from what I originally planned. I answered the best way I knew how. "5,775 souls on *Steinbeck* at this time. Give or take."

"Good heavens! It would take a small armada to rescue them all. It's quite impossible, Mister Gabriel. However, in the port of Perthland, you may find sufficient help there. We shall make sail to Perthland when the winds allow. There you shall disembark. There you shall raise your inquiry."

"We could at least return and rescue a few. That way they'll all know there's hope."

The captain spun and walked little circles as though deep thought. "So, tell me, young lad. After we collect those whom you hope to collect, what then?"

"Then north to Australia. That was our original plan. We hoped Australia would be the best place for us to settle."

"Australia!"

"We know we could thrive there," Eli put in.

"Why, Mister Raphael, Australia is no longer. It hasn't been Australia since The Fall.

"Australia is gone?"

"Not gone. Just . . . err. . . changed. It is now known as The Province of Australee. The coastlines are not as you might think. The province consists of some islands. No longer is it the large land mass of yesteryear. The great seep destroyed most everything."

"The great seep?"

"The Great Seep, Mister Gabriel. The oceans from the north after The Fall. The entire length and breadth of what was once Australia became inundated. What is left are the islands of today. If you decide to venture there, you must take care. Australee is not a place for the unwary. There are many dangers. Much animal life has been changed forever due to the effects of radiation. Some aggressive animals have increased in their aggressive nature. Some have mutated into great beasts. And that, my dear fellow, is just the beginning."

I took a breath and sat down. I didn't know what to make of it. I'd set my heart on a vision. Now the vision was fading away. The

hard truth of the matter became clear. It wasn't the paradise I originally thought. But one thing was for sure. We had to return to the
south. Chloe. After that, we'd adapt and change to anything.

It was as though Captain Bass knew the news of Australee had
an adverse effect on me. "Incidentally, we opened dead man's
chest," Captain Bass said, changing the subject. "Inside, we found
items of most interest. And some of great value. One of the items
we found is a journal. Perhaps you might enjoy some light reading, Mister Gabriel. Over a tot of rum? Or porter wine if rum isn't
to your taste."

"And about going south? You haven't given a straight yes or
no answer."

I became short with our captain. But I needed to know, one
way or another. I needed an answer. Right now.

"I will need some more time to ponder this whole affair. However, read to me the dead man's journal, and I promise you shall
have your answer."

And just like that, it occurred to me. Our captain didn't read.

Chapter Seven

Picking up the Trail

IN THE MORNING, AFTER A FULL NIGHT OF uninterrupted sleep, I arrived at Captain Bass's great cabin. I was safe on *Victory*. I felt as though, after Chloe's rescue, I could've easily stayed on board to be part of *Victory's* crew. It was a tantalizing prospect. However, I couldn't swim. But I also knew most sailors during the days of old regarded the ability to swim as a bad omen. Maybe I wasn't far from the sea-dogs who were on-board, considering my upbringing.

Taking the opportunity for another breath, I knocked on the great cabin door.

Captain Bass's voice immediately responded, "Enter . . ."

On entering, a silhouette outlined Captain Bass against the early morning sunlight entering through several lavishly decorated windows. There was the sweet smell of lavender in the air, and I thought it was an attempt to cover up the much more horrible odors emanating from other parts of the ship.

"Welcome," Captain Bass said as he stepped from behind his desk and met me in the middle of the floor. For some reason I felt I needed to salute. Before I could, Captain Bass's hand was held out, and I took it and shook. Before I knew it, I was seated in an almost worn out old-style chair. It smelt of the same plush leather that was on *Steinbeck*, and when I sat, the chair almost wrapped around me.

On a side table to my left, under an electric lamp, were a pile of tattered pages, some in different dimensions, most with rips and dog-ears; all had smudging and discolorations in various shapes and sizes. I was also quite certain at least a few pages were bloodstained. I wondered what to do with it. But I wondered even more about the electric lamp.

"Electricity?" I asked, then became lost for words.

"We have a small wind turbine installed on the poop deck. Yes, I know. But we adhere to the tradition whenever possible. The small amount of electricity is for emergencies. Now, back to the task at hand, shall we?"

It wasn't easy to shrug off, but I reached and picked up the stack of papers. Closer inspection revealed no page numbers at all. It was as though the journal was nothing more than a collection of writing, where the writer used scraps of paper whenever and wherever he could find them. But then I looked at it from a different angle. Maybe it wasn't penned out of laziness. Maybe the writer wrote his entries on any piece of paper he could find, purely because there simply *was* nothing else. Looking at it in that light changed everything. I now felt the *need* to read it.

I picked up the unruly wad of papers and placed them in my lap.

"What do you make of this, Mister Gabriel?" The Captain's words interrupted me. "Do you think the dead man who was in the water could be the author of this journal?"

I lifted my eyes to find the captain standing, gazing down at me with a childlike eagerness in his eyes.

"Almost certainly," I said. "If it was in the dead guy's possession, then he must be the writer."

After a long silent pause, it seemed as though the captain's eagerness that was once there abruptly abandoned him. He spun, placed his hands behind his back and peered out of great cabin window. "Then I'm afraid we have . . . fucked it up, as it were."

"How do you mean?"

"The eagle figurine," he said, facing me again. "When you read the journal, you shall find reference to it."

"I'm sorry, Captain Bass. I assumed you couldn't read. I assumed that's why you asked me to . . ."

"There's an old saying," Captain Bass laughed. "Never assume anything. It'll make an ass out of you. I need a powerful mind. I need your help. After I read the first few pages of the journal, it became clear to me; we are missing this eagle figurine. It was missing from dead man's chest. So, the question remains. Where it is?"

After thinking about it, "Maybe it was in the dead guy's pocket?"

"My assumption also. But now this fellow has gone to the deep. There isn't a man on this ship who can swim much less dive into the depths without the proper equipment. If the figurine is down there, the only way to reach it is with the appropriate apparatus, which we do not have. We are quite literally between the devil and the deep blue sea. If we set sail to Perthland to procure the diving equipment we need, we'll lose our position. But if we don't, we're not able to dive."

"Why is the figurine so important?"

"Read on, Mister Gabriel. Read on."

* * *

Entry 722.

A spear of light sometimes rushes through it, casting a rainbow of colours. It's so refreshing to see colours again. Sometimes I find myself staring at it for hours. Sometimes it flashes. Sometimes it glints. Sometimes it sparkles, depending on the time of day. But it never moves. It sits there, frozen in time, sunrise after sunrise, nightfall after nightfall.

I pick it up occasionally. I dust it down. I polish it up. Then, I set it back down and stare at it all over again. The crystal figurine of an eagle, static, yet mesmerising in its beauty eats up my attention until the next time I get the chance to spruce it up. When my folks were alive, they said it was probably the most valuable find ever. They said it was even more valuable than its weight in crackle. More priceless than the Crown Jewels of England before the bombs fell. Those jewels are now gone. Under the waters somewhere, so they said . . .

"What's crackle? And I've never seen this kind of spelling before. Is it a dialect?"

"My dear fellow. Crackle is essentially super hard glass formed in the immense compression of a nuclear explosion. Its hardness makes it perfect for making tools and weapons. Its rarity gives it value. Therefore, they use it as currency between the colonies. They use crackle for the purchase of most anything. Oh, and your second question. I'm afraid I don't know what you're talking about. This person appears to be highly educated because most dwellers outside the colonies can't read, much less spell. But, read on, if you please."

. . . When my folks were alive, they said they could only guess from where the eagle figurine came. There were stories, but no one knew for sure. The scrounger who sold it to me showed me there were bones to go with it. Bones, with a significance. She even expressed an urgency that the eagle figurine and bones must stay together. Whatever the cost . . .

"A scrounger?"

"Good god, man! Just read, will you?"

. . . She introduced herself as Charlotte, and she was eager to offer her name. It was rare for a female scrounger to turn up, and the first in my experience. Having the pleasure of owning something so delicate, so beautiful, is something to fight over. Something to cheat death over. I'll guard it forever, bones and all. I still wonder to this day, why she offered those things to someone like me.

"You're Michael the Protector," she told me. One-how did she know my name? And two-I've never been a protector of anything except my own skin. But anyway. The bones and eagle figurine only cost me nine shards of crackle and a half measure of water. A bargain.

I never stop wondering about the scroungers. They only live short lives from what I can imagine. Out there in the waste, due to the radiation, they'd spend their time mostly in pain. But doing what they do, they're probably the richest individuals still walking. Only those knowing their fate would ever consider going into Fool's Desert. And the odd thing is this. Most scroungers don't usually survive long enough to see where their wealth will take them. They're mad. They're all mad. The lot of them. But without them, there'd be no crackle and no way to purchase supplies. But Charlotte; her face so fresh. Her complexion so perfect. No scratches. No lesions. No sign of discomfort or pain as though she'd never spent any time in the waste at all. I ask myself, how is this possible? And how was it possible to evade the Takers?

I rested the journal in my lap. I looked across the great cabin to a captain who was completely comfortable in his chair, tot of rum - as he called it - in his grip, even though it was early in the morning. "Anything the matter?" the captain asked.

"There's something that comes to mind."

"Go on."

"Charlotte. She had some human bones with the figurine and wanted them to stay together. Why? Also, she appeared to be without the signs of radiation sickness that others share. How?"

"Both valid questions, Mister Gabriel. I am as uncertain how to answer these as you are, I'm afraid. But we have the bones. They were in dead man's chest. Now you're beginning to understand how important it is that we have the figurine."

"And what about these so-called Takers?"

Captain Bass raised himself from his chair and once again stood at the window. He peered out at the same time taking a swig from his glass. "Let me bring you into the light, as it were," Captain Bass said as he took a sidestep and returned to his delicately crafted decanter. "Takers are quite simply our enemy. They will kill anyone to get anything. And due to this, the meek are usually the ones who go without and are the ones who fight for their survival.

"Many decades ago, an ad-hoc government was formed. It was the first attempt at bringing order to the people. During those years, the Takers were mere tax collectors. But, the habit of 'taking' became their prime directive. The juvenile government collapsed as a result. Now, the Takers will take anything at all. They will slit the throat of anybody and do their damnedest to get anything they deem valuable. If you thought you could find a place to settle on the land far away from the Takers, you would be wrong, Mister Gabriel. They are everywhere. Including the high seas. Mark my words. There shall come the day when you shall see this enemy up close and personal."

Before continuing to read, I let Captain Bass's words linger in my mind for a while. He certainly painted a picture which had a profound effect. Even though I didn't know my enemy up close and personal, as Captain Bass put it, I felt as though I was now familiar with them. I wanted to know more, and somehow, I knew what was coming in the next few pages.

. . . They take everything from the corpses they leave behind. Guns are rare. Bullets are even rarer. The Takers had them and no one else. They're out there lurking. They settle among the dust and colourless landscape. They're among the blackened tree trunks and the blackened branches. Blackened branches that forever point up to an endlessly greyed out sky. The fact that I'm alive today is only through the death of the other. And now, those Takers have me on their blood list. They won't stop until they find me.

One day they will. One day my body will be split apart and dismembered. They'll use their crackle encrusted bludgeons to do it. They'll save their bullets for killing scroungers. So, I hide. I shelter. Forever peering, forever looking over my shoulder, never looking straight on, never staying too long, traveling only at night and never, ever, on a full moon . . .

Suddenly, an interruption to my reading. The sounds of rushed footfalls thumped down the staircase and stopped at the great cabin door. Then an urgent knock.

"Enter!" Captain Bass yelled as though he was most annoyed.

"Pardon Captain," William Fletcher said as he was halfway through the door. "Enemy man o' war sighted. She flies *Excelsior's* colors."

Captain Bass immediately clasped both hands behind his back and turned his attention through the great cabin window. "Damn them. Damn their hides," Captain Bass said before spinning and locking his eyes with mine. "The Takers are here for the flesh from our bones, Mister Gabriel. If we engage them, we'll lose our standing position, and we'll lose the prospect of recovering that eagle figurine. If we don't engage them, we're a duck shoot."

With his tot of rum still grasped tightly in his hand, Captain Bass spun on his heel and faced his first officer. "Where away, Mister Fletcher?"

"She's comin' from the nor-east."

"And the weather gauge?"

"It's not in our favor, Captain. *Excelsior's* got the 'eadwind to which we ain't."

It was as though the captain needed to think fast and weigh up his options. Find the eagle or go to war. I could almost see the words on his facial expression as he paced around his great cabin, eyes down tracing the long oak floorboards. I thought a hard choice needed to be made. Much was at stake. Oddly, I found myself in a sort of relief that it wasn't a choice that I had to make. I wasn't a captain and *Victory* wasn't my ship.

"Very well, Mister Fletcher," Captain Bass said almost under his breath. "Beat to quarters, if you please."

"Aye, aye, Captain." Then just as quick as he arrived, William Fletcher was gone.

Captain Bass spun and faced me. There was an enormous disappointment in his expression, and I knew it in my heart what he was thinking. We will never retrieve the eagle figurine from the depths.

"It appears, Mister Gabriel, you're about to meet our enemy for the very first time. Let's give them hell, shall we?"

Chapter Eight

The Seven

FROM HIS GREAT CABIN, I FOLLOWED Captain Bass up the steep flight of mahogany stairs. As we approached the commotion that was churning up top, my mind returned to Jason and Eli. I realized for the first time I hadn't seen them since daybreak. With all the urgency going on, I wondered where they were and in what jobs they'd found themselves. As I thought it, I heard the snare drums rattling away, calling men to their battle stations. I imagined the sea-dogs I'd once thought about were in the midst of being transformed from the unruly mob of liquor drinking sailors, into finely tuned men at arms. I realized war changes men in ways only soldiers and sailors could understand. Somewhere in my gut, I knew I was about to find out how.

"Captain Bass," I called out after him. "Captain Bass, sir."

"Come, come, Mister Gabriel. No time to waste. This way if you please."

Stepping out onto the quarter-deck, it was a scene straight out of a classic maritime novel. Huge sails were already deployed and were with the wind. Men were running here and there, but at the same time, they scurried with purpose, not panic. It was a cleverly put together choreography of movements. Everyone knew their place. Everyone jumped to their posts and stood fast. At the same time, Captain Bass strutted up and down the quarter-deck as though to make a final inspection. With a set of steely eyes hard-set against an expression of determination, he settled at his post next to the ship's helm and the coxswain who had the task of pointing the bowsprit to where *Victory* needed to be. After all hands were at their posts, Captain Bass bellowed out his orders.

"Lieutenant Bradley! Sharpshooters aloft, if you will!"

"Aye, aye, Captain!"

Moments later, red-coated marines hurried themselves up masts with muskets in hand. It was then I saw the outline of my brother disappear with them. He'd found his place among the men, and I had to be honest; it suited him. I smiled a little to my-self as I saw him almost with seasoned ability climb the rigging up the main mast. One of the marines extended a telescope and after placing it back in its pouch yelled, "*Excelsior* ahoy!"

The captain smiled briefly and looked at me over his left shoulder. "She's a fine ship, Mister Gabriel, but she must be dealt with."

Immediately, Captain Bass turned and faced Master's Mate, "Raise our colors, Mister Tennant, if you please."

In the same breath without a pause, "Mister Finch! Run out the starboard battery. Aim chain and nail to flesh above decks. Eighteen pounders low on her hull. Make it so."

"Aye, aye, sir."

"Come up on the wind," the captain ordered his coxswain. "Lay us alongside the bastards, Mister Brice. With one broadside, we shall put her alongside Davey Jones' locker."

I looked up to the crow's nest; to a marine who had his telescope trained on *Excelsior*. His next shouted words changed everything. "Torpedo in the water! Tor-pe-do-in-the-wa-ter!"

In an instant without appearing to think about it, the captain responded. "Hard to starboard Mister Brice! Hard to starboard!"

As the ship took its time responding to the helm, I ran to the starboard rail and looked out. I saw it with my own eyes, the telltale trail in the water that was bearing down, heading straight toward us. I knew in my heart what Captain Bass was doing. I hoped *Victory* would narrow her target footprint in time. As she turned at a screaming slow pace, someone behind me yelled out, "All hands! Brace for impact!"

I needed to get myself to another part of the ship. I needed to get myself away from the blast zone as far as I could get. My legs betrayed me, and I couldn't move. I heard the torpedo drilling through the water with its bow wave forming in front of its warhead like a hammer. I watched on thinking at the same time; this is the end.

The torpedo came drilling through the water, so close I heard the sound of its electric motor. It barely skimmed *Victory's* starboard timbers with a touch so light; it was just a mere kiss. Without exploding as I'd expected, the torpedo passed harmlessly away.

The men roared their happiness at the same time the captain screamed from his post. "If they feel the need to fight with twentieth-century weapons, we'll answer it, by god! We'll answer it and send them to their deaths!"

Looking out to sea, I saw several small waves forming and dipping as though a pod of porpoises were at play beneath the surface. They moved with great speed toward the Takers Ship *Excelsior,* and I knew, these dolphin-like creatures weren't even close to what I at first assumed.

In an arrowhead formation with the albino leading, the group of orcas breached the water and crashed down in what I assumed was intimidation. Then they appeared to dive down deep, and I could no longer see the outlines of their huge bodies. Looking on, I could see the silhouettes of men on *Excelsior* begin to scurry in all directions. It was like seeing an old-fashioned silent movie; the ones I'd watched back on *Steinbeck.*

From where I stood, I saw the water near *Excelsior* rise slightly. Then a huge white Killer Whale slammed into *Excelsior's* larboard hull with enough energy to tip her briefly on her side.

As the Takers Ship righted herself, the booms of guns erupted from her decks in answer to the onslaught. Two orcas at the exact same time struck *Excelsior* amidships and again sent her over on her side. This time men on deck were brutally cast off and flung out into the water.

As *Excelsior* righted herself once more, the sea around her hull frothed with screaming, yelling men. Four Killer Whales as though in synchronicity to each other breached the surface and crashed down on them. After several repeated bombings, the boiling white water became a ghastly tinge of red. The urgent screams of men died slowly as three orcas, albino at the head, crashed with an almighty blow into Excelsior's hull, sending her capsized. The water bubbled and gurgled momentarily before *Excelsior's* stern raised high and she slowly disappeared beneath the surface.

Excelsior was gone. She was laid beside Davey Jones' locker, as Captain Bass had predicted. The water where she was last seen became still and silent. The seven orcas had vanished. And all the while, there was not a single peep from anyone on-board *Victory*. All were as silent as the day itself, including the captain. They were as though stunned, not able to move.

I thought it was up to me to break the silence. "Shit!"

Saying that one word had the same effect of a dozen. Behind me, a little snicker broke into laughter before the entire crew began to rejoice and celebrate the fact no one had lost limbs.

* * *

After the battle, I again found myself with Captain Bass's company in his great cabin. I winced with the pain in my broken shoulder as I lowered myself into the same old leather chair where I'd sat down before things went awry.

"Is it any better?" The captain said pointing his finger while holding his glass of rum both at the same time.

"It's coming along, I think. Still hurts like a bitch if I make sudden moves." As soon as I said it, I knew the captain mostly ignored what I said. His expression told me he was elsewhere. "What say you of those Killer Whales, Mister Gabriel?" Captain Bass asked as he returned to his chair and sat heavily down.

"I don't know what to tell you, Captain."

"Henry," the captain put in. "Please call me Henry. You're no longer on detail here. You and your brother are guests on board *Victory* as from this moment. I'd very much like to consider you as a friend."

"And Eli?"

"He's chosen to spend his time with our surgeon Doctor Hamell."

Just then, it occurred to me. "Oh? You think *I* had something to do with the orcas?"

"Well if you didn't, it does seem quite the coincidence, wouldn't you agree?"

For some reason, I left the conversation there. Maybe I thought it wouldn't hurt for the captain to believe what he was already believing. Maybe it would also bring better negotiating power to the table when we get to talking more about heading south for Chloe. It seemed whenever I brought up the subject, Captain Bass danced away from it. If I was a friend, as he said I was, perhaps he'd be more willing. I decided I'd cement the relationship first by giving him more reading time with dead man's journal. After which, there'd be no more dancing around the subject. I'd go at it full force until Captain Bass relented and took us back to Antarctica.

After taking some rum, I placed the glass to the side and picked up the wad of unruly papers. Captain Bass looked at me with eyes, eager to know what was written next. His expression said something almost childlike. It was as though this hardened man at arms had a soft spot for what might well turn out to be a treasure hunt. Then I realized this whole scenario was getting to be similar to any classic pirate story. Sometimes I wish I hadn't read so many books.

Entry 722 Supplemental

Last evening, a scrounger turned up with a book. After handing it over, I took it and pushed the dust away from the jacket. The Holy Bible was etched into the cover in what I thought could be real silver . . .

I put the papers in my lap and looked away.

"What is it, Richard?"

"What's a *Holy Bible*? Is it some kind of old classic?"

There was silence. I noticed the shock over the captain's expression as he pointed with a trembling finger toward the bookcase. There it was. *The Holy Bible* with all its embellishment on the spine was right there. But the silence ensued. I thought about asking my question again. I had no need.

"Richard. I'm both flabbergasted and staggered at the same time. This isn't a joke, is it? You truly have not read the good book on the holy scriptures?"

"I'm afraid I don't know what that is." It seemed as though the captain wasn't listening to me. To get that kind of reaction, however, I realized this *Holy Bible* must've been somewhat important. I decided I'd pursue this at a later time. But for now, a tactful ignorance was required, and it was back to the unruly pages to continue with the reading.

Chapter Nine

The Lost Ones

. . . At first, I thought the book was an offering, and I handed the old guy a few shards of crackle for his trouble. He pushed my hand away and then gave me two shards to have me read it to him. So, I read it, passing the entire night under my last few sticks of wax. As the first rays of sunlight pierced the horizon, the old scrounger got to his feet, nodded with thanks, and left. I found him a day later just down the hill. He'd taken a shard of crackle to his own throat. What could I do? The man was dead, and his flesh was too far gone. I couldn't use it. The flies were having a feast on his bloated body, so I turned my attention to the flies. In my mind, they were protein, but the bastards were too bloody fast. Then I thought about the scrounger's stuff. No point in not using it, so I took it. I now have a few extra shards of crackle I can use for trade, plus a skin of water, a fresh pair of boots that, tomorrow, I will modify slightly to fit my feet. Some other things; a dingo skin, salted red-belly-black meat, and a couple of old tins

containing what might be either corned beef or dog food. Rare as
rare. In any case, there'd be a good time to crack it open; in an
emergency when things get hard, and I know they will. What a
surprise; the old bastard had candles and not told me. Prick!

I put the papers in my lap, and I was compelled to again look
away. The man's story was starting to get to me.

"Richard. Whatever could be the matter?"

"I never knew about those hardships. I thought things were
tough where I came from. These people are eating each other to
survive?"

"Some do. Most don't. Those who live in the colonies will
never stoop to such abomination. But the Takers . . . My boy, they
are different humans to the civilized. As you've seen with your
own eyes, out on the oceans, Takers have ships bent on taking
souls for their meat."

"They're *all* cannibals?"

"Every last one of them, yes. Horrible to think about, wouldn't
you say?"

So, there it was. If we'd lost against *Excelsior*, we'd all be meat
for the eating. I shuddered in my spot thinking about it. But somehow, I cast that aside and kept going.

. . . I remember the old man telling me the waste was given other
names to begin with. The Big Empty. The Hole. The Black Death,
Fool's Desert, among others. Now, it's 'the waste.' It best de-
scribes what's out there. Nothing. Wind. Dust. Emptiness.

I learned to survive by perfecting the art of boiling my own
urine to purify it a little. It doesn't matter how much I try; the stuff

never tastes like real water. It always has that aftertaste that stays at the back of the throat and never leaves. I dream of a scrounger turning up one day with a condenser I can use. I'd pay whatever the asking. We used to have one when I was a kid. I knocked it off the table by accident, and it fell to the floor, smashing into little pieces. The old man broke my arm for my troubles. That broken arm never healed straight. It serves as a reminder to this day not to fuck up.

Real water I only ever drink if I don't make enough urine. It's a science knowing when to drink water or boil up a kettle of piss.

Lucky for the rain we get, even though you can't drink it straight away. When it rains, it comes down grey as the clouds it comes from. At night, rainwater has a strange glow. I save some of it in a container to see at night if I decide it's better to save on wax sticks. I still don't know how I'll get along once my supply of water purifiers run out. If I don't drink water, I won't piss. What happens after that, I don't know. That bloody condenser again. Wish I never smashed it.

Entry 723.

Gonna make this one quick. Running out of paper. Gonna have to find some from somewhere. And new pens too, else I'll be writing with charcoal. Hate that shit.

Another scrounger came through last evening. This guy with some kind of tribal facial tattoos and he appeared to be much younger than most. I was really hoping he had something I could use. I'd give my left nut for a new shifter. I bloody hate rust. After I asked him inside so I could start a barter, I noticed how bad his clothes reeked of diesel and the smell immediately took me back to a time when I was a kid. That said one thing. He must've come from somewhere that had diesel-powered electricity. I asked him from where did he come. He said east. Nothing more, like it was some kind of secret. I wasn't gonna let this guy get away without telling me the whole of the truth. I thought the place he came from couldn't have been far. Diesel fumes don't stick around on clothes for long. Not unless he was drenched in the stuff. If he was drenched in it, that said he obviously came from somewhere that had lots of it. So, me being me, I pressed him for the rest of his story.

After I gave this guy a palm full of pumpkin seeds which I never had any success with, I saw him loosen up a bit. Even so, I had to work harder. I had to do something that went against everything I believed in. I told him my name, hoping he would do the same. It worked. Michael, I said sticking out my hand. He took it and shook with one word. Temothy.

I thought he doesn't know how to pronounce his own name. "Don't you mean Timothy?"

"That's what I said, bro. Temothy."

I shook my head and thought maybe he had some kind of speaking impairment going on.

From there, things started to come and he finally 'fessed up.

Timothy claimed he came fourteen nights' stride from the east. A place called Newman. He said his clan had been there since Pre-Fall. Already, my mind went into bullshit alert mode. I said to Timothy, "Fourteen nights to the east is under the waters." I knew that from info I got from past scroungers. Then I pulled out my blade and flashed it about so he could see I was in *no mood for the bullshit. Then he did something I wasn't expecting. From a back pocket, he pulled a wad of something I'd never seen before, only heard about. The old man once told me about pho-to-graphs. So, imagine my surprise when I finally saw them. He passed them over and sure enough, ten or so pictures showing people at Pre-Fall, prepping for the coming of the bombs. Imagine my surprise when I could see what they were living in. A big area of buildings and sheds of different shapes and sizes. One picture showed someone up high on a mill, driven by the winds apparently, which Timothy reckoned helped make electricity and also pumped up waters from the ground. Imagine my surprise to see things of colour. Trees, plants, flowers—and animals that they called horses and cows.*

Sceptical, I asked, "Those animals still there?" knowing he'd have to be spinning the bullshit if he said they were still alive. He shook his head and said no. Then he added, "Gran and Pop were the last to see thim. But their mit is stell in our dip friz." He looked down and I could see the tears come to his eyes. I prompted further and he went on to explain about the generators. It seems Timothy's clan were on their last generator when it quit. Timothy reckoned it must've been a fuel blockage. He took the fuel lines apart, but he didn't have the nous to get all the lines sorted so the engine could restart. Now I know why he was drenched in diesel. It all made sense.

"Did you bleed the fuel system?" I asked him. "Diesel engines won't fire if there's air in there."

He looked up at me with these pleading eyes that almost made me sick. "You know how to fex et?"

"We have one of those generators here," I said. "But there's no fuel. There hasn't been for as long as I can remember. We had oil and used it to light up at night. But that ran dry too." I went on. "That old generator doesn't even crank anymore. Even if I had oil and diesel fuel, it'd make no difference now."

"But do you know how to fex et?" He repeated it again, looking up at me with his glossy, fucking pleading bullshit eyes.

"Yeah. Bleed the fuel system and it'll work," I told him. Then it struck me to what he was getting at. Timothy was hinting at the propect for me to go with him back to his place to repair it. For some reason, I looked at his hands, and I remembered the handshake. Timothy's hands were smooth and no rough bits at all. Suddenly, Timothy stood up and asked me properly. "I'll give you anything you want," he said. "If you fex et, you can stay with us for as long as you like. We have food and supplies—everytheng you nid."

I must admit—the prospect of leaving this place was very tempting. After all, what's left for me here? And I've never been fourteen nights east. If anything, if the guy was bullshitting, I'd finally get to see the edge of the waters. From there, I'd make up my own mind where to head, and leave this fucker in the dust where he belongs. There was only one thing stopping me from committing to anything. Takers. Then the thought really hit home.

Three nights east is a Takers' garrison. That's as far as I've ever gone. Even then it was too close for comfort. Too close to getting my head swiped clean from my shoulders. It was while I was out there, I encountered that lone Taker and killed the bastard outright. So, I asked Timothy how he got past the garrison undetected. If he did come from that far east, highly unlikely he'd gotten past The Takers alive. Now I'm thinking the bullshit was laid on thick as that rare sweet stuff they call honey. Yeah, just the thought of honey makes my eyes water. I'm just saying.

"Underground," he said. "Them up top. Me below."

It was a surprise just as much as it was a warning in my head. It made me cough and laugh, both at the same time. Yeah, I thought. Now the bullshit tap was turned fully on. We were on first name basis. I stuffed up again. Now I'm thinking I'll have to kill the bastard before he gets away.

So straight away I lunged forward at him. I put a hand around his throat and the tip of my blade just above his left kidney. Immediately his hands went up and he started to shake. Really fucking scared I thought this guy was. I looked into his eyes, pausing for a second, deciding whether or not to push the blade into his back. There was no bullshit there I could see. After a moment or two with no words, I relaxed a little and I sat down again, but my crackle blade was still ready to make a strike if I had to use it. "Underground?" I said. "Never heard of anything underground. And the Takers would know about it. They know everything out there."

"Not thes," Timothy said. "We've cammoed et so they can't find et." A stunted smile curled on his lips before he added, "We heaped all our toilet business there, so the Takers stay away."

I narrowed my eyes at him, willing him to speak more.

"Et's an old silver mine," he told me. "It goes right under the Takers place and et goes out the other ind to the gully."

"Go on," I said. "You're not convincing me yet and I don't much take to bull-shitters."

"Et's true. If you come, our place will sit you up for life. I just nid the generators to work."

I narrowed my eyes a bit more. "You just said, I."

He looked blankly, said nothing.

"You said, I. Not we. So, you're implying you're by yourself. You said we, before." I got up and charged at him, stopping so the tip of my nose just touched his.

He shrunk back. "No, I mint to say, wi. Just said I because I am here by myself. But we're numbers back at Newman."

"How many?" I shouted. He said two hundred and twenty-two without hesitation. It was the fact he said it without hesitation that made me wonder if there was truth to his words. Surely no one could drag a number from the sky so quick. And certainly, not a number such as two hundred and twenty-two. A hundred? A hundred and fifty? If he'd said that number, I'd have thought it was made up. But the two hundred and twenty-two said truth. So, I sat back again and tapped the tip of my razor-sharp crackle blade on the toe of my boot while I thought things over. Already, my mind had other questions to ask, if only to bring about some kind of clarity—if only to settle my mind. So far, there were things that didn't add up. Like the part about Newman being fourteen nights to the east when the silver mine was only three. If there was truth there, that meant they'd dragged their shit to the mine to keep away Takers. That meant at least eleven nights trudging the stuff. That was far beyond any belief. It was his last chance to set things straight. He'd better have a good answer, or he's stuffed. Plain and simple.

"We camp there sometimes," he said after I asked him.

"So, you've got food stores there?"

Timothy nodded sharply. Fair enough I thought. If there's food stores there, I'd have a supply if things went to shit. One down, one to go. Then, there was the question of the diesel fuel. How could they have enough of it to last all this time? I reckoned they'd need an endless supply. That's something unheard of. Then, the oil. They'd need that too. I asked him where he got it. As far as I was concerned, this answer was his life or death.

"We trade diesel fuel and oil for mit," he said. "From traders, from up north."

"North! No-one's up there," I yelled at him. "That's all radioactive. Up there, you'd melt before you get to glow green." This time Timothy was right out at the ragged edge of my patience. I held up my blade again and twisted it in the candlelight so he could see I was losing it.

"You're wrong," Timothy said. "They've trucks and all sorts up there. They truck in our fuel and take mit away." Then he dropped his gaze. "That's how it was. We haven't heard from the Northerners in ages and our fuel is running low. That's why I'm out here. I've bin looking for new trade and seeing about getting ourselves back on our fit. Without the generators going, our mit stores will turn and we won't last long."

"Trucks," I said. "Never seen one. Stories. Just bloody stories."

"Not stories. They're real."

"How long has it been since these northerners last came?"

"About two hundred days."

I got up and walked away. I left him there to stew for a bit. No one up north could survive. Every scrounger I ever met had the same thing to say about the place. Now I'm thinking if there were northerners, they'd had to have a way of surviving. I couldn't help it. The thought of people actually living up there drilled into my logical brain. It wasn't possible and it didn't make any sense. So, I asked Timothy what made them so different that they could survive the radiation sickness. Timothy replied by saying he didn't know why they were able to survive. He went on by explaining the northerners all had one thing in common. Orange hair. White skin. Lots of freckles. And they all looked the same. As soon as he said it, my body shook from the inside out. Timothy's orange-headed friends exactly resembled a story my Pop once told me before he passed. Ambers. Some called them 'The Lost Ones.' People who were genetically altered to survive radioactivity. I asked Timothy if he'd heard about The Lost Ones. He said no he never. My mouth went suddenly dry and I said nothing more on it, at the same time thinking I might investigate the so-called northerners that could turn out to be The Lost Ones that my Pop described. It all depends on what happens after I fix his bloody generator.

So, I sat there and I ogled him a little. I wanted to make him feel uncomfortable. Maybe he'll spill some more, I kept thinking. I wasn't going to commit to going back with him until I had everything sorted in my head. No room for mistakes around here. Then he said something that made perfect sense. It was his words that finally made my mind up.

"Hell is an empty place. The devil and his demons are all here."

Chapter Ten

A Box of Stuff

Entry 723 Supplemental.

Almost packed. Timothy sleeps. The guy's knackered I reckon. A fourteen-night trek across the waste does things to the man, and I'm not talking about exhaustion, although that's something else to consider on top of everything else. There's things out there that'd make a man's blood freeze, over and I've only ever been three nights across. Looking at Timothy still makes me wonder how he managed to trek so far and still be alive. Luck is so rare, and he must possess a heap of the stuff to get him out here unscathed.

I've fashioned what I call a bug-out-sleigh that I can drag along. I reckon we'll take turns dragging it. I've had many a scrounger come through. Not one of them had a set of wheels on offer. Sad, isn't it? Not even wheels out there. So, the plan is for one to drag our stuff, the other goes behind and rubs out the tracks in the dust so if there's Takers they can't find us. Fourteen nights' trek will turn into twenty, I'm sure of it. Paper. Need more bloody paper. We'll wait for next sundown before we get going.

Entry 724.

Dawn. We're hunkered at the silver mine Timothy talked about. Thought I'd take the opportunity to pen a while as he busies himself answering nature's call. It's appropriate considering the huge pile of human waste dumped here. What he said was true. The stench by itself is enormous and enough to keep anything living away, not just the Takers.

Our travels across the waste were for the most part without any incident. I must admit—I'm relieved. There were lots of bones from many small animals that were already picked clean. That doesn't mean we didn't try because we did. Any small scrap left over is a blessing and any tiny morsel meant going further or perish. I saw bull ants for the first time in years. Not many. Just a dozen or so. And at night. Miraculous just by itself. Needless to say, we weren't about to pass up the opportunity for a protein boost. Timothy was about to put one in his mouth that was still alive. I said, "Timothy, you bloody idiot. At least pop the head first." He gave me that blank stare of his. It seems he's never ate one before. Then I went on and told him about bull ant bites inside the mouth. That's one nasty fucked up pain if you've never felt it. He smiled politely. I heard the bull ant head go 'pop', then it was gone. "Thanks," he said. Just like that. Simple and without any emotion. Then he did something that really got up my nose. I saw *his eyes compress, and he spat it back out in his hand. The fuck-wit. "Tastes awful," he said. I said, "We're not doing it for the taste. You wanna survive, don't you?" He shrugged a pause and licked it back up, at the same time wincing from the bitterness. After a few moments spent scrounging for more, and none were around, it was time to move on.*

While trudging, dragging the bug-out-sleigh behind me, Timothy in the rear kicked our drag tracks into non-existence, my head got to think about those bloody Takers. We were in prime territory for their numbers. We have weapons to take on close-up foes but we don't have any capability at all to answer the ranged weapons they'd have. But through the darkness, throughout the night, no-one was out and about. The old man's training came in handy. I still surprise myself sometimes.

We cracked open a tin after we got here. I broke the tip of my crackle blade. Jeez that made me angry. It took forever to find enough crackle and ages for me to make. What made matters worse was the discovery of cat food in the tin. Not dog food. Bloody cat food. That stuff stinks and the fish taste will stay in my mouth even after drinking a few gulps of boiled piss. I hope the rest of the day doesn't turn out crap. What a start so far.

I can't see the opening to the mine just yet. Timothy reckons we need to move all the human excrement to one side. The opening is underneath apparently. Lovely! Something I'm hugely looking forward to. Just saying.

Check back with a supplemental in a few. Timothy's decided to wipe his arse with a sheet of my writing paper! I reckon this day will have its hazards. I've already decided.

Entry 724. Supplemental.

We're inside. About five thousand strides down the horizontal shaft, we came to a large open area where there're other shafts heading off. It's a junction where all the other mineshafts connect. And, there's daylight here. A shaft goes straight up and reaches the surface letting light through. When we were on approach to this area, Timothy put a finger to his lips and gestured for silence. We had to pick up the bug-out-sleigh and carry it. Then he pointed up top indicating something. I figured out we were right under an area the Takers used to dispose of their rubbish. We had to remain silent; else they'd hear us messing about without any trouble. It was both amazing and disheartening at the same time. Directly under the shaft going up is a great pile of stinking Takers scraps and rubbish. It suddenly occurred to me this is the food supply Timothy was talking about. For some reason, I pictured something else in my mind. I pictured stacks of stored clean water. Shelves of tinned non-perishable food. Racks of packets and so on. Even knives and forks to eat it with. But this? Jesus Christ!

A closer inspection of the rubbish heap in the centre of the large area reveals something else about the Takers. They didn't eat everything. They chucked away stuff that, if it was me, I'd have microscopically cleaned. This pile of rubbish has stuff in it that can keep a man on his feet forever.

I quietly moved over to the heap and started to poke around a bit. Timothy moved silently beside me and pushed his mouth up to my ear. My mind went, "Hey mate, don't even think about it." But then he whispered into my ear, so softly that I'm sure no one would hear even if they were standing right next to us. "Fresh stuff coming," he said. "Just wait a bit." I froze. The word fresh isn't in my vocabulary, but the tantalising prospect of something fresh couldn't be ignored. So I waited. We both did. We hunkered down without a peep. I looked up into the light and waited as though some God was about to send something down through the hole. My mouth began to water. I sucked back saliva and waited.

Sure enough, it wasn't long. Something came through the hole. Whatever it was, it landed on the heap and rolled down the side. Timothy smiled and moved forward at the same time as gesturing for me to stay still. I realised if he made a noise, it was bad enough. If we both made noises, we'd end up in a state. He came back a little bit later holding something in his hands and offered it. Some small animal, half eaten. Lots of meat still left on the bones--and it was cooked. My heart beat hard in my chest and my mouth watered like the tides out past fourteen nights' stride. I took it from Timothy and I took a bite of the purest, softest, sweetest, most delicious meat I'd ever tasted. My eyes filled with tears. I sat back and enjoyed it with a delight I'd never known.

More came through from up top. Timothy was right. We could've easily stayed forever, and it was hard to consider the fact we'd have to get going pretty soon. With my mouth, full of the wonderful tastes that danced around for a while and melted away, I happened to ask in a whisper right down low, "What is this?"

"Checkin," whispered Timothy with a smile beaming across his greasy face.

"What? Is it like some kind of small roo? Like wallaby?" My mind traced back to when there were some around that the old man caught for us kids. Those were the days all right. Timothy looked at me with some kind of expression that said I must've been on Mars. "Et's Checkin. Haven't you had et before?"

"No," I said. It didn't bloody matter. I was ever so grateful. Now I know a place where the risks are so high, but the payoff is worth it. Funny, after I had that thought, anger raged inside me. Takers had this stuff while the rest of us go begging. It wasn't right.

I'd eaten until I was full up and couldn't eat anymore. I can't remember the last time my belly felt heavy and bloated. Now, all I want to do is sleep. Even now, as I sit and write under the dim light, I can see Timothy fighting his drowsiness. It's not an option. We must at least find ourselves a good part of the way down the end of the shaft. If we sleep here and snore, those up top would know. That would end up as a major shit fight.

Entry 725.

It was at least another five thousand strides away from the location that gave us our last meal. I have to add that five thousand or so of those strides were made with an almost crippling cramp under my ribcage, made worse by having to carry the bug-out-sleigh. Thank god we don't have to do that anymore.

We didn't talk much on the way down the shaft. I was quite content with my own thoughts. But Timothy said something that brought me back to the reality.

"Wanna see my treasures?" he asked.

It was the word 'treasures' that sparked my interest. Of course.

He pointed just up ahead of where we were. "Just up there. Wanna see?"

Then it occurred to me how lucky this guy was. Timothy had all the luck of the Gods on his side. However, I was immediately thinking what an idiot. If he had treasures, surely, he'd have the need to keep it to himself. What made him so sure I wouldn't rip him across the throat? Of course, I wouldn't, having come this far. But what if it was someone else other than me? He'd be dead, and the treasure somewhere else. So, I answered him. "Treasure huh? Okay, let's see what you got."

There was a slight depression in the side of the tunnel where we stopped after another thirty odd strides. It didn't look out of the ordinary and perhaps that's why Timothy's treasures were still there. Timothy reached into the depression and cleared away a few loose rocks. Then, he cleared some larger rocks that showed the opening to a small chamber that was cut into the wall. Probably some kind of exploration tunnel started there and then became abandoned for some reason. Further into the chamber and Timothy cleared dust and debris away from what looked like a large plastic container. When he pulled it away from a micro landslide, I recognised it as a military footlocker. I had one exactly the same back at my hometown, Kumarina. My Pop once told me they were used by the local militia and were big enough to store several changes of uniforms, a blanket or two and other things.

After Timothy opened the military footlocker, I was absolutely, positively, without a doubt, gobsmacked. The first thing Timothy retrieved was something tiny. Something wrapped in what looked like a faded yellow wrapper. It had writing on it and I could just make out the words *Juicy Fruit*. Timothy said it was chewing gum. He placed it in my hand and I ran my fingers over what felt like a ribcage of some sort.

"There's pieces in the packet. You put et in your mouth and chew on et," he said.

"Why?"

Then he looked at me oddly. "Dunno why. Et just es. People used to do et. But I reckon et'd be more like chewing on sandstone by now."

"So why keep it?"

"Because et's worth something. And anytheng thet's worth something you kip."

He reached into the trunk and pulled out something else. A small box that looked like it was at one time made from wood. The writing on the box said 'Flor De Tobacos, Habana.' He opened it and handed it over. "These are for smoking,"

"Like cigarettes? They're bloody huge."

Timothy nodded at the same time quickly closing the box and putting it back in the footlocker, adding, "I've smoked one and et made me seck for a day. Trust me Michael, you don't want to smoke thim."

What he said made sense. If we got ourselves captured by the Takers, the big cigarettes by themselves could save our lives in barter. Maybe. The next thing he pulled out was a huge slab of crackle, measuring five hands wide and four hands deep. So big, it took effort to retrieve. I reckoned there was enough of the stuff to buy supplies for a thousand days. But under the slab of crackle was the biggest surprise of all. Timothy reached in and grabbed something wrapped in a tattered red cloth. The red cloth smelt of some kind of sweetness and had white printed patterns and a strange emblem of some description. A picture of a dagger with a lightning bolt in a strange triangular shape going around it. Inside was something heavy and metallic. Timothy unraveled it and held it up. A Pre-Fall handgun. My eyes watered. I couldn't believe it.

Timothy's treasures he had safely tucked away were exactly what he reckoned. There were loads of other items contained in the footlocker, but the gun was most precious. How he'd got it and then kept it out of Takers' hands was incredible to say the least. But at the same time, was useless without ammo, and there wasn't any. He had a lone bullet in the footlocker wrapped up in some old paper. The bullet resembled something that could've been fired from a cannon, not from a handgun.

"Pre-Fall fefty-cal," he said smiling again. "Ef only we had something to fire et."

He started packing things away back in the footlocker, but I was reluctant to give up the handgun. It felt balanced and weighty in my hands. It was like a precision instrument meant for performing the task of death. Timothy put his hand out and waited for me to hand it back. I paused. "What'll you take for it?" I asked him as I held it up to the light. That's when I saw it. An inscription on the handle. 'Donald P Bosco.'

"Not for sale," Timothy said plain and simple. Then he stuck his hand out for it like some little spoilt brat.

"Everything's for sale," I told him. "Don't give me the shits. There's something I can trade."

He stood up and wrenched the handgun from me. Then wrapped it back up, repeating his words not for sale. It was at this time I started to wonder about Timothy. He'd come across as meek and mild. The sort of bloke who could be easily played. Now he seemed harder. Almost seasoned. Or was he just stalling for the best possible asking price. So, I stood there and watched him for a while. He wasn't in a hurry to pack the gun away. Yeah, he's a player alright. He was on a mission for a sale. I could see it. But what was his asking?

The moment I went to the bug-out-sleigh and started fumbling through my items, Timothy stopped doing what he was doing. The game had begun, and his body language showed it. I consider myself as seasoned as the next when it comes to dealing.

I read all the signs, and I wasn't about to let the prospect of own-
ing a gun get away. The problem was I reckoned Timothy had
enough crackle, and a few more shards was unlikely to sway him.
I had to come up with something he'd want. More than that, some-
thing he'd need. So, I reluctantly took out something he'd most
likely desire. I knew he wasn't good at fixing stuff. If he had any
nous, those diesel generators wouldn't be such a problem. So, I
was happy to give up my torque wrench and crowbar, thinking
it'd be a good trade. He plainly said without expression, "Need
to try harder." Bastard. He's playing the hard game. So, I quickly
added a small paper sachet of Pre-Fall tomato seeds. I'd tried to
grow them. It seems I didn't have what it took to get them going.
From what Timothy said about where he came, he'd make good
use of them.

Timothy smiled brightly when I handed them over. He knew
the value of seeds. I paid good crackle to get them and now my
investment was going to pay off. But the bastard still wanted
more. "How about your eagle?" he asked. My heart sank. That
was something I wasn't about to let go. The dealing suddenly hit
the side of a stone wall and left me feeling as though everything
was lost.

He must've noticed my hesitation. "Tell you what," he put in.
"I'll kip et here with my treasures, and et'll be safe. You'll never
have to worry about et. Et'll stay away from the Takers."

"The bones have to stay with it," I said after much thought.
"It's important they stay together."

"Why?"

"Just is." I shrugged. I was even going to tell him about Charlotte but stopped myself, thinking the information wasn't relevant and the less he knew, the better. In my mind, I already decided to come and get it back after I fix his damn generator. How would the idiot know?

As soon I had that thought, Timothy responded. "Don't even think of coming back to get it, Michael. Only I know how to retrieve it without setting off the trap. If you attempt to get it later, everything will be destroyed." He then pointed down to a metallic box that was slightly U-shaped and set back in the depression just behind the footlocker. I'd only ever seen one before. Claymore. I knew they spit out death quick as a click of the tongue. The C4 explosion was bad enough. The ball bearings had the ability of ripping anything in half. It looked ready to slice and dice just sitting there, but Timothy had it attached to something only he knew about. I think I just lost my beloved figurine forever. Or returning his gun into his hands was the only other option. He won. I lost. Plain and simple.

Chapter Eleven

Small Things

Entry 726.

After finally getting to the end of the mineshaft and emerging into a gully exactly as Timothy described, it took more than a few moments for my eyes to adjust to the daylight. Ahead of us, rocky hills jut upward on either side. Sandstone boulders sit there as if they'd been delicately placed into position by some giant being. The place is alive with the sounds of insects and creatures I'd never heard before. An abundance of protein and any man can live here forever. If there is water here it'd give me reason enough to stay. I'd be able to survive easily.

As I sit here writing, Timothy is nursing some horrible sores on his feet. It wasn't until after I saw him limping along while wrestling with the bug-out-sleigh, that I asked him when was the last time he took off his boots? He looked at me with bug eyes and said he didn't know, only to add it was a long time. Shit. The bloody idiot.

"Didn't you notice how I took my boots off every time we stopped?"

"Yeah," Timothy said. "Your fit stenk. Thet's bad enough. I couldn't do both of us at the same time."

Jesus H Christ!

Next thing, a bird call. Some kind of bird I didn't recognise from a position high above the bank to our left. Timothy sprung up and began to prance around. Takers! I had the gun and began to wish hard I had the ammo for it. It may as well had been something to throw if it came down to it. Useless.

Timothy answered the bird call with an exact sound he had made by pushing his fingers to his lips and blowing. He smiled and for the first time I saw how yellowed his teeth were. A few heads bobbed up from behind a couple of rocks about forty strides up the embankment. "Over here," Timothy yelled out. I pounced on Timothy to silence his excitement once and for all, but it was too late.

"Relax Michael, they're my clan."

After the heads-up top became bodies, they began to shimmy down the embankment toward us, Timothy met them halfway and greeted them by touching his nose to theirs. I found this way of saying hello to be quite odd. I kept myself way back until I knew everything was okay.

Timothy introduced one of them as his sister, Cherith, which was hard to pronounce at first until I got used to it. She appeared younger than Timothy and her complexion was surprisingly fresh. She had the same facial tattoos as Timothy that curled around her left cheek and eye. The other was a brother and ran by the name of Seth who also had virtually the same facial tattoos only a little more expressive in the design. I commented on the tattoos and Seth answered, "Where we're from, we all have 'em, bro."

Turns out, when we depart this place, we'll all get the chance to carry Timothy. His feet are truly stuffed. The bloody idiot.

Entry 727.

We trudged the gully about ten thousand strides east. Carrying Timothy was already the task we never wanted. If I wasn't dragging, dragging, dragging, I'd have him on my back while Seth took over the bug-out-sleigh, Cherith erasing drag tracks from behind. Then we'd all change our positions again after another thousand strides or so. It was hard work. Added to that, Cherith is one tough girl, no doubt about it. When it was her turn to take Timothy on her back, she did it like a man. Flabbergasted, I was.

I'd never consider the trudging in full daylight. The heat is a killer. I drank twice as much retched fluid compared to at night. But Seth assures there'd be no threat this far east from the Takers. He seems to think if there're contacts, they'd be easy enough to deal with. So far none. Can't help thinking that's just more arse than class. I also can't help but wonder if Seth ever had the pleasure of Takers company. He's too complacent for my liking. I wonder if there's something about Seth under the surface.

Something that carries with his complacency. Guess I'll find out soon enough.

I had my boots off for a time while we stopped to rest, and judging by the condition of my feet, I hoped our destination wouldn't be too far away. The sores between my toes, even though not half as bad as Timothy's, were already in the established stages of trench-foot. Timothy's trench-foot is full blown. He'll have a battle keeping his feet attached to his legs, I reckon. With no hope of an antibiotic, I fear he'll turn gangrene. All because the fucker was too damn lazy to take off his boots. Then what? We chop his feet off to save his life. The more I think about it, the more I wonder about his number of days. Then, I think about something else entirely different.

Without Timothy alive, there's next to no chance of retrieving my figurine. I must keep him alive. No question. After we get to Newman, after I fix the generator, I must go shopping out in the waste. My shopping list will be short. Antibiotic, antibiotic and antibiotics. Oh, and it'd be nice for at least one bloody bullet for my future handgun.

I'm now somewhat reluctantly Timothy's bodyguard. That is, until I get my figurine back. After that, I don't care much. I'm sure Timothy's clan will continue without too much trouble. Guess what? I'll be somewhere else. Where that'll be is anyone's guess.

Enough said. I'm out of paper. Time to get going. The Sun is about to dip below. Time to trek through the night.

Chapter Twelve

A Journey Begins

THE WEIGHT OF THE LAST TATTERED and possibly blood-stained sheet of paper felt much heavier than it truly was. I'd read a lot of books over the years. I was well accustomed to the anticlimax one feels at the end of a good read, but this was something else. In my mind, my internal voice kept telling me, 'This can't be the end of it. There must be more.' If that was the case, where was it? And what would it take to get hold of it?

After having read what was written by Michael, who was an obviously educated individual, I found myself torn in half by the new questions the journal raised. The urgency to head south and rescue Chloe hadn't wavered. But I found myself also wanting to know the whereabouts of these so-called Lost Ones and also, to learn the fate of what happened to Michael and Timothy. I realized I'd never know without having access to more of Michael's writings. If it existed, was it possible to launch into an investigation and find out where the rest of it was? Or perhaps there may be the risk of starting something I'd regret. Either way, how could I ignore the adventure? And where would that adventure lead?

"Richard. Pray tell what you're thinking," Captain Bass said. "If it's the same as what I have in my head, I'm afraid we're both in a spot of bother, are we not?"

"In my head, I'm thinking there're too many questions and not enough answers. When that happens, I get the itches. One—What's the significance with the relics' relationship to each other? And why must they stay together? Two—Who is Charlotte? And why did she refer to the journal's author as 'Michael the Protector?' Three-There was a gun in dead man's chest. Where is it now? Four-Who are The Lost Ones? And why are they lost? Shall I go on?"

"Err . . . No. Stop there before you do yourself a brain hemorrhage."

I went on. "It'd be nice to know who the bones belong to. I'd like to think we could do the decent thing and return them to the right family. And! Once we retrieve the figurine, we should find out its history and where it came from."

"Young man! You're beginning to drown in the details. Let's finish one thing at a time."

"Need a whiteboard," I responded. "Everything needs organizing in a way we don't leave anything out."

"Richard . . ."

"We'll need portable recording devices . . ."

"Richard!"

"We'll need more men . . ."

"RICHARD"

"What?"

"Just stop, will you? We're not living in the times before The Fall. We shall never have the resources to go at this as though we've been given some government grant. My boy, everything we do must have a near invisible footprint. Trust me on this. Let us take some time and think what needs doing first."

"Chloe is first."

"And it shall be done."

Finally, firm confirmation from the captain. We were at last about to set sail for Antarctica. I should've been high on the happiness. I should've run from the great cabin, up the stairs to the ship's rail and shouted out her name. I should've shouted 'Chloe, I'm coming for you.' But I didn't. It seemed no matter how hard I tried, I couldn't get my head away from the journal. And, as soon as I realized it, I felt shame tear me into two pieces. How I hated it. But how could I help it?

The journal mentioned 'Ambers,' and in my mind, the word 'Ambers' rang true in some strange way. A memory from somewhere. Distant, going way back to when I was a kid. But it was a foggy memory. I tried hard to recover it. It wouldn't come.

"So, pray tell. Who do you think is the dead man?" the captain interrupted my thoughts.

"Dead man is either Michael or Timothy. It's a slim chance it could be anybody else."

"My deduction also, dear boy. Do you think it is possible that we shall ever find out for certain?"

"That depends."

The shame of it all. I almost felt a sense of disgrace that something else had crept into my life and was threatening to take me away from the one person I loved so dearly. But somehow, I managed to bite it all back. Somehow, I knew it in my heart that my future was about to change so drastically.

I got up from my chair and without any consideration at all, I walked past Captain Bass as though he wasn't there. I could almost feel his eyes upon me as I was about to help myself to another glass of rum from the decanter. My internal dialogue sounded off. This wasn't me. How could I be so ignorant and empty of manners? I spun and immediately apologized to the captain. "Crap, I'm so sorry. May I?"

"But of course. There's plenty."

Just then, something rocketed through my brain, sending off tiny shockwaves as a sudden realization leapt into my conscience mind. *But of course, There's plenty . . .* It occurred to me that I was having the luxury of drinking rum when there shouldn't have been any. From what I learned, only the Takers would have such a luxury. And the captain said it himself. There was plenty. An incredible sinking feeling swept over me. Maybe I'd gone from a situation that was bad enough, into a situation that was truly fucked-up. From this moment on, I decided that a good measure of caution must be taken.

"And how, may I ask, do we manage such a task?" the captain broke into my thoughts.

"I'm sorry, Captain. Where were we?"

"The dead man. The figurine. How do we retrieve them? We do not have the equipment, my boy. Only in Perthland will we ever find such items. That has a twofold disadvantage. One cannot expect to procure such items without drawing attention to oneself. And drawing attention to oneself means The Takers will know. Should that happen, our attempt at diving for the eagle has come to naught and the eagle figurine will inevitably fall into the wrong hands."

And there it was. A warning bell. I must play this with care.

I quickly changed the subject. "This rum. Where did it come from?"

I saw the captain's eyes narrow. He paused long enough to think about what he was about to say. The fact that he paused was another warning. Then his hardened expression melted away and he began to laugh. "You think . . . Oh, my dear boy. How could you think . . . I'm dumbfounded . . . I don't know what to say."

"That doesn't answer my question."

"Richard. Calm down, will you? This can be explained as easily as having a piss off the end of the bowsprit."

I said nothing. I assumed my expression said all the words necessary. The captain immediately stepped across the floor to a very heavy looking sea chest. Lifting up the lid, he beckoned me closer. Inside the sea chest was what I thought was some kind of solidified oil. After thinking about it, I realized I was looking at the material Michael wrote about in his journal. Crackle. And the sea chest was full of it.

"Crackle," the captain said, confirming all of my thoughts. "My boy, there is enough here to purchase most anything from the colonies for many years to come."

"And where did you get that!" I said. I wasn't totally convinced. Our captain would need to explain a whole lot more before he could take away my suspicions. But I also realized if I was in the presence of The Takers, I'd perhaps be dead by now. Jason and Eli as well. However, if I *was* in the company of The Takers, what could I do about it? Fight my way out? To where? I was more trapped on *Victory* than I ever was on *Steinbeck*.

Captain Bass took a big chunk of crackle out of the sea chest and gave it to me. I felt the cold weight in my hand. I saw my own reflection in the surface and then I thought about how it was made. All those lives. All those billions of people. All gone. Wiped out when the bombs fell. Crackle has the blood of billions of souls compressed into it. Billions of birthdays. Billions of Independence Days. Billions of Thanksgivings. Billions of first walks, first talks, first dances, first kisses, all gone. I realized it and the first thing I wanted to do was smash it into a million fragments. But instead I fell to my knees. I felt something ripping up through my body I'd never felt before. What was it? Was it the pain and suffering of all those people? Was I somehow transmuting their anguish? Billions upon billions of citizens of Earth? I suddenly felt as though every tear ever shed was now falling from my eyes.

* * *

I felt a hand land gently on my shoulder and I realized Captain Bass and his *Victory* could not have been part of any Taker stronghold or fleet. I kept telling myself, it just wasn't possible. We'd be dead. But what he said next cemented our partnership and our cooperation in this coming venture for the eagle and the Lost Ones.

"You've read about it yourself in dead man's journal. You've read about the scroungers."

I nodded.

"That's much the same as what we do on *Victory*. But instead, we do it on the high seas. The more Takers ships we raid and sink, the more goods we're able to transport back to the colonies. The everyday folk can therefore survive a little longer. We help them. As much as we can. But it doesn't hurt to give *Victory's* crew some luxuries for their labors. That's our rum. It came from The Takers. And our business to the colonies still stands, Richard. So we must make haste and do whatever needs doing so we might find ourselves in Perthland again. The people there depend upon us."

With my mind settled, I began to think what our next steps must be. "In that case, Henry, we must be on our way. Tonight. Without any further delay." I was thinking about Chloe, but I was also thinking about what lay beneath the surface of the seas and how we could retrieve it. Then an idea came.

"*Steinbeck* has a two-man submersible there for the taking," I said. "There'll be no need to purchase diving equipment at Perthland." But something I didn't think about made me halt. How many years had it been since the submersible was ever used? Or was it ever used at all? One thing I knew about electronics. If not constantly maintained, electronics will fail. Plain. Simple. I wasn't, however, about to tell that to our captain. After we make sail, it could turn out to be an issue resulting in turning around the ship.

"Richard, my boy. If we move, we lose our location to where the eagle figurine was last seen."

"We don't have to be exactly accurate. Mark our current location on the ship's charts and when we return, the submersible will take us to where we need to be. Now. Let's get going."

* * *

I didn't realize how difficult it was navigating below decks at night until I tried it. Having had a few rums made things more difficult. Being injured with a broken shoulder and a bruised knee cap that was made worse with the ship's rolling, just made everything virtually impossible. But I did eventually make it to my allotted space between two cannons. Arriving there, both Eli and Jason were tucked in their hammocks fast asleep.

I did my best getting into my hammock as stealthily as possible. The potato soup and damper, as the captain called it, that was delivered to the great cabin, rolled around in my belly as I heaved myself up and in. I was silent, all the way up until my body went one way and my shoulder went the other. F-U-C-K!

"Ditch! Where've you been, Ditch?"

Oh crap! "Captain's great cabin. Jase, I have to tell you something."

Over the next couple of hours, I put Jason and Eli well into the picture. I'd told them everything I'd learned and read about. As I explained it, Jason never interrupted me. The fact Jason didn't interrupt said everything about his interest. And the fact Eli was also wordless meant he must've fallen asleep. Or did he? But both also reacted negatively the same as each other when I told them about the idea with the submersible. Both launched into hearty laughter as though I'd finally lost my mind.

"Ditch. It'll never work. And if it does work, how're we ever going to get it from *Steinbeck* knowing what's instore when we get there?"

"What do you think is going to happen?" I asked.

There was silence for a couple of moments. It didn't appear anybody knew for sure.

"We're on an armed vessel," I said. "When was the last time you saw guns of any type on *Steinbeck?* We've also got small arms. All they've got are batons and tear gas. Yeah, I get it. Our firearms are over three hundred years old. But they still pack a punch. And in my mind, I say bullets will always win over fists."

* * *

We discussed all our options and came up with a solid workable plan, passing in most of the night. Just before dawn, a plan was nutted out and it was time to get some much-needed sleep. I had no idea how close we were to Antarctica, or how many hours must pass before we finally drop anchor. The only clue to tell me was the growing length of each day. Already, the sense of time I was well accustomed to was gone. Living in a world which had a twenty-four-hour cycle of night and day had thrown my stable body clock out the window. After sun-up, our objectives will be heard in the captain's quarters where we'll receive a yay or nay from Captain Bass and his officers.

Once I found myself comfortable in my hammock, I closed my eyes and went over everything in my head. After arriving back at the Ross Ice Shelf, it would be important for Jason, Eli and myself to remain on board *Victory*. We'd left *Steinbeck* as prisoners, sentenced to death. If we were seen, it was mutually assumed between us that we'd be again taken captive. So instead, a party of men chosen by Captain Bass would disembark *Victory* and make contact with Skipper, making him aware that *Victory* had arrived on a rescue mission to relocate all souls to Australee.

Skipper would then be invited aboard *Victory* to inspect the ship's capacity to transport human cargo. He would also be encouraged to draft a lottery for the first transport. It would all be discussed at a formal dinner at the Captain's table in his great cabin.

The plan would ramp up with the capture and imprisonment of Skipper while partaking in evening mess. He'd be held prisoner on *Victory* for a ransom. That ransom would be the sum total of a lone two-man submersible delivered directly to the *HMS Victory* within twenty-four hours. That was the plan. How much simpler could it be? There was only one thing that worried me. What if Skipper no longer had the popularity vote? Certainly, he was on the top of the hate lists that a majority of *Steinbeck's* inhabitants carried around inside their minds. Perhaps a ransom wouldn't work for that reason. Nobody could give a shit about him. Then what?

A plan B must be put in place. For some reason, I lightly shuddered thinking what that might entail. Whatever the outcome, however, it was discussed that it will be with the good intention of everyone on board *Victory,* that as many souls as possible are transported, with the intention of the armed vessel to return as many times as required to evacuate the rest.

Chapter Thirteen

A Higher Purpose

I OPENED MY EYES. I'D BEEN TRANSPORTED to a place among crowds of people. High up on a stage, I sat overlooking them all. So many people were jumping and cheering in time to the beat. The beat I played. I played the beat loud. I played it hard.

Kickdrum, snare. Kickdrum, snare. Kickdrum, snare, kick-kick. Snare.

Rimshots. All rimshots. I played in my style. None of that syncopated bullshit. None of the traditionally mastered art of parra-diddle-parra-diddle. None of the technically perfect rolls and beats that are divided sixty-four times into the four beats to a bar time signature. No. I was raw. I was powerful. And-they-loved-it.

Kickdrum, snare. Kickdrum, snare. Kickdrum, snare, kick-kick. Snare.

To my left through the curtain, someone arrived on stage. A woman I thought looked familiar. But there was no face. Only her back toward me. Could it be that I knew her? The crowd went crazy! But I played on. The same beat. The same heavy beat. Rim-shots, baby. Rimshots. Four tom-toms on a rack in front of me. I didn't touch them. I was the last of the groove heavy hitters. I laid down the groove.

Kickdrum, snare. Kickdrum snare. Kickdrum snare, kick-kick. Snare.

From my right, another entered on stage. Someone I didn't rec-ognize. A bald-headed guy with a bad limp shimmied over to the Marshall stack and grabbed his axe, whipped it up, and plugged in the cord. The Marshall stack responded with an earsplitting squelch. The crowd went wild! But I played on.

Kickdrum, snare. Kickdrum snare. Kickdrum snare, kick-kick. Snare.

On my left, someone I didn't recognize arrived on stage. A female with long black flowing hair. The hourglass body of a Hol-lywood movie star. Skin tight leathers shiny and black as her long locks that went all the way down to her ass. She strutted over to the Marshall stack and picked up her axe. She plugged it in. An-other ear-splitting squelch but I played on.

Kickdrum, snare. Kickdrum snare. Kickdrum snare, kick-kick. Snare.

The crowd went nuts.

In the light, I managed to see the back of the bald guy's head. A tattoo. An eagle. A white eagle with a sword. Then he started grinding on his axe. The earsplitting sound through my fold back speaker was immense. All of a sudden, I could no longer hear my own beat. The sound guy! Tell him to turn up my kit! Before I screw-up! Before it's too late.

Kickdrum, snare. Kickdrum snare. Kickdrum snare, kick-kick. Snare.

The crowd went wild. Women started to take off their shirts. Some riding their boyfriend's shoulders while they showed their tits to the world. Screaming and jumping. Jumping and shouting while the band played. While I lay down my heavy, heavy, groove.

Then.

The front man stopped.

The chick in black stopped.

The woman I thought I might know stopped.

The crowd no longer shouted and screamed.

There's just me and the beat.

Kickdrum, snare. Kickdrum snare. Kickdrum snare, kick-kick. Snare.

The bald guy with the eagle tattoo and what I thought must be a fake leg turned and looked at me. "Ladies and gentlemen, a big round of applause for our drummer who will be travelling north into danger. Who knows if he will survive? He might die, ladies and gentlemen. He might die."

The crowd again went nuts. But this time, I knew it was all for me.

The rock chick dressed in black put her hand on her belly and began to laugh. She stepped up to the mic. "Ladies and gentlemen. I'm Teresa. This is Nathan and we're The Angels of Mercy!" Her strange accent. I thought she must be Arabic.

The crowd went completely out of their minds.

Then Teresa turned to look at me. She whispered so quietly, placing her hand over her mic at the same time. Somehow I heard her above the crowd. Somehow, I heard her above everything. "Richard, go north. Those Lost. Find them. Find them, Richard. Follow the path and the Moon won't fall. Follow the path and the Moon won't fall. Follow the path and the Moon won't fall."

The woman with her back toward me I thought I knew collapsed on the stage.

I woke up sweating. Panting. Dizzied. I was almost about to scream out.

I didn't know how or why but a hard realization came. Something in the pit of my stomach told me Chloe had died. I leapt out of my bunk with such energy I left my calico sling behind. I raced for the steps and flew up and out into the daylight. I ran for the ship's rail, already feeling ready to purge anything that might exist down in the depths of my guts. When I got there, the violent rush up my throat was immense. I tasted the acid bile as it pushed up my throat and out.

"NOOO!"

I shouted and two voices bounced back from the icebergs that littered the place.

"CHLOE! NOOO!"

I slid down from the rail and hit the deck, feeling heavy with my head about to explode in pain. I sat on the ship's deck with my head in my hands. My hands on my knees. Curled up almost like an embryo. Somehow, I didn't know how it was possible. I didn't know how it could *ever* be possible. I had to be sure. I moved my arm around. A little at first. Then I made big circles. My shoulder and my knee were completely healed.

* * *

Morning mess consisted of a damper with cheese from a goat and a large mug of black liquid that was called coffee. The coffee was hard to get used to at the beginning but as I consumed more of it, I found myself becoming addicted to it. I also found that coffee was a great remedy for a sore head. An old sailor sitting opposite at the table, eyed me with a grin, " 'Ung over, are we? That coffee will sort ya out. Trust me. The more of it inside ya, the better. So, drink that coffee. Drink it all up."

I didn't know what he meant about a 'ung over,' as he put it. That being what it was, I put my trust in the old sailor and drank several cups before leaving the table. He was right. The pain in my head left, even though my heart rate picked up in speed to a level equal to what might be the case had I been running. I felt a little sweaty and light headed. But there was no pain. Coffee. What a wonder.

We organized to meet in the captain's quarters shortly after mess. Jason, Eli and myself, along with first officer, William Fletcher, Surgeon Cristian Hamell and Master at Arms Thomas Brice sat around an oval table that shone and reflected the early morning light. I couldn't help but run my hands over it. It felt cold. It smelt like a hundred years. It looked as though it was made from a rich, dark, mahogany, the same kind of wood that was used as the trimming in Skipper's quarters. It made me think that perhaps it was a tradition to use mahogany in such ways. It was easy to think of trivial things. I found myself thinking of the inconsequential if only to take my mind away from the ugliness I felt in my heart. It appeared to work. I hung my head and searched for other unimportant things that I could focus on. But before I could, Captain Bass finally appeared at the doorway.

Captain Bass eyed me curiously as he sat himself down at the table. "No sling, Richard? Are you sure?"

"It seems I'm now all healed up. How about that?"

Captain Bass's eyes went immediately to Christian Hamell and then to Eli. They had no words. Eli managed a shrug. Christian Hamell shook his head a little as though he was as befuddled as ever.

"You've been drinking far too much coffee, Richard. It blocks the pain receptors, but you may well still be as injured. Mind you be careful. You could do more harm to yourself than you can imagine."

I smiled a little to myself as I reflected on the dream. In my mind, I told myself it was nothing more than that. A bad dream. That's it. Nothing more. Chloe is all right. There is nothing to worry about. I kept saying it, over and over. If I kept saying it enough, I'd start to believe it. And that was the reason why I told nobody about what I'd seen.

The plan we'd nutted out was put before the Captain. It was a big ask to assume he'd agree to use his men while Jason, Eli and myself lay low. But he did see sense in what we had planned. By the time our meeting was concluded, everyone knew what they needed to do. Jason called it our plan A. By calling it that, it implied there must be a plan B. There wasn't a plan B. Simply because I supposed nothing else could've worked.

Before leaving the table, there was only one concern left in my mind. It was the fact we weren't going anywhere in a hurry. With the absence of the prevailing winds, we'd found ourselves becalmed, as the captain had put it. The winds could pick up again in an hour, or they might not pick up for days. There was no choice but to wait it out. Or was there?

"Can I ask a question?"

I saw that the captain was ready to leave. He sat himself back down and eyed me. "But of course. What is it?"

"What would it take to move the ship under oars?"

"We only have the two longboats, Richard. If we tethered *Victory*, we'd still need a lot more man power and many more oars. I'm afraid we're stranded until such time as there's a change in the weather conditions."

* * *

I heard them up there. Seabirds. Gulls, and maybe the elusive albatross. I rubbed my eyes awake as the light of a new day dazzled my senses. Vapor shot away from my every breath. It was a clue I couldn't ignore. I bounced out of my hammock without a sound, taking extra care not to wake Jason. I shimmied around a cannon and poked my head out of a porthole to be sure we'd made land. We were home. Finally.

Chloe.

I hope you're alright.

Out on the glass-like water that sparkled with the early morning sun, the familiar craggy peaks of icebergs littered the sea in sporadic gangs. *There*, was the ice shelf. *There*, was the *Steinbeck*. But billows of black smoke rose in a funnel, reaching high then sharply trailing off at ninety degrees. I felt the contents in my stomach begin to curdle and separate. The hard realization. Nothing was all right.

"Jason."

Jason woke up as his usual grumpy self.

"Jase. Something's wrong," I said.

After Jason and Eli saw the black smoke emanating from *Steinbeck*, I realized our plan A was trashed. There was no plan B. It was with urgency, however, that a landing party must be put to shore. To find out what had happened. To find Chloe.

Eli put his head further outside the porthole and looked up. I noticed his skin paled. Pulling his head back in he looked as shocked as ever. "We're still at close-reef."

Jason and I exchanged our glances of bewilderment. "How did we get here, Ditch? There's no wind. And the sails are still tied up."

Chapter Fourteen

Sunken City

EVEN THOUGH THE QUARTER DECK WAS crowded with men, and the deck was abuzz with activity, I felt heavily forlorn standing at the starboard rail, looking out across the choppy waters. Behind me, the prevailing winds had returned, and it filled every sail. *Victory* pitched and rolled, cutting noisily through the waves. All hands got on with what needed doing; pulling at ropes, scaling the rigging, tying this, untying that, pulling and pushing as though they were truly born into the craft of sailing such a huge vessel.

And me?

I was alone as ever.

If there were a hundred men around me, I was sure it would still feel as though I was standing, looking out, feeling isolated and cut off from everything.

Thinking it over, what had happened on *Steinbeck* was completely unexpected. And I kept thinking back to that damned dream. The Angels of Mercy, they'd called themselves. If this was mercy, it was a bad joke and there was no humor about it at any angle. But still the memory of the dream lingered in my mind, and it felt as real as taking a piss off the bowsprit, as our captain had put it.

Everyone on *Steinbeck* was dead. There was no denying how it happened. The rampage came early. Among the dead were my wife and unborn child. We stepped over body after body in the search for Chloe. Bodies which had been savagely bashed to almost beyond any possible means of recognition. I'd never seen such carnage. I fear the image of those poor souls will stay with me forever.

Jason and Eli started their search for Chloe from the flight deck. William Fletcher, Captain Bass and I decided it would be better to start below decks. I found Chloe where I thought she'd most likely be. She was with my mother in her stateroom which had been set alight. Both had died in the fire. They were burned so badly it was impossible to hold them in my arms one last time. As I knelt down beside my wife, I noticed she'd used something to scratch the letter 'R' in the metal floor. My first initial. She was thinking of me when she died. How it hurt me to see it.

We managed to take their bodies from *Steinbeck*, up the hill past Emert's Turn to the cemetery. I said goodbye to Chloe and my mother with all the strength I had left. But no matter how much I tried, I couldn't swallow down the feeling of anger at myself for their abandonment. I hated myself terribly for doing that to them.

But even so, above everything that had happened, we managed to procure what we needed. What *they* needed. The two-man submersible.

Every time I see the submersible sitting on *Victory's* poop deck in such contrast between what was old, and what was very-very old, the cost of getting it there chills me. I was no longer happy about it. How could I be? I'd lost so much. And it cost so much. It no longer mattered about what it was going to be used for. The eagle figurine could stay where it was. The dead man's journal; I swore the next time I saw it, I'd put a match to it. And the lost ones could damned-well stay lost.

I stood at the starboard rail, the toe of my boot just slightly hanging over the edge. What would it take? To take one step too far? One step and I could go to sleep. My tired mind. I was so tired of thinking. Sleep would be nice. And I thought wherever I go from here, perhaps I'd find Chloe again. There'd be little effort just to step over the rail and step off the edge. A little effort and much relief.

As I swung my leg up and over the rail, I grabbed a rope and held myself there for a moment. What was I waiting for? Let go of the rope, I told myself. Just let go. I loosened my grip slightly. Looking down in the water was a huge creature I knew I'd seen before. The same all white orca who'd pushed the slab of ice north. The same all white orca who'd sunk the Takers' ship. And it was rumored this orca was one of several who saved *Victory* from being becalmed. I loosened my grip fully, and I fell.

I didn't know how it was at all possible. The need for oxygen while under the water never mattered. I grabbed onto an orca dorsal fin and rode.

The great white orca pulled me down, all the way down. I felt my ears want to burst. I felt as though a hundred men were sitting on my chest. But still, we went down. I looked on. The water darkened as we dove and out of the darkness, the hulks of what were once shops that I'd only ever seen in pictures appeared out of the murk. It was as though a thick fog had rolled in and had covered everything. Then out of the gloominess emerged broken buildings with shattered windows. Roads that had been smashed to pieces. Cars and trucks lay on their sides and on their roofs with their doors left flung open to somebody who'd never show up.

The orca took me further.

We passed a couple of street side signs. One said, 'Battery Point' and I knew it in my heart this was once the Hobart in Tasmania that I'd read so much about. We followed a sign that said, 'Elizabeth Street'. The orca took me into the city center, and out the other side to a bridge that arose from the bottom of the sea like a dead giant. The sign on approach said, 'Tasman Bridge.' We followed the bridge to the other side through suburbs of housing estates were normal folk must've once lived.

Skeletons lay everywhere.

Human bones were stacked in the middle of roads, in suburban yards, in open doorways, in cars that were piled with suitcases. Suitcases that were still tied down.

Skeletons of the young and the old. Babies in prams. All of which seemed frozen in time. It was as though these souls were attempting to take shelter or were trying to escape. Then I knew what I was seeing. I was witnessing the last minutes on Earth as The Great Seep washed through. People everywhere tried desperately to get away. But to where? Nobody had any chance at all. There were signs of panic and madness everywhere I looked.

The orca took me to a clearing, and in the middle of the clearing was one single skeleton dressed in the same clothes I'd seen on that day we'd nearly perished on the ice. I knew we had arrived at where the submersible was supposed to take us. I knew we'd found the dead man.

As we got there, the orca slowed to a stop. I almost instinctively put my hand out and plunged it into his pocket. My fingers curled around something. It was no eagle figurine. I pulled away a big wad of what I knew were papers. The wad of papers looked exactly the same as what I'd already read, and I knew it was more of dead man's journal. In my mind, I decided I must now find the eagle. I darted around the dead man's clothes. I worked them over, zealously. I searched every pocket more than once, more than twice but there was no eagle.

* * *

I broke the surface and took oxygen like I'd never needed it more. The water was choppy, *Victory* was at close-reef, and I knew they'd responded to a 'man overboard.' How was I going to tell the captain what had happened? A hundred thoughts in a split second drilled through my mind. But in my hand, I grasped the wad of papers. It was living proof of where I'd been.

With the water seething around me, I grabbed the rope which someone had flung down. When I finally got to the top, I was greeted unceremoniously with a ferocious punch to the jaw. I found myself flat on my back and my brother standing over me. I knew if I got up again, he'd have another go. So, I got to my feet. And down I went again. I got to my feet and this time someone was hanging onto Jason. My brother's face was red. Fury, I knew, raged inside him. I couldn't blame him. I wanted to exit, taking the easy option. If it was me, I'd have done the same thing. He could've beat on me as much as he wanted, it didn't matter. When this all unravels, it'll be worth it.

* * *

It took almost a week to painstakingly dry out each single page. Jason, Eli and myself met daily in the captain's great cabin where each page had its own place to dry. I had to hold myself back from the urge of reading as I went. Had I attempted to read a page while it was still wet, I ran the risk of putting my damn finger through it. So I lay out each page separately and put them back together only when they again became stable.

The day came when the journal was put back together. I couldn't help but feel a certain eagerness building inside me. Jason and Eli tried to hide their excitement as best they could but failed. Even Captain Bass appeared impatient to get going. I guess we all knew that we'd finally find out more of what happened to Michael and Timothy, perhaps even find out what had happened to the figurine and uncover clues that may lead to its whereabouts. The question remained, however, whether there was enough to lead us to it? And if so, what would it take to recover it.

Chapter Fifteen

Charlotte

I MET CAPTAIN BASS IN THE GREAT CABIN to continue my reading commitment, but this time I had an audience. Eli and Jason stopped whatever they were supposed to be doing and joined us. It felt very odd. It felt almost as though I was a teacher and these eager faces staring up at me belonged to my pupils. As I picked up the papers and held them, I made sure one final time they were all bone dry. Happy with that, I started at the top of the first page being aware that my brother and the doctor, as well as our captain, appeared to be almost salivating. They eyed me excitedly as though I was holding up a big cut of prime meat. I also found myself wanting to get going if only for the reprieve I'd get from my other much darker thoughts. I wanted to escape all the hurt and upset and this was an opportunity. I was so glad the relief was only seconds away.

Dropping my eyes on the first sheet that was as badly dog-eared and tattered as the first part of the journal, I was pleased the writing continued at entry 728. If it didn't, that meant there was a hole in time which might've led to the possibility of missing vital clues.

Entry 728.

Newman is everything Timothy described. The entire place from what I can tell is walled up and it resembles some kind of fort. The walls are as high as thirty hands in some places and it's made of odd scraps of wood and other materials that they've collected. Rusted tin sheet, pieces of gyprock, wire, steel, slabs of concrete and even great chunks of asphalt. From the outside, it looks like a junk pile. And everything's lashed into place with ropes, hooks, nails, and screws. But it's strong. Seth assures me, it'll stand up to any Takers raid.

"What about the trucks, Timothy told me about? If the northerners have them like he says, that means the Takers have them as well. They can smash through the barriers."

"The Takers don't have thim. Only carts drawn by their droppers."

"Droppers?"

"People thet work for thim. They call thim droppers because when they drop dead, they get eaten."

"Slaves?"

"Sort of. They give thim labour but they're more for food. And the Ambers from up north haven't bin down here in a while. Even if the Takers attack us with ranged weapons they'd get

nowhere. We've got contingencies in place for an evint like that. You're safe, Michael. There's no nid to worry."

Tracking the edges of the sentry walls as Seth calls them, we came to an opening and heads popped up from behind a pile of rusted forty four galon drums. After greeting the sentry guards and making ourselves known, I stepped down a flight of rickety steel stairs and into a darkened musty smelling tunnel. It was my turn to carry Timothy. I put him on my back for the 101st time and I was so sick of it, I felt glad that it wasn't for much longer. It doesn't matter what anybody tells me. I still reckon Timothy won't last long without medication. It's up to me now. I'll have to get them and sort him out. If he dies, I'll lose my eagle. That's just not happening.

Climbing the steps at the other end of the tunnel and emerging again into the sunlight, I looked out over rows and rows of green.

Green!

I've never seen it before. There's crops just like Timothy described as far as I could see. The crops swayed in the breeze and rippled like liquid. Seth told me it's corn but they also grow wheat, barley, and rye. There's vegetables, the same as those I tried so hard to nurture and get going but failed. Tomatoes. Pumpkin. Celery. Even horse radish. What a surprise.

As I adjusted my eyes trying to believe what I was seeing, Cherith grabbed Timothy off my back and took him away. Timothy said nothing, the bastard. Not even a thanks. He just disappeared into the distance, not a word said.

Seth grabbed my attention just as I was about to shout out 'thanks for nothing.' He pointed to the far east side of the compound to a hill that rose up from the flatlands. "See that?" he said. "That's our fertiliser pile. Horse shet, cow shet, donkey shet, chook shet, pig shet, but no people shet. We're not like the Takers. We don't put people shet on our crops. Thengs grow because we prep the land and we have water. After harvest, we turn and rotate the paddocks. We don't plant the same seed in the same paddock twice."

That was when the first warning sounded off in my head. I should've listened to my gut instinct. Timothy told me these people only have meat in deep freeze. That's why they needed their generator fixed. So then, where did they get all that manure? Their animals are supposedly dead. My mind went, 'Turn the fuck around and run, you wanker.' I couldn't. I was too far from the sentry tunnel. I had no idea what kind of weapons these people might have. They might have guns and ammo. They might even have bolts and crossbows. They might have anything. If I made a run for it, I was sure they'd either tackle me, or shoot me as I ran.

As soon as I thought about it, the second warning ricocheted around in my brain. Nobody has firearms but the Takers. What made Seth think they could stand up to them? The only thing that can answer a gun fight is more guns. A horrible thought came to mind. Maybe I'm now in more shit than I know.

Entry 729

I thought it'd be better to play out what needs playing out and make a break for it when I got close enough to the tunnel. An old memory told me, 'If you hold your hand out long enough, you'll catch bird shit.' The trick is not to hold your hand out. Keep everything to yourself. And this is what I'm doing right now. I swallowed all my suspicions. I said nothing to nobody.

After they'd taken my stuff away; my belongings and precious gun with a single 50 cal bullet, they'd given me a place to sleep in one of the farm sheds. Something in my head told me I might not see those things again, and I worked hard trying to force my mind to think positive thoughts. But Timothy is a bloody liar. The place stinks of cows. And it doesn't take much intelligence to work out they've fed them only yesterday. It made me wonder about the generator. Do they even have one?

Entry 730

This guy called Murk turned up and said he was to take me to my workstation. Workstation? What? Was I some kind of slave now? That being what it was, Murk wasn't a guy you'd mess with. The guy is beefier than a Brahmin. And probably twice as angry. I said to Murk, "There's a diesel generator that needs fixing. That's why I'm here."

He laughed and said, "Yeah, that's what Temothy tells all of thim. He even wears the right kind of diesel perfume when he goes out looking for droppers."

Droppers! Shit!

As soon as he said it, Murk tightly gripped my upper arm. I thought my blood was going to squeeze out of my eyes. Pretty soon after that, there were more of us so-called droppers. I saw them hunkered down, swinging sickles, chained together in long lines. None of them were smiling. None of them even talked about anything. The next thing I knew; I was added to the chain and doing the same damn thing.

Swinging a sickle is a pain in the arse. Under the beating sun, it's twice as bad.

I tried to make small talk with one of the other droppers. He was reluctant to say anything. He kept on swinging that sickle, at the same time acting as though he was deaf and dumb. I felt Murk's big curled up fist between my shoulder blades and I got the message to shut the hell up.

Entry 731

A new day of swinging a damn sickle awaits me. At least it's a way of getting out of this stinking barn. I wasn't alone this time. Last night, several of us were dropped off like pieces of litter in this stinking cow shed. Before the sun went down, they threw some plastic plates under the big wooden door. They'd made us a heap of what the chain masters call clag. They also pushed a container of brown bore water toward us before shutting and locking up for the night.

With the heavy chains off my limbs, I grabbed my plate of clag and found a place to eat away from everyone else. I hoed into it with my fingers, thinking at the same time what I must've looked like from the outside. Here we all were tucking into something that was made from crushed wheat and water. To be honest, I'm pretty sure this clag could be used like glue to stick things together. But eating it was better than nothing. I ate all my clag and washed it down with that wretched brown bore water.

After I'd finished my plate, I pushed some dirty hay into a heap and thought it was well enough off the ground to get a good night's sleep. Before I knew it, one of the other droppers was scoping my plate for possible leftovers. I only left the tiniest amount. I was gonna save it for breakfast. But when he got close enough, I thought maybe I could finally talk to somebody.

"What's your name. I'm Michael."

This guy looked at me a little startled as though nobody had ever attempted to talk to him before. Then he pointed to his mouth.

"What's wrong with your mouth?" I asked him.

He opened up and showed me. These guys don't have a tongue. He showed me in sign language what happens to new droppers. They cut their tongues out! The takers like their food supply nice and quiet.

Fuck!

Now what?

I got up and tested every possible escape route I could find. The place is solid. The ground is much too hard and compacted to dig a tunnel with my bare hands. The only way out is through that big door.

I grabbed the handles and gave it a big shake. "Let me out of here!"

I did it again but the droppers behind me seemed to be amused, making a laughing sound that wasn't quite a laugh. It was very spooky.

"Let me OUT!"

I screamed it a few times to nobody. The sun started to go down and night time came.

Entry 732

They came in just after sun up. Murk burst through the big heavy barnyard door with another behind him, wearing doctor's garb that was so grimy and dirty; it was hard to tell it was supposed to be white. Without any hesitation, they went straight for me. Murk grabbed me. I tried to fight him off. I had no strength. The other guy held out his huge rusty knife. I knew what was coming. I was going to lose the ability to speak.

Murk grabbed my hair and forced my head back. "Get on your knees, dropper!"

I fought him. I fought him hard. Murk's big hands tried to force my mouth open. My head spun. My brain went, 'fight him, fight him, fight him.' I clenched my teeth has hard as I could. But I was fading. I relaxed a little. My mouth opened slightly. Murk's fat fingers entered my mouth. I felt his flesh. I felt his bone. I bit down hard, and I instantly tasted that coppery taste. His bone went 'crack.' I bit down and spat away Murk's big fingers. He reeled back, screaming like a little girl.

The hit I got across the face was aided by an implement. My skin peeled back and opened up. The wetness oozing out was hard to mistake for anything else other than my blood. It ran down my face and neck, and by the time it reached my shoulder it had already gotten cold. There was nothing further I could do. They can take out my damn tongue. They'll never stop me writing.

That guy with the dirty whites got down and did what he came for. I knew Murk would help out even though he was down a good hand. I felt fingers dart and rummage around inside my mouth. Then the blast of pain shot down my throat and into my stomach.

Entry 733

I thought I'd be dead by now. Three weeks fighting an infection and only today am I able to write something. Eating nothing but clag and drinking stinking water somehow kept me going. Today, I join my gang and work the fields. I wonder if this is going to be for the last time. I feel like I've been cheated. Why can't I just die?

Entry 734

I've lost the sense of time. I have no idea how long I've been here. Maybe a lifetime and a bit more. More new droppers arrived. More tongues were cut out. More dead droppers were laid on the backs of carts and pulled away by the Takers walking food supply.

Entry 735
I thought I saw someone familiar. Was I dreaming?

At sentry wall mending detail, I happened to get my eyes on a scrounger who'd turned up to sell wares. I cast my mind back and I remembered who this scrounger was. It was Charlotte, of all people. The young scrounger with a face like an angel. The scrounger who sold me the eagle figurine and bones. I would've shouted something. Anything to grab her attention. But now, I can't say anything to anybody that they would understand. Now, words don't mean anything. She probably wouldn't have recognised me anyway. I've lost so much weight and my hair's fallen out. I've lost most of my teeth. I don't need them to eat clag, so I can't complain. Maybe tomorrow at sentry wall mending detail, Charlotte might be there again. This time I'll let her know I'm around.

Entry 736

A funeral was held for Timothy. He'd died from infections to both legs, I heard them saying. His feet were so bad they had no choice but to amputate. I should be happy he's gone but I'm not. One— I don't know how I'm ever going to get my things back. Two— I've resigned to the fact that I'm never going to get out of here. I'll die soon and I'll end up on a Takers' dinner plate.

Entry 737

A party of Takers arrived for their weekly collection of dead droppers. There was something different this time. They didn't bother to enter the sentry tunnel as they usually do. And from what I could tell, they all seemed to be on edge about something.

But that was before something DID happen.

From my workstation outside the Newman compound, I heard a low earthy rumble and it seemed to be coming from a distance to the north. It was a mechanical noise and something I'd never heard before. Dust clouds were kicked up high in the desert sky. After it got close enough, something in my head told me they were the trucks from the north I'd heard so much about. And they'd picked a bad time to arrive at Newman.

The Takers scattered toward the sentry tunnel, instantly taking cover behind several forty-four gallon drums, and concrete barriers. Almost involuntarily, I turned to seek refuge behind ancient roadside debris. I pulled at my chain and it wouldn't budge. As a member of a gang of seven droppers, it was useless. It was as though my gang knew it was an opportunity to gain their own freedom; to die where they stood. The idiots were reluctant to go anywhere that might be safe. I stood there, agog, out in the open, knowing shit was about to go down.

Several Newman dwellers raced with arms raised towards the incoming fleet of Ambers. It was an attempt to warn them off, but far too late. By the time the Newman dwellers got away by forty strides, the Takers opened fire and cut them down as they ran.

A Taker popped up from behind cover, holding a missile launcher. The tracer of a missile screeched across the sky, then struck an inbound fuel tanker. The tanker exploded, tipped over on its side and erupted in a cloud of black smoke. Several Newman folks screamed at the Takers to stop the madness. Then a

Taker, without any nuisance, drew his pistol and shot a guy who complained.

The rest of the Ambers' fleet rushed to a stop and were immediately peppered with small arms fire. The Ambers' vehicles turned long, slow, U-turns and headed off in the direction they came. More Newman residents emerged from out of the sentry tunnel, two of whom, almost point blank, were shot in the head.

From out of nowhere, that familiar face I'd recognised as Charlotte entered the affray. I didn't know where she came from and it didn't matter. Lightning fast, as though non-human, she retrieved her long recurved blade from her bejewelled cross-draw sheath. Instantly, as if she wasn't affected by the forces of gravity, she moved swiftly between them, mowing down Takers one by one until they all had been relieved of limbs and heads.

I rubbed my eyes, not believing what I'd seen, but as I looked skyward I caught sight of an enormous eagle. The eagle joined more of their kind to become seven; one of which was entirely, and completely the colour of white.

I lifted my eyes from the journal amid the sounds of an almost childlike objection. Clearly, both Jason and Eli could've stayed and listened all night, but I was fast losing my ability to read aloud. My voice was getting croaky and my words were becoming more like mumbles. Apart from that, I had to stem the barrage of new questions that were beginning to emerge.

"What is it, Richard?" Captain Bass asked. "You're looking more befuddled than you were during our last reading."

I was forced to hold my breath and think about what I was going to say next. Yes, I was still enthusiastic as ever to find the crystal eagle but I was also weary. "I hate it when you think there might be an answer, more questions arise. It means there's more work involved and more trudging to do."

"Oh?" Captain Bass got up from his chair and headed for his decanter. "This is unlike you, if you don't mind me saying. I've only known you for a short time and already I see you as an adventurer. Now, it feels as though you're ready to give up."

"It's not that. It's not that at all."

"So pray tell what you mean?"

"It's to do with Charlotte," I said. "She seemed to have this power. This ability. But even so, she appeared to avoid the cruelty of how the droppers were treated. Why did she let them live like that when it's clear she could've helped them? But also this. Michael saw several eagles, one of which was all white."

"Your point?"

I took a breath. I knew this wasn't going to be easy. "The orcas. Seven of them," I said. "Just the same as the seven eagles . . ."

"One of which was all white," Eli said straight away.

"There's a correlation, do you think?" Captain Bass asked in a tone as though he was genuinely mystified.

"There's a correlation, all right. And this also has something to do with the relics, and the reason for them to stay together. We must find the crystal eagle, Captain Bass. Whatever the cost. Whatever the human endeavor. And in my mind, the more I read of this journal, the more it feels like we're on a race with time."

"There's more in the journal," Eli put in. "Maybe Charlotte *did* help the droppers. We won't know for sure until we have the whole story."

Eli was right. Of course it could've been exactly as he said. That question, however, would go unanswered for tonight. We all needed sleep. We all needed our wits about us. We were on the edge of discovering something that was fated to reveal itself. To all of us. Maybe a destiny. I felt it to the core of my body. I wondered if Eli and Jason felt the same. I wondered if Captain Bass felt it as well. What he said next confirmed my feelings.

"You're albino just as much as the orca and the eagle," Captain Bass said, just as I thought it was good time to head off to my allotted hammock. And as he said it, something went through my mind at the speed of light that I didn't at first want to acknowledge; but perhaps subconsciously I already did. Maybe I knew it from the time the orca took me down in the ocean. It was as though we were both somehow joined.

"You haven't read the *Holy Bible*," Captain Bass continued. "So you wouldn't be aware of the *Old Testament* and the seven archangels either. Perhaps some further reading is on the table."

I didn't know what to make of it. But there was a part of me that just couldn't let it go. Curiosity sparked up and I was no longer tired. I was alert and alive, finding myself leaning in toward Captain Bass as he went on explaining.

"There're seven of them. The messengers - and hands of God. Michael the Protector . . ." *There it was. Michael the Protector as Charlotte had called him.* ". . . Gabriel the Messenger, Raphael the Healer, Jophiel the Creator, Uriel the Guardian of Beasts, Azrael, the Angel of Death, and Chamuel the Keeper of the Light. Their job? The fight for the righteous and the battle against evil on earth."

After Captain Bass had said it, he simply turned and headed for a refill of rum. "There was one other," he went on. "The fallen angel. Lucifer was cast out of the kingdom of God. Cast out because Lucifer wanted to be God unto himself. So he was given a choice. Accept God as his creator or he can be God elsewhere. So for Lucifer, he chose the latter. He is God of Evil, or the Prince of Darkness as most are aware.

"So, young Mister Gabriel. You're albino, and your name suggests you're more connected than you might think. Same with you, young Jason. To be honest, all three of you are. Eli here shares the name Raphael. A healer no less! Coincidence? I say not! The more I think about it, after what's been put before all of us, there's a mission revealing itself that is turning out to be vastly more important that we can imagine."

Shit!

My head thumped as the realization came. It all made sense. It all made perfect sense. On *Steinbeck*, we all shared the names of these seven archangels. We didn't know it. We weren't aware of it. And perhaps someone sharing the name of Lucifer decided it was better to do away with and erase any literature or reference to *The Holy Bible* or to *The Old Testament*. It might have been a completely different story living there had we all known the significance. And now, only three *Steinbeck* dwellers survive. Fate or Destiny? I felt it was turning out that way. Now, with every fiber of my being. Sleep would have to wait. I grabbed the journal.

Chapter Sixteen

They Can Go and Eat Themselves

Entry 738

On the outside of the compound, us droppers were detailed to clean up the mess. Picking up body parts wasn't what I had on my wish list for the day. But instead of burying or burning the Takers' remains, Seth chose to have everything placed in containers and stored in deep freeze. The thing was, I couldn't have cared less even if we were going to grind those body parts into a powder and use them as blood and bone fertilizer. But then I realized Seth planned to put the body parts in with the next export of dead droppers, so the Takers can literally go and eat themselves. A bit of poetic justice if that was the case. The sad thing was, I'd never know what the outcome would be.

As I bent over the huge trough that held the Taker grossness, one my chain members tapped me on the back. He pushed his finger up to his lips in a sign of 'shush.' It was a little odd knowing we couldn't form or mouth verbal words even if we needed to, but that was beside the case. It was his way of warning me to be quiet because our gang master had his back turned and he was just a little beyond the range of quiet noises.

My chain member held out his hand, and in it, was a key. It was the key that can set all of us droppers free.

I signed to him, "Where in the heck did you get that?"

He signed back, "I picked Murk's pocket."

"Shit!" I signed. "He'll know soon enough. We're all gonna die."

My dropper friend just shook his head slightly and smiled. His hands were already unchained. Without any further delay, he pushed the key into my hand and he took off. I thought I was a fast runner. This guy ran like the wind. It was then I realized why he took off in a big hurry. Murk gave chase. Murk didn't have a weapon. They don't give out weapons to gang masters, simply because there's not enough to go around. So, on foot, our sixth dropper was gone, and with big Murk chasing him down.

I saw the opportunity. I didn't waste my time. The key in my hand found my lock and I was free. The other droppers? Who gave a shit? I gave them the key. I was outta there!

I ran as hard as I could go, back toward the west. But it wasn't long before my malnutrition caught up with me and running at full force slowed to an uneven non-rhythmical lollop. But I was by this time far enough away that I wasn't able to be seen *by the other Newmaners, or the other gangs of droppers who were always on work detail outside the compound.*

Now was the time to get back into survival mode. It was still full sunlight. And one of the things I never do is walk the waste-land while I can see things at any distance. The general rule of surviving the flat-lands is, if I can see them, they can see me. I needed to get to cover and hole up until night. Then I could start thinking about how I'll get my stuff out of the footlocker without being blown to pieces.

Entry 739

I'm at the gully before the entrance to the silver mine. I'm a little nervous. If the worst happens, these will be my last words.

That was the end of reading all the journal. But we all agreed that Michael's life didn't end in the tunnel after he retrieved his belongings. If he was blown to pieces, as he put it in his writing, his skeletal remains wouldn't have ended up floating on the ocean. So, the question was, what happened, and where do *we* go from here?

"We shall make haste and sail for Perthland," Captain Bass said with one finger pointing into the air. "From there, we shall see about getting your backsides to this place they call Newman. I think, if you're ever going to find the relic, you should start there."

"You're not coming with us?" Eli put in.

"I have a ship. But you shall have my support when we dock in Fremantle."

I was a little disappointed that Captain Bass wouldn't join us on the journey, but I agreed we needed to start at Perthland if we were to ever stand a chance. We also needed a map and see for ourselves where Newman really is. "Do we have a map of the area?"

"Absolutely." Captain Bass stepped behind his desk and opened a drawer that I could see contained large rolls of sea charts. He retrieved an old looking map and printed underneath several islands were the words, 'The Province of Australee.' There was no resemblance at all to the maps of Australia that I'd seen in *Steinbeck's* Library. For the first time, I saw what had happened to the continent of Australia after The Great Seep had killed so many millions. It was a sobering sight. The thought of all those lives lost almost made me ill. I had to stem my anger and put it away. Now wasn't the time to transmute the pain of millions of people.

Captain Bass unrolled the map across his desk and placed a candle holder on one edge to hold it down. Eli stepped closer and placed his hand down to hold the map open. Already my mind wondered how we could ever get there.

I discovered Newman was virtually in the center of the land mass called West Australee. And right in the middle of an area known as Fool's Desert. The map also showed several Takers' outposts. To get there from Perthland, we'd have to traverse Fool's Desert while avoiding Taker contacts but that wasn't all. Newman was also in close proximity to Great Crater. An area which the map showed as being highly radioactive. "The coast to the east of Newman is far too radioactive," I said. "And there're too many Takers' outposts to the west. To the north we have the Irradiated Badlands. And Fool's Desert just south of that. Newman looks truly boxed in."

"That leaves Perthland as our *only* option," Jason said as he studied the map closer.

"I agree but how do we get to Newman from the south?" I asked after a moment of looking things over.

"There is one option," Captain Bass responded. "There's a caravan that departs Perthland and travels the old Trans Access Track to the north. Perhaps it might be a good idea to . . . err . . . tag along, as it were."

* * *

The Port of Perthland came into view as the sun's rays pierced the horizon to the east. For my eyes, it was a beautiful thing. I'd made it. Land. And not only that, my chance to make a new start finally started to feel real. As soon as I had that thought, Chloe's sweet face appeared in my mind. A few seconds ago, I was happy and looking forward to the adventure. Now, all I felt was hurt and guilt all over again.

"Looks like we made it, Ditch."

"Yeah. Looks like we made it," I said to my brother as he stepped up behind me.

Jason eyed me and it was as though he knew what my mind was thinking. "Rick. It just turned out that way. You're gonna have to get over it. You've gotta get your head clear for what's coming up."

My brother was right. But the hurt still lived in my heart for Chloe and my mother. Part of being human is hurting. And part of being human is learning to live with it until time takes the hurt away.

"Time, little brother. Time is the healer." Jason said it exactly as I was thinking it. I looked at him and gave him a smile. "Don't ask me why. But something tells me more hurt is coming. More hurt for me to get over, huh?"

After thinking about it, Jason replied, "I'm not going any-where, Ditch. I'll bury you. Not you, me. Got it?"

Not saying anymore on the subject, I thought of Chloe and I promised myself that whatever the future holds, she'd always be in my heart. I would always remember her. I'll always be thankful for the memories we have of being together.

* * *

As *Victory* docked in Fremantle after being hauled into place by what appeared to be a timely old diesel tug, the first thing I noticed was the noise. I wasn't accustomed to so many people shouting over the top of each other. Then I realized what all the shouting was about. There was a market at the end of the docks. People were making their living from selling wares as soon as goods were delivered. Goods that came in on ships.

It wasn't too long before a crowd of Perthlanders arrived at *Victory's* dockside. Then I remembered the discussion I had with our captain about the commodities she brings to the colonies. They were items that had been taken from the Takers. As I looked out among the dozens of messily dressed individuals with cheerful faces, it was as though they were all there waiting for the ship to unload. It turned out I was right. In the next moment, a sudden burst of activity toward the rear of *Victory's* quarter deck told me the unloading had already begun.

Captain Bass appeared behind me and placed his hand on my shoulder. "This is what we live for, young lad. This is what makes it all worthwhile. Seeing their happy faces and knowing they can get along a little longer with the items we bring them. And I don't mind saying that most of these things were stolen from them in the first instance. It brings a whole new meaning to the word 'justice,' wouldn't you agree?"

I *did* agree. It was heartwarming to see. "Robin Hood."

"What was that, Richard?"

"That's who you are to them. You're Robin Hood. You take from the Takers and give to the colonies."

"Well perhaps you might be correct. But let's not dilly-dally any longer. We have a caravan to find and you three have a whole lot of distance to cover. But first, you'll need cooler clothing. It's hotter out there than you can ever imagine. Oh, and another thing. I feel it's vitally important for the bones to stay on *Victory*. They'll be safe behind our cannon. When you find the eagle figurine, make your way back to Perthland and wait for me."

I agreed. Jason and Eli agreed. It seemed like a logical thing to do. But at the same time, I was surprised that Captain Bass wanted to go out of his way to help us. I pictured Jason and Eli with me as we learned all about our new environment. But this captain was not only willing to go ashore and show us where things were in Perthland, but he'd already decided to negotiate with the caravan driver on our behalf.

* * *

Captain Bass issued us with calico purses full of the stuff they called crackle. Judging by the weight, I guessed there was enough to purchase anything we needed. I was almost about to object to the amount Captain Bass had given us, oddly thinking it was too much. I offered my purse back, which he politely refused, then Captain Bass pointed with a finger back to *Victory's* poop deck. "Your two-man submersible. Consider it sold. And I'm afraid you'll need every shard you have for this journey. I'm not doing you any favors. I gave you fair price for what I've purchased. Let's leave it at that, shall we?"

"You're a good man, Henry Bass. A good and decent man."

"And that, my dear boy, is why I cannot leave my ship. Let it be said, though, I am mildly jealous of you for the journey you're about to embark upon. Perhaps I've been at sea a little too long. But business is business. This is what I've chosen to do."

"And they all depend on your expeditions."

"That they do, young Mister Gabriel. That, they do."

Heading down the worn looking timber decking of the docklands, a mixture of odors attacked my senses. The smell of fresh cuts of meat from a butcher's stand, mixed with the strong stench of a fishmonger's stall. The dye used for coloring clothing and leather; the heavy smell of cheeses in a stall where goats were kept in timber and wire enclosures. The cackling noises of poultry and geese and boxes and boxes of eggs on display. And above all the smells and animal noises, were the loud voices of the stall holders, hollering out their special prices for the day.

"Get ya fresh chook here! Lop the head yaself and save! Only four shards!"

"Damper! Get ya damper while it's hot. One shard for damper. Two shards for three!"

It was then I noticed someone staring straight at me through the crowds of rushing people. A woman dressed in earthy colored cottons with flowing black hair all the way to her waist. And her complexion; so milky white and perfect. Her eyes, black as a cold winter's night. It was in that moment, impossible as it was, I was sure I'd met her before, but where? Then I remembered the dream. She was Teresa. But that was even more impossible.

I left Eli, Jason and Captain Bass at the poultry stand and rushed through the crowd to catch up with her. "Teresa! Wait!" But she was gone as I reached the place I'd seen her. I slowly scanned a full three-sixty. "Damn it!" She wasn't anywhere to be seen. For the sake of one last time, I scanned again. This time slower. "Where are you?" Just as I thought I was hallucinating and about to give up, Teresa appeared again, standing just outside what I thought was a hut with fine looking glass-blown art pieces on display in the windows. She walked through the door to the inside. At last I knew where she went. "Wait! Teresa! Wait!"

PART TWO

THE LONG WALK

Chapter Seventeen

The Vanishing

I PUNCHED THROUGH THE DOOR. "Teresa!" As my eyes adjusted to the glinting of glass trinkets everywhere, I found myself alone standing in the middle of the floor, surrounded by shelves upon shelves of intricately-blown glass creations. I wondered if there was a back door. Teresa could've found an exit to the outside. There was no back door I could find. Teresa had vanished into nothingness. And yet, in a far corner, a lanky old man with a crooked arm, wearing jeweler's headgear sat eyes down in a cubicle oblivious to anything. On his cluttered desk were art pieces in various stages of completion. He looked up and eyed me curiously. His long grey beard was tied into several plaits with little bows at each end and jiggled as he spoke. "Can I help you, mate?"

"Teresa. There was a woman . . ."

The man took his headgear off and eyed me, this time appearing to be genuinely surprised. "You've got the wrong place. Try the house of ill repute on Cliff Street. If you're after the company of a woman, there's plenty to choose from."

"No," I said. "I was outside. I saw her come through the door. This door."

"You're mistaken. I've been here all morning and no customers yet. But be my guest. Have a browse. There may be something here that you might like. These hands make everything here. Take two, and I'll give you a special deal."

I was in no mood for shopping, but how could I resist such beautiful work. On the shelves were sculptures of unicorns, penguins, bulls, and horses. Dioramas of domestic pets they called dogs and cats. Creatures of the sea including sharks and dolphins. Even birds of prey like the condor and the eagle. But when I saw the eagle sitting there on the shelf, something inside me immediately snapped to attention. I went to the shelf. I picked it up. The glass eagle with its wings spread out was beautifully created; awe-inspiring.

"It's an exact copy of the real one that's made from rock crystal called *The Angel of Bunjil*," the old man said as I held up the eagle to the light. "It's as exact as I could get it, I suppose. That there, is one of the first sculptures I've made, going back nearly forty years ago. I'm sorry. It's not for sale."

"If this is a copy, the real one must be truly magnificent. Can I see it?"

"Unfortunately, I don't have it. That's why I'd never forgive myself if I sold my sculpture. It's the only record of my recollection. One day my memory will fail me. If I still have this sculpture, I hope I won't be so challenged. There's a story with her. A story written in a journal."

"Journal?" I couldn't believe what I was hearing. "Are you sure?"

"Of course, I'm sure," the old man said. "But it's not complete. There're pages missing. For almost half of my life, I often wondered if I'd ever one day have the chance of seeing the entire journal from start to finish."

The old man paused, then eyed me more intensely than before. He took a step back, put his hand to his chin and for some reason seemed to hold his breath. I saw a slight smile curl on his lips. He put his eyes down and let out a huge sigh that could never be misread. It was a sigh of relief. "It's the journal of the one they called 'Michael the Protector'," he continued. "And after all these years, something deep inside me is telling me you have the missing pages of that same journal. I'm not mistaken, am I?"

I didn't know what I must've looked like to him. I tried to hold my composure and not seem so excited, even though inside I was going completely nuts. If he had the last part of the same journal that I'd spent the previous weeks poring over . . .

"Are you okay? You look like you've seen a ghost."

"I'm albino. I always look like I've seen a ghost. The real crystal eagle. *The Angel of Bunjil*. If you know where it is, please tell me how I can find it. I need it. We all need it."

In that split second, Jason and Eli along with Captain Bass burst into the shop; beads of perspiration glistened on their faces. "Mother of penguins!" Jason spat. "You're like a little kid. You gonna tell me where you're going next time? Disappearing around here isn't an option, Ditch!"

Jason grabbed my arm, but I pulled away. I told him to look around the place. Then I showed him the glass eagle. In that moment, everything changed. I told Jason, Eli and Captain Bass everything the shop owner had told me. They were no longer in such a hurry to get away to the caravan.

Captain Bass approached the shop owner, appearing to do his best not to seem so utterly eager even though I knew he was feeling as excited as I was. He held his hand out to the old man. "I'm Captain Henry Bass of His Majesty's Ship of the Line, *Victory*."

"Marty," the old man said and shook the captain's hand. "Marty McBride."

I was getting anxious. I felt like asking Marty, 'Where's the eagle, where's journal, and can I have them?' But I knew that wasn't going to do any good. In the next split second, Captain Bass asked Marty, "Where's this journal and may we please have it?"

Oh no. I held my breath. Now we were going to be refused.

"You don't have to ask," Marty said. "I was going to offer you the journal anyway. But please do me the honor of letting me see it one last time in its complete form; how it should've been before everything went bad. After all these years, this day has finally arrived. Now, it's best to let it go."

Before I was able to add anything further, Eli butted in. "Have you seen the crystal eagle? We need information. It's of utmost importance that we find it?"

"So, everyone keeps saying," Marty McBride said as he got up from his chair and placed both his palms on his desk. From his body language, it appeared from the outside at least; he was in regret. "But before we go down this road, there is something I must say to clear my conscience. I've had to bear this weight for forty years. This seems like a good time to let it all go.

"I was a Taker. I'm not proud of it. I was one of those pieces of shit. Some might say I grew a conscience when I was out raiding. I suddenly realized the life wasn't for me. I stopped going out on raids. I stopped taking things just for the sake of taking them. Every time I ate something, I became sick. So, they locked me up. I became a prisoner; a dropper. But I escaped. I absconded. I made my own life down here in Perthland. But, always looking over my shoulder and sleeping with an eye open does things to a man. My health has paid a heavy price for it. I'm now on the Takers' blood list. If they capture me, I'll die by the way of the blood eagle. I'm not afraid of death. I've stared death in the eyes more than a few times. But, the blood eagle; it's not the way I'd like to leave this life. That's why I make these little pieces of art. So, your question was, have I seen it? Yes, I have. Not only that, I know where it is right now. That being what it is, I'm guessing you've also recovered the Sacred Bones?"

Captain Bass pointed toward the docks. "We have the Sacred Bones and they're safe on *Victory*."

"Well then," Marty said. "Let's make things happen."

* * *

With the new twist to the entire situation, Captain Bass thought it was a good idea for all of us to regroup back on-board *Victory*. I couldn't help but be amused as I saw Marty's facial expressions. After he'd stepped across the gangway and onto *Victory's* quarter deck, it was rather like seeing a child light up for the first time after receiving a birthday present.

Being taken by surprise so suddenly caused Marty to almost drop an intricately decorated wooden box which he'd brought with him. I guessed what was in it. The glass eagle he'd made. He juggled the box in both hands before he caught it again. A near miss but it was heartwarming to see Marty's eyes full of joy. His happiness was quite contagious, and it almost made me get a little misty.

I was happy also in most part because, in my grip, was the rest of Michael's story. With the entire journal safe in our hands, I knew it would give us the extra clarity we needed to search for the crystal eagle called, *The Angel of Bunjil*. And as a bonus, we also had an actual first-hand account in the mind of this person we took onboard. What more could we ask for? With his forth-coming information, we could put firm plans into place to find it, and I knew it in my heart that it was just a matter of time until the complete mystery unraveled. In the back of my mind, however, I also knew that all of us were being guided in some way, one step at a time by something I couldn't quite comprehend. I shivered slightly thinking about it. How can a person in a dream become real and then, disappear? But to answer that question, I'd need also to answer the question of the orcas. And then there was eve-rything that was in Michael's writings. My brain pounded with the blood from each heartbeat. Maybe there'd be the day when everything made sense. I had to let it go for now.

* * *

By 1900 hours, my job of showing Marty around the ship was complete. And by 1930 hours, we'd all found ourselves at the captain's table for evening meal. I was seated at the table with Eli to my left, Jason to my right. Captain Bass was seated at his usual position at the head of the table. On his right was First Officer William Fletcher, then Surgeon Cristian Hamel. Lastly, taking up the guest of honor end of the table, master craftsman extraordinaire, Marty McBride.

Tonight's affair was a silver service at the Captain's pleasure, to which everyone at the table was impeccably dressed for the occasion. Ship's officers wore their decorative navy blues which were pressed with precision and were meticulously made lint free. For some reason, our captain had also issued Eli and myself with naval officer's uniforms; rank of ensign. For Jason, he'd climbed back into the red, royal marines uniform he'd donned during the tussle with the Takers ship, *Excelsior.*

With *Victory* being freshly resupplied, I wondered what might be served up instead of the normal damper or dumplings, goat's cheese, oranges or lemons. I wasn't, however, prepared for a meal that consisted of lamb and mashed potato with gravy. The potato and gravy weren't unfamiliar. I'd never had the lamb before. It was the very best meal I'd ever had the pleasure of enjoying. After finishing such a satisfying meal, I started to wonder if our captain was putting on a show for the benefit of our newcomer. I thought perhaps Captain Bass was softening Marty up. Then I thought I was seeing something that was out of context to everything else that was in front of me. Was our captain gay? As soon as I had the thought, I thrust it to the back of my mind. Surely not. But then, why not? What difference would it have made? And it certainly was no business of mine. The captain had every right to his happiness. It didn't matter at all where he found it. But my suspicions of Captain Bass putting on a show to soften our guest a little was confirmed after we'd all retreated to his great cabin.

* * *

In my mind, I still remembered vividly how Michael had written about the time he and Timothy opened his box of treasures. Of one of the many items was a box of Cuban cigars. As I thought about it, here in front of me was a captain enjoying a cigar with his guests, complete with a crystal glass of rum. What I saw with my own eyes was a Jules Verne novel. Everyone was small talking to each other. But nothing substantial about our quest was forthcoming. I decided to change all that.

"So don't keep us in any more suspense. Please let me read some of the pages in Michael's journal," I said rather loudly over everyone. It was a subject that played heavily on my mind even through the act of enjoying such a gorgeous dinner. I decided I wasn't about to retire to my hammock without knowing more about Michael. Now that I'd almost rudely silenced everyone in the room, I was about to hear it for the first time.

Marty looked down at his empty glass and twiddled the stem back and forth in his fingers. He then handed the glass up for a refill which Captain Bass willingly obliged him. He took a breath before sitting down in the same chair that I'd sat in while reading to Captain Bass. He picked up the pages that were in a ragged pile to his left. As he handed me the pages, his voice lowered. "You'd better prepare yourselves for this."

Chapter Eighteen

Prophecy

MARTY MCBRIDE MADE HIMSELF comfortable in his chair, hitching an ankle up to his knee and taking up his glass of rum. After drawing an audible breath, he began to speak with words that seemed heavier than only moments ago. "As you'll find after reading the final pages of Michael's journal, the prophecy of the *Angel of Bunjil* and the Sacred Bones will only come to pass after the relics are reunited and returned to their rightful keepers. That being what it is, I'm compelled, now, to tell you the *complete* story."

Here it was — the moment of truth. Now was the time we'd find out about all the intricate details we'd missed. I was looking forward to settling my mind, and I could go to my hammock have a decent night's sleep.

"Rosemary Keene, a survivor of The Fall, wrote her memoir called *The Book of Hearts*," Marty explained. "Before the bombs, Rosemary was a nurse who'd worked at a secret location in the

Northern Territory of Australia as it was known back then. She was part of an elite group of individuals who'd been given an exit strategy away from the coming destruction."

"What elite group of individuals?" Jason asked.

"Ambers. These people were genetically created to resist the effects of radiation and so, therefore, they'd become a master race on Earth. Keene also goes on to write about a group of Ambers who failed to exfiltrate from danger, and are now known as The Lost Ones.

"On that final day, Keene chose not to use her ticket to safety. She tells of her incredible story of survival, and not only that, how she endured the after-effects, the radiation fallout, and most amazingly, how she endured the wash-over, also known as The Great Seep. But in Rosemary Keene's account, she describes the death of Nathan Masters and today, her story; *The Book of Hearts* has become a legend.

"One set of relics you have with you on this ship are known as The Sacred Bones. They belong to Nathan Masters. Some years before the Fall Wars, Nathan Masters operated as a special forces soldier who was given the task of rearing an orphaned ten-year-old girl named Angel—a girl who possessed special abilities."

"What special abilities," Eli asked.

"Angel had the power to heal, and also, she possessed a heightened sense of perception, more so than what's deemed the typical level human of awareness. After the bombs fell, Nathan Masters contracted radiation sickness and died from the effects."

"If Angel was a healer, why didn't she heal him?" I asked. "If she had these abilities as you say, it seems logical that she'd do just that."

Marty immediately held up his hand and carried on. "In *The Book of Hearts*, Rosemary Keene explains how Angel *wanted* to heal Nathan. The legend also describes Angel's pain. She was torn between being healer and friend. She knew Nathan wanted to die. As hard as the decision was - she let Nathan go in peace. It meant Nathan could finally be reunited in death with his long-lost love, Teresa."

"Teresa?" Captain Bass asked. "The same Teresa as in young Mister Gabriel's dream, no less?"

Marty looked directly at me. His inquiring eyes drilled into my bones. "Did she have long black hair and black pupils, so black; you could see your reflection in them from across the room?"

I nodded. "What happened to Teresa? In my dream, she was a young woman. That means she was young when she died."

"Nathan Masters killed her. He shot her in the head, point blank."

I immediately recoiled in my chair. I couldn't imagine any reason why Nathan would do such a thing if he and Teresa were in love. But just as I had those wonderings, Marty enlightened me a little.

"Nathan didn't have a choice in the matter. He was made to do it. Nathan Masters was held captive by a group of thugs who called themselves the Guardianship of Milestone. And today, these thugs are the Takers. They're the direct descendants of the original arseholes.

"According to Rosemary Keene's account, the crystal eagle figurine known today as *The Angel of Bunjil* was given to Angel as a birthday present from her partner, Jenny. But unbeknown to Angel, Jenny wasn't just human. Jenny was something else completely extraordinary. Jenny was also Charlotte, an eagle who Angel had befriended as a child. And Charlotte was . . . and still is, the Angel of Death, Azrael."

"Angel carried the crystal figurine with her right up until the time Nathan Masters passed away. When he died, Angel placed the figurine on Nathan's body, and she made a vow that she'd return and give him the burial he deserved."

"Where did she go?" I asked. "Where did all of them go?"

"Unfortunately, there's no record of where they exfiltrated to in Rosemary Keene's memoir. But she wrote about the prophecy of their return that will come to pass once the Sacred Bones and the *Angel of Bunjil* are reunited and returned to The Lost Ones."

"And that's the reason the Takers seek to destroy the relics," Jason said. "No relics, no prophecy."

Marty McBride nodded vigorously. "When the Ambers return, there'll be one mighty showdown between good and evil on Earth."

As the evening went on, I became a little cautious about our guest. It seemed every time we wanted to know more about the possible location of the *Angel of Bunjil*, Marty stepped further and further away from giving us the direct information that we needed. It was a little odd for Marty to be so aloof knowing he'd seen the crystal figurine with his own eyes. Even if it was long ago, the information would've given us a starting point. But Marty held back on giving us anything. Why?

By 2317 hours, I'd had enough, so I asked Marty directly. Loudly. Over everyone in the room. "Marty, do you know where the *Angel of Bunjil* is or don't you? It's not a trick question, it's a straight yes or no answer."

Everyone in Captain Bass' great cabin held their tongues. Only sounds of cracking and creaking emanated from oak timbers as the ship moved on the waters. I knew I'd said the same as what everyone was thinking. Maybe I was a little rude. It was late and my weary eyes needed to be shut down.

Marty appeared to hold his breath, looking a little annoyed while he placed his empty glass on the mahogany side table. "I could answer you in a way you'd like to hear it right now. Or, I could let Michael give you your answer through his writing. Which would you have?"

Marty was right. Not only did he put me back in my place, it made sense to wait until the entire story was made known. Now I had a choice. Go grab some sleep or stay up for the night with some light reading. Of course, I chose to stay up.

Chapter Nineteen

Marty

Entry 740

I'm glad I'm able to write. It's been a while. Getting hold of paper and then finding something to write with seems harder now than it used to be. I have to do it out of sight. I have to do it when they think I'm doing other things. Other things they get me to do. At least they have me work outside and I'm no longer trapped in that room. It's a room where nightmares live. It's a room that contains the most horrifying things my eyes have seen. My biggest wish is for the ability to un-see. But in that room down below the ground, they're there. The not quite dying; not quite living. The ones who've been selected for their meat. The ones who've had parts taken from them, but they still live. They say nothing but make noises. They make noises and cry. They cry in their pain and their anguish. They're fresh food for the Takers. The Takers feed them. They take parts of them away, and they slowly die.

Entry 741

I think about it all the time. Why did I enter the silver mine after I heard their voices? I could've stopped. I could've stepped back and thought about something else. Maybe there was another way in. I didn't explore it. How could I have done things differently? But no. I waltzed straight into the obvious. I blasted down the tunnel, running noisily toward their voices. But I had to. I had no choice. They were going to take my things. I had to save them. And then, the explosion.

I thrust my hands up to my ears. The shockwave almost knocked me over. I could see it. The footlocker was on the ground. It hadn't been damaged. But bodies lay there. It was too late for them. I ran toward it and I was so glad that everything wasn't destroyed. The next thing I thought of was to get away before more came. And more did come.

I ran as hard as I could with my footlocker in my arms. I ran to the west entrance, past the great stack of rubbish where I'd once eaten to my fill. I could see it. There in the distance. The light at the end of the tunnel. I nearly got there. Nearly.

"Stop! Or you're dead!" The voice reached my ears. Then the unmistakable ca-clink of a weapon being cocked. I stopped where I was.

"Put it on the ground!"

I did exactly that. I put the footlocker down at my feet, and I raised my hands.

"What's your name and where ya from!"

I couldn't say anything. How could I? But I managed to make a mumble.

"What's the matter with you! Can't ya talk!"

I shook my head. I wondered if he could see my reaction in the darkness of the tunnel. I shook my head again even harder.

"Well, looky-look. We've got a runaway dropper. Which camp ya from, dropper!"

I mouthed something. Whatever the heck it was.

"Oh. Can't speak huh? That's right. I forgot! Your tongue was on someone's dinner plate. Ha-ha-ha."

What a smartarse. My anger started to burn. But just as I was able to get physically violent, a sharp thud from between my shoulder blades sent me over onto my hands and knees. From there, I can't remember anything.

Entry 742

Once, I ran from seven chain members. Now I'm chained to twelve. They keep us working in the day. They keep us working pulling things. Pushing things. Picking up things and carrying things to places. It's mundane and meaningless. A purpose of our labors must be somewhere, but I can't see it. They don't eat greens, so they don't grow them. They don't grow them so there's no sickle to swing. So, they get us to pick up things and put them down. Pick them up again and put them down again. All day. Every day. Day in. Day out.

At night they throw us in a hole — no ladder to climb down. If we break a leg, we'll get sent to that room of unspeakable horrors. It's too high to climb. It's too hard to dig. So, we wait in the hole until the sun comes up again.

In the darkness while in the hole, I felt someone next to me. I felt his hands touch my hands. I immediately pulled my hands away. He grabbed them again and pulled them toward him. I didn't know what he was wanting, but if he was wanting what I was thinking, what would it have hurt? and who would know about it? Maybe it wouldn't be that bad. Maybe I just had to let myself go. Maybe it would save me from insanity. But as he took my hands again, it wasn't that at all. It was a way to learn a new language. By the touch of a hand, we worked out how to communicate. Before the week was out, we were having conversations.

Entry 743

My new friend on the chain said his name is Marty McBride. Each night after they throw us in the hole, we talk about anything at all. Using our hands, we can tell each other stories. We can take ourselves away to somewhere in our imagination and share our experiences. We can cheer each other up if we're sad. We can silently laugh together at things that are funny. We can even be mad at each other if we say something wrong. But Marty told me something tonight that took me by surprise. Marty told me he kmows a way to escape.

Entry 744

The bastards must have sensed something. They put Marty and me at the opposite ends of the chain. Now, I don't get to talk to him when we rest for clag. I'm so pissed off right now; I can't write.

Entry 745

In the hole, Marty grabbed my hands, and we started to talk about our plans. We'd have to time it right. But I said to Marty, I can't go if I don't have my eagle. And I can't go if I don't have my Sacred Bones.

"What are they?" he asked by twisting and touching my hands.

I told him the entire story up to the minute. By the time I was finished, my hands felt like I'd dragged them through sand.

Marty agreed. My things were much too important to leave behind. So now our escape would have to include their recovery. The question was, how?

Entry 746

Picking up things. Putting things down. Does it ever end? But just before clag time, the same things happen every day. They get us to pick up concrete blocks and place them into a pile. The chain master always takes his seat and puts tobacco into his pipe. He always puts his shotgun within reach to his left. He always wears the keys on a big ring on his right hip. He always opens a can of bully beef or beans and starts to eat it in front of us. He always smiles before each mouthful. He always finishes each can and folds the lid over to the outside of the tin. He always puts the can on a piece of concrete to his right. It was the same set of actions every, single, day, without fail. So, Marty and I built our plans around this sequence of events.

Entry 747

Marty and I ran from that place after we got ourselves free. We're now out of sight in an old creek bed far west of the silver mine. And I'm so glad we've been able to get my things. The Takers had taken stuff out of the footlocker. But they'd left the eagle and bones. Why? I don't know and I don't care. Not only that, we now have a shotgun and ammo. I don't know if it was just plain old luck, but it bloody-well seemed that way. The shot gun took a bit of getting used to but as soon as I pressed the trigger a couple of times, I worked out what that shotgun could do.

The bad news. Some of the Takers are dead and if they find us, we'll get executed by the blood eagle. A nasty way to die.

We'll take off again after sundown and we should reach my home before dawn.

Entry 748

Home again but it's not good. They raided my house. They took everything. There's nothing left here but a hulk of a place. My most precious backup food supplies and water are gone. All my tools. All my furniture. All my belongings. If it was too heavy to carry, they'd smashed it to pieces. There's debris all over the place. Fuck I'm angry. But Marty says we can start a new life at a place he knows about. It's another twenty nights stride west of here. He says it's on the coast and there're people living together in a community. I've never lived with other people before. And I've never lived in a community. Maybe they won't like me. Maybe I won't like them. But it sounds much better than staying here in this dump. To think it used to be my home. Bastards!

I'll gather what I can gather, and we'll start west after sundown.

Entry 749

Marty makes everything look so easy. There're bugs when we need them. If we find small animal bones, there'll be stuff left on them. Sometimes there'll be live echidnas wandering and it's just a matter of getting past their sharp spines, and then they're food. Once there were five in a row. Five! We ate like Takers that night. But water. Yeah, pissing again. Gees. I didn't have to do that when we were chowing on clag three times a day. How those bad things can get forgotten so quickly.

Marty says three more nights and we should be there!

Entry 750

It was so sad to see Marty's hopes drop so suddenly. After we came over the top of the hill that overlooked the community of Kalbarri, it wasn't long before we both realised it had been taken over by FUCKING-BLOODY-TAKERS!

Entry 751

We made camp on the hill for the night. I had so many pieces of paper in my pockets, I decided to lighten the load and leave a big wad of my journal in the footlocker. Marty and I spoke for a while with our hands. I was surprised that he wanted just to give in and go down there knowing he'd be placed on another freaking chain, or worse, die by blood eagle. But the thing was, it meant we didn't have to drink our own urine. And to be totally honest, I was getting so sick and tired of carrying the bloody footlocker even though it was a lot lighter than it used to be. So, Marty's idea of just getting it over was slightly attractive in that respect. But we also had the shotgun, and I thought, how about if we go down there and kill as many of them before they kill us?

Marty didn't grab my hands to reply. He just walked over, picked up the shotgun and tossed it as far as he could get it. Then he sat down next to me and for the first time in my life I saw a grown man sulk. I used to do that when I was . . . five?

He grabbed my hands and said, "Can I have a look at your eagle figurine?"

Without a reply, I opened the footlocker and gave it to him. He studied it for a while, then asked if he could keep it in his shirt pocket. For good luck, so he asked.

"Sure. No problem. Be my guest," I replied.

Marty then squeezed it into the top breast pocket of his checked western shirt. It looked a little odd. It looked like he had a breast. I grabbed his hand and said, "What happened to your other boob?" He laughed and I was glad I was able to cheer him up. Then he looked at me all serious. "Let's go," he said with his hands.

"Where?"

He pointed down the hill, then grabbed my hands, "let's take down as many of the bastards as we can." Then he started beating on his chest. He must've remembered what was in his pocket. He grabbed it out, smiled, and gave the eagle back to me. This time Marty picked up my footlocker and started down the hill. I placed the eagle in my pocket and grabbed the shotgun on the way past thinking at the same time, 'I'm gonna be dead soon, but it'll be fun getting there.'

Marty and I were a bit more than halfway down the hill when someone noticed our approach. There was yelling and carryings on in the distance but worse than that; there were voices behind us. Two Takers were on the chase towards us coming at us down the hill. I stopped and crouched behind some post-fall debris and I waited until they were in shotgun range. Spinning around, I signalled to Marty, "Run Marty, Run!" Which he did. He picked up the pace, footlocker and all. But he was running right into the arms of the Takers who were down there already waiting for him.

If I could've screamed something I would've. I would've screamed for him to run to the coast. "No Marty. Run to the coast and find a boat. Don't die. Save yourself." But it didn't matter how much I wanted to yell out to him, I couldn't. I wasn't capable. But Marty kept going.

I turned my attention back to the Takers who were almost on top of me. I popped up from behind cover and blew the bastards away! The wind blew their cloud of blood all over me. Some, I got in my mouth and I spat the filth away.

Spinning back toward Marty, he was almost out of sight, but it was as though he'd heard my thoughts. Marty had veered off to the right and headed for the coast. He'd find a boat and he'd wait for me if I lived. If I knew my friend Marty, that's what he'd do.

I cracked my shotgun and loaded more shells. Now, I was in no mood for the bullshit. I headed downhill toward the Taker stronghold. I touched my eagle figurine in my pocket for good luck, wondering at the same time how many Takers I could take out before I died.

Just as I was about to take the fight to the Takers, I felt an enormous amount of air pressure all over me. The downforce almost pinned me into place. I looked up, saw it, and I knew I wasn't alone in this fight. The huge eagle landed on the ground in front of me, it was no longer an eagle. My breath left me as I saw the young and fresh face of Charlotte.

"Michael. Go south," Charlotte said. "Go south, now."

"But Marty . . ."

"Your friend no longer lives. You must go south from here and take The Angel of Bunjil."

"The Sacred Bones, I must have them too."

"The Sacred Bones will find you again. Go. Do not look back. You may hear it, but you shall not bear witness as I slay with my sword."

I turned away from Charlotte and faced south, amidst the sounds of booms and explosions to my rear and I suddenly realised I was again able to speak words verbally using my own voice.

Chapter Twenty

Confession

I SAW IT IN HIS EYES, THE PAIN HE MUST'VE felt back then. After I'd read the final words in the journal, I knew why he'd chosen to hold off on telling us anything. How Michael must've loved Marty. Marty McBride was dead and had died a long time ago. Now, it was obvious who this humble glass-blower was. It was also clear about the dead man we'd found floating in the water. But just as shocking as the truth was, it was also a relief not only to me but, to Michael who was seated in front of us with red-rimmed eyes, appearing to hold back a wave sadness.

"Michael the Protector," I said.

"For over forty years, yes."

"You could've told us back at your shop," Jason said.

"I agree. But others have asked for the whereabouts of *The Angel of Bunjil* after they visited my shop. I didn't know who they were. I invented a cover story, and it stuck with me all these years. For all I knew, those who've asked for it were Takers. Even though we're safe from raids in Perthland, I remained cautious.

Takers have infiltrators in both genders. We've caught several of them over the years. I was doing my job at protecting."

Captain Bass walked over to Michael and kneeled before him. "I'm honored and privileged, sir, to make your acquaintance."

As Captain Bass said it, Michael burst into tears.

* * *

I tried hard to imagine it, but I could never appreciate what forty years of carrying pain and suffering could do to a man. Michael shed those many years of sadness in less than an hour. After he'd finished, he sighed and politely asked for another glass of the captain's fine rum. "Of course, there's the question of *The Angel of Bunjil* and where to find it," he said with words that felt a little happier."

I still had the pangs of sorrow for Michael inside me. Even though Michael was about to let us finally know where to find *The Angel of Bunjil*, the sadness of his story still played heavily on my mind. I wasn't as eager as I once was to find the crystal eagle. It was almost as though I didn't care anymore. My mind stepped back to all the loss we've had to endure over this journey. My mother. Chloe. How I missed Chloe. Our unborn child I'd never meet. I remembered how I felt as I stood at the rail and looked out over the water. My motivation to end everything was strong, and I remembered how I was just a moment away from peace. I could've been with Chloe again. Perhaps I could've even been with our baby.

Michael broke through my thoughts by holding up the wooden box he'd brought with him. The glass eagle was most likely an offering of gratitude to our captain which I knew he'd love and give pride of place in his great cabin. I realized it was a very generous gesture of friendship. I remembered Michael telling me it wasn't for sale. Now he was giving our captain something that was most precious. I was misty-eyed before. Now, I was tearing up and trying desperately not to become a blubbering mess.

Michael opened the box and smiled. "I haven't seen this in so many years," he said at the same time as drawing the eagle out. But it was no glass eagle.

My legs wobbled a little. Eli let out a gasp. Jason said, Shit! Captain Bass dropped his glass of rum, and it smashed on the timber floor. Michael had *The Angel of Bunjil* with him all this time. And it was as beautiful as everything we'd learned. The eagle posed with its wings spread out; a gold inclusion ran diagonally through it from the base to a flared wing tip. We were all stunned into silence.

* * *

Not able to sleep, I left my hammock, and I navigated my way up the steps to the quarter deck to get some air. The smell of coal wafted in on the soft breeze which carried a briskness that caused the skin on my forearms to prickle. Ordinarily, I wouldn't have noticed the cold. I thought I might be finally acclimatizing to the new environment.

The view from *Victory* across Perthland at night was beautiful with the light of candles and lanterns dancing through windows and on poles. I wondered what it must've looked like before The Fall when electricity was everywhere. Maybe one day in the future, the people of Perthland might have electricity again, and it'd become as second nature as just breathing. Maybe one day, humans would learn to treat technology with respect and not hurt the planet. Ultimately, that was the reason humans had got the entire world into the mess it is now. But as soon as I had that thought, I realized I'd not had the experience of a world before The Fall, and I could only imagine what it was like. Reading about things, however, was not as real as living it. I'd have to settle for what my imagination could provide.

Eli stepped up behind me which caused me to startle. He apologized then said, "You can't sleep either, huh?"

"Me? No. I have so many things in my head right now; I don't know if I'll ever have the pleasure of sleeping again. I keep thinking of the next phase, and I don't know why we haven't thoroughly thought of it before. How, exactly, are we ever going to contact the Ambers in the north?"

"Our minds were on other things."

"That's right, Eli. But now, we're left with the dilemma."

"You're talking about the radiation?"

I nodded. "It's scary. Every time I think I might have a solution, the fact that there's radiation up there that can fry anything living blows my ideas away."

Eli paused for a while and said nothing. He stepped up to the rail and looked out. "It's peaceful out there, isn't it?"

I agreed. "Those people in their beds tonight don't have to worry about when the next Takers raid might come. That's the only reason why its peaceful, Eli. The entire populous of Australee should be able to sleep in peace. But it's not that way. Not yet anyway. What will Australee be like after the prophecy comes to pass, I wonder? Will it be for the good and for the better? Or will the Takers find a way back and all this that we're going through now will be for nothing."

"We don't have the power to see into the future," Eli said. "All we've got to work with is the here and now. We'll find a way to contact the Ambers. The answer is out there somewhere. After we've done our duty, what happens after that, we have no control over. So, you're giving yourself extra to worry about when there's no need."

Eli was right as usual. And I kept forgetting about the divine help we've received that I was only starting to fully understand. Perhaps we'll get more guidance from the archangels as time goes on. But I also thought that I must be careful and not take for granted anything from that moment on.

* * *

After breaking fast on damper and eggs from a chicken, we all met in the captain's great cabin and I knew in my heart that by the time we left there, there'd be a firm action plan put into place and I'd no longer have to endure the nights spent tossing around in my hammock. Not only was it not doing my health any good, but it also meant I'd stop getting kicked by Jason who was always nearby.

As I stepped through the great cabin door, Captain Bass was already in deep discussions with Michael, and I saw them both bent over the map of The Province of Australee. Eli was with them, standing arms folded with a hand to his chin looking on as intent as ever. But as I looked around, I couldn't see Jason.

Captain Bass stepped from behind his desk and met me in the middle of the floor, looking as cheerful as a cherub. "Come. Come, dear boy. I think you may enjoy hearing what we've discovered."

"Where's Jason?"

"I've sent him on an errand with William Fletcher. He'll be back shortly, I assure you. Come."

I approached the map, and I saw that plot lines had already been marked out. It appeared that there was much discussed already without my presence. I was a little disappointed but knowing time was of the essence, I let it go.

Behind the captain's table, Michael's footlocker was left open, and inside it, I could see the crystal eagle and the Sacred Bones were placed together. Finally, the relics were reunited, and I reflected a little on what was known as the legend according to Rosemary Keene's account in *The Book of Hearts*. *The Angel of Bunjil* rested once again with the body of Nathan Masters. Captain Bass noticed my eyes on the footlocker. He smiled warmly as though he too was relieved that we were able to bring the reunion of the relics to a conclusion. But somewhere in the back of my mind, I knew we'd won a battle and the war was yet to be decided.

Just as I had the thought, the door opened, and Jason stepped through holding a gadget which I already knew about. A yellow box with a handle that made clicking, squelching noises. A Geiger Counter. It was nice to have, but it still didn't fix the problem. "What? Are we to draw straws to see who goes north?"

"We've already decided," Eli said. "It's going to be me."

"What? You can't. You're our doctor!"

"Haven't you noticed, Richard? I was the only one who ever got close enough to the McMurdo ruins without getting sick. What does that tell you? And, I have the same skin and hair as an Amber. Coincidence? I don't think so. All the Raphaels on *Steinbeck* could've done the same thing. I think we shared the same gene as those of the Lost Ones."

"Wishful thinking," I said. "Can't you see that? You're getting swept away with the adventure. It's making you see things that aren't there."

"Ditch!"

"You have no proof that you can survive the radioactivity and you won't have proof until it's too late."

"DITCH"

"I won't let this happen . . . I won't . . ."

I felt Captain Bass' hand land on my shoulder. "Richard, we've decided. We're ready to go and go we must. We weigh anchor at the hour of ten. We shall sail north as far as we can go until the Geiger Counter tells us it's no longer safe, and then, Eli takes it from there. It's settled."

Chapter Twenty-One

Death from Above

VICTORY'S SAILS BELLOWED OUT and strained with the gusty winds that whipped up from the south. Monstrous seas crashed over her decks—sailors dashed and scurried through wash after wash with their obvious seasoned ability. None of them tripped or slipped or stumbled or fell. It was as though they ran around with sandpaper stuck to the soles of their shoes. But in times like these, they wore no shoes at all. In prep for the southerly gales, they roughed the bottoms of their feet with corn husk.

Hours after the winds had died; after emptying the contents of my stomach over the starboard rail about seven hundred times, the raging seas settled into a subtle swell, allowing everyone one on board to get some much-needed respite from *Victory's* severe pitching and rolling. As I stood there, looking out, there was no longer any sign of land. I was alarmed and thought the wind had taken us far away from where we were supposed to be. Captain Bass joined me at the rail and with only a few words; he took away my concerns and swapped them with something else to worry over. "Don't worry your head, young Richard. If we can't see the land from here, it means the Takers can't see us. We must be out of sight because if they know where we are, they can use their artillery guns to sink us."

"Artillery?"

"Howitzers, Richard. They have them in positions along the west coast of West Australee. You thought the north was fraught with danger from radiation. That might be the case. But getting there is equally as perilous. We must all have our wits about us." Captain Bass slapped me hard on my back and stepped away. But after he'd left my side; a low drilling sound flew overhead. As the object hit the water off the larboard bow, it exploded sending up sheets water high into the sky. I looked up as shrapnel tore through the sails. Pieces of timber rained down from the masts and yardarms. Then another shell flew; drilling overhead with the same awful sound.

Captain Bass spun and immediately commanded his crew. "All hands! All hands! Battle stations! Mister Fletcher! Beat to quarters!"

"Aye, aye Captain," William Fletcher said, then spun and shouted to the crew, "We shall beat to quarters!"

Within the minute, a lone drummer began beating on his snare drum, and the quarter-deck came alive with activity.

Captain Bass took up his position near the helm. "Evasive maneuvers! Mister Brice. Evasive maneuvers, god-damn it! Mister Finch! Run up all batteries if you please!"

Victory lurched violently sideways as another massive explosion erupted out of the water sending a monster wave shooting straight up. "All hands brace!" The leeward side of the wave hit *Victory* with an incredible crunch, sending skillful sailors off their feet. Some fell from yardarms and crashed into the deck with an audible snap from their limbs.

Another shell came in drilling across the sky. I involuntarily got down and thrust my hands to my ears. The incoming shell struck *Victory* amidships, exploding like a hammer from the gods, splintering timbers and sending men through the air; their blood instantly turned the spray of salty water a ghastly shade of violet.

"Mister Brice! Get that helm hard over! Hard over! Do you understand me, Mister Brice!"

"Trying, Captain."

It all went racing through my mind. We were so far from shore we couldn't see it. But they saw us. How?

I raced over to the captain's side and shouted over the noise of explosions and rushing, shouting men. "They're using radar to track us. It could be x-band marine radar. It doesn't matter if we can't see the shoreline, Captain Bass. They can see us on their scanners."

"It doesn't make any sense, Richard. How is this possible?"

"They used the same radar tracking system on the *Steinbeck*. We must move further out to sea. We have to get *Victory* out of range."

Immediately, Captain Bass commanded his coxswain. "Mister Brice! West by southwest if you please!"

"Aye, aye!"

Another shell found *Victory* and exploded on impact, sending massive solid oak boards skyward as though they were mere matchsticks. In that instant, I knew it was the end for the once proud flagship of the British Royal Navy.

The Footlocker!

It went screaming through my mind. I need to get there. Right now.

Without any explanation to the captain, I turned on my heel and bolted for the stairs. Just as I got there, a shell dropped from the sky and struck the quarter-deck, top dead center. Instantly, the detonation caused the ship to dome upward and explode with debris sent screaming up, licking the sky with deadly shrapnel. I flew down the stairs to the great cabin, hoping like crazy it was intact when I got there.

To my rear, I heard men shouting the words I never wanted to hear. "Abandon ship! A-BAN-DON-SHIP!"

Another almighty explosion ripped through the ship, and I heard the cracking of masts as they collapsed onto the decks; men I knew had become trapped under the huge timbers and were badly injured or dead. Those still alive screamed out their anguish.

"Abandon SHIP! The ship is sinking! Abandon ship!"

"Away with the longboats! Away with the fucking longboats!"

In the great cabin, I opened the footlocker. I grabbed some of the Sacred Bones. I grabbed *The Angel of Bunjil,* and I thrust them deep into my shirt. As I looked through the great cabin window from the rear of the ship, the stern; once high up from the sea was now almost at sea level. The ship began to keel over. I had but moments to get to a longboat. I ran like I'd never run before.

On the quarter-deck, Captain Bass strutted back and forth. He helped his sailors get to the safety of the longboats, as yet another explosion violently rocked the ship. This time, a gaping hole opened before me, and I could see down through *Victory's* decks to the water's surface below.

"Richard! Get in the longboat!"

"You're coming too, Captain Bass. None of that, 'captain goes down with ship' bullshit."

"Richard. Just go, will you?"

"You first! Then me!"

"Just go!" Captain Bass shoved me over the edge. I fell half in the water and half in the longboat. I saw Jason's face, and I was glad he was okay. I saw Eli's shocked face behind him. Another shell drilled overhead, and this time, it missed and fell into the water a good distance away. After the shell exploded, a wave pushed up and almost caused *Victory* to stand true again. It as though it was meant to be *Victory's* last wave. *Victory* slunk back down into the water lower than she was before. Voices of men behind me screamed. "She's goin' down!"

I looked over to where *Victory* lay on her side. On the rail, I saw Captain Bass holding on and dangling in the air. His facial expression was void of any emotion as the hulk of *Victory* gurgled her last breath and slowly sunk under the surface, taking Captain Bass with her.

There was no way I could believe what had just happened. "NOOO!"

I ripped off my shirt. The things I had stashed in there fell onto the longboat floor. I got myself to the edge about to leap into the sea. Jason grabbed me and hauled me back. "Leave it, Ditch! He's gone. Captain Bass has gone!"

* * *

We'd been floating on the sea for what seemed like hours. The shelling had ceased. The ocean had calmed. And an air of sadness had descended upon us. No-one spoke. I wondered how long the shell shock might last. But in the back of my mind, I knew we were all still ducks in a duck shoot, as Captain Bass had once put it. We needed to get as far out to sea as possible. I was aware of the ability of x-band radar. It not only picked up seagoing vessels, but the x-band system also picked up much smaller objects. I wondered how much time we had before the shelling started again. With a bit of luck, perhaps we were already in the area of radar where it exceeded the range of the Takers' howitzers. It was the only sliver of hope we had left.

Around me, the men who were lucky to survive the onslaught sat calmly as one volunteer began a roll call. After the roll call, we discovered we'd lost more than half the crew. To make matters worse, we had no oars. Crew hastily put the longboats into the sea. Out of the panic and the madness, the oars somehow never made it into the hands of the men. We were bedraggled and beaten, crammed into two longboats that were roped together, floating aimlessly in an ocean, floating wherever the current took us. I was certain the question in everyone's mind was, how long could we last?

Out of the corner of my eye, I saw something under water. I leaned over the edge of the longboat and looked down into the depths below to confirm my suspicions. I wondered for a second, could it be one of the orcas? I couldn't help but think they'd turned up much too late. I was almost angry, and I felt betrayed. But after looking harder into the water, I realized it couldn't have been an orca. Orcas aren't yellow where this object appeared the same shade of yellow that I'd seen before. Suddenly, I was lighter. And when the object broke the surface, everyone rose from their seats in the longboats and cheered.

The yellow two-man submersible that once belonged on *Stein-beck* appeared from below the surface. After the hatch opened, a smiling Captain Henry Bass protruded. "You there, young lad. Pass me that rope, if you please."

I got myself to the edge of the longboat and happily shouted to Captain Bass. "I thought the submersible would never work!"

"Turns out, young Richard, all that was wrong were flat batteries. We charged them with the wind turbine on Victory's poop deck. Do you remember me telling you we installed it for emergencies? Hmm?"

With the longboats tethered together, and our captain towing them in a steady northeasterly direction, it was with no doubt in my mind our mission would have to proceed over-land. We'd have to take a long walk.

* * *

We reached the west coast of West Australee without incident. As we approached land, I could see in everyone's eyes how nervous they were feeling. If I was on the outside of my body and looking in, I was sure my eyes would've reflected the same concerns. But disembarking the longboat and hitting the sandy shore, I looked around, and there seemed to be nobody anywhere.

"Where do you think we are?" I said as I found a higher position to see into the distance.

"We appear to have luck greatly on our side," Captain Bass responded. "Judging by the elements of land that I've come to know, I'd say we're in the vicinity north of Drummond Cove and somewhere south of a place called Horrocks. If that's the case, it's a short distance north to the Horrocks trading post. With a bit of luck, we should be able to pick up supplies before we take our journey inland."

"The Takers run the Horrocks trading post," Michael put in.

"Yes, I'm aware of that, Michael. You must stay out of sight and far away from the area. Nonetheless, they'll trade with persons such as I even though at exorbitant prices. The bad news is, one never knows if the Takers will take those items away when you're no more than two hundred yards up the street. We'll need to take extra precautions. Perhaps I'll go it alone at first while the rest of you stay back. We shall then see what happens."

The long walk was confirmed but expected. I readied my mind for the journey. Already, the sun's heat bit deep into my skin; I've never felt so hot. I wondered how long it would be before my skin turned into a raging inferno. Being albino, both Jason and I were completely at the sun's mercy, more so than the others. Maybe if we're lucky, this place called Horrocks might have suitable long sleeved clothing that may give us the protection we needed. But just as I thought it, I realized it was impossible. We had no crackle. No crackle meant no supplies.

"Captain Bass. You forget we have nothing to purchase supplies. We're not able to get supplies if . . ."

Captain Bass cut in as though preempting the end of my sentence. "We have crackle, dear boy. It's in the form of something else at this moment. I'm quite sure the submersible will get us what we need. What use is it now?"

I wasn't totally happy, but I knew it was our only option. Trading the submersible with the Takers just felt odd. It felt wrong. It was almost as weird as doing trade with them in the first place. But what choice did we have? From what I'd read in Michael's journal, we were about to traverse a most unforgiving land. Without the right preparation, we'd all die. Plain and simple.

Captain Bass was finally able to do a more accurate headcount, and with the loss of so many men, he named the beach 'Mandown Beach' in their honor. We all worked together to gather and piled up sandstone rocks to form a pyramid which stood eighteen hands high. First Officer William Fletcher said a few final words as we all stood somberly with our heads bowed.

Chapter Twenty-Two

The Angel that Made Me

WE MADE CAMP ON MANDOWN BEACH. Captain Bass and William Fletcher left in the submersible and headed north to the Takers trading post known as Horrocks. Our instructions were to stay camped until our captain and his first officer made their way back. They would either have the supplies with them, and we could immediately begin the trek to the east, or we'd be invited to the trading post and take up trade as we saw fit.

As the hours dragged on, I began to wonder if resorting to making contact with our enemy was a good idea at all. These people were responsible for the deaths of at least thirty members of our crew. And here we were, walking up to them in the hope they'll trade. It was almost an insult. My anger raged inside me all over again. As I played in the sand, doodling with a stick, the reasons we were all there in the first place seemed to be distant in my mind. I was beginning to lose hope, and I felt trapped.

More hours had passed, and the sun sat low on the horizon to the west. A cool breeze whipped up and was cold enough to cause me to shiver. I looked over to Michael who'd fashioned a carry bag out of a piece of his calico shirt. In the bag; along with the *Angel of Bunjil*, he carried the only Sacred Bone we had left which we both thought was a femur. I smiled a little and thought that Michael will always be the protector until this journey concludes. I was almost jealous, only because I was no longer on the roster for their care.

The sailors of other ranks got together and collected enough sticks for a fire. Soon after, a bonfire raged roughly three hundred yards away from where I sat doodling. Everyone including Eli and Jason crowded around the fire and began to sing what they called ditties. Everything felt so relaxed and peaceful. But as the sun sank fully under the horizon and stars began to appear, I began to wonder about the amount of time Captain Bass and William Fletcher were taking.

"Michael!" I shouted and waved him over.

Michael made his way up the beach sat heavily down beside me. He handed me the bag containing the *Angel of Bunjil* and Sacred Bone. I took it from him, and I placed the bag down at my side and put my hand on it. I reflected a little and looked back at what had taken place in my life to bring me to this point. All the people I've loved, and then they were torn away. But as I sat there and reminisced, I noticed Eli was no longer around the bonfire. Jason, however, joined in with the sailors as they sung their sometimes-strange ditties.

"Eli was there with them," I said. "But he's not there anymore."

"Oh that," Michael snickered under his breath. "Eli went to see a man about a dog."

"What?"

"He's answering nature's call. He said he had to go, most urgent. I told him, 'why're you telling me?' He said, he had to tell somebody in case somebody needed to know where he was. Then I told him the slang term for it. He was mystified. Just like you."

"That's a good one. I'll have to remember it. Go and see a man about a dog doesn't sound anything like taking a dump. How did they come up with that?"

Then in the distance, from somewhere south of where we were, three flashes lit up the twilight sky.

"What was that? Did you see it?"

"See what?" Michael said.

As soon as Michael answered me, three dull thuds, one after the other rang out. In my heart, I knew what they were. The burst of lights were muzzle flashes. The low rumbling thuds came from the barrels of howitzers. But around the campfire; over their singing, Jason and the others would've never seen the flashes or heard the burst of fire. I looked up, and I saw shell tracers streaking across the sky towards us. Michael looked up at the same time. "Shit!"

Shit!

"Jason!" I screamed out.

But he and the sailors kept on with their singing, oblivious to anything.

"JASON! RUN!" I screamed out louder than before.

I got up. Just as I commanded my legs to run toward the fire, Michael grabbed my shirt tail and pulled me back "No, Rick. It's too late!"

I stood there willing for it not to happen. Jason noticed I was staring straight at him. He waved at me; then innocently beckoned me over. I couldn't help but watch the tracer as it drilled in across the sky then, instantly, the shells exploded on impact. Jason and all who were around the fire were gone.

"JASON!"

"Rick. Quickly. We have to get to cover."

Michael grabbed my arm and forced me to run in the direction away from where the bonfire was reduced to a huge gaping crater in the middle of the beach. As we ran, Eli popped up from behind a dune and beckoned us over to him. There was no more artillery — only the eerie silence with the thick smell of exploded ordnance hanging on the cool seaside air.

* * *

At sunrise, there was still no sign of Captain Bass and William Fletcher. But I'd had enough. My anger for the Takers now burned inside me. Retribution pumped around my body, and I was sure I could do the damage of a thousand men. I got myself out of that hole where we'd found cover. I clenched my fists and rose to the highest point on top of the dune. If I were a wolf, I'd have certainly howled loud enough to be heard across oceans. But I was no wolf. I was a mad-man. I was enraged, and my anger gave me the power to kill any Taker I put my eyes on. My blood was steam. My biceps were pistons. My fists were hammers. Show me a Taker. Steer me toward him. Let me slowly take his body apart. Let me rip the head from his shoulder.

"Richard. Give me your burden. Do not harbor such anger."

As soon as I heard the voice, it was as though it was speaking inside me. I spun around, then spun some more. There was no one I could see. "Who are you! Why did you let them kill my brother!"

"I am you, and you are me. We are one. You and I are one, Richard Gabriel."

"Why-did-you-let-them-kill-my-brother!"

"There can only be one true heart. Give me your burden. Give it to me now."

I fell to my knees and felt sickness rip up from the pit of my stomach. I threw up something black and ugly looking like crude oil over the sand. I felt a hand on my back as I threw up more. But after it was done, my hate had left me. I was no longer furious. It was as though everything I ever hated in my life no longer mattered. A new peace had descended. I was lighter. I was stronger. I felt like I could walk any desert unchallenged.

"Richard. Is everything okay?" Eli met me at the top of the dune. "You were sick? You'd better let me examine you. Black bile usually means internal injuries."

"I'm fine, Eli. But Captain Bass and William Fletcher have been captured. We need to rescue them."

* * *

Even though he'd been away from the area for nearly forty years, Michael knew the area better than Eli and me. We stayed close to the water and tracked the beach north. By close to mid-day when the sun had already turned my white skin a fiery shade of red, Michael assured us that the Takers trading post was just around the next bend. The question I had in my head was, what in the heck were we supposed to do? We had no weapons. We had nothing but fists. They had guns. They even had artillery. My internal dialogue told me it was going to get ugly and we'd come off worse than any Taker. But Michael still seemed confident we'd find a way.

As we came around the edge of a dune, I saw two Takers, one male, and one female, swimming naked in the ocean. On the sand were their belongings. I was convinced from where I was standing; I could see a rifle was among the items that lay in the sun on towels.

Before I could say anything, Eli picked up his feet and ran. He bolted toward the Takers belongings, and when he got there, he grabbed up the Takers' rifle. I saw him as he cocked what I thought was an M4 assault rifle. Eli ran toward the Takers who were swimming in the waves and opened fire. Within a moment, the wash from waves brought two dead bodies onto the shore. Both Michael and I exchanged our shocked glances. Who I saw wasn't Eli. I didn't know who that guy was.

"Why the fuck did you do that, Eli? We could've had something to trade. The two Takers for Captain Bass and William Fletcher. But now that's not possible."

"They had towels, Richard. Towels! When was the last time *you* had a damn towel? Huh?"

What was going on? Two people were dead over the fact they had towels. Was this beach turning us into mad-men? Nonetheless, they were the enemy. And these assholes took Jason. I immediately thought back to the archangel Gabriel and my anger was no more. And now, we not only had their weapon, but at least one of us could use their outfit.

After gathering up the Takers clothing, we worked out that the woman's outfit was out of the question, but we could use the leather for other purposes. It'd be a complete waste to leave them on the beach. It was agreed that Michael had the privilege of wearing the Takers' leather and canvas outfit. It seemed to fit him perfectly even though I argued my point one last time.

"I still think I should be the one to infiltrate and find out where they have Captain Bass."

"No," Eli said. "Richard, you may not be white anymore. But you're the same shade of red as a Red Delicious apple. You'd stick out. And we don't go around 'sticking out' when we're infiltrating. I can't do it either. I look too much like an Amber. It must be Michael."

"So, stay here and wait until I get back," Michael added.

* * *

"I know where they're being held," Michael said as he suddenly returned to where we were hiding. "But it's not good. They're on the Takers blood list. If we don't get to them in time, they'll die by blood eagle. It's to do with something about Captain Bass and a wind turbine generator. They think he stole it from them."

"Shit!" Eli said. "So, what do we do next?"

"We go and break them out, of course. But getting there. It's a long way east of here. Twenty nights stride."

I thought about it for a while. "The same place you talk about in your journal?"

Michael nodded slowly. It was as though, suddenly, his memories returned. I saw it in his eyes; he disengaged from reality. He returned to his torment and haunting. I grabbed him by both shoulders and shook. I shook hard. He looked at me with eyes that said nothing at all. I shook again. "Michael!"

After a moment, Michael returned from where he'd gone. His pupils were again full of life. "I'll go back the trading post and get some water and supplies. I don't expect you guys to do the same things I've had to do in the past. The desert isn't a nice place, and without the right preparations, people can die. Easy as that."

Chapter Twenty-Three

One Flew into Fool's Desert

MICHAEL LED THE WAY INTO THE GREY and dusty desert, armed with an M4 assault rifle firmly placed at his hip. I strode behind him, humping two gallons of water in opaque plastic bottles on a long stick across my shoulders. Eli was in the rear, swiping footprints into nothingness with a hunk of old fence paling and a scrap of rag.

As we walked, my thoughts returned to Captain Bass and his first officer. Then something horrible occurred to me. There was no doubt in my mind they'd both be turned into mutes; in the same way they'd once done to Michael. But I couldn't imagine how bad it was for Captain Bass. What good is a captain who couldn't command his men? Just thinking about it made me feel so sad. And he wasn't even aware that his men were gone.

I thought the stars at night in Antarctica were beautiful. I'd realized that all my life, I'd taken for granted the months of an uninterrupted jeweled night sky. In the desert, I couldn't take my eyes away from the band of the Milky Way, nebulae, and clusters of stars that formed into galaxies. I wondered if there was other life out there. I wondered if they'd evolved into intelligent beings and evolved like humans. I wondered if they started to make mistakes and changed the course of their planet's environment. I wondered if they turned into power crazy, greedy, hurtful sons o' bitches who'd ended up nuking their world into oblivion. Maybe it was a course of passage that all intelligent life must traverse. Maybe intelligent life needs to virtually annihilate itself before the ones who're left realize how wrong they were. And I wondered if it was the same everywhere. I looked up, and I wondered.

I realized that looking up, and walking along, was never a good idea. Michael had stopped in front of me, and I crashed into the back of him. Michael gestured with his hand for Eli and me to get down. We did, but I also wondered why he crouched down so suddenly. "What is it?" I asked.

"It's dinner for the next two nights. But only if we're lucky."

I peered into the distance, but clearly, Michael had better skills than me. Eli worked his vision and said he saw nothing.

Michael looked back over his shoulder and sighed. "I'll need to teach you night vision skills. Concentrate your field of vision a little left or a little right, and you'll see things with more clarity.

It's to do with using your rod cells which are more tuned for seeing at night; as compared with your cone cells which are tuned for seeing during the day."

I didn't know what the heck he was talking about.

"Try it. See that tree trunk over there."

I nodded "Yeah, I see it."

"Now look slightly away from it."

He was right. "Holy crap!"

"Magic," Michael said. "But you need at least twenty minutes of total darkness before it develops. If you get white light into your eyes, you're stuffed. You'll need another twenty minutes before it comes back. I'm surprised you blokes didn't know about it considering the part of the world from where you came. Six months in a year of darkness; you'd have to be using your rods."

"We had electric lights," Eli added. "We stayed on board *Steinbeck* during winter. But even so, by the time the sun came up again, I was treating many of our people for severe cabin fever and melancholy."

I patted Michael on the back. "I think I see it now. A kangaroo?"

"You wish. There're no kangaroos anymore. Just these . . . things, that look like them. They're carnivores. Man-eaters. We call them 'Rad Roos.' Kangaroos have mutated over the decades since The Fall. If you see one of these beasts during the day, run. Run as fast as you can. It's the only hope you have left. If they get you, they'll rip your guts open with their nine-inch claws. If you can't find a tree high enough in time, you're dead. The thing is, you'll never see one by itself. They're pack animals. Kill one of them; you'd better hope you can kill more. They'll all turn on you. They'll seek you out and hunt you down. But there's a technique to hunt them. You get them to all turn on themselves."

"How?"

"I found out that they don't like being hit in the head. They think one of the pack has picked a fight. So then, they'll fight each other until one gets killed. You must get close enough so you can throw a rock. If you miss, you'd better have a tree close by so you can get to safety. Even then, they'll wait for you to come down. Or they'll hide and make you think they're gone."

"Mother of penguins! Is it worth it?" Eli asked.

"Well, if you want my opinion, dying of starvation is worse. At least if you get done by a Rad Roo, it's guaranteed to be quick."

"We have our rifle," I said. "We have a better chance if we shot one."

"No. Our ammo is valuable. We don't waste it on Rad Roos. And we're not taking one down either. The fact they're here means they're on a hunt. There's prey in the area. It can be anything from dingoes to echidnas. That's good for us. We'll leave the Rad Roos alone."

We waited in the shadows of the shrubbery for the mob of Rad Roos to move on. It meant we could get up and continue our journey, or hunt the creatures the Rad Roos were interested in. But they seemed to be quite contented staying where they were. We were stuck. No way forward. No way back. "How much ammo?" I asked Michael.

Michael quietly took the magazine out and held it in his hand. "By the weight, I think about nine rounds. Give or take. And no, we're not shooting them. We wait. Patiently."

I sighed and turned to check on Eli, but he was gone. I spun and tapped Michael on the back. "Eli's gone!"

"What! The bloody idiot! Didn't I just say . . ."

Just as Michael had said it, I saw out of my night vision someone protrude from the bushes fifty yards in front of where we were. Eli had a huge rock in his hand. He launched it, and it struck a Rad Roo square in the back of the head. The Rad Roo shook its head and then looked around at the rest of its mob for the aggressor. The spat was on. Two huge Rad Roo males squared off and danced around as though they were world heavyweight boxers. Then one got up on its tail and kicked out with its huge claws. His opponent did the same, but this time connected. The injured Rad Roo let out a terrible scream that sounded like a mother in the final stages of labor. The beating went on.

Eli made it back to where we were. I spun around and saw his face in the pale moonlight. "That wasn't so bad," he said. "We'll have fresh food after these big roos do what they need to do. Then we'll go and clean up."

But just over his shoulder, I saw a set of huge canines glinting and glistening.

"RRUN!"

I'd never ran so fast or so hard. My heart pumped like the rattle of a snare drum. As I ran, I looked for a suitable tree. I saw one and thought I could make it. Behind me, I heard the padded hopping of a Rad Roo closing in. I reached up with my hands to grab a branch. My foot snagged something in the ground, and I went down skidding on my face as the Rad Roo bounced over my head.

Getting myself up on my hands, I saw the roo do a turn in the dirt before it stopped momentarily and sized me up. The tree was my chance, and the big branch was just above my head. I had to get there. I had to jump up at least twenty hands high. My life depended on it. As soon as I got up, the Rad Roo was coming at me like a furious bull. I jumped. I couldn't quite make it. The tips of my fingers only just missed the life-giving tree. I fell again, realizing there was nothing else I could do. I was too late. I put my hands over my eyes.

A burst of gunfire rang out and hit the Rad Roo which skidded to a stop right at my feet.

"Get in that tree!" Michael shouted from somewhere. "There's more. Get up in there!"

Then more gunfire rang out as I again jumped and this time; I grabbed hold of a branch. I climbed up and out of danger.

* * *

Remembering what Michael had told us about the Rad Roos, I stayed up in the tree until full sunlight, and with the sunshine, I could see the carnage of dead Rad Roo carcasses that littered the area. I counted them — seven dead Rad Roos. Michael was already skinning one of them with a crackle blade he'd scored from dead Takers. I couldn't see where Eli was, and I hoped he was okay.

Getting out of the tree, I approached Michael, and I could already see how unhappy he was. I said a few words which went ignored. It wasn't until after I asked Michael if he knew where Eli had gone until he said anything at all.

"I don't really care, Rick. I'm so fucking pissed off right now, I don't know what to tell you."

Then Eli, as though hearing his name, emerged from the bushes. Michael charged at him; crackle blade held over his head. I got in the middle of them. "Hey! Calm down! This is *not* how we're gonna get our brothers out of imprisonment. Calm down!"

It took a bit of effort, but I got there in the end. I managed to avert a disaster between Michael and Eli. But what I saw next broke my heart — the water bottles I'd been carrying lay on the ground in the distance. The Rad Roos must've used their claws to puncture them and then they'd helped themselves to the most precious items we had.

"Yeah," Michael said. "We've got meat. We've got skins. We've even got sinew for making things. But what a price! No water. One bullet left. It's back to drinking piss. You blokes will now know what it's like to do those things. I've tried hard not to do them again. There's no choice now. Eli, you bloody idiot. Why didn't you just let me handle it?"

"Easy," I said. "Let's not do this again."

"You know what?" Michael went on. "After this is over, I'm going back to my own place. The place where I grew up. At least I know how to survive. Not like you two. You're fucking hopeless."

"I'm sorry," Eli offered. "I thought . . ."

"You thought! What did you think, Eli? Did you think it would be easy? Wake up sunshine; nothing is easy out here. Everywhere you go, there's something or somebody who wants to kill you. Let me give you a little lesson in life in Fool's Desert. Every time you eat something, be thankful because there may not be anymore. Every time you drink something, be thankful because you're not drinking your own piss. But now we have no water, and only ONE bullet left, it'll be a miracle that we'll even make it to the Takers' garrison. So wise up. Listen to what I say. Do what I get you to do. And we might just get there. Is that all right with you!"

Michael turned his back and immediately got on with skinning the Rad Roo carcass. As Eli stood there after being firmly put in his place, I started stripping the meat from the bones of the Rad Roo, wondering at the same time, how it would taste after we cooked it.

I couldn't help wondering about Eli. First the Takers on the beach, then this. He was becoming unstable and hard to trust. For now, I thought I'd keep those feelings to myself.

Chapter Twenty-Four

Fletcher

WE ARRIVED AT THE TAKERS' ENCAMPMENT
under cover of night, much to Michael's contentment. It also
meant we could rest up before sunrise in roughly two hours. It'd
give us the time to sort things out in our minds and to figure out
what to do next. Along the journey, I hoped we'd use the time to
work out a tangible plan, but that wasn't the case. The last nine
nights of trekking was empty of anything verbal apart from what
needed to be said to get by. After we finally arrived, I was so
weary, all I wanted to do was lie down and go to sleep. I was sure
Eli felt the same. Over the last sixty miles, we strode with Eli
complaining bitterly about his hunger. Oddly, he didn't complain
as much when we needed to drink our urine just to survive.

Michael was right. He'd once written in his journal that trekking across Fool's Desert for twenty-three nights does things to a
man. It wasn't until after I'd taken my shirt off to let it air dry
from my perspiration, I noticed how much weight had come off
my bones. I realized I was much too weak even to consider

mounting a rescue using what Michael had called, 'extreme violence.' I already knew deep inside my mind that the rescue would never work if we all got physical and went in there all gung-ho. Not only did we have just one round of ammo left; time was against us, and in our state of health, going in there looking for a frenzy of bloodletting was asking for trouble. I also began to realize that the visit from Archangel Gabriel had somehow gifted me with a way of seeing things differently. Although I didn't know exactly what it was, I knew I was on the verge of learning something extraordinary.

As we sat in the shadow of the Takers' stronghold that was positioned up high on a hill, Michael pointed to the base of the hill, and he assured us the opening to the silver mine might still be there. Even though the entrance was covered in desert weeds and shrubbery, the telltale indent near the entrance could still be seen.

We hunkered down in a ditch and got ourselves away from any possibility of getting busted. Ditches; I hated them. I hoped it was the last time that I smelt the desert and the dust right up to my face. But this time, Michael didn't attempt to get any rest. While Eli snored heavily in the background, I heard Michael saying things under his breath. I thought he saw things; maybe he hallucinated due to the effects of dehydration. After I asked him what he was talking about, Michael shut up and looked at me with the same eyes my brother had given me all that time ago. There was hopelessness sitting there behind Michael's eyes, even though he tried to hide it by looking down and away. It was the exact same reaction that immediately took me back to the time with Jason while sitting on the edge of *Steinbeck's* flight deck as we discussed options for escaping the blackout.

Michael looked up at me and said, "This is it, Rick. This is how we go out. The mongrel bastards win every time."

After Michael said those words, something inside me suddenly erupted and came alive. I couldn't have disagreed more. I locked eye contact with him. "When we go in there to liberate Captain Bass and William Fletcher, it's not going to be the outcome any of us are expecting. Their liberation isn't going to be by extreme violence as you keep saying. I don't know why I know this. I just know it. I want you to get your head back in the game, Michael. We have a job to do, and we need you. We must succeed. And we will succeed. All we have to do is turn up at the Takers' gate and knock. What happens after that has already been fated, and we have no control over it."

"Well, look at you," Michael said, smiling a little. "What happened? Are you giving me pep talks now? This wasn't you a few days ago. But you know what? You're right. Whatever happens, is whatever happens."

* * *

"Are you sure you want to do it this way?" Eli asked me, then rubbed his eyes as though he didn't believe what he was hearing.

"I'm sure. Just trust me with this one. Everything will work out. But before we go, we'll stash everything here. The relics, the rifle; everything."

After I dug a hole in the sand and buried our belongings with the relics, I placed a sandstone rock that was in the shape of a heart on top of it, so it'd be easy to find. I looked at Michael and nodded. He returned my nod with a nervous looking smile.

We had no need for the silver mine. It may as well have not even been there. Instead, all three of us walked with conviction up the track to reach the Takers' garrison main gate. My heart was pumping, and I swore it was in my mouth, but I kept going. We all kept going in an arrowhead formation; me leading, Michael to my right, Eli to my left. We walked up the hill and stopped in front of a huge steel gate which had coils of rusty razor wire running the length of the top, and continued along the garrison's old bluestone walls, disappearing away into the distance.

I walked up to the gate, and I was almost overwhelmed with the stench of death that emerged from the garrison. With one hand, I covered my nose and mouth. With the other, I smacked the gate with the heel of my hand, which resulted in a deep clang and an echo, and I knew that someone in there would've heard it. The gate squealed noisily open by roughly four hands. The surprised stare of a musclebound freak of a Taker gazed straight at me. "What the fuck do you blokes want. Fuck off, before I put a bullet through you."

"I'm Gabriel," I said. "This is Michael and Raphael."

"So what? I said fuck off before I put a bullet through your heads. You've got three seconds. ONE."

I sucked back a huge gulp of air. "It's in your best interest to release the two men who you're holding. Henry Bass and William Fletcher."

"TWO. And don't make me fucking laugh. Fuck off. Last chance."

"Release them right now. I demand it. *Your* last chance."

"Right!"

The rusty steel gate slid fully open with an ear-piercing squeal.

"Do what I do," I said over my shoulder to Eli and Michael. "And whatever happens, don't move. Just hold still."

I got on my knees and put my hands on my head. Eli and Michael did the same.

"I hope you're right," Michael whispered.

They sprung from behind the rusty steel gate and came at us. The big guy who'd told us to fuck off came at me and landed a hard punch to the side of my head. I heard a loud crack. It wasn't what I was expecting. The big guy reeled back screaming in agony, holding and shaking his hand.

"Mutha-Fukka!" he yelled at the same time as he examined his broken hand and busted fingers.

In an instant, another massive Taker came for me. He wound up a huge baseball bat which I saw was modified with nails to do more damage. He lifted it high above my head and he brought it down with mammoth force. The baseball bat snapped and broke into a thousand splinters. The big Taker looked at the remnants of the bat he was holding in his hand and tossed it over his shoulder; then he retrieved his pistol from his holster. After cocking the weapon, he came at me and held the barrel point blank to my face.

"You can use that weapon," I said. "But what if that bullet doesn't come out? What if your gun explodes in your hand? But let's not discuss it. Go ahead and pull that trigger. It's the only way we'll find out."

Fear; I had none of it. But I saw it on his face, the big Taker thought about pulling the trigger. I had no idea if he'd kill me and it didn't matter. From my peripheral vision, I could see eagles circling on the wind. There were seven of them that I could make out. So, without any trepidation, I knew what was about to occur.

In the next moment, the two big Takers spun and left us where we were. They disappeared behind the gate and then slammed it closed.

I heard Eli mutter the words, 'mother of penguins,' under his breath.

"What now?" Michael asked.

I looked up and caught sight of the seven eagles which were circling, speeding up into tighter circles, as though they were making themselves ready. "Well for one, let's all get up off our knees," I answered Michael. "No reason we should ever do that again. So now, we'll wait, and we'll see what happens next."

* * *

We waited for long enough to think we were forgotten, as the seven eagles above us flew tighter and tighter circles. During the time we were there, it was easy to hear screams of pain and suffering coming from somewhere on the other side of the gate. It was incredibly difficult to stand there and do nothing to help them. As soon as I felt the anger rise, I remembered Gabriel's words and I looked up again. Six eagles now flew in a circle where the albino hovered in the center. If someone told me the white eagle was looking directly at me, I would've believed it. And as soon as I saw it hovering, the anger I once felt was gone.

The gate squealed opened by four hands, and they'd pushed someone through the aperture. William Fletcher fell on the ground as though he was only semiconscious. But it wasn't William Fletcher. It was a man who'd had pieces taken from him with unspeakable ruthlessness.

I read the words in Michael's journal about that room of appalling horrors. After I saw with my own eyes what these people did to fellow humans, the true revulsion touched me in a way that cut deep into my soul. It'd be easy to give up like the scrounger who took a shard of crackle to his own throat. It'd be easy to turn away, find a patch of ground, raise some crops, survive and not think about anything anymore. But this? *This* must stop, and *we* must make it happen. I looked up again, and all the eagles had stopped circling. They were all hovering, line abreast as though they waited for me to command them.

I took a breath and instructed my legs to walk towards William Fletcher who seemed lifeless on the ground. As I walked, the gate squealed open again and, in my mind, I thought Captain Bass was next to step through. I held my breath and waited, knowing well he'd be as injured, if not more, than William Fletcher. But instead of Captain Bass, a young woman with bright red hair and freckled complexion was thrust outward, and the gate behind her squealed closed.

The three of us rushed urgently to the gate. I looked down upon William Fletcher's face. His eyes were taken out. And judging by the lack of sounds and the amount of blood coming out of him, they'd also taken his tongue. The stumps of both arms were wrapped in blood-soaked rags, and they didn't even bother with his missing foot.

While Eli was busy with William Fletcher and making him as comfortable as he could, I caught sight of Michael's expression. He looked as though he was ready to blow up. As soon as he turned away, I knew he was on a mission to destroy whatever he could destroy. But I grabbed him in time. I pointed skyward. "Their day is here, Michael." It seemed to settle him down. It seemed to take away his anger and pain.

After a moment, the woman with red hair introduced herself as Abigail. She said the Takers had no use for her anymore and seeing as William Fletcher wasn't able to talk, it was her job to let us know the whereabouts of Henry Bass.

"He's at Newman," she told us. "They said his body was too old and his meat would be tough. They've put him on a caravan and sent him east."

Just as I realized it, Michael confirmed it with his next words. He went on to explain that Newman was the place they'd kept him on a chain before he made his escape. But I needed no reminding. I also realized that Michael knew where Newman was and how long it would take to get there. I looked back down to William Fletcher. It was impossible for someone so injured to travel such distances. He'd never make the journey. I thought about it in my mind. I knew Eli was thinking the same, and I was sure Michael was with us. There was no need for words. I could see it in their eyes.

We retrieved our belongings from where we'd buried them, and I used our last round of ammunition to take William Fletcher's pain away.

After we'd buried William Fletcher in the same place we'd once buried our things, we shouldered our belongings, and I looked up for the last time. The seven eagles still hovered line abreast, and I realized they were waiting until the four of us were finished in the area. Michael approached me and said, "It's important that you don't look back, Rick."

"What'll happen if I do?"

"Just don't, is all. Trust me."

As we began our long walk toward the east, the sounds of complete chaos and destruction erupted behind me and was hard to ignore. It seemed even harder not to look over my shoulder. I nearly did. But Michael stopped me. We walked away from the sounds of explosions, and bursts of fire. The screams of terror and anguish. It was a sound I'll always remember.

Suddenly I thought about Abigail. It felt like slow motion as I spun and desperately shaded my eyes. "Abigail! No!" It was too late. Abigail gave in to the temptation and turned around. I caught sight of her facial expression as she became frozen in time. In an instant, she was no longer living. I reached out and touched her with the tip of my finger. Abigail had become a statue made of something harder than ash and something softer than rock. I took a breath and put my head down. I faced east and walked on.

Chapter Twenty-Six

Nothing Is How It Seems

I CAUGHT MYSELF THINKING THAT if Michael had made it the first time across Fool's Desert, it must've been more ass than class. But Michael surprised me by his knowledge of the area and by the demonstration of his survival skills. The desert bloodwood gave us food, but by also using the sap, we were able to heal the sores and blisters that were always a side effect of constant walking. We used the sap also as a repellant from marauding Rad Roos. The Rad Roos hated bloodwood trees and stayed away from them. By using the sap, we sent out a message to all Rad Roos in the desert that we were nothing more than walking bloodwood trees.

Michael also knew where there was water in the far east of Fool's Desert. In the middle of grey dusty nothing for miles everywhere, Michael took us directly to an oasis of water which gave us life and energy when we needed it the most. As I fell into the earthy smelling cool water, I smacked my face a few times to make sure I was fully conscious and not dreaming.

While we were at the water hole, we began to discuss our options for when we arrived at Newman. My memory of Michael's journal told me it was a place filled with danger. The Newman people appeared to only look after their own. I saw them in my mind as a tribe, and everyone on the outside of their compound was considered a threat. Maybe they were even worse than the Takers. As I thought it over, it appeared The Fall had reduced any surviving human inhabitants down to the rules of tribal warfare. But Michael assured us that if we played the part of scroungers selling wares, we'd not find ourselves dropped on a chain or offered up as food to the Takers.

"What do we sell?" I asked Michael. "We've got nothing but these Rad Roo skins."

"That's why I insisted on skinning them," Michael said. "They're worth good crackle out here, and they're always in demand. The demand is high only because people get killed if they specifically go out hunting Rad Roos."

"And you think this will get us inside the compound?"

"It won't work. Scroungers sell other things. They'll see right through us," Eli put in.

Michael put up his hand. "It'll work out. Let me do the talking."

I thought about it for a while, but it still didn't sit well with me. Then I realized Michael's motivation. "You're going for unfinished business, aren't you? After all these years, you think Murk is still there?"

"He could be."

"Could be? You risk jeopardizing our mission because you want payback?"

"He's got my gun, and I want it back."

"That was forty years ago, Michael. Things have changed. Forget about the unfinished business. We're there for Captain Bass. We negotiate for his release. Maybe we can use the Rad Roo skins as payment seeing they're in demand. We get Captain Bass out. We continue north to make contact with the Ambers. End of discussion."

After I'd said it, I saw it in Michael's body language that he was never going to leave it at that. But there was something else that played on my mind. After we leave Newman, then what? Do we all trek north into the Irradiated Badlands? Do we all die from radiation sickness?

"There's no need to leave Newman," Michael said at the same time I was thinking about it. "The Ambers deliver diesel to Newman, remember?"

We stayed at the water hole for longer than we planned. It wasn't a good idea. It gave us a false sense of security. It also meant we'd have to stride the final stretch in daylight. But Michael made waterskins out of Rad Roo hide and sinew. Finally, we were able to carry water on our long walk.

* * *

By the time we were within reach of Newman, our water was long gone. Along the way, we tried to save as much water as we could, but it was hopeless. The waterskins Michael made leaked worse than *Steinbeck's* lifeboats, and everything was lost. With not having water for what seemed days, nothing could've described us more accurately than walking skeletons arriving on death's door.

From out of the flatlands, in the middle of the day, the mirage of Newman's compound walls came into view. I struggled to pick up my feet and place them. My shoulders drooped, and my arms failed to swing. Eli was somewhere behind me. I heard his footfalls slide then drop into the desert dust. I watched Michael in front of me. I kept willing him forward, hoping he wouldn't fall. If he went down, I wasn't sure there was a way I could help him.

Slowly, and painfully, we trudged on.

I heard Eli as he hit the dirt hard. I spun, and I saw him spread-eagled with an arm raised.

I got myself back there and kneeled at his side. "Eli. Are you okay?"

After I'd said it, it seemed like a dumb thing to ask. But Eli responded with one word only. The same word I had in my mind for the past twenty-thousand strides. "Th-Thirsty."

"Michael," I yelled. "Michael, stop."

It was as though Michael didn't hear me or he didn't have the energy to fight his forward momentum. He kept up his steps going forward.

"Michael!"

As soon as I said it, I saw him stop. I thought he might turn around. He didn't. His body slowly fell forward, and he face-planted the earth.

"SHIT!"

Somehow, I got up off the ground. I didn't want to leave Michael and Eli. I had no choice. Before heading for Newman, I covered Eli and Michael with a Rad Roo skins, hoping that would make a difference. Hoping it would help keep the sun from burning them.

The mirage blurred in the distance. I squinted my eyes then relaxed them. I squinted them again and tried to breathe. Every breath I sucked back felt as though it weighed a ton. I willed every step forward and down, forward and down. I pushed my hips in front of my legs hoping like crazy that gravity would take over and move everything else. Gravity. The very second, I thought of it . . .

* * *

I felt hands patting my face. I heard a voice. A female voice. A muted voice. I tried to open my eyes. My eyelids ignored my efforts. I felt cooling water on my body. I felt cooling water all over me. I knew, somewhere in my core; I was dead.

The female voice said it again. The same words again. But it was like hearing her from a distance. She was speaking to me from the other side of the desert. But I knew her voice was sweet and lovely. I couldn't understand her words, but it was like hearing a song. I felt myself floating toward her. Her sweet and lovely voice. Chloe. Chloe's voice.

"Open your eyes," Chloe said. "Open your eyes, Ricky."

I tried to open them. But I wanted the opposite. I wanted to sleep; I was so tired. Sleep. How wonderful and beautiful is sleep? Dream on . . . Dream on . . .

"Open your eyes Ricky!"

I felt hands on my face — a sharp slap.

I opened my eyes.

The light was immense as it dazzled my senses. I saw a blurred outline of someone standing there. I saw a blurred shape and her hair, so dark. I closed my eyes.

"Richard. Wake up Richard . . . You must wake up."

More water over me. So lovely, the water.

I saw her again, that woman with long black hair and eyes so black they were the center of galaxies.

Then, I felt a sharp thud to the side of my face.

I opened my eyes wide, and I shook my head. I looked up to the woman standing there. She smiled down at me. I saw her take in a huge breath of air. A huge sigh. "Well you sure know how to worry someone, don't you? Welcome back."

"W-Where am I? What happened?"

The woman said nothing. She stepped to my side and lifted my head off the pillow to allow me to drink. I took a sip then wanted more. I wanted so much more.

"Hey. Easy there." The woman took the cup away. My body kept drinking from it. "I'm here to look after you. I'm Cherith. And you need your rest."

As soon as she told me her name, I knew where I was, and I realized how bad I was in it. I'd gone from something terrible, headlong into something truly screwed up. I tried to get up. Cherith pushed me back down. "Rest. You need to rest."

"Eli . . . Michael . . . Where are they?"

She said nothing.

I asked it again. "Eli and Michael. They were with me. Where are they?"

She again avoided my question but asked for my name.

"I'm Richard. Richard Gabriel."

Cherith stepped to my side and quickly changed my IV drip, all the while smiling her beaming white pins. She touched the top of my hand as she walked away.

"My things. My bag with my belongings," I said after her.

Cherith stopped and faced me. "We've locked your items away for safe keeping. When you're better, you may have them back." She smiled briefly before adding, "Seth will see you in a while. But rest for now."

After she'd gone, I instantly checked the drawer to my side. There was nothing in there. Something at the back of my mind told me they weren't going to give my precious items back to me in a hurry. I relaxed as much as I could. I relaxed, but at the same time, I wondered about Eli and Michael. Then blackness came.

* * *

Seth closed the door quietly behind him and eyed me intensely as he walked with light footsteps toward me. By the time he pulled out a chair and sat by my side, I knew it in my heart that Eli and

Michael had died. I expected Seth to speak, but I also knew what he was thinking. It wasn't about the death of my friends. He sat there eyeing me as though he was wondering if I was strong enough to pull my own weight on a chain.

Seth leaned forward in his chair before he said anything. He put his hands together and rubbed them as though he was cold. "We did everything we could, I'm sorry. You friends were both deceased when we found them out there. But one of your friends wasn't a stranger. I met him a long time ago. Michael."

Things went through my mind — many things. I should've felt nothing but sadness. I didn't have the time. I needed my belongings back, and I needed to get the heck out of the place.

"Thank you, Seth. And thank you for everything. Now, If I could please have my things back, I'll get going, and I'll burden you no longer."

"Burden? Not at all. Please stay. Stay as long as you like. When you're strong enough and feel up to it, you may like to help out in the fields. In return, we'll give you lodging and meals. Meet our people. Join our community. Perhaps you might like to stay forever. Our home is your home."

"Thanks. But no thanks. I'll have my things back if you don't mind."

"What's the hurry?"

"What's the hurry? How about being locked on a chain and made to work like a slave. How about having my tongue cut out? That's two reasons. There's more."

Seth sat back and laughed. Sick bastard. Then he said something that shook every atom in my body.

"Yes, we've read Michael's journal. We've all read it. That man had an imagination that entertained everyone here. We had no books. But Michael gave to this community in ways nobody else could. He was an entertainer — a fiction writer. In his journal, he even gave the people of Newman their own unique accent. I asked him where he came up with the idea. Michael said he'd read a bunch of books about the Maoris in New Zealand and their history before The Fall. He got the idea from those books. Michael gave everyone Maori tattoos in his journal. Do you see any on me? Hmm?"

I studied Seth for a moment and thought about everything he'd said. "I need a moment."

"Sure. I'll leave you be. I can show you more of Michael's work if you like. He's written many books which are works of fiction based on fact. We keep them for entertainment. We've kept them for over forty years."

What was I supposed to do with this information? Was I supposed to believe it?

"What about Murk?" I asked.

Seth smiled and leaned forward in his chair. Over his shoulder, he called out Murk's name. In the next moment, the door opened, and a thinly built middle-aged guy wearing clinical whites stepped through.

"This is Murk," Seth said. "Murk, this is our new guest, Richard Gabriel."

Murk stepped over to me and offered his hand. I took it and shook. "You don't fit the description I've read about."

Murk smiled and said, "Pain in the arse, that fella. Sad that he's dead though."

"Michael was good at stretching the details and distorting the truth," Seth went on. "I asked Michael once. I said, Michael, why is it that you can never write how things really are? Do you know what he replied? He said, because the world is a stage. So, I'm glad we've got that off our chests. It's good that you're getting better, Richard. I'll be showing you around the compound soon enough."

Seth got up from his chair and turned to leave.

"Can I see them?" I asked. "Eli and Michael. Can I see where you've buried them?"

"Of course. Rest for now."

But there was something else that bothered me. Captain Henry Bass.

Chapter Twenty-Seven

Orientation

FROM THE WINDOW, AS I LOOKED around the place, it was exactly as Michael described in his journal. But there were no gangs of slaves. There were no chain masters. There were no armed guards. There were no screams of terror. Everything Michael had led me to believe about this place couldn't have been further from reality. My eyes scanned the area, and I saw teams of workers in fields of green with their bare backs in the sun, glistening with sweat. It made every bit of difference to see them working because they wanted to work. Their body language showed it. They loved what they did. They enjoyed it. And there were no shackles or restraints of any kind.

After I climbed into my clothes and walked the small passageway to the outside, I stopped to take in the sweet air. It was gorgeous, smelling of fresh garden aromas that I'd never experienced before. The compound was huge and much bigger than the picture I had in my mind. To my left, I saw the fields of corn Michael had written about, stretching to the far end of the compound. Beyond that, I could see the shapes of buildings and barns and a mill that was driven by the winds; the same kind I'd learned in books describing Holland. In front of me was a collection of gardens consisting of various varieties of vegetables. At the far end of the gardens, I heard the cackle of chickens and geese. Another large building behind the shack where they'd kept chickens I assumed was for livestock.

On my right, I saw a collection of small buildings stretching to the far end of the compound, and people walked and talked with each other in what seemed a relaxed atmosphere. Some sat on chairs and enjoying the sun. Others talked over fences while holding mugs and enjoying whatever they were drinking. I heard the sounds of small engines and I saw something that took my breath away. People were using small engine powered implements to cut grass and shape it down. I was mesmerized by everything I'd seen. But a strange white square structure stuck out of the ground near the windmill. I wondered what that might be used for. I remembered Seth had asked me if I'd like to stay forever. I thought it was a good possibility that it might be the case.

"Good morning, Richard. Feeling better?" Cherith said from behind me. "Would you like some coffee?"

"Coffee?" The last time I'd had coffee was on the *Victory*. So many things had happened over the journey. I'd traveled so far and done so many things. Many people had died. My friends. My family. Everyone I knew. Now I was getting coffee? "Yeah. Coffee. I think I'd like that a lot."

On the verandah, I sat down in a long wicker lounge which smelled a little old and musty, but for some reason, it felt like home. My eyes filled with tears as I looked around. I became overwhelmed with the happiness I saw everywhere. I looked from one corner of the compound to the next. Was I dreaming? Was this for real?

Cherith met me on the verandah with two mugs. "It's got milk in it. I thought you looked like a white coffee kind of guy," she said smiling, as she handed me a mug.

"Are you making fun of me because I'm albino?"

Cherith giggled and looked away.

"I've never had milk. I've had goats' cheese but not milk." I started to realize how limited my horizons actually were. I took a sip of my coffee, and I enjoyed the taste. It was strange. It didn't have the same kick as the coffee I had on *Victory*, but it was pleasant.

"So, Seth will be showing you around. You'll meet all our clan. You'll even meet an old sea captain who recently joined us. He takes the children after school and tells them about his seagoing adventures."

As soon as Cherith said it, I knew who she was talking about and what a relief he wasn't dead. "Henry Bass?"

Cherith eyed me curiously. "Oh. You must be the Richard he talks about."

"I hope he tells you all good things about me. But changing the subject, what is that big white square thing sticking out of the ground over there?"

"That's is our outdoor cinema. Tonight, we're watching *Big Country* with Gregory Peck and Jean Simmons. It's one of my favorite movies. But I can't go, unfortunately."

"Why can't you go? You're free to do whatever you want. Just go and see it."

"Well, it's because I don't have a date," Cherith said then blushed a little.

I was almost going to tell Cherith how happily married I was, and that dating wasn't an option. But as soon as I thought it, I realized for the first time that I'd never see Chloe again. I was no longer married. Suddenly, it was as though I now had the time to properly mourn the loss of my wife. But having found myself in such a wonderful place, I saw myself settling in this sanctuary called Newman. But something else appeared in the back of my mind. *The Angel of Bunjil* and the Sacred Bone. My mission. I must not let good things cloud my judgment. I had a job to do first. Then I could come back and join the Newman dwellers.

"Cherith."

"Yes?"

"I'd love to go and see a movie with you."

But before Cherith had the chance to add anything else, a familiar voice shouted my name from a distance away. "Richard! Could it be you, dear boy?"

I couldn't believe my ears. "Captain Bass!"

I launched myself from the verandah and ran to Captain Bass who limped and walked aided by a walking cane toward me. When I got there, he took my hand and shook it vigorously. "Oh, I'm so glad to see you, dear boy; I'm so glad indeed."

But after our greeting had concluded I caught Captain Bass eyeing over my shoulder as though he was expecting to see the others. How could I tell him there were none? His facial expression dropped from being happy to being concerned. "All of them?" he asked slowly.

I nodded. I had no words.

"The entire crew? All of my men?"

I nodded again.

"Jason . . . Eli and Michael?"

Tears backed up in my eyes. I could no longer hold them.

"Good heavens! I . . . I . . . am so sorry, dear Richard."

"As am I, Captain Bass. But the Takers encampment has been destroyed. They're no longer there. We've given William Fletcher a proper burial. They'd done too much damage to him."

Captain Bass lowered himself to the ground and sat. It was as though his legs just gave way from under him. I sat on the ground with him and waited for him to return from his thoughts. When he did return, it wasn't anything I expected.

"All of the Takers from the central garrison are gone, did you say?"

"There's nothing left of their encampment. They won't bother the Newman dwellers anymore. The people here can live freely without fear."

"But my dear boy, now that the Takers are gone, it's much worse than you realize. The people here had a ceasefire agreement. Now that the garrison has been destroyed, the agreement is no longer. Newman is now open slather for the taking. There's a war coming, Richard. Once other Takers' outposts learn about the destruction of the central garrison, they'll come in the numbers. We must now prepare the people. At once, before it's too late!"

* * *

I didn't mind watching an old black and white movie. And the sounds of crickets and frogs in the background didn't seem to take away from the atmosphere. There were roughly sixty people at the outdoor cinema seated on blankets and in foldaway chairs. We'd all brought little containers with garlic and lime with cloves to keep mosquitos away. I had no idea what mosquitos were until Cherith told me. But after I felt their sting and heard their drone, I believed every word Cherith had said.

I would've enjoyed the movie more than I did. I found my mind on the things Captain Bass was concerned about. I wondered how much time it would take for the word to get around each Takers' outpost. Then I tried to calculate the time it would take for them to react. It didn't matter how many times I'd tossed it around in my head; there were so many variables to consider; I ended up with completely different answers.

As Cherith and I sat on a blanket and the scent of everyone's homemade mosquito repellant was thick in the air, my thoughts returned to another place and another time which now seemed so far away. I wondered what Chloe had gone through. I wondered what my mother had gone though. Their final waking moments was sure to have been catastrophic for them; not just horrific. Here I was enjoying a movie, at the same time knowing what they had to endure. And I wasn't there to do anything about it. Suddenly I felt violently ill. I made my quick excuses and I returned to my quarters before my physical sickness became something ugly which I had no control over.

* * *

My orientation of the compound with Seth ended at my small but comfortable and functional farmhand quarters. Seth urged me to stay on for a second time as more hands were needed for the coming corn harvest. How could I deny him? Considering the welcome I've had so far, how could I not agree? But Seth didn't know about the destroyed Takers' central garrison. I wondered what his reaction might be after Captain Bass and I explain what had happened, and worse, what's likely to happen in the coming short future. It was agreed between Captain Bass and myself, that nothing should be said until such time as we both meet with Seth in his office to discuss what needs to be done next. As Seth smiled and walked away, leaving me at my door, I felt an urge to spill everything. It took everything bit of will to hold it back.

Chapter Twenty-Eight

Take That

OVER THE LOUDSPEAKER, EVERYONE was woken by a song called *'Bright Side of the Road,'* I didn't know who it was by, and nobody seemed to know for sure. At first, it was a nice way to get out of bed. By day five, I wished someone would play something else. By day ten, the song no longer did anything for me. But even though, it was effective as an alarm clock for everyone who needed to get ready for work.

We continued with strengthening the fortifications around the Newman compound and all the while, I hoped with all my heart that the Takers wouldn't come while we were vulnerable.

Cherith met me at the south wall. As I worked with adding new material to the fortification, the wall was reaching new heights.

"Hey, come down from there," Cherith shouted as she looked up and cupped a hand over her brow.

After I'd got myself down from the ladder, Cherith handed me a tall glass of cool water, which I took and guzzled down. I didn't notice how incredibly thirsty I was until I started to drink. Cherith must've read my mind. I sat down in the shade and wiped the buildup of sweat and dirt from my forehead. Cherith sat beside me. But as she lowered herself down, I noticed from her body language that something was on her mind and was upsetting her.

"What is it?" I asked her as I playfully put my arm around her and tried to cheer her up.

Cherith wasn't one to mess around with her words. She came out and said exactly what was on her mind without any delay. "How do you think we'll go?"

I thought about it for a while. I was almost going to fluff things up, so it'd be easier to digest. But if I knew Cherith, she'd not settle for anything fluffed up. I told her, word for word, how I thought things would go. "We don't stand a chance, Cherith. We'll be overrun before the battle even gets started. And that's why we're putting so much time into getting the last resort bunker ready. I think shelter in the bunker is the only chance left for saving the families and the children."

"So, we climb down into a hole. We're good for how long? A week?"

"Two weeks."

"Okay. Two weeks, and then what? Will the Takers be gone by then?"

"That's the plan. When they're gone . . ."

"What, exactly." Cherith got up, stood back and folded her arms. "What should we do, Ricky? What? And what about you?"

I couldn't answer her although I wished I could. I wished hard I could see into the future and tell her no harm would come to her and the kids. I wished I could tell her I'd be okay and so would everyone else. But I knew by the end of the coming war, many of us would die, myself included. What other choice was there? We had to prepare the best way we knew how. I drew back to the words from someone who'd told me a long time ago; hope for the best but expect the worst.

* * *

Using huge horse-drawn carts that were made from old flatbed trucks with the cabins cut off, we collected ancient Post-Fall debris from Old Newman town center and used anything else we could find to make our compound stronger than it ever was. New to our compound were strategically positioned watchtowers which doubled as sniper nests if they were needed. With the new fortifications almost complete, I guesstimated that in two days of hard work, Newman's security would rival any Takers' outpost. The problem was, however, the lack of any significant firepower.

The weapons we had available ranged from a small number of antique bolt action rifles and only one of them was fitted with a scope — handguns and revolvers which were useless only because we had a limited reserve of ammunition. Everything else we had at our disposal were string weapons; bows, crossbows, and slingshots. But we had an ample supply of hand to hand fighting weapons. We had shields, knives, and swords made by our blacksmith from collected scraps of high carbon steel. We had bludgeons encrusted with razor-sharp shards of crackle. We even had garrotes made from the wire of an abandoned broken up piano we'd come across in Old Newman. As I went over it in my mind, if the Takers breach the wall, we'd give them a good showdown but, in the end, it was inevitable we'd be defeated. Every one of us would die.

In the center of the compound, the last resort bunker was complete. We supplied the bunker with enough water and food for the families to last for two weeks, which was exactly as I calculated. The entrance to the bunker was cleverly disguised under a row of outhouses, and it would take someone with intelligence to work out where to locate the entrance and how to breach it. I judged by what I already knew about Takers; the families would be safe until their supplies ran out.

On my list of things to get done were to help build an array of trebuchets. We'd need to position them at locations around the compound, in areas where we thought the Takers would begin their assault. Three huge trebuchets that were made out of reclaimed scrap stood ominously; thirty hands high, ready to do the damage. We needed more. The more, the better. Somewhere in the back of my mind, I had the image of 39-caliber howitzer shells raining down on us, and I tried not to think about it. The truth was, we were so unevenly matched, it would take nothing short of a miracle to stand up to the Takers and fight them until they were all dead.

I stood atop the central watchtower with my binoculars as guys outside the compound south wall placed markers where I needed them to go. I commanded the trebuchet operator on the ground in front of me, "Loose when ready."

The trebuchet swung its massive arm. A bag of flour was sent skyward, and I watched through my binoculars where it hit the ground. "Marker," I flag signaled the guys out there. Immediately, two guys ran and placed debris and rocks marking the location of the impact.

* * *

By the end of the day, the area outside the south wall of the compound had been target-marked, and the three trebuchets we had were set up with the correct trajectories. Just as I was finishing up and ready to climb down from the watchtower, I looked out to the north. I saw a group of eagles hugging the terrain, flying low and coming toward me.

"No. We're not ready," I said loudly to myself.

The white eagle led the formation as they approached, but there were more than the seven I'd seen before. Two had joined the seven to become nine. A black eagle, as black as a crow, and I knew, an American Bald Eagle, much larger than the rest, flew with them bringing up the rear. I cast my memory back to the dream that still lived vividly in my mind. Could it be these newcomers to the seven were the Angels of Mercy? They cried out with ear piercing eagle cries, passing over the top of me in arrowhead formation. As the eagles disappeared into the southern sky, my heart plummeted, and I knew the Takers were about to launch their attack. From the top of the central watchtower, I urgently grabbed a leather cord with my shaking hands and rang the bell. "Get the children!" I screamed. "Get the families and the children to the bunker. Now!"

By the time I reached the ground, men and women scurried madly with crying children in their arms as they raced for shelter. "Get the children to safety!" I kept screaming. Cherith ran up behind me. I spun and eyed her urgently. "What're you doing! Get to the bunker!"

"I wanted to give you something," Cherith said, at the same time wiping her tears away.

Cherith handed me something heavy wrapped in what I thought was a red bandana. After I unwrapped it, I held the pistol in my hand. A pistol with an inscription. *'Donald P Bosco.'*

Out of all the panic and madness around me, I was somehow surprised. "This is Michael's gun."

Cherith nodded. "It's fully loaded. I've been saving bullets as I've found them. I always knew Michael's gun was for a purpose. It's today, Rick. Make every bullet count." She pulled me into her arms and kissed me. Then I watched her as she spun and raced for the bunker.

Now, I turned and fixed my mind on what needed doing.

After I checked for rounds and cocked the weapon, I slipped the pistol behind the small of my back. I raced to my quarters and busted through the door. I picked up my rifle with the twenty-times scope and shouldered it. With time running out, I raced for the south watchtower.

Getting to the watchtower, three trebuchets were pushed to the boundary walls and were loaded with explosive bags of nails and anything else we could find that might do serious harm. I climbed the ladder and raised my binoculars. I waited. Archers made their way up ladders and took up position along the rim of the southern wall. They loaded their bows with explosive tipped arrows. The compound behind me grew silent as those who were about to fight held their position.

We all held still and silent.

Through my binoculars, I watched for signs of movement to the south.

Then.

They came.

The first line of Takers stopped just outside of Old Newman town center. I saw through the lenses of my binoculars they were roughly a thousand strong. Where are the eagles? I couldn't see them. But the Takers had all halted their advance. It wasn't long before I found out why.

A long series of low rolling booms rang out from somewhere in the far southern distance. As soon as I heard them, all the horrors I had in my head became a reality.

Howitzers!

"STAND-TO! STAND-TO!" I screamed. "TAKE COVER! INCOMING! TAKE COVER!"

I got myself to the ground as quickly as I could. Unshouldering my rifle, I bolted for the south wall. Howitzer shells screamed and drilled through the sky. An enormous explosion in front of me, knocked me off my feet as the south wall took a direct hit. Men were shredded, momentarily turning the sky a cloud of blood red. As bodies and parts of bodies landed around me, some were still alive and screamed out in pain. I ran to one man who was minus both his legs. I pushed my hands up to his stumps to stop the bleeding. "MEDIC! M-E-D-I-C!" I screamed at the same time another shell landed in the middle of the compound and exploded, sending the central watchtower toppling to the ground.

"M-E-D-I-C!" I screamed through the smoke and the blood.

Doc Drouin ran to my side. "I've got this. Go!"

Another shell drilled through the sky and exploded on impact with incredible force. I knew this time it was the east wall. Through the smoke a distance away, I saw the outline of Captain Bass, and I knew he had his detachment on the trebuchets ready to go.

Men were screaming from the west. I saw Takers already breaching the wall. Gunfire broke out. I raced to get there. As I ran, I retrieved my pistol. I raised my weapon and caught sight of Takers pulling themselves over the wall and down. I aimed and fired. Takers' heads snapped backward as their dead bodies fell to the ground. I continued to fire. More Takers fell.

From out of nowhere, nine eagles landed in front of me then instantly they transformed into human forms. One of the archangels faced me. "Get to the west watchtower. Do not look upon the face of the white archangel, Gabriel." Then she drew her sword and was gone. An angel with the tattoo of a white eagle and sword on the back of his head, spun and burned his eyes into me. He gave me a wink, reached and drew his recurved kukri, then disappeared into the smoke, thrusting his blade through invading Takers. I stood awestruck as the angels dispersed into the fray, slaying as they went. Running for the watchtower, I popped the heads of Takers who were in my way.

I climbed the west watchtower. And at the top, I saw what seemed several thousand Takers who were all sprinting across the desert, heading our way. Raising my rifle, I shot down Takers as they ran, sniping in quick secession until my ammo ran out. Dropping the rifle, I grabbed my sidearm and fired in rapid fire. Knowing my ammo was finite, I killed as many Takers as I could.

A tremor shook the platform at my feet. A deep rumble rose up through the watchtower, and into my body. Out in the south, dust rose up high into the air. As I turned to face the west, I raised my binoculars. I couldn't believe what I was seeing. A stampede of Rad Roos bore down on the thousands-strong Takers.

Just as I saw the Rad Roos from the west, from the north, the thunder of mechanical beasts cut through the noise of battle. The outlines of trucks raced across the desert pan. Trucks and tankers, and I knew . . . I knew they could be none other than the Ambers who we'd spent so many days and months in the hope of tracking down. The Lost Ones had arrived.

I faced west again to the sounds of men being ripped to pieces. Rad Roos, thousands of them, encircled Takers and closed in. One by one, Takers were ripped apart by the Rad Roos' nine-inch claws. The desert became a sea of blood with Takers' body parts abstractly strewn as far as I was able to see. But in their numbers, the Takers kept coming.

Trucks and tankers rushed vociferously to a stop. Ambers sprang from doors, shouldering weapons I'd only ever heard about. Then they lit the place up. The Ambers ripped into the Takers, letting them have it with their M134 miniguns. The multi-barreled guns spun at high speed and glowed red hot, spitting death and destruction wherever the Ambers pointed them. The Ambers walked slowly in lines abreast with their miniguns setting the place ablaze, cutting down Takers as they advanced. I watched on, and I saw Takers literally cut in half and then immediately shredded with the many hundreds of thousands of high-speed projectiles coming from the M134s

Rad Roos from the south and the west and the east. Ambers from the north. The Takers who were left alive and who were able to run dropped their weapons, turned, and bolted. The people of Newman roared their happiness. By the end, what was left over was a ghastly battlefield of the dead and the dying, in a sea of gore stretching to the horizon in each direction.

Chapter Twenty-Nine

Aftermath

I DIDN'T KNOW WHAT I'D DO IF I HAD to listen to that song again. I made sure I was up early and far enough away from the loudspeakers. As the sun broke through the horizon to the east, I stood beside the gaping hole that was left in the compound wall. The break of day brought with it the true horror of war.

Ravens. Millions of them. They'd descended on the battlefield, and it was as though they were there to take the souls of the dead to some dark place. The battlefield was alive with the ravens' squawking and screeching, as they got busy with their pecking and prodding. For as far as it was possible to see, the ground before me seemed to be alive with shimmering waves of black upon red.

I hadn't come to the east of the compound to gloat about our victory over the Takers. A victory, yes. But somehow, I knew there'd be more. Our triumph was over a single battle; and not a war. Somewhere in my heart, I felt there'd be the day when the righteous descends upon evil in one final conflict. When that day would come was anybody's guess. They shall have their day of reckoning. They shall be made to pay for their crimes.

On the east side of the compound, I kneeled in front of Eli's grave. In a way, I was glad Eli never had to deal with the horrors of last night. I was equally glad for Jason whose grave had been placed without a body next to Eli's. But, if only I could visit Chloe's place of rest one last time. Perhaps one day I might have the opportunity to travel back to Antarctica, even if it's only to visit Chloe and my mother for one last time.

I put my hand down on Jason's resting place. Even though his body wasn't there, I knew his spirit would be wherever I chose it to be. "This is goodbye, brother. I'll see you on the other side, huh?"

I got up and turned away. With a sigh, in my mind at least, I began to continue the long walk.

* * *

We spent the next five full days collecting bodies and body parts, piling them into heaps and setting them on fire. I would've liked to have seen the entire battlefield cleaned, but with so many of the dead to deal with, it was virtually impossible. Apart from the immediate area of the compound, the Ravens were left with the task of cleaning what we were unable to handle. But, if we'd never had help from the Ambers, the task of cleaning up would've taken much longer than it did. I was thankful to them. We all were. It meant the people of Newman could get back to their lives and not have to worry about disease.

At the end of each day, tired and exhausted, I retreated to my quarters knowing the next day would come, and it would play out in much the same way. By day six, however, life began to return to normal with the Newman dwellers. As for me, I had a job to finish.

I met Seth during the morning of the seventh day. After Seth handed over my calico bag containing *The Angel of Bunjil* and the Sacred Bone, there was only one thing left to do. And that was to hand the relics over to the Ambers before they left and returned north. My job would be over. I would've finished what I started. But, after that, what? I couldn't help but feel empty with that thought running around my head. I'd thought about staying in Newman only superficially. Now, I had to make up my mind one way or another.

In the early afternoon, I'd met a tall and slender looking Amber who shared the same bright red hair, fair skin, and freckles as the rest of them. He introduced himself as George De Niro and took my hand, shaking it with a grip so firm, he momentarily cut off the blood supply from the rest of my body. George was in charge of the Ambers' convoy and said he makes the trip once a year from Amberton in the north to Newman and then back; and has been doing it for the past forty years. After I handed over the relics, George opened the bag, and it was like he'd been reunited with a long-lost friend. He put a hand to his face and took a step back. "This is wonderful!" he said happily. And the smile on his face was priceless enough for me to leave everything right there. But my quest was never going to end at that moment.

"I'm grateful and happy to see the relics. I'll hand them to our high priests after we return."

After he said it, I knew I wasn't going to be happy until I saw the very end of the journey with my own eyes. "If you must give the relics to your high priests, then I will be the one to do it. I've come so far, and I've been through so much. I'd like to be the one to take the relics to them."

George took a few moments to think about what I'd said. "If you come with us, you'll die."

I nodded. "I'm aware of that."

"You'll die in pain."

I nodded again. "I know what pain is."

"Come with me," George said.

I followed George to the west wall. Before we reached the entrance tunnel, he told me to wait. George stepped away and left me there but returned a few moments later with something yellow and plastic in his hands. "Put this on. It won't save you, but it'll slow down the onset of radiation sickness. You'll have time to hand the relics to the high priests."

"I'll die after that?"

George nodded slowly. "You've got balls. I gotta hand it to you. We'll all hope for your quick death. But we must go right now."

Cherith. I needed to at least tell her that . . . "I'll be a moment. I just need to . . ."

"We have to go now," George said urgently. "If you want to live long enough, we must leave. Our vehicles are all highly radioactive. You've already taken a big count. So, put on that rad suit and let's go."

* * *

The Amber's convoy of three troop trucks, three flatbeds, and two diesel tankers left Newman in the afternoon of the seventh day. I rode shotgun with George in a huge tanker as it bounced heavily over the ruts and potholes that were abundant in the ancient postfall highways. As I rode with George, my mind returned to Cherith and how I was forcefully torn away. I regretted it. I wished I'd had the chance to say a proper goodbye. Cherith might spend the rest of her life wondering what had happened to me. But then, something else came to mind.

As I thought back to Michael's journal, I remembered the time he'd met Cherith and Seth for the first time after he and Timothy weren't far from the silver mine. That was forty years ago. Give or take, as Michael had said. But forty years ago, Seth and Cherith were adults. That would've made them at least seventy years of age the last time I saw them. But Cherith was never in her seventies. She looked like she was still in the prime of her youth. The same went for Seth. As I thought it over in my mind, it just didn't make any sense. Then something else. I hadn't seen anybody at Newman that I considered elderly.

"Stop the truck!" I yelled. "I need to go back."

George shot me a sideways glare. "There's not enough time."

"Stop! Stop the truck! Right now!"

George shoved the brake pedal down hard. The truck lurched to a stop amid the sounds of rushing air. "What is it?" George asked.

"We need to go back. It's urgent!"

After a big sigh, George grabbed the mic and announced over the radio that we were turning around, and the rest of the convoy must continue straight on. "We'll catch up with them, but this had better be a good reason to go back. I'm just saying."

After George pulled up outside of Newman, my heart fell to my feet. My breath was wrenched away. There was nobody at Newman. It was as though ghosts had lived there. There were no crops of corn. No vegetables. No chicken and geese. Not even cattle. The buildings in Newman were like nobody had lived there in centuries. Everything was derelict and half fallen over. Through my shock, I wasn't able to feel my dismay. So, what, in the heck, had gone on in Newman? Was everything I went through all in my head?

George put his hand on my shoulder. "Come on. We need to go."

* * *

I remained silent for the rest of the journey north. Partly because I still couldn't figure Newman out. And partly because I was wearing a rad suit, and nobody could hear me if I didn't shout as loud as I could. And I was sick of the shouting.

As we got further north, I noticed the changes in the landscape, and I knew it was the radiation which had caused such ugliness on the planet. We went from flat colorless nothing to flat colorless deadly nothing. I could feel it on my skin how much deadlier things were getting with every mile we drove. I wondered if I'd be dead by now if I wasn't wearing any protection. Either way, it no longer mattered. The only thing I wished to do now was to finish my quest. Any moment spent alive after that was a bonus. Just as I had that thought, I coughed hard inside my rad suit. My face shield became an ugliness of phlegm mixed with spots of blood. I lifted my hand to take my hood down so I could at least clean it.

"No!" George responded just in time. "Don't take it off. Just deal with it. It's going to be worse by the time we get there."

For the next several hours, I sat there looking at my own blood sputum. But hey. Death was coming. What did I care?

* * *

We finally reached Amberton before the sun was due to rise. As George drove the tanker through the empty streets which were filled with the same post-fall debris, I'd seen everywhere else, we passed a huge aged and pockmarked sign that said, *'Welcome to Darwin. Estab. 1874.'*

It was obvious now. In recent years, the Darwin I'd once learned about had now become Amberton.

The truck wound its way around streets that got tighter and tighter—streets which had been modified or cleaned up or changed to suit the needs of the Ambers. When George pulled the tanker to a stop, the headlights briefly illuminated the convoy we'd left behind. George switched the engine off. "We're home!" he said smiling. "Come on. The faster we get underground, the faster we'll get you away from the radiation, and then you can take that suit off."

Getting out of the truck, an old cottage caught my eye with a sign that seemed even older. *'Charlotte Station.'* I wondered if there was a correlation between where I was and the angel in Michael's journal. But by the time we were at a steel doorway behind the cottage, I left that thought behind.

Chapter Thirty

Arrival

PEERING DOWN INTO THE DARKENED stairwell, it beckoned as I stepped down. It was as though I was looking down into my own grave. Already, my breathing was heavy, and my throat felt like I'd swallowed a handful of sand. I did my best to ignore the sensation of fire in my extremities. I did my best to ignore all the symptoms. I had a job to get done. I *must* deliver the relics and see my journey at its end. I peered down into the darkened stairwell, and I stepped down.

George grabbed the lid of an electrical box to his left and flipped it up. After he'd flicked a few switches, the lights from below sprang to life and showed the stairwell going down even deeper. My tired and worn out boots clicked on the metal steps that went down for roughly a hundred hands and arrived at a couple of steel sliding doors.

George invited me to push the button with a simple hand gesture. "Go ahead," he said. "After this, you get to take off that rad suit."

After I'd pushed the button, the door slid open. At first, I thought it was an elevator like those I'd seen in movies. But after George stepped in front of me and entered the chamber, he showed me what to do. He put his arms out to his side. Immediately, he was awash with jets of water and air. After he was done and walked through to the other side, he gestured with a hand for me to enter the chamber and to do the same.

If anything, I was glad my rad suit was washed clean from the outside. But I was still looking through blood-snot after I'd been jet blasted. Nonetheless, the room on the other side of the decontamination chamber was an area to change into clean clothing. I took off that damn rad suit and tossed it aside. George passed me something fresh to put on. After changing into something that smelled fresh, I decided to leave my red bandana on my head, and I put my pistol back behind the small of my back. "I thought you guys were resistant to radiation," I said as I shouldered the bag containing the relics, and as George finished up putting on what he called his vault suit.

"We are. But our food won't grow if it's contaminated. Everything we need to survive is underground. The radiation can't get to it. It's imperative everything is clean, clean, clean. C'mon. Let's go."

It seemed a little odd to have animals underground. That was the height of cruelty. After I asked George about the Ambers' meat and protein supplies, things began to get a little weird.

"We're vegans," George said. "Our protein comes from the things we grow. We don't do animal meat of any kind. Unlike the Takers who'd eat their own given a chance."

As we walked the underground corridors that resembled a spider's web, my mind went back to Michael's journal. According to Michael, the reason the Ambers went to Newman was to drop off diesel and pick up meat. Now I'm finding out they're vegans? But nothing could've prepared me for what George said after I challenged him.

"The high priests sent us to Newman."

"Why?"

"To look for you, Richard Gabriel. The battle of Newman was prophesized by our high priests. And after the battle, the relics would find us. It was always said the relics would appear out of the hands of the white one. *You* are the white one. After all these years and decades, the prophecy of *The Angel of Bunjil* is about to come to fruition."

* * *

By the time we reached the main area of the underground commune, I was staggered by the size. I couldn't imagine how the Ambers had built such a massive structure underground. The span of the dome was enormous. The cathedral by itself reached as high as several hundred hands up. It was a place for all the Ambers to congregate and socialize. It was also the hub where all corridors connected. I stood high up on a landing and looked down to see the population of Amberton going about their business as though it was a day the same as any other. But one of the Ambers must've noticed me as I began my journey down the steps. Before I knew it, one by one, they began to stop what they were doing. One of them pointed. "The white one," she said loudly. Then everyone began to chant the words, "Bunjil, Bunjil, Bunjil."

Arriving at the bottom of the staircase, I began to move through them, and the crowd opened as I walked between them. It seemed an awkward time to begin a coughing fit, but I couldn't have helped it. This time as I coughed hard into my hand, I couldn't ignore the amount of blood. And I couldn't ignore what I was feeling. Someone had lit a fire underneath me. It was the first time I noticed the blood blisters all over my arms. I knew time was getting away.

In the center of the cathedral was a priestly structure. It was magnetic, pulling me toward it. I approached the center where two huge columns stood like obelisks reaching up roughly eighty hands. Standing beside the columns were five Ambers dressed in long gold garments which flowed out and dragged along the floor. The five turned to face me. I unshouldered the bag containing the relics, trying hard to stem another bout of coughing which I only just managed. Opening the bag, I gave over the contents; the crystal figurine and the human bone. My journey and my epic mission were over.

The high priests nodded before taking the relics and placing them down on a small altar. Immediately, bright blue light glowed between the huge obelisks, and a vibration pulsed deep into my body.

People behind me chanted. "Bunjil, Bunjil, Bunjil."

Louder and louder, they chanted. The light grew brighter. I shaded my eyes with the back of my hands and saw an outline of someone coming through. Then more appeared.

A woman with long flowing dark and greying hair, dressed in what appeared to be black rubber appeared through the blue light. She quickly studied the area, then turned to help others as they came through. By the time it was over, more than a hundred Ambers had passed through the light and appeared to be stunned with their new surroundings. The chanting from behind me had ceased. The high priests had stepped away. The woman dressed in black made her way toward me. Eyeing me intensely with her piercing eyes, she reached and took the red bandana off my head. "That doesn't belong to you. Where did you get it?"

I didn't know how to react. I did the best I could. "My gun was wrapped in it."

"Your gun? Show me."

I took the gun from behind my back and gave it to her. She read the inscription engraved on it. "Bosco . . ." she said with sadness. She swayed slightly before her legs collapsed from under her. I tried to reach out and grab her as she fell. The high priests immediately stopped me.

The woman bent her head forward and began to weep. Someone else of Amber appearance but much older stepped up behind the woman and placed his hand on her shoulder.

"I'm okay, Scotty. I just need a moment. It's a little more than I can handle."

"Angel. Take as much time as ya need, love. We've all been through this crap for a reason. Now, we're about to show 'em why, eh?"

* * *

The pain was such that I could no longer stand. They'd given me a soft and comfortable bed; and medication to help relieve the fire that raged in every corner of my body. But despite everything – despite all the suffering and loss, despite the pain I was feeling; I was somehow at peace.

Angel Bunjil reached out with her hand, lightly hovering it above my chest. Scotty-Blue reached and slowly took her hand away. "No, love. Let 'im go. After what 'es been through, 'e needs 'is rest, eh?" They both stood there, looking down at me as I closed my eyes for the last time.

TO BE CONTINUED . . .

LATE 2020

ABOUT THE AUTHOR

Carl Lakeland lives with his wife in the sleepy town of Snake Valley, 36 kilometres south west of Ballarat in Australia.

Lakeland grew up during the early seventies western suburbs of Sydney. Having enlisted into the military at the age of seventeen, he draws on his experience to create powerful and engaging speculative fiction

"Sometimes, I can't let things be," says Lakeland. "I write stories with passion that others might see as being obsessive. I live and breathe it. I dream it when I sleep. But I never write down my dreams. If I can't remember those things I've dreamt, they're not important enough."

Carl Lakeland's stories revolve around the element of 'what if?' He pushes the boundaries of his stories to the edge of the *Official Secrets Act,* which will have the reader wondering about the aspect of creative licence, or the possibility of fact in his writing. Either way, the reader will be left to make up their own mind. His books are fast paced, edge of your seat thrillers which are distinctively written in a way that will have the reader guessing which way the story is about to head.

"As a writer, unpredictability is key essence. If I write something that can be foreseen in coming chapters, it's not good enough. I will scrap it. My goal is to keep the reader wondering, even sometimes to the detriment of my good guys!"

Catch up with me at carllakeland.com